The Complete Ruritanian Romances

The Prisoner of Zenda, Rupert of Hentzau, and The Heart of Princess Osra

Anthony Hope

i

TABLE OF CONTENTS

THE PRISONER OF ZENDA

RUPERT OF HENTZAU

THE HEART OF PRINCESS OSRA

CHAPTER 1

The Rassendylls—With a Word on the Elphbergs

"I wonder when in the world you're going to do anything, Rudolf?" said my brother's wife. "My dear Rose," I answered, laying down my egg-spoon, "why in the world should I do anything? My position is a comfortable one. I have an income nearly sufficient for my wants (no one's income is ever quite sufficient, you know), I enjoy an enviable social position: I am brother to Lord Burlesdon, and brother-in-law to that charming lady, his countess. Behold, it is enough!"

"You are nine-and-twenty," she observed, "and you've done nothing but—"

"Knock about? It is true. Our family doesn't need to do things."

This remark of mine rather annoyed Rose, for everybody knows (and therefore there can be no harm in referring to the fact) that, pretty and accomplished as she herself is, her family is hardly of the same standing as the Rassendylls. Besides her attractions, she possessed a large fortune, and my brother Robert was wise enough not to mind about her ancestry. Ancestry is, in fact, a matter concerning which the next observation of Rose's has some truth.

"Good families are generally worse than any others," she said.

Upon this I stroked my hair: I knew quite well what she meant.

"I'm so glad Robert's is black!" she cried.

At this moment Robert (who rises at seven and works before breakfast) came in. He glanced at his wife: her cheek was slightly flushed; he patted it caressingly.

"What's the matter, my dear?" he asked.

"She objects to my doing nothing and having red hair," said I, in an injured tone.

"Oh! of course he can't help his hair," admitted Rose.

"It generally crops out once in a generation," said my brother. "So does the nose. Rudolf has got them both."

"I wish they didn't crop out," said Rose, still flushed.

"I rather like them myself," said I, and, rising, I bowed to the portrait of Countess Amelia.

My brother's wife uttered an exclamation of impatience.

"I wish you'd take that picture away, Robert," said she.

"My dear!" he cried.

"Good heavens!" I added.

"Then it might be forgotten," she continued.

"Hardly—with Rudolf about," said Robert, shaking his head.

"Why should it be forgotten?" I asked.

"Rudolf!" exclaimed my brother's wife, blushing very prettily.

I laughed, and went on with my egg. At least I had shelved the question of what (if anything) I ought to do. And, by way of closing the discussion—and also, I must admit, of exasperating my strict little sister-in-law a trifle more—I observed:

"I rather like being an Elphberg myself."

When I read a story, I skip the explanations; yet the moment I begin to write one, I find that I must have an explanation. For it is manifest that I must explain why my sister-in-law was vexed with my nose and hair, and why I ventured to call myself an Elphberg. For eminent as, I must protest, the Rassendylls have been for many generations, yet participation in their blood of course does not, at first sight, justify the boast of a connection with the grander stock of the Elphbergs or a claim to be one of that Royal House. For what relationship is there between Ruritania and Burlesdon, between the Palace at Strelsau or the Castle of Zenda and Number 305 Park Lane, W.?

Well then—and I must premise that I am going, perforce, to rake up the very scandal which my dear Lady Burlesdon wishes forgotten—in the year 1733, George II. sitting then on the throne, peace reigning for the moment, and the King and the Prince of Wales being not yet at loggerheads, there came on a visit to the English Court a certain prince, who was afterwards known to history as Rudolf the Third of Ruritania. The prince was a tall, handsome young fellow, marked (maybe marred, it is not for me to say) by a somewhat unusually long, sharp and straight nose, and a mass of dark-red hair—in fact, the nose and the hair which have stamped the Elphbergs time out of mind. He stayed some months in England, where he was most courteously received; yet, in the end, he left rather under a cloud. For he fought a duel (it was considered highly well bred of him to waive all question of his rank) with a nobleman, well known in the society of the day, not only for his own merits, but as the husband of a very beautiful wife. In that duel Prince Rudolf received a severe wound, and, recovering therefrom, was adroitly smuggled off by the Ruritanian ambassador, who had found him a pretty handful. The nobleman was not wounded in the duel; but the morning being raw and damp on the occasion of the meeting, he contracted a severe chill, and, failing to throw it off, he died some six months after the departure of Prince Rudolf, without having found leisure to adjust his relations with his wife—who, after another two months, bore an heir to the title and estates of the family of Burlesdon. This lady was the Countess Amelia, whose picture my sister-in-law wished to remove from the drawing-room in Park Lane; and her husband was James, fifth Earl of Burlesdon and twenty-second Baron Rassendyll, both in the peerage of England, and a Knight of the Garter. As for Rudolf, he went back to Ruritania, married a wife, and ascended the throne, whereon his progeny in the direct line have sat from then till this very hour—with one short interval. And, finally, if you walk through the picture galleries at Burlesdon, among the fifty portraits or so of the last century and a half, you will find five or six, including that of the sixth earl, distinguished by long, sharp, straight noses and a quantity of dark-red hair; these five or six have also blue eyes, whereas among the Rassendylls dark eyes are the commoner.

That is the explanation, and I am glad to have finished it: the blemishes on honourable lineage are a delicate subject, and certainly this heredity we hear so much about is the finest scandalmonger in the world; it laughs at discretion, and writes strange entries between the lines of the "Peerages".

It will be observed that my sister-in-law, with a want of logic that must have been peculiar to herself (since we are no longer allowed to lay it to the charge of her sex), treated my complexion almost as an offence for which I was responsible, hastening to assume from that external sign inward qualities of which I protest my entire innocence; and this unjust inference she sought to buttress by pointing to the uselessness of the life I had led. Well, be that as it may, I had picked up a good deal of pleasure and a good deal of knowledge. I had been to a German school and a German university, and spoke German as readily and perfectly as English; I was thoroughly at home in French; I had a smattering of Italian and enough Spanish to swear by. I was, I believe, a strong, though hardly fine swordsman and a good shot. I could ride anything that had a back to sit on; and my head was as cool a one as you could find, for all its flaming cover. If you say that I ought to have spent my time in useful labour, I am out of Court and have nothing to say, save that my parents had no business to leave me two thousand pounds a year and a roving disposition.

"The difference between you and Robert," said my sister-in-law, who often (bless her!) speaks on a platform, and oftener still as if she were on one, "is that he recognizes the duties of his position, and you see the opportunities of yours."

"To a man of spirit, my dear Rose," I answered, "opportunities are duties."

"Nonsense!" said she, tossing her head; and after a moment she went on: "Now, here's Sir Jacob Borrodaile offering you exactly what you might be equal to."

"A thousand thanks!" I murmured.

"He's to have an Embassy in six months, and Robert says he is sure that he'll take you as an attache. Do take it, Rudolf—to please me."

Now, when my sister-in-law puts the matter in that way, wrinkling her pretty brows, twisting her little hands, and growing wistful in the eyes, all on account of an idle scamp like myself, for whom she has no natural responsibility, I am visited with compunction. Moreover, I thought it possible that I could pass the time in the position suggested with some tolerable amusement. Therefore I said:

"My dear sister, if in six months' time no unforeseen obstacle has arisen, and Sir Jacob invites me, hang me if I don't go with Sir Jacob!"

"Oh, Rudolf, how good of you! I am glad!"

"Where's he going to?"

"He doesn't know yet; but it's sure to be a good Embassy."

"Madame," said I, "for your sake I'll go, if it's no more than a beggarly Legation. When I do a thing, I don't do it by halves."

My promise, then, was given; but six months are six months, and seem an eternity, and, inasmuch as they stretched between me and my prospective industry (I suppose attaches are industrious; but I know not, for I never became attache to Sir Jacob or anybody else), I cast about for some desirable mode of spending them. And it occurred to me suddenly that I would visit Ruritania. It may seem strange that I had never visited that country yet; but my father (in spite of a sneaking fondness for the Elphbergs, which led him to give me, his second son, the famous Elphberg name of Rudolf) had always been averse from my going, and, since his death, my brother, prompted by Rose, had accepted the family tradition which taught that a wide berth was to be given to that country. But the moment Ruritania had come into my head I was eaten up with a curiosity to see it. After all, red hair and long noses are not confined to the House of Elphberg, and the old story seemed a preposterously insufficient reason for debarring myself from acquaintance with a highly interesting and important kingdom, one which had played no small part in European history, and might do the like again under the sway of a young and vigorous ruler, such as the new King was rumoured to be. My determination was clinched by reading in The Times that Rudolf the Fifth was to be crowned at Strelsau in the course of the next three weeks, and that great magnificence was to mark the occasion. At once I made up my mind to be present, and began my preparations. But, inasmuch as it has never been my practice to furnish my relatives with an itinerary of my journeys and in this case I anticipated opposition to my wishes, I gave out that I was going for a ramble in the Tyrol—an old haunt of mine—and propitiated Rose's wrath by declaring that I intended to study the political and social problems of the interesting community which dwells in that neighbourhood.

"Perhaps," I hinted darkly, "there may be an outcome of the expedition."

"What do you mean?" she asked.

"Well," said I carelessly, "there seems a gap that might be filled by an exhaustive work on—"

"Oh! will you write a book?" she cried, clapping her hands. "That would be splendid, wouldn't it, Robert?"

"It's the best of introductions to political life nowadays," observed my brother, who has, by the way, introduced himself in this manner several times over. Burlesdon on Ancient Theories and Modern Facts and The Ultimate Outcome, by a Political Student, are both works of recognized eminence.

"I believe you are right, Bob, my boy," said I.

"Now promise you'll do it," said Rose earnestly.

"No, I won't promise; but if I find enough material, I will."

"That's fair enough," said Robert.

"Oh, material doesn't matter!" she said, pouting.

But this time she could get no more than a qualified promise out of me. To tell the truth, I would have wagered a handsome sum that the story of my expedition that summer would stain no paper and spoil not a single pen. And that shows how little we know what the future holds; for here I am, fulfilling my qualified promise, and writing, as I never thought to write, a book—though it will hardly serve as an introduction to political life, and has not a jot to do with the Tyrol.

Neither would it, I fear, please Lady Burlesdon, if I were to submit it to her critical eye—a step which I have no intention of taking.

CHAPTER 2

Concerning the Colour of Men's Hair

It was a maxim of my Uncle William's that no man should pass through Paris without spending four-and-twenty hours there. My uncle spoke out of a ripe experience of the world, and I honoured his advice by putting up for a day and a night at "The Continental" on my way to—the Tyrol. I called on George Featherly at the Embassy, and we had a bit of dinner together at Durand's, and afterwards dropped in to the Opera; and after that we had a little supper, and after that we called on Bertram Bertrand, a versifier of some repute and Paris correspondent to The Critic. He had a very comfortable suite of rooms, and we found some pleasant fellows smoking and talking. It struck me, however, that Bertram himself was absent and in low spirits, and when everybody except ourselves had gone, I rallied him on his moping preoccupation. He fenced with me for a while, but at last, flinging himself on a sofa, he exclaimed:

"Very well; have it your own way. I am in love—infernally in love!"

"Oh, you'll write the better poetry," said I, by way of consolation.

He ruffled his hair with his hand and smoked furiously. George Featherly, standing with his back to the mantelpiece, smiled unkindly.

"If it's the old affair," said he, "you may as well throw it up, Bert. She's leaving Paris tomorrow."

"I know that," snapped Bertram.

"Not that it would make any difference if she stayed," pursued the relentless George. "She flies higher than the paper trade, my boy!"

"Hang her!" said Bertram.

"It would make it more interesting for me," I ventured to observe, "if I knew who you were talking about."

"Antoinette Mauban," said George.

"De Mauban," growled Bertram.

"Oho!" said I, passing by the question of the `de'. "You don't mean to say, Bert—?"

"Can't you let me alone?"

"Where's she going to?" I asked, for the lady was something of a celebrity.

George jingled his money, smiled cruelly at poor Bertram, and answered pleasantly:

"Nobody knows. By the way, Bert, I met a great man at her house the other night—at least, about a month ago. Did you ever meet him—the Duke of Strelsau?"

"Yes, I did," growled Bertram.

"An extremely accomplished man, I thought him."

It was not hard to see that George's references to the duke were intended to aggravate poor Bertram's sufferings, so that I drew the inference that the duke had distinguished Madame de Mauban by his attentions. She was a widow, rich, handsome, and, according to repute, ambitious. It was quite possible that she, as George put it, was flying as high as a personage who was everything he could be, short of enjoying strictly royal rank: for the duke was the son of the late King of Ruritania by a second and morganatic marriage, and half-brother to the new King. He had been his father's favourite, and it had occasioned some unfavourable comment when he had been created a duke, with a title derived from no less a city than the capital itself. His mother had been of good, but not exalted, birth.

"He's not in Paris now, is he?" I asked.

"Oh no! He's gone back to be present at the King's coronation; a ceremony which, I should say, he'll not enjoy much. But, Bert, old man, don't despair! He won't marry the fair Antoinette—at least, not unless another plan comes to nothing. Still perhaps she—" He paused and added, with a laugh: "Royal attentions are hard to resist—you know that, don't you, Rudolf?"

"Confound you!" said I; and rising, I left the hapless Bertram in George's hands and went home to bed.

The next day George Featherly went with me to the station, where I took a ticket for Dresden.

"Going to see the pictures?" asked George, with a grin.

George is an inveterate gossip, and had I told him that I was off to Ruritania, the news would have been in London in three days and in Park Lane in a week. I was, therefore, about to return an evasive answer, when he saved my conscience by leaving me suddenly and darting across the platform. Following him with my eyes, I saw him lift his hat and accost a graceful, fashionably dressed woman who had just appeared from the booking-office. She was, perhaps, a year or two over thirty, tall, dark, and of rather full figure. As George talked, I saw her glance at me, and my vanity was hurt by the thought that, muffled in a fur coat and a neck-wrapper (for it was a chilly April day) and wearing a soft travelling hat pulled down to my ears, I must be looking very far from my best. A moment later, George rejoined me.

"You've got a charming travelling companion," he said. "That's poor Bert Bertrand's goddess, Antoinette de Mauban, and, like you, she's going to Dresden—also, no doubt, to see the pictures. It's very queer, though, that she doesn't at present desire the honour of your acquaintance."

"I didn't ask to be introduced," I observed, a little annoyed.

"Well, I offered to bring you to her; but she said, 'Another time.' Never mind, old fellow, perhaps there'll be a smash, and you'll have a chance of rescuing her and cutting out the Duke of Strelsau!"

No smash, however, happened, either to me or to Madame de Mauban. I can speak for her as confidently as for myself; for when, after a night's rest in Dresden, I continued my journey, she got into the same train. Understanding that she wished to be let alone, I avoided her carefully, but I saw that she went the same way as I did to the very end of my journey, and I took opportunities of having a good look at her, when I could do so unobserved.

As soon as we reached the Ruritanian frontier (where the old officer who presided over the Custom House favoured me with such a stare that I felt surer than before of my Elphberg physiognomy), I bought the papers, and found in them news which affected my movements. For some reason, which was not clearly explained, and seemed to be something of a mystery, the date of the coronation had been suddenly advanced, and the ceremony was to take place on the next day but one. The whole country seemed in a stir about it, and it was evident that Strelsau was thronged. Rooms were all let and hotels overflowing; there would be very little chance of my obtaining a lodging, and I should certainly have to pay an exorbitant charge for it. I made up my mind to stop at Zenda, a small town fifty miles short of the capital, and about ten from the frontier. My train reached there in the evening; I would spend the next day, Tuesday, in a wander over the hills, which were said to be very fine, and in taking a glance at the famous Castle, and go over by train to Strelsau on the Wednesday morning, returning at night to sleep at Zenda.

Accordingly at Zenda I got out, and as the train passed where I stood on the platform, I saw my friend Madame de Mauban in her place; clearly she was going through to Strelsau, having, with more providence than I could boast, secured apartments there. I smiled to think how surprised George Featherly would have been to know that she and I had been fellow travellers for so long.

I was very kindly received at the hotel—it was really no more than an inn—kept by a fat old lady and her two daughters. They were good, quiet people, and seemed very little interested in the great doings at Strelsau. The old lady's hero was the duke, for he was now, under the late King's will, master of the Zenda estates and of the Castle, which rose grandly on its steep hill at the end of the valley a mile or so from the inn. The old lady, indeed, did not hesitate to express regret that the duke was not on the throne, instead of his brother.

"We know Duke Michael," said she. "He has always lived among us; every Ruritanian knows Duke Michael. But the King is almost a stranger; he has been so much abroad, not one in ten knows him even by sight."

"And now," chimed in one of the young women, "they say he has shaved off his beard, so that no one at all knows him."

"Shaved his beard!" exclaimed her mother. "Who says so?"

"Johann, the duke's keeper. He has seen the King."

"Ah, yes. The King, sir, is now at the duke's hunting-lodge in the forest here; from here he goes to Strelsau to be crowned on Wednesday morning."

I was interested to hear this, and made up my mind to walk next day in the direction of the lodge, on the chance of coming across the King. The old lady ran on garrulously:

"Ah, and I wish he would stay at his hunting—that and wine (and one thing more) are all he loves, they say—and suffer our duke to be crowned on Wednesday. That I wish, and I don't care who knows it."

"Hush, mother!" urged the daughters.

"Oh, there's many to think as I do!" cried the old woman stubbornly.

I threw myself back in my deep armchair, and laughed at her zeal.

"For my part," said the younger and prettier of the two daughters, a fair, buxom, smiling wench, "I hate Black Michael! A red Elphberg for me, mother! The King, they say, is as red as a fox or as—"

And she laughed mischievously as she cast a glance at me, and tossed her head at her sister's reproving face.

"Many a man has cursed their red hair before now," muttered the old lady—and I remembered James, fifth Earl of Burlesdon.

"But never a woman!" cried the girl.

"Ay, and women, when it was too late," was the stern answer, reducing the girl to silence and blushes.

"How comes the King here?" I asked, to break an embarrassed silence. "It is the duke's land here, you say."

"The duke invited him, sir, to rest here till Wednesday. The duke is at Strelsau, preparing the King's reception."

"Then they're friends?"

"None better," said the old lady.

But my rosy damsel tossed her head again; she was not to be repressed for long, and she broke out again:

"Ay, they love one another as men do who want the same place and the same wife!"

The old woman glowered; but the last words pricked my curiosity, and I interposed before she could begin scolding:

"What, the same wife, too! How's that, young lady?"

"All the world knows that Black Michael—well then, mother, the duke—would give his soul to marry his cousin, the Princess Flavia, and that she is to be the queen."

"Upon my word," said I, "I begin to be sorry for your duke. But if a man will be a younger son, why he must take what the elder leaves, and be as thankful to God as he can;" and, thinking of myself, I shrugged my shoulders and laughed. And then I thought also of Antoinette de Mauban and her journey to Strelsau.

"It's little dealing Black Michael has with—" began the girl, braving her mother's anger; but as she spoke a heavy step sounded on the floor, and a gruff voice asked in a threatening tone: "Who talks of 'Black Michael' in his Highness's own burgh?"

The girl gave a little shriek, half of fright—half, I think, of amusement.

"You'll not tell of me, Johann?" she said.

"See where your chatter leads," said the old lady.

The man who had spoken came forward.

"We have company, Johann," said my hostess, and the fellow plucked off his cap. A moment later he saw me, and, to my amazement, he started back a step, as though he had seen something wonderful.

"What ails you, Johann?" asked the elder girl. "This is a gentleman on his travels, come to see the coronation."

The man had recovered himself, but he was staring at me with an intense, searching, almost fierce glance.

"Good evening to you," said I.

"Good evening, sir," he muttered, still scrutinizing me, and the merry girl began to laugh as she called—

"See, Johann, it is the colour you love! He started to see your hair, sir. It's not the colour we see most of here in Zenda."

"I crave your pardon, sir," stammered the fellow, with puzzled eyes. "I expected to see no one."

"Give him a glass to drink my health in; and I'll bid you good night, and thanks to you, ladies, for your courtesy and pleasant conversation."

So speaking, I rose to my feet, and with a slight bow turned to the door. The young girl ran to light me on the way, and the man fell back to let me pass, his eyes still fixed on me. The moment I was by, he started a step forward, asking:

"Pray, sir, do you know our King?"

"I never saw him," said I. "I hope to do so on Wednesday."

He said no more, but I felt his eyes following me till the door closed behind me. My saucy conductor, looking over her shoulder at me as she preceded me upstairs, said:

"There's no pleasing Master Johann for one of your colour, sir."

"He prefers yours, maybe?" I suggested.

"I meant, sir, in a man," she answered, with a coquettish glance.

"What," asked I, taking hold of the other side of the candlestick, "does colour matter in a man?"

"Nay, but I love yours—it's the Elphberg red."

"Colour in a man," said I, "is a matter of no more moment than that!"—and I gave her something of no value.

"God send the kitchen door be shut!" said she.

"Amen!" said I, and left her.

In fact, however, as I now know, colour is sometimes of considerable moment to a man.

CHAPTER 3

A Merry Evening with a Distant Relative

I was not so unreasonable as to be prejudiced against the duke's keeper because he disliked my complexion; and if I had been, his most civil and obliging conduct (as it seemed to me to be) next morning would have disarmed me. Hearing that I was bound for Strelsau, he came to see me while I was breakfasting, and told me that a sister of his who had married a well-to-do tradesman and lived in the capital, had invited him to occupy a room in her house. He had gladly accepted, but now found that his duties would not permit of his absence. He begged therefore that, if such humble (though, as he added, clean and comfortable) lodgings would satisfy me, I would take his place. He pledged his sister's acquiescence, and urged the inconvenience and crowding to which I should be subject in my journeys to and from Strelsau the next day. I accepted his offer without a moment's hesitation, and he went off to telegraph to his sister, while I packed up and prepared to take the next train. But I still hankered after the forest and the hunting-lodge, and when my little maid told me that I could, by walking ten miles or so through the forest, hit the railway at a roadside station, I decided to send my luggage direct to the address which Johann had given, take my walk, and follow to Strelsau myself. Johann had gone off and was not aware of the change in my plans; but, as its only effect was to delay my arrival at his sister's for a few hours, there was no reason for troubling to inform him of it. Doubtless the good lady would waste no anxiety on my account.

I took an early luncheon, and, having bidden my kind entertainers farewell, promising to return to them on my way home, I set out to climb the hill that led to the Castle, and thence to the forest of Zenda. Half an hour's leisurely walking brought me to the Castle. It had been a fortress in old days, and the ancient keep was still in good preservation and very imposing. Behind it stood another portion of the original castle, and behind that again, and separated from it by a deep and broad moat, which ran all round the old buildings, was a handsome modern chateau, erected by the last king, and now forming the country residence of the Duke of Strelsau. The old and the new portions were connected by a drawbridge, and this indirect mode of access formed the only passage between the old building and the outer world; but leading to the modern chateau there was a broad and handsome avenue. It was an ideal residence: when "Black Michael" desired company, he could dwell in his chateau; if a fit of misanthropy seized him, he had merely to cross the bridge and draw it up after him (it ran on rollers), and nothing short of a regiment and a train of artillery could fetch him out. I went on my way, glad that poor Black Michael, though he could not have the throne or the princess, had, at least, as fine a residence as any prince in Europe.

Soon I entered the forest, and walked on for an hour or more in its cool sombre shade. The great trees enlaced with one another over my head, and the sunshine stole through in patches as bright as diamonds, and hardly bigger. I was enchanted with the place, and, finding a felled tree-trunk, propped my back against it, and stretching my legs out gave myself up to undisturbed contemplation of the solemn beauty of the woods and to the comfort of a good cigar. And when the cigar was finished and I had (I suppose) inhaled as much beauty as I could, I went off into the most delightful sleep, regardless of my train to Strelsau and of the fast-waning afternoon. To remember a train in such a spot would have been rank sacrilege. Instead of that, I fell to dreaming that I was married to the Princess Flavia and dwelt in the Castle of Zenda, and beguiled whole days with my love in the glades of the forest—which made a very pleasant dream. In fact, I was just impressing a fervent kiss on the charming lips of the princess, when I heard (and the voice seemed at first a part of the dream) someone exclaim, in rough strident tones.

"Why, the devil's in it! Shave him, and he'd be the King!"

The idea seemed whimsical enough for a dream: by the sacrifice of my heavy moustache and carefully pointed imperial, I was to be transformed into a monarch! I was about to kiss the princess again, when I arrived (very reluctantly) at the conclusion that I was awake.

I opened my eyes, and found two men regarding me with much curiosity. Both wore shooting costumes and carried guns. One was rather short and very stoutly built, with a big bullet-shaped head, a bristly grey moustache, and small pale-blue eyes, a trifle bloodshot. The other was a slender young fellow, of middle height, dark in complexion, and bearing himself with grace and distinction. I set the one down as an old soldier: the other for a gentleman accustomed to move in good society, but not unused to military life either. It turned out afterwards that my guess was a good one.

The elder man approached me, beckoning the younger to follow. He did so, courteously raising his hat. I rose slowly to my feet.

"He's the height, too!" I heard the elder murmur, as he surveyed my six feet two inches of stature. Then, with a cavalier touch of the cap, he addressed me:

"May I ask your name?"

"As you have taken the first step in the acquaintance, gentlemen," said I, with a smile, "suppose you give me a lead in the matter of names."

The young man stepped forward with a pleasant smile.

"This," said he, "is Colonel Sapt, and I am called Fritz von Tarlenheim: we are both in the service of the King of Ruritania."

I bowed and, baring my head, answered:

"I am Rudolf Rassendyll. I am a traveller from England; and once for a year or two I held a commission from her Majesty the Queen."

"Then we are all brethren of the sword," answered Tarlenheim, holding out his hand, which I took readily.

"Rassendyll, Rassendyll!" muttered Colonel Sapt; then a gleam of intelligence flitted across his face.

"By Heaven!" he cried, "you're of the Burlesdons?"

"My brother is now Lord Burlesdon," said I.

"Thy head betrayeth thee," he chuckled, pointing to my uncovered poll. "Why, Fritz, you know the story?"

The young man glanced apologetically at me. He felt a delicacy which my sister-in-law would have admired. To put him at his ease, I remarked with a smile:

"Ah! the story is known here as well as among us, it seems."

"Known!" cried Sapt. "If you stay here, the deuce a man in all Ruritania will doubt of it—or a woman either."

I began to feel uncomfortable. Had I realized what a very plainly written pedigree I carried about with me, I should have thought long before I visited Ruritania. However, I was in for it now.

At this moment a ringing voice sounded from the wood behind us:

"Fritz, Fritz! where are you, man?"

Tarlenheim started, and said hastily:

"It's the King!"

Old Sapt chuckled again.

Then a young man jumped out from behind the trunk of a tree and stood beside us. As I looked at him, I uttered an astonished cry; and he, seeing me, drew back in sudden wonder. Saving the hair on my face and a manner of conscious dignity which his position gave him, saving also that he lacked perhaps half an inch—nay, less than that, but still something—of my height, the King of Ruritania might have been Rudolf Rassendyll, and I, Rudolf, the King. For an instant we stood motionless, looking at one another. Then I bared my head again and bowed respectfully. The King found his voice, and asked in bewilderment:

"Colonel—Fritz—who is this gentleman?"

I was about to answer, when Colonel Sapt stepped between the King and me, and began to talk to his Majesty in a low growl. The King towered over Sapt, and, as he listened, his eyes now and again sought mine. I looked at him long and carefully. The likeness was certainly astonishing, though I saw the points of difference also. The King's face was slightly more fleshy than mine, the oval of its contour the least trifle more pronounced, and, as I fancied,

9

his mouth lacking something of the firmness (or obstinacy) which was to be gathered from my close-shutting lips. But, for all that, and above all minor distinctions, the likeness rose striking, salient, wonderful.

Sapt ceased speaking, and the King still frowned. Then, gradually, the corners of his mouth began to twitch, his nose came down (as mine does when I laugh), his eyes twinkled, and, behold! he burst into the merriest fit of irrepressible laughter, which rang through the woods and proclaimed him a jovial soul.

"Well met, cousin!" he cried, stepping up to me, clapping me on the back, and laughing still. "You must forgive me if I was taken aback. A man doesn't expect to see double at this time of day, eh, Fritz?"

"I must pray pardon, sire, for my presumption," said I. "I trust it will not forfeit your Majesty's favour."

"By Heaven! you'll always enjoy the King's countenance," he laughed, "whether I like it or not; and, sir, I shall very gladly add to it what services I can. Where are you travelling to?"

"To Strelsau, sire—to the coronation."

The King looked at his friends: he still smiled, though his expression hinted some uneasiness. But the humorous side of the matter caught him again.

"Fritz, Fritz!" he cried, "a thousand crowns for a sight of brother Michael's face when he sees a pair of us!" and the merry laugh rang out again.

"Seriously," observed Fritz von Tarlenheim, "I question Mr. Rassendyll's wisdom in visiting Strelsau just now."

The King lit a cigarette.

"Well, Sapt?" said he, questioningly.

"He mustn't go," growled the old fellow.

"Come, colonel, you mean that I should be in Mr. Rassendyll's debt, if—"

"Oh, ay! wrap it up in the right way," said Sapt, hauling a great pipe out of his pocket.

"Enough, sire," said I. "I'll leave Ruritania today."

"No, by thunder, you shan't—and that's sans phrase, as Sapt likes it. For you shall dine with me tonight, happen what will afterwards. Come, man, you don't meet a new relation every day!"

"We dine sparingly tonight," said Fritz von Tarlenheim.

"Not we—with our new cousin for a guest!" cried the King; and, as Fritz shrugged his shoulders, he added: "Oh! I'll remember our early start, Fritz."

"So will I—tomorrow morning," said old Sapt, pulling at his pipe.

"O wise old Sapt!" cried the King. "Come, Mr. Rassendyll—by the way, what name did they give you?"

"Your Majesty's," I answered, bowing.

"Well, that shows they weren't ashamed of us," he laughed. "Come, then, cousin Rudolf; I've got no house of my own here, but my dear brother Michael lends us a place of his, and we'll make shift to entertain you there;" and he put his arm through mine and, signing to the others to accompany us, walked me off, westerly, through the forest.

We walked for more than half an hour, and the King smoked cigarettes and chattered incessantly. He was full of interest in my family, laughed heartily when I told him of the portraits with Elphberg hair in our galleries, and yet more heartily when he heard that my expedition to Ruritania was a secret one.

"You have to visit your disreputable cousin on the sly, have you?" said he.

Suddenly emerging from the wood, we came on a small and rude hunting-lodge. It was a one-storey building, a sort of bungalow, built entirely of wood. As we approached it, a little man in a plain livery came out to meet us. The only other person I saw about the place was a fat elderly woman, whom I afterwards discovered to be the mother of Johann, the duke's keeper.

"Well, is dinner ready, Josef?" asked the King.

The little servant informed us that it was, and we soon sat down to a plentiful meal. The fare was plain enough: the King ate heartily, Fritz von Tarlenheim delicately, old Sapt voraciously. I played a good knife and fork, as my custom is; the King noticed my performance with approval.

"We're all good trenchermen, we Elphbergs," said he. "But what?—we're eating dry! Wine, Josef! wine, man! Are we beasts, to eat without drinking? Are we cattle, Josef?"

At this reproof Josef hastened to load the table with bottles.

"Remember tomorrow!" said Fritz.

"Ay—tomorrow!" said old Sapt.

The King drained a bumper to his "Cousin Rudolf," as he was gracious—or merry—enough to call me; and I drank its fellow to the "Elphberg Red," whereat he laughed loudly.

Now, be the meat what it might, the wine we drank was beyond all price or praise, and we did it justice. Fritz ventured once to stay the King's hand.

"What?" cried the King. "Remember you start before I do, Master Fritz—you must be more sparing by two hours than I."

Fritz saw that I did not understand.

"The colonel and I," he explained, "leave here at six: we ride down to Zenda and return with the guard of honour to fetch the King at eight, and then we all ride together to the station."

"Hang that same guard!" growled Sapt.

"Oh! it's very civil of my brother to ask the honour for his regiment," said the King. "Come, cousin, you need not start early. Another bottle, man!"

I had another bottle—or, rather, a part of one, for the larger half travelled quickly down his Majesty's throat. Fritz gave up his attempts at persuasion: from persuading, he fell to being persuaded, and soon we were all of us as full of wine as we had any right to be. The King began talking of what he would do in the future, old Sapt of what he had done in the past, Fritz of some beautiful girl or other, and I of the wonderful merits of the Elphberg dynasty. We all talked at once, and followed to the letter Sapt's exhortation to let the morrow take care of itself.

At last the King set down his glass and leant back in his chair.

"I have drunk enough," said he.

"Far be it from me to contradict the King," said I.

Indeed, his remark was most absolutely true—so far as it went.

While I yet spoke, Josef came and set before the King a marvellous old wicker-covered flagon. It had lain so long in some darkened cellar that it seemed to blink in the candlelight.

"His Highness the Duke of Strelsau bade me set this wine before the King, when the King was weary of all other wines, and pray the King to drink, for the love that he bears his brother."

"Well done, Black Michael!" said the King. "Out with the cork, Josef. Hang him! Did he think I'd flinch from his bottle?"

The bottle was opened, and Josef filled the King's glass. The King tasted it. Then, with a solemnity born of the hour and his own condition, he looked round on us:

"Gentlemen, my friends—Rudolf, my cousin ('tis a scandalous story, Rudolf, on my honour!), everything is yours to the half of Ruritania. But ask me not for a single drop of this divine bottle, which I will drink to the health of that—that sly knave, my brother, Black Michael."

And the King seized the bottle and turned it over his mouth, and drained it and flung it from him, and laid his head on his arms on the table.

And we drank pleasant dreams to his Majesty—and that is all I remember of the evening. Perhaps it is enough.

CHAPTER 4

The King Keeps His Appointment

Whether I had slept a minute or a year I knew not. I awoke with a start and a shiver; my face, hair and clothes dripped water, and opposite me stood old Sapt, a sneering smile on his face and an empty bucket in his hand. On the table by him sat Fritz von Tarlenheim, pale as a ghost and black as a crow under the eyes.

I leapt to my feet in anger.

"Your joke goes too far, sir!" I cried.

"Tut, man, we've no time for quarrelling. Nothing else would rouse you. It's five o'clock."

"I'll thank you, Colonel Sapt—" I began again, hot in spirit, though I was uncommonly cold in body.

"Rassendyll," interrupted Fritz, getting down from the table and taking my arm, "look here."

The King lay full length on the floor. His face was red as his hair, and he breathed heavily. Sapt, the disrespectful old dog, kicked him sharply. He did not stir, nor was there any break in his breathing. I saw that his face and head were wet with water, as were mine.

"We've spent half an hour on him," said Fritz.

"He drank three times what either of you did," growled Sapt.

I knelt down and felt his pulse. It was alarmingly languid and slow. We three looked at one another.

"Was it drugged—that last bottle?" I asked in a whisper.

"I don't know," said Sapt.

"We must get a doctor."

"There's none within ten miles, and a thousand doctors wouldn't take him to Strelsau today. I know the look of it. He'll not move for six or seven hours yet."

"But the coronation!" I cried in horror.

Fritz shrugged his shoulders, as I began to see was his habit on most occasions.

"We must send word that he's ill," he said.

"I suppose so," said I.

Old Sapt, who seemed as fresh as a daisy, had lit his pipe and was puffing hard at it.

"If he's not crowned today," said he, "I'll lay a crown he's never crowned."

"But heavens, why?"

"The whole nation's there to meet him; half the army—ay, and Black Michael at the head. Shall we send word that the King's drunk?"

"That he's ill," said I, in correction.

"Ill!" echoed Sapt, with a scornful laugh. "They know his illnesses too well. He's been 'ill' before!"

"Well, we must chance what they think," said Fritz helplessly. "I'll carry the news and make the best of it."

Sapt raised his hand.

"Tell me," said he. "Do you think the King was drugged?"

"I do," said I.

"And who drugged him?"

"That damned hound, Black Michael," said Fritz between his teeth.

"Ay," said Sapt, "that he might not come to be crowned. Rassendyll here doesn't know our pretty Michael. What think you, Fritz, has Michael no king ready? Has half Strelsau no other candidate? As God's alive, man the throne's lost if the King show himself not in Strelsau today. I know Black Michael."

"We could carry him there," said I.

"And a very pretty picture he makes," sneered Sapt.

Fritz von Tarlenheim buried his face in his hands. The King breathed loudly and heavily. Sapt stirred him again with his foot.

"The drunken dog!" he said; "but he's an Elphberg and the son of his father, and may I rot in hell before Black Michael sits in his place!"

For a moment or two we were all silent; then Sapt, knitting his bushy grey brows, took his pipe from his mouth and said to me:

"As a man grows old he believes in Fate. Fate sent you here. Fate sends you now to Strelsau."

I staggered back, murmuring "Good God!"

Fritz looked up with an eager, bewildered gaze.

"Impossible!" I muttered. "I should be known."

"It's a risk—against a certainty," said Sapt. "If you shave, I'll wager you'll not be known. Are you afraid?"

"Sir!"

"Come, lad, there, there; but it's your life, you know, if you're known—and mine—and Fritz's here. But, if you don't go, I swear to you Black Michael will sit tonight on the throne, and the King lie in prison or his grave."

"The King would never forgive it," I stammered.

"Are we women? Who cares for his forgiveness?"

The clock ticked fifty times, and sixty and seventy times, as I stood in thought. Then I suppose a look came over my face, for old Sapt caught me by the hand, crying:

"You'll go?"

"Yes, I'll go," said I, and I turned my eyes on the prostrate figure of the King on the floor.

"Tonight," Sapt went on in a hasty whisper, "we are to lodge in the Palace. The moment they leave us you and I will mount our horses—Fritz must stay there and guard the King's room—and ride here at a gallop. The King will be ready—Josef will tell him—and he must ride back with me to Strelsau, and you ride as if the devil were behind you to the frontier."

I took it all in in a second, and nodded my head.

"There's a chance," said Fritz, with his first sign of hopefulness.

"If I escape detection," said I.

"If we're detected," said Sapt. "I'll send Black Michael down below before I go myself, so help me heaven! Sit in that chair, man."

I obeyed him.

He darted from the room, calling "Josef! Josef!" In three minutes he was back, and Josef with him. The latter carried a jug of hot water, soap and razors. He was trembling as Sapt told him how the land lay, and bade him shave me.

Suddenly Fritz smote on his thigh:

"But the guard! They'll know! they'll know!"

"Pooh! We shan't wait for the guard. We'll ride to Hofbau and catch a train there. When they come, the bird'll be flown."

"But the King?"

"The King will be in the wine-cellar. I'm going to carry him there now."

"If they find him?"

"They won't. How should they? Josef will put them off."

"But—"

Sapt stamped his foot.

"We're not playing," he roared. "My God! don't I know the risk? If they do find him, he's no worse off than if he isn't crowned today in Strelsau."

So speaking, he flung the door open and, stooping, put forth a strength I did not dream he had, and lifted the King in his hands. And as he did so, the old woman, Johann the keeper's mother, stood in the doorway. For a moment she stood, then she turned on her heel, without a sign of surprise, and clattered down the passage.

"Has she heard?" cried Fritz.

"I'll shut her mouth!" said Sapt grimly, and he bore off the King in his arms.

For me, I sat down in an armchair, and as I sat there, half-dazed, Josef clipped and scraped me till my moustache and imperial were things of the past and my face was as bare as the King's. And when Fritz saw me thus he drew a long breath and exclaimed:—

"By Jove, we shall do it!"

It was six o'clock now, and we had no time to lose. Sapt hurried me into the King's room, and I dressed myself in the uniform of a colonel of the Guard, finding time as I slipped on the King's boots to ask Sapt what he had done with the old woman.

"She swore she'd heard nothing," said he; "but to make sure I tied her legs together and put a handkerchief in her mouth and bound her hands, and locked her up in the coal-cellar, next door to the King. Josef will look after them both later on."

Then I burst out laughing, and even old Sapt grimly smiled.

"I fancy," said he, "that when Josef tells them the King is gone they'll think it is because we smelt a rat. For you may swear Black Michael doesn't expect to see him in Strelsau today."

I put the King's helmet on my head. Old Sapt handed me the King's sword, looking at me long and carefully.

"Thank God, he shaved his beard!" he exclaimed.

"Why did he?" I asked.

"Because Princess Flavia said he grazed her cheek when he was graciously pleased to give her a cousinly kiss. Come though, we must ride."

"Is all safe here?"

"Nothing's safe anywhere," said Sapt, "but we can make it no safer."

Fritz now rejoined us in the uniform of a captain in the same regiment as that to which my dress belonged. In four minutes Sapt had arrayed himself in his uniform. Josef called that the horses were ready. We jumped on their backs and started at a rapid trot. The game had begun. What would the issue of it be?

The cool morning air cleared my head, and I was able to take in all Sapt said to me. He was wonderful. Fritz hardly spoke, riding like a man asleep, but Sapt, without another word for the King, began at once to instruct me most minutely in the history of my past life, of my family, of my tastes, pursuits, weaknesses, friends, companions, and servants. He told me the etiquette of the Ruritanian Court, promising to be constantly at my elbow to point out everybody whom I ought to know, and give me hints with what degree of favour to greet them.

"By the way," he said, "you're a Catholic, I suppose?"

"Not I," I answered.

"Lord, he's a heretic!" groaned Sapt, and forthwith he fell to a rudimentary lesson in the practices and observances of the Romish faith.

"Luckily," said he, "you won't be expected to know much, for the King's notoriously lax and careless about such matters. But you must be as civil as butter to the Cardinal. We hope to win him over, because he and Michael have a standing quarrel about their precedence."

We were by now at the station. Fritz had recovered nerve enough to explain to the astonished station master that the King had changed his plans. The train steamed up. We got into a first-class carriage, and Sapt, leaning back on the cushions, went on with his lesson. I looked at my watch—the King's watch it was, of course. It was just eight.

"I wonder if they've gone to look for us," I said.

"I hope they won't find the King," said Fritz nervously, and this time it was Sapt who shrugged his shoulders.

The train travelled well, and at half-past nine, looking out of the window, I saw the towers and spires of a great city.

"Your capital, my liege," grinned old Sapt, with a wave of his hand, and, leaning forward, he laid his finger on my pulse. "A little too quick," said he, in his grumbling tone.

"I'm not made of stone!" I exclaimed.

"You'll do," said he, with a nod. "We must say Fritz here has caught the ague. Drain your flask, Fritz, for heaven's sake, boy!"

Fritz did as he was bid.

"We're an hour early," said Sapt. "We'll send word forward for your Majesty's arrival, for there'll be no one here to meet us yet. And meanwhile—"

"Meanwhile," said I, "the King'll be hanged if he doesn't have some breakfast."

Old Sapt chuckled, and held out his hand.

"You're an Elphberg, every inch of you," said he. Then he paused, and looking at us, said quietly, "God send we may be alive tonight!"

"Amen!" said Fritz von Tarlenheim.

The train stopped. Fritz and Sapt leapt out, uncovered, and held the door for me. I choked down a lump that rose in my throat, settled my helmet firmly on my head, and (I'm not ashamed to say it) breathed a short prayer to God. Then I stepped on the platform of the station at Strelsau.

A moment later, all was bustle and confusion: men hurrying up, hats in hand, and hurrying off again; men conducting me to the buffet; men mounting and riding in hot haste to the quarters of the troops, to the Cathedral, to the residence of Duke Michael. Even as I swallowed the last drop of my cup of coffee, the bells throughout all the city broke out into a joyful peal, and the sound of a military band and of men cheering smote upon my ear.

King Rudolf the Fifth was in his good city of Strelsau! And they shouted outside—

"God save the King!"

Old Sapt's mouth wrinkled into a smile.

"God save 'em both!" he whispered. "Courage, lad!" and I felt his hand press my knee.

CHAPTER 5

The Adventures of an Understudy

With Fritz von Tarlenheim and Colonel Sapt close behind me, I stepped out of the buffet on to the platform. The last thing I did was to feel if my revolver were handy and my sword loose in the scabbard. A gay group of officers and high dignitaries stood awaiting me, at their head a tall old man, covered with medals, and of military bearing. He wore the yellow and red ribbon of the Red Rose of Ruritania—which, by the way, decorated my unworthy breast also. "Marshal Strakencz," whispered Sapt, and I knew that I was in the presence of the most famous veteran of the Ruritanian army.

Just behind the Marshal stood a short spare man, in flowing robes of black and crimson. "The Chancellor of the Kingdom," whispered Sapt.

The Marshal greeted me in a few loyal words, and proceeded to deliver an apology from the Duke of Strelsau. The duke, it seemed, had been afflicted with a sudden indisposition which made it impossible for him to come to the station, but he craved leave to await his Majesty at the Cathedral. I expressed my concern, accepted the Marshal's excuses very suavely, and received the compliments of a large number of distinguished personages. No one betrayed the least suspicion, and I felt my nerve returning and the agitated beating of my heart subsiding. But Fritz was still pale, and his hand shook like a leaf as he extended it to the Marshal.

Presently we formed procession and took our way to the door of the station. Here I mounted my horse, the Marshal holding my stirrup. The civil dignitaries went off to their carriages, and I started to ride through the streets with the Marshal on my right and Sapt (who, as my chief aide-de-camp, was entitled to the place) on my left. The city of Strelsau is partly old and partly new. Spacious modern boulevards and residential quarters surround and embrace the narrow, tortuous, and picturesque streets of the original town. In the outer circles the upper classes live; in the inner the shops are situated; and, behind their prosperous fronts, lie hidden populous but wretched lanes and alleys, filled with a poverty-stricken, turbulent, and (in large measure) criminal class. These social and local divisions corresponded, as I knew from Sapt's information, to another division more important to me. The New Town was for the King; but to the Old Town Michael of Strelsau was a hope, a hero, and a darling.

The scene was very brilliant as we passed along the Grand Boulevard and on to the great square where the Royal Palace stood. Here I was in the midst of my devoted adherents. Every house was hung with red and bedecked with flags and mottoes. The streets were lined with raised seats on each side, and I passed along, bowing this way and that, under a shower of cheers, blessings, and waving handkerchiefs. The balconies were full of gaily dressed ladies, who clapped their hands and curtsied and threw their brightest glances at me. A torrent of red roses fell on me; one bloom lodged in my horse's mane, and I took it and stuck it in my coat. The Marshal smiled grimly. I had stolen some glances at his face, but he was too impassive to show me whether his sympathies were with me or not.

"The red rose for the Elphbergs, Marshal," said I gaily, and he nodded.

I have written "gaily," and a strange word it must seem. But the truth is, that I was drunk with excitement. At that moment I believed—I almost believed—that I was in very truth the King; and, with a look of laughing triumph, I raised my eyes to the beauty-laden balconies again . . . and then I started. For, looking down on me, with her handsome face and proud smile, was the lady who had been my fellow traveller—Antoinette de Mauban; and I saw her also start, and her lips moved, and she leant forward and gazed at me. And I, collecting myself, met her eyes full and square, while again I felt my revolver. Suppose she had cried aloud, "That's not the King!"

Well, we went by; and then the Marshal, turning round in his saddle, waved his hand, and the Cuirassiers closed round us, so that the crowd could not come near me. We were leaving my quarter and entering Duke Michael's, and this action of the Marshal's showed me more clearly than words what the state of feeling in the town must be. But if Fate made me a King, the least I could do was to play the part handsomely.

"Why this change in our order, Marshal?" said I.

The Marshal bit his white moustache.

"It is more prudent, sire," he murmured.

I drew rein.

"Let those in front ride on," said I, "till they are fifty yards ahead. But do you, Marshal, and Colonel Sapt and my friends, wait here till I have ridden fifty yards. And see that no one is nearer to me. I will have my people see that their King trusts them."

Sapt laid his hand on my arm. I shook him off. The Marshal hesitated.

"Am I not understood?" said I; and, biting his moustache again, he gave the orders. I saw old Sapt smiling into his beard, but he shook his head at me. If I had been killed in open day in the streets of Strelsau, Sapt's position would have been a difficult one.

Perhaps I ought to say that I was dressed all in white, except my boots. I wore a silver helmet with gilt ornaments, and the broad ribbon of the Rose looked well across my chest. I should be paying a poor compliment to the King if I did not set modesty aside and admit that I made a very fine figure. So the people thought; for when I, riding alone, entered the dingy, sparsely decorated, sombre streets of the Old Town, there was first a murmur, then a cheer, and a woman, from a window above a cookshop, cried the old local saying:

"If he's red, he's right!" whereat I laughed and took off my helmet that she might see that I was of the right colour and they cheered me again at that.

It was more interesting riding thus alone, for I heard the comments of the crowd.

"He looks paler than his wont," said one.

"You'd look pale if you lived as he does," was the highly disrespectful retort.

16

"He's a bigger man than I thought," said another.

"So he had a good jaw under that beard after all," commented a third.

"The pictures of him aren't handsome enough," declared a pretty girl, taking great care that I should hear. No doubt it was mere flattery.

But, in spite of these signs of approval and interest, the mass of the people received me in silence and with sullen looks, and my dear brother's portrait ornamented most of the windows—which was an ironical sort of greeting to the King. I was quite glad that he had been spared the unpleasant sight. He was a man of quick temper, and perhaps he would not have taken it so placidly as I did.

At last we were at the Cathedral. Its great grey front, embellished with hundreds of statues and boasting a pair of the finest oak doors in Europe, rose for the first time before me, and the sudden sense of my audacity almost overcame me. Everything was in a mist as I dismounted. I saw the Marshal and Sapt dimly, and dimly the throng of gorgeously robed priests who awaited me. And my eyes were still dim as I walked up the great nave, with the pealing of the organ in my ears. I saw nothing of the brilliant throng that filled it, I hardly distinguished the stately figure of the Cardinal as he rose from the archiepiscopal throne to greet me. Two faces only stood out side by side clearly before my eyes—the face of a girl, pale and lovely, surmounted by a crown of the glorious Elphberg hair (for in a woman it is glorious), and the face of a man, whose full-blooded red cheeks, black hair, and dark deep eyes told me that at last I was in presence of my brother, Black Michael. And when he saw me his red cheeks went pale all in a moment, and his helmet fell with a clatter on the floor. Till that moment I believe that he had not realized that the King was in very truth come to Strelsau.

Of what followed next I remember nothing. I knelt before the altar and the Cardinal anointed my head. Then I rose to my feet, and stretched out my hand and took from him the crown of Ruritania and set it on my head, and I swore the old oath of the King; and (if it were a sin, may it be forgiven me) I received the Holy Sacrament there before them all. Then the great organ pealed out again, the Marshal bade the heralds proclaim me, and Rudolf the Fifth was crowned King; of which imposing ceremony an excellent picture hangs now in my dining-room. The portrait of the King is very good.

Then the lady with the pale face and the glorious hair, her train held by two pages, stepped from her place and came to where I stood. And a herald cried:

"Her Royal Highness the Princess Flavia!"

She curtsied low, and put her hand under mine and raised my hand and kissed it. And for an instant I thought what I had best do. Then I drew her to me and kissed her twice on the cheek, and she blushed red, and—then his Eminence the Cardinal Archbishop slipped in front of Black Michael, and kissed my hand and presented me with a letter from the Pope—the first and last which I have received from that exalted quarter!

And then came the Duke of Strelsau. His step trembled, I swear, and he looked to the right and to the left, as a man looks who thinks on flight; and his face was patched with red and white, and his hand shook so that it jumped under mine, and I felt his lips dry and parched. And I glanced at Sapt, who was smiling again into his beard, and, resolutely doing my duty in that station of life to which I had been marvellously called, I took my dear Michael by both hands and kissed him on the cheek. I think we were both glad when that was over!

But neither in the face of the princess nor in that of any other did I see the least doubt or questioning. Yet, had I and the King stood side by side, she could have told us in an instant, or, at least, on a little consideration. But neither she nor anyone else dreamed or imagined that I could be other than the King. So the likeness served, and for an hour I stood there, feeling as weary and blasé as though I had been a king all my life; and everybody kissed my hand, and the ambassadors paid me their respects, among them old Lord Topham, at whose house in Grosvenor Square I had danced a score of times. Thank heaven, the old man was as blind as a bat, and did not claim my acquaintance.

Then back we went through the streets to the Palace, and I heard them cheering Black Michael; but he, Fritz told me, sat biting his nails like a man in a reverie, and even his own friends said that he should have made a braver show. I was in a carriage now, side by side with the Princess Flavia, and a rough fellow cried out:

"And when's the wedding?" and as he spoke another struck him in the face, crying "Long live Duke Michael!" and the princess coloured—it was an admirable tint—and looked straight in front of her.

Now I felt in a difficulty, because I had forgotten to ask Sapt the state of my affections, or how far matters had gone between the princess and myself. Frankly, had I been the King, the further they had gone the better should I have been pleased. For I am not a slow-blooded man, and I had not kissed Princess Flavia's cheek for nothing. These thoughts passed through my head, but, not being sure of my ground, I said nothing; and in a moment or two the princess, recovering her equanimity, turned to me.

"Do you know, Rudolf," said she, "you look somehow different today?"

The fact was not surprising, but the remark was disquieting.

"You look," she went on, "more sober, more sedate; you're almost careworn, and I declare you're thinner. Surely it's not possible that you've begun to take anything seriously?"

The princess seemed to hold of the King much the same opinion that Lady Burlesdon held of me.

I braced myself up to the conversation.

"Would that please you?" I asked softly.

"Oh, you know my views," said she, turning her eyes away.

"Whatever pleases you I try to do," I said; and, as I saw her smile and blush, I thought that I was playing the King's hand very well for him. So I continued and what I said was perfectly true:

"I assure you, my dear cousin, that nothing in my life has affected me more than the reception I've been greeted with today."

She smiled brightly, but in an instant grew grave again, and whispered:

"Did you notice Michael?"

"Yes," said I, adding, "he wasn't enjoying himself."

"Do be careful!" she went on. "You don't—indeed you don't—keep enough watch on him. You know—"

"I know," said I, "that he wants what I've got."

"Yes. Hush!"

Then—and I can't justify it, for I committed the King far beyond what I had a right to do—I suppose she carried me off my feet—I went on:

"And perhaps also something which I haven't got yet, but hope to win some day."

This was my answer. Had I been the King, I should have thought it encouraging:

"Haven't you enough responsibilities on you for one day, cousin?"

Bang, bang! Blare, blare! We were at the Palace. Guns were firing and trumpets blowing. Rows of lackeys stood waiting, and, handing the princess up the broad marble staircase, I took formal possession, as a crowned King, of the House of my ancestors, and sat down at my own table, with my cousin on my right hand, on her other side Black Michael, and on my left his Eminence the Cardinal. Behind my chair stood Sapt; and at the end of the table, I saw Fritz von Tarlenheim drain to the bottom his glass of champagne rather sooner than he decently should.

I wondered what the King of Ruritania was doing.

CHAPTER 6

We were in the King's dressing-room—Fritz von Tarlenheim, Sapt, and I. I flung myself exhausted into an armchair. Sapt lit his pipe. He uttered no congratulations on the marvellous success of our wild risk, but his whole bearing was eloquent of satisfaction. The triumph, aided perhaps by good wine, had made a new man of Fritz.

"What a day for you to remember!" he cried. "Gad, I'd like to be King for twelve hours myself! But, Rassendyll, you mustn't throw your heart too much into the part. I don't wonder Black Michael looked blacker than ever—you and the princess had so much to say to one another."

"How beautiful she is!" I exclaimed.

"Never mind the woman," growled Sapt. "Are you ready to start?"

"Yes," said I, with a sigh.

It was five o'clock, and at twelve I should be no more than Rudolf Rassendyll. I remarked on it in a joking tone.

"You'll be lucky," observed Sapt grimly, "if you're not the late Rudolf Rassendyll. By Heaven! I feel my head wobbling on my shoulders every minute you're in the city. Do you know, friend, that Michael has had news from Zenda? He went into a room alone to read it—and he came out looking like a man dazed."

"I'm ready," said I, this news making me none the more eager to linger.

Sapt sat down.

"I must write us an order to leave the city. Michael's Governor, you know, and we must be prepared for hindrances. You must sign the order."

"My dear colonel, I've not been bred a forger!"

Out of his pocket Sapt produced a piece of paper.

"There's the King's signature," he said, "and here," he went on, after another search in his pocket, "is some tracing paper. If you can't manage a 'Rudolf' in ten minutes, why—I can."

"Your education has been more comprehensive than mine," said I. "You write it."

And a very tolerable forgery did this versatile hero produce.

"Now, Fritz," said he, "the King goes to bed. He is upset. No one is to see him till nine o'clock tomorrow. You understand—no one?"

"I understand," answered Fritz.

"Michael may come, and claim immediate audience. You'll answer that only princes of the blood are entitled to it."

"That'll annoy Michael," laughed Fritz.

"You quite understand?" asked Sapt again. "If the door of this room is opened while we're away, you're not to be alive to tell us about it."

"I need no schooling, colonel," said Fritz, a trifle haughtily.

"Here, wrap yourself in this big cloak," Sapt continued to me, "and put on this flat cap. My orderly rides with me to the hunting-lodge tonight."

"There's an obstacle," I observed. "The horse doesn't live that can carry me forty miles."

"Oh, yes, he does—two of him: one here—one at the lodge. Now, are you ready?"

"I'm ready," said I.

Fritz held out his hand.

"In case," said he; and we shook hands heartily.

"Damn your sentiment!" growled Sapt. "Come along."

He went, not to the door, but to a panel in the wall.

"In the old King's time," said he, "I knew this way well."

I followed him, and we walked, as I should estimate, near two hundred yards along a narrow passage. Then we came to a stout oak door. Sapt unlocked it. We passed through, and found ourselves in a quiet street that ran along the back of the Palace gardens. A man was waiting for us with two horses. One was a magnificent bay, up to any weight; the other a sturdy brown. Sapt signed to me to mount the bay. Without a word to the man, we mounted and rode away. The town was full of noise and merriment, but we took secluded ways. My cloak was wrapped over half my face; the capacious flat cap hid every lock of my tell-tale hair. By Sapt's directions, I crouched on my saddle, and rode with such a round back as I hope never to exhibit on a horse again. Down a long narrow lane we went, meeting some wanderers and some roisterers; and, as we rode, we heard the Cathedral bells still clanging out their welcome to the King. It was half-past six, and still light. At last we came to the city wall and to a gate.

"Have your weapon ready," whispered Sapt. "We must stop his mouth, if he talks."

I put my hand on my revolver. Sapt hailed the doorkeeper. The stars fought for us! A little girl of fourteen tripped out.

"Please, sir, father's gone to see the King."

"He'd better have stayed here," said Sapt to me, grinning.

"But he said I wasn't to open the gate, sir."

"Did he, my dear?" said Sapt, dismounting. "Then give me the key."

The key was in the child's hand. Sapt gave her a crown.

"Here's an order from the King. Show it to your father. Orderly, open the gate!"

I leapt down. Between us we rolled back the great gate, led our horses out, and closed it again. "I shall be sorry for the doorkeeper if Michael finds out that he wasn't there. Now then, lad, for a canter. We mustn't go too fast while we're near the town."

Once, however, outside the city, we ran little danger, for everybody else was inside, merry-making; and as the evening fell we quickened our pace, my splendid horse bounding along under me as though I had been a feather. It was a fine night, and presently the moon appeared. We talked little on the way, and chiefly about the progress we were making.

"I wonder what the duke's despatches told him," said I, once.

"Ay, I wonder!" responded Sapt.

We stopped for a draught of wine and to bait our horses, losing half an hour thus. I dared not go into the inn, and stayed with the horses in the stable. Then we went ahead again, and had covered some five-and-twenty miles, when Sapt abruptly stopped.

"Hark!" he cried.

I listened. Away, far behind us, in the still of the evening—it was just half-past nine—we heard the beat of horses' hoofs. The wind blowing strong behind us, carried the sound. I glanced at Sapt.

"Come on!" he cried, and spurred his horse into a gallop. When we next paused to listen, the hoof-beats were not audible, and we relaxed our pace. Then we heard them again. Sapt jumped down and laid his ear to the ground.

"There are two," he said. "They're only a mile behind. Thank God the road curves in and out, and the wind's our way."

We galloped on. We seemed to be holding our own. We had entered the outskirts of the forest of Zenda, and the trees, closing in behind us as the track zigged and zagged, prevented us seeing our pursuers, and them from seeing us.

Another half-hour brought us to a divide of the road. Sapt drew rein.

"To the right is our road," he said. "To the left, to the Castle. Each about eight miles. Get down."

"But they'll be on us!" I cried.

"Get down!" he repeated brusquely; and I obeyed. The wood was dense up to the very edge of the road. We led our horses into the covert, bound handkerchiefs over their eyes, and stood beside them.

"You want to see who they are?" I whispered.

"Ay, and where they're going," he answered.

I saw that his revolver was in his hand.

Nearer and nearer came the hoofs. The moon shone out now clear and full, so that the road was white with it. The ground was hard, and we had left no traces.

"Here they come!" whispered Sapt.

"It's the duke!"

"I thought so," he answered.

It was the duke; and with him a burly fellow whom I knew well, and who had cause to know me afterwards—Max Holf, brother to Johann the keeper, and body-servant to his Highness. They were up to us: the duke reined up. I saw Sapt's finger curl lovingly towards the trigger. I believe he would have given ten years of his life for a shot; and he could have picked off Black Michael as easily as I could a barn-door fowl in a farmyard. I laid my hand on his arm. He nodded reassuringly: he was always ready to sacrifice inclination to duty.

"Which way?" asked Black Michael.

"To the Castle, your Highness," urged his companion. "There we shall learn the truth."

For an instant the duke hesitated.

"I thought I heard hoofs," said he.

"I think not, your Highness."

"Why shouldn't we go to the lodge?"

"I fear a trap. If all is well, why go to the lodge? If not, it's a snare to trap us."

Suddenly the duke's horse neighed. In an instant we folded our cloaks close round our horses' heads, and, holding them thus, covered the duke and his attendant with our revolvers. If they had found us, they had been dead men, or our prisoners.

Michael waited a moment longer. Then he cried:

"To Zenda, then!" and setting spurs to his horse, galloped on.

Sapt raised his weapon after him, and there was such an expression of wistful regret on his face that I had much ado not to burst out laughing.

For ten minutes we stayed where we were.

"You see," said Sapt, "they've sent him news that all is well."

"What does that mean?" I asked.

"God knows," said Sapt, frowning heavily. "But it's brought him from Strelsau in a rare puzzle."

Then we mounted, and rode as fast as our weary horses could lay their feet to the ground. For those last eight miles we spoke no more. Our minds were full of apprehension. "All is well." What did it mean? Was all well with the King?

At last the lodge came in sight. Spurring our horses to a last gallop, we rode up to the gate. All was still and quiet. Not a soul came to meet us. We dismounted in haste. Suddenly Sapt caught me by the arm.

"Look there!" he said, pointing to the ground.

I looked down. At my feet lay five or six silk handkerchiefs, torn and slashed and rent. I turned to him questioningly.

"They're what I tied the old woman up with," said he. "Fasten the horses, and come along."

The handle of the door turned without resistance. We passed into the room which had been the scene of last night's bout. It was still strewn with the remnants of our meal and with empty bottles.

"Come on," cried Sapt, whose marvellous composure had at last almost given way.

We rushed down the passage towards the cellars. The door of the coal-cellar stood wide open.

"They found the old woman," said I.

"You might have known that from the handkerchiefs," he said.

Then we came opposite the door of the wine-cellar. It was shut. It looked in all respects as it had looked when we left it that morning.

"Come, it's all right," said I.

A loud oath from Sapt rang out. His face turned pale, and he pointed again at the floor. From under the door a red stain had spread over the floor of the passage and dried there. Sapt sank against the opposite wall. I tried the door. It was locked.

"Where's Josef?" muttered Sapt.

"Where's the King?" I responded.

Sapt took out a flask and put it to his lips. I ran back to the dining-room, and seized a heavy poker from the fireplace. In my terror and excitement I rained blows on the lock of the door, and I fired a cartridge into it. It gave way, and the door swung open.

"Give me a light," said I; but Sapt still leant against the wall.

He was, of course, more moved than I, for he loved his master. Afraid for himself he was not—no man ever saw him that; but to think what might lie in that dark cellar was enough to turn any man's face pale. I went myself, and took a silver candlestick from the dining-table and struck a light, and, as I returned, I felt the hot wax drip on my naked hand as the candle swayed to and fro; so that I cannot afford to despise Colonel Sapt for his agitation.

I came to the door of the cellar. The red stain turning more and more to a dull brown, stretched inside. I walked two yards into the cellar, and held the candle high above my head. I saw the full bins of wine; I saw spiders crawling on the walls; I saw, too, a couple of empty bottles lying on the floor; and then, away in the corner, I saw the body of a man, lying flat on his back, with his arms stretched wide, and a crimson gash across his throat. I walked to him and knelt down beside him, and commended to God the soul of a faithful man. For it was the body of Josef, the little servant, slain in guarding the King.

I felt a hand on my shoulders, and, turning, saw Sapt, eyes glaring and terror-struck, beside me.

"The King? My God! the King?" he whispered hoarsely.

I threw the candle's gleam over every inch of the cellar.

"The King is not here," said I.

CHAPTER 7

His Majesty Sleeps in Strelsau

I put my arm round Sapt's waist and supported him out of the cellar, drawing the battered door close after me. For ten minutes or more we sat silent in the dining-room. Then old Sapt rubbed his knuckles into his eyes, gave one great gasp, and was himself again. As the clock on the mantelpiece struck one he stamped his foot on the floor, saying:

"They've got the King!"

"Yes," said I, "'all's well!' as Black Michael's despatch said. What a moment it must have been for him when the royal salutes fired at Strelsau this morning! I wonder when he got the message?"

"It must have been sent in the morning," said Sapt. "They must have sent it before news of your arrival at Strelsau reached Zenda—I suppose it came from Zenda."

"And he's carried it about all day!" I exclaimed. "Upon my honour, I'm not the only man who's had a trying day! What did he think, Sapt?"

"What does that matter? What does he think, lad, now?"

I rose to my feet.

"We must get back," I said, "and rouse every soldier in Strelsau. We ought to be in pursuit of Michael before midday."

Old Sapt pulled out his pipe and carefully lit it from the candle which guttered on the table.

"The King may be murdered while we sit here!" I urged.

22

Sapt smoked on for a moment in silence.

"That cursed old woman!" he broke out. "She must have attracted their attention somehow. I see the game. They came up to kidnap the King, and—as I say—somehow they found him. If you hadn't gone to Strelsau, you and I and Fritz had been in heaven by now!"

"And the King?"

"Who knows where the King is now?" he asked.

"Come, let's be off!" said I; but he sat still. And suddenly he burst into one of his grating chuckles:

"By Jove, we've shaken up Black Michael!"

"Come, come!" I repeated impatiently.

"And we'll shake him up a bit more," he added, a cunning smile broadening on his wrinkled, weather-beaten face, and his teeth working on an end of his grizzled moustache. "Ay, lad, we'll go back to Strelsau. The King shall be in his capital again tomorrow."

"The King?"

"The crowned King!"

"You're mad!" I cried.

"If we go back and tell the trick we played, what would you give for our lives?"

"Just what they're worth," said I.

"And for the King's throne? Do you think that the nobles and the people will enjoy being fooled as you've fooled them? Do you think they'll love a King who was too drunk to be crowned, and sent a servant to personate him?"

"He was drugged—and I'm no servant."

"Mine will be Black Michael's version."

He rose, came to me, and laid his hand on my shoulder.

"Lad," he said, "if you play the man, you may save the King yet. Go back and keep his throne warm for him."

"But the duke knows—the villains he has employed know—"

"Ay, but they can't speak!" roared Sapt in grim triumph.

"We've got 'em! How can they denounce you without denouncing themselves? This is not the King, because we kidnapped the King and murdered his servant. Can they say that?"

The position flashed on me. Whether Michael knew me or not, he could not speak. Unless he produced the King, what could he do? And if he produced the King, where was he? For a moment I was carried away headlong; but in an instant the difficulties came strong upon me.

"I must be found out," I urged.

"Perhaps; but every hour's something. Above all, we must have a King in Strelsau, or the city will be Michael's in four-and-twenty hours, and what would the King's life be worth then— or his throne? Lad, you must do it!"

"Suppose they kill the King?"

"They'll kill him, if you don't."

"Sapt, suppose they have killed the King?"

"Then, by heaven, you're as good an Elphberg as Black Michael, and you shall reign in Ruritania! But I don't believe they have; nor will they kill him if you're on the throne. Will they kill him, to put you in?"

It was a wild plan—wilder even and more hopeless than the trick we had already carried through; but as I listened to Sapt I saw the strong points in our game. And then I was a young man and I loved action, and I was offered such a hand in such a game as perhaps never man played yet.

"I shall be found out," I said.

"Perhaps," said Sapt. "Come! to Strelsau! We shall be caught like rats in a trap if we stay here."

"Sapt," I cried, "I'll try it!"

23

"Well played!" said he. "I hope they've left us the horses. I'll go and see."

"We must bury that poor fellow," said I.

"No time," said Sapt.

"I'll do it."

"Hang you!" he grinned. "I make you a King, and—Well, do it. Go and fetch him, while I look to the horses. He can't lie very deep, but I doubt if he'll care about that. Poor little Josef! He was an honest bit of a man."

He went out, and I went to the cellar. I raised poor Josef in my arms and bore him into the passage and thence towards the door of the house. Just inside I laid him down, remembering that I must find spades for our task. At this instant Sapt came up.

"The horses are all right; there's the own brother to the one that brought you here. But you may save yourself that job."

"I'll not go before he's buried."

"Yes, you will."

"Not I, Colonel Sapt; not for all Ruritania."

"You fool!" said he. "Come here."

He drew me to the door. The moon was sinking, but about three hundred yards away, coming along the road from Zenda, I made out a party of men. There were seven or eight of them; four were on horseback and the rest were walking, and I saw that they carried long implements, which I guessed to be spades and mattocks, on their shoulders.

"They'll save you the trouble," said Sapt. "Come along."

He was right. The approaching party must, beyond doubt, be Duke Michael's men, come to remove the traces of their evil work. I hesitated no longer, but an irresistible desire seized me. Pointing to the corpse of poor little Josef, I said to Sapt:

"Colonel, we ought to strike a blow for him!"

"You'd like to give him some company, eh! But it's too risky work, your Majesty."

"I must have a slap at 'em," said I.

Sapt wavered.

"Well," said he, "it's not business, you know; but you've been good boy—and if we come to grief, why, hang me, it'll save us lot of thinking! I'll show you how to touch them."

He cautiously closed the open chink of the door.

Then we retreated through the house and made our way to the back entrance. Here our horses were standing. A carriage-drive swept all round the lodge.

"Revolver ready?" asked Sapt.

"No; steel for me," said I.

"Gad, you're thirsty tonight," chuckled Sapt. "So be it."

We mounted, drawing our swords, and waited silently for a minute or two. Then we heard the tramp of men on the drive the other side of the house. They came to a stand, and one cried:

"Now then, fetch him out!"

"Now!" whispered Sapt.

Driving the spurs into our horses, we rushed at a gallop round the house, and in a moment we were among the ruffians. Sapt told me afterwards that he killed a man, and I believe him; but I saw no more of him. With a cut, I split the head of a fellow on a brown horse, and he fell to the ground. Then I found myself opposite a big man, and I was half conscious of another to my right. It was too warm to stay, and with a simultaneous action I drove my spurs into my horse again and my sword full into the big man's breast. His bullet whizzed past my ear—I could almost swear it touched it. I wrenched at the sword, but it would not come, and I dropped it and galloped after Sapt, whom I now saw about twenty yards ahead. I waved my hand in farewell, and dropped it a second later with a yell, for a bullet had grazed my finger and I felt the blood. Old Sapt turned round in the saddle. Someone fired again, but they had no rifles, and we were out of range. Sapt fell to laughing.

"That's one to me and two to you, with decent luck," said he. "Little Josef will have company."

"Ay, they'll be a partie carree," said I. My blood was up, and I rejoiced to have killed them.

"Well, a pleasant night's work to the rest!" said he. "I wonder if they noticed you?"

"The big fellow did; as I stuck him I heard him cry, 'The King!'"

"Good! good! Oh, we'll give Black Michael some work before we've done!"

Pausing an instant, we made a bandage for my wounded finger, which was bleeding freely and ached severely, the bone being much bruised. Then we rode on, asking of our good horses all that was in them. The excitement of the fight and of our great resolve died away, and we rode in gloomy silence. Day broke clear and cold. We found a farmer just up, and made him give us sustenance for ourselves and our horses. I, feigning a toothache, muffled my face closely. Then ahead again, till Strelsau lay before us. It was eight o'clock or nearing nine, and the gates were all open, as they always were save when the duke's caprice or intrigues shut them. We rode in by the same way as we had come out the evening before, all four of us—the men and the horses—wearied and jaded. The streets were even quieter than when we had gone: everyone was sleeping off last night's revelry, and we met hardly a soul till we reached the little gate of the Palace. There Sapt's old groom was waiting for us.

"Is all well, sir?" he asked.

"All's well," said Sapt, and the man, coming to me, took my hand to kiss.

"The King's hurt!" he cried.

"It's nothing," said I, as I dismounted; "I caught my finger in the door."

"Remember—silence!" said Sapt. "Ah! but, my good Freyler, I do not need to tell you that!" The old fellow shrugged his shoulders.

"All young men like to ride abroad now and again, why not the King?" said he; and Sapt's laugh left his opinion of my motives undisturbed.

"You should always trust a man," observed Sapt, fitting the key in the lock, "just as far as you must."

We went in and reached the dressing-room. Flinging open the door, we saw Fritz von Tarlenheim stretched, fully dressed, on the sofa. He seemed to have been sleeping, but our entry woke him. He leapt to his feet, gave one glance at me, and with a joyful cry, threw himself on his knees before me.

"Thank God, sire! thank God, you're safe!" he cried, stretching his hand up to catch hold of mine.

I confess that I was moved. This King, whatever his faults, made people love him. For a moment I could not bear to speak or break the poor fellow's illusion. But tough old Sapt had no such feeling. He slapped his hand on his thigh delightedly.

"Bravo, lad!" cried he. "We shall do!"

Fritz looked up in bewilderment. I held out my hand.

"You're wounded, sire!" he exclaimed.

"It's only a scratch," said I, "but—" I paused.

He rose to his feet with a bewildered air. Holding my hand, he looked me up and down, and down and up. Then suddenly he dropped my hand and reeled back.

"Where's the King? Where's the King?" he cried.

"Hush, you fool!" hissed Sapt. "Not so loud! Here's the King!"

A knock sounded on the door. Sapt seized me by the hand.

"Here, quick, to the bedroom! Off with your cap and boots. Get into bed. Cover everything up."

I did as I was bid. A moment later Sapt looked in, nodded, grinned, and introduced an extremely smart and deferential young gentleman, who came up to my bedside, bowing again and again, and informed me that he was of the household of the Princess Flavia, and that her Royal Highness had sent him especially to enquire how the King's health was after the fatigues which his Majesty had undergone yesterday.

"My best thanks, sir, to my cousin," said I; "and tell her Royal Highness that I was never better in my life."

"The King," added old Sapt (who, I began to find, loved a good lie for its own sake), "has slept without a break all night."

The young gentleman (he reminded me of "Osric" in Hamlet) bowed himself out again. The farce was over, and Fritz von Tarlenheim's pale face recalled us to reality—though, in faith, the farce had to be reality for us now.

"Is the King dead?" he whispered.

"Please God, no," said I. "But he's in the hands of Black Michael!"

CHAPTER 8

A Fair Cousin and a Dark Brother

A real king's life is perhaps a hard one; but a pretended king's is, I warrant, much harder. On the next day, Sapt instructed me in my duties—what I ought to do and what I ought to know—for three hours; then I snatched breakfast, with Sapt still opposite me, telling me that the King always took white wine in the morning and was known to detest all highly seasoned dishes. Then came the Chancellor, for another three hours; and to him I had to explain that the hurt to my finger (we turned that bullet to happy account) prevented me from writing— whence arose great to-do, hunting of precedents and so forth, ending in my "making my mark," and the Chancellor attesting it with a superfluity of solemn oaths. Then the French ambassador was introduced, to present his credentials; here my ignorance was of no importance, as the King would have been equally raw to the business (we worked through the whole corps diplomatique in the next few days, a demise of the Crown necessitating all this bother).

Then, at last, I was left alone. I called my new servant (we had chosen, to succeed poor Josef, a young man who had never known the King), had a brandy-and-soda brought to me, and observed to Sapt that I trusted that I might now have a rest. Fritz von Tarlenheim was standing by.

"By heaven!" he cried, "we waste time. Aren't we going to throw Black Michael by the heels?"

"Gently, my son, gently," said Sapt, knitting his brows. "It would be a pleasure, but it might cost us dear. Would Michael fall and leave the King alive?"

"And," I suggested, "while the King is here in Strelsau, on his throne, what grievance has he against his dear brother Michael?"

"Are we to do nothing, then?"

"We're to do nothing stupid," growled Sapt.

"In fact, Fritz," said I, "I am reminded of a situation in one of our English plays—The Critic—have you heard of it? Or, if you like, of two men, each covering the other with a revolver. For I can't expose Michael without exposing myself—"

"And the King," put in Sapt.

"And, hang me if Michael won't expose himself, if he tries to expose me!"

"It's very pretty," said old Sapt.

"If I'm found out," I pursued, "I will make a clean breast of it, and fight it out with the duke; but at present I'm waiting for a move from him."

"He'll kill the King," said Fritz.

"Not he," said Sapt.

"Half of the Six are in Strelsau," said Fritz.

"Only half? You're sure?" asked Sapt eagerly.

"Yes—only half."

"Then the King's alive, for the other three are guarding him!" cried Sapt.

"Yes—you're right!" exclaimed Fritz, his face brightening. "If the King were dead and buried, they'd all be here with Michael. You know Michael's back, colonel?"

"I know, curse him!"

"Gentlemen, gentlemen," said I, "who are the Six?"

"I think you'll make their acquaintance soon," said Sapt. "They are six gentlemen whom Michael maintains in his household: they belong to him body and soul. There are three Ruritanians; then there's a Frenchman, a Belgian, and one of your countrymen."

"They'd all cut a throat if Michael told them," said Fritz.

"Perhaps they'll cut mine," I suggested.

"Nothing more likely," agreed Sapt. "Who are here, Fritz?"

"De Gautet, Bersonin, and Detchard."

"The foreigners! It's as plain as a pikestaff. He's brought them, and left the Ruritanians with the King; that's because he wants to commit the Ruritanians as deep as he can."

"They were none of them among our friends at the lodge, then?" I asked.

"I wish they had been," said Sapt wistfully. "They had been, not six, but four, by now."

I had already developed one attribute of royalty—a feeling that I need not reveal all my mind or my secret designs even to my intimate friends. I had fully resolved on my course of action. I meant to make myself as popular as I could, and at the same time to show no disfavour to Michael. By these means I hoped to allay the hostility of his adherents, and make it appear, if an open conflict came about, that he was ungrateful and not oppressed.

Yet an open conflict was not what I hoped for.

The King's interest demanded secrecy; and while secrecy lasted, I had a fine game to play in Strelsau, Michael should not grow stronger for delay!

I ordered my horse, and, attended by Fritz von Tarlenheim, rode in the grand new avenue of the Royal Park, returning all the salutes which I received with punctilious politeness. Then I rode through a few of the streets, stopped and bought flowers of a pretty girl, paying her with a piece of gold; and then, having attracted the desired amount of attention (for I had a trail of half a thousand people after me), I rode to the residence of the Princess Flavia, and asked if she would receive me. This step created much interest, and was met with shouts of approval. The princess was very popular, and the Chancellor himself had not scrupled to hint to me that the more I pressed my suit, and the more rapidly I brought it to a prosperous conclusion, the stronger should I be in the affection of my subjects. The Chancellor, of course, did not understand the difficulties which lay in the way of following his loyal and excellent advice. However, I thought I could do no harm by calling; and in this view Fritz supported me with a cordiality that surprised me, until he confessed that he also had his motives for liking a visit to the princess's house, which motive was no other than a great desire to see the princess's lady-in-waiting and bosom friend, the Countess Helga von Strofzin.

Etiquette seconded Fritz's hopes. While I was ushered into the princess's room, he remained with the countess in the ante-chamber: in spite of the people and servants who were hanging about, I doubt not that they managed a tete-a-tete; but I had no leisure to think of them, for I was playing the most delicate move in all my difficult game. I had to keep the princess devoted to me—and yet indifferent to me: I had to show affection for her—and not feel it. I had to make love for another, and that to a girl who—princess or no princess—was the most beautiful I had ever seen. Well, I braced myself to the task, made no easier by the charming embarrassment with which I was received. How I succeeded in carrying out my programme will appear hereafter.

"You are gaining golden laurels," she said. "You are like the prince in Shakespeare who was transformed by becoming king. But I'm forgetting you are King, sire."

"I ask you to speak nothing but what your heart tells you—and to call me nothing but my name."

She looked at me for a moment.

"Then I'm glad and proud, Rudolf," said she. "Why, as I told you, your very face is changed."

I acknowledged the compliment, but I disliked the topic; so I said:

"My brother is back, I hear. He made an excursion, didn't he?"

"Yes, he is here," she said, frowning a little.

"He can't stay long from Strelsau, it seems," I observed, smiling. "Well, we are all glad to see him. The nearer he is, the better."

The princess glanced at me with a gleam of amusement in her eyes.

"Why, cousin? Is it that you can—?"

"See better what he's doing? Perhaps," said I. "And why are you glad?"

"I didn't say I was glad," she answered.

"Some people say so for you."

"There are many insolent people," she said, with delightful haughtiness.

"Possibly you mean that I am one?"

"Your Majesty could not be," she said, curtseying in feigned deference, but adding, mischievously, after a pause: "Unless, that is—"

"Well, unless what?"

"Unless you tell me that I mind a snap of my fingers where the Duke of Strelsau is."

Really, I wished that I had been the King.

"You don't care where cousin Michael—"

"Ah, cousin Michael! I call him the Duke of Strelsau."

"You call him Michael when you meet him?"

"Yes—by the orders of your father."

"I see. And now by mine?"

"If those are your orders."

"Oh, decidedly! We must all be pleasant to our dear Michael."

"You order me to receive his friends, too, I suppose?"

"The Six?"

"You call them that, too?"

"To be in the fashion, I do. But I order you to receive no one unless you like."

"Except yourself?"

"I pray for myself. I could not order."

As I spoke, there came a cheer from the street. The princess ran to the window.

"It is he!" she cried. "It is—the Duke of Strelsau!"

I smiled, but said nothing. She returned to her seat. For a few moments we sat in silence. The noise outside subsided, but I heard the tread of feet in the ante-room. I began to talk on general subjects. This went on for some minutes. I wondered what had become of Michael, but it did not seem to be for me to interfere. All at once, to my great surprise, Flavia, clasping her hands asked in an agitated voice:

"Are you wise to make him angry?"

"What? Who? How am I making him angry?"

"Why, by keeping him waiting."

"My dear cousin, I don't want to keep him—"

"Well, then, is he to come in?"

"Of course, if you wish it."

She looked at me curiously.

"How funny you are," she said. "Of course no one could be announced while I was with you."

Here was a charming attribute of royalty!

28

"An excellent etiquette!" I cried. "But I had clean forgotten it; and if I were alone with someone else, couldn't you be announced?"

"You know as well as I do. I could be, because I am of the Blood;" and she still looked puzzled.

"I never could remember all these silly rules," said I, rather feebly, as I inwardly cursed Fritz for not posting me up. "But I'll repair my fault."

I jumped up, flung open the door, and advanced into the ante-room. Michael was sitting at a table, a heavy frown on his face. Everyone else was standing, save that impudent young dog Fritz, who was lounging easily in an armchair, and flirting with the Countess Helga. He leapt up as I entered, with a deferential alacrity that lent point to his former nonchalance. I had no difficulty in understanding that the duke might not like young Fritz.

I held out my hand, Michael took it, and I embraced him. Then I drew him with me into the inner room.

"Brother," I said, "if I had known you were here, you should not have waited a moment before I asked the princess to permit me to bring you to her."

He thanked me, but coldly. The man had many qualities, but he could not hide his feelings. A mere stranger could have seen that he hated me, and hated worse to see me with Princess Flavia; yet I am persuaded that he tried to conceal both feelings, and, further, that he tried to persuade me that he believed I was verily the King. I did not know, of course; but, unless the King were an impostor, at once cleverer and more audacious than I (and I began to think something of myself in that role), Michael could not believe that. And, if he didn't, how he must have loathed paying me deference, and hearing my "Michael" and my "Flavia!"

"Your hand is hurt, sire," he observed, with concern.

"Yes, I was playing a game with a mongrel dog" (I meant to stir him), "and you know, brother, such have uncertain tempers."

He smiled sourly, and his dark eyes rested on me for a moment.

"But is there no danger from the bite?" cried Flavia anxiously.

"None from this," said I. "If I gave him a chance to bite deeper, it would be different, cousin."

"But surely he has been destroyed?" said she.

"Not yet. We're waiting to see if his bite is harmful."

"And if it is?" asked Michael, with his sour smile.

"He'll be knocked on the head, brother," said I.

"You won't play with him any more?" urged Flavia.

"Perhaps I shall."

"He might bite again."

"Doubtless he'll try," said I, smiling.

Then, fearing Michael would say something which I must appear to resent (for, though I might show him my hate, I must seem to be full of favour), I began to compliment him on the magnificent condition of his regiment, and of their loyal greeting to me on the day of my coronation. Thence I passed to a rapturous description of the hunting-lodge which he had lent me. But he rose suddenly to his feet. His temper was failing him, and, with an excuse, he said farewell. However, as he reached the door he stopped, saying:

"Three friends of mine are very anxious to have the honour of being presented to you, sire. They are here in the ante-chamber."

I joined him directly, passing my arm through his. The look on his face was honey to me. We entered the ante-chamber in fraternal fashion. Michael beckoned, and three men came forward.

"These gentlemen," said Michael, with a stately courtesy which, to do him justice, he could assume with perfect grace and ease, "are the loyalest and most devoted of your Majesty's servants, and are my very faithful and attached friends."

"On the last ground as much as the first," said I, "I am very pleased to see them."

29

They came one by one and kissed my hand—De Gautet, a tall lean fellow, with hair standing straight up and waxed moustache; Bersonin, the Belgian, a portly man of middle height with a bald head (though he was not far past thirty); and last, the Englishman, Detchard, a narrow-faced fellow, with close-cut fair hair and a bronzed complexion. He was a finely made man, broad in the shoulder and slender in the hips. A good fighter, but a crooked customer, I put him down for. I spoke to him in English, with a slight foreign accent, and I swear the fellow smiled, though he hid the smile in an instant.

"So Mr. Detchard is in the secret," thought I.

Having got rid of my dear brother and his friends, I returned to make my adieu to my cousin. She was standing at the door. I bade her farewell, taking her hand in mine.

"Rudolf," she said, very low, "be careful, won't you?"

"Of what?"

"You know—I can't say. But think what your life is to—"

"Well to—?"

"To Ruritania."

Was I right to play the part, or wrong to play the part? I know not: evil lay both ways, and I dared not tell her the truth.

"Only to Ruritania?" I asked softly.

A sudden flush spread over her incomparable face.

"To your friends, too," she said.

"Friends?"

"And to your cousin," she whispered, "and loving servant."

I could not speak. I kissed her hand, and went out cursing myself.

Outside I found Master Fritz, quite reckless of the footmen, playing at cat's-cradle with the Countess Helga.

"Hang it!" said he, "we can't always be plotting. Love claims his share."

"I'm inclined to think he does," said I; and Fritz, who had been by my side, dropped respectfully behind.

CHAPTER 9

A New Use for a Tea-table

If I were to detail the ordinary events of my daily life at this time, they might prove instructive to people who are not familiar with the inside of palaces; if I revealed some of the secrets I learnt, they might prove of interest to the statesmen of Europe. I intend to do neither of these things. I should be between the Scylla of dullness and the Charybdis of indiscretion, and I feel that I had far better confine myself strictly to the underground drama which was being played beneath the surface of Ruritanian politics. I need only say that the secret of my imposture defied detection. I made mistakes. I had bad minutes: it needed all the tact and graciousness whereof I was master to smooth over some apparent lapses of memory and unmindfulness of old acquaintances of which I was guilty. But I escaped, and I attribute my escape, as I have said before, most of all, to the very audacity of the enterprise. It is my belief that, given the necessary physical likeness, it was far easier to pretend to be King of Ruritania than it would have been to personate my next-door neighbour. One day Sapt came into my room. He threw me a letter, saying:

"That's for you—a woman's hand, I think. But I've some news for you first."

"What's that?"

"The King's at the Castle of Zenda," said he.

"How do you know?"

"Because the other half of Michael's Six are there. I had enquiries made, and they're all there—Lauengram, Krafstein, and young Rupert Hentzau: three rogues, too, on my honour, as fine as live in Ruritania."

"Well?"

"Well, Fritz wants you to march to the Castle with horse, foot, and artillery."

"And drag the moat?" I asked.

"That would be about it," grinned Sapt, "and we shouldn't find the King's body then."

"You think it's certain he's there?"

"Very probable. Besides the fact of those three being there, the drawbridge is kept up, and no one goes in without an order from young Hentzau or Black Michael himself. We must tie Fritz up."

"I'll go to Zenda," said I.

"You're mad."

"Some day."

"Oh, perhaps. You'll very likely stay there though, if you do."

"That may be, my friend," said I carelessly.

"His Majesty looks sulky," observed Sapt. "How's the love affair?"

"Damn you, hold your tongue!" I said.

He looked at me for a moment, then he lit his pipe. It was quite true that I was in a bad temper, and I went on perversely:

"Wherever I go, I'm dogged by half a dozen fellows."

"I know you are; I send 'em," he replied composedly.

"What for?"

"Well," said Sapt, puffing away, "it wouldn't be exactly inconvenient for Black Michael if you disappeared. With you gone, the old game that we stopped would be played—or he'd have a shot at it."

"I can take care of myself."

"De Gautet, Bersonin, and Detchard are in Strelsau; and any one of them, lad, would cut your throat as readily—as readily as I would Black Michael's, and a deal more treacherously. What's the letter?"

I opened it and read it aloud:

"If the King desires to know what it deeply concerns the King to know, let him do as this letter bids him. At the end of the New Avenue there stands a house in large grounds. The house has a portico, with a statue of a nymph on it. A wall encloses the garden; there is a gate in the wall at the back. At twelve o'clock tonight, if the King enters alone by that gate, turns to the right, and walks twenty yards, he will find a summerhouse, approached by a flight of six steps. If he mounts and enters, he will find someone who will tell him what touches most dearly his life and his throne. This is written by a faithful friend. He must be alone. If he neglects the invitation his life will be in danger. Let him show this to no one, or he will ruin a woman who loves him: Black Michael does not pardon."

"No," observed Sapt, as I ended, "but he can dictate a very pretty letter."

I had arrived at the same conclusion, and was about to throw the letter away, when I saw there was more writing on the other side.

"Hallo! there's some more."

"If you hesitate," the writer continued, "consult Colonel Sapt—"

"Eh," exclaimed that gentleman, genuinely astonished. "Does she take me for a greater fool than you?"

I waved to him to be silent.

"Ask him what woman would do most to prevent the duke from marrying his cousin, and therefore most to prevent him becoming king? And ask if her name begins with—A?"

I sprang to my feet. Sapt laid down his pipe.

"Antoinette de Mauban, by heaven!" I cried.

"How do you know?" asked Sapt.

I told him what I knew of the lady, and how I knew it. He nodded.

"It's so far true that she's had a great row with Michael," said he, thoughtfully.

"If she would, she could be useful," I said.

"I believe, though, that Michael wrote that letter."

"So do I, but I mean to know for certain. I shall go, Sapt."

"No, I shall go," said he.

"You may go as far as the gate."

"I shall go to the summer-house."

"I'm hanged if you shall!"

I rose and leant my back against the mantelpiece.

"Sapt, I believe in that woman, and I shall go."

"I don't believe in any woman," said Sapt, "and you shan't go."

"I either go to the summer-house or back to England," said I.

Sapt began to know exactly how far he could lead or drive, and when he must follow.

"We're playing against time," I added. "Every day we leave the King where he is there is fresh risk. Every day I masquerade like this, there is fresh risk. Sapt, we must play high; we must force the game."

"So be it," he said, with a sigh.

To cut the story short, at half-past eleven that night Sapt and I mounted our horses. Fritz was again left on guard, our destination not being revealed to him. It was a very dark night. I wore no sword, but I carried a revolver, a long knife, and a bull's-eye lantern. We arrived outside the gate. I dismounted. Sapt held out his hand.

"I shall wait here," he said. "If I hear a shot, I'll—"

"Stay where you are; it's the King's only chance. You mustn't come to grief too."

"You're right, lad. Good luck!"

I pressed the little gate. It yielded, and I found myself in a wild sort of shrubbery. There was a grass-grown path and, turning to the right as I had been bidden, I followed it cautiously. My lantern was closed, the revolver was in my hand. I heard not a sound. Presently a large dark object loomed out of the gloom ahead of me. It was the summer-house. Reaching the steps, I mounted them and found myself confronted by a weak, rickety wooden door, which hung upon the latch. I pushed it open and walked in. A woman flew to me and seized my hand.

"Shut the door," she whispered.

I obeyed and turned the light of my lantern on her. She was in evening dress, arrayed very sumptuously, and her dark striking beauty was marvellously displayed in the glare of the bull's-eye. The summer-house was a bare little room, furnished only with a couple of chairs and a small iron table, such as one sees in a tea garden or an open-air cafe.

"Don't talk," she said. "We've no time. Listen! I know you, Mr. Rassendyll. I wrote that letter at the duke's orders."

"So I thought," said I.

"In twenty minutes three men will be here to kill you."

"Three—the three?"

"Yes. You must be gone by then. If not, tonight you'll be killed—"

"Or they will."

"Listen, listen! When you're killed, your body will be taken to a low quarter of the town. It will be found there. Michael will at once arrest all your friends—Colonel Sapt and Captain von Tarlenheim first—proclaim a state of siege in Strelsau, and send a messenger to Zenda. The other three will murder the King in the Castle, and the duke will proclaim either himself or the princess—himself, if he is strong enough. Anyhow, he'll marry her, and become king in fact, and soon in name. Do you see?"

"It's a pretty plot. But why, madame, do you—?"

"Say I'm a Christian—or say I'm jealous. My God! shall I see him marry her? Now go; but remember—this is what I have to tell you—that never, by night or by day, are you safe. Three men follow you as a guard. Is it not so? Well, three follow them; Michael's three are never two hundred yards from you. Your life is not worth a moment if ever they find you alone. Now go. Stay, the gate will be guarded by now. Go down softly, go past the summer-house, on for a hundred yards, and you'll find a ladder against the wall. Get over it, and fly for your life."

"And you?" I asked.

"I have my game to play too. If he finds out what I have done, we shall not meet again. If not, I may yet—But never mind. Go at once."

"But what will you tell him?"

"That you never came—that you saw through the trick."

I took her hand and kissed it.

"Madame," said I, "you have served the King well tonight. Where is he in the Castle?"

She sank her voice to a fearful whisper. I listened eagerly.

"Across the drawbridge you come to a heavy door; behind that lies—Hark! What's that?"

There were steps outside.

"They're coming! They're too soon! Heavens! they're too soon!" and she turned pale as death.

"They seem to me," said I, "to be in the nick of time."

"Close your lantern. See, there's a chink in the door. Can you see them?"

I put my eye to the chink. On the lowest step I saw three dim figures. I cocked my revolver. Antoinette hastily laid her hand on mine.

"You may kill one," said she. "But what then?"

A voice came from outside—a voice that spoke perfect English.

"Mr. Rassendyll," it said.

I made no answer.

"We want to talk to you. Will you promise not to shoot till we've done?"

"Have I the pleasure of addressing Mr. Detchard?" I said.

"Never mind names."

"Then let mine alone."

"All right, sire. I've an offer for you."

I still had my eye to the chink. The three had mounted two steps more; three revolvers pointed full at the door.

"Will you let us in? We pledge our honour to observe the truce."

"Don't trust them," whispered Antoinette.

"We can speak through the door," said I.

"But you might open it and fire," objected Detchard; "and though we should finish you, you might finish one of us. Will you give your honour not to fire while we talk?"

"Don't trust them," whispered Antoinette again.

A sudden idea struck me. I considered it for a moment. It seemed feasible.

"I give my honour not to fire before you do," said I; "but I won't let you in. Stand outside and talk."

"That's sensible," he said.

The three mounted the last step, and stood just outside the door. I laid my ear to the chink. I could hear no words, but Detchard's head was close to that of the taller of his companions (De Gautet, I guessed).

"H'm! Private communications," thought I. Then I said aloud:

"Well, gentlemen, what's the offer?"

"A safe-conduct to the frontier, and fifty thousand pounds English."

"No, no," whispered Antoinette in the lowest of whispers. "They are treacherous."

"That seems handsome," said I, reconnoitering through the chink. They were all close together, just outside the door now.

I had probed the hearts of the ruffians, and I did not need Antoinette's warning. They meant to "rush" me as soon as I was engaged in talk.

"Give me a minute to consider," said I; and I thought I heard a laugh outside.

I turned to Antoinette.

"Stand up close to the wall, out of the line of fire from the door," I whispered.

"What are you going to do?" she asked in fright.

"You'll see," said I.

I took up the little iron table. It was not very heavy for a man of my strength, and I held it by the legs. The top, protruding in front of me, made a complete screen for my head and body. I fastened my closed lantern to my belt and put my revolver in a handy pocket. Suddenly I saw the door move ever so slightly—perhaps it was the wind, perhaps it was a hand trying it outside.

I drew back as far as I could from the door, holding the table in the position that I have described. Then I called out:

"Gentlemen, I accept your offer, relying on your honour. If you will open the door—"

"Open it yourself," said Detchard.

"It opens outwards," said I. "Stand back a little, gentlemen, or I shall hit you when I open it."

I went and fumbled with the latch. Then I stole back to my place on tiptoe.

"I can't open it!" I cried. "The latch has caught."

"Tut! I'll open it!" cried Detchard. "Nonsense, Bersonin, why not? Are you afraid of one man?"

I smiled to myself. An instant later the door was flung back. The gleam of a lantern showed me the three close together outside, their revolvers levelled. With a shout, I charged at my utmost pace across the summer-house and through the doorway. Three shots rang out and battered into my shield. Another moment, and I leapt out and the table caught them full and square, and in a tumbling, swearing, struggling mass, they and I and that brave table, rolled down the steps of the summerhouse to the ground below. Antoinette de Mauban shrieked, but I rose to my feet, laughing aloud.

De Gautet and Bersonin lay like men stunned. Detchard was under the table, but, as I rose, he pushed it from him and fired again. I raised my revolver and took a snap shot; I heard him curse, and then I ran like a hare, laughing as I went, past the summer-house and along by the wall. I heard steps behind me, and turning round I fired again for luck. The steps ceased.

"Please God," said I, "she told me the truth about the ladder!" for the wall was high and topped with iron spikes.

Yes, there it was. I was up and over in a minute. Doubling back, I saw the horses; then I heard a shot. It was Sapt. He had heard us, and was battling and raging with the locked gate, hammering it and firing into the keyhole like a man possessed. He had quite forgotten that he was not to take part in the fight. Whereat I laughed again, and said, as I clapped him on the shoulder:

"Come home to bed, old chap. I've got the finest tea-table story that ever you heard!"

He started and cried: "You're safe!" and wrung my hand. But a moment later he added: "And what the devil are you laughing at?"

"Four gentlemen round a tea-table," said I, laughing still, for it had been uncommonly ludicrous to see the formidable three altogether routed and scattered with no more deadly weapon than an ordinary tea-table.

Moreover, you will observe that I had honourably kept my word, and not fired till they did.

CHAPTER 10

A Great Chance for a Villain

It was the custom that the Prefect of Police should send every afternoon a report to me on the condition of the capital and the feeling of the people: the document included also an account of the movements of any persons whom the police had received instructions to watch. Since I had been in Strelsau, Sapt had been in the habit of reading the report and telling me any items of interest which it might contain. On the day after my adventure in the summer-house, he came in as I was playing a hand of ecarte with Fritz von Tarlenheim.

"The report is rather full of interest this afternoon," he observed, sitting down.

"Do you find," I asked, "any mention of a certain fracas?"

He shook his head with a smile.

"I find this first," he said: "'His Highness the Duke of Strelsau left the city (so far as it appears, suddenly), accompanied by several of his household. His destination is believed to be the Castle of Zenda, but the party travelled by road and not by train. MM De Gautet, Bersonin, and Detchard followed an hour later, the last-named carrying his arm in a sling. The cause of his wound is not known, but it is suspected that he has fought a duel, probably incidental to a love affair.'"

"That is remotely true," I observed, very well pleased to find that I had left my mark on the fellow.

"Then we come to this," pursued Sapt: "'Madame de Mauban, whose movements have been watched according to instructions, left by train at midday. She took a ticket for Dresden—'"

"It's an old habit of hers," said I.

"'The Dresden train stops at Zenda.' An acute fellow, this. And finally listen to this: 'The state of feeling in the city is not satisfactory. The King is much criticized' (you know, he's told to be quite frank) 'for taking no steps about his marriage. From enquiries among the entourage of the Princess Flavia, her Royal Highness is believed to be deeply offended by the remissness of his Majesty. The common people are coupling her name with that of the Duke of Strelsau, and the duke gains much popularity from the suggestion.' I have caused the announcement that the King gives a ball tonight in honour of the princess to be widely diffused, and the effect is good."

"That is news to me," said I.

"Oh, the preparations are all made!" laughed Fritz. "I've seen to that."

Sapt turned to me and said, in a sharp, decisive voice:

"You must make love to her tonight, you know."

"I think it is very likely I shall, if I see her alone," said I. "Hang it, Sapt, you don't suppose I find it difficult?"

Fritz whistled a bar or two; then he said: "You'll find it only too easy. Look here, I hate telling you this, but I must. The Countess Helga told me that the princess had become most attached to the King. Since the coronation, her feelings have undergone a marked development. It's quite true that she is deeply wounded by the King's apparent neglect."

"Here's a kettle of fish!" I groaned.

"Tut, tut!" said Sapt. "I suppose you've made pretty speeches to a girl before now? That's all she wants."

Fritz, himself a lover, understood better my distress. He laid his hand on my shoulder, but said nothing.

"I think, though," pursued that cold-blooded old Sapt, "that you'd better make your offer tonight."

"Good heavens!"

"Or, any rate, go near it: and I shall send a 'semi-official' to the papers."

"I'll do nothing of the sort—no more will you!" said I. "I utterly refuse to take part in making a fool of the princess."

Sapt looked at me with his small keen eyes. A slow cunning smile passed over his face.

"All right, lad, all right," said he. "We mustn't press you too hard. Soothe her down a bit, if you can, you know. Now for Michael!"

"Oh, damn Michael!" said I. "He'll do tomorrow. Here, Fritz, come for a stroll in the garden."

Sapt at once yielded. His rough manner covered a wonderful tact—and as I came to recognize more and more, a remarkable knowledge of human nature. Why did he urge me so little about the princess? Because he knew that her beauty and my ardour would carry me further than all his arguments—and that the less I thought about the thing, the more likely was I to do it. He must have seen the unhappiness he might bring on the princess; but that went for nothing with him. Can I say, confidently, that he was wrong? If the King were restored, the princess must turn to him, either knowing or not knowing the change. And if the King were not restored to us? It was a subject that we had never yet spoken of. But I had an idea that, in such a case, Sapt meant to seat me on the throne of Ruritania for the term of my life. He would have set Satan himself there sooner than that pupil of his, Black Michael.

The ball was a sumptuous affair. I opened it by dancing a quadrille with Flavia: then I waltzed with her. Curious eyes and eager whispers attended us. We went in to supper; and, half way through, I, half mad by then, for her glance had answered mine, and her quick breathing met my stammered sentences—I rose in my place before all the brilliant crowd, and taking the Red Rose that I wore, flung the ribbon with its jewelled badge round her neck. In a tumult of applause I sat down: I saw Sapt smiling over his wine, and Fritz frowning. The rest of the meal passed in silence; neither Flavia nor I could speak. Fritz touched me on the shoulder, and I rose, gave her my arm, and walked down the hall into a little room, where coffee was served to us. The gentlemen and ladies in attendance withdrew, and we were alone.

The little room had French windows opening on the gardens. The night was fine, cool, and fragrant. Flavia sat down, and I stood opposite her. I was struggling with myself: if she had not looked at me, I believe that even then I should have won my fight. But suddenly, involuntarily, she gave me one brief glance—a glance of question, hurriedly turned aside; a blush that the question had ever come spread over her cheek, and she caught her breath. Ah, if you had seen her! I forgot the King in Zenda. I forgot the King in Strelsau. She was a princess—and I an impostor. Do you think I remembered that? I threw myself on my knee and seized her hands in mine. I said nothing. Why should I? The soft sounds of the night set my wooing to a wordless melody, as I pressed my kisses on her lips.

She pushed me from her, crying suddenly:

"Ah! is it true? or is it only because you must?"

"It's true!" I said, in low smothered tones—"true that I love you more than life—or truth—or honour!"

She set no meaning to my words, treating them as one of love's sweet extravagances. She came close to me, and whispered:

"Oh, if you were not the King! Then I could show you how I love you! How is it that I love you now, Rudolf?"

"Now?"

"Yes—just lately. I—I never did before."

Pure triumph filled me. It was I—Rudolf Rassendyll—who had won her! I caught her round the waist.

"You didn't love me before?" I asked.

She looked up into my face, smiling, as she whispered:

"It must have been your Crown. I felt it first on the Coronation Day."

"Never before?" I asked eagerly.

She laughed low.

"You speak as if you would be pleased to hear me say 'Yes' to that," she said.

"Would 'Yes' be true?"

"Yes," I just heard her breathe, and she went on in an instant: "Be careful, Rudolf; be careful, dear. He will be mad now."

"What, Michael? If Michael were the worst—"

"What worse is there?"

There was yet a chance for me. Controlling myself with a mighty effort, I took my hands off her and stood a yard or two away. I remember now the note of the wind in the elm trees outside.

"If I were not the King," I began, "if I were only a private gentleman—"

Before I could finish, her hand was in mine.

"If you were a convict in the prison of Strelsau, you would be my King," she said.

And under my breath I groaned, "God forgive me!" and, holding her hand in mine, I said again:

"If I were not the King—"

"Hush, hush!" she whispered. "I don't deserve it—I don't deserve to be doubted. Ah, Rudolf! does a woman who marries without love look on the man as I look on you?"

And she hid her face from me.

For more than a minute we stood there together; and I, even with my arm about her, summoned up what honour and conscience her beauty and the toils that I was in had left me.

"Flavia," I said, in a strange dry voice that seemed not my own, "I am not—"

As I spoke—as she raised her eyes to me—there was a heavy step on the gravel outside, and a man appeared at the window. A little cry burst from Flavia, as she sprang back from me. My half-finished sentence died on my lips. Sapt stood there, bowing low, but with a stern frown on his face.

"A thousand pardons, sire," said he, "but his Eminence the Cardinal has waited this quarter of an hour to offer his respectful adieu to your Majesty."

I met his eye full and square; and I read in it an angry warning. How long he had been a listener I knew not, but he had come in upon us in the nick of time.

"We must not keep his Eminence waiting," said I.

But Flavia, in whose love there lay no shame, with radiant eyes and blushing face, held out her hand to Sapt. She said nothing, but no man could have missed her meaning, who had ever seen a woman in the exultation of love. A sour, yet sad, smile passed over the old soldier's face, and there was tenderness in his voice, as bending to kiss her hand, he said:

"In joy and sorrow, in good times and bad, God save your Royal Highness!"

He paused and added, glancing at me and drawing himself up to military erectness:

"But, before all comes the King—God save the King!"

And Flavia caught at my hand and kissed it, murmuring:

"Amen! Good God, Amen!"

We went into the ballroom again. Forced to receive adieus, I was separated from Flavia: everyone, when they left me, went to her. Sapt was out and in of the throng, and where he had been, glances, smiles, and whispers were rife. I doubted not that, true to his relentless purpose, he was spreading the news that he had learnt. To uphold the Crown and beat Black Michael—that was his one resolve. Flavia, myself—ay, and the real King in Zenda, were pieces in his game; and pawns have no business with passions. Not even at the walls of the Palace did he stop; for when at last I handed Flavia down the broad marble steps and into her carriage, there was a great crowd awaiting us, and we were welcomed with deafening cheers. What could I do? Had I spoken then, they would have refused to believe that I was not the King; they might have believed that the King had run mad. By Sapt's devices and my own ungoverned passion I had been forced on, and the way back had closed behind me; and the passion still drove me in the same direction as the devices seduced me. I faced all Strelsau that night as the King and the accepted suitor of the Princess Flavia.

At last, at three in the morning, when the cold light of dawning day began to steal in, I was in my dressing-room, and Sapt alone was with me. I sat like a man dazed, staring into the fire; he puffed at his pipe; Fritz was gone to bed, having almost refused to speak to me. On the table by me lay a rose; it had been in Flavia's dress, and, as we parted, she had kissed it and given it to me.

Sapt advanced his hand towards the rose, but, with a quick movement, I shut mine down upon it.

"That's mine," I said, "not yours—nor the King's either."

"We struck a good blow for the King tonight," said he.

I turned on him fiercely.

"What's to prevent me striking a blow for myself?" I said.

He nodded his head.

"I know what's in your mind," he said. "Yes, lad; but you're bound in honour."

"Have you left me any honour?"

"Oh, come, to play a little trick on a girl—"

"You can spare me that. Colonel Sapt, if you would not have me utterly a villain—if you would not have your King rot in Zenda, while Michael and I play for the great stake outside— You follow me?"

"Ay, I follow you."

"We must act, and quickly! You saw tonight—you heard—tonight—"

"I did," said he.

"Your cursed acuteness told you what I should do. Well, leave me here a week—and there's another problem for you. Do you find the answer?"

"Yes, I find it," he answered, frowning heavily. "But if you did that, you'd have to fight me first—and kill me."

"Well, and if I had—or a score of men? I tell you, I could raise all Strelsau on you in an hour, and choke you with your lies—yes, your mad lies—in your mouth."

"It's gospel truth," he said—"thanks to my advice you could."

"I could marry the princess, and send Michael and his brother together to—"

"I'm not denying it, lad," said he.

"Then, in God's name," I cried, stretching out my hands to him, "let us go to Zenda and crush this Michael and bring the King back to his own again." The old fellow stood and looked at me for full a minute.

"And the princess?" he said.

I bowed my head to meet my hands, and crushed the rose between my fingers and my lips.

I felt his hand on my shoulder, and his voice sounded husky as he whispered low in my ear: "Before God, you're the finest Elphberg of them all. But I have eaten of the King's bread, and I am the King's servant. Come, we will go to Zenda!"

And I looked up and caught him by the hand. And the eyes of both of us were wet.

CHAPTER 11

Hunting a Very Big Boar

The terrible temptation which was assailing me will now be understood. I would so force Michael's hand that he must kill the King. I was in a position to bid him defiance and tighten my grasp on the crown—not for its own sake, but because the King of Ruritania was to wed the Princess Flavia. What of Sapt and Fritz? Ah! but a man cannot be held to write down in cold blood the wild and black thoughts that storm his brain when an uncontrolled passion has battered a breach for them. Yet, unless he sets up as a saint, he need not hate himself for them. He is better employed, as it humbly seems to me, in giving thanks that power to resist was vouchsafed to him, than in fretting over wicked impulses which come unsought and extort an unwilling hospitality from the weakness of our nature.

It was a fine bright morning when I walked, unattended, to the princess's house, carrying a nosegay in my hand. Policy made excuses for love, and every attention that I paid her, while it riveted my own chains, bound closer to me the people of the great city, who worshipped her. I found Fritz's inamorata, the Countess Helga, gathering blooms in the garden for her mistress's wear, and prevailed on her to take mine in their place. The girl was rosy with happiness, for Fritz, in his turn, had not wasted his evening, and no dark shadow hung over his wooing, save the hatred which the Duke of Strelsau was known to bear him.

"And that," she said, with a mischievous smile, "your Majesty has made of no moment. Yes, I will take the flowers; shall I tell you, sire, what is the first thing the princess does with them?" We were talking on a broad terrace that ran along the back of the house, and a window above our heads stood open.

"Madame!" cried the countess merrily, and Flavia herself looked out. I bared my head and bowed. She wore a white gown, and her hair was loosely gathered in a knot. She kissed her hand to me, crying:

"Bring the King up, Helga; I'll give him some coffee."

The countess, with a gay glance, led the way, and took me into Flavia's morning-room. And, left alone, we greeted one another as lovers are wont. Then the princess laid two letters before me. One was from Black Michael—a most courteous request that she would honour him by spending a day at his Castle of Zenda, as had been her custom once a year in the summer, when the place and its gardens were in the height of their great beauty. I threw the letter down in disgust, and Flavia laughed at me. Then, growing grave again, she pointed to the other sheet.

"I don't know who that comes from," she said. "Read it."

I knew in a moment. There was no signature at all this time, but the handwriting was the same as that which had told me of the snare in the summer-house: it was Antoinette de Mauban's.

"I have no cause to love you," it ran, "but God forbid that you should fall into the power of the duke. Accept no invitations of his. Go nowhere without a large guard—a regiment is not too much to make you safe. Show this, if you can, to him who reigns in Strelsau."

"Why doesn't it say 'the King'?" asked Flavia, leaning over my shoulder, so that the ripple of her hair played on my cheek. "Is it a hoax?"

"As you value life, and more than life, my queen," I said, "obey it to the very letter. A regiment shall camp round your house today. See that you do not go out unless well guarded."

"An order, sire?" she asked, a little rebellious.

"Yes, an order, madame—if you love me."

"Ah!" she cried; and I could not but kiss her.

"You know who sent it?" she asked.

"I guess," said I. "It is from a good friend—and I fear, an unhappy woman. You must be ill, Flavia, and unable to go to Zenda. Make your excuses as cold and formal as you like."

"So you feel strong enough to anger Michael?" she said, with a proud smile.

"I'm strong enough for anything, while you are safe," said I.

Soon I tore myself away from her, and then, without consulting Sapt, I took my way to the house of Marshal Strakencz. I had seen something of the old general, and I liked and trusted him. Sapt was less enthusiastic, but I had learnt by now that Sapt was best pleased when he could do everything, and jealousy played some part in his views. As things were now, I had more work than Sapt and Fritz could manage, for they must come with me to Zenda, and I wanted a man to guard what I loved most in all the world, and suffer me to set about my task of releasing the King with a quiet mind.

The Marshal received me with most loyal kindness. To some extent, I took him into my confidence. I charged him with the care of the princess, looking him full and significantly in the face as I bade him let no one from her cousin the duke approach her, unless he himself were there and a dozen of his men with him.

"You may be right, sire," said he, shaking his grey head sadly. "I have known better men than the duke do worse things than that for love."

I could quite appreciate the remark, but I said:

"There's something beside love, Marshal. Love's for the heart; is there nothing my brother might like for his head?"

"I pray that you wrong him, sire."

"Marshal, I'm leaving Strelsau for a few days. Every evening I will send a courier to you. If for three days none comes, you will publish an order which I will give you, depriving Duke Michael of the governorship of Strelsau and appointing you in his place. You will declare a state of siege. Then you will send word to Michael that you demand an audience of the King—You follow me?"

"Ay, sire."

"—In twenty-four hours. If he does not produce the King" (I laid my hand on his knee), "then the King is dead, and you will proclaim the next heir. You know who that is?"

"The Princess Flavia."

"And swear to me, on your faith and honour and by the fear of the living God, that you will stand by her to the death, and kill that reptile, and seat her where I sit now."

"On my faith and honour, and by the fear of God, I swear it! And may Almighty God preserve your Majesty, for I think that you go on an errand of danger."

"I hope that no life more precious than mine may be demanded," said I, rising. Then I held out my hand to him.

"Marshal," I said, "in days to come, it may be—I know not—that you will hear strange things of the man who speaks to you now. Let him be what he may, and who he may, what say you of the manner in which he has borne himself as King in Strelsau?"

The old man, holding my hand, spoke to me, man to man.

"I have known many of the Elphbergs," said he, "and I have seen you. And, happen what may, you have borne yourself as a wise King and a brave man; ay, and you have proved as courteous a gentleman and as gallant a lover as any that have been of the House."

"Be that my epitaph," said I, "when the time comes that another sits on the throne of Ruritania."

"God send a far day, and may I not see it!" said he.

I was much moved, and the Marshal's worn face twitched. I sat down and wrote my order.

"I can hardly yet write," said I; "my finger is stiff still."

It was, in fact, the first time that I had ventured to write more than a signature; and in spite of the pains I had taken to learn the King's hand, I was not yet perfect in it.

"Indeed, sire," he said, "it differs a little from your ordinary handwriting. It is unfortunate, for it may lead to a suspicion of forgery."

"Marshal," said I, with a laugh, "what use are the guns of Strelsau, if they can't assuage a little suspicion?"

He smiled grimly, and took the paper.

"Colonel Sapt and Fritz von Tarlenheim go with me," I continued.

"You go to seek the duke?" he asked in a low tone.

"Yes, the duke, and someone else of whom I have need, and who is at Zenda," I replied.

"I wish I could go with you," he cried, tugging at his white moustache. "I'd like to strike a blow for you and your crown."

"I leave you what is more than my life and more than my crown," said I, "because you are the man I trust more than all other in Ruritania."

"I will deliver her to you safe and sound," said he, "and, failing that, I will make her queen."

We parted, and I returned to the Palace and told Sapt and Fritz what I had done. Sapt had a few faults to find and a few grumbles to utter. This was merely what I expected, for Sapt liked to be consulted beforehand, not informed afterwards; but on the whole he approved of my plans, and his spirits rose high as the hour of action drew nearer and nearer. Fritz, too, was ready; though he, poor fellow, risked more than Sapt did, for he was a lover, and his happiness hung in the scale. Yet how I envied him! For the triumphant issue which would crown him with happiness and unite him to his mistress, the success for which we were bound to hope and strive and struggle, meant to me sorrow more certain and greater than if I were doomed to fail. He understood something of this, for when we were alone (save for old Sapt, who was smoking at the other end of the room) he passed his arm through mine, saying:

"It's hard for you. Don't think I don't trust you; I know you have nothing but true thoughts in your heart."

But I turned away from him, thankful that he could not see what my heart held, but only be witness to the deeds that my hands were to do.

Yet even he did not understand, for he had not dared to lift his eyes to the Princess Flavia, as I had lifted mine.

Our plans were now all made, even as we proceeded to carry them out, and as they will hereafter appear. The next morning we were to start on the hunting excursion. I had made all arrangements for being absent, and now there was only one thing left to do—the hardest, the most heart-breaking. As evening fell, I drove through the busy streets to Flavia's residence. I was recognized as I went and heartily cheered. I played my part, and made shift to look the happy lover. In spite of my depression, I was almost amused at the coolness and delicate hauteur with which my sweet lover received me. She had heard that the King was leaving Strelsau on a hunting expedition.

"I regret that we cannot amuse your Majesty here in Strelsau," she said, tapping her foot lightly on the floor. "I would have offered you more entertainment, but I was foolish enough to think—"

"Well, what?" I asked, leaning over her.

"That just for a day or two after—after last night—you might be happy without much gaiety;" and she turned pettishly from me, as she added, "I hope the boars will be more engrossing."

"I'm going after a very big boar," said I; and, because I could not help it, I began to play with her hair, but she moved her head away.

"Are you offended with me?" I asked, in feigned surprise, for I could not resist tormenting her a little. I had never seen her angry, and every fresh aspect of her was a delight to me.

"What right have I to be offended? True, you said last night that every hour away from me was wasted. But a very big boar! that's a different thing."

"Perhaps the boar will hunt me," I suggested. "Perhaps, Flavia, he'll catch me."

She made no answer.

"You are not touched even by that danger?"

Still she said nothing; and I, stealing round, found her eyes full of tears.

"You weep for my danger?"

Then she spoke very low:

"This is like what you used to be; but not like the King—the King I—I have come to love!"

With a sudden great groan, I caught her to my heart.

"My darling!" I cried, forgetting everything but her, "did you dream that I left you to go hunting?"

"What then, Rudolf? Ah! you're not going—?"

"Well, it is hunting. I go to seek Michael in his lair."

She had turned very pale.

"So, you see, sweet, I was not so poor a lover as you thought me. I shall not be long gone."

"You will write to me, Rudolf?"

I was weak, but I could not say a word to stir suspicion in her.

41

"I'll send you all my heart every day," said I.

"And you'll run no danger?"

"None that I need not."

"And when will you be back? Ah, how long will it be!"

"When shall I be back?" I repeated.

"Yes, yes! Don't be long, dear, don't be long. I shan't sleep while you're away."

"I don't know when I shall be back," said I.

"Soon, Rudolf, soon?"

"God knows, my darling. But, if never—"

"Hush, hush!" and she pressed her lips to mine.

"If never," I whispered, "you must take my place; you'll be the only one of the House then. You must reign, and not weep for me."

For a moment she drew herself up like a very queen.

"Yes, I will!" she said. "I will reign. I will do my part though all my life will be empty and my heart dead; yet I'll do it!"

She paused, and sinking against me again, wailed softly.

"Come soon! come soon!"

Carried away, I cried loudly:

"As God lives, I—yes, I myself—will see you once more before I die!"

"What do you mean?" she exclaimed, with wondering eyes; but I had no answer for her, and she gazed at me with her wondering eyes.

I dared not ask her to forget, she would have found it an insult. I could not tell her then who and what I was. She was weeping, and I had but to dry her tears.

"Shall a man not come back to the loveliest lady in all the wide world?" said I. "A thousand Michaels should not keep me from you!"

She clung to me, a little comforted.

"You won't let Michael hurt you?"

"No, sweetheart."

"Or keep you from me?"

"No, sweetheart."

"Nor anyone else?"

And again I answered:

"No, sweetheart."

Yet there was one—not Michael—who, if he lived, must keep me from her; and for whose life I was going forth to stake my own. And his figure—the lithe, buoyant figure I had met in the woods of Zenda—the dull, inert mass I had left in the cellar of the hunting-lodge— seemed to rise, double-shaped, before me, and to come between us, thrusting itself in even where she lay, pale, exhausted, fainting, in my arms, and yet looking up at me with those eyes that bore such love as I have never seen, and haunt me now, and will till the ground closes over me—and (who knows?) perhaps beyond.

CHAPTER 12

I Receive a Visitor and Bait a Hook

About five miles from Zenda—on the opposite side from that on which the Castle is situated, there lies a large tract of wood. It is rising ground, and in the centre of the demesne, on the top of the hill, stands a fine modern chateau, the property of a distant kinsman of Fritz's, the Count Stanislas von Tarlenheim. Count Stanislas himself was a student and a recluse. He seldom visited the house, and had, on Fritz's request, very readily and courteously offered me its hospitality for myself and my party. This, then, was our destination; chosen ostensibly for the sake of the boar-hunting (for the wood was carefully preserved, and boars, once common all over Ruritania, were still to be found there in considerable numbers), really because it brought us within striking distance of the Duke of Strelsau's more magnificent dwelling on the other side of the town. A large party of servants, with horses and luggage, started early in the morning; we followed at midday, travelling by train for thirty miles, and then mounting our horses to ride the remaining distance to the chateau.

We were a gallant party. Besides Sapt and Fritz, I was accompanied by ten gentlemen: every one of them had been carefully chosen, and no less carefully sounded, by my two friends, and all were devotedly attached to the person of the King. They were told a part of the truth; the attempt on my life in the summer-house was revealed to them, as a spur to their loyalty and an incitement against Michael. They were also informed that a friend of the King's was suspected to be forcibly confined within the Castle of Zenda. His rescue was one of the objects of the expedition; but, it was added, the King's main desire was to carry into effect certain steps against his treacherous brother, as to the precise nature of which they could not at present be further enlightened. Enough that the King commanded their services, and would rely on their devotion when occasion arose to call for it. Young, well-bred, brave, and loyal, they asked no more: they were ready to prove their dutiful obedience, and prayed for a fight as the best and most exhilarating mode of showing it.

Thus the scene was shifted from Strelsau to the chateau of Tarlenheim and Castle of Zenda, which frowned at us across the valley. I tried to shift my thoughts also, to forget my love, and to bend all my energies to the task before me. It was to get the King out of the Castle alive. Force was useless: in some trick lay the chance; and I had already an inkling of what we must do. But I was terribly hampered by the publicity which attended my movements. Michael must know by now of my expedition; and I knew Michael too well to suppose that his eyes would be blinded by the feint of the boar-hunt. He would understand very well what the real quarry was. That, however, must be risked—that and all it might mean; for Sapt, no less than myself, recognized that the present state of things had become unendurable. And there was one thing that I dared to calculate on—not, as I now know, without warrant. It was this— that Black Michael would not believe that I meant well by the King. He could not appreciate—I will not say an honest man, for the thoughts of my own heart have been revealed—but a man acting honestly. He saw my opportunity as I had seen it, as Sapt had seen it; he knew the princess—nay (and I declare that a sneaking sort of pity for him invaded me), in his way he loved her; he would think that Sapt and Fritz could be bribed, so the bribe was large enough. Thinking thus, would he kill the King, my rival and my danger? Ay, verily, that he would, with as little compunction as he would kill a rat. But he would kill Rudolf Rassendyll first, if he could; and nothing but the certainty of being utterly damned by the release of the King alive and his restoration to the throne would drive him to throw away the trump card which he held in reserve to baulk the supposed game of the impudent impostor Rassendyll. Musing on all this as I rode along, I took courage.

Michael knew of my coming, sure enough. I had not been in the house an hour, when an imposing Embassy arrived from him. He did not quite reach the impudence of sending my would-be assassins, but he sent the other three of his famous Six—the three Ruritanian gentlemen—Lauengram, Krafstein, and Rupert Hentzau. A fine, strapping trio they were, splendidly horsed and admirably equipped. Young Rupert, who looked a dare-devil, and could not have been more than twenty-two or twenty-three, took the lead, and made us the neatest speech, wherein my devoted subject and loving brother Michael of Strelsau, prayed me to pardon him for not paying his addresses in person, and, further, for not putting his Castle at my disposal; the reason for both of these apparent derelictions being that he and several of his servants lay sick of scarlet fever, and were in a very sad, and also a very infectious state. So declared young Rupert with an insolent smile on his curling upper lip and a toss of his thick hair—he was a handsome villain, and the gossip ran that many a lady had troubled her heart for him already.

"If my brother has scarlet fever," said I, "he is nearer my complexion than he is wont to be, my lord. I trust he does not suffer?"

"He is able to attend to his affairs, sire."

"I hope all beneath your roof are not sick. What of my good friends, De Gautet, Bersonin, and Detchard? I heard the last had suffered a hurt."

Lauengram and Krafstein looked glum and uneasy, but young Rupert's smile grew broader. "He hopes soon to find a medicine for it, sire," he answered.

And I burst out laughing, for I knew what medicine Detchard longed for—it is called Revenge.

"You will dine with us, gentlemen?" I asked.

Young Rupert was profuse in apologies. They had urgent duties at the Castle.

"Then," said I, with a wave of my hand, "to our next meeting, gentlemen. May it make us better acquainted."

"We will pray your Majesty for an early opportunity," quoth Rupert airily; and he strode past Sapt with such jeering scorn on his face that I saw the old fellow clench his fist and scowl black as night.

For my part, if a man must needs be a knave, I would have him a debonair knave, and I liked Rupert Hentzau better than his long-faced, close-eyed companions. It makes your sin no worse, as I conceive, to do it a la mode and stylishly.

Now it was a curious thing that on this first night, instead of eating the excellent dinner my cooks had prepared for me, I must needs leave my gentlemen to eat it alone, under Sapt's presiding care, and ride myself with Fritz to the town of Zenda and a certain little inn that I knew of. There was little danger in the excursion; the evenings were long and light, and the road this side of Zenda well frequented. So off we rode, with a groom behind us. I muffled myself up in a big cloak.

"Fritz," said I, as we entered the town, "there's an uncommonly pretty girl at this inn."

"How do you know?" he asked.

"Because I've been there," said I.

"Since—?" he began.

"No. Before," said I.

"But they'll recognize you?"

"Well, of course they will. Now, don't argue, my good fellow, but listen to me. We're two gentlemen of the King's household, and one of us has a toothache. The other will order a private room and dinner, and, further, a bottle of the best wine for the sufferer. And if he be as clever a fellow as I take him for, the pretty girl and no other will wait on us."

"What if she won't?" objected Fritz.

"My dear Fritz," said I, "if she won't for you, she will for me."

We were at the inn. Nothing of me but my eyes was visible as I walked in. The landlady received us; two minutes later, my little friend (ever, I fear me, on the look-out for such guests as might prove amusing) made her appearance. Dinner and the wine were ordered. I sat down in the private room. A minute later Fritz came in.

"She's coming," he said.

"If she were not, I should have to doubt the Countess Helga's taste."

She came in. I gave her time to set the wine down—I didn't want it dropped. Fritz poured out a glass and gave it to me.

"Is the gentleman in great pain?" the girl asked, sympathetically.

"The gentleman is no worse than when he saw you last," said I, throwing away my cloak. She started, with a little shriek. Then she cried:

"It was the King, then! I told mother so the moment I saw his picture. Oh, sir, forgive me!"

"Faith, you gave me nothing that hurt much," said I.

"But the things we said!"

"I forgive them for the thing you did."

"I must go and tell mother."

"Stop," said I, assuming a graver air. "We are not here for sport tonight. Go and bring dinner, and not a word of the King being here."

She came back in a few minutes, looking grave, yet very curious.

"Well, how is Johann?" I asked, beginning my dinner.

"Oh, that fellow, sir—my lord King, I mean!"

"'Sir' will do, please. How is he?"

"We hardly see him now, sir."

"And why not?"

"I told him he came too often, sir," said she, tossing her head.

"So he sulks and stays away?"

"Yes, sir."

"But you could bring him back?" I suggested with a smile.

"Perhaps I could," said she.

"I know your powers, you see," said I, and she blushed with pleasure.

"It's not only that, sir, that keeps him away. He's very busy at the Castle."

"But there's no shooting on now."

"No, sir; but he's in charge of the house."

"Johann turned housemaid?"

The little girl was brimming over with gossip.

"Well, there are no others," said she. "There's not a woman there—not as a servant, I mean. They do say—but perhaps it's false, sir."

"Let's have it for what it's worth," said I.

"Indeed, I'm ashamed to tell you, sir."

"Oh, see, I'm looking at the ceiling."

"They do say there is a lady there, sir; but, except for her, there's not a woman in the place. And Johann has to wait on the gentlemen."

"Poor Johann! He must be overworked. Yet I'm sure he could find half an hour to come and see you."

"It would depend on the time, sir, perhaps."

"Do you love him?" I asked.

"Not I, sir."

"And you wish to serve the King?"

"Yes, sir."

"Then tell him to meet you at the second milestone out of Zenda tomorrow evening at ten o'clock. Say you'll be there and will walk home with him."

"Do you mean him harm, sir?"

"Not if he will do as I bid him. But I think I've told you enough, my pretty maid. See that you do as I bid you. And, mind, no one is to know that the King has been here."

I spoke a little sternly, for there is seldom harm in infusing a little fear into a woman's liking for you, and I softened the effect by giving her a handsome present. Then we dined, and, wrapping my cloak about my face, with Fritz leading the way, we went downstairs to our horses again.

It was but half-past eight, and hardly yet dark; the streets were full for such a quiet little place, and I could see that gossip was all agog. With the King on one side and the duke on the other, Zenda felt itself the centre of all Ruritania. We jogged gently through the town, but set our horses to a sharper pace when we reached the open country.

"You want to catch this fellow Johann?" asked Fritz.

45

"Ay, and I fancy I've baited the hook right. Our little Delilah will bring our Samson. It is not enough, Fritz, to have no women in a house, though brother Michael shows some wisdom there. If you want safety, you must have none within fifty miles."

"None nearer than Strelsau, for instance," said poor Fritz, with a lovelorn sigh.

We reached the avenue of the chateau, and were soon at the house. As the hoofs of our horses sounded on the gravel, Sapt rushed out to meet us.

"Thank God, you're safe!" he cried. "Have you seen anything of them?"

"Of whom?" I asked, dismounting.

He drew us aside, that the grooms might not hear.

"Lad," he said to me, "you must not ride about here, unless with half a dozen of us. You know among our men a tall young fellow, Bernenstein by name?"

I knew him. He was a fine strapping young man, almost of my height, and of light complexion.

"He lies in his room upstairs, with a bullet through his arm."

"The deuce he does!"

"After dinner he strolled out alone, and went a mile or so into the wood; and as he walked, he thought he saw three men among the trees; and one levelled a gun at him. He had no weapon, and he started at a run back towards the house. But one of them fired, and he was hit, and had much ado to reach here before he fainted. By good luck, they feared to pursue him nearer the house."

He paused and added:

"Lad, the bullet was meant for you."

"It is very likely," said I, "and it's first blood to brother Michael."

"I wonder which three it was," said Fritz.

"Well, Sapt," I said, "I went out tonight for no idle purpose, as you shall hear. But there's one thing in my mind."

"What's that?" he asked.

"Why this," I answered. "That I shall ill requite the very great honours Ruritania has done me if I depart from it leaving one of those Six alive—neither with the help of God, will I."

And Sapt shook my hand on that.

CHAPTER 13

An Improvement on Jacob's Ladder

In the morning of the day after that on which I swore my oath against the Six, I gave certain orders, and then rested in greater contentment than I had known for some time. I was at work; and work, though it cannot cure love, is yet a narcotic to it; so that Sapt, who grew feverish, marvelled to see me sprawling in an armchair in the sunshine, listening to one of my friends who sang me amorous songs in a mellow voice and induced in me a pleasing melancholy. Thus was I engaged when young Rupert Hentzau, who feared neither man nor devil, and rode through the demesne—where every tree might hide a marksman, for all he knew—as though it had been the park at Strelsau, cantered up to where I lay, bowing with burlesque deference, and craving private speech with me in order to deliver a message from the Duke of Strelsau. I made all withdraw, and then he said, seating himself by me:

"The King is in love, it seems?"

"Not with life, my lord," said I, smiling.

"It is well," he rejoined. "Come, we are alone, Rassendyll—"

I rose to a sitting posture.

"What's the matter?" he asked.

"I was about to call one of my gentlemen to bring your horse, my lord. If you do not know how to address the King, my brother must find another messenger."

"Why keep up the farce?" he asked, negligently dusting his boot with his glove.

"Because it is not finished yet; and meanwhile I'll choose my own name."

"Oh, so be it! Yet I spoke in love for you; for indeed you are a man after my own heart."

"Saving my poor honesty," said I, "maybe I am. But that I keep faith with men, and honour with women, maybe I am, my lord."

He darted a glance at me—a glance of anger.

"Is your mother dead?" said I.

"Ay, she's dead."

"She may thank God," said I, and I heard him curse me softly. "Well, what's the message?" I continued.

I had touched him on the raw, for all the world knew he had broken his mother's heart and flaunted his mistresses in her house; and his airy manner was gone for the moment.

"The duke offers you more than I would," he growled. "A halter for you, sire, was my suggestion. But he offers you safe-conduct across the frontier and a million crowns."

"I prefer your offer, my lord, if I am bound to one."

"You refuse?"

"Of course."

"I told Michael you would;" and the villain, his temper restored, gave me the sunniest of smiles. "The fact is, between ourselves," he continued, "Michael doesn't understand a gentleman."

I began to laugh.

"And you?" I asked.

"I do," he said. "Well, well, the halter be it."

"I'm sorry you won't live to see it," I observed.

"Has his Majesty done me the honour to fasten a particular quarrel on me?"

"I would you were a few years older, though."

"Oh, God gives years, but the devil gives increase," laughed he. "I can hold my own."

"How is your prisoner?" I asked.

"The K——?"

"Your prisoner."

"I forgot your wishes, sire. Well, he is alive."

He rose to his feet; I imitated him. Then, with a smile, he said:

"And the pretty princess? Faith, I'll wager the next Elphberg will be red enough, for all that Black Michael will be called his father."

I sprang a step towards him, clenching my hand. He did not move an inch, and his lip curled in insolent amusement.

"Go, while your skin's whole!" I muttered. He had repaid me with interest my hit about his mother.

Then came the most audacious thing I have known in my life. My friends were some thirty yards away. Rupert called to a groom to bring him his horse, and dismissed the fellow with a crown. The horse stood near. I stood still, suspecting nothing. Rupert made as though to mount; then he suddenly turned to me: his left hand resting in his belt, his right outstretched:

"Shake hands," he said.

I bowed, and did as he had foreseen—I put my hands behind me. Quicker than thought, his left hand darted out at me, and a small dagger flashed in the air; he struck me in the left shoulder—had I not swerved, it had been my heart. With a cry, I staggered back. Without touching the stirrup, he leapt upon his horse and was off like an arrow, pursued by cries and revolver shots—the last as useless as the first—and I sank into my chair, bleeding profusely, as I watched the devil's brat disappear down the long avenue. My friends surrounded me, and then I fainted.

I suppose that I was put to bed, and there lay, unconscious, or half conscious, for many hours; for it was night when I awoke to my full mind, and found Fritz beside me. I was weak and weary, but he bade me be of good cheer, saying that my wound would soon heal, and that meanwhile all had gone well, for Johann, the keeper, had fallen into the snare we had laid for him, and was even now in the house.

"And the queer thing is," pursued Fritz, "that I fancy he's not altogether sorry to find himself here. He seems to think that when Black Michael has brought off his coup, witnesses of how it was effected—saving, of course, the Six themselves—will not be at a premium."

This idea argued a shrewdness in our captive which led me to build hopes on his assistance. I ordered him to be brought in at once. Sapt conducted him, and set him in a chair by my bedside. He was sullen, and afraid; but, to say truth, after young Rupert's exploit, we also had our fears, and, if he got as far as possible from Sapt's formidable six-shooter, Sapt kept him as far as he could from me. Moreover, when he came in his hands were bound, but that I would not suffer.

I need not stay to recount the safeguards and rewards we promised the fellow—all of which were honourably observed and paid, so that he lives now in prosperity (though where I may not mention); and we were the more free inasmuch as we soon learnt that he was rather a weak man than a wicked, and had acted throughout this matter more from fear of the duke and of his own brother Max than for any love of what was done. But he had persuaded all of his loyalty; and though not in their secret counsels, was yet, by his knowledge of their dispositions within the Castle, able to lay bare before us the very heart of their devices. And here, in brief, is his story:

Below the level of the ground in the Castle, approached by a flight of stone steps which abutted on the end of the drawbridge, were situated two small rooms, cut out of the rock itself. The outer of the two had no windows, but was always lighted with candles; the inner had one square window, which gave upon the moat. In the outer room there lay always, day and night, three of the Six; and the instructions of Duke Michael were, that on any attack being made on the outer room, the three were to defend the door of it so long as they could without risk to themselves. But, so soon as the door should be in danger of being forced, then Rupert Hentzau or Detchard (for one of these two was always there) should leave the others to hold it as long as they could, and himself pass into the inner room, and, without more ado, kill the King who lay there, well-treated indeed, but without weapons, and with his arms confined in fine steel chains, which did not allow him to move his elbow more than three inches from his side. Thus, before the outer door were stormed, the King would be dead. And his body? For his body would be evidence as damning as himself.

"Nay, sir," said Johann, "his Highness has thought of that. While the two hold the outer room, the one who has killed the King unlocks the bars in the square window (they turn on a hinge). The window now gives no light, for its mouth is choked by a great pipe of earthenware; and this pipe, which is large enough to let pass through it the body of a man, passes into the moat, coming to an end immediately above the surface of the water, so that there is no perceptible interval between water and pipe. The King being dead, his murderer swiftly ties a weight to the body, and, dragging it to the window, raises it by a pulley (for, lest the weight should prove too great, Detchard has provided one) till it is level with the mouth of the pipe. He inserts the feet in the pipe, and pushes the body down. Silently, without splash or sound, it falls into the water and thence to the bottom of the moat, which is twenty feet deep thereabouts. This done, the murderer cries loudly, 'All's well!' and himself slides down the pipe; and the others, if they can and the attack is not too hot, run to the inner room and, seeking a moment's delay, bar the door, and in their turn slide down. And though the King rises not from the bottom, they rise and swim round to the other side, where the orders are for men to wait them with ropes, to haul them out, and horses. And here, if things go ill, the duke will join them and seek safety by riding; but if all goes well, they will return to the Castle, and have their enemies in a trap. That, sir, is the plan of his Highness for the disposal of the King in case of need. But it is not to be used till the last; for, as we all know, he is not minded to kill the King unless he can, before or soon after, kill you also, sir. Now, sir, I have spoken the truth, as God is my witness, and I pray you to shield me from the vengeance of Duke Michael; for if, after he knows what I have done, I fall into his hands, I shall pray for one thing out of all the world—a speedy death, and that I shall not obtain from him!"

The fellow's story was rudely told, but our questions supplemented his narrative. What he had told us applied to an armed attack; but if suspicions were aroused, and there came overwhelming force—such, for instance, as I, the King, could bring—the idea of resistance would be abandoned; the King would be quietly murdered and slid down the pipe. And— here comes an ingenious touch—one of the Six would take his place in the cell, and, on the entrance of the searchers, loudly demand release and redress; and Michael, being summoned, would confess to hasty action, but he would say the man had angered him by seeking the favour of a lady in the Castle (this was Antoinette de Mauban) and he had confined him there, as he conceived he, as Lord of Zenda, had right to do. But he was now, on receiving his apology, content to let him go, and so end the gossip which, to his Highness's annoyance, had arisen concerning a prisoner in Zenda, and had given his visitors the trouble of this enquiry. The visitors, baffled, would retire, and Michael could, at his leisure, dispose of the body of the King.

Sapt, Fritz, and I in my bed, looked round on one another in horror and bewilderment at the cruelty and cunning of the plan. Whether I went in peace or in war, openly at the head of a corps, or secretly by a stealthy assault, the King would be dead before I could come near him. If Michael were stronger and overcame my party, there would be an end. But if I were stronger, I should have no way to punish him, no means of proving any guilt in him without proving my own guilt also. On the other hand, I should be left as King (ah! for a moment my pulse quickened) and it would be for the future to witness the final struggle between him and me. He seemed to have made triumph possible and ruin impossible. At the worst, he would stand as well as he had stood before I crossed his path—with but one man between him and the throne, and that man an impostor; at best, there would be none left to stand against him. I had begun to think that Black Michael was over fond of leaving the fighting to his friends; but now I acknowledged that the brains, if not the arms, of the conspiracy were his.

"Does the King know this?" I asked.

"I and my brother," answered Johann, "put up the pipe, under the orders of my Lord of Hentzau. He was on guard that day, and the King asked my lord what it meant. 'Faith,' he answered, with his airy laugh, 'it's a new improvement on the ladder of Jacob, whereby, as you have read, sire, men pass from the earth to heaven. We thought it not meet that your Majesty should go, in case, sire, you must go, by the common route. So we have made you a pretty private passage where the vulgar cannot stare at you or incommode your passage. That, sire, is the meaning of that pipe.' And he laughed and bowed, and prayed the King's leave to replenish the King's glass—for the King was at supper. And the King, though he is a brave man, as are all of his House, grew red and then white as he looked on the pipe and at the merry devil who mocked him. Ah, sir" (and the fellow shuddered), "it is not easy to sleep quiet in the Castle of Zenda, for all of them would as soon cut a man's throat as play a game at cards; and my Lord Rupert would choose it sooner for a pastime than any other—ay, sooner than he would ruin a woman, though that he loves also."

The man ceased, and I bade Fritz take him away and have him carefully guarded; and, turning to him, I added:

"If anyone asks you if there is a prisoner in Zenda, you may answer 'Yes.' But if any asks who the prisoner is, do not answer. For all my promises will not save you if any man here learns from you the truth as to the prisoner of Zenda. I'll kill you like a dog if the thing be so much as breathed within the house!"

Then, when he was gone, I looked at Sapt.

"It's a hard nut!" said I.

"So hard," said he, shaking his grizzled head, "that as I think, this time next year is like to find you still King of Ruritania!" and he broke out into curses on Michael's cunning.

I lay back on my pillows.

"There seems to me," I observed, "to be two ways by which the King can come out of Zenda alive. One is by treachery in the duke's followers."

"You can leave that out," said Sapt.

"I hope not," I rejoined, "because the other I was about to mention is—by a miracle from heaven!"

CHAPTER 14

A Night Outside the Castle

It would have surprised the good people of Ruritania to know of the foregoing talk; for, according to the official reports, I had suffered a grievous and dangerous hurt from an accidental spear-thrust, received in the course of my sport. I caused the bulletins to be of a very serious character, and created great public excitement, whereby three things occurred: first, I gravely offended the medical faculty of Strelsau by refusing to summon to my bedside any of them, save a young man, a friend of Fritz's, whom we could trust; secondly, I received word from Marshal Strakencz that my orders seemed to have no more weight than his, and that the Princess Flavia was leaving for Tarlenheim under his unwilling escort (news whereat I strove not to be glad and proud); and thirdly, my brother, the Duke of Strelsau, although too well informed to believe the account of the origin of my sickness, was yet persuaded by the reports and by my seeming inactivity that I was in truth incapable of action, and that my life was in some danger. This I learnt from the man Johann, whom I was compelled to trust and send back to Zenda, where, by the way, Rupert Hentzau had him soundly flogged for daring to smirch the morals of Zenda by staying out all night in the pursuits of love. This, from Rupert, Johann deeply resented, and the duke's approval of it did more to bind the keeper to my side than all my promises.

On Flavia's arrival I cannot dwell. Her joy at finding me up and well, instead of on my back and fighting with death, makes a picture that even now dances before my eyes till they grow too dim to see it; and her reproaches that I had not trusted even her must excuse the means I took to quiet them. In truth, to have her with me once more was like a taste of heaven to a damned soul, the sweeter for the inevitable doom that was to follow; and I rejoiced in being able to waste two whole days with her. And when I had wasted two days, the Duke of Strelsau arranged a hunting-party.

The stroke was near now. For Sapt and I, after anxious consultations, had resolved that we must risk a blow, our resolution being clinched by Johann's news that the King grew peaked, pale, and ill, and that his health was breaking down under his rigorous confinement. Now a man—be he king or no king—may as well die swiftly and as becomes a gentleman, from bullet or thrust, as rot his life out in a cellar! That thought made prompt action advisable in the interests of the King; from my own point of view, it grew more and more necessary. For Strakencz urged on me the need of a speedy marriage, and my own inclinations seconded him with such terrible insistence that I feared for my resolution. I do not believe that I should have done the deed I dreamt of; but I might have come to flight, and my flight would have ruined the cause. And—yes, I am no saint (ask my little sister-in-law), and worse still might have happened.

It is perhaps as strange a thing as has ever been in the history of a country that the King's brother and the King's personator, in a time of profound outward peace, near a placid, undisturbed country town, under semblance of amity, should wage a desperate war for the person and life of the King. Yet such was the struggle that began now between Zenda and Tarlenheim. When I look back on the time, I seem to myself to have been half mad. Sapt has told me that I suffered no interference and listened to no remonstrances; and if ever a King of Ruritania ruled like a despot, I was, in those days, the man. Look where I would, I saw nothing that made life sweet to me, and I took my life in my hand and carried it carelessly as a man dangles an old glove. At first they strove to guard me, to keep me safe, to persuade me not to expose myself; but when they saw how I was set, there grew up among them—whether they knew the truth or not—a feeling that Fate ruled the issue, and that I must be left to play my game with Michael my own way.

Late next night I rose from table, where Flavia had sat by me, and conducted her to the door of her apartments. There I kissed her hand, and bade her sleep sound and wake to happy days. Then I changed my clothes and went out. Sapt and Fritz were waiting for me with six men and the horses. Over his saddle Sapt carried a long coil of rope, and both were heavily armed. I had with me a short stout cudgel and a long knife. Making a circuit, we avoided the town, and in an hour found ourselves slowly mounting the hill that led to the Castle of Zenda. The night was dark and very stormy; gusts of wind and spits of rain caught us as we breasted the incline, and the great trees moaned and sighed. When we came to a thick clump, about a quarter of a mile from the Castle, we bade our six friends hide there with the horses. Sapt had a whistle, and they could rejoin us in a few moments if danger came: but, up to now, we had met no one. I hoped that Michael was still off his guard, believing me to be safe in bed. However that might be, we gained the top of the hill without accident, and found ourselves on the edge of the moat where it sweeps under the road, separating the Old Castle from it. A tree stood on the edge of the bank, and Sapt, silently and diligently, set to make fast the rope. I stripped off my boots, took a pull at a flask of brandy, loosened the knife in its sheath, and took the cudgel between my teeth. Then I shook hands with my friends, not heeding a last look of entreaty from Fritz, and laid hold of the rope. I was going to have a look at "Jacob's Ladder."

Gently I lowered myself into the water. Though the night was wild, the day had been warm and bright, and the water was not cold. I struck out, and began to swim round the great walls which frowned above me. I could see only three yards ahead; I had then good hopes of not being seen, as I crept along close under the damp, moss-grown masonry. There were lights from the new part of the Castle on the other side, and now and again I heard laughter and merry shouts. I fancied I recognized young Rupert Hentzau's ringing tones, and pictured him flushed with wine. Recalling my thoughts to the business in hand, I rested a moment. If Johann's description were right, I must be near the window now. Very slowly I moved; and out of the darkness ahead loomed a shape. It was the pipe, curving from the window to the water: about four feet of its surface were displayed; it was as big round as two men. I was about to approach it, when I saw something else, and my heart stood still. The nose of a boat protruded beyond the pipe on the other side; and listening intently, I heard a slight shuffle— as of a man shifting his position. Who was the man who guarded Michael's invention? Was he awake or was he asleep? I felt if my knife were ready, and trod water; as I did so, I found bottom under my feet. The foundations of the Castle extended some fifteen inches, making a ledge; and I stood on it, out of water from my armpits upwards. Then I crouched and peered through the darkness under the pipe, where, curving, it left a space.

There was a man in the boat. A rifle lay by him—I saw the gleam of the barrel. Here was the sentinel! He sat very still. I listened; he breathed heavily, regularly, monotonously. By heaven, he slept! Kneeling on the shelf, I drew forward under the pipe till my face was within two feet of his. He was a big man, I saw. It was Max Holf, the brother of Johann. My hand stole to my belt, and I drew out my knife. Of all the deeds of my life, I love the least to think of this, and whether it were the act of a man or a traitor I will not ask. I said to myself: "It is war—and the King's life is the stake." And I raised myself from beneath the pipe and stood up by the boat, which lay moored by the ledge. Holding my breath, I marked the spot and raised my arm. The great fellow stirred. He opened his eyes—wide, wider. He grasped in terror at my face and clutched at his rifle. I struck home. And I heard the chorus of a love-song from the opposite bank.

Leaving him where he lay, a huddled mass, I turned to "Jacob's Ladder." My time was short. This fellow's turn of watching might be over directly, and relief would come. Leaning over the pipe, I examined it, from the end near the water to the topmost extremity where it passed, or seemed to pass, through the masonry of the wall. There was no break in it, no chink. Dropping on my knees, I tested the under side. And my breath went quick and fast, for on this lower side, where the pipe should have clung close to the masonry, there was a gleam of light! That light must come from the cell of the King! I set my shoulder against the pipe and exerted my strength. The chink widened a very, very little, and hastily I desisted; I had done enough to show that the pipe was not fixed in the masonry at the lower side.

Then I heard a voice—a harsh, grating voice:

"Well, sire, if you have had enough of my society, I will leave you to repose; but I must fasten the little ornaments first."

It was Detchard! I caught the English accent in a moment.

"Have you anything to ask, sire, before we part?"

The King's voice followed. It was his, though it was faint and hollow—different from the merry tones I had heard in the glades of the forest.

"Pray my brother," said the King, "to kill me. I am dying by inches here."

"The duke does not desire your death, sire—yet," sneered Detchard; "when he does behold your path to heaven!"

The King answered:

"So be it! And now, if your orders allow it, pray leave me."

"May you dream of paradise!" said the ruffian.

The light disappeared. I heard the bolts of the door run home. And then I heard the sobs of the King. He was alone, as he thought. Who dares mock at him?

I did not venture to speak to him. The risk of some exclamation escaping him in surprise was too great. I dared do nothing that night; and my task now was to get myself away in safety, and to carry off the carcass of the dead man. To leave him there would tell too much. Casting loose the boat, I got in. The wind was blowing a gale now, and there was little danger of oars being heard. I rowed swiftly round to where my friends waited. I had just reached the spot, when a loud whistle sounded over the moat behind me.

"Hullo, Max!" I heard shouted.

I hailed Sapt in a low tone. The rope came down. I tied it round the corpse, and then went up it myself.

"Whistle you too," I whispered, "for our men, and haul in the line. No talk now."

They hauled up the body. Just as it reached the road, three men on horseback swept round from the front of the Castle. We saw them; but, being on foot ourselves, we escaped their notice. But we heard our men coming up with a shout.

"The devil, but it's dark!" cried a ringing voice.

It was young Rupert. A moment later, shots rang out. Our people had met them. I started forward at a run, Sapt and Fritz following me.

"Thrust, thrust!" cried Rupert again, and a loud groan following told that he himself was not behind-hand.

"I'm done, Rupert!" cried a voice. "They're three to one. Save yourself!"

I ran on, holding my cudgel in my hand. Suddenly a horse came towards me. A man was on it, leaning over his shoulder.

"Are you cooked too, Krafstein?" he cried.

52

There was no answer.

I sprang to the horse's head. It was Rupert Hentzau.

"At last!" I cried.

For we seemed to have him. He had only his sword in his hand. My men were hot upon him; Sapt and Fritz were running up. I had outstripped them; but if they got close enough to fire, he must die or surrender.

"At last!" I cried.

"It's the play-actor!" cried he, slashing at my cudgel. He cut it clean in two; and, judging discretion better than death, I ducked my head and (I blush to tell it) scampered for my life. The devil was in Rupert Hentzau; for he put spurs to his horse, and I, turning to look, saw him ride, full gallop, to the edge of the moat and leap in, while the shots of our party fell thick round him like hail. With one gleam of moonlight we should have riddled him with balls; but, in the darkness, he won to the corner of the Castle, and vanished from our sight.

"The deuce take him!" grinned Sapt.

"It's a pity," said I, "that he's a villain. Whom have we got?"

We had Lauengram and Krafstein: they lay dead; and, concealment being no longer possible, we flung them, with Max, into the moat; and, drawing together in a compact body, rode off down the hill. And, in our midst, went the bodies of three gallant gentlemen. Thus we travelled home, heavy at heart for the death of our friends, sore uneasy concerning the King, and cut to the quick that young Rupert had played yet another winning hand with us.

For my own part, I was vexed and angry that I had killed no man in open fight, but only stabbed a knave in his sleep. And I did not love to hear Rupert call me a play-actor.

CHAPTER 15

I Talk with a Tempter

Ruritania is not England, or the quarrel between Duke Michael and myself could not have gone on, with the extraordinary incidents which marked it, without more public notice being directed to it. Duels were frequent among all the upper classes, and private quarrels between great men kept the old habit of spreading to their friends and dependents. Nevertheless, after the affray which I have just related, such reports began to circulate that I felt it necessary to be on my guard. The death of the gentlemen involved could not be hidden from their relatives. I issued a stern order, declaring that duelling had attained unprecedented licence (the Chancellor drew up the document for me, and very well he did it), and forbidding it save in the gravest cases. I sent a public and stately apology to Michael, and he returned a deferential and courteous reply to me; for our one point of union was—and it underlay all our differences and induced an unwilling harmony between our actions—that we could neither of us afford to throw our cards on the table. He, as well as I, was a "play-actor", and, hating one another, we combined to dupe public opinion. Unfortunately, however, the necessity for concealment involved the necessity of delay: the King might die in his prison, or even be spirited off somewhere else; it could not be helped. For a little while I was compelled to observe a truce, and my only consolation was that Flavia most warmly approved of my edict against duelling, and, when I expressed delight at having won her favour, prayed me, if her favour were any motive to me, to prohibit the practice altogether.

"Wait till we are married," said I, smiling.

Not the least peculiar result of the truce and of the secrecy which dictated it was that the town of Zenda became in the day-time—I would not have trusted far to its protection by night—a sort of neutral zone, where both parties could safely go; and I, riding down one day with Flavia and Sapt, had an encounter with an acquaintance, which presented a ludicrous side, but was at the same time embarrassing. As I rode along, I met a dignified looking person driving in a two-horsed carriage. He stopped his horses, got out, and approached me, bowing low. I recognized the Head of the Strelsau Police.

"Your Majesty's ordinance as to duelling is receiving our best attention," he assured me.

If the best attention involved his presence in Zenda, I determined at once to dispense with it.

"Is that what brings you to Zenda, Prefect?" I asked.

"Why no, sire; I am here because I desired to oblige the British Ambassador."

"What's the British Ambassador doing dans cette galere?" said I, carelessly.

"A young countryman of his, sire—a man of some position—is missing. His friends have not heard from him for two months, and there is reason to believe that he was last seen in Zenda."

Flavia was paying little attention. I dared not look at Sapt.

"What reason?"

"A friend of his in Paris—a certain M. Featherly—has given us information which makes it possible that he came here, and the officials of the railway recollect his name on some luggage."

"What was his name?"

"Rassendyll, sire," he answered; and I saw that the name meant nothing to him. But, glancing at Flavia, he lowered his voice, as he went on: "It is thought that he may have followed a lady here. Has your Majesty heard of a certain Madame de Mauban?"

"Why, yes," said I, my eye involuntarily travelling towards the Castle.

"She arrived in Ruritania about the same time as this Rassendyll."

I caught the Prefect's glance; he was regarding me with enquiry writ large on his face.

"Sapt," said I, "I must speak a word to the Prefect. Will you ride on a few paces with the princess?" And I added to the Prefect: "Come, sir, what do you mean?"

He drew close to me, and I bent in the saddle.

"If he were in love with the lady?" he whispered. "Nothing has been heard of him for two months;" and this time it was the eye of the Prefect which travelled towards the Castle.

"Yes, the lady is there," I said quietly. "But I don't suppose Mr. Rassendyll—is that the name?—is."

"The duke," he whispered, "does not like rivals, sire."

"You're right there," said I, with all sincerity. "But surely you hint at a very grave charge?"

He spread his hands out in apology. I whispered in his ear:

"This is a grave matter. Go back to Strelsau—"

"But, sire, if I have a clue here?"

"Go back to Strelsau," I repeated. "Tell the Ambassador that you have a clue, but that you must be left alone for a week or two. Meanwhile, I'll charge myself with looking into the matter."

"The Ambassador is very pressing, sir."

"You must quiet him. Come, sir; you see that if your suspicions are correct, it is an affair in which we must move with caution. We can have no scandal. Mind you return tonight."

He promised to obey me, and I rode on to rejoin my companions, a little easier in my mind. Enquiries after me must be stopped at all hazards for a week or two; and this clever official had come surprisingly near the truth. His impression might be useful some day, but if he acted on it now it might mean the worse to the King. Heartily did I curse George Featherly for not holding his tongue.

"Well," asked Flavia, "have you finished your business?"

"Most satisfactorily," said I. "Come, shall we turn round? We are almost trenching on my brother's territory."

We were, in fact, at the extreme end of the town, just where the hills begin to mount towards the Castle. We cast our eyes up, admiring the massive beauty of the old walls, and we saw a cortege winding slowly down the hill. On it came.

"Let us go back," said Sapt.

"I should like to stay," said Flavia; and I reined my horse beside hers.

We could distinguish the approaching party now. There came first two mounted servants in black uniforms, relieved only by a silver badge. These were followed by a car drawn by four horses: on it, under a heavy pall, lay a coffin; behind it rode a man in plain black clothes, carrying his hat in his hand. Sapt uncovered, and we stood waiting, Flavia keeping by me and laying her hand on my arm.

"It is one of the gentlemen killed in the quarrel, I expect," she said.

I beckoned to a groom.

"Ride and ask whom they escort," I ordered.

He rode up to the servants, and I saw him pass on to the gentleman who rode behind.

"It's Rupert of Hentzau," whispered Sapt.

Rupert it was, and directly afterwards, waving to the procession to stand still, Rupert trotted up to me. He was in a frock-coat, tightly buttoned, and trousers. He wore an aspect of sadness, and he bowed with profound respect. Yet suddenly he smiled, and I smiled too, for old Sapt's hand lay in his left breast-pocket, and Rupert and I both guessed what lay in the hand inside the pocket.

"Your Majesty asks whom we escort," said Rupert. "It is my dear friend, Albert of Lauengram."

"Sir," said I, "no one regrets the unfortunate affair more than I. My ordinance, which I mean to have obeyed, is witness to it."

"Poor fellow!" said Flavia softly, and I saw Rupert's eyes flash at her. Whereat I grew red; for, if I had my way, Rupert Hentzau should not have defiled her by so much as a glance. Yet he did it and dared to let admiration be seen in his look.

"Your Majesty's words are gracious," he said. "I grieve for my friend. Yet, sire, others must soon lie as he lies now."

"It is a thing we all do well to remember, my lord," I rejoined.

"Even kings, sire," said Rupert, in a moralizing tone; and old Sapt swore softly by my side.

"It is true," said I. "How fares my brother, my lord?"

"He is better, sire."

"I am rejoiced."

"He hopes soon to leave for Strelsau, when his health is secured."

"He is only convalescent then?"

"There remain one or two small troubles," answered the insolent fellow, in the mildest tone in the world.

"Express my earnest hope," said Flavia, "that they may soon cease to trouble him."

"Your Royal Highness's wish is, humbly, my own," said Rupert, with a bold glance that brought a blush to Flavia's cheek.

I bowed; and Rupert, bowing lower, backed his horse and signed to his party to proceed. With a sudden impulse, I rode after him. He turned swiftly, fearing that, even in the presence of the dead and before a lady's eyes, I meant him mischief.

"You fought as a brave man the other night," I said. "Come, you are young, sir. If you will deliver your prisoner alive to me, you shall come to no hurt."

He looked at me with a mocking smile; but suddenly he rode nearer to me.

"I'm unarmed," he said; "and our old Sapt there could pick me off in a minute."

"I'm not afraid," said I.

"No, curse you!" he answered. "Look here, I made you a proposal from the duke once."

"I'll hear nothing from Black Michael," said I.

"Then hear one from me." He lowered his voice to a whisper. "Attack the Castle boldly. Let Sapt and Tarlenheim lead."

"Go on," said I.

"Arrange the time with me."

"I have such confidence in you, my lord!"

"Tut! I'm talking business now. Sapt there and Fritz will fall; Black Michael will fall—"

"What!"

"—Black Michael will fall, like the dog he is; the prisoner, as you call him, will go by 'Jacob's Ladder'—ah, you know that!—to hell! Two men will be left—I, Rupert Hentzau, and you, the King of Ruritania."

He paused, and then, in a voice that quivered with eagerness, added:

"Isn't that a hand to play?—a throne and your princess! And for me, say a competence and your Majesty's gratitude."

"Surely," I exclaimed, "while you're above ground, hell wants its master!"

"Well, think it over," he said. "And, look you, it would take more than a scruple or two to keep me from yonder girl," and his evil eye flashed again at her I loved.

"Get out of my reach!" said I; and yet in a moment I began to laugh for the very audacity of it.

"Would you turn against your master?" I asked.

He swore at Michael for being what the offspring of a legal, though morganatic, union should not be called, and said to me in an almost confidential and apparently friendly tone:

"He gets in my way, you know. He's a jealous brute! Faith, I nearly stuck a knife into him last night; he came most cursedly mal a propos!"

My temper was well under control now; I was learning something.

"A lady?" I asked negligently.

"Ay, and a beauty," he nodded. "But you've seen her."

"Ah! was it at a tea-party, when some of your friends got on the wrong side of the table?"

"What can you expect of fools like Detchard and De Gautet? I wish I'd been there."

"And the duke interferes?"

"Well," said Rupert meditatively, "that's hardly a fair way of putting it, perhaps. I want to interfere."

"And she prefers the duke?"

"Ay, the silly creature! Ah, well, you think about my plan," and, with a bow, he pricked his horse and trotted after the body of his friend.

I went back to Flavia and Sapt, pondering on the strangeness of the man. Wicked men I have known in plenty, but Rupert Hentzau remains unique in my experience. And if there be another anywhere, let him be caught and hanged out of hand. So say I!

"He's very handsome, isn't he?" said Flavia.

Well, of course, she didn't know him as I did; yet I was put out, for I thought his bold glances would have made her angry. But my dear Flavia was a woman, and so—she was not put out. On the contrary, she thought young Rupert very handsome—as, beyond question, the ruffian was.

"And how sad he looked at his friend's death!" said she.

"He'll have better reason to be sad at his own," observed Sapt, with a grim smile.

As for me, I grew sulky; unreasonable it was perhaps, for what better business had I to look at her with love than had even Rupert's lustful eyes? And sulky I remained till, as evening fell and we rode up to Tarlenheim, Sapt having fallen behind in case anyone should be following us, Flavia, riding close beside me, said softly, with a little half-ashamed laugh:

"Unless you smile, Rudolf, I cry. Why are you angry?"

"It was something that fellow said to me," said I, but I was smiling as we reached the door and dismounted.

There a servant handed me a note: it was unaddressed.

"Is it for me?" I asked.

"Yes, sire; a boy brought it."

I tore it open:

Johann carries this for me. I warned you once. In the name of God, and if you are a man, rescue me from this den of murderers!—A. de M.

I handed it to Sapt; but all that the tough old soul said in reply to this piteous appeal was: "Whose fault brought her there?"

Nevertheless, not being faultless myself, I took leave to pity Antoinette de Mauban.

CHAPTER 16

A Desperate Plan

As I had ridden publicly in Zenda, and had talked there with Rupert Hentzau, of course all pretence of illness was at an end. I marked the effect on the garrison of Zenda: they ceased to be seen abroad; and any of my men who went near the Castle reported that the utmost vigilance prevailed there. Touched as I was by Madame de Mauban's appeal, I seemed as powerless to befriend her as I had proved to help the King. Michael bade me defiance; and although he too had been seen outside the walls, with more disregard for appearances than he had hitherto shown, he did not take the trouble to send any excuse for his failure to wait on the King. Time ran on in inactivity, when every moment was pressing; for not only was I faced with the new danger which the stir about my disappearance brought on me, but great murmurs had arisen in Strelsau at my continued absence from the city. They had been greater, but for the knowledge that Flavia was with me; and for this reason I suffered her to stay, though I hated to have her where danger was, and though every day of our present sweet intercourse strained my endurance almost to breaking. As a final blow, nothing would content my advisers, Strakencz and the Chancellor (who came out from Strelsau to make an urgent representation to me), save that I should appoint a day for the public solemnization of my betrothal, a ceremony which in Ruritania is well nigh as binding and great a thing as the marriage itself. And this—with Flavia sitting by me—I was forced to do, setting a date a fortnight ahead, and appointing the Cathedral in Strelsau as the place. And this formal act being published far and wide, caused great joy throughout the kingdom, and was the talk of all tongues; so that I reckoned there were but two men who chafed at it—I mean Black Michael and myself; and but one who did not know of it—that one the man whose name I bore, the King of Ruritania.

In truth, I heard something of the way the news was received in the Castle; for after an interval of three days, the man Johann, greedy for more money, though fearful for his life, again found means to visit us. He had been waiting on the duke when the tidings came. Black Michael's face had grown blacker still, and he had sworn savagely; nor was he better pleased when young Rupert took oath that I meant to do as I said, and turning to Madame de Mauban, wished her joy on a rival gone. Michael's hand stole towards his sword (said Johann), but not a bit did Rupert care; for he rallied the duke on having made a better King than had reigned for years past in Ruritania. "And," said he, with a meaning bow to his exasperated master, "the devil sends the princess a finer man than heaven had marked out for her, by my soul, it does!" Then Michael harshly bade him hold his tongue, and leave them; but Rupert must needs first kiss madame's hand, which he did as though he loved her, while Michael glared at him.

This was the lighter side of the fellow's news; but more serious came behind, and it was plain that if time pressed at Tarlenheim, it pressed none the less fiercely at Zenda. For the King was very sick: Johann had seen him, and he was wasted and hardly able to move. "There could be no thought of taking another for him now." So alarmed were they, that they had sent for a physician from Strelsau; and the physician having been introduced into the King's cell, had come forth pale and trembling, and urgently prayed the duke to let him go back and meddle no more in the affair; but the duke would not, and held him there a prisoner, telling him his life was safe if the King lived while the duke desired and died when the duke desired— not otherwise. And, persuaded by the physician, they had allowed Madame de Mauban to visit the King and give him such attendance as his state needed, and as only a woman can give. Yet his life hung in the balance; and I was still strong and whole and free. Wherefore great gloom reigned at Zenda; and save when they quarrelled, to which they were very prone, they hardly spoke. But the deeper the depression of the rest, young Rupert went about Satan's work with a smile in his eye and a song on his lip; and laughed "fit to burst" (said Johann) because the duke always set Detchard to guard the King when Madame de Mauban was in the cell—which precaution was, indeed, not unwise in my careful brother. Thus Johann told his tale and seized his crowns. Yet he besought us to allow him to stay with us in Tarlenheim, and not venture his head again in the lion's den; but we had need of him there, and, although I refused to constrain him, I prevailed on him by increased rewards to go back and carry tidings to Madame de Mauban that I was working for her, and that, if she could, she should speak one word of comfort to the King. For while suspense is bad for the sick, yet despair is worse still, and it might be that the King lay dying of mere hopelessness, for I could learn of no definite disease that afflicted him.

"And how do they guard the King now?" I asked, remembering that two of the Six were dead, and Max Holf also.

"Detchard and Bersonin watch by night, Rupert Hentzau and De Gautet by day, sir," he answered.

"Only two at a time?"

"Ay, sir; but the others rest in a room just above, and are within sound of a cry or a whistle."

"A room just above? I didn't know of that. Is there any communication between it and the room where they watch?"

"No, sir. You must go down a few stairs and through the door by the drawbridge, and so to where the King is lodged."

"And that door is locked?"

"Only the four lords have keys, sir."

I drew nearer to him.

"And have they keys of the grating?" I asked in a low whisper.

"I think, sir, only Detchard and Rupert."

"Where does the duke lodge?"

"In the chateau, on the first floor. His apartments are on the right as you go towards the drawbridge."

"And Madame de Mauban?"

"Just opposite, on the left. But her door is locked after she has entered."

"To keep her in?"

"Doubtless, sir."

"Perhaps for another reason?"

"It is possible."

"And the duke, I suppose, has the key?"

"Yes. And the drawbridge is drawn back at night, and of that, too, the duke holds the key, so that it cannot be run across the moat without application to him."

"And where do you sleep?"

"In the entrance hall of the chateau, with five servants."

"Armed?"

"They have pikes, sir, but no firearms. The duke will not trust them with firearms."

58

Then at last I took the matter boldly in my hands. I had failed once at "Jacob's Ladder;" I should fail again there. I must make the attack from the other side.

"I have promised you twenty thousand crowns," said I. "You shall have fifty thousand if you will do what I ask of you tomorrow night. But, first, do those servants know who your prisoner is?"

"No, sir. They believe him to be some private enemy of the duke's."

"And they would not doubt that I am the King?"

"How should they?" he asked.

"Look to this, then. Tomorrow, at two in the morning exactly, fling open the front door of the chateau. Don't fail by an instant."

"Shall you be there, sir?"

"Ask no questions. Do what I tell you. Say the hall is close, or what you will. That is all I ask of you."

"And may I escape by the door, sir, when I have opened it?"

"Yes, as quick as your legs will carry you. One thing more. Carry this note to madame—oh, it's in French, you can't read it—and charge her, for the sake of all our lives, not to fail in what it orders."

The man was trembling but I had to trust to what he had of courage and to what he had of honesty. I dared not wait, for I feared that the King would die.

When the fellow was gone, I called Sapt and Fritz to me, and unfolded the plan that I had formed. Sapt shook his head over it.

"Why can't you wait?" he asked.

"The King may die."

"Michael will be forced to act before that."

"Then," said I, "the King may live."

"Well, and if he does?"

"For a fortnight?" I asked simply.

And Sapt bit his moustache.

Suddenly Fritz von Tarlenheim laid his hand on my shoulder.

"Let us go and make the attempt," said he.

"I mean you to go—don't be afraid," said I.

"Ay, but do you stay here, and take care of the princess."

A gleam came into old Sapt's eye.

"We should have Michael one way or the other then," he chuckled; "whereas if you go and are killed with the King, what will become of those of us who are left?"

"They will serve Queen Flavia," said I, "and I would to God I could be one of them."

A pause followed. Old Sapt broke it by saying sadly, yet with an unmeant drollery that set Fritz and me laughing:

"Why didn't old Rudolf the Third marry your—great-grandmother, was it?"

"Come," said I, "it is the King we are thinking about."

"It is true," said Fritz.

"Moreover," I went on, "I have been an impostor for the profit of another, but I will not be one for my own; and if the King is not alive and on his throne before the day of betrothal comes, I will tell the truth, come what may."

"You shall go, lad," said Sapt.

Here is the plan I had made. A strong party under Sapt's command was to steal up to the door of the chateau. If discovered prematurely, they were to kill anyone who found them—with their swords, for I wanted no noise of firing. If all went well, they would be at the door when Johann opened it. They were to rush in and secure the servants if their mere presence and the use of the King's name were not enough. At the same moment—and on this hinged the plan—a woman's cry was to ring out loud and shrill from Antoinette de Mauban's chamber. Again and again she was to cry: "Help, help! Michael, help!" and then to utter the name of young Rupert Hentzau. Then, as we hoped, Michael, in fury, would rush out of his apartments opposite, and fall alive into the hands of Sapt. Still the cries would go on; and my men would let down the drawbridge; and it would be strange if Rupert, hearing his name thus taken in vain, did not descend from where he slept and seek to cross. De Gautet might or might not come with him: that must be left to chance.

And when Rupert set his foot on the drawbridge? There was my part: for I was minded for another swim in the moat; and, lest I should grow weary, I had resolved to take with me a small wooden ladder, on which I could rest my arms in the water—and my feet when I left it. I would rear it against the wall just by the bridge; and when the bridge was across, I would stealthily creep on to it—and then if Rupert or De Gautet crossed in safety, it would be my misfortune, not my fault. They dead, two men only would remain; and for them we must trust to the confusion we had created and to a sudden rush. We should have the keys of the door that led to the all-important rooms. Perhaps they would rush out. If they stood by their orders, then the King's life hung on the swiftness with which we could force the outer door; and I thanked God that not Rupert Hentzau watched, but Detchard. For though Detchard was a cool man, relentless, and no coward, he had neither the dash nor the recklessness of Rupert. Moreover, he, if any one of them, really loved Black Michael, and it might be that he would leave Bersonin to guard the King, and rush across the bridge to take part in the affray on the other side.

So I planned—desperately. And, that our enemy might be the better lulled to security, I gave orders that our residence should be brilliantly lighted from top to bottom, as though we were engaged in revelry; and should so be kept all night, with music playing and people moving to and fro. Strakencz would be there, and he was to conceal our departure, if he could, from Flavia. And if we came not again by the morning, he was to march, openly and in force to the Castle, and demand the person of the King; if Black Michael were not there, as I did not think he would be, the Marshal would take Flavia with him, as swiftly as he could, to Strelsau, and there proclaim Black Michael's treachery and the probable death of the King, and rally all that there was honest and true round the banner of the princess. And, to say truth, this was what I thought most likely to happen. For I had great doubts whether either the King or Black Michael or I had more than a day to live. Well, if Black Michael died, and if I, the play-actor, slew Rupert Hentzau with my own hand, and then died myself, it might be that Fate would deal as lightly with Ruritania as could be hoped, notwithstanding that she demanded the life of the King—and to her dealing thus with me, I was in no temper to make objection. It was late when we rose from conference, and I betook me to the princess's apartments. She was pensive that evening; yet, when I left her, she flung her arms about me and grew, for an instant, bashfully radiant as she slipped a ring on my finger. I was wearing the King's ring; but I had also on my little finger a plain band of gold engraved with the motto of our family: "Nil Quae Feci." This I took off and put on her, and signed to her to let me go. And she, understanding, stood away and watched me with dimmed eyes.

"Wear that ring, even though you wear another when you are queen," I said.

"Whatever else I wear, this I will wear till I die and after," said she, as she kissed the ring.

CHAPTER 17

Young Rupert's Midnight Diversions

The night came fine and clear. I had prayed for dirty weather, such as had favoured my previous voyage in the moat, but Fortune was this time against me. Still I reckoned that by keeping close under the wall and in the shadow I could escape detection from the windows of the chateau that looked out on the scene of my efforts. If they searched the moat, indeed, my scheme must fail; but I did not think they would. They had made "Jacob's Ladder" secure against attack. Johann had himself helped to fix it closely to the masonry on the under side, so that it could not now be moved from below any more than from above. An assault with explosives or a long battering with picks alone could displace it, and the noise involved in either of these operations put them out of the question. What harm, then, could a man do in the moat? I trusted that Black Michael, putting this query to himself, would answer confidently, "None;" while, even if Johann meant treachery, he did not know my scheme, and would doubtless expect to see me, at the head of my friends, before the front entrance to the chateau. There, I said to Sapt, was the real danger. "And there," I added, "you shall be. Doesn't that content you?"

But it did not. Dearly would he have liked to come with me, had I not utterly refused to take him. One man might escape notice, to double the party more than doubled the risk; and when he ventured to hint once again that my life was too valuable, I, knowing the secret thought he clung to, sternly bade him be silent, assuring him that unless the King lived through the night, I would not live through it either.

At twelve o'clock, Sapt's command left the chateau of Tarlenheim and struck off to the right, riding by unfrequented roads, and avoiding the town of Zenda. If all went well, they would be in front of the Castle by about a quarter to two. Leaving their horses half a mile off, they were to steal up to the entrance and hold themselves in readiness for the opening of the door. If the door were not opened by two, they were to send Fritz von Tarlenheim round to the other side of the Castle. I would meet him there if I were alive, and we would consult whether to storm the Castle or not. If I were not there, they were to return with all speed to Tarlenheim, rouse the Marshal, and march in force to Zenda. For if not there, I should be dead; and I knew that the King would not be alive five minutes after I ceased to breathe. I must now leave Sapt and his friends, and relate how I myself proceeded on this eventful night. I went out on the good horse which had carried me, on the night of the coronation, back from the hunting-lodge to Strelsau. I carried a revolver in the saddle and my sword. I was covered with a large cloak, and under this I wore a warm, tight-fitting woollen jersey, a pair of knickerbockers, thick stockings, and light canvas shoes. I had rubbed myself thoroughly with oil, and I carried a large flask of whisky. The night was warm, but I might probably be immersed a long while, and it was necessary to take every precaution against cold: for cold not only saps a man's courage if he has to die, but impairs his energy if others have to die, and, finally, gives him rheumatics, if it be God's will that he lives. Also I tied round my body a length of thin but stout cord, and I did not forget my ladder. I, starting after Sapt, took a shorter route, skirting the town to the left, and found myself in the outskirts of the forest at about half-past twelve. I tied my horse up in a thick clump of trees, leaving the revolver in its pocket in the saddle—it would be no use to me—and, ladder in hand, made my way to the edge of the moat. Here I unwound my rope from about my waist, bound it securely round the trunk of a tree on the bank, and let myself down. The Castle clock struck a quarter to one as I felt the water under me and began to swim round the keep, pushing the ladder before me, and hugging the Castle wall. Thus voyaging, I came to my old friend, "Jacob's Ladder," and felt the ledge of the masonry under me. I crouched down in the shadow of the great pipe—I tried to stir it, but it was quite immovable—and waited. I remember that my predominant feeling was neither anxiety for the King nor longing for Flavia, but an intense desire to smoke; and this craving, of course, I could not gratify.

The drawbridge was still in its place. I saw its airy, slight framework above me, some ten yards to my right, as I crouched with my back against the wall of the King's cell. I made out a window two yards my side of it and nearly on the same level. That, if Johann spoke true, must belong to the duke's apartments; and on the other side, in about the same relative position, must be Madame de Mauban's window. Women are careless, forgetful creatures. I prayed that she might not forget that she was to be the victim of a brutal attempt at two o'clock precisely. I was rather amused at the part I had assigned to my young friend Rupert Hentzau; but I owed him a stroke—for, even as I sat, my shoulder ached where he had, with an audacity that seemed half to hide his treachery, struck at me, in the sight of all my friends, on the terrace at Tarlenheim.

Suddenly the duke's window grew bright. The shutters were not closed, and the interior became partially visible to me as I cautiously raised myself till I stood on tiptoe. Thus placed, my range of sight embraced a yard or more inside the window, while the radius of light did not reach me. The window was flung open and someone looked out. I marked Antoinette de Mauban's graceful figure, and, though her face was in shadow, the fine outline of her head was revealed against the light behind. I longed to cry softly, "Remember!" but I dared not—and happily, for a moment later a man came up and stood by her. He tried to put his arm round her waist, but with a swift motion she sprang away and leant against the shutter, her profile towards me. I made out who the newcomer was: it was young Rupert. A low laugh from him made me sure, as he leant forward, stretching out his hand towards her.

"Gently, gently!" I murmured. "You're too soon, my boy!"

His head was close to hers. I suppose he whispered to her, for I saw her point to the moat, and I heard her say, in slow and distinct tones:

"I had rather throw myself out of this window!"

He came close up to the window and looked out.

"It looks cold," said he. "Come, Antoinette, are you serious?"

She made no answer so far as I heard; and he, smiting his hand petulantly on the window-sill, went on, in the voice of some spoilt child:

"Hang Black Michael! Isn't the princess enough for him? Is he to have everything? What the devil do you see in Black Michael?"

"If I told him what you say—" she began.

"Well, tell him," said Rupert, carelessly; and, catching her off her guard, he sprang forward and kissed her, laughing, and crying, "There's something to tell him!"

If I had kept my revolver with me, I should have been very sorely tempted. Being spared the temptation, I merely added this new score to his account.

"Though, faith," said Rupert, "it's little he cares. He's mad about the princess, you know. He talks of nothing but cutting the play-actor's throat."

Didn't he, indeed?

"And if I do it for him, what do you think he's promised me?"

The unhappy woman raised her hands above her head, in prayer or in despair.

"But I detest waiting," said Rupert; and I saw that he was about to lay his hand on her again, when there was a noise of a door in the room opening, and a harsh voice cried:

"What are you doing here, sir?"

Rupert turned his back to the window, bowed low, and said, in his loud, merry tones:

"Apologizing for your absence, sir. Could I leave the lady alone?"

The newcomer must be Black Michael. I saw him directly, as he advanced towards the window. He caught young Rupert by the arm.

"The moat would hold more than the King!" said he, with a significant gesture.

"Does your Highness threaten me?" asked Rupert.

"A threat is more warning than most men get from me."

"Yet," observed Rupert, "Rudolf Rassendyll has been much threatened, and yet lives!"

"Am I in fault because my servants bungle?" asked Michael scornfully.

"Your Highness has run no risk of bungling!" sneered Rupert.

It was telling the duke that he shirked danger as plain as ever I have heard a man told. Black Michael had self-control. I dare say he scowled—it was a great regret to me that I could not see their faces better—but his voice was even and calm, as he answered:

"Enough, enough! We mustn't quarrel, Rupert. Are Detchard and Bersonin at their posts?"

"They are, sir."

"I need you no more."

"Nay, I'm not oppressed with fatigue," said Rupert.

"Pray, sir, leave us," said Michael, more impatiently. "In ten minutes the drawbridge will be drawn back, and I presume you have no wish to swim to your bed."

Rupert's figure disappeared. I heard the door open and shut again. Michael and Antoinette de Mauban were left together. To my chagrin, the duke laid his hand on the window and closed it. He stood talking to Antoinette for a moment or two. She shook her head, and he turned impatiently away. She left the window. The door sounded again, and Black Michael closed the shutters.

"De Gautet, De Gautet, man!" sounded from the drawbridge. "Unless you want a bath before your bed, come along!"

It was Rupert's voice, coming from the end of the drawbridge. A moment later he and De Gautet stepped out on the bridge. Rupert's arm was through De Gautet's, and in the middle of the bridge he detained his companion and leant over. I dropped behind the shelter of "Jacob's Ladder."

Then Master Rupert had a little sport. He took from De Gautet a bottle which he carried, and put it to his lips.

"Hardly a drop!" he cried discontentedly, and flung it in the moat.

It fell, as I judged from the sound and the circles on the water, within a yard of the pipe. And Rupert, taking out his revolver, began to shoot at it. The first two shots missed the bottle, but hit the pipe. The third shattered the bottle. I hoped that the young ruffian would be content; but he emptied the other barrels at the pipe, and one, skimming over the pipe, whistled through my hair as I crouched on the other side.

"'Ware bridge!" a voice cried, to my relief.

Rupert and De Gautet cried, "A moment!" and ran across. The bridge was drawn back, and all became still. The clock struck a quarter-past one. I rose and stretched myself and yawned. I think some ten minutes had passed when I heard a slight noise to my right. I peered over the pipe, and saw a dark figure standing in the gateway that led to the bridge. It was a man. By the careless, graceful poise, I guessed it to be Rupert again. He held a sword in his hand, and he stood motionless for a minute or two. Wild thoughts ran through me. On what mischief was the young fiend bent now? Then he laughed low to himself; then he turned his face to the wall, took a step in my direction, and, to my surprise, began to climb down the wall. In an instant I saw that there must be steps in the wall; it was plain. They were cut into or affixed to the wall, at intervals of about eighteen inches. Rupert set his foot on the lower one. Then he placed his sword between his teeth, turned round, and noiselessly let himself into the water. Had it been a matter of my life only, I would have swum to meet him. Dearly would I have loved to fight it out with him then and there—with steel, on a fine night, and none to come between us. But there was the King! I restrained myself, but I could not bridle my swift breathing, and I watched him with the intensest eagerness.

He swam leisurely and quietly across. There were more steps up on the other side, and he climbed them. When he set foot in the gateway, standing on the drawn-back bridge, he felt in his pocket and took something out. I heard him unlock the door. I could hear no noise of its closing behind him. He vanished from my sight.

Abandoning my ladder—I saw I did not need it now—I swam to the side of the bridge and climbed half way up the steps. There I hung with my sword in my hand, listening eagerly. The duke's room was shuttered and dark. There was a light in the window on the opposite side of the bridge. Not a sound broke the silence, till half-past one chimed from the great clock in the tower of the chateau.

There were other plots than mine afoot in the Castle that night.

CHAPTER 18

The Forcing of the Trap

The position wherein I stood does not appear very favourable to thought; yet for the next moment or two I thought profoundly. I had, I told myself, scored one point. Be Rupert Hentzau's errand what it might, and the villainy he was engaged on what it would, I had scored one point. He was on the other side of the moat from the King, and it would be by no fault of mine if ever he set foot on the same side again. I had three left to deal with: two on guard and De Gautet in his bed. Ah, if I had the keys! I would have risked everything and attacked Detchard and Bersonin before their friends could join them. But I was powerless. I must wait till the coming of my friends enticed someone to cross the bridge—someone with the keys. And I waited, as it seemed, for half an hour, really for about five minutes, before the next act in the rapid drama began.

All was still on the other side. The duke's room remained inscrutable behind its shutters. The light burnt steadily in Madame de Mauban's window. Then I heard the faintest, faintest sound: it came from behind the door which led to the drawbridge on the other side of the moat. It but just reached my ear, yet I could not be mistaken as to what it was. It was made by a key being turned very carefully and slowly. Who was turning it? And of what room was it the key? There leapt before my eyes the picture of young Rupert, with the key in one hand, his sword in the other, and an evil smile on his face. But I did not know what door it was, nor on which of his favourite pursuits young Rupert was spending the hours of that night.

I was soon to be enlightened, for the next moment—before my friends could be near the chateau door—before Johann the keeper would have thought to nerve himself for his task—there was a sudden crash from the room with the lighted window. It sounded as though someone had flung down a lamp; and the window went dark and black. At the same instant a cry rang out, shrill in the night: "Help, help! Michael, help!" and was followed by a shriek of utter terror.

I was tingling in every nerve. I stood on the topmost step, clinging to the threshold of the gate with my right hand and holding my sword in my left. Suddenly I perceived that the gateway was broader than the bridge; there was a dark corner on the opposite side where a man could stand. I darted across and stood there. Thus placed, I commanded the path, and no man could pass between the chateau and the old Castle till he had tried conclusions with me.

There was another shriek. Then a door was flung open and clanged against the wall, and I heard the handle of a door savagely twisted.

"Open the door! In God's name, what's the matter?" cried a voice—the voice of Black Michael himself.

He was answered by the very words I had written in my letter.

"Help, Michael—Hentzau!"

A fierce oath rang out from the duke, and with a loud thud he threw himself against the door. At the same moment I heard a window above my head open, and a voice cried: "What's the matter?" and I heard a man's hasty footsteps. I grasped my sword. If De Gautet came my way, the Six would be less by one more.

Then I heard the clash of crossed swords and a tramp of feet and—I cannot tell the thing so quickly as it happened, for all seemed to come at once. There was an angry cry from madame's room, the cry of a wounded man; the window was flung open; young Rupert stood there sword in hand. He turned his back, and I saw his body go forward to the lunge.

"Ah, Johann, there's one for you! Come on, Michael!"

Johann was there, then—come to the rescue of the duke! How would he open the door for me? For I feared that Rupert had slain him.

"Help!" cried the duke's voice, faint and husky.

I heard a step on the stairs above me; and I heard a stir down to my left, in the direction of the King's cell. But, before anything happened on my side of the moat, I saw five or six men round young Rupert in the embrasure of madame's window. Three or four times he lunged with incomparable dash and dexterity. For an instant they fell back, leaving a ring round him. He leapt on the parapet of the window, laughing as he leapt, and waving his sword in his hand. He was drunk with blood, and he laughed again wildly as he flung himself headlong into the moat.

What became of him then? I did not see: for as he leapt, De Gautet's lean face looked out through the door by me, and, without a second's hesitation, I struck at him with all the strength God had given me, and he fell dead in the doorway without a word or a groan. I dropped on my knees by him. Where were the keys? I found myself muttering: "The keys, man, the keys?" as though he had been yet alive and could listen; and when I could not find them, I—God forgive me!—I believe I struck a dead man's face.

At last I had them. There were but three. Seizing the largest, I felt the lock of the door that led to the cell. I fitted in the key. It was right. The lock turned. I drew the door close behind me and locked it as noiselessly as I could, putting the key in my pocket.

I found myself at the top of a flight of steep stone stairs. An oil lamp burnt dimly in the bracket. I took it down and held it in my hand; and I stood and listened.

"What in the devil can it be?" I heard a voice say.

It came from behind a door that faced me at the bottom of the stairs.

And another answered:

"Shall we kill him?"

I strained to hear the answer, and could have sobbed with relief when Detchard's voice came grating and cold:

"Wait a bit. There'll be trouble if we strike too soon."

There was a moment's silence. Then I heard the bolt of the door cautiously drawn back. Instantly I put out the light I held, replacing the lamp in the bracket.

"It's dark—the lamp's out. Have you a light?" said the other voice—Bersonin's.

No doubt they had a light, but they should not use it. It was come to the crisis now, and I rushed down the steps and flung myself against the door. Bersonin had unbolted it and it gave way before me. The Belgian stood there sword in hand, and Detchard was sitting on a couch at the side of the room. In astonishment at seeing me, Bersonin recoiled; Detchard jumped to his sword. I rushed madly at the Belgian: he gave way before me, and I drove him up against the wall. He was no swordsman, though he fought bravely, and in a moment he lay on the floor before me. I turned—Detchard was not there. Faithful to his orders, he had not risked a fight with me, but had rushed straight to the door of the King's room, opened it and slammed it behind him. Even now he was at his work inside.

And surely he would have killed the King, and perhaps me also, had it not been for one devoted man who gave his life for the King. For when I forced the door, the sight I saw was this: the King stood in the corner of the room: broken by his sickness, he could do nothing; his fettered hands moved uselessly up and down, and he was laughing horribly in half-mad delirium. Detchard and the doctor were together in the middle of the room; and the doctor had flung himself on the murderer, pinning his hands to his sides for an instant. Then Detchard wrenched himself free from the feeble grip, and, as I entered, drove his sword through the hapless man. Then he turned on me, crying:

"At last!"

We were sword to sword. By blessed chance, neither he nor Bersonin had been wearing their revolvers. I found them afterwards, ready loaded, on the mantelpiece of the outer room: it was hard by the door, ready to their hands, but my sudden rush in had cut off access to them. Yes, we were man to man: and we began to fight, silently, sternly, and hard. Yet I remember little of it, save that the man was my match with the sword—nay, and more, for he knew more tricks than I; and that he forced me back against the bars that guarded the entrance to "Jacob's Ladder." And I saw a smile on his face, and he wounded me in the left arm.

No glory do I take for that contest. I believe that the man would have mastered me and slain me, and then done his butcher's work, for he was the most skilful swordsman I have ever met; but even as he pressed me hard, the half-mad, wasted, wan creature in the corner leapt high in lunatic mirth, shrieking:

"It's cousin Rudolf! Cousin Rudolf! I'll help you, cousin Rudolf!" and catching up a chair in his hands (he could but just lift it from the ground and hold it uselessly before him) he came towards us. Hope came to me. "Come on!" I cried. "Come on! Drive it against his legs." Detchard replied with a savage thrust. He all but had me.

"Come on! Come on, man!" I cried. "Come and share the fun!"

And the King laughed gleefully, and came on, pushing his chair before him.

With an oath Detchard skipped back, and, before I knew what he was doing, had turned his sword against the King. He made one fierce cut at the King, and the King, with a piteous cry, dropped where he stood. The stout ruffian turned to face me again. But his own hand had prepared his destruction: for in turning he trod in the pool of blood that flowed from the dead physician. He slipped; he fell. Like a dart I was upon him. I caught him by the throat, and before he could recover himself I drove my point through his neck, and with a stifled curse he fell across the body of his victim.

Was the King dead? It was my first thought. I rushed to where he lay. Ay, it seemed as if he were dead, for he had a great gash across his forehead, and he lay still in a huddled heap on the floor. I dropped on my knees beside him, and leant my ear down to hear if he breathed. But before I could there was a loud rattle from the outside. I knew the sound: the drawbridge was being pushed out. A moment later it rang home against the wall on my side of the moat. I should be caught in a trap and the King with me, if he yet lived. He must take his chance, to live or die. I took my sword, and passed into the outer room. Who were pushing the drawbridge out—my men? If so, all was well. My eye fell on the revolvers, and I seized one; and paused to listen in the doorway of the outer room. To listen, say I? Yes, and to get my breath: and I tore my shirt and twisted a strip of it round my bleeding arm; and stood listening again. I would have given the world to hear Sapt's voice. For I was faint, spent, and weary. And that wild-cat Rupert Hentzau was yet at large in the Castle. Yet, because I could better defend the narrow door at the top of the stairs than the wider entrance to the room, I dragged myself up the steps, and stood behind it listening.

What was the sound? Again a strange one for the place and time. An easy, scornful, merry laugh—the laugh of young Rupert Hentzau! I could scarcely believe that a sane man would laugh. Yet the laugh told me that my men had not come; for they must have shot Rupert ere now, if they had come. And the clock struck half-past two! My God! The door had not been opened! They had gone to the bank! They had not found me! They had gone by now back to Tarlenheim, with the news of the King's death—and mine. Well, it would be true before they got there. Was not Rupert laughing in triumph?

For a moment, I sank, unnerved, against the door. Then I started up alert again, for Rupert cried scornfully:

"Well, the bridge is there! Come over it! And in God's name, let's see Black Michael. Keep back, you curs! Michael, come and fight for her!"

If it were a three-cornered fight, I might yet bear my part. I turned the key in the door and looked out.

CHAPTER 19

66

For a moment I could see nothing, for the glare of lanterns and torches caught me full in the eyes from the other side of the bridge. But soon the scene grew clear: and it was a strange scene. The bridge was in its place. At the far end of it stood a group of the duke's servants; two or three carried the lights which had dazzled me, three or four held pikes in rest. They were huddled together; their weapons were protruded before them; their faces were pale and agitated. To put it plainly, they looked in as arrant a fright as I have seen men look, and they gazed apprehensively at a man who stood in the middle of the bridge, sword in hand. Rupert Hentzau was in his trousers and shirt; the white linen was stained with blood, but his easy, buoyant pose told me that he was himself either not touched at all or merely scratched. There he stood, holding the bridge against them, and daring them to come on; or, rather, bidding them send Black Michael to him; and they, having no firearms, cowered before the desperate man and dared not attack him. They whispered to one another; and in the backmost rank, I saw my friend Johann, leaning against the portal of the door and stanching with a handkerchief the blood which flowed from a wound in his cheek.

By marvellous chance, I was master. The cravens would oppose me no more than they dared attack Rupert. I had but to raise my revolver, and I sent him to his account with his sins on his head. He did not so much as know that I was there. I did nothing—why, I hardly know to this day. I had killed one man stealthily that night, and another by luck rather than skill—perhaps it was that. Again, villain as the man was, I did not relish being one of a crowd against him—perhaps it was that. But stronger than either of these restrained feelings came a curiosity and a fascination which held me spellbound, watching for the outcome of the scene.

"Michael, you dog! Michael! If you can stand, come on!" cried Rupert; and he advanced a step, the group shrinking back a little before him. "Michael, you bastard! Come on!"

The answer to his taunts came in the wild cry of a woman:

"He's dead! My God, he's dead!"

"Dead!" shouted Rupert. "I struck better than I knew!" and he laughed triumphantly. Then he went on: "Down with your weapons there! I'm your master now! Down with them, I say!"

I believe they would have obeyed, but as he spoke came new things. First, there arose a distant sound, as of shouts and knockings from the other side of the chateau. My heart leapt. It must be my men, come by a happy disobedience to seek me. The noise continued, but none of the rest seemed to heed it. Their attention was chained by what now happened before their eyes. The group of servants parted and a woman staggered on to the bridge. Antoinette de Mauban was in a loose white robe, her dark hair streamed over her shoulders, her face was ghastly pale, and her eyes gleamed wildly in the light of the torches. In her shaking hand she held a revolver, and, as she tottered forward, she fired it at Rupert Hentzau. The ball missed him, and struck the woodwork over my head.

"Faith, madame," laughed Rupert, "had your eyes been no more deadly than your shooting, I had not been in this scrape—nor Black Michael in hell—tonight!"

She took no notice of his words. With a wonderful effort, she calmed herself till she stood still and rigid. Then very slowly and deliberately she began to raise her arm again, taking most careful aim.

He would be mad to risk it. He must rush on her, chancing the bullet, or retreat towards me. I covered him with my weapon.

He did neither. Before she had got her aim, he bowed in his most graceful fashion, cried "I can't kill where I've kissed," and before she or I could stop him, laid his hand on the parapet of the bridge, and lightly leapt into the moat.

At that very moment I heard a rush of feet, and a voice I knew—Sapt's—cry: "God! it's the duke—dead!" Then I knew that the King needed me no more, and throwing down my revolver, I sprang out on the bridge. There was a cry of wild wonder, "The King!" and then

I, like Rupert of Hentzau, sword in hand, vaulted over the parapet, intent on finishing my quarrel with him where I saw his curly head fifteen yards off in the water of the moat.

He swam swiftly and easily. I was weary and half crippled with my wounded arm. I could not gain on him. For a time I made no sound, but as we rounded the corner of the old keep I cried:

"Stop, Rupert, stop!"

I saw him look over his shoulder, but he swam on. He was under the bank now, searching, as I guessed, for a spot that he could climb. I knew there to be none—but there was my rope, which would still be hanging where I had left it. He would come to where it was before I could. Perhaps he would miss it—perhaps he would find it; and if he drew it up after him, he would get a good start of me. I put forth all my remaining strength and pressed on. At last I began to gain on him; for he, occupied with his search, unconsciously slackened his pace.

Ah, he had found it! A low shout of triumph came from him. He laid hold of it and began to haul himself up. I was near enough to hear him mutter: "How the devil comes this here?" I was at the rope, and he, hanging in mid air, saw me, but I could not reach him.

"Hullo! who's here?" he cried in startled tones.

For a moment, I believe, he took me for the King—I dare say I was pale enough to lend colour to the thought; but an instant later he cried:

"Why it's the play-actor! How come you here, man?"

And so saying he gained the bank.

I laid hold of the rope, but I paused. He stood on the bank, sword in hand, and he could cut my head open or spit me through the heart as I came up. I let go the rope.

"Never mind," said I; "but as I am here, I think I'll stay."

He smiled down on me.

"These women are the deuce—" he began; when suddenly the great bell of the Castle started to ring furiously, and a loud shout reached us from the moat.

Rupert smiled again, and waved his hand to me.

"I should like a turn with you, but it's a little too hot!" said he, and he disappeared from above me.

In an instant, without thinking of danger, I laid my hand to the rope. I was up. I saw him thirty yards off, running like a deer towards the shelter of the forest. For once Rupert Hentzau had chosen discretion for his part. I laid my feet to the ground and rushed after him, calling to him to stand. He would not. Unwounded and vigorous, he gained on me at every step; but, forgetting everything in the world except him and my thirst for his blood, I pressed on, and soon the deep shades of the forest of Zenda engulfed us both, pursued and pursuer.

It was three o'clock now, and day was dawning. I was on a long straight grass avenue, and a hundred yards ahead ran young Rupert, his curls waving in the fresh breeze. I was weary and panting; he looked over his shoulder and waved his hand again to me. He was mocking me, for he saw he had the pace of me. I was forced to pause for breath. A moment later, Rupert turned sharply to the right and was lost from my sight.

I thought all was over, and in deep vexation sank on the ground. But I was up again directly, for a scream rang through the forest—a woman's scream. Putting forth the last of my strength, I ran on to the place where he had turned out of my sight, and, turning also, I saw him again. But alas! I could not touch him. He was in the act of lifting a girl down from her horse; doubtless it was her scream that I heard. She looked like a small farmer's or a peasant's daughter, and she carried a basket on her arm. Probably she was on her way to the early market at Zenda. Her horse was a stout, well shaped animal. Master Rupert lifted her down amid her shrieks—the sight of him frightened her; but he treated her gently, laughed, kissed her, and gave her money. Then he jumped on the horse, sitting sideways like a woman; and then he waited for me. I, on my part, waited for him.

Presently he rode towards me, keeping his distance, however. He lifted up his hand, saying: "What did you in the Castle?"

"I killed three of your friends," said I.

"What! You got to the cells?"

"Yes."

"And the King?"

"He was hurt by Detchard before I killed Detchard, but I pray that he lives."

"You fool!" said Rupert, pleasantly.

"One thing more I did."

"And what's that?"

"I spared your life. I was behind you on the bridge, with a revolver in my hand."

"No? Faith, I was between two fires!"

"Get off your horse," I cried, "and fight like a man."

"Before a lady!" said he, pointing to the girl. "Fie, your Majesty!"

Then in my rage, hardly knowing what I did, I rushed at him. For a moment he seemed to waver. Then he reined his horse in and stood waiting for me. On I went in my folly. I seized the bridle and I struck at him. He parried and thrust at me. I fell back a pace and rushed at him again; and this time I reached his face and laid his cheek open, and darted back almost before he could strike me. He seemed almost dazed at the fierceness of my attack; otherwise I think he must have killed me. I sank on my knee panting, expecting him to ride at me. And so he would have done, and then and there, I doubt not, one or both of us would have died; but at the moment there came a shout from behind us, and, looking round, I saw, just at the turn of the avenue, a man on a horse. He was riding hard, and he carried a revolver in his hand. It was Fritz von Tarlenheim, my faithful friend. Rupert saw him, and knew that the game was up. He checked his rush at me and flung his leg over the saddle, but yet for just a moment he waited. Leaning forward, he tossed his hair off his forehead and smiled, and said: "Au revoir, Rudolf Rassendyll!"

Then, with his cheek streaming blood, but his lips laughing and his body swaying with ease and grace, he bowed to me; and he bowed to the farm-girl, who had drawn near in trembling fascination, and he waved his hand to Fritz, who was just within range and let fly a shot at him. The ball came nigh doing its work, for it struck the sword he held, and he dropped the sword with an oath, wringing his fingers and clapped his heels hard on his horse's belly, and rode away at a gallop.

And I watched him go down the long avenue, riding as though he rode for his pleasure and singing as he went, for all there was that gash in his cheek.

Once again he turned to wave his hand, and then the gloom of thickets swallowed him and he was lost from our sight. Thus he vanished—reckless and wary, graceful and graceless, handsome, debonair, vile, and unconquered. And I flung my sword passionately on the ground and cried to Fritz to ride after him. But Fritz stopped his horse, and leapt down and ran to me, and knelt, putting his arm about me. And indeed it was time, for the wound that Detchard had given me was broken forth afresh, and my blood was staining the ground.

"Then give me the horse!" I cried, staggering to my feet and throwing his arms off me. And the strength of my rage carried me so far as where the horse stood, and then I fell prone beside it. And Fritz knelt by me again.

"Fritz!" I said.

"Ay, friend—dear friend!" he said, tender as a woman.

"Is the King alive?"

He took his handkerchief and wiped my lips, and bent and kissed me on the forehead.

"Thanks to the most gallant gentleman that lives," said he softly, "the King is alive!"

The little farm-girl stood by us, weeping for fright and wide-eyed for wonder; for she had seen me at Zenda; and was not I, pallid, dripping, foul, and bloody as I was—yet was not I the King?

And when I heard that the King was alive, I strove to cry "Hurrah!" But I could not speak, and I laid my head back in Fritz's arms and closed my eyes, and I groaned; and then, lest Fritz should do me wrong in his thoughts, I opened my eyes and tried to say "Hurrah!" again. But I could not. And being very tired, and now very cold, I huddled myself close up to Fritz, to get the warmth of him, and shut my eyes again and went to sleep.

CHAPTER 20

The Prisoner and the King

In order to a full understanding of what had occurred in the Castle of Zenda, it is necessary to supplement my account of what I myself saw and did on that night by relating briefly what I afterwards learnt from Fritz and Madame de Mauban. The story told by the latter explained clearly how it happened that the cry which I had arranged as a stratagem and a sham had come, in dreadful reality, before its time, and had thus, as it seemed at the moment, ruined our hopes, while in the end it had favoured them. The unhappy woman, fired, I believe by a genuine attachment to the Duke of Strelsau, no less than by the dazzling prospects which a dominion over him opened before her eyes, had followed him at his request from Paris to Ruritania. He was a man of strong passions, but of stronger will, and his cool head ruled both. He was content to take all and give nothing. When she arrived, she was not long in finding that she had a rival in the Princess Flavia; rendered desperate, she stood at nothing which might give, or keep for her, her power over the duke. As I say, he took and gave not. Simultaneously, Antoinette found herself entangled in his audacious schemes. Unwilling to abandon him, bound to him by the chains of shame and hope, yet she would not be a decoy, nor, at his bidding, lure me to death. Hence the letters of warning she had written. Whether the lines she sent to Flavia were inspired by good or bad feeling, by jealousy or by pity, I do not know; but here also she served us well. When the duke went to Zenda, she accompanied him; and here for the first time she learnt the full measure of his cruelty, and was touched with compassion for the unfortunate King. From this time she was with us; yet, from what she told me, I know that she still (as women will) loved Michael, and trusted to gain his life, if not his pardon, from the King, as the reward for her assistance. His triumph she did not desire, for she loathed his crime, and loathed yet more fiercely what would be the prize of it—his marriage with his cousin, Princess Flavia.

At Zenda new forces came into play—the lust and daring of young Rupert. He was caught by her beauty, perhaps; perhaps it was enough for him that she belonged to another man, and that she hated him. For many days there had been quarrels and ill will between him and the duke, and the scene which I had witnessed in the duke's room was but one of many. Rupert's proposals to me, of which she had, of course, been ignorant, in no way surprised her when I related them; she had herself warned Michael against Rupert, even when she was calling on me to deliver her from both of them. On this night, then, Rupert had determined to have his will. When she had gone to her room, he, having furnished himself with a key to it, had made his entrance. Her cries had brought the duke, and there in the dark room, while she screamed, the men had fought; and Rupert, having wounded his master with a mortal blow, had, on the servants rushing in, escaped through the window as I have described. The duke's blood, spurting out, had stained his opponent's shirt; but Rupert, not knowing that he had dealt Michael his death, was eager to finish the encounter. How he meant to deal with the other three of the band, I know not. I dare say he did not think, for the killing of Michael was not premeditated. Antoinette, left alone with the duke, had tried to stanch his wound, and thus was she busied till he died; and then, hearing Rupert's taunts, she had come forth to avenge him. Me she had not seen, nor did she till I darted out of my ambush, and leapt after Rupert into the moat.

The same moment found my friends on the scene. They had reached the chateau in due time, and waited ready by the door. But Johann, swept with the rest to the rescue of the duke, did not open it; nay, he took a part against Rupert, putting himself forward more bravely than any in his anxiety to avert suspicion; and he had received a wound, in the embrasure of the window. Till nearly half-past two Sapt waited; then, following my orders, he had sent Fritz to search the banks of the moat. I was not there. Hastening back, Fritz told Sapt; and Sapt was for following orders still, and riding at full speed back to Tarlenheim; while Fritz would not hear of abandoning me, let me have ordered what I would. On this they disputed some few minutes; then Sapt, persuaded by Fritz, detached a party under Bernenstein to gallop back to Tarlenheim and bring up the marshal, while the rest fell to on the great door of the chateau. For several minutes it resisted them; then, just as Antoinette de Mauban fired at Rupert of Hentzau on the bridge, they broke in, eight of them in all: and the first door they came to was the door of Michael's room; and Michael lay dead across the threshold, with a sword-thrust through his breast. Sapt cried out at his death, as I had heard, and they rushed on the servants; but these, in fear, dropped their weapons, and Antoinette flung herself weeping at Sapt's feet. And all she cried was that I had been at the end of the bridge and leapt off. "What of the prisoner?" asked Sapt; but she shook her head. Then Sapt and Fritz, with the gentlemen behind them, crossed the bridge, slowly, warily, and without noise; and Fritz stumbled over the body of De Gautet in the way of the door. They felt him and found him dead.

Then they consulted, listening eagerly for any sound from the cells below; but there came none, and they were greatly afraid that the King's guards had killed him, and having pushed his body through the great pipe, had escaped the same way themselves. Yet, because I had been seen here, they had still some hope (thus indeed Fritz, in his friendship, told me); and going back to Michael's body, pushing aside Antoinette, who prayed by it, they found a key to the door which I had locked, and opened the door. The staircase was dark, and they would not use a torch at first, lest they should be more exposed to fire. But soon Fritz cried: "The door down there is open! See, there is light!" So they went on boldly, and found none to oppose them. And when they came to the outer room and saw the Belgian, Bersonin, lying dead, they thanked God, Sapt saying: "Ay, he has been here." Then rushing into the King's cell, they found Detchard lying dead across the dead physician, and the King on his back with his chair by him. And Fritz cried: "He's dead!" and Sapt drove all out of the room except Fritz, and knelt down by the King; and, having learnt more of wounds and the sign of death than I, he soon knew that the King was not dead, nor, if properly attended, would die. And they covered his face and carried him to Duke Michael's room, and laid him there; and Antoinette rose from praying by the body of the duke and went to bathe the King's head and dress his wounds, till a doctor came. And Sapt, seeing I had been there, and having heard Antoinette's story, sent Fritz to search the moat and then the forest. He dared send no one else. And Fritz found my horse, and feared the worst. Then, as I have told, he found me, guided by the shout with which I had called on Rupert to stop and face me. And I think a man has never been more glad to find his own brother alive than was Fritz to come on me; so that, in love and anxiety for me, he thought nothing of a thing so great as would have been the death of Rupert Hentzau. Yet, had Fritz killed him, I should have grudged it.

The enterprise of the King's rescue being thus prosperously concluded, it lay on Colonel Sapt to secure secrecy as to the King ever having been in need of rescue. Antoinette de Mauban and Johann the keeper (who, indeed, was too much hurt to be wagging his tongue just now) were sworn to reveal nothing; and Fritz went forth to find—not the King, but the unnamed friend of the King, who had lain in Zenda and flashed for a moment before the dazed eyes of Duke Michael's servants on the drawbridge. The metamorphosis had happened; and the King, wounded almost to death by the attacks of the gaolers who guarded his friend, had at last overcome them, and rested now, wounded but alive, in Black Michael's own room in the Castle. There he had been carried, his face covered with a cloak, from the cell; and thence orders issued, that if his friend were found, he should be brought directly and privately to the

71

King, and that meanwhile messengers should ride at full speed to Tarlenheim, to tell Marshall Strakencz to assure the princess of the King's safety and to come himself with all speed to greet the King. The princess was enjoined to remain at Tarlenheim, and there await her cousin's coming or his further injunctions. Thus the King would come to his own again, having wrought brave deeds, and escaped, almost by a miracle, the treacherous assault of his unnatural brother.

This ingenious arrangement of my long-headed old friend prospered in every way, save where it encountered a force that often defeats the most cunning schemes. I mean nothing else than the pleasure of a woman. For, let her cousin and sovereign send what command he chose (or Colonel Sapt chose for him), and let Marshal Strakencz insist as he would, the Princess Flavia was in no way minded to rest at Tarlenheim while her lover lay wounded at Zenda; and when the Marshal, with a small suite, rode forth from Tarlenheim on the way to Zenda, the princess's carriage followed immediately behind, and in this order they passed through the town, where the report was already rife that the King, going the night before to remonstrate with his brother, in all friendliness, for that he held one of the King's friends in confinement in the Castle, had been most traitorously set upon; that there had been a desperate conflict; that the duke was slain with several of his gentlemen; and that the King, wounded as he was, had seized and held the Castle of Zenda. All of which talk made, as may be supposed, a mighty excitement: and the wires were set in motion, and the tidings came to Strelsau only just after orders had been sent thither to parade the troops and overawe the dissatisfied quarters of the town with a display of force.

Thus the Princess Flavia came to Zenda. And as she drove up the hill, with the Marshal riding by the wheel and still imploring her to return in obedience to the King's orders, Fritz von Tarlenheim, with the prisoner of Zenda, came to the edge of the forest. I had revived from my swoon, and walked, resting on Fritz's arm; and looking out from the cover of the trees, I saw the princess. Suddenly understanding from a glance at my companion's face that we must not meet her, I sank on my knees behind a clump of bushes. But there was one whom we had forgotten, but who followed us, and was not disposed to let slip the chance of earning a smile and maybe a crown or two; and, while we lay hidden, the little farm-girl came by us and ran to the princess, curtseying and crying:

"Madame, the King is here—in the bushes! May I guide you to him, madame?"

"Nonsense, child!" said old Strakencz; "the King lies wounded in the Castle."

"Yes, sir, he's wounded, I know; but he's there—with Count Fritz—and not at the Castle," she persisted.

"Is he in two places, or are there two Kings?" asked Flavia, bewildered. "And how should he be there?"

"He pursued a gentleman, madame, and they fought till Count Fritz came; and the other gentleman took my father's horse from me and rode away; but the King is here with Count Fritz. Why, madame, is there another man in Ruritania like the King?"

"No, my child," said Flavia softly (I was told it afterwards), and she smiled and gave the girl money. "I will go and see this gentleman," and she rose to alight from the carriage.

But at this moment Sapt came riding from the Castle, and, seeing the princess, made the best of a bad job, and cried to her that the King was well tended and in no danger.

"In the Castle?" she asked.

"Where else, madame?" said he, bowing.

"But this girl says he is yonder—with Count Fritz."

Sapt turned his eyes on the child with an incredulous smile.

"Every fine gentleman is a King to such," said he.

"Why, he's as like the King as one pea to another, madame!" cried the girl, a little shaken but still obstinate.

Sapt started round. The old Marshal's face asked unspoken questions. Flavia's glance was no less eloquent. Suspicion spread quick.

72

"I'll ride myself and see this man," said Sapt hastily.

"Nay, I'll come myself," said the princess.

"Then come alone," he whispered.

And she, obedient to the strange hinting in his face, prayed the Marshal and the rest to wait; and she and Sapt came on foot towards where we lay, Sapt waving to the farm-girl to keep at a distance. And when I saw them coming, I sat in a sad heap on the ground, and buried my face in my hands. I could not look at her. Fritz knelt by me, laying his hand on my shoulder. "Speak low, whatever you say," I heard Sapt whisper as they came up; and the next thing I heard was a low cry—half of joy, half of fear—from the princess:

"It is he! Are you hurt?"

And she fell on the ground by me, and gently pulled my hands away; but I kept my eyes to the ground.

"It is the King!" she said. "Pray, Colonel Sapt, tell me where lay the wit of the joke you played on me?"

We answered none of us; we three were silent before her. Regardless of them, she threw her arms round my neck and kissed me. Then Sapt spoke in a low hoarse whisper:

"It is not the King. Don't kiss him; he's not the King."

She drew back for a moment; then, with an arm still round my neck, she asked, in superb indignation:

"Do I not know my love? Rudolf my love!"

"It is not the King," said old Sapt again; and a sudden sob broke from tender-hearted Fritz. It was the sob that told her no comedy was afoot.

"He is the King!" she cried. "It is the King's face—the King's ring—my ring! It is my love!"

"Your love, madame," said old Sapt, "but not the King. The King is there in the Castle. This gentleman—"

"Look at me, Rudolf! look at me!" she cried, taking my face between her hands. "Why do you let them torment me? Tell me what it means!"

Then I spoke, gazing into her eyes.

"God forgive me, madame!" I said. "I am not the King!"

I felt her hands clutch my cheeks. She gazed at me as never man's face was scanned yet. And I, silent again, saw wonder born, and doubt grow, and terror spring to life as she looked. And very gradually the grasp of her hands slackened; she turned to Sapt, to Fritz, and back to me: then suddenly she reeled forward and fell in my arms; and with a great cry of pain I gathered her to me and kissed her lips. Sapt laid his hand on my arm. I looked up in his face. And I laid her softly on the ground, and stood up, looking on her, cursing heaven that young Rupert's sword had spared me for this sharper pang.

CHAPTER 21

If love were all!

It was night, and I was in the cell wherein the King had lain in the Castle of Zenda. The great pipe that Rupert of Hentzau had nicknamed "Jacob's Ladder" was gone, and the lights in the room across the moat twinkled in the darkness. All was still; the din and clash of strife were gone. I had spent the day hidden in the forest, from the time when Fritz had led me off, leaving Sapt with the princess. Under cover of dusk, muffled up, I had been brought to the Castle and lodged where I now lay. Though three men had died there—two of them by my hand—I was not troubled by ghosts. I had thrown myself on a pallet by the window, and was looking out on the black water; Johann, the keeper, still pale from his wound, but not much

73

hurt besides, had brought me supper. He told me that the King was doing well, that he had seen the princess; that she and he, Sapt and Fritz, had been long together. Marshal Strakencz was gone to Strelsau; Black Michael lay in his coffin, and Antoinette de Mauban watched by him; had I not heard, from the chapel, priests singing mass for him?

Outside there were strange rumours afloat. Some said that the prisoner of Zenda was dead; some, that he had vanished yet alive; some, that he was a friend who had served the King well in some adventure in England; others, that he had discovered the Duke's plots, and had therefore been kidnapped by him. One or two shrewd fellows shook their heads and said only that they would say nothing, but they had suspicions that more was to be known than was known, if Colonel Sapt would tell all he knew.

Thus Johann chattered till I sent him away and lay there alone, thinking, not of the future, but—as a man is wont to do when stirring things have happened to him—rehearsing the events of the past weeks, and wondering how strangely they had fallen out. And above me, in the stillness of the night, I heard the standards flapping against their poles, for Black Michael's banner hung there half-mast high, and above it the royal flag of Ruritania, floating for one night more over my head. Habit grows so quick, that only by an effort did I recollect that it floated no longer for me.

Presently Fritz von Tarlenheim came into the room. I was standing then by the window; the glass was opened, and I was idly fingering the cement which clung to the masonry where "Jacob's Ladder" had been. He told me briefly that the King wanted me, and together we crossed the drawbridge and entered the room that had been Black Michael's.

The King was lying there in bed; our doctor from Tarlenheim was in attendance on him, and whispered to me that my visit must be brief. The King held out his hand and shook mine. Fritz and the doctor withdrew to the window.

I took the King's ring from my finger and placed it on his.

"I have tried not to dishonour it, sire," said I.

"I can't talk much to you," he said, in a weak voice. "I have had a great fight with Sapt and the Marshal—for we have told the Marshal everything. I wanted to take you to Strelsau and keep you with me, and tell everyone of what you had done; and you would have been my best and nearest friend, Cousin Rudolf. But they tell me I must not, and that the secret must be kept—if kept it can be."

"They are right, sire. Let me go. My work here is done."

"Yes, it is done, as no man but you could have done it. When they see me again, I shall have my beard on; I shall—yes, faith, I shall be wasted with sickness. They will not wonder that the King looks changed in face. Cousin, I shall try to let them find him changed in nothing else. You have shown me how to play the King."

"Sire," said I. "I can take no praise from you. It is by the narrowest grace of God that I was not a worse traitor than your brother."

He turned inquiring eyes on me; but a sick man shrinks from puzzles, and he had no strength to question me. His glance fell on Flavia's ring, which I wore. I thought he would question me about it; but, after fingering it idly, he let his head fall on his pillow.

"I don't know when I shall see you again," he said faintly, almost listlessly.

"If I can ever serve you again, sire," I answered.

His eyelids closed. Fritz came with the doctor. I kissed the King's hand, and let Fritz lead me away. I have never seen the King since.

Outside, Fritz turned, not to the right, back towards the drawbridge, but to the left, and without speaking led me upstairs, through a handsome corridor in the chateau.

"Where are we going?" I asked.

Looking away from me, Fritz answered:

"She has sent for you. When it is over, come back to the bridge. I'll wait for you there."

"What does she want?" said I, breathing quickly.

He shook his head.

"Does she know everything?"

"Yes, everything."

He opened a door, and gently pushing me in, closed it behind me. I found myself in a drawing-room, small and richly furnished. At first I thought that I was alone, for the light that came from a pair of shaded candles on the mantelpiece was very dim. But presently I discerned a woman's figure standing by the window. I knew it was the princess, and I walked up to her, fell on one knee, and carried the hand that hung by her side to my lips. She neither moved nor spoke. I rose to my feet, and, piercing the gloom with my eager eyes, saw her pale face and the gleam of her hair, and before I knew, I spoke softly:

"Flavia!"

She trembled a little, and looked round. Then she darted to me, taking hold of me.

"Don't stand, don't stand! No, you mustn't! You're hurt! Sit down—here, here!"

She made me sit on a sofa, and put her hand on my forehead.

"How hot your head is," she said, sinking on her knees by me. Then she laid her head against me, and I heard her murmur: "My darling, how hot your head is!"

Somehow love gives even to a dull man the knowledge of his lover's heart. I had come to humble myself and pray pardon for my presumption; but what I said now was:

"I love you with all my heart and soul!"

For what troubled and shamed her? Not her love for me, but the fear that I had counterfeited the lover as I had acted the King, and taken her kisses with a smothered smile.

"With all my life and heart," said I, as she clung to me. "Always, from the first moment I saw you in the Cathedral! There has been but one woman in the world to me—and there will be no other. But God forgive me the wrong I've done you!"

"They made you do it!" she said quickly; and she added, raising her head and looking in my eyes: "It might have made no difference if I'd known it. It was always you, never the King!"

"I meant to tell you," said I. "I was going to on the night of the ball in Strelsau, when Sapt interrupted me. After that, I couldn't—I couldn't risk losing you before—before—I must! My darling, for you I nearly left the King to die!"

"I know, I know! What are we to do now, Rudolf?"

I put my arm round her and held her up while I said:

"I am going away tonight."

"Ah, no, no!" she cried. "Not tonight!"

"I must go tonight, before more people have seen me. And how would you have me stay, sweetheart, except—?"

"If I could come with you!" she whispered very low.

"My God!" said I roughly, "don't talk about that!" and I thrust her a little back from me.

"Why not? I love you. You are as good a gentleman as the King!"

Then I was false to all that I should have held by. For I caught her in my arms and prayed her, in words that I will not write, to come with me, daring all Ruritania to take her from me. And for a while she listened, with wondering, dazzled eyes. But as her eyes looked on me, I grew ashamed, and my voice died away in broken murmurs and stammerings, and at last I was silent.

She drew herself away from me and stood against the wall, while I sat on the edge of the sofa, trembling in every limb, knowing what I had done—loathing it, obstinate not to undo it. So we rested a long time.

"I am mad!" I said sullenly.

"I love your madness, dear," she answered.

Her face was away from me, but I caught the sparkle of a tear on her cheek. I clutched the sofa with my hand and held myself there.

"Is love the only thing?" she asked, in low, sweet tones that seemed to bring a calm even to my wrung heart. "If love were the only thing, I would follow you—in rags, if need be—to the world's end; for you hold my heart in the hollow of your hand! But is love the only thing?"

I made no answer. It gives me shame now to think that I would not help her.

She came near me and laid her hand on my shoulder. I put my hand up and held hers.

"I know people write and talk as if it were. Perhaps, for some, Fate lets it be. Ah, if I were one of them! But if love had been the only thing, you would have let the King die in his cell."

I kissed her hand.

"Honour binds a woman too, Rudolf. My honour lies in being true to my country and my House. I don't know why God has let me love you; but I know that I must stay."

Still I said nothing; and she, pausing a while, then went on:

"Your ring will always be on my finger, your heart in my heart, the touch of your lips on mine. But you must go and I must stay. Perhaps I must do what it kills me to think of doing."

I knew what she meant, and a shiver ran through me. But I could not utterly fail her. I rose and took her hand.

"Do what you will, or what you must," I said. "I think God shows His purposes to such as you. My part is lighter; for your ring shall be on my finger and your heart in mine, and no touch save of your lips will ever be on mine. So, may God comfort you, my darling!"

There struck on our ears the sound of singing. The priests in the chapel were singing masses for the souls of those who lay dead. They seemed to chant a requiem over our buried joy, to pray forgiveness for our love that would not die. The soft, sweet, pitiful music rose and fell as we stood opposite one another, her hands in mine.

"My queen and my beauty!" said I.

"My lover and true knight!" she said. "Perhaps we shall never see one another again. Kiss me, my dear, and go!"

I kissed her as she bade me; but at the last she clung to me, whispering nothing but my name, and that over and over again—and again—and again; and then I left her.

Rapidly I walked down to the bridge. Sapt and Fritz were waiting for me. Under their directions I changed my dress, and muffling my face, as I had done more than once before, I mounted with them at the door of the Castle, and we three rode through the night and on to the breaking day, and found ourselves at a little roadside station just over the border of Ruritania. The train was not quite due, and I walked with them in a meadow by a little brook while we waited for it. They promised to send me all news; they overwhelmed me with kindness—even old Sapt was touched to gentleness, while Fritz was half unmanned. I listened in a kind of dream to all they said. "Rudolf! Rudolf! Rudolf!" still rang in my ears—a burden of sorrow and of love. At last they saw that I could not heed them, and we walked up and down in silence, till Fritz touched me on the arm, and I saw, a mile or more away, the blue smoke of the train. Then I held out a hand to each of them.

"We are all but half-men this morning," said I, smiling. "But we have been men, eh, Sapt and Fritz, old friends? We have run a good course between us."

"We have defeated traitors and set the King firm on his throne," said Sapt.

Then Fritz von Tarlenheim suddenly, before I could discern his purpose or stay him, uncovered his head and bent as he used to do, and kissed my hand; and as I snatched it away, he said, trying to laugh:

"Heaven doesn't always make the right men kings!"

Old Sapt twisted his mouth as he wrung my hand.

"The devil has his share in most things," said he.

The people at the station looked curiously at the tall man with the muffled face, but we took no notice of their glances. I stood with my two friends and waited till the train came up to us. Then we shook hands again, saying nothing; and both this time—and, indeed, from old Sapt it seemed strange—bared their heads, and so stood still till the train bore me away from their sight. So that it was thought some great man travelled privately for his pleasure from the little station that morning; whereas, in truth it was only I, Rudolf Rassendyll, an English gentleman, a cadet of a good house, but a man of no wealth nor position, nor of much rank. They would have been disappointed to know that. Yet had they known all they would have looked more curiously still. For, be I what I might now, I had been for three months a King, which, if not a thing to be proud of, is at least an experience to have undergone. Doubtless I should have thought more of it, had there not echoed through the air, from the towers of Zenda that we were leaving far away, into my ears and into my heart the cry of a woman's love—"Rudolf! Rudolf! Rudolf!"

Hark! I hear it now!

CHAPTER 22

Present, Past—and Future?

The details of my return home can have but little interest. I went straight to the Tyrol and spent a quiet fortnight—mostly on my back, for a severe chill developed itself; and I was also the victim of a nervous reaction, which made me weak as a baby. As soon as I had reached my quarters, I sent an apparently careless postcard to my brother, announcing my good health and prospective return. That would serve to satisfy the inquiries as to my whereabouts, which were probably still vexing the Prefect of the Police of Strelsau. I let my moustache and imperial grow again; and as hair comes quickly on my face, they were respectable, though not luxuriant, by the time that I landed myself in Paris and called on my friend George Featherly. My interview with him was chiefly remarkable for the number of unwilling but necessary falsehoods that I told; and I rallied him unmercifully when he told me that he had made up his mind that I had gone in the track of Madame de Mauban to Strelsau. The lady, it appeared, was back in Paris, but was living in great seclusion—a fact for which gossip found no difficulty in accounting. Did not all the world know of the treachery and death of Duke Michael? Nevertheless, George bade Bertram Bertrand be of good cheer, "for," said he flippantly, "a live poet is better than a dead duke." Then he turned on me and asked:

"What have you been doing to your moustache?"

"To tell the truth," I answered, assuming a sly air, "a man now and then has reasons for wishing to alter his appearance. But it's coming on very well again."

"What? Then I wasn't so far out! If not the fair Antoinette, there was a charmer?"

"There is always a charmer," said I, sententiously.

But George would not be satisfied till he had wormed out of me (he took much pride in his ingenuity) an absolutely imaginary love-affair, attended with the proper soupçon of scandal, which had kept me all this time in the peaceful regions of the Tyrol. In return for this narrative, George regaled me with a great deal of what he called "inside information" (known only to diplomatists), as to the true course of events in Ruritania, the plots and counterplots. In his opinion, he told me, with a significant nod, there was more to be said for Black Michael than the public supposed; and he hinted at a well-founded suspicion that the mysterious prisoner of Zenda, concerning whom a good many paragraphs had appeared, was not a man at all, but (here I had much ado not to smile) a woman disguised as a man; and that strife between the King and his brother for this imaginary lady's favour was at the bottom of their quarrel.

"Perhaps it was Madame de Mauban herself," I suggested.

"No!" said George decisively, "Antoinette de Mauban was jealous of her, and betrayed the duke to the King for that reason. And, to confirm what I say, it's well known that the Princess Flavia is now extremely cold to the King, after having been most affectionate."

At this point I changed the subject, and escaped from George's "inspired" delusions. But if diplomatists never know anything more than they had succeeded in finding out in this instance, they appear to me to be somewhat expensive luxuries.

While in Paris I wrote to Antoinette, though I did not venture to call upon her. I received in return a very affecting letter, in which she assured me that the King's generosity and kindness, no less than her regard for me, bound her conscience to absolute secrecy. She expressed the intention of settling in the country, and withdrawing herself entirely from society. Whether she carried out her designs, I have never heard; but as I have not met her, or heard news of her up to this time, it is probable that she did. There is no doubt that she was deeply attached to the Duke of Strelsau; and her conduct at the time of his death proved that no knowledge of the man's real character was enough to root her regard for him out of her heart.

I had one more battle left to fight—a battle that would, I knew, be severe, and was bound to end in my complete defeat. Was I not back from the Tyrol, without having made any study of its inhabitants, institutions, scenery, fauna, flora, or other features? Had I not simply wasted my time in my usual frivolous, good-for-nothing way? That was the aspect of the matter which, I was obliged to admit, would present itself to my sister-in-law; and against a verdict based on such evidence, I had really no defence to offer. It may be supposed, then, that I presented myself in Park Lane in a shamefaced, sheepish fashion. On the whole, my reception was not so alarming as I had feared. It turned out that I had done, not what Rose wished, but—the next best thing—what she prophesied. She had declared that I should make no notes, record no observations, gather no materials. My brother, on the other hand, had been weak enough to maintain that a serious resolve had at length animated me.

When I returned empty-handed, Rose was so occupied in triumphing over Burlesdon that she let me down quite easily, devoting the greater part of her reproaches to my failure to advertise my friends of my whereabouts.

"We've wasted a lot of time trying to find you," she said.

"I know you have," said I. "Half our ambassadors have led weary lives on my account. George Featherly told me so. But why should you have been anxious? I can take care of myself."

"Oh, it wasn't that," she cried scornfully, "but I wanted to tell you about Sir Jacob Borrodaile. You know, he's got an Embassy—at least, he will have in a month—and he wrote to say he hoped you would go with him."

"Where's he going to?"

"He's going to succeed Lord Topham at Strelsau," said she. "You couldn't have a nicer place, short of Paris."

"Strelsau! H'm!" said I, glancing at my brother.

"Oh, that doesn't matter!" exclaimed Rose impatiently. "Now, you will go, won't you?"

"I don't know that I care about it!"

"Oh, you're too exasperating!"

"And I don't think I can go to Strelsau. My dear Rose, would it be—suitable?"

"Oh, nobody remembers that horrid old story now."

Upon this, I took out of my pocket a portrait of the King of Ruritania. It had been taken a month or two before he ascended the throne. She could not miss my point when I said, putting it into her hands:

"In case you've not seen, or not noticed, a picture of Rudolf V, there he is. Don't you think they might recall the story, if I appeared at the Court of Ruritania?"

My sister-in-law looked at the portrait, and then at me.

"Good gracious!" she said, and flung the photograph down on the table.

"What do you say, Bob?" I asked.

Burlesdon got up, went to a corner of the room, and searched in a heap of newspapers. Presently he came back with a copy of the Illustrated London News. Opening the paper, he displayed a double-page engraving of the Coronation of Rudolf V at Strelsau. The photograph and the picture he laid side by side. I sat at the table fronting them; and, as I looked, I grew absorbed. My eye travelled from my own portrait to Sapt, to Strakencz, to the rich robes of the Cardinal, to Black Michael's face, to the stately figure of the princess by his side. Long I looked and eagerly. I was roused by my brother's hand on my shoulder. He was gazing down at me with a puzzled expression.

"It's a remarkable likeness, you see," said I. "I really think I had better not go to Ruritania." Rose, though half convinced, would not abandon her position.

"It's just an excuse," she said pettishly. "You don't want to do anything. Why, you might become an ambassador!"

"I don't think I want to be an ambassador," said I.

"It's more than you ever will be," she retorted.

That is very likely true, but it is not more than I have been.

The idea of being an ambassador could scarcely dazzle me. I had been a king!

So pretty Rose left us in dudgeon; and Burlesdon, lighting a cigarette, looked at me still with that curious gaze.

"That picture in the paper—" he said.

"Well, what of it? It shows that the King of Ruritania and your humble servant are as like as two peas."

My brother shook his head.

"I suppose so," he said. "But I should know you from the man in the photograph."

"And not from the picture in the paper?"

"I should know the photograph from the picture: the picture's very like the photograph, but—"

"Well?"

"It's more like you!" said my brother.

My brother is a good man and true—so that, for all that he is a married man and mighty fond of his wife, he should know any secret of mine. But this secret was not mine, and I could not tell it to him.

"I don't think it's so much like me as the photograph," said I boldly. "But, anyhow, Bob, I won't go to Strelsau."

"No, don't go to Strelsau, Rudolf," said he.

And whether he suspects anything, or has a glimmer of the truth, I do not know. If he has, he keeps it to himself, and he and I never refer to it. And we let Sir Jacob Borrodaile find another attache.

Since all these events whose history I have set down happened I have lived a very quiet life at a small house which I have taken in the country. The ordinary ambitions and aims of men in my position seem to me dull and unattractive. I have little fancy for the whirl of society, and none for the jostle of politics. Lady Burlesdon utterly despairs of me; my neighbours think me an indolent, dreamy, unsociable fellow. Yet I am a young man; and sometimes I have a fancy—the superstitious would call it a presentiment—that my part in life is not yet altogether played; that, somehow and some day, I shall mix again in great affairs, I shall again spin policies in a busy brain, match my wits against my enemies', brace my muscles to fight a good fight and strike stout blows. Such is the tissue of my thoughts as, with gun or rod in hand, I wander through the woods or by the side of the stream. Whether the fancy will be fulfilled, I cannot tell—still less whether the scene that, led by memory, I lay for my new exploits will be the true one—for I love to see myself once again in the crowded streets of Strelsau, or beneath the frowning keep of the Castle of Zenda.

Thus led, my broodings leave the future, and turn back on the past. Shapes rise before me in long array—the wild first revel with the King, the rush with my brave tea-table, the night in the moat, the pursuit in the forest: my friends and my foes, the people who learnt to love and honour me, the desperate men who tried to kill me. And, from amidst these last, comes one who alone of all of them yet moves on earth, though where I know not, yet plans (as I do not doubt) wickedness, yet turns women's hearts to softness and men's to fear and hate. Where is young Rupert of Hentzau—the boy who came so nigh to beating me? When his name comes into my head, I feel my hand grip and the blood move quicker through my veins: and the hint of Fate—the presentiment—seems to grow stronger and more definite, and to whisper insistently in my ear that I have yet a hand to play with young Rupert; therefore I exercise myself in arms, and seek to put off the day when the vigour of youth must leave me. One break comes every year in my quiet life. Then I go to Dresden, and there I am met by my dear friend and companion, Fritz von Tarlenheim. Last time, his pretty wife Helga came, and a lusty crowing baby with her. And for a week Fritz and I are together, and I hear all of what falls out in Strelsau; and in the evenings, as we walk and smoke together, we talk of Sapt, and of the King, and often of young Rupert; and, as the hours grow small, at last we speak of Flavia. For every year Fritz carries with him to Dresden a little box; in it lies a red rose, and round the stalk of the rose is a slip of paper with the words written: "Rudolf—Flavia—always." And the like I send back by him. That message, and the wearing of the rings, are all that now bind me and the Queen of Ruritania. For—nobler, as I hold her, for the act—she has followed where her duty to her country and her House led her, and is the wife of the King, uniting his subjects to him by the love they bear to her, giving peace and quiet days to thousands by her self-sacrifice. There are moments when I dare not think of it, but there are others when I rise in spirit to where she ever dwells; then I can thank God that I love the noblest lady in the world, the most gracious and beautiful, and that there was nothing in my love that made her fall short in her high duty.

Shall I see her face again—the pale face and the glorious hair? Of that I know nothing; Fate has no hint, my heart no presentiment. I do not know. In this world, perhaps—nay, it is likely—never. And can it be that somewhere, in a manner whereof our flesh-bound minds have no apprehension, she and I will be together again, with nothing to come between us, nothing to forbid our love? That I know not, nor wiser heads than mine. But if it be never—if I can never hold sweet converse again with her, or look upon her face, or know from her her love; why, then, this side the grave, I will live as becomes the man whom she loves; and, for the other side, I must pray a dreamless sleep.

CHAPTER I. THE QUEEN'S GOOD-BY

A man who has lived in the world, marking how every act, although in itself perhaps light and insignificant, may become the source of consequences that spread far and wide, and flow for years or centuries, could scarcely feel secure in reckoning that with the death of the Duke of Strelsau and the restoration of King Rudolf to liberty and his throne, there would end, for good and all, the troubles born of Black Michael's daring conspiracy. The stakes had been high, the struggle keen; the edge of passion had been sharpened, and the seeds of enmity sown. Yet Michael, having struck for the crown, had paid for the blow with his life: should there not then be an end? Michael was dead, the Princess her cousin's wife, the story in safe keeping, and Mr. Rassendyll's face seen no more in Ruritania. Should there not then be an end? So said I to my friend the Constable of Zenda, as we talked by the bedside of Marshal Strakencz. The old man, already nearing the death that soon after robbed us of his aid and counsel, bowed his head in assent: in the aged and ailing the love of peace breeds hope of it. But Colonel Sapt tugged at his gray moustache, and twisted his black cigar in his mouth, saying, "You're very sanguine, friend Fritz. But is Rupert of Hentzau dead? I had not heard it."

Well said, and like old Sapt! Yet the man is little without the opportunity, and Rupert by himself could hardly have troubled our repose. Hampered by his own guilt, he dared not set his foot in the kingdom from which by rare good luck he had escaped, but wandered to and fro over Europe, making a living by his wits, and, as some said, adding to his resources by gallantries for which he did not refuse substantial recompense. But he kept himself constantly before our eyes, and never ceased to contrive how he might gain permission to return and enjoy the estates to which his uncle's death had entitled him. The chief agent through whom he had the effrontery to approach the king was his relative, the Count of Luzau-Rischenheim, a young man of high rank and great wealth who was devoted to Rupert. The count fulfilled his mission well: acknowledging Rupert's heavy offences, he put forward in his behalf the pleas of youth and of the predominant influence which Duke Michael had exercised over his adherent, and promised, in words so significant as to betray Rupert's own dictation, a future fidelity no less discreet than hearty. "Give me my price and I'll hold my tongue," seemed to come in Rupert's off-hand accents through his cousin's deferential lips. As may be supposed, however, the king and those who advised him in the matter, knowing too well the manner of man the Count of Hentzau was, were not inclined to give ear to his ambassador's prayer. We kept firm hold on Master Rupert's revenues, and as good watch as we could on his movements; for we were most firmly determined that he should never return to Ruritania. Perhaps we might have obtained his extradition and hanged him on the score of his crimes; but in these days every rogue who deserves no better than to be strung up to the nearest tree must have what they call a fair trial; and we feared that, if Rupert were handed over to our police and arraigned before the courts at Strelsau, the secret which we guarded so sedulously would become the gossip of all the city, ay, and of all Europe. So Rupert went unpunished except by banishment and the impounding of his rents.

Yet Sapt was in the right about him. Helpless as he seemed, he did not for an instant abandon the contest. He lived in the faith that his chance would come, and from day to day was ready for its coming. He schemed against us as we schemed to protect ourselves from him; if we watched him, he kept his eye on us. His ascendency over Luzau-Rischenheim grew markedly greater after a visit which his cousin paid to him in Paris. From this time the young count began to supply him with resources. Thus armed, he gathered instruments round him and organized a system of espionage that carried to his ears all our actions and the whole position of affairs at court. He knew, far more accurately than anyone else outside the royal circle, the measures taken for the government of the kingdom and the considerations that dictated the royal policy. More than this, he possessed himself of every detail concerning the king's health, although the utmost reticence was observed on this subject. Had his discoveries stopped there, they would have been vexatious and disquieting, but perhaps of little serious harm. They went further. Set on the track by his acquaintance with what had passed during Mr. Rassendyll's tenure of the throne, he penetrated the secret which had been kept successfully from the king himself. In the knowledge of it he found the opportunity for which he had waited; in its bold use he discerned his chance. I cannot say whether he were influenced more strongly by his desire to reestablish his position in the kingdom or by the grudge he bore against Mr. Rassendyll. He loved power and money; dearly he loved revenge also. No doubt both motives worked together, and he was rejoiced to find that the weapon put into his hand had a double edge; with one he hoped to cut his own path clear; with the other, to wound the man he hated through the woman whom that man loved. In fine, the Count of Hentzau, shrewdly discerning the feeling that existed between the queen and Rudolf Rassendyll, set his spies to work, and was rewarded by discovering the object of my yearly meetings with Mr. Rassendyll. At least he conjectured the nature of my errand; this was enough for him. Head and hand were soon busy in turning the knowledge to account; scruples of the heart never stood in Rupert's way.

The marriage which had set all Ruritania on fire with joy and formed in the people's eyes the visible triumph over Black Michael and his fellow-conspirators was now three years old. For three years the Princess Flavia had been queen. I am come by now to the age when a man should look out on life with an eye undimmed by the mists of passion. My love-making days are over; yet there is nothing for which I am more thankful to Almighty God than the gift of my wife's love. In storm it has been my anchor, and in clear skies my star. But we common folk are free to follow our hearts; am I an old fool for saying that he is a fool who follows anything else? Our liberty is not for princes. We need wait for no future world to balance the luck of men; even here there is an equipoise. From the highly placed a price is exacted for their state, their wealth, and their honors, as heavy as these are great; to the poor, what is to us mean and of no sweetness may appear decked in the robes of pleasure and delight. Well, if it were not so, who could sleep at nights? The burden laid on Queen Flavia I knew, and know, so well as a man can know it. I think it needs a woman to know it fully; for even now my wife's eyes fill with tears when we speak of it. Yet she bore it, and if she failed in anything, I wonder that it was in so little. For it was not only that she had never loved the king and had loved another with all her heart. The king's health, shattered by the horror and rigors of his imprisonment in the castle of Zenda, soon broke utterly. He lived, indeed; nay, he shot and hunted, and kept in his hand some measure, at least, of government. But always from the day of his release he was a fretful invalid, different utterly from the gay and jovial prince whom Michael's villains had caught in the shooting lodge. There was worse than this. As time went on, the first impulse of gratitude and admiration that he had felt towards Mr. Rassendyll died away. He came to brood more and more on what had passed while he was a prisoner; he was possessed not only by a haunting dread of Rupert of Hentzau, at whose hands he had suffered so greatly, but also by a morbid, half mad jealousy of Mr. Rassendyll. Rudolf had played the hero while he lay helpless. Rudolf's were the exploits for which his own people cheered him in his own capital. Rudolf's were the laurels that crowned his impatient brow. He had enough nobility to resent his borrowed credit, without the fortitude to endure it manfully. And the hateful comparison struck him nearer home. Sapt would tell him bluntly that Rudolf did this or that, set this precedent or that, laid down this or the other policy, and that the king could do no better than follow in Rudolf's steps. Mr. Rassendyll's name seldom passed his wife's lips, but when she spoke of him it was as one speaks of a great man who is dead, belittling all the living by the shadow of his name. I do not believe that the king discerned that truth which his wife spent her days in hiding from him; yet he was uneasy if Rudolf's name were mentioned by Sapt or myself, and from the queen's mouth he could not bear it. I have seen him fall into fits of passion on the mere sound of it; for he lost control of himself on what seemed slight provocation.

Moved by this disquieting jealousy, he sought continually to exact from the queen proofs of love and care beyond what most husbands can boast of, or, in my humble judgment, make good their right to, always asking of her what in his heart he feared was not hers to give. Much she did in pity and in duty; but in some moments, being but human and herself a woman of high temper, she failed; then the slight rebuff or involuntary coldness was magnified by a sick man's fancy into great offence or studied insult, and nothing that she could do would atone for it. Thus they, who had never in truth come together, drifted yet further apart; he was alone in his sickness and suspicion, she in her sorrows and her memories. There was no child to bridge the gulf between them, and although she was his queen and his wife, she grew almost a stranger to him. So he seemed to will that it should be.

Thus, worse than widowed, she lived for three years; and once only in each year she sent three words to the man she loved, and received from him three words in answer. Then her strength failed her. A pitiful scene had occurred in which the king peevishly upbraided her in regard to some trivial matter—the occasion escapes my memory—speaking to her before others words that even alone she could not have listened to with dignity. I was there, and Sapt; the colonel's small eyes had gleamed in anger. "I should like to shut his mouth for him," I heard him mutter, for the king's waywardness had well-nigh worn out even his devotion. The thing, of which I will say no more, happened a day or two before I was to set out to meet Mr. Rassendyll. I was to seek him this time at Wintenberg, for I had been recognized the year before at Dresden; and Wintenberg, being a smaller place and less in the way of chance visitors, was deemed safer. I remember well how she was when she called me into her own room, a few hours after she had left the king. She stood by the table; the box was on it, and I knew well that the red rose and the message were within. But there was more to-day. Without preface she broke into the subject of my errand.

"I must write to him," she said. "I can't bear it, I must write. My dear friend Fritz, you will carry it safely for me, won't you? And he must write to me. And you'll bring that safely, won't you? Ah, Fritz, I know I'm wrong, but I'm starved, starved, starved! And it's for the last time. For I know now that if I send anything, I must send more. So after this time I won't send at all. But I must say good-by to him; I must have his good-by to carry me through my life. This once, then, Fritz, do it for me."

The tears rolled down her cheeks, which to-day were flushed out of their paleness to a stormy red; her eyes defied me even while they pleaded. I bent my head and kissed her hand.

"With God's help I'll carry it safely and bring his safely, my queen," said I.

"And tell me how he looks. Look at him closely, Fritz. See if he is well and seems strong. Oh, and make him merry and happy! Bring that smile to his lips, Fritz, and the merry twinkle to his eyes. When you speak of me, see if he—if he looks as if he still loved me." But then she broke off, crying, "But don't tell him I said that. He'd be grieved if I doubted his love. I don't doubt it; I don't, indeed; but still tell me how he looks when you speak of me, won't you, Fritz? See, here's the letter."

Taking it from her bosom, she kissed it before she gave it to me. Then she added a thousand cautions, how I was to carry her letter, how I was to go and how return, and how I was to run no danger, because my wife Helga loved me as well as she would have loved her husband had Heaven been kinder. "At least, almost as I should, Fritz," she said, now between smiles and tears. She would not believe that any woman could love as she loved.

I left the queen and went to prepare for my journey. I used to take only one servant with me, and I had chosen a different man each year. None of them had known that I met Mr. Rassendyll, but supposed that I was engaged on the private business which I made my pretext for obtaining leave of absence from the king. This time I had determined to take with me a Swiss youth who had entered my service only a few weeks before. His name was Bauer; he seemed a stolid, somewhat stupid fellow, but as honest as the day and very obliging.

He had come to me well recommended, and I had not hesitated to engage him. I chose him for my companion now, chiefly because he was a foreigner and therefore less likely to gossip with the other servants when we returned. I do not pretend to much cleverness, but I confess that it vexes me to remember how that stout, guileless-looking youth made a fool of me. For Rupert knew that I had met Mr. Rassendyll the year before at Dresden; Rupert was keeping a watchful eye on all that passed in Strelsau; Rupert had procured the fellow his fine testimonials and sent him to me, in the hope that he would chance on something of advantage to his employer. My resolve to take him to Wintenberg may have been hoped for, but could scarcely have been counted on; it was the added luck that waits so often on the plans of a clever schemer.

Going to take leave of the king, I found him huddled over the fire. The day was not cold, but the damp chill of his dungeon seemed to have penetrated to the very core of his bones. He was annoyed at my going, and questioned me peevishly about the business that occasioned my journey. I parried his curiosity as I best could, but did not succeed in appeasing his ill-humor. Half ashamed of his recent outburst, half-anxious to justify it to himself, he cried fretfully:

"Business! Yes, any business is a good enough excuse for leaving me! By Heaven, I wonder if a king was ever served so badly as I am! Why did you trouble to get me out of Zenda? Nobody wants me, nobody cares whether I live or die."

To reason with such a mood was impossible. I could only assure him that I would hasten my return by all possible means.

"Yes, pray do," said he. "I want somebody to look after me. Who knows what that villain Rupert may attempt against me? And I can't defend myself can I? I'm not Rudolf Rassendyll, am I?"

Thus, with a mixture of plaintiveness and malice, he scolded me. At last I stood silent, waiting till he should be pleased to dismiss me. At any rate I was thankful that he entertained no suspicion as to my errand. Had I spoken a word of Mr. Rassendyll he would not have let me go. He had fallen foul of me before on learning that I was in communication with Rudolf; so completely had jealousy destroyed gratitude in his breast. If he had known what I carried, I do not think that he could have hated his preserver more. Very likely some such feeling was natural enough; it was none the less painful to perceive.

On leaving the king's presence, I sought out the Constable of Zenda. He knew my errand; and, sitting down beside him, I told him of the letter I carried, and arranged how to apprise him of my fortune surely and quickly. He was not in a good humor that day: the king had ruffled him also, and Colonel Sapt had no great reserve of patience.

"If we haven't cut one another's throats before then, we shall all be at Zenda by the time you arrive at Wintenberg," he said. "The court moves there to-morrow, and I shall be there as long as the king is."

He paused, and then added: "Destroy the letter if there's any danger."

I nodded my head.

"And destroy yourself with it, if there's the only way," he went on with a surly smile. "Heaven knows why she must send such a silly message at all; but since she must, she'd better have sent me with it."

I knew that Sapt was in the way of jeering at all sentiment, and I took no notice of the terms that he applied to the queen's farewell. I contented myself with answering the last part of what he said.

"No, it's better you should be here," I urged. "For if I should lose the letter—though there's little chance of it—you could prevent it from coming to the king."

"I could try," he grinned. "But on my life, to run the chance for a letter's sake! A letter's a poor thing to risk the peace of a kingdom for."

"Unhappily," said I, "it's the only thing that a messenger can well carry."

"Off with you, then," grumbled the colonel. "Tell Rassendyll from me that he did well. But tell him to do something more. Let 'em say good-by and have done with it. Good God, is he going to waste all his life thinking of a woman he never sees?" Sapt's air was full of indignation.

"What more is he to do?" I asked. "Isn't his work here done?"

"Ay, it's done. Perhaps it's done," he answered. "At least he has given us back our good king." To lay on the king the full blame for what he was would have been rank injustice. Sapt was not guilty of it, but his disappointment was bitter that all our efforts had secured no better ruler for Ruritania. Sapt could serve, but he liked his master to be a man.

"Ay, I'm afraid the lad's work here is done," he said, as I shook him by the hand. Then a sudden light came in his eyes. "Perhaps not," he muttered. "Who knows?"

A man need not, I hope, be deemed uxorious for liking a quiet dinner alone with his wife before he starts on a long journey. Such, at least, was my fancy; and I was annoyed to find that Helga's cousin, Anton von Strofzin, had invited himself to share our meal and our farewell. He conversed with his usual airy emptiness on all the topics that were supplying Strelsau with gossip. There were rumors that the king was ill; that the queen was angry at being carried off to Zenda; that the archbishop meant to preach against low dresses; that the chancellor was to be dismissed; that his daughter was to be married; and so forth. I heard without listening. But the last bit of his budget caught my wandering attention.

"They were betting at the club," said Anton, "that Rupert of Hentzau would be recalled. Have you heard anything about it, Fritz?"

If I had known anything, it is needless to say that I should not have confided it to Anton. But the suggested step was so utterly at variance with the king's intentions that I made no difficulty about contradicting the report with an authoritative air. Anton heard me with a judicial wrinkle on his smooth brow.

"That's all very well," said he, "and I dare say you're bound to say so. All I know is that Rischenheim dropped a hint to Colonel Markel a day or two ago."

"Rischenheim believes what he hopes," said I.

"And where's he gone?" cried Anton, exultantly. "Why has he suddenly left Strelsau? I tell you he's gone to meet Rupert, and I'll bet you what you like he carries some proposal. Ah, you don't know everything, Fritz, my boy?"

It was indeed true that I did not know everything. I made haste to admit as much. "I didn't even know that the count was gone, much less why he's gone," said I.

"You see?" exclaimed Anton. And he added, patronizingly, "You should keep your ears open, my boy; then you might be worth what the king pays you."

"No less, I trust," said I, "for he pays me nothing." Indeed, at this time I held no office save the honorary position of chamberlain to Her Majesty. Any advice the king needed from me was asked and given unofficially.

Anton went off, persuaded that he had scored a point against me. I could not see where. It was possible that the Count of Luzau-Rischenheim had gone to meet his cousin, equally possible that no such business claimed his care. At any rate, the matter was not for me. I had a more pressing affair in hand. Dismissing the whole thing from my mind, I bade the butler tell Bauer to go forward with my luggage and to let my carriage be at the door in good time. Helga had busied herself, since our guest's departure, in preparing small comforts for my journey; now she came to me to say good-by. Although she tried to hide all signs of it, I detected an uneasiness in her manner. She did not like these errands of mine, imagining dangers and risks of which I saw no likelihood. I would not give in to her mood, and, as I kissed her, I bade her expect me back in a few days' time. Not even to her did I speak of the new and more dangerous burden that I carried, although I was aware that she enjoyed a full measure of the queen's confidence.

"My love to King Rudolf, the real King Rudolf," said she. "Though you carry what will make him think little of my love."

"I have no desire he should think too much of it, sweet," said I. She caught me by the hands, and looked up in my face.

"What a friend you are, aren't you, Fritz?" said she. "You worship Mr. Rassendyll. I know you think I should worship him too, if he asked me. Well, I shouldn't. I am foolish enough to have my own idol." All my modesty did not let me doubt who her idol might be. Suddenly she drew near to me and whispered in my ear. I think that our own happiness brought to her a sudden keen sympathy with her mistress.

"Make him send her a loving message, Fritz," she whispered. "Something that will comfort her. Her idol can't be with her as mine is with me."

"Yes, he'll send something to comfort her," I answered. "And God keep you, my dear."

For he would surely send an answer to the letter that I carried, and that answer I was sworn to bring safely to her. So I set out in good heart, bearing in the pocket of my coat the little box and the queen's good-by. And, as Colonel Sapt said to me, both I would destroy, if need were—ay, and myself with them. A man did not serve Queen Flavia with divided mind.

CHAPTER II. A STATION WITHOUT A CAB

The arrangements for my meeting with Mr. Rassendyll had been carefully made by correspondence before he left England. He was to be at the Golden Lion Hotel at eleven o'clock on the night of the 15th of October. I reckoned to arrive in the town between eight and nine on the same evening, to proceed to another hotel, and, on pretence of taking a stroll, slip out and call on him at the appointed hour. I should then fulfil my commission, take his answer, and enjoy the rare pleasure of a long talk with him. Early the next morning he would have left Wintenberg, and I should be on my way back to Strelsau. I knew that he would not fail to keep his appointment, and I was perfectly confident of being able to carry out the programme punctually; I had, however, taken the precaution of obtaining a week's leave of absence, in case any unforeseen accident should delay my return. Conscious of having done all I could to guard against misunderstanding or mishap, I got into the train in a tolerably peaceful frame of mind. The box was in my inner pocket, the letter in a portemonnaie. I could feel them both with my hand. I was not in uniform, but I took my revolver. Although I had no reason to anticipate any difficulties, I did not forget that what I carried must be protected at all hazards and all costs.

The weary night journey wore itself away. Bauer came to me in the morning, performed his small services, repacked my hand-bag, procured me some coffee, and left me. It was then about eight o'clock; we had arrived at a station of some importance and were not to stop again till mid-day. I saw Bauer enter the second-class compartment in which he was traveling, and settled down in my own coupe. I think it was at this moment that the thought of Rischenheim came again into my head, and I found myself wondering why he clung to the hopeless idea of compassing Rupert's return and what business had taken him from Strelsau. But I made little of the matter, and, drowsy from a broken night's rest, soon fell into a doze. I was alone in the carriage and could sleep without fear or danger. I was awakened by our noontide halt. Here I saw Bauer again. After taking a basin of soup, I went to the telegraph bureau to send a message to my wife; the receipt of it would not merely set her mind at case, but would also ensure word of my safe progress reaching the queen. As I entered the bureau I met Bauer coming out of it. He seemed rather startled at our encounter, but told me readily enough that he had been telegraphing for rooms at Wintenberg, a very needless precaution, since there was no danger of the hotel being full. In fact I was annoyed, as I especially wished to avoid calling attention to my arrival. However, the mischief was done, and to rebuke my servant might have aggravated it by setting his wits at work to find out my motive for secrecy.

So I said nothing, but passed by him with a nod. When the whole circumstances came to light, I had reason to suppose that besides his message to the inn-keeper, Bauer sent one of a character and to a quarter unsuspected by me.

We stopped once again before reaching Wintenberg. I put my head out of the window to look about me, and saw Bauer standing near the luggage van. He ran to me eagerly, asking whether I required anything. I told him "nothing"; but instead of going away, he began to talk to me. Growing weary of him, I returned to my seat and waited impatiently for the train to go on. There was a further delay of five minutes, and then we started.

"Thank goodness!" I exclaimed, leaning back comfortably in my seat and taking a cigar from my case.

But in a moment the cigar rolled unheeded on to the floor, as I sprang eagerly to my feet and darted to the window. For just as we were clearing the station, I saw being carried past the carriage, on the shoulders of a porter, a bag which looked very much like mine. Bauer had been in charge of my bag, and it had been put in the van under his directions. It seemed unlikely that it should be taken out now by any mistake. Yet the bag I saw was very like the bag I owned. But I was not sure, and could have done nothing had I been sure. We were not to stop again before Wintenberg, and, with my luggage or without it, I myself must be in the town that evening.

We arrived punctual to our appointed time. I sat in the carriage a moment or two, expecting Bauer to open the door and relieve me of my small baggage. He did not come, so I got out. It seemed that I had few fellow-passengers, and these were quickly disappearing on foot or in carriages and carts that waited outside the station. I stood looking for my servant and my luggage. The evening was mild; I was encumbered with my hand-bag and a heavy fur coat. There were no signs either of Bauer or of baggage. I stayed where I was for five or six minutes. The guard of the train had disappeared, but presently I observed the station-master; he seemed to be taking a last glance round the premises. Going up to him I asked whether he had seen my servant; he could give me no news of him. I had no luggage ticket, for mine had been in Bauer's hands; but I prevailed on him to allow me to look at the baggage which had arrived; my property was not among it. The station-master was inclined, I think, to be a little skeptical as to the existence both of bag and of servant. His only suggestion was that the man must have been left behind accidentally. I pointed out that in this case he would not have had the bag with him, but that it would have come on in the train. The station-master admitted the force of my argument; he shrugged his shoulders and spread his hands out; he was evidently at the end of his resources.

Now, for the first time and with sudden force, a doubt of Bauer's fidelity thrust itself into my mind. I remembered how little I knew of the fellow and how great my charge was. Three rapid movements of my hand assured me that letter, box, and revolver were in their respective places. If Bauer had gone hunting in the bag, he had drawn a blank. The station-master noticed nothing; he was stating at the dim gas lamp that hung from the roof. I turned to him. "Well, tell him when he comes——" I began.

"He won't come to-night, now," interrupted the stationmaster, none too politely. "No other train arrives to-night."

"Tell him when he does come to follow me at once to the Wintenbergerhof. I'm going there immediately." For time was short, and I did not wish to keep Mr. Rassendyll waiting. Besides, in my new-born nervousness, I was anxious to accomplish my errand as soon as might be. What had become of Bauer? The thought returned, and now with it another, that seemed to connect itself in some subtle way with my present position: why and whither had the Count of Luzau-Rischenheim set out from Strelsau a day before I started on my journey to Wintenberg?

"If he comes I'll tell him," said the station-master, and as he spoke he looked round the yard.

There was not a cab to be seen! I knew that the station lay on the extreme outskirts of the town, for I had passed through Wintenberg on my wedding journey, nearly three years before. The trouble involved in walking, and the further waste of time, put the cap on my irritation. "Why don't you have enough cabs?" I asked angrily.

"There are plenty generally, sir," he answered more civilly, with an apologetic air. "There would be to-night but for an accident."

Another accident! This expedition of mine seemed doomed to be the sport of chance.

"Just before your train arrived," he continued, "a local came in. As a rule, hardly anybody comes by it, but to-night a number of men—oh, twenty or five-and-twenty, I should think—got out. I collected their tickets myself, and they all came from the first station on the line. Well, that's not so strange, for there's a good beer-garden there. But, curiously enough, every one of them hired a separate cab and drove off, laughing and shouting to one another as they went. That's how it happens that there were only one or two cabs left when your train came in, and they were snapped up at once."

Taken alone, this occurrence was nothing; but I asked myself whether the conspiracy that had robbed me of my servant had deprived me of a vehicle also.

"What sort of men were they?" I asked.

"All sorts of men, sir," answered the station-master, "but most of them were shabby-looking fellows. I wondered where some of them had got the money for their ride."

The vague feeling of uneasiness which had already attacked me grew stronger. Although I fought against it, calling myself an old woman and a coward, I must confess to an impulse which almost made me beg the station-master's company on my walk; but, besides being ashamed to exhibit a timidity apparently groundless, I was reluctant to draw attention to myself in any way. I would not for the world have it supposed that I carried anything of value.

"Well, there's no help for it," said I, and, buttoning my heavy coat about me, I took my hand-bag and stick in one hand, and asked my way to the hotel. My misfortunes had broken down the station-master's indifference, and he directed me in a sympathetic tone.

"Straight along the road, sir," said he, "between the poplars, for hard on half a mile; then the houses begin, and your hotel is in the first square you come to, on the right."

I thanked him curtly (for I had not quite forgiven him his earlier incivility), and started on my walk, weighed down by my big coat and the handbag. When I left the lighted station yard I realized that the evening had fallen very dark, and the shade of the tall lank trees intensified the gloom. I could hardly see my way, and went timidly, with frequent stumbles over the uneven stones of the road. The lamps were dim, few, and widely separated; so far as company was concerned, I might have been a thousand miles from an inhabited house. In spite of myself, the thought of danger persistently assailed my mind. I began to review every circumstance of my journey, twisting the trivial into some ominous shape, magnifying the significance of everything which might justly seem suspicious, studying in the light of my new apprehensions every expression of Bauer's face and every word that had fallen from his lips. I could not persuade myself into security. I carried the queen's letter, and—well, I would have given much to have old Sapt or Rudolf Rassendyll by my side.

Now, when a man suspects danger, let him not spend his time in asking whether there be really danger or in upbraiding himself for timidity, but let him face his cowardice, and act as though the danger were real. If I had followed that rule and kept my eyes about me, scanning the sides of the road and the ground in front of my feet, instead of losing myself in a maze of reflection, I might have had time to avoid the trap, or at least to get my hand to my revolver and make a fight for it; or, indeed, in the last resort, to destroy what I carried before harm came to it. But my mind was preoccupied, and the whole thing seemed to happen in a minute. At the very moment that I had declared to myself the vanity of my fears and determined to be resolute in banishing them, I heard voices—a low, strained whispering; I saw two or three figures in the shadow of the poplars by the wayside. An instant later, a dart was made at me. While I could fly I would not fight; with a sudden forward plunge I eluded the men who rushed at me, and started at a run towards the lights of the town and the shapes of the houses, now distant about a quarter of a mile. Perhaps I ran twenty yards, perhaps fifty; I do not know. I heard the steps behind me, quick as my own. Then I fell headlong on the road— tripped up! I understood. They had stretched a rope across my path; as I fell a man bounded up from either side, and I found the rope slack under my body. There I lay on my face; a man knelt on me, others held either hand; my face was pressed into the mud of the road, and I was like to have been stifled; my hand-bag had whizzed away from me. Then a voice said: "Turn him over."

I knew the voice; it was a confirmation of the fears which I had lately been at such pains to banish. It justified the forecast of Anton von Strofzin, and explained the wager of the Count of Luzau-Rischenheim—for it was Rischenheim's voice.

They caught hold of me and began to turn me on my back. Here I saw a chance, and with a great heave of my body I flung them from me. For a short instant I was free; my impetuous attack seemed to have startled the enemy; I gathered myself up on my knees. But my advantage was not to last long. Another man, whom I had not seen, sprang suddenly on me like a bullet from a catapult. His fierce onset overthrew me; I was stretched on the ground again, on my back now, and my throat was clutched viciously in strong fingers. At the same moment my arms were again seized and pinned. The face of the man on my chest bent down towards mine, and through the darkness I discerned the features of Rupert of Hentzau. He was panting with the sudden exertion and the intense force with which he held me, but he was smiling also; and when he saw by my eyes that I knew him, he laughed softly in triumph. Then came Rischenheim's voice again.

"Where's the bag he carried? It may be in the bag."

"You fool, he'll have it about him," said Rupert, scornfully. "Hold him fast while I search."

On either side my hands were still pinned fast. Rupert's left hand did not leave my throat, but his free right hand began to dart about me, feeling, probing, and rummaging. I lay quite helpless and in the bitterness of great consternation. Rupert found my revolver, drew it out with a gibe, and handed it to Rischenheim, who was now standing beside him. Then he felt the box, he drew it out, his eyes sparkled. He set his knee hard on my chest, so that I could scarcely breathe; then he ventured to loose my throat, and tore the box open eagerly.

"Bring a light here," he cried. Another ruffian came with a dark-lantern, whose glow he turned on the box. Rupert opened it, and when he saw what was inside, he laughed again, and stowed it away in his pocket.

"Quick, quick!" urged Rischenheim. "We've got what we wanted, and somebody may come at any moment."

A brief hope comforted me. The loss of the box was a calamity, but I would pardon fortune if only the letter escaped capture. Rupert might have suspected that I carried some such token as the box, but he could not know of the letter. Would he listen to Rischenheim? No. The Count of Hentzau did things thoroughly.

"We may as well overhaul him a bit more," said he, and resumed his search. My hope vanished, for now he was bound to come upon the letter.

Another instant brought him to it. He snatched the pocketbook, and, motioning impatiently to the man to hold the lantern nearer, he began to examine the contents. I remember well the look of his face as the fierce white light threw it up against the darkness in its clear pallor and high-bred comeliness, with its curling lips and scornful eyes. He had the letter now, and a gleam of joy danced in his eyes as he tore it open. A hasty glance showed him what his prize was; then, coolly and deliberately he settled himself to read, regarding neither Rischenheim's nervous hurry nor my desperate, angry glance that glared up at him. He read leisurely, as though he had been in an armchair in his own house; the lips smiled and curled as he read the last words that the queen had written to her lover. He had indeed come on more than he thought.

Rischenheim laid a hand on his shoulder.

"Quick, Rupert, quick," he urged again, in a voice full of agitation.

"Let me alone, man. I haven't read anything so amusing for a long while," answered Rupert. Then he burst into a laugh, crying, "Look, look!" and pointing to the foot of the last page of the letter. I was mad with anger; my fury gave me new strength. In his enjoyment of what he read Rupert had grown careless; his knee pressed more lightly on me, and as he showed Rischenheim the passage in the letter that caused him so much amusement he turned his head away for an instant. My chance had come. With a sudden movement I displaced him, and with a desperate wrench I freed my right hand. Darting it out, I snatched at the letter. Rupert, alarmed for his treasure, sprang back and off me. I also sprang up on my feet, hurling away the fellow who had gripped my other hand. For a moment I stood facing Rupert; then I darted on him. He was too quick for me; he dodged behind the man with the lantern and hurled the fellow forward against me. The lantern fell on the ground.

"Give me your stick!" I heard Rupert say. "Where is it? That's right!"

Then came Rischenheim's voice again, imploring and timid:

"Rupert, you promised not to kill him."

The only answer was a short, fierce laugh. I hurled away the man who had been thrust into my arms and sprang forward. I saw Rupert of Hentzau; his hand was raised above his head and held a stout club. I do not know what followed; there came—all in a confused blur of instant sequence—an oath from Rupert, a rush from me, a scuffle, as though some one sought to hold him back; then he was on me; I felt a great thud on my forehead, and I felt nothing more. Again I was on my back, with a terrible pain in my head, and a dull, dreamy consciousness of a knot of men standing over me, talking eagerly to one another.

I could not hear what they were saying; I had no great desire to hear. I fancied, somehow, that they were talking about me; they looked at me and moved their hands towards me now and again. I heard Rupert's laugh, and saw his club poised over me; then Rischenheim caught him by the wrist. I know now that Rischenheim was reminding his cousin that he had promised not to kill me, that Rupert's oath did not weigh a straw in the scales, but that he was held back only by a doubt whether I alive or my dead body would be more inconvenient to dispose of. Yet then I did not understand, but lay there listless. And presently the talking forms seemed to cease their talking; they grew blurred and dim, running into one another, and all mingling together to form one great shapeless creature that seemed to murmur and gibber over me, some such monster as a man sees in his dreams. I hated to see it, and closed my eyes; its murmurings and gibberings haunted my ears for awhile, making me restless and unhappy; then they died away. Their going made me happy; I sighed in contentment; and everything became as though it were not.

Yet I had one more vision, breaking suddenly across my unconsciousness. A bold, rich voice rang out, "By God, I will!"

"No, no," cried another. Then, "What's that?" There was a rush of feet, the cries of men who met in anger or excitement, the crack of a shot and of another quickly following, oaths, and scuffling. Then came the sound of feet flying. I could not make it out; I grew weary with the puzzle of it. Would they not be quiet? Quiet was what I wanted. At last they grew quiet; I closed my eyes again. The pain was less now; they were quiet; I could sleep.

When a man looks back on the past, reviewing in his mind the chances Fortune has given and the calls she has made, he always torments himself by thinking that he could have done other and better than in fact he did. Even now I lie awake at night sometimes, making clever plans by which I could have thwarted Rupert's schemes. In these musings I am very acute; Anton von Strofzin's idle talk furnishes me with many a clue, and I draw inferences sure and swift as a detective in the story books. Bauer is my tool, I am not his. I lay Rischenheim by the heels, send Rupert howling off with a ball in his arm, and carry my precious burden in triumph to Mr. Rassendyll. By the time I have played the whole game I am indeed proud of myself. Yet in truth—in daylight truth—I fear that, unless Heaven sent me a fresh set of brains, I should be caught in much the same way again. Though not by that fellow Bauer, I swear! Well, there it was. They had made a fool of me. I lay on the road with a bloody head, and Rupert of Hentzau had the queen's letter.

CHAPTER III. AGAIN TO ZENDA

By Heaven's care, or—since a man may be over-apt to arrogate to himself great share of such attention—by good luck, I had not to trust for my life to the slender thread of an oath sworn by Rupert of Hentzau. The visions of my dazed brain were transmutations of reality; the scuffle, the rush, the retreat were not all dream.

There is an honest fellow now living in Wintenberg comfortably and at his ease by reason that his wagon chanced to come lumbering along with three or four stout lads in it at the moment when Rupert was meditating a second and murderous blow. Seeing the group of us, the good carrier and his lads leapt down and rushed on my assailants. One of the thieves, they said, was for fighting it out—I could guess who that was—and called on the rest to stand; but they, more prudent, laid hands on him, and, in spite of his oaths, hustled him off along the road towards the station. Open country lay there and the promise of safety. My new friends set off in pursuit; but a couple of revolver shots, heard by me, but not understood, awoke their caution. Good Samaritans, but not men of war, they returned to where I lay senseless on the ground, congratulating themselves and me that an enemy so well armed should run and not stand his ground. They forced a drink of rough wine down my throat, and in a minute or two I opened my eyes. They were for carrying me to a hospital; I would have none of it. As soon as things grew clear to me again and I knew where I was, I did nothing but repeat in urgent tones, "The Golden Lion, The Golden Lion! Twenty crowns to carry me to the Golden Lion."

Perceiving that I knew my own business and where I wished to go, one picked up my hand-bag and the rest hoisted me into their wagon and set out for the hotel where Rudolf Rassendyll was. The one thought my broken head held was to get to him as soon as might be and tell him how I had been fool enough to let myself be robbed of the queen's letter.

He was there. He stood on the threshold of the inn, waiting for me, as it seemed, although it was not yet the hour of my appointment. As they drew me up to the door, I saw his tall, straight figure and his red hair by the light of the hall lamps. By Heaven, I felt as a lost child must on sight of his mother! I stretched out my hand to him, over the side of the wagon, murmuring, "I've lost it."

He started at the words, and sprang forward to me. Then he turned quickly to the carrier. "This gentleman is my friend," he said. "Give him to me. I'll speak to you later." He waited while I was lifted down from the wagon into the arms that he held ready for me, and himself carried me across the threshold. I was quite clear in the head by now and understood all that passed. There were one or two people in the hall, but Mr. Rassendyll took no heed of them. He bore me quickly upstairs and into his sitting-room. There he set me down in an arm-chair, and stood opposite to me. He was smiling, but anxiety was awake in his eyes.

"I've lost it," I said again, looking up at him pitifully enough.

"That's all right," said he, nodding. "Will you wait, or can you tell me?"

"Yes, but give me some brandy," said I.

Rudolf gave me a little brandy mixed in a great deal of water, and then I made shift to tell him. Though faint, I was not confused, and I gave my story in brief, hurried, yet sufficient words. He made no sign till I mentioned the letter. Then his face changed.

"A letter, too?" he exclaimed, in a strange mixture of increased apprehension and unlooked-for joy.

"Yes, a letter, too; she wrote a letter, and I carried that as well as the box. I've lost them both, Rudolf. God help me, I've lost them both! Rupert has the letter too!" I think I must have been weak and unmanned from the blow I had received, for my composure broke down here. Rudolf stepped up to me and wrung me by the hand. I mastered myself again and looked in his face as he stood in thought, his hand caressing the strong curve of his clean-shaven chin. Now that I was with him again it seemed as though I had never lost him; as though we were still together in Strelsau or at Tarlenheim, planning how to hoodwink Black Michael, send Rupert of Hentzau to his own place, and bring the king back to his throne. For Mr. Rassendyll, as he stood before me now, was changed in nothing since our last meeting, nor indeed since he reigned in Strelsau, save that a few flecks of gray spotted his hair.

My battered head ached most consumedly. Mr. Rassendyll rang the bell twice, and a short, thickset man of middle age appeared; he wore a suit of tweed, and had the air of smartness and respectability which marks English servants.

"James," said Rudolf, "this gentleman has hurt his head. Look after it."

James went out. In a few minutes he was back, with water, basin, towels, and bandages. Bending over me, he began to wash and tend my wound very deftly. Rudolf was walking up and down.

"Done the head, James?" he asked, after a few moments.

"Yes, sir," answered the servant, gathering together his appliances.

"Telegraph forms, then."

James went out, and was back with the forms in an instant.

"Be ready when I ring," said Rudolf. And he added, turning to me, "Any easier, Fritz?"

"I can listen to you now," I said.

"I see their game," said he. "One or other of them, Rupert or this Rischenheim, will try to get to the king with the letter."

I sprang to my feet.

"They mustn't," I cried, and I reeled back into my chair, with a feeling as if a red-hot poker were being run through my head.

"Much you can do to stop 'em, old fellow," smiled Rudolf, pausing to press my hand as he went by. "They won't trust the post, you know. One will go. Now which?" He stood facing me with a thoughtful frown on his face.

I did not know, but I thought that Rischenheim would go. It was a great risk for Rupert to trust himself in the kingdom, and he knew that the king would not easily be persuaded to receive him, however startling might be the business he professed as his errand. On the other hand, nothing was known against Rischenheim, while his rank would secure, and indeed entitle, him to an early audience. Therefore I concluded that Rischenheim would go with the letter, or, if Rupert would not let that out of his possession, with the news of the letter.

"Or a copy," suggested Rassendyll. "Well, Rischenheim or Rupert will be on his way by to-morrow morning, or is on his way to-night."

Again I tried to rise, for I was on fire to prevent the fatal consequences of my stupidity. Rudolf thrust me back in my chair, saying, "No, no." Then he sat down at the table and took up the telegraph forms.

"You and Sapt arranged a cipher, I suppose?" he asked.

"Yes. You write the message, and I'll put it into the cipher."

"This is what I've written: 'Document lost. Let nobody see him if possible. Wire who asks.' I don't like to make it plainer: most ciphers can be read, you know."

"Not ours," said I.

"Well, but will that do?" asked Rudolf, with an unconvinced smile.

"Yes, I think he'll understand it." And I wrote it again in the cipher; it was as much as I could do to hold the pen.

The bell was rung again, and James appeared in an instant.

"Send this," said Rudolf.

"The offices will be shut, sir."

"James, James!"

"Very good, sir; but it may take an hour to get one open."

"I'll give you half an hour. Have you money?"

"Yes, sir."

"And now," added Rudolf, turning to me, "you'd better go to bed."

I do not recollect what I answered, for my faintness came upon me again, and I remember only that Rudolf himself helped me into his own bed. I slept, but I do not think he so much as lay down on the sofa; chancing to awake once or twice, I heard him pacing about. But towards morning I slept heavily, and I did not know what he was doing then. At eight o'clock James entered and roused me. He said that a doctor was to be at the hotel in half an hour, but that Mr. Rassendyll would like to see me for a few minutes if I felt equal to business. I begged James to summon his master at once. Whether I were equal or unequal, the business had to be done.

Rudolf came, calm and serene. Danger and the need for exertion acted on him like a draught of good wine on a seasoned drinker. He was not only himself, but more than himself: his excellences enhanced, the indolence that marred him in quiet hours sloughed off. But to-day there was something more; I can only describe it as a kind of radiance. I have seen it on the faces of young sparks when the lady they love comes through the ball-room door, and I have seen it glow more softly in a girl's eyes when some fellow who seemed to me nothing out of the ordinary asked her for a dance. That strange gleam was on Rudolf's face as he stood by my bedside. I dare say it used to be on mine when I went courting.

"Fritz, old friend," said he, "there's an answer from Sapt. I'll lay the telegraph offices were stirred in Zenda as well as James stirred them here in Wintenberg! And what do you think? Rischenheim asked for an audience before he left Strelsau."

I raised myself on my elbow in the bed.

"You understand?" he went on. "He left on Monday. To-day's Wednesday. The king has granted him an audience at four on Friday. Well, then——"

"They counted on success," I cried, "and Rischenheim takes the letter!"

"A copy, if I know Rupert of Hentzau. Yes, it was well laid. I like the men taking all the cabs! How much ahead had they, now."

I did not know that, though I had no more doubt than he that Rupert's hand was in the business.

"Well," he continued, "I am going to wire to Sapt to put Rischenheim off for twelve hours if he can; failing that, to get the king away from Zenda."

"But Rischenheim must have his audience sooner or later," I objected.

"Sooner or later—there's the world's difference between them!" cried Rudolf Rassendyll. He sat down on the bed by me, and went on in quick, decisive words: "You can't move for a day or two. Send my message to Sapt. Tell him to keep you informed of what happens. As soon as you can travel, go to Strelsau, and let Sapt know directly you arrive. We shall want your help."

"And what are you going to do?" I cried, staring at him.

He looked at me for a moment, and his face was crossed by conflicting feelings. I saw resolve there, obstinacy, and the scorn of danger; fun, too, and merriment; and, lastly, the same radiance I spoke of. He had been smoking a cigarette; now he threw the end of it into the grate and rose from the bed where he had been sitting.

"I'm going to Zenda," said he.

"To Zenda!" I cried, amazed.

"Yes," said Rudolf. "I'm going again to Zenda, Fritz, old fellow. By heaven, I knew it would come, and now it has come!"

"But to do what?"

"I shall overtake Rischenheim or be hot on his heels. If he gets there first, Sapt will keep him waiting till I come; and if I come, he shall never see the king. Yes, if I come in time—" He broke into a sudden laugh. "What!" he cried, "have I lost my likeness? Can't I still play the king? Yes, if I come in time, Rischenheim shall have his audience of the king of Zenda, and the king will be very gracious to him, and the king will take his copy of the letter from him! Oh, Rischenheim shall have an audience of King Rudolf in the castle of Zenda, never fear!" He stood, looking to see how I received his plan; but amazed at the boldness of it, I could only lie back and gasp.

Rudolf's excitement left him as suddenly as it had come; he was again the cool, shrewd, nonchalant Englishman, as, lighting another cigarette, he proceeded:

"You see, there are two of them, Rupert and Rischenheim. Now you can't move for a day or two, that's certain. But there must be two of us there in Ruritania. Rischenheim is to try first; but if he fails, Rupert will risk everything and break through to the king's presence. Give him five minutes with the king, and the mischief's done! Very well, then; Sapt must keep Rupert at bay while I tackle Rischenheim. As soon as you can move, go to Strelsau, and let Sapt know where you are."

"But if you're seen, if you're found out?"

"Better I than the queen's letter," said he. Then he laid his hand on my arm and said, quite quietly, "If the letter gets to the king, I and I only can do what must be done."

I did not know what he meant; perhaps it was that he would carry off the queen sooner than leave her alone after her letter was known; but there was another possible meaning that I, a loyal subject, dared not inquire into. Yet I made no answer, for I was above all and first of all the queen's servant. Still I cannot believe that he meant harm to the king.

"Come, Fritz," he cried, "don't look so glum. This is not so great an affair as the other, and we brought that through safe." I suppose I still looked doubtful, for he added, with a sort of impatience, "Well, I'm going, anyhow. Heavens, man, am I to sit here while that letter is carried to the king?"

I understood his feeling, and knew that he held life a light thing compared with the recovery of Queen Flavia's letter. I ceased to urge him. When I assented to his wishes, every shadow vanished from his face, and he began to discuss the details of the plan with business-like brevity.

"I shall leave James with you," said Rudolf. "He'll be very useful, and you can rely on him absolutely. Any message that you dare trust to no other conveyance, give to him; he'll carry it. He can shoot, too." He rose as he spoke. "I'll look in before I start," he added, "and hear what the doctor says about you."

I lay there, thinking, as men sick and weary in body will, of the dangers and the desperate nature of the risk, rather than of the hope which its boldness would have inspired in a healthy, active brain. I distrusted the rapid inference that Rudolf had drawn from Sapt's telegram, telling myself that it was based on too slender a foundation. Well, there I was wrong, and I am glad now to pay that tribute to his discernment. The first steps of Rupert's scheme were laid as Rudolf had conjectured: Rischenheim had started, even while I lay there, for Zenda, carrying on his person a copy of the queen's farewell letter and armed for his enterprise by his right of audience with the king. So far we were right, then; for the rest we were in darkness, not knowing or being able even to guess where Rupert would choose to await the result of the first cast, or what precautions he had taken against the failure of his envoy. But although in total obscurity as to his future plans, I traced his past actions, and subsequent knowledge has shown that I was right. Bauer was the tool; a couple of florins apiece had hired the fellows who, conceiving that they were playing a part in some practical joke, had taken all the cabs at the station. Rupert had reckoned that I should linger looking for my servant and luggage, and thus miss my last chance of a vehicle. If, however, I had obtained one, the attack would still have been made, although, of course, under much greater difficulties. Finally—and of this at the time I knew nothing—had I evaded them and got safe to port with my cargo, the plot

94

would have been changed. Rupert's attention would then have been diverted from me to Rudolf; counting on love overcoming prudence, he reckoned that Mr. Rassendyll would not at once destroy what the queen sent, and had arranged to track his steps from Wintenberg till an opportunity offered of robbing him of his treasure. The scheme, as I know it, was full of audacious cunning, and required large resources—the former Rupert himself supplied; for the second he was indebted to his cousin and slave, the Count of Luzau-Rischenheim.

My meditations were interrupted by the arrival of the doctor. He hummed and ha'd over me, but to my surprise asked me no questions as to the cause of my misfortune, and did not, as I had feared, suggest that his efforts should be seconded by those of the police. On the contrary, he appeared, from an unobtrusive hint or two, to be anxious that I should know that his discretion could be trusted.

"You must not think of moving for a couple of days," he said; "but then, I think we can get you away without danger and quite quietly."

I thanked him; he promised to look in again; I murmured something about his fee.

"Oh, thank you, that is all settled," he said. "Your friend Herr Schmidt has seen to it, and, my dear sir, most liberally."

He was hardly gone when 'my friend Herr Schmidt'—alias Rudolf Rassendyll—was back. He laughed a little when I told him how discreet the doctor had been.

"You see," he explained, "he thinks you've been very indiscreet. I was obliged, my dear Fritz, to take some liberties with your character. However, it's odds against the matter coming to your wife's ears."

"But couldn't we have laid the others by the heels?"

"With the letter on Rupert? My dear fellow, you're very ill."

I laughed at myself, and forgave Rudolf his trick, though I think that he might have made my fictitious inamorata something more than a baker's wife. It would have cost no more to make her a countess, and the doctor would have looked with more respect on me. However, Rudolf had said that the baker broke my head with his rolling-pin, and thus the story rests in the doctor's mind to this day.

"Well, I'm off," said Rudolf.

"But where?"

"Why, to that same little station where two good friends parted from me once before. Fritz, where's Rupert gone?"

"I wish we knew."

"I lay he won't be far off."

"Are you armed?"

"The six-shooter. Well, yes, since you press me, a knife, too; but only if he uses one. You'll let Sapt know when you come?"

"Yes; and I come the moment I can stand?"

"As if you need tell me that, old fellow!"

"Where do you go from the station?"

"To Zenda, through the forest," he answered. "I shall reach the station about nine to-morrow night, Thursday. Unless Rischenheim has got the audience sooner than was arranged, I shall be in time."

"How will you get hold of Sapt?"

"We must leave something to the minute."

"God bless you, Rudolf."

"The king sha'n't have the letter, Fritz."

There was a moment's silence as we shook hands. Then that soft yet bright look came in his eyes again. He looked down at me, and caught me regarding him with a smile that I know was not unkind.

"I never thought I should see her again," he said. "I think I shall now, Fritz. To have a turn with that boy and to see her again—it's worth something."

"How will you see her?"

Rudolf laughed, and I laughed too. He caught my hand again. I think that he was anxious to infect me with his gayety and confidence. But I could not answer to the appeal of his eyes. There was a motive in him that found no place in me—a great longing, the prospect or hope of whose sudden fulfilment dwarfed danger and banished despair. He saw that I detected its presence in him and perceived how it filled his mind.

"But the letter comes before all," said he. "I expected to die without seeing her; I will die without seeing her, if I must, to save the letter."

"I know you will," said I.

He pressed my hand again. As he turned away, James came with his noiseless, quick step into the room.

"The carriage is at the door, sir," said he.

"Look after the count, James," said Rudolf. "Don't leave him till he sends you away."

"Very well, sir."

I raised myself in bed.

"Here's luck," I cried, catching up the lemonade James had brought me, and taking a gulp of it.

"Please God," said Rudolf, with a shrug.

And he was gone to his work and his reward—to save the queen's letter and to see the queen's face. Thus he went a second time to Zenda.

CHAPTER IV. AN EDDY ON THE MOAT

On the evening of Thursday, the sixteenth of October, the Constable of Zenda was very much out of humor; he has since confessed as much. To risk the peace of a palace for the sake of a lover's greeting had never been wisdom to his mind, and he had been sorely impatient with "that fool Fritz's" yearly pilgrimage. The letter of farewell had been an added folly, pregnant with chances of disaster. Now disaster, or the danger of it, had come. The curt, mysterious telegram from Wintenberg, which told him so little, at least told him that. It ordered him—and he did not know even whose the order was—to delay Rischenheim's audience, or, if he could not, to get the king away from Zenda: why he was to act thus was not disclosed to him. But he knew as well as I that Rischenheim was completely in Rupert's hands, and he could not fail to guess that something had gone wrong at Wintenberg, and that Rischenheim came to tell the king some news that the king must not hear. His task sounded simple, but it was not easy; for he did not know where Rischenheim was, and so could not prevent his coming; besides, the king had been very pleased to learn of the count's approaching visit, since he desired to talk with him on the subject of a certain breed of dogs, which the count bred with great, his Majesty with only indifferent success; therefore he had declared that nothing should interfere with his reception of Rischenheim. In vain Sapt told him that a large boar had been seen in the forest, and that a fine day's sport might be expected if he would hunt next day. "I shouldn't be back in time to see Rischenheim," said the king.

"Your Majesty would be back by nightfall," suggested Sapt.

"I should be too tired to talk to him, and I've a great deal to discuss."

"You could sleep at the hunting-lodge, sire, and ride back to receive the count next morning."

"I'm anxious to see him as soon as may be." Then he looked up at Sapt with a sick man's quick suspicion. "Why shouldn't I see him?" he asked.

"It's a pity to miss the boar, sire," was all Sapt's plea. The king made light of it.

"Curse the boar!" said he. "I want to know how he gets the dogs' coats so fine."

As the king spoke a servant entered, carrying a telegram for Sapt. The colonel took it and put it in his pocket.

"Read it," said the king. He had dined and was about to go to bed, it being nearly ten o'clock.

"It will keep, sire," answered Sapt, who did not know but that it might be from Wintenberg.

"Read it," insisted the king testily. "It may be from Rischenheim. Perhaps he can get here sooner. I should like to know about those dogs. Read it, I beg."

Sapt could do nothing but read it. He had taken to spectacles lately, and he spent a long while adjusting them and thinking what he should do if the message were not fit for the king's ear. "Be quick, man, be quick!" urged the irritable king.

Sapt had got the envelope open at last, and relief, mingled with perplexity, showed in his face. "Your Majesty guessed wonderfully well. Rischenheim can be here at eight to-morrow morning," he said, looking up.

"Capital!" cried the king. "He shall breakfast with me at nine, and I'll have a ride after the boar when we've done our business. Now are you satisfied?"

"Perfectly, sire," said Sapt, biting his moustache.

The king rose with a yawn, and bade the colonel good-night. "He must have some trick I don't know with those dogs," he remarked, as he went out. And "Damn the dogs!" cried Colonel Sapt the moment that the door was shut behind his Majesty.

But the colonel was not a man to accept defeat easily. The audience that he had been instructed to postpone was advanced; the king, whom he had been told to get away from Zenda, would not go till he had seen Rischenheim. Still there are many ways of preventing a meeting. Some are by fraud; these it is no injustice to Sapt to say that he had tried; some are by force, and the colonel was being driven to the conclusion that one of these must be his resort.

"Though the king," he mused, with a grin, "will be furious if anything happens to Rischenheim before he's told him about the dogs."

Yet he fell to racking his brains to find a means by which the count might be rendered incapable of performing the service so desired by the king and of carrying out his own purpose in seeking an audience. Nothing save assassination suggested itself to the constable; a quarrel and a duel offered no security; and Sapt was not Black Michael, and had no band of ruffians to join him in an apparently unprovoked kidnapping of a distinguished nobleman.

"I can think of nothing," muttered Sapt, rising from his chair and moving across towards the window in search of the fresh air that a man so often thinks will give him a fresh idea. He was in his own quarters, that room of the new chateau which opens on to the moat immediately to the right of the drawbridge as you face the old castle; it was the room which Duke Michael had occupied, and almost opposite to the spot where the great pipe had connected the window of the king's dungeon with the waters of the moat. The bridge was down now, for peaceful days had come to Zenda; the pipe was gone, and the dungeon's window, though still barred, was uncovered. The night was clear and fine, and the still water gleamed fitfully as the moon, half-full, escaped from or was hidden by passing clouds. Sapt stood staring out gloomily, beating his knuckles on the stone sill. The fresh air was there, but the fresh idea tarried.

Suddenly the constable bent forward, craning his head out and down, far as he could stretch it, towards the water. What he had seen, or seemed dimly to see, is a sight common enough on the surface of water—large circular eddies, widening from a centre; a stone thrown in makes them, or a fish on the rise. But Sapt had thrown no stone, and the fish in the moat were few and not rising then. The light was behind Sapt, and threw his figure into bold relief. The royal apartments looked out the other way; there were no lights in the windows this side the bridge, although beyond it the guards' lodgings and the servants' offices still showed a light here and there. Sapt waited till the eddies ceased. Then he heard the faintest sound, as of a large body let very gently into the water; a moment later, from the moat right below him, a man's head emerged.

"Sapt!" said a voice, low but distinct.

The old colonel started, and, resting both hands on the sill, bent further out, till he seemed in danger of overbalancing.

"Quick—to the ledge on the other side. You know," said the voice, and the head turned; with quick, quiet strokes the man crossed the moat till he was hidden in the triangle of deep shade formed by the meeting of the drawbridge and the old castle wall. Sapt watched him go, almost stupefied by the sudden wonder of hearing that voice come to him out of the stillness of the night. For the king was abed; and who spoke in that voice save the king and one other?

Then, with a curse at himself for his delay, he turned and walked quickly across the room. Opening the door, he found himself in the passage. But here he ran right into the arms of young Bernenstein, the officer of the guard, who was going his rounds. Sapt knew and trusted him, for he had been with us all through the siege of Zenda, when Michael kept the king a prisoner, and he bore marks given him by Rupert of Hentzau's ruffians. He now held a commission as lieutenant in the cuirassiers of the King's Guard.

He noticed Sapt's bearing, for he cried out in a low voice, "Anything wrong, sir?"

"Bernenstein, my boy, the castle's all right about here. Go round to the front, and, hang you, stay there," said Sapt.

The officer stared, as well he might. Sapt caught him by the arm.

"No, stay here. See, stand by the door there that leads to the royal apartments. Stand there, and let nobody pass. You understand?"

"Yes, sir."

"And whatever you hear, don't look round."

Bernenstein's bewilderment grew greater; but Sapt was constable, and on Sapt's shoulders lay the responsibility for the safety of Zenda and all in it.

"Very well, sir," he said, with a submissive shrug, and he drew his sword and stood by the door; he could obey, although he could not understand.

Sapt ran on. Opening the gate that led to the bridge, he sped across. Then, stepping on one side and turning his face to the wall, he descended the steps that gave foothold down to the ledge running six or eight inches above the water. He also was now in the triangle of deep darkness, yet he knew that a man was there, who stood straight and tall, rising above his own height. And he felt his hand caught in a sudden grip. Rudolf Rassendyll was there, in his wet drawers and socks.

"Is it you?" he whispered.

"Yes," answered Rudolf; "I swam round from the other side and got here. Then I threw in a bit of mortar, but I wasn't sure I'd roused you, and I didn't dare shout, so I followed it myself. Lay hold of me a minute while I get on my breeches: I didn't want to get wet, so I carried my clothes in a bundle. Hold me tight, it's slippery."

"In God's name what brings you here?" whispered Sapt, catching Rudolf by the arm as he was directed.

"The queen's service. When does Rischenheim come?"

"To-morrow at eight."

"The deuce! That's earlier than I thought. And the king?"

"Is here and determined to see him. It's impossible to move him from it."

There was a moment's silence; Rudolf drew his shirt over his head and tucked it into his trousers. "Give me the jacket and waistcoat," he said. "I feel deuced damp underneath, though."

"You'll soon get dry," grinned Sapt. "You'll be kept moving, you see."

"I've lost my hat."

"Seems to me you've lost your head too."

"You'll find me both, eh, Sapt?"

"As good as your own, anyhow," growled the constable.

"Now the boots, and I'm ready." Then he asked quickly, "Has the king seen or heard from Rischenheim?"

"Neither, except through me."

"Then why is he so set on seeing him?"

"To find out what gives dogs smooth coats."

"You're serious? Hang you, I can't see your face."

"Absolutely."

"All's well, then. Has he got a beard now?"

"Yes."

"Confound him! Can't you take me anywhere to talk?"

"What the deuce are you here at all for?"

"To meet Rischenheim."

"To meet—?"

"Yes. Sapt, he's got a copy of the queen's letter."

Sapt twirled his moustache.

"I've always said as much," he remarked in tones of satisfaction. He need not have said it; he would have been more than human not to think it.

"Where can you take me to?" asked Rudolf impatiently.

"Any room with a door and a lock to it," answered old Sapt. "I command here, and when I say 'Stay out'—well, they don't come in."

"Not the king?"

"The king is in bed. Come along," and the constable set his toe on the lowest step.

"Is there nobody about?" asked Rudolf, catching his arm.

"Bernenstein; but he will keep his back toward us."

"Your discipline is still good, then, Colonel?"

"Pretty well for these days, your Majesty," grunted Sapt, as he reached the level of the bridge. Having crossed, they entered the chateau. The passage was empty, save for Bernenstein, whose broad back barred the way from the royal apartments.

"In here," whispered Sapt, laying his hand on the door of the room whence he had come.

"All right," answered Rudolf. Bernenstein's hand twitched, but he did not look round. There was discipline in the castle of Zenda.

But as Sapt was half-way through the door and Rudolf about to follow him, the other door, that which Bernenstein guarded, was softly yet swiftly opened. Bernenstein's sword was in rest in an instant. A muttered oath from Sapt and Rudolf's quick snatch at his breath greeted the interruption. Bernenstein did not look round, but his sword fell to his side. In the doorway stood Queen Flavia, all in white; and now her face turned white as her dress. For her eyes had fallen on Rudolf Rassendyll. For a moment the four stood thus; then Rudolf passed Sapt, thrust Bernenstein's brawny shoulders (the young man had not looked round) out of the way, and, falling on his knee before the queen, seized her hand and kissed it. Bernenstein could see now without looking round, and if astonishment could kill, he would have been a dead man that instant. He fairly reeled and leant against the wall, his mouth hanging open. For the king was in bed, and had a beard; yet there was the king, fully dressed and clean shaven, and he was kissing the queen's hand, while she gazed down on him in a struggle between amazement, fright, and joy. A soldier should be prepared for anything, but I cannot be hard on young Bernenstein's bewilderment.

Yet there was in truth nothing strange in the queen seeking to see old Sapt that night, nor in her guessing where he would most probably be found. For she had asked him three times whether news had come from Wintenberg and each time he had put her off with excuses. Quick to forbode evil, and conscious of the pledge to fortune that she had given in her letter, she had determined to know from him whether there were really cause for alarm, and had stolen, undetected, from her apartments to seek him. What filled her at once with unbearable apprehension and incredulous joy was to find Rudolf present in actual flesh and blood, no longer in sad longing dreams or visions, and to feel his live lips on her hand.

Lovers count neither time nor danger; but Sapt counted both, and no more than a moment had passed before, with eager imperative gestures, he beckoned them to enter the room. The queen obeyed, and Rudolf followed her.

"Let nobody in, and don't say a word to anybody," whispered Sapt, as he entered, leaving Bernenstein outside. The young man was half-dazed still, but he had sense to read the expression in the constable's eyes and to learn from it that he must give his life sooner than let the door be opened. So with drawn sword he stood on guard.

It was eleven o'clock when the queen came, and midnight had struck from the great clock of the castle before the door opened again and Sapt came out. His sword was not drawn, but he had his revolver in his hand. He shut the door silently after him and began at once to talk in low, earnest, quick tones to Bernenstein. Bernenstein listened intently and without interrupting. Sapt's story ran on for eight or nine minutes. Then he paused, before asking: "You understand now?"

"Yes, it is wonderful," said the young man, drawing in his breath.

"Pooh!" said Sapt. "Nothing is wonderful: some things are unusual."

Bernenstein was not convinced, and shrugged his shoulders in protest.

"Well?" said the constable, with a quick glance at him.

"I would die for the queen, sir," he answered, clicking his heels together as though on parade.

"Good," said Sapt. "Then listen," and he began again to talk. Bernenstein nodded from time to time. "You'll meet him at the gate," said the constable, "and bring him straight here. He's not to go anywhere else, you understand me?"

"Perfectly, Colonel," smiled young Bernenstein.

"The king will be in this room—the king. You know who is the king?"

"Perfectly, Colonel."

"And when the interview is ended, and we go to breakfast—"

"I know who will be the king then. Yes, Colonel."

"Good. But we do him no harm unless—"

"It is necessary."

"Precisely."

Sapt turned away with a little sigh. Bernenstein was an apt pupil, but the colonel was exhausted by so much explanation. He knocked softly at the door of the room. The queen's voice bade him enter, and he passed in. Bernenstein was left alone again in the passage, pondering over what he had heard and rehearsing the part that it now fell to him to play. As he thought he may well have raised his head proudly. The service seemed so great and the honor so high, that he almost wished he could die in the performing of his role. It would be a finer death than his soldier's dreams had dared to picture.

At one o'clock Colonel Sapt came out. "Go to bed till six," said he to Bernenstein.

"I'm not sleepy."

"No, but you will be at eight if you don't sleep now."

"Is the queen coming out, Colonel?"

"In a minute, Lieutenant."

"I should like to kiss her hand."

"Well, if you think it worth waiting a quarter of an hour for!" said Sapt, with a slight smile.

"You said a minute, sir."

"So did she," answered the constable.

Nevertheless it was a quarter of an hour before Rudolf Rassendyll opened the door and the queen appeared on the threshold. She was very pale, and she had been crying, but her eyes were happy and her air firm. The moment he saw her, young Bernenstein fell on his knee and raised her hand to his lips.

"To the death, madame," said he, in a trembling voice.

"I knew it, sir," she answered graciously. Then she looked round on the three of them. "Gentlemen," said she, "my servants and dear friends, with you, and with Fritz who lies wounded in Wintenberg, rest my honor and my life; for I will not live if the letter reaches the king."

"The king shall not have it, madame," said Colonel Sapt. He took her hand in his and patted it with a clumsy gentleness; smiling, she extended it again to young Bernenstein, in mark of her favor. They two then stood at the salute, while Rudolf walked with her to the end of the passage. There for a moment she and he stood together; the others turned their eyes away and thus did not see her suddenly stoop and cover his hand with her kisses. He tried to draw it away, not thinking it fit that she should kiss his hand, but she seemed as though she could not let it go. Yet at last, still with her eyes on his, she passed backwards through the door, and he shut it after her.

"Now to business," said Colonel Sapt dryly; and Rudolf laughed a little.

Rudolf passed into the room. Sapt went to the king's apartments, and asked the physician whether his Majesty were sleeping well. Receiving reassuring news of the royal slumbers, he proceeded to the quarters of the king's body-servant, knocked up the sleepy wretch, and ordered breakfast for the king and the Count of Luzau-Rischenheim at nine o'clock precisely, in the morning-room that looked out over the avenue leading to the entrance to the new chateau. This done, he returned to the room where Rudolf was, carried a chair into the passage, bade Rudolf lock the door, sat down, revolver in hand, and himself went to sleep. Young Bernenstein was in bed just now, taken faint, and the constable himself was acting as his substitute; that was to be the story, if a story were needed. Thus the hours from two to six passed that morning in the castle of Zenda.

At six the constable awoke and knocked at the door; Rudolf Rassendyll opened it.

"Slept well?" asked Sapt.

"Not a wink," answered Rudolf cheerfully.

"I thought you had more nerve."

"It wasn't want of nerve that kept me awake," said Mr. Rassendyll.

Sapt, with a pitying shrug, looked round. The curtains of the window were half-drawn. The table was moved near to the wall, and the arm-chair by it was well in shadow, being quite close to the curtains.

"There's plenty of room for you behind," said Rudolf; "And when Rischenheim is seated in his chair opposite to mine, you can put your barrel against his head by just stretching out your hand. And of course I can do the same."

"Yes, it looks well enough," said Sapt, with an approving nod. "What about the beard?"

"Bernenstein is to tell him you've shaved this morning."

"Will he believe that?"

"Why not? For his own sake he'd better believe everything."

"And if we have to kill him?"

"We must run for it. The king would be furious."

"He's fond of him?"

"You forget. He wants to know about the dogs."

"True. You'll be in your place in time?"

"Of course."

Rudolf Rassendyll took a turn up and down the room. It was easy to see that the events of the night had disturbed him. Sapt's thoughts were running in a different channel.

"When we've done with this fellow, we must find Rupert," said he.

Rudolf started.

"Rupert? Rupert? True; I forgot. Of course we must," said he confusedly.

Sapt looked scornful; he knew that his companion's mind had been occupied with the queen. But his remarks—if he had meditated any—were interrupted by the clock striking seven.

"He'll be here in an hour," said he.

101

"We're ready for him," answered Rudolf Rassendyll. With the thought of action his eyes grew bright and his brow smooth again. He and old Sapt looked at one another, and they both smiled.

"Like old times, isn't it, Sapt?"

"Aye, sire, like the reign of good King Rudolf."

Thus they made ready for the Count of Luzau-Rischenheim, while my cursed wound held me a prisoner at Wintenberg. It is still a sorrow to me that I know what passed that morning only by report, and had not the honor of bearing a part in it. Still, her Majesty did not forget me, but remembered that I would have taken my share, had fortune allowed. Indeed I would most eagerly.

CHAPTER V. AN AUDIENCE OF THE KING

Having come thus far in the story that I set out to tell, I have half a mind to lay down my pen, and leave untold how from the moment that Mr. Rassendyll came again to Zenda a fury of chance seemed to catch us all in a whirlwind, carrying us whither we would not, and ever driving us onwards to fresh enterprises, breathing into us a recklessness that stood at no obstacle, and a devotion to the queen and to the man she loved that swept away all other feeling. The ancients held there to be a fate which would have its fill, though women wept and men died, and none could tell whose was the guilt nor who fell innocent. Thus did they blindly wrong God's providence. Yet, save that we are taught to believe that all is ruled, we are as blind as they, and are still left wondering why all that is true and generous and love's own fruit must turn so often to woe and shame, exacting tears and blood. For myself I would leave the thing untold, lest a word of it should seem to stain her whom I serve; it is by her own command I write, that all may one day, in time's fullness, be truly known, and those condemn who are without sin, while they pity whose own hearts have fought the equal fight. So much for her and him; for us less needs be said. It was not ours to weigh her actions; we served her; him we had served. She was our queen; we bore Heaven a grudge that he was not our king. The worst of what befell was not of our own planning, no, nor of our hoping. It came a thunderbolt from the hand of Rupert, flung carelessly between a curse and a laugh; its coming entangled us more tightly in the net of circumstances. Then there arose in us that strange and overpowering desire of which I must tell later, filling us with a zeal to accomplish our purpose, and to force Mr. Rassendyll himself into the way we chose. Led by this star, we pressed on through the darkness, until at length the deeper darkness fell that stayed our steps. We also stand for judgment, even as she and he. So I will write; but I will write plainly and briefly, setting down what I must, and no more, yet seeking to give truly the picture of that time, and to preserve as long as may be the portrait of the man whose like I have not known. Yet the fear is always upon me that, failing to show him as he was, I may fail also in gaining an understanding of how he wrought on us, one and all, till his cause became in all things the right, and to seat him where he should be our highest duty and our nearest wish. For he said little, and that straight to the purpose; no high-flown words of his live in my memory. And he asked nothing for himself. Yet his speech and his eyes went straight to men's hearts and women's, so that they held their lives in an eager attendance on his bidding. Do I rave? Then Sapt was a raver too, for Sapt was foremost in the business.

At ten minutes to eight o'clock, young Bernenstein, very admirably and smartly accoutred, took his stand outside the main entrance of the castle. He wore a confident air that became almost a swagger as he strolled to and fro past the motionless sentries. He had not long to wait. On the stroke of eight a gentleman, well-horsed but entirely unattended, rode up the carriage drive. Bernenstein, crying "Ah, it is the count!" ran to meet him. Rischenheim dismounted, holding out his hand to the young officer.

"My dear Bernenstein!" said he, for they were acquainted with one another.

"You're punctual, my dear Rischenheim, and it's lucky, for the king awaits you most impatiently."

"I didn't expect to find him up so soon," remarked Rischenheim.

"Up! He's been up these two hours. Indeed we've had the devil of a time of it. Treat him carefully, my dear Count; he's in one of his troublesome humors. For example—but I mustn't keep you waiting. Pray follow me."

"No, but pray tell me. Otherwise I might say something unfortunate."

"Well, he woke at six; and when the barber came to trim his beard there were—imagine it, Count!—no less than seven gray hairs." The king fell into a passion. "Take it off!" he said. "Take it off. I won't have a gray beard! Take it off!' Well what would you? A man is free to be shaved if he chooses, so much more a king. So it's taken off."

"His beard!"

"His beard, my dear Count." Then, after thanking Heaven it was gone, and declaring he looked ten years younger, he cried, "The Count of Luzau-Rischenheim breakfasts with me to-day: what is there for breakfast?" And he had the chef out his of bed and—"But, by heavens, I shall get into trouble if I stop here chattering. He's waiting most eagerly for you. Come along." And Bernenstein, passing his arm through the count's, walked him rapidly into the castle.

The Count of Luzau-Rischenheim was a young man; he was no more versed in affairs of this kind than Bernenstein, and it cannot be said that he showed so much aptitude for them. He was decidedly pale this morning; his manner was uneasy, and his hands trembled. He did not lack courage, but that rarer virtue, coolness; and the importance—or perhaps the shame—of his mission upset the balance of his nerves. Hardly noting where he went, he allowed Bernenstein to lead him quickly and directly towards the room where Rudolf Rassendyll was, not doubting that he was being conducted to the king's presence.

"Breakfast is ordered for nine," said Bernenstein, "but he wants to see you before. He has something important to say; and you perhaps have the same?"

"I? Oh, no. A small matter; but—er—of a private nature."

"Quite so, quite so. Oh, I don't ask any questions, my dear Count."

"Shall I find the king alone?" asked Rischenheim nervously.

"I don't think you'll find anybody with him; no, nobody, I think," answered Bernenstein, with a grave and reassuring air.

They arrived now at the door. Here Bernenstein paused.

"I am ordered to wait outside till his Majesty summons me," he said in a low voice, as though he feared that the irritable king would hear him. "I'll open the door and announce you. Pray keep him in a good temper, for all our sakes." And he flung the door open, saying, "Sire, the Count of Luzau-Rischenheim has the honor to wait on your Majesty." With this he shut the door promptly, and stood against it. Nor did he move, save once, and then only to take out his revolver and carefully inspect it.

The count advanced, bowing low, and striving to conceal a visible agitation. He saw the king in his arm-chair; the king wore a suit of brown tweeds (none the better for being crushed into a bundle the night before); his face was in deep shadow, but Rischenheim perceived that the beard was indeed gone. The king held out his hand to Rischenheim, and motioned him to sit in a chair just opposite to him and within a foot of the window-curtains.

"I'm delighted to see you, my lord," said the king.

Rischenheim looked up. Rudolf's voice had once been so like the king's that no man could tell the difference, but in the last year or two the king's had grown weaker, and Rischenheim seemed to be struck by the vigor of the tones in which he was addressed. As he looked up, there was a slight movement in the curtains by him; it died away when the count gave no further signs of suspicion, but Rudolf had noticed his surprise: the voice, when it next spoke, was subdued.

"Most delighted," pursued Mr. Rassendyll. "For I am pestered beyond endurance about those dogs. I can't get the coats right, I've tried everything, but they won't come as I wish. Now, yours are magnificent."

"You are very good, sire. But I ventured to ask an audience in order to—"

"Positively you must tell me about the dogs. And before Sapt comes, for I want nobody to hear but myself."

"Your Majesty expects Colonel Sapt?"

"In about twenty minutes," said the king, with a glance at the clock on the mantelpiece.

At this Rischenheim became all on fire to get his errand done before Sapt appeared.

"The coats of your dogs," pursued the king, "grow so beautifully—"

"A thousand pardons, sire, but—"

"Long and silky, that I despair of—"

"I have a most urgent and important matter," persisted Rischenheim in agony.

Rudolf threw himself back in his chair with a peevish air. "Well, if you must, you must. What is this great affair, Count? Let us have it over, and then you can tell me about the dogs."

Rischenheim looked round the room. There was nobody; the curtains were still; the king's left hand caressed his beardless chin; the right was hidden from his visitor by the small table that stood between them.

"Sire, my cousin, the Count of Hentzau, has entrusted me with a message."

Rudolf suddenly assumed a stern air.

"I can hold no communication, directly or indirectly, with the Count of Hentzau," said he.

"Pardon me, sire, pardon me. A document has come into the count's hands which is of vital importance to your Majesty."

"The Count of Hentzau, my lord, has incurred my heaviest displeasure."

"Sire, it is in the hopes of atoning for his offences that he has sent me here to-day. There is a conspiracy against your Majesty's honor."

"By whom, my lord?" asked Rudolf, in cold and doubting tones.

"By those who are very near your Majesty's person and very high in your Majesty's love."

"Name them."

"Sire, I dare not. You would not believe me. But your Majesty will believe written evidence."

"Show it me, and quickly. We may be interrupted."

"Sire, I have a copy—"

"Oh, a copy, my lord?" sneered Rudolf.

"My cousin has the original, and will forward it at your Majesty's command. A copy of a letter of her Majesty's—"

"Of the queen's?"

"Yes, sire. It is addressed to—" Rischenheim paused.

"Well, my lord, to whom?"

"To a Mr. Rudolf Rassendyll."

Now Rudolf played his part well. He did not feign indifference, but allowed his voice to tremble with emotion as he stretched out his hand and said in a hoarse whisper, "Give it me, give it me."

Rischenheim's eyes sparkled. His shot had told: the king's attention was his; the coats of the dogs were forgotten. Plainly he had stirred the suspicions and jealousy of the king.

"My cousin," he continued, "conceives it his duty to lay the letter before your Majesty. He obtained it—"

"A curse on how he got it! Give it me!"

Rischenheim unbuttoned his coat, then his waistcoat. The head of a revolver showed in a belt round his waist. He undid the flap of a pocket in the lining of his waistcoat, and he began to draw out a sheet of paper.

But Rudolf, great as his powers of self-control were, was but human. When he saw the paper, he leant forward, half rising from his chair. As a result, his face came beyond the shadow of the curtain, and the full morning light beat on it. As Rischenheim took the paper out, he looked up. He saw the face that glared so eagerly at him; his eyes met Rassendyll's: a sudden suspicion seized him, for the face, though the king's face in every feature, bore a stern resolution and witnessed a vigor that were not the king's. In that instant the truth, or a hint of it, flashed across his mind. He gave a half-articulate cry; in one hand he crumpled up the paper, the other flew to his revolver. But he was too late. Rudolf's left hand encircled his hand and the paper in an iron grip; Rudolf's revolver was on his temple; and an arm was stretched out from behind the curtain, holding another barrel full before his eyes, while a dry voice said, "You'd best take it quietly." Then Sapt stepped out.

Rischenheim had no words to meet the sudden transformation of the interview. He seemed to be able to do nothing but stare at Rudolf Rassendyll. Sapt wasted no time. He snatched the count's revolver and stowed it in his own pocket.

"Now take the paper," said he to Rudolf, and his barrel held Rischenheim motionless while Rudolf wrenched the precious document from his fingers. "Look if it's the right one. No, don't read it through; just look. Is it right? That's good. Now put your revolver to his head again. I'm going to search him. Stand up, sir."

They compelled the count to stand up, and Sapt subjected him to a search that made the concealment of another copy, or of any other document, impossible. Then they let him sit down again. His eyes seemed fascinated by Rudolf Rassendyll.

"Yet you've seen me before, I think," smiled Rudolf. "I seem to remember you as a boy in Strelsau when I was there. Now tell us, sir, where did you leave this cousin of yours?" For the plan was to find out from Rischenheim where Rupert was, and to set off in pursuit of Rupert as soon as they had disposed of Rischenheim.

But even as Rudolf spoke there was a violent knock at the door. Rudolf sprang to open it. Sapt and his revolver kept their places. Bernenstein was on the threshold, open-mouthed.

"The king's servant has just gone by. He's looking for Colonel Sapt. The King has been walking in the drive, and learnt from a sentry of Rischenheim's arrival. I told the man that you had taken the count for a stroll round the castle, and I did not know where you were. He says that the king may come himself at any moment."

Sapt considered for one short instant; then he was back by the prisoner's side.

"We must talk again later on," he said, in low quick tones. "Now you're going to breakfast with the king. I shall be there, and Bernenstein. Remember, not a word of your errand, not a word of this gentleman! At a word, a sign, a hint, a gesture, a motion, as God lives, I'll put a bullet through your head, and a thousand kings sha'n't stop me. Rudolf, get behind the curtain. If there's an alarm you must jump through the window into the moat and swim for it."

"All right," said Rudolf Rassendyll. "I can read my letter there."

"Burn it, you fool."

"When I've read it I'll eat it, if you like, but not before."

Bernenstein looked in again. "Quick, quick! The man will be back," he whispered.

"Bernenstein, did you hear what I said to the count?"

"Yes, I heard."

"Then you know your part. Now, gentlemen, to the king."

"Well," said an angry voice outside, "I wondered how long I was to be kept waiting."

Rudolf Rassendyll skipped behind the curtain. Sapt's revolver slipped into a handy pocket. Rischenheim stood with arms dangling by his side and his waistcoat half unbuttoned. Young Bernenstein was bowing low on the threshold, and protesting that the king's servant had but just gone, and that they were on the point of waiting on his Majesty. Then the king walked in, pale and full-bearded.

"Ah, Count," said he, "I'm glad to see you. If they had told me you were here, you shouldn't have waited a minute. You're very dark in here, Sapt. Why don't you draw back the curtains?" and the king moved towards the curtain behind which Rudolf was.

"Allow me, sire," cried Sapt, darting past him and laying a hand on the curtain.

A malicious gleam of pleasure shot into Rischenheim's eyes. "In truth, sire," continued the constable, his hand on the curtain, "we were so interested in what the count was saying about his dogs—"

"By heaven, I forgot!" cried the king. "Yes, yes, the dogs. Now tell me, Count—"

"Your pardon, sire," put in young Bernenstein, "but breakfast waits."

"Yes, yes. Well, then, we'll have them together—breakfast and the dogs. Come along, Count." The king passed his arm through Rischenheim's, adding to Bernenstein, "Lead the way, Lieutenant; and you, Colonel, come with us."

They went out. Sapt stopped and locked the door behind him. "Why do you lock the door, Colonel?" asked the king.

"There are some papers in my drawer there, sire."

"But why not lock the drawer?

"I have lost the key, sire, like the fool I am," said the colonel.

The Count of Luzau-Rischenheim did not make a very good breakfast. He sat opposite to the king. Colonel Sapt placed himself at the back of the king's chair, and Rischenheim saw the muzzle of a revolver resting on the top of the chair just behind his Majesty's right ear. Bernenstein stood in soldierly rigidity by the door; Rischenheim looked round at him once and met a most significant gaze.

"You're eating nothing," said the king. "I hope you're not indisposed?"

"I am a little upset, sire," stammered Rischenheim, and truly enough.

"Well, tell me about the dogs—while I eat, for I'm hungry."

Rischenheim began to disclose his secret. His statement was decidedly wanting in clearness. The king grew impatient.

"I don't understand," said he testily, and he pushed his chair back so quickly that Sapt skipped away, and hid the revolver behind his back.

"Sire—" cried Rischenheim, half rising. A cough from Lieutenant von Bernenstein interrupted him.

"Tell it me all over again," said the king. Rischenheim did as he was bid.

"Ah, I understand a little better now. Do you see, Sapt?" and he turned his head round towards the constable. Sapt had just time to whisk the revolver away. The count lent forward towards the king. Lieutenant von Bernenstein coughed. The count sank back again.

"Perfectly, sire," said Colonel Sapt. "I understand all the count wishes to convey to your Majesty."

"Well, I understand about half," said the king with a laugh. "But perhaps that'll be enough."

"I think quite enough, sire," answered Sapt with a smile. The important matter of the dogs being thus disposed of, the king recollected that the count had asked for an audience on a matter of business.

"Now, what did you wish to say to me?" he asked, with a weary air. The dogs had been more interesting.

Rischenheim looked at Sapt. The revolver was in its place; Bernenstein coughed again. Yet he saw a chance.

"Your pardon, sire," said he, "but we are not alone."

The king lifted his eyebrows.

"Is the business so private?" he asked.

"I should prefer to tell it to your Majesty alone," pleaded the count.

Now Sapt was resolved not to leave Rischenheim alone with the king, for, although the count, being robbed of his evidence could do little harm concerning the letter, he would doubtless tell the king that Rudolf Rassendyll was in the castle. He leant now over the king's shoulder, and said with a sneer:

"Messages from Rupert of Hentzau are too exalted matters for my poor ears, it seems."

The king flushed red.

"Is that your business, my lord?" he asked Rischenheim sternly.

"Your Majesty does not know what my cousin—"

"It is the old plea?" interrupted the king. "He wants to come back? Is that all, or is there anything else?"

A moment's silence followed the king's words. Sapt looked full at Rischenheim, and smiled as he slightly raised his right hand and showed the revolver. Bernenstein coughed twice. Rischenheim sat twisting his fingers. He understood that, cost what it might, they would not let him declare his errand to the king or betray Mr. Rassendyll's presence. He cleared his throat and opened his mouth as if to speak, but still he remained silent.

"Well, my lord, is it the old story or something new," asked the king impatiently.

Again Rischenheim sat silent.

"Are you dumb, my lord?" cried the king most impatiently.

"It—it is only what you call the old story, sire."

"Then let me say that you have treated me very badly in obtaining an audience of me for any such purpose," said the king. "You knew my decision, and your cousin knows it." Thus speaking, the king rose; Sapt's revolver slid into his pocket; but Lieutenant von Bernenstein drew his sword and stood at the salute; he also coughed.

"My dear Rischenheim," pursued the king more kindly, "I can allow for your natural affection. But, believe me, in this case it misleads you. Do me the favor not to open this subject again to me."

Rischenheim, humiliated and angry, could do nothing but bow in acknowledgment of the king's rebuke.

"Colonel Sapt, see that the count is well entertained. My horse should be at the door by now. Farewell, Count. Bernenstein, give me your arm."

Bernenstein shot a rapid glance at the constable. Sapt nodded reassuringly. Bernenstein sheathed his sword and gave his arm to the king. They passed through the door, and Bernenstein closed it with a backward push of his hand. But at this moment Rischenheim, goaded to fury and desperate at the trick played on him—seeing, moreover, that he had now only one man to deal with—made a sudden rush at the door. He reached it, and his hand was on the door-knob. But Sapt was upon him, and Sapt's revolver was at his ear.

In the passage the king stopped.

"What are they doing in there?" he asked, hearing the noise of the quick movements.

"I don't know, sire," said Bernenstein, and he took a step forward.

"No, stop a minute, Lieutenant; you're pulling me along!"

"A thousand pardons, sire."

"I hear nothing more now." And there was nothing to hear, for the two now stood dead silent inside the door.

"Nor I, sire. Will your Majesty go on?" And Bernenstein took another step.

"You're determined I shall," said the king with a laugh, and he let the young officer lead him away.

Inside the room, Rischenheim stood with his back against the door. He was panting for breath, and his face was flushed and working with excitement. Opposite to him stood Sapt, revolver in hand.

"Till you get to heaven, my lord," said the constable, "you'll never be nearer to it than you were in that moment. If you had opened the door, I'd have shot you through the head."

As he spoke there came a knock at the door.

"Open it," he said brusquely to Rischenheim. With a muttered curse the count obeyed him. A servant stood outside with a telegram on a salver.

"Take it," whispered Sapt, and Rischenheim put out his hand.

"Your pardon, my lord, but this has arrived for you," said the man respectfully.

"Take it," whispered Sapt again.

"Give it me," muttered Rischenheim confusedly; and he took the envelope.

The servant bowed and shut the door.

"Open it," commanded Sapt.

"God's curse on you!" cried Rischenheim in a voice that choked with passion.

"Eh? Oh, you can have no secrets from so good a friend as I am, my lord. Be quick and open it."

The count began to open it.

"If you tear it up, or crumple it, I'll shoot you," said Sapt quietly. "You know you can trust my word. Now read it."

"By God, I won't read it."

"Read it, I tell you, or say your prayers."

The muzzle was within a foot of his head. He unfolded the telegram. Then he looked at Sapt.

"Read," said the constable.

"I don't understand what it means," grumbled Rischenheim.

"Possibly I may be able to help you."

"It's nothing but—"

"Read, my lord, read!"

Then he read, and this was the telegram: "Holf, 19 Konigstrasse."

"A thousand thanks, my lord. And—the place it's despatched from?"

"Strelsau."

"Just turn it so that I can see. Oh, I don't doubt you, but seeing is believing. Ah, thanks. It's as you say. You're puzzled what it means, Count?"

"I don't know at all what it means!"

"How strange! Because I can guess so well."

"You are very acute, sir."

"It seems to me a simple thing to guess, my lord."

"And pray," said Rischenheim, endeavoring to assume an easy and sarcastic air, "what does your wisdom tell you that the message means?"

"I think, my lord, that the message is an address."

"An address! I never thought of that. But I know no Holf."

"I don't think it's Holf's address."

"Whose, then?" asked Rischenheim, biting his nail, and looking furtively at the constable.

"Why," said Sapt, "the present address of Count Rupert of Hentzau."

As he spoke, he fixed his eyes on the eyes of Rischenheim. He gave a short, sharp laugh, then put his revolver in his pocket and bowed to the count.

"In truth, you are very convenient, my dear Count," said he.

CHAPTER VI. THE TASK OF THE QUEEN'S SERVANTS

THE doctor who attended me at Wintenberg was not only discreet, but also indulgent; perhaps he had the sense to see that little benefit would come to a sick man from fretting in helplessness on his back, when he was on fire to be afoot. I fear he thought the baker's rolling-pin was in my mind, but at any rate I extorted a consent from him, and was on my way home from Wintenberg not much more than twelve hours after Rudolf Rassendyll left me. Thus I arrived at my own house in Strelsau on the same Friday morning that witnessed the Count of Luzau-Rischenheim's two-fold interview with the king at the Castle of Zenda. The moment

I had arrived, I sent James, whose assistance had been, and continued to be, in all respects most valuable, to despatch a message to the constable, acquainting him with my whereabouts, and putting myself entirely at his disposal. Sapt received this message while a council of war was being held, and the information it gave aided not a little in the arrangements that the constable and Rudolf Rassendyll made. What these were I must now relate, although, I fear, at the risk of some tediousness.

Yet that council of war in Zenda was held under no common circumstances. Cowed as Rischenheim appeared, they dared not let him out of their sight. Rudolf could not leave the room into which Sapt had locked him; the king's absence was to be short, and before he came again Rudolf must be gone, Rischenheim safely disposed of, and measures taken against the original letter reaching the hands for which the intercepted copy had been destined. The room was a large one. In the corner farthest from the door sat Rischenheim, disarmed, dispirited, to all seeming ready to throw up his dangerous game and acquiesce in any terms presented to him. Just inside the door, guarding it, if need should be, with their lives, were the other three, Bernenstein merry and triumphant, Sapt blunt and cool, Rudolf calm and clear-headed. The queen awaited the result of their deliberations in her apartments, ready to act as they directed, but determined to see Rudolf before he left the castle. They conversed together in low tones. Presently Sapt took paper and wrote. This first message was to me, and it bade me come to Zenda that afternoon; another head and another pair of hands were sadly needed. Then followed more deliberation; Rudolf took up the talking now, for his was the bold plan on which they consulted. Sapt twirled his moustache, smiling doubtfully.

"Yes, yes," murmured young Bernenstein, his eyes alight with excitement.

"It's dangerous, but the best thing," said Rudolf, carefully sinking his voice yet lower, lest the prisoner should catch the lightest word of what he said. "It involves my staying here till the evening. Is that possible?"

"No; but you can leave here and hide in the forest till I join you," said Sapt.

"Till we join you," corrected Bernenstein eagerly.

"No," said the constable, "you must look after our friend here. Come, Lieutenant, it's all in the queen's service."

"Besides," added Rudolf with a smile, "neither the colonel nor I would let you have a chance at Rupert. He's our game, isn't he, Sapt?"

The colonel nodded. Rudolf in his turn took paper, and here is the message that he wrote:

"Holf, 19, Konigstrasse, Strelsau.—All well. He has what I had, but wishes to see what you have. He and I will be at the hunting-lodge at ten this evening. Bring it and meet us. The business is unsuspected.—R."

Rudolf threw the paper across to Sapt; Bernenstein leant over the constable's shoulder and read it eagerly.

"I doubt if it would bring me," grinned old Sapt, throwing the paper down.

"It'll bring Rupert to Hentzau. Why not? He'll know that the king will wish to meet him unknown to the queen, and also unknown to you, Sapt, since you were my friend: what place more likely for the king to choose than his hunting-lodge, where he is accustomed to go when he wishes to be alone? The message will bring him, depend on it. Why, man, Rupert would come even if he suspected; and why should he suspect?"

"They may have a cipher, he and Rischenheim," objected Sapt.

"No, or Rupert would have sent the address in it," retorted Rudolf quickly.

"Then—when he comes?" asked Bernenstein.

"He finds such a king as Rischenheim found, and Sapt, here, at his elbow."

"But he'll know you," objected Bernenstein.

"Ay, I think he'll know me," said Rudolf with a smile. "Meanwhile we send for Fritz to come here and look after the king."

"And Rischenheim?"

"That's your share, Lieutenant. Sapt, is any one at Tarlenheim?"

"No. Count Stanislas has put it at Fritz's disposal."

"Good; then Fritz's two friends, the Count of Luzau-Rischenheim and Lieutenant von Bernenstein, will ride over there to-day. The constable of Zenda will give the lieutenant twenty-four hours' leave of absence, and the two gentlemen will pass the day and sleep at the chateau. They will pass the day side by side, Bernenstein, not losing sight of one another for an instant, and they will pass the night in the same room. And one of them will not close his eyes nor take his hand off the butt of his revolver."

"Very good, sir," said young Bernenstein.

"If he tries to escape or give any alarm, shoot him through the head, ride to the frontier, get to safe hiding, and, if you can, let us know."

"Yes," said Bernenstein simply. Sapt had chosen well, and the young officer made nothing of the peril and ruin that her Majesty's service might ask of him.

A restless movement and a weary sigh from Rischenheim attracted their attention. He had strained his ears to listen till his head ached, but the talkers had been careful, and he had heard nothing that threw light on their deliberations. He had now given up his vain attempt, and sat in listless inattention, sunk in an apathy.

"I don't think he'll give you much trouble," whispered Sapt to Bernenstein, with a jerk of his thumb towards the captive.

"Act as if he were likely to give you much," urged Rudolf, laying his hand on the lieutenant's arm.

"Yes, that's a wise man's advice," nodded the constable approvingly. "We were well governed, Lieutenant, when this Rudolf was king."

"Wasn't I also his loyal subject?" asked young Bernenstein.

"Yes, wounded in my service," added Rudolf; for he remembered how the boy—he was little more then—had been fired upon in the park of Tarlenheim, being taken for Mr. Rassendyll himself.

Thus their plans were laid. If they could defeat Rupert, they would have Rischenheim at their mercy. If they could keep Rischenheim out of the way while they used his name in their trick, they had a strong chance of deluding and killing Rupert. Yes, of killing him; for that and nothing less was their purpose, as the constable of Zenda himself has told me.

"We would have stood on no ceremony," he said. "The queen's honor was at stake, and the fellow himself an assassin."

Bernenstein rose and went out. He was gone about half an hour, being employed in despatching the telegrams to Strelsau. Rudolf and Sapt used the interval to explain to Rischenheim what they proposed to do with him. They asked no pledge, and he offered none. He heard what they said with a dulled uninterested air. When asked if he would go without resistance, he laughed a bitter laugh. "How can I resist?" he asked. "I should have a bullet through my head."

"Why, without doubt," said Colonel Sapt. "My lord, you are very sensible."

"Let me advise you, my lord," said Rudolf, looking down on him kindly enough, "if you come safe through this affair, to add honor to your prudence, and chivalry to your honor. There is still time for you to become a gentleman."

He turned away, followed by a glance of anger from the count and a grating chuckle from old Sapt.

A few moments later Bernenstein returned. His errand was done, and horses for himself and Rischenheim were at the gate of the castle. After a few final words and clasp of the hand from Rudolf, the lieutenant motioned to his prisoner to accompany him, and they two walked out together, being to all appearance willing companions and in perfect friendliness with one another. The queen herself watched them go from the windows of her apartment, and noticed that Bernenstein rode half a pace behind, and that his free hand rested on the revolver by his side.

It was now well on in the morning, and the risk of Rudolf's sojourn in the castle grew greater with every moment. Yet he was resolved to see the queen before he went. This interview presented no great difficulties, since her Majesty was in the habit of coming to the constable's room to take his advice or to consult with him. The hardest task was to contrive afterwards a free and unnoticed escape for Mr. Rassendyll. To meet this necessity, the constable issued orders that the company of guards which garrisoned the castle should parade at one o'clock in the park, and that the servants should all, after their dinner, be granted permission to watch the manoeuvres. By this means he counted on drawing off any curious eyes and allowing Rudolf to reach the forest unobserved. They appointed a rendezvous in a handy and sheltered spot; the one thing which they were compelled to trust to fortune was Rudolf's success in evading chance encounters while he waited. Mr. Rassendyll himself was confident of his ability to conceal his presence, or, if need were, so to hide his face that no strange tale of the king being seen wandering, alone and beardless, should reach the ears of the castle or the town.

While Sapt was making his arrangements, Queen Flavia came to the room where Rudolf Rassendyll was. It was then nearing twelve, and young Bernenstein had been gone half an hour. Sapt attended her to the door, set a sentry at the end of the passage with orders that her Majesty should on no pretence be disturbed, promised her very audibly to return as soon as he possibly could, and respectfully closed the door after she had entered. The constable was well aware of the value in a secret business of doing openly all that can safely be done with openness.

All of what passed at that interview I do not know, but a part Queen Flavia herself told to me, or rather to Helga, my wife; for although it was meant to reach my ear, yet to me, a man, she would not disclose it directly. First she learnt from Mr. Rassendyll the plans that had been made, and, although she trembled at the danger that he must run in meeting Rupert of Hentzau, she had such love of him and such a trust in his powers that she seemed to doubt little of his success. But she began to reproach herself for having brought him into this peril by writing her letter. At this he took from his pocket the copy that Rischenheim had carried. He had found time to read it, and now before her eyes he kissed it.

"Had I as many lives as there are words, my queen," he said softly, "for each word I would gladly give a life."

"Ah, Rudolf, but you've only one life, and that more mine than yours. Did you think we should ever meet again?"

"I didn't know," said he; and now they were standing opposite one another.

"But I knew," she said, her eyes shining brightly; "I knew always that we should meet once more. Not how, nor where, but just that we should. So I lived, Rudolf."

"God bless you!" he said.

"Yes, I lived through it all."

He pressed her hand, knowing what that phrase meant and must mean for her.

"Will it last forever?" she asked, suddenly gripping his hand tightly. But a moment later she went on: "No, no, I mustn't make you unhappy, Rudolf. I'm half glad I wrote the letter, and half glad they stole it. It's so sweet to have you fighting for me, for me only this time, Rudolf—not for the king, for me!"

"Sweet indeed, my dearest lady. Don't be afraid: we shall win."

"You will win, yes. And then you'll go?" And, dropping his hand, she covered her face with hers.

"I mustn't kiss your face," said he, "but your hands I may kiss," and he kissed her hands as they were pressed against her face.

"You wear my ring," she murmured through her fingers, "always?"

"Why, yes," he said, with a little laugh of wonder at her question.

"And there is—no one else?"

"My queen!" said he, laughing again.

"No, I knew really, Rudolf, I knew really," and now her hands flew out towards him, imploring his pardon. Then she began to speak quickly: "Rudolf, last night I had a dream about you, a strange dream. I seemed to be in Strelsau, and all the people were talking about the king. It was you they meant; you were the king. At last you were the king, and I was your queen. But I could see you only very dimly; you were somewhere, but I could not make out where; just sometimes your face came. Then I tried to tell you that you were king—yes, and Colonel Sapt and Fritz tried to tell you; the people, too, called out that you were king. What did it mean? But your face, when I saw it, was unmoved, and very pale, and you seemed not to hear what we said, not even what I said. It almost seemed as if you were dead, and yet king. Ah, you mustn't die, even to be king," and she laid a hand on his shoulder.

"Sweetheart," said he gently, "in dreams desires and fears blend in strange visions, so I seemed to you to be both a king and a dead man; but I'm not a king, and I am a very healthy fellow. Yet a thousand thanks to my dearest queen for dreaming of me."

"No, but what could it mean?" she asked again.

"What does it mean when I dream always of you, except that I always love you?"

"Was it only that?" she said, still unconvinced.

What more passed between them I do not know. I think that the queen told my wife more, but women will sometimes keep women's secrets even from their husbands; though they love us, yet we are always in some sort the common enemy, against whom they join hands. Well, I would not look too far into such secrets, for to know must be, I suppose, to blame, and who is himself so blameless that in such a case he would be free with his censures?

Yet much cannot have passed, for almost close on their talk about the dream came Colonel Sapt, saying that the guards were in line, and all the women streamed out to watch them, while the men followed, lest the gay uniforms should make them forgotten. Certainly a quiet fell over the old castle, that only the constable's curt tones broke, as he bade Rudolf come by the back way to the stables and mount his horse.

"There's no time to lose," said Sapt, and his eye seemed to grudge the queen even one more word with the man she loved.

But Rudolf was not to be hurried into leaving her in such a fashion. He clapped the constable on the shoulder, laughing, and bidding him think of what he would for a moment; then he went again to the queen and would have knelt before her, but that she would not suffer, and they stood with hands locked. Then suddenly she drew him to her and kissed his forehead, saying: "God go with you, Rudolf my knight."

Thus she turned away, letting him go. He walked towards the door; but a sound arrested his steps, and he waited in the middle of the room, his eyes on the door. Old Sapt flew to the threshold, his sword half-way out of its sheath. There was a step coming down the passage, and the feet stopped outside the door.

"Is it the king?" whispered Rudolf.

"I don't know," said Sapt.

"No, it's not the king," came in unhesitating certainty from Queen Flavia.

They waited: a low knock sounded on the door. Still for a moment they waited. The knock was repeated urgently.

"We must open," said Sapt. "Behind the curtain with you, Rudolf."

The queen sat down, and Sapt piled a heap of papers before her, that it might seem as though he and she transacted business. But his precautions were interrupted by a hoarse, eager, low cry from outside, "Quick! in God's name, quick!"

They knew the voice for Bernenstein's. The queen sprang up, Rudolf came out, Sapt turned the key. The lieutenant entered, hurried, breathless, pale.

"Well?" asked Sapt.

"He has got away?" cried Rudolf, guessing in a moment the misfortune that had brought Bernenstein back.

"Yes, he's got away. Just as we left the town and reached the open road towards Tarlenheim, he said, 'Are we going to walk all the way? I was not loath to go quicker, and we broke into a trot. But I—ah, what a pestilent fool I am!'"

"Never mind that—go on."

"Why, I was thinking of him and my task, and having a bullet ready for him, and—"

"Of everything except your horse?" guessed Sapt, with a grim smile.

"Yes; and the horse pecked and stumbled, and I fell forward on his neck. I put out my arm to recover myself, and—I jerked my revolver on to the ground."

"And he saw?"

"He saw, curse him. For a second he waited; then he smiled, and turned, and dug his spurs in and was off, straight across country towards Strelsau. Well, I was off my horse in a moment, and I fired three times after him."

"You hit?" asked Rudolf.

"I think so. He shifted the reins from one hand to the other and wrung his arm. I mounted and made after him, but his horse was better than mine and he gained ground. We began to meet people, too, and I didn't dare to fire again. So I left him and rode here to tell you. Never employ me again, Constable, so long as you live," and the young man's face was twisted with misery and shame, as, forgetting the queen's presence, he sank despondently into a chair.

Sapt took no notice of his self-reproaches. But Rudolf went and laid a hand on his shoulder. "It was an accident," he said. "No blame to you."

The queen rose and walked towards him; Bernenstein sprang to his feet.

"Sir," said she, "it is not success but effort that should gain thanks," and she held out her hand.

Well, he was young; I do not laugh at the sob that escaped his lips as he turned his head.

"Let me try something else!" he implored.

"Mr. Rassendyll," said the queen, "you'll do my pleasure by employing this gentleman in my further service. I am already deep in his debt, and would be deeper." There was a moment's silence.

"Well, but what's to be done?" asked Colonel Sapt. "He's gone to Strelsau."

"He'll stop Rupert," mused Mr. Rassendyll. "He may or he mayn't."

"It's odds that he will."

"We must provide for both."

Sapt and Rudolf looked at one another.

"You must be here!" asked Rudolf of the constable. "Well, I'll go to Strelsau." His smile broke out. "That is, if Bernenstein'll lend me a hat."

The queen made no sound; but she came and laid her hand on his arm. He looked at her, smiling still.

"Yes, I'll go to Strelsau," said he, "and I'll find Rupert, ay, and Rischenheim too, if they're in the city."

"Take me with you," cried Bernenstein eagerly.

Rudolf glanced at Sapt. The constable shook his head. Bernenstein's face fell.

"It's not that, boy," said old Sapt, half in kindness, half in impatience. "We want you here. Suppose Rupert comes here with Rischenheim!"

The idea was new, but the event was by no means unlikely.

"But you'll be here, Constable," urged Bernenstein, "and Fritz von Tarlenheim will arrive in an hour."

"Ay, young man," said Sapt, nodding his head; "but when I fight Rupert of Hentzau, I like to have a man to spare," and he grinned broadly, being no whit afraid of what Bernenstein might think of his courage. "Now go and get him a hat," he added, and the lieutenant ran off on the errand.

But the queen cried:

"Are you sending Rudolf alone, then—alone against two?"

113

"Yes, madam, if I may command the campaign," said Sapt. "I take it he should be equal to the task."

He could not know the feelings of the queen's heart. She dashed her hand across her eyes, and turned in mute entreaty to Rudolf Rassendyll.

"I must go," he said softly. "We can't spare Bernenstein, and I mustn't stay here."

She said no more. Rudolf walked across to Sapt.

"Take me to the stables. Is the horse good? I daren't take the train. Ah, here's the lieutenant and the hat."

"The horse'll get you there to-night," said Sapt. "Come along. Bernenstein, stay with the queen."

At the threshold Rudolf paused, and, turning his head, glanced once at Queen Flavia, who stood still as a statue, watching him go. Then he followed the constable, who brought him where the horse was. Sapt's devices for securing freedom from observation had served well, and Rudolf mounted unmolested.

"The hat doesn't fit very well," said Rudolf.

"Like a crown better, eh?" suggested the colonel.

Rudolf laughed as he asked, "Well, what are my orders?"

"Ride round by the moat to the road at the back; then through the forest to Hofbau; you know your way after that. You mustn't reach Strelsau till it's dark. Then, if you want a shelter—"

"To Fritz von Tarlenheim's, yes! From there I shall go straight to the address."

"Ay. And—Rudolf!"

"Yes?"

"Make an end of him this time."

"Please God. But if he goes to the lodge? He will, unless Rischenheim stops him."

"I'll be there in case—but I think Rischenheim will stop him."

"If he comes here?"

"Young Bernenstein will die before he suffers him to reach the king."

"Sapt!"

"Ay?"

"Be kind to her."

"Bless the man, yes!"

"Good-by."

"And good luck."

At a swift canter Rudolf darted round the drive that led from the stables, by the moat, to the old forest road behind; five minutes brought him within the shelter of the trees, and he rode on confidently, meeting nobody, save here and there a yokel, who, seeing a man ride hard with his head averted, took no more notice of him than to wish that he himself could ride abroad instead of being bound to work. Thus Rudolf Rassendyll set out again for the walls of Strelsau, through the forest of Zenda. And ahead of him, with an hour's start, galloped the Count of Luzau-Rischenheim, again a man, and a man with resolution, resentment, and revenge in his heart.

The game was afoot now; who could tell the issue of it?

CHAPTER VII. THE MESSAGE OF SIMON THE HUNTSMAN

I RECEIVED the telegram sent to me by the Constable of Zenda at my own house in Strelsau about one o'clock. It is needless to say that I made immediate preparations to obey his summons. My wife indeed protested—and I must admit with some show of reason—that I was unfit to endure further fatigues, and that my bed was the only proper place for me. I could not listen; and James, Mr. Rassendyll's servant, being informed of the summons, was at my elbow with a card of the trains from Strelsau to Zenda, without waiting for any order from me. I had talked to this man in the course of our journey, and discovered that he had been in the service of Lord Topham, formerly British Ambassador to the Court of Ruritania. How far he was acquainted with the secrets of his present master, I did not know, but his familiarity with the city and the country made him of great use to me. We discovered, to our annoyance, that no train left till four o'clock, and then only a slow one; the result was that we could not arrive at the castle till past six o'clock. This hour was not absolutely too late, but I was of course eager to be on the scene of action as early as possible.

"You'd better see if you can get a special, my lord," James suggested; "I'll run on to the station and arrange about it."

I agreed. Since I was known to be often employed in the king's service, I could take a special train without exciting remark. James set out, and about a quarter of an hour later I got into my carriage to drive to the station. Just as the horses were about to start, however, the butler approached me.

"I beg your pardon, my lord," said he, "but Bauer didn't return with your lordship. Is he coming back?"

"No," said I. "Bauer was grossly impertinent on the journey, and I dismissed him."

"Those foreign men are never to be trusted, my lord. And your lordship's bag?"

"What, hasn't it come?" I cried. "I told him to send it."

"It's not arrived, my lord."

"Can the rogue have stolen it?" I exclaimed indignantly.

"If your lordship wishes it, I will mention the matter to the police."

I appeared to consider this proposal.

"Wait till I come back," I ended by saying. "The bag may come, and I have no reason to doubt the fellow's honesty."

This, I thought, would be the end of my connection with Master Bauer. He had served Rupert's turn, and would now disappear from the scene. Indeed it may be that Rupert would have liked to dispense with further aid from him; but he had few whom he could trust, and was compelled to employ those few more than once. At any rate he had not done with Bauer, and I very soon received proof of the fact. My house is a couple of miles from the station, and we have to pass through a considerable part of the old town, where the streets are narrow and tortuous and progress necessarily slow. We had just entered the Konigstrasse (and it must be remembered that I had at that time no reason for attaching any special significance to this locality), and were waiting impatiently for a heavy dray to move out of our path, when my coachman, who had overheard the butler's conversation with me, leant down from his box with an air of lively excitement.

"My lord," he cried, "there's Bauer—there, passing the butcher's shop!"

I sprang up in the carriage; the man's back was towards me, and he was threading his way through the people with a quick, stealthy tread. I believe he must have seen me, and was slinking away as fast as he could. I was not sure of him, but the coachman banished my doubt by saying, "It's Bauer—it's certainly Bauer, my lord."

I hardly stayed to form a resolution. If I could catch this fellow or even see where he went, a most important clue as to Rupert's doings and whereabouts might be put into my hand. I leapt out of the carriage, bidding the man wait, and at once started in pursuit of my former servant. I heard the coachman laugh: he thought, no doubt, that anxiety for the missing bag inspired such eager haste.

The numbers of the houses in the Konigstrasse begin, as anybody familiar with Strelsau will remember, at the end adjoining the station. The street being a long one, intersecting almost the entire length of the old town, I was, when I set out after Bauer, opposite number 300 or thereabouts, and distant nearly three-quarters of a mile from that important number nineteen, towards which Bauer was hurrying like a rabbit to its burrow. I knew nothing and thought nothing of where he was going; to me nineteen was no more than eighteen or twenty; my only desire was to overtake him. I had no clear idea of what I meant to do when I caught him, but I had some hazy notion of intimidating him into giving up his secret by the threat of an accusation of theft. In fact, he had stolen my bag. After him I went; and he knew that I was after him. I saw him turn his face over his shoulder, and then bustle on faster. Neither of us, pursued or pursuer, dared quite to run; as it was, our eager strides and our carelessness of collisions created more than enough attention. But I had one advantage. Most folk in Strelsau knew me, and many got out of my way who were by no means inclined to pay a like civility to Bauer. Thus I began to gain on him, in spite of his haste; I had started fifty yards behind, but as we neared the end of the street and saw the station ahead of us, not more than twenty separated me from him. Then an annoying thing happened. I ran full into a stout old gentleman; Bauer had run into him before, and he was standing, as people will, staring in resentful astonishment at his first assailant's retreating figure. The second collision immensely increased his vexation; for me it had yet worse consequences; for when I disentangled myself, Bauer was gone! There was not a sign of him; I looked up: the number of the house above me was twenty-three; but the door was shut. I walked on a few paces, past twenty-two, past twenty-one—and up to nineteen. Nineteen was an old house, with a dirty, dilapidated front and an air almost dissipated. It was a shop where provisions of the cheaper sort were on view in the window, things that one has never eaten but has heard of people eating. The shop-door stood open, but there was nothing to connect Bauer with the house. Muttering an oath in my exasperation, I was about to pass on, when an old woman put her head out of the door and looked round. I was full in front of her. I am sure that the old woman started slightly, and I think that I did. For I knew her and she knew me. She was old Mother Holf, one of whose sons, Johann, had betrayed to us the secret of the dungeon at Zenda, while the other had died by Mr. Rassendyll's hand by the side of the great pipe that masked the king's window. Her presence might mean nothing, yet it seemed at once to connect the house with the secret of the past and the crisis of the present.

She recovered herself in a moment, and curtseyed to me.

"Ah, Mother Holf," said I, "how long is it since you set up shop in Strelsau?"

"About six months, my lord," she answered, with a composed air and arms akimbo.

"I have not come across you before," said I, looking keenly at her.

"Such a poor little shop as mine would not be likely to secure your lordship's patronage," she answered, in a humility that seemed only half genuine.

I looked up at the windows. They were all closed and had their wooden lattices shut. The house was devoid of any signs of life.

"You've a good house here, mother, though it wants a splash of paint," said I. "Do you live all alone in it with your daughter?" For Max was dead and Johann abroad, and the old woman had, as far as I knew, no other children.

"Sometimes; sometimes not," said she. "I let lodgings to single men when I can."

"Full now?"

"Not a soul, worse luck, my lord." Then I shot an arrow at a venture.

"The man who came in just now, then, was he only a customer?"

"I wish a customer had come in, but there has been nobody," she replied in surprised tones. I looked full in her eyes; she met mine with a blinking imperturbability. There is no face so inscrutable as a clever old woman's when she is on her guard. And her fat body barred the entrance; I could not so much as see inside, while the window, choked full with pigs' trotters and such-like dainties, helped me very little. If the fox were there, he had got to earth and I could not dig him out.

At this moment I saw James approaching hurriedly. He was looking up the street, no doubt seeking my carriage and chafing at its delay. An instant later he saw me.

"My lord," he said, "your train will be ready in five minutes; if it doesn't start then, the line must be closed for another half-hour."

I perceived a faint smile on the old woman's face. I was sure then that I was on the track of Bauer, and probably of more than Bauer. But my first duty was to obey orders and get to Zenda. Besides, I could not force my way in, there in open daylight, without a scandal that would have set all the long ears in Strelsau aprick. I turned away reluctantly. I did not even know for certain that Bauer was within, and thus had no information of value to carry with me.

"If your lordship would kindly recommend me—" said the old hag.

"Yes, I'll recommend you," said I. "I'll recommend you to be careful whom you take for lodgers. There are queer fish about, mother."

"I take the money beforehand," she retorted with a grin; and I was as sure that she was in the plot as of my own existence.

There was nothing to be done; James's face urged me towards the station. I turned away. But at this instant a loud, merry laugh sounded from inside the house. I started, and this time violently. The old woman's brow contracted in a frown, and her lips twitched for a moment; then her face regained its composure; but I knew the laugh, and she must have guessed that I knew it. Instantly I tried to appear as though I had noticed nothing. I nodded to her carelessly, and bidding James follow me, set out for the station. But as we reached the platform, I laid my hand on his shoulder, saying:

"The Count of Hentzau is in that house, James."

He looked at me without surprise; he was as hard to stir to wonder as old Sapt himself.

"Indeed, sir. Shall I stay and watch?"

"No, come with me," I answered. To tell the truth, I thought that to leave him alone in Strelsau to watch that house was in all likelihood to sign his death warrant, and I shrank from imposing the duty on him. Rudolf might send him if he would; I dared not. So we got into our train, and I suppose that my coachman, when he had looked long enough for me, went home. I forgot to ask him afterwards. Very likely he thought it a fine joke to see his master hunting a truant servant and a truant bag through the streets in broad daylight. Had he known the truth, he would have been as interested, though, maybe, less amused.

I arrived at the town of Zenda at half-past three, and was in the castle before four. I may pass over the most kind and gracious words with which the queen received me. Every sight of her face and every sound of her voice bound a man closer to her service, and now she made me feel that I was a poor fellow to have lost her letter and yet to be alive. But she would hear nothing of such talk, choosing rather to praise the little I had done than to blame the great thing in which I had failed. Dismissed from her presence, I flew open-mouthed to Sapt. I found him in his room with Bernenstein, and had the satisfaction of learning that my news of Rupert's whereabouts was confirmed by his information. I was also made acquainted with all that had been done, even as I have already related it, from the first successful trick played on Rischenheim to the moment of his unfortunate escape. But my face grew long and apprehensive when I heard that Rudolf Rassendyll had gone alone to Strelsau to put his head in that lion's mouth in the Konigstrasse.

"There will be three of them there—Rupert, Rischenheim, and my rascal Bauer," said I.

"As to Rupert, we don't know," Sapt reminded me. "He'll be there if Rischenheim arrives in time to tell him the truth. But we have also to be ready for him here, and at the hunting lodge. Well, we're ready for him wherever he is: Rudolf will be in Strelsau, you and I will ride to the lodge, and Bernenstein will be here with the queen."

"Only one here?" I asked.

"Ay, but a good one," said the constable, clapping Bernenstein on the shoulder. "We sha'n't be gone above four hours, and those while the king is safe in his bed. Bernenstein has only to refuse access to him, and stand to that with his life till we come back. You're equal to that, eh, Lieutenant?"

I am, by nature, a cautious man, and prone to look at the dark side of every prospect and the risks of every enterprise; but I could not see what better dispositions were possible against the attack that threatened us. Yet I was sorely uneasy concerning Mr. Rassendyll.

Now, after all our stir and runnings to and fro, came an hour or two of peace. We employed the time in having a good meal, and it was past five when, our repast finished, we sat back in our chairs enjoying cigars. James had waited on us, quietly usurping the office of the constable's own servant, and thus we had been able to talk freely. The man's calm confidence in his master and his master's fortune also went far to comfort me.

"The king should be back soon," said Sapt at last, with a glance at his big, old-fashioned silver watch. "Thank God, he'll be too tired to sit up long. We shall be free by nine o'clock, Fritz. I wish young Rupert would come to the lodge!" And the colonel's face expressed a lively pleasure at the idea.

Six o'clock struck, and the king did not appear. A few moments later, a message came from the queen, requesting our presence on the terrace in front of the chateau. The place commanded a view of the road by which the king would ride back, and we found the queen walking restlessly up and down, considerably disquieted by the lateness of his return. In such a position as ours, every unusual or unforeseen incident magnifies its possible meaning, and invests itself with a sinister importance which would at ordinary times seem absurd. We three shared the queen's feelings, and forgetting the many chances of the chase, any one of which would amply account for the king's delay, fell to speculating on remote possibilities of disaster. He might have met Rischenheim—though they had ridden in opposite directions; Rupert might have intercepted him—though no means could have brought Rupert to the forest so early. Our fears defeated common sense, and our conjectures outran possibility. Sapt was the first to recover from this foolish mood, and he rated us soundly, not sparing even the queen herself. With a laugh we regained some of our equanimity, and felt rather ashamed of our weakness.

"Still it's strange that he doesn't come," murmured the queen, shading her eyes with her hand, and looking along the road to where the dark masses of the forest trees bounded our view. It was already dusk, but not so dark but that we could have seen the king's party as soon as it came into the open.

If the king's delay seemed strange at six, it was stranger at seven, and by eight most strange. We had long since ceased to talk lightly; by now we had lapsed into silence. Sapt's scoldings had died away. The queen, wrapped in her furs (for it was very cold), sat sometimes on a seat, but oftener paced restlessly to and fro. Evening had fallen. We did not know what to do, nor even whether we ought to do anything. Sapt would not own to sharing our worst apprehensions, but his gloomy silence in face of our surmises witnessed that he was in his heart as disturbed as we were. For my part I had come to the end of my endurance, and I cried, "For God's sake, let's act! Shall I go and seek him?"

"A needle in a bundle of hay," said Sapt with a shrug.

But at this instant my ear caught the sound of horses cantering on the road from the forest; at the same moment Bernenstein cried, "Here they come!" The queen paused, and we gathered round her. The horse-hoofs came nearer. Now we made out the figures of three men: they were the king's huntsmen, and they rode along merrily, singing a hunting chorus. The sound of it brought relief to us; so far at least there was no disaster. But why was not the king with them?

"The king is probably tired, and is following more slowly, madam," suggested Bernenstein.

This explanation seemed very probable, and the lieutenant and I, as ready to be hopeful on slight grounds as fearful on small provocation, joyfully accepted it. Sapt, less easily turned to either mood, said, "Ay, but let us hear," and raising his voice, called to the huntsmen, who had now arrived in the avenue. One of them, the king's chief huntsman Simon, gorgeous in his uniform of green and gold, came swaggering along, and bowed low to the queen.

"Well, Simon, where is the king?" she asked, trying to smile.

"The king, madam, has sent a message by me to your majesty."

"Pray, deliver it to me, Simon."

"I will, madam. The king has enjoyed fine sport; and, indeed, madam, if I may say so for myself, a better run.—"

"You may say, friend Simon," interrupted the constable, tapping him on the shoulder, "anything you like for yourself, but, as a matter of etiquette, the king's message should come first."

"Oh, ay, Constable," said Simon. "You're always so down on a man, aren't you? Well, then, madam, the king has enjoyed fine sport. For we started a boar at eleven, and—"

"Is this the king's message, Simon?" asked the queen, smiling in genuine amusement, but impatiently.

"Why, no, madam, not precisely his majesty's message."

"Then get to it, man, in Heaven's name," growled Sapt testily. For here were we four (the queen, too, one of us!) on tenterhooks, while the fool boasted about the sport that he had shown the king. For every boar in the forest Simon took as much credit as though he, and not Almighty God, had made the animal. It is the way with such fellows.

Simon became a little confused under the combined influence of his own seductive memories and Sapt's brusque exhortations.

"As I was saying, madam," he resumed, "the boar led us a long way, but at last the hounds pulled him down, and his majesty himself gave the coup de grace. Well, then it was very late."

"It's no earlier now," grumbled the constable.

"And the king, although indeed, madam, his majesty was so gracious as to say that no huntsman whom his majesty had ever had, had given his majesty—"

"God help us!" groaned the constable.

Simon shot an apprehensive apologetic glance at Colonel Sapt. The constable was frowning ferociously. In spite of the serious matters in hand I could not forbear a smile, while young Bernenstein broke into an audible laugh, which he tried to smother with his hand.

"Yes, the king was very tired, Simon?" said the queen, at once encouraging him and bringing him back to the point with a woman's skill.

"Yes, madam, the king was very tired; and as we chanced to kill near the hunting-lodge—"

I do not know whether Simon noticed any change in the manner of his audience. But the queen looked up with parted lips, and I believe that we three all drew a step nearer him. Sapt did not interrupt this time.

"Yes, madam, the king was very tired, and as we chanced to kill near the hunting-lodge, the king bade us carry our quarry there, and come back to dress it to-morrow; so we obeyed, and here we are—that is, except Herbert, my brother, who stayed with the king by his majesty's orders. Because, madam, Herbert is a handy fellow, and my good mother taught him to cook a steak and—"

"Stayed where with the king?" roared Sapt.

"Why, at the hunting-lodge, Constable. The king stays there to-night, and will ride back to-morrow morning with Herbert. That, madam, is the king's message."

We had come to it at last, and it was something to come to. Simon gazed from face to face. I saw him, and I understood at once that our feelings must be speaking too plainly. So I took on myself to dismiss him, saying:

"Thanks, Simon, thanks: we understand."

He bowed to the queen; she roused herself, and added her thanks to mine. Simon withdrew, looking still a little puzzled.

After we were left alone, there was a moment's silence. Then I said:

"Suppose Rupert—"

The Constable of Zenda broke in with a short laugh.

"On my life," said he, "how things fall out! We say he will go to the hunting-lodge, and—he goes!"

"If Rupert goes—if Rischenheim doesn't stop him!" I urged again.

The queen rose from her seat and stretched out her hands towards us.

"Gentlemen, my letter!" said she.

Sapt wasted no time.

"Bernenstein," said he, "you stay here as we arranged. Nothing is altered. Horses for Fritz and myself in five minutes."

Bernenstein turned and shot like an arrow along the terrace towards the stables.

"Nothing is altered, madam," said Sapt, "except that we must be there before Count Rupert." I looked at my watch. It was twenty minutes past nine. Simon's cursed chatter had lost a quarter of an hour. I opened my lips to speak. A glance from Sapt's eyes told me that he discerned what I was about to say. I was silent.

"You'll be in time?" asked the queen, with clasped hands and frightened eyes.

"Assuredly, madam," returned Sapt with a bow.

"You won't let him reach the king?"

"Why, no, madam," said Sapt with a smile.

"From my heart, gentlemen," she said in a trembling voice, "from my heart—"

"Here are the horses," cried Sapt. He snatched her hand, brushed it with his grizzly moustache, and—well, I am not sure I heard, and I can hardly believe what I think I heard. But I will set it down for what it is worth. I think he said, "Bless your sweet face, we'll do it." At any rate she drew back with a little cry of surprise, and I saw the tears standing in her eyes. I kissed her hand also; then we mounted, and we started, and we rode, as if the devil were behind us, for the hunting-lodge.

But I turned once to watch her standing on the terrace, with young Bernenstein's tall figure beside her.

"Can we be in time?" said I. It was what I had meant to say before.

"I think not, but, by God, we'll try," said Colonel Sapt. And I knew why he had not let me speak.

Suddenly there was a sound behind us of a horse at the gallop. Our heads flew round in the ready apprehension of men on a perilous errand. The hoofs drew near, for the unknown rode with reckless haste.

"We had best see what it is," said the constable, pulling up.

A second more, and the horseman was beside us. Sapt swore an oath, half in amusement, half in vexation.

"Why, is it you, James?" I cried.

"Yes, sir," answered Rudolf Rassendyll's servant.

"What the devil do you want?" asked Sapt.

"I came to attend on the Count von Tarlenheim, sir."

"I did not give you any orders, James."

"No, sir. But Mr. Rassendyll told me not to leave you, unless you sent me away. So I made haste to follow you."

Then Sapt cried: "Deuce take it, what horse is that?"

"The best in the stables, so far as I could see, sir. I was afraid of not overtaking you." Sapt tugged his moustaches, scowled, but finally laughed.

"Much obliged for your compliment," said he. "The horse is mine."

"Indeed, sir?" said James with respectful interest.

For a moment we were all silent. Then Sapt laughed again.

"Forward!" said he, and the three of us dashed into the forest.

CHAPTER VIII. THE TEMPER OF BORIS THE HOUND

Looking back now, in the light of the information I have gathered, I am able to trace very clearly, and almost hour by hour, the events of this day, and to understand how chance, laying hold of our cunning plan and mocking our wiliness, twisted and turned our device to a predetermined but undreamt-of issue, of which we were most guiltless in thought or intent. Had the king not gone to the hunting-lodge, our design would have found the fulfilment we looked for; had Rischenheim succeeded in warning Rupert of Hentzau, we should have stood where we were. Fate or fortune would have it otherwise. The king, being weary, went to the lodge, and Rischenheim failed in warning his cousin. It was a narrow failure, for Rupert, as his laugh told me, was in the house in the Konigstrasse when I set out from Strelsau, and Rischenheim arrived there at half past four. He had taken the train at a roadside station, and thus easily outstripped Mr. Rassendyll, who, not daring to show his face, was forced to ride all the way and enter the city under cover of night. But Rischenheim had not dared to send a warning, for he knew that we were in possession of the address and did not know what steps we might have taken to intercept messages. Therefore he was obliged to carry the news himself; when he came his man was gone. Indeed Rupert must have left the house almost immediately after I was safe away from the city. He was determined to be in good time for his appointment; his only enemies were not in Strelsau; there was no warrant on which he could be apprehended; and, although his connection with Black Michael was a matter of popular gossip, he felt himself safe from arrest by virtue of the secret that protected him. Accordingly he walked out of the house, went to the station, took his ticket to Hofbau, and, traveling by the four o'clock train, reached his destination about half-past five. He must have passed the train in which Rischenheim traveled; the first news the latter had of his departure was from a porter at the station, who, having recognized the Count of Hentzau, ventured to congratulate Rischenheim on his cousin's return. Rischenheim made no answer, but hurried in great agitation to the house in the Konigstrasse, where the old woman Holf confirmed the tidings. Then he passed through a period of great irresolution. Loyalty to Rupert urged that he should follow him and share the perils into which his cousin was hastening. But caution whispered that he was not irrevocably committed, that nothing overt yet connected him with Rupert's schemes, and that we who knew the truth should be well content to purchase his silence as to the trick we had played by granting him immunity. His fears won the day, and, like the irresolute man he was, he determined to wait in Strelsau till he heard the issue of the meeting at the lodge. If Rupert were disposed of there, he had something to offer us in return for peace; if his cousin escaped, he would be in the Konigstrasse, prepared to second the further plans of the desperate adventurer. In any event his skin was safe, and I presume to think that this weighed a little with him; for excuse he had the wound which Bernenstein had given him, and which rendered his right arm entirely useless; had he gone then, he would have been a most inefficient ally.

Of all this we, as we rode through the forest, knew nothing. We might guess, conjecture, hope, or fear; but our certain knowledge stopped with Rischenheim's start for the capital and Rupert's presence there at three o'clock. The pair might have met or might have missed. We had to act as though they had missed and Rupert were gone to meet the king. But we were late. The consciousness of that pressed upon us, although we evaded further mention of it; it made us spur and drive our horses as quickly, ay, and a little more quickly, than safety allowed. Once James's horse stumbled in the darkness and its rider was thrown; more than once a low bough hanging over the path nearly swept me, dead or stunned, from my seat. Sapt paid no attention to these mishaps or threatened mishaps. He had taken the lead, and, sitting well down in his saddle, rode ahead, turning neither to right nor left, never slackening his pace, sparing neither himself nor his beast. James and I were side by side behind him. We rode in silence, finding nothing to say to one another. My mind was full of a picture—the picture of Rupert with his easy smile handing to the king the queen's letter. For the hour of the rendezvous was past. If that image had been translated into reality, what must we do? To kill

Rupert would satisfy revenge, but of what other avail would it be when the king had read the letter? I am ashamed to say that I found myself girding at Mr. Rassendyll for happening on a plan which the course of events had turned into a trap for ourselves and not for Rupert of Hentzau.

Suddenly Sapt, turning his head for the first time, pointed in front of him. The lodge was before us; we saw it looming dimly a quarter of a mile off. Sapt reined in his horse, and we followed his example. All dismounted, we tied our horses to trees and went forward at a quick, silent walk. Our idea was that Sapt should enter on pretext of having been sent by the queen to attend to her husband's comfort and arrange for his return without further fatigue next day. If Rupert had come and gone, the king's demeanor would probably betray the fact; if he had not yet come, I and James, patrolling outside, would bar his passage. There was a third possibility; he might be even now with the king. Our course in such a case we left unsettled; so far as I had any plan, it was to kill Rupert and to convince the king that the letter was a forgery—a desperate hope, so desperate that we turned our eyes away from the possibility which would make it our only resource.

We were now very near the hunting-lodge, being about forty yards from the front of it. All at once Sapt threw himself on his stomach on the ground.

"Give me a match," he whispered.

James struck a light, and, the night being still, the flame burnt brightly: it showed us the mark of a horse's hoof, apparently quite fresh, and leading away from the lodge. We rose and went on, following the tracks by the aid of more matches till we reached a tree twenty yards from the door. Here the hoof marks ceased; but beyond there was a double track of human feet in the soft black earth; a man had gone thence to the house and returned from the house thither. On the right of the tree were more hoof-marks, leading up to it and then ceasing. A man had ridden up from the right, dismounted, gone on foot to the house, returned to the tree, remounted, and ridden away along the track by which we had approached.

"It may be somebody else," said I; but I do not think that we any of us doubted in our hearts that the tracks were made by the coming of Hentzau. Then the king had the letter; the mischief was done. We were too late.

Yet we did not hesitate. Since disaster had come, it must be faced. Mr. Rassendyll's servant and I followed the constable of Zenda up to the door, or within a few feet of it. Here Sapt, who was in uniform, loosened his sword in its sheath; James and I looked to our revolvers. There were no lights visible in the lodge; the door was shut; everything was still. Sapt knocked softly with his knuckles, but there was no answer from within. He laid hold of the handle and turned it; the door opened, and the passage lay dark and apparently empty before us.

"You stay here, as we arranged," whispered the colonel. "Give me the matches, and I'll go in."

James handed him the box of matches, and he crossed the threshold. For a yard or two we saw him plainly, then his figure grew dim and indistinct. I heard nothing except my own hard breathing. But in a moment there was another sound—a muffled exclamation, and a noise of a man stumbling; a sword, too, clattered on the stones of the passage. We looked at one another; the noise did not produce any answering stir in the house; then came the sharp little explosion of a match struck on its box; next we heard Sapt raising himself, his scabbard scraping along the stones; his footsteps came towards us, and in a second he appeared at the door.

"What was it?" I whispered.

"I fell," said Sapt.

"Over what?"

"Come and see. James, stay here."

I followed the constable for the distance of eight or ten feet along the passage.

"Isn't there a lamp anywhere?" I asked.

"We can see enough with a match," he answered. "Here, this is what I fell over."

Even before the match was struck I saw a dark body lying across the passage.

"A dead man?" I guessed instantly.

"Why, no," said Sapt, striking a light: "a dead dog, Fritz." An exclamation of wonder escaped me as I fell on my knees. At the same instant Sapt muttered, "Ay, there's a lamp," and, stretching up his hand to a little oil lamp that stood on a bracket, he lit it, took it down, and held it over the body. It served to give a fair, though unsteady, light, and enabled us to see what lay in the passage.

"It's Boris, the boar-hound," said I, still in a whisper, although there was no sign of any listeners.

I knew the dog well; he was the king's favorite, and always accompanied him when he went hunting. He was obedient to every word of the king's, but of a rather uncertain temper towards the rest of the world. However, de mortuis nil nisi bonum; there he lay dead in the passage. Sapt put his hand on the beast's head. There was a bullet-hole right through his forehead. I nodded, and in my turn pointed to the dog's right shoulder, which was shattered by another ball.

"And see here," said the constable. "Have a pull at this."

I looked where his hand now was. In the dog's mouth was a piece of gray cloth, and on the piece of gray cloth was a horn coat-button. I took hold of the cloth and pulled. Boris held on even in death. Sapt drew his sword, and, inserting the point of it between the dog's teeth, parted them enough for me to draw out the piece of cloth.

"You'd better put it in your pocket," said the constable. "Now come along;" and, holding the lamp in one hand and his sword (which he did not resheathe) in the other, he stepped over the body of the boar-hound, and I followed him.

We were now in front of the door of the room where Rudolf Rassendyll had supped with us on the day of his first coming to Ruritania, and whence he had set out to be crowned in Strelsau. On the right of it was the room where the king slept, and farther along in the same direction the kitchen and the cellars. The officer or officers in attendance on the king used to sleep on the other side of the dining-room.

"We must explore, I suppose," said Sapt. In spite of his outward calmness, I caught in his voice the ring of excitement rising and ill-repressed. But at this moment we heard from the passage on our left (as we faced the door) a low moan, and then a dragging sound, as if a man were crawling along the floor, painfully trailing his limbs after him. Sapt held the lamp in that direction, and we saw Herbert the forester, pale-faced and wide-eyed, raised from the ground on his two hands, while his legs stretched behind him and his stomach rested on the flags.

"Who is it?" he said in a faint voice.

"Why, man, you know us," said the constable, stepping up to him. "What's happened here?" The poor fellow was very faint, and, I think, wandered a little in his brain.

"I've got it, sir," he murmured; "I've got it, fair and straight. No more hunting for me, sir. I've got it here in the stomach. Oh, my God!" He let his head fall with a thud on the floor.

I ran and raised him. Kneeling on one knee, I propped his head against my leg.

"Tell us about it," commanded Sapt in a curt, crisp voice while I got the man into the easiest position that I could contrive.

In slow, struggling tones he began his story, repeating here, omitting there, often confusing the order of his narrative, oftener still arresting it while he waited for fresh strength. Yet we were not impatient, but heard without a thought of time. I looked round once at a sound, and found that James, anxious about us, had stolen along the passage and joined us. Sapt took no notice of him, nor of anything save the words that dropped in irregular utterance from the stricken man's lips. Here is the story, a strange instance of the turning of a great event on a small cause.

The king had eaten a little supper, and, having gone to his bedroom, had stretched himself on the bed and fallen asleep without undressing. Herbert was clearing the dining-table and performing similar duties, when suddenly (thus he told it) he found a man standing beside him. He did not know (he was new to the king's service) who the unexpected visitor was, but he was of middle height, dark, handsome, and "looked a gentleman all over." He was dressed in a shooting-tunic, and a revolver was thrust through the belt of it. One hand rested on the belt, while the other held a small square box.

"Tell the king I am here. He expects me," said the stranger. Herbert, alarmed at the suddenness and silence of the stranger's approach, and guiltily conscious of having left the door unbolted, drew back. He was unarmed, but, being a stout fellow, was prepared to defend his master as best he could. Rupert—beyond doubt it was Rupert—laughed lightly, saying again, "Man, he expects me. Go and tell him," and sat himself on the table, swinging his leg. Herbert, influenced by the visitor's air of command, began to retreat towards the bedroom, keeping his face towards Rupert.

"If the king asks more, tell him I have the packet and the letter," said Rupert. The man bowed and passed into the bedroom. The king was asleep; when roused he seemed to know nothing of letter or packet, and to expect no visitor. Herbert's ready fears revived; he whispered that the stranger carried a revolver. Whatever the king's faults might be—and God forbid that I should speak hardly of him whom fate used so hardly—he was no coward. He sprang from his bed; at the same moment the great boar-hound uncoiled himself and came from beneath, yawning and fawning. But in an instant the beast caught the scent of a stranger: his ears pricked and he gave a low growl, as he looked up in his master's face. Then Rupert of Hentzau, weary perhaps of waiting, perhaps only doubtful whether his message would be properly delivered, appeared in the doorway.

The king was unarmed, and Herbert in no better plight; their hunting weapons were in the adjoining room, and Rupert seemed to bar the way. I have said that the king was no coward, yet I think, that the sight of Rupert, bringing back the memory of his torments in the dungeon, half cowed him; for he shrank back crying, "You!" The hound, in subtle understanding of his master's movement, growled angrily.

"You expected me, sire?" said Rupert with a bow; but he smiled. I know that the sight of the king's alarm pleased him. To inspire terror was his delight, and it does not come to every man to strike fear into the heart of a king and an Elphberg. It had come more than once to Rupert of Hentzau.

"No," muttered the king. Then, recovering his composure a little, he said angrily, "How dare you come here?"

"You didn't expect me?" cried Rupert, and in an instant the thought of a trap seemed to flash across his alert mind. He drew the revolver halfway from his belt, probably in a scarcely conscious movement, born of the desire to assure himself of its presence. With a cry of alarm Herbert flung himself before the king, who sank back on the bed. Rupert, puzzled, vexed, yet half-amused (for he smiled still, the man said), took a step forward, crying out something about Rischenheim—what, Herbert could not tell us.

"Keep back," exclaimed the king. "Keep back."

Rupert paused; then, as though with a sudden thought, he held up the box that was in his left hand, saying:

"Well, look at this sire, and we'll talk afterwards," and he stretched out his hand with the box in it.

Now the king stood on a razor's edge, for the king whispered to Herbert, "What is it? Go and take it."

But Herbert hesitated, fearing to leave the king, whom his body now protected as though with a shield. Rupert's impatience overcame him: if there were a trap, every moment's delay doubled his danger. With a scornful laugh he exclaimed, "Catch it, then, if you're afraid to come for it," and he flung the packet to Herbert or the king, or which of them might chance to catch it.

This insolence had a strange result. In an instant, with a fierce growl and a mighty bound, Boris was at the stranger's throat. Rupert had not seen or had not heeded the dog. A startled oath rang out from him. He snatched the revolver from his belt and fired at his assailant. This shot must have broken the beast's shoulder, but it only half arrested his spring. His great weight was still hurled on Rupert's chest, and bore him back on his knee. The packet that he had flung lay unheeded. The king, wild with alarm and furious with anger at his favorite's fate, jumped up and ran past Rupert into the next room. Herbert followed; even as they went Rupert flung the wounded, weakened beast from him and darted to the doorway. He found himself facing Herbert, who held a boar-spear, and the king, who had a double-barreled hunting-gun. He raised his left hand, Herbert said—no doubt he still asked a hearing—but the king leveled his weapon. With a spring Rupert gained the shelter of the door, the bullet sped by him, and buried itself in the wall of the room. Then Herbert was at him with the boar-spear. Explanations must wait now: it was life or death; without hesitation Rupert fired at Herbert, bringing him to the ground with a mortal wound. The king's gun was at his shoulder again.

"You damned fool!" roared Rupert, "if you must have it, take it," and gun and revolver rang out at the same moment. But Rupert—never did his nerve fail him—hit, the king missed; Herbert saw the count stand for an instant with his smoking barrel in his hand, looking at the king, who lay on the ground. Then Rupert walked towards the door. I wish I had seen his face then! Did he frown or smile? Was triumph or chagrin uppermost? Remorse? Not he!

He reached the door and passed through. That was the last Herbert saw of him; but the fourth actor in the drama, the wordless player whose part had been so momentous, took the stage. Limping along, now whining in sharp agony, now growling in fierce anger, with blood flowing but hair bristling, the hound Boris dragged himself across the room, through the door, after Rupert of Hentzau. Herbert listened, raising his head from the ground. There was a growl, an oath, the sound of the scuffle. Rupert must have turned in time to receive the dog's spring. The beast, maimed and crippled by his shattered shoulder, did not reach his enemy's face, but his teeth tore away the bit of cloth that we had found held in the vise of his jaws. Then came another shot, a laugh, retreating steps, and a door slammed. With that last sound Herbert woke to the fact of the count's escape; with weary efforts he dragged himself into the passage. The idea that he could go on if he got a drink of brandy turned him in the direction of the cellar. But his strength failed, and he sank down where we found him, not knowing whether the king were dead or still alive, and unable even to make his way back to the room where his master lay stretched on the ground.

I had listened to the story, bound as though by a spell. Halfway through, James's hand had crept to my arm and rested there; when Herbert finished I heard the little man licking his lips, again and again slapping his tongue against them. Then I looked at Sapt. He was as pale as a ghost, and the lines on his face seemed to have grown deeper. He glanced up, and met my regard. Neither of us spoke; we exchanged thoughts with our eyes. "This is our work," we said to one another. "It was our trap, these are our victims." I cannot even now think of that hour, for by our act the king lay dead.

But was he dead? I seized Sapt by the arm. His glance questioned me.

"The king," I whispered hoarsely.

"Yes, the king," he returned.

Facing round, we walked to the door of the dining-room. Here I turned suddenly faint, and clutched at the constable. He held me up, and pushed the door wide open. The smell of powder was in the room; it seemed as if the smoke hung about, curling in dim coils round the chandelier which gave a subdued light. James had the lamp now, and followed us with it. But the king was not there. A sudden hope filled me. He had not been killed then! I regained strength, and darted across towards the inside room. Here too the light was dim, and I turned to beckon for the lamp. Sapt and James came together, and stood peering over my shoulder in the doorway.

The king lay prone on the floor, face downwards, near the bed. He had crawled there, seeking for some place to rest, as we supposed. He did not move. We watched him for a moment;

the silence seemed deeper than silence could be. At last, moved by a common impulse, we stepped forward, but timidly, as though we approached the throne of Death himself. I was the first to kneel by the king and raise his head. Blood had flowed from his lips, but it had ceased to flow now. He was dead.

I felt Sapt's hand on my shoulder. Looking up, I saw his other hand stretched out towards the ground. I turned my eyes where he pointed. There, in the king's hand, stained with the king's blood, was the box that I had carried to Wintenberg and Rupert of Hentzau had brought to the lodge that night. It was not rest, but the box that the dying king had sought in his last moment. I bent, and lifting his hand unclasped the fingers, still limp and warm.

Sapt bent down with sudden eagerness. "Is it open?" he whispered.

The string was round it; the sealing-wax was unbroken. The secret had outlived the king, and he had gone to his death unknowing. All at once—I cannot tell why—I put my hand over my eyes; I found my eyelashes were wet.

"Is it open?" asked Sapt again, for in the dim light he could not see.

"No," I answered.

"Thank God!" said he. And, for Sapt's, the voice was soft.

CHAPTER IX. THE KING IN THE HUNTING LODGE

THE moment with its shock and tumult of feeling brings one judgment, later reflection another. Among the sins of Rupert of Hentzau I do not assign the first and greatest place to his killing of the king. It was, indeed, the act of a reckless man who stood at nothing and held nothing sacred; but when I consider Herbert's story, and trace how the deed came to be done and the impulsion of circumstances that led to it, it seems to have been in some sort thrust upon him by the same perverse fate that dogged our steps. He had meant the king no harm— indeed it may be argued that, from whatever motive, he had sought to serve him—and save under the sudden stress of self-defense he had done him none. The king's unlooked-for ignorance of his errand, Herbert's honest hasty zeal, the temper of Boris the hound, had forced on him an act unmeditated and utterly against his interest. His whole guilt lay in preferring the king's death to his own—a crime perhaps in most men, but hardly deserving a place in Rupert's catalogue. All this I can admit now, but on that night, with the dead body lying there before us, with the story piteously told by Herbert's faltering voice fresh in our ears, it was hard to allow any such extenuation. Our hearts cried out for vengeance, although we ourselves served the king no more. Nay, it may well be that we hoped to stifle some reproach of our own consciences by a louder clamor against another's sin, or longed to offer some belated empty atonement to our dead master by executing swift justice on the man who had killed him. I cannot tell fully what the others felt, but in me at least the dominant impulse was to waste not a moment in proclaiming the crime and raising the whole country in pursuit of Rupert, so that every man in Ruritania should quit his work, his pleasure, or his bed, and make it his concern to take the Count of Hentzau, alive or dead. I remember that I walked over to where Sapt was sitting, and caught him by the arm, saying:

"We must raise the alarm. If you'll go to Zenda, I'll start for Strelsau."

"The alarm?" said he, looking up at me and tugging his moustache.

"Yes: when the news is known, every man in the kingdom will be on the lookout for him, and he can't escape."

"So that he'd be taken?" asked the constable.

"Yes, to a certainty," I cried, hot in excitement and emotion. Sapt glanced across at Mr. Rassendyll's servant. James had, with my help, raised the king's body on to the bed, and had aided the wounded forester to reach a couch. He stood now near the constable, in his usual unobtrusive readiness. He did not speak, but I saw a look of understanding in his eyes as he nodded his head to Colonel Sapt. They were well matched, that pair, hard to move, hard to shake, not to be turned from the purpose in their minds and the matter that lay to their hands.

"Yes, he'd probably be taken or killed," said Sapt.

"Then let's do it!" I cried.

"With the queen's letter on him," said Colonel Sapt.

I had forgotten.

"We have the box, he has the letter still," said Sapt.

I could have laughed even at that moment. He had left the box (whether from haste or heedlessness or malice, we could not tell), but the letter was on him. Taken alive, he would use that powerful weapon to save his life or satisfy his anger; if it were found on his body, its evidence would speak loud and clear to all the world. Again he was protected by his crime: while he had the letter, he must be kept inviolate from all attack except at our own hands. We desired his death, but we must be his body-guard and die in his defense rather than let any other but ourselves come at him. No open means must be used, and no allies sought. All this rushed to my mind at Sapt's words, and I saw what the constable and James had never forgotten. But what to do I could not see. For the King of Ruritania lay dead.

An hour or more had passed since our discovery, and it was now close on midnight. Had all gone well we ought by this time to have been far on our road back to the castle; by this time Rupert must be miles away from where he had killed the king; already Mr. Rassendyll would be seeking his enemy in Strelsau.

"But what are we to do about—about that, then?" I asked, pointing with my finger through the doorway towards the bed.

Sapt gave a last tug at his moustache, then crossed his hands on the hilt of the sword between his knees, and leant forward in his chair.

"Nothing, he said," looking at my face. "Until we have the letter, nothing."

"But it's impossible!" I cried.

"Why, no, Fritz," he answered thoughtfully. "It's not possible yet; it may become so. But if we can catch Rupert in the next day, or even in the next two days, it's not impossible. Only let me have the letter, and I'll account for the concealment. What? Is the fact that crimes are known never concealed, for fear of putting the criminal on his guard?"

"You'll be able to make a story, sir," James put in, with a grave but reassuring air.

"Yes, James, I shall be able to make a story, or your master will make one for me. But, by God, story or no story, the letter mustn't be found. Let them say we killed him ourselves if they like, but—"

I seized his hand and gripped it.

"You don't doubt I'm with you?" I asked.

"Not for a moment, Fritz," he answered.

"Then how can we do it?"

We drew nearer together; Sapt and I sat, while James leant over Sapt's chair.

The oil in the lamp was almost exhausted, and the light burnt very dim. Now and again poor Herbert, for whom our skill could do nothing, gave a slight moan. I am ashamed to remember how little we thought of him, but great schemes make the actors in them careless of humanity; the life of a man goes for nothing against a point in the game. Except for his groans—and they grew fainter and less frequent—our voices alone broke the silence of the little lodge.

"The queen must know," said Sapt. "Let her stay at Zenda and give out that the king is at the lodge for a day or two longer. Then you, Fritz—for you must ride to the castle at once—and Bernenstein must get to Strelsau as quick as you can, and find Rudolf Rassendyll. You three ought to be able to track young Rupert down and get the letter from him. If he's not in the city, you must catch Rischenheim, and force him to say where he is; we know Rischenheim can be persuaded. If Rupert's there, I need give no advice either to you or to Rudolf."

"And you?"

"James and I stay here. If any one comes whom we can keep out, the king is ill. If rumors get about, and great folk come, why, they must enter."

"But the body?"

"This morning, when you're gone, we shall make a temporary grave. I dare say two," and he jerked his thumb towards poor Herbert.

"Or even," he added, with his grim smile, "three—for our friend Boris, too, must be out of sight."

"You'll bury the king?"

"Not so deep but that we can take him out again, poor fellow. Well, Fritz, have you a better plan?"

I had no plan, and I was not in love with Sapt's plan. Yet it offered us four and twenty hours. For that time, at least, it seemed as if the secret could be kept. Beyond that we could hardly hope for success; after that we must produce the king; dead or alive, the king must be seen. Yet it might be that before the respite ran out Rupert would be ours. In fine, what else could be chosen? For now a greater peril threatened than that against which we had at the first sought to guard. Then the worst we feared was that the letter should come to the king's hands. That could never be. But it would be a worse thing if it were found on Rupert, and all the kingdom, nay, all Europe, know that it was written in the hand of her who was now, in her own right, Queen of Ruritania. To save her from that, no chance was too desperate, no scheme too perilous; yes, if, as Sapt said, we ourselves were held to answer for the king's death, still we must go on. I, through whose negligence the whole train of disaster had been laid, was the last man to hesitate. In all honesty, I held my life due and forfeit, should it be demanded of me—my life and, before the world, my honor.

So the plan was made. A grave was to be dug ready for the king; if need arose, his body should be laid in it, and the place chosen was under the floor of the wine-cellar. When death came to poor Herbert, he could lie in the yard behind the house; for Boris they meditated a resting-place under the tree where our horses were tethered. There was nothing to keep me, and I rose; but as I rose, I heard the forester's voice call plaintively for me. The unlucky fellow knew me well, and now cried to me to sit by him. I think Sapt wanted me to leave him, but I could not refuse his last request, even though it consumed some precious minutes. He was very near his end, and, sitting by him, I did my best to soothe his passing. His fortitude was good to see, and I believe that we all at last found new courage for our enterprise from seeing how this humble man met death. At least even the constable ceased to show impatience, and let me stay till I could close the sufferer's eyes.

But thus time went, and it was nearly five in the morning before I bade them farewell and mounted my horse. They took theirs and led them away to the stables behind the lodge; I waved my hand and galloped off on my return to the castle. Day was dawning, and the air was fresh and pure. The new light brought new hope; fears seemed to vanish before it; my nerves were strung to effort and to confidence. My horse moved freely under me and carried me easily along the grassy avenues. It was hard then to be utterly despondent, hard to doubt skill of brain, strength of hand, or fortune's favor.

The castle came in sight, and I hailed it with a glad cry that echoed among the trees. But a moment later I gave an exclamation of surprise, and raised myself a little from the saddle while I gazed earnestly at the summit of the keep. The flag staff was naked; the royal standard that had flapped in the wind last night was gone. But by immemorial custom the flag flew on the keep when the king or the queen was at the castle. It would fly for Rudolf V. no more; but why did it not proclaim and honor the presence of Queen Flavia? I sat down in my saddle and spurred my horse to the top of his speed. We had been buffeted by fate sorely, but now I feared yet another blow.

In a quarter of an hour more I was at the door. A servant ran out, and I dismounted leisurely and easily. Pulling off my gloves, I dusted my boots with them, turned to the stableman and bade him look to the horse, and then said to the footman:

"As soon as the queen is dressed, find out if she can see me. I have a message from his Majesty."

The fellow looked a little puzzled, but at this moment Hermann, the king's major-domo, came to the door.

"Isn't the constable with you, my lord?" he asked.

"No, the constable remains at the lodge with the king," said I carelessly, though I was very far from careless. "I have a message for her Majesty, Hermann. Find out from some of the women when she will receive me."

"The queen's not here," said he. "Indeed we've had a lively time, my lord. At five o'clock she came out, ready dressed, from her room, sent for Lieutenant von Bernenstein, and announced that she was about to set out from the castle. As you know, the mail train passes here at six." Hermann took out his watch. "Yes, the queen must just have left the station."

"Where for?" I asked, with a shrug for the woman's whim. "Why, for Strelsau. She gave no reasons for going, and took with her only one lady, Lieutenant von Bernenstein being in attendance. It was a bustle, if you like, with everybody to be roused and got out of bed, and a carriage to be made ready, and messages to go to the station, and—"

"She gave no reasons?"

"None, my lord. She left with me a letter to the constable, which she ordered me to give to his own hands as soon as he arrived at the castle. She said it contained a message of importance, which the constable was to convey to the king, and that it must be intrusted to nobody except Colonel Sapt himself. I wonder, my lord, that you didn't notice that the flag was hauled down."

"Tut, man, I wasn't staring at the keep. Give me the letter." For I saw that the clue to this fresh puzzle must lie under the cover of Sapt's letter. That letter I must myself carry to Sapt, and without loss of time.

"Give you the letter, my lord? But, pardon me, you're not the constable." He laughed a little.

"Why, no," said I, mustering a smile. "It's true that I'm not the constable, but I'm going to the constable. I had the king's orders to rejoin him as soon as I had seen the queen, and since her Majesty isn't here, I shall return to the lodge directly a fresh horse can be saddled for me. And the constable's at the lodge. Come, the letter!"

"I can't give it you, my lord. Her Majesty's orders were positive."

"Nonsense! If she had known I should come and not the constable, she would have told me to carry it to him."

"I don't know about that, my lord: her orders were plain, and she doesn't like being disobeyed."

The stableman had led the horse away, the footman had disappeared, Hermann and I were alone. "Give me the letter," I said; and I know that my self-control failed, and eagerness was plain in my voice. Plain it was, and Hermann took alarm. He started back, clapping his hand to the breast of his laced coat. The gesture betrayed where the letter was; I was past prudence; I sprang on him and wrenched his hand away, catching him by the throat with my other hand. Diving into his pocket, I got the letter. Then I suddenly loosed hold of him, for his eyes were starting out of his head. I took out a couple of gold pieces and gave them to him.

"It's urgent, you fool," said I. "Hold your tongue about it." And without waiting to study his amazed red face, I turned and ran towards the stable. In five minutes I was on a fresh horse, in six I was clear of the castle, heading back fast as I could go for the hunting-lodge. Even now Hermann remembers the grip I gave him—though doubtless he has long spent the pieces of gold.

When I reached the end of this second journey, I came in for the obsequies of Boris. James was just patting the ground under the tree with a mattock when I rode up; Sapt was standing by, smoking his pipe. The boots of both were stained and sticky with mud. I flung myself from my saddle and blurted out my news. The constable snatched at his letter with an oath;

James leveled the ground with careful accuracy; I do not remember doing anything except wiping my forehead and feeling very hungry.

"Good Lord, she's gone after him!" said Sapt, as he read. Then he handed me the letter.

I will not set out what the queen wrote. The purport seemed to us, who did not share her feelings, pathetic indeed and moving, but in the end (to speak plainly) folly. She had tried to endure her sojourn at Zenda, she said; but it drove her mad. She could not rest; she did not know how we fared, nor how those in Strelsau; for hours she had lain awake; then at last falling asleep, she had dreamt.

"I had had the same dream before. Now it came again. I saw him so plain. He seemed to me to be king, and to be called king. But he did not answer nor move. He seemed dead; and I could not rest." So she wrote, ever excusing herself, ever repeating how something drew her to Strelsau, telling her that she must go if she would see "him whom you know," alive again. "And I must see him—ah, I must see him! If the king has had the letter, I am ruined already. If he has not, tell him what you will or what you can contrive. I must go. It came a second time, and all so plain. I saw him; I tell you I saw him. Ah, I must see him again. I swear that I will only see him once. He's in danger—I know he's in danger; or what does the dream mean? Bernenstein will go with me, and I shall see him. Do, do forgive me: I can't stay, the dream was so plain." Thus she ended, seeming, poor lady, half frantic with the visions that her own troubled brain and desolate heart had conjured up to torment her. I did not know that she had before told Mr. Rassendyll himself of this strange dream; though I lay small store by such matters, believing that we ourselves make our dreams, fashioning out of the fears and hopes of to-day what seems to come by night in the guise of a mysterious revelation. Yet there are some things that a man cannot understand, and I do not profess to measure with my mind the ways of God.

However, not why the queen went, but that she had gone, concerned us. We had returned to the house now, and James, remembering that men must eat though kings die, was getting us some breakfast. In fact, I had great need of food, being utterly worn out; and they, after their labors, were hardly less weary. As we ate, we talked; and it was plain to us that I also must go to Strelsau. There, in the city, the drama must be played out. There was Rudolf, there Rischenheim, there in all likelihood Rupert of Hentzau, there now the queen. And of these Rupert alone, or perhaps Rischenheim also, knew that the king was dead, and how the issue of last night had shaped itself under the compelling hand of wayward fortune. The king lay in peace on his bed, his grave was dug; Sapt and James held the secret with solemn faith and ready lives. To Strelsau I must go to tell the queen that she was widowed, and to aim the stroke at young Rupert's heart.

At nine in the morning I started from the lodge. I was bound to ride to Hofbau and there wait for a train which would carry me to the capital. From Hofbau I could send a message, but the message must announce only my own coming, not the news I carried. To Sapt, thanks to the cipher, I could send word at any time, and he bade me ask Mr. Rassendyll whether he should come to our aid, or stay where he was.

"A day must decide the whole thing," he said. "We can't conceal the king's death long. For God's sake, Fritz, make an end of that young villain, and get the letter."

So, wasting no time in farewells, I set out. By ten o'clock I was at Hofbau, for I rode furiously. From there I sent to Bernenstein at the palace word of my coming. But there I was delayed. There was no train for an hour.

"I'll ride," I cried to myself, only to remember the next moment that, if I rode, I should come to my journey's end much later. There was nothing for it but to wait, and it may be imagined in what mood I waited. Every minute seemed an hour, and I know not to this day how the hour wore itself away. I ate, I drank, I smoked, I walked, sat, and stood. The stationmaster knew me, and thought I had gone mad, till I told him that I carried most important despatches from the king, and that the delay imperiled great interests. Then he became sympathetic; but what could he do? No special train was to be had at a roadside station: I must wait; and wait, somehow, and without blowing my brains out, I did.

At last I was in the train; now indeed we moved, and I came nearer. An hour's run brought me in sight of the city. Then, to my unutterable wrath, we were stopped, and waited motionless twenty minutes or half an hour. At last we started again; had we not, I should have jumped out and run, for to sit longer would have driven me mad. Now we entered the station. With a great effort I calmed myself. I lolled back in my seat; when we stopped I sat there till a porter opened the door. In lazy leisureliness I bade him get me a cab, and followed him across the station. He held the door for me, and, giving him his douceur, I set my foot on the step.

"Tell him to drive to the palace," said I, "and be quick. I'm late already, thanks to this cursed train."

"The old mare'll soon take you there, sir," said the driver. I jumped in. But at this moment I saw a man on the platform beckoning with his hand and hastening towards me. The cabman also saw him and waited. I dared not tell him to drive on, for I feared to betray any undue haste, and it would have looked strange not to spare a moment to my wife's cousin, Anton von Strofzin. He came up, holding out his hand delicately gloved in pearl-gray kid, for young Anton was a leader of the Strelsau dandies.

"Ah, my dear Fritz!" said he. "I am glad I hold no appointment at court. How dreadfully active you all are! I thought you were settled at Zenda for a month?"

"The queen changed her mind suddenly," said I, smiling. "Ladies do, as you know well, you who know all about them."

My compliment, or insinuation, produced a pleased smile and a gallant twirling of his moustache.

"Well, I thought you'd be here soon," he said, "but I didn't know that the queen had come."

"You didn't? Then why did you look for me?"

He opened his eyes a little in languid, elegant surprise. "Oh, I supposed you'd be on duty, or something, and have to come. Aren't you in attendance?"

"On the queen? No, not just now."

"But on the king?"

"Why, yes," said I, and I leaned forward. "At least I'm engaged now on the king's business."

"Precisely," said he. "So I thought you'd come, as soon as I heard that the king was here."

It may be that I ought to have preserved my composure. But I am not Sapt nor Rudolf Rassendyll.

"The king here?" I gasped, clutching him by the arm.

"Of course. You didn't know? Yes, he's in town."

But I heeded him no more. For a moment I could not speak, then I cried to the cabman:

"To the palace. And drive like the devil!"

We shot away, leaving Anton open-mouthed in wonder. For me, I sank back on the cushions, fairly aghast. The king lay dead in the hunting-lodge, but the king was in his capital!

Of course, the truth soon flashed through my mind, but it brought no comfort. Rudolf Rassendyll was in Strelsau. He had been seen by somebody and taken for the king. But comfort? What comfort was there, now that the king was dead and could never come to the rescue of his counterfeit?

In fact, the truth was worse than I conceived. Had I known it all, I might well have yielded to despair. For not by the chance, uncertain sight of a passer-by, not by mere rumor which might have been sturdily denied, not by the evidence of one only or of two, was the king's presence in the city known. That day, by the witness of a crowd of people, by his own claim and his own voice, ay, and by the assent of the queen herself, Mr. Rassendyll was taken to be the king in Strelsau, while neither he nor Queen Flavia knew that the king was dead. I must now relate the strange and perverse succession of events which forced them to employ a resource so dangerous and face a peril so immense. Yet, great and perilous as they knew the risk to be even when they dared it, in the light of what they did not know it was more fearful and more fatal still.

CHAPTER X. THE KING IN STRELSAU

MR. RASSENDYLL reached Strelsau from Zenda without accident about nine o'clock in the evening of the same day as that which witnessed the tragedy of the hunting-lodge. He could have arrived sooner, but prudence did not allow him to enter the populous suburbs of the town till the darkness guarded him from notice. The gates of the city were no longer shut at sunset, as they had used to be in the days when Duke Michael was governor, and Rudolf passed them without difficulty. Fortunately the night, fine where we were, was wet and stormy at Strelsau; thus there were few people in the streets, and he was able to gain the door of my house still unremarked. Here, of course, a danger presented itself. None of my servants were in the secret; only my wife, in whom the queen herself had confided, knew Rudolf, and she did not expect to see him, since she was ignorant of the recent course of events. Rudolf was quite alive to the peril, and regretted the absence of his faithful attendant, who could have cleared the way for him. The pouring rain gave him an excuse for twisting a scarf about his face and pulling his coat-collar up to his ears, while the gusts of wind made the cramming of his hat low down over his eyes no more than a natural precaution against its loss. Thus masked from curious eyes, he drew rein before my door, and, having dismounted, rang the bell. When the butler came a strange hoarse voice, half-stifled by folds of scarf, asked for the countess, alleging for pretext a message from myself. The man hesitated, as well he might, to leave the stranger alone with the door open and the contents of the hall at his mercy. Murmuring an apology in case his visitor should prove to be a gentleman, he shut the door and went in search of his mistress. His description of the untimely caller at once roused my wife's quick wit; she had heard from me how Rudolf had ridden once from Strelsau to the hunting-lodge with muffled face; a very tall man with his face wrapped in a scarf and his hat over his eyes, who came with a private message, suggested to her at least a possibility of Mr. Rassendyll's arrival. Helga will never admit that she is clever, yet I find she discovers from me what she wants to know, and I suspect hides successfully the small matters of which she in her wifely discretion deems I had best remain ignorant. Being able thus to manage me, she was equal to coping with the butler. She laid aside her embroidery most composedly.

"Ah, yes," she said, "I know the gentleman. Surely you haven't left him out in the rain?" She was anxious lest Rudolf's features should have been exposed too long to the light of the hall-lamps.

The butler stammered an apology, explaining his fears for our goods and the impossibility of distinguishing social rank on a dark night. Helga cut him short with an impatient gesture, crying, "How stupid of you!" and herself ran quickly down and opened the door—a little way only, though. The first sight of Mr. Rassendyll confirmed her suspicions; in a moment, she said, she knew his eyes.

"It is you, then?" she cried. "And my foolish servant has left you in the rain! Pray come in. Oh, but your horse!" She turned to the penitent butler, who had followed her downstairs. "Take the baron's horse round to the stables," she said.

"I will send some one at once, my lady."

"No, no, take it yourself—take it at once. I'll look after the baron."

Reluctantly and ruefully the fat fellow stepped out into the storm. Rudolf drew back and let him pass, then he entered quickly, to find himself alone with Helga in the hall. With a finger on her lips, she led him swiftly into a small sitting-room on the ground floor, which I used as a sort of office or place of business. It looked out on the street, and the rain could be heard driving against the broad panes of the window. Rudolf turned to her with a smile, and, bowing, kissed her hand.

"The baron what, my dear countess?" he inquired.

"He won't ask," said she with a shrug. "Do tell me what brings you here, and what has happened."

He told her very briefly all he knew. She hid bravely her alarm at hearing that I might perhaps meet Rupert at the lodge, and at once listened to what Rudolf wanted of her.

"Can I get out of the house, and, if need be, back again unnoticed?" he asked.

"The door is locked at night, and only Fritz and the butler have keys."

Mr. Rassendyll's eye traveled to the window of the room.

"I haven't grown so fat that I can't get through there," said he. "So we'd better not trouble the butler. He'd talk, you know."

"I will sit here all night and keep everybody from the room."

"I may come back pursued if I bungle my work and an alarm is raised."

"Your work?" she asked, shrinking back a little.

"Yes," said he. "Don't ask what it is, Countess. It is in the queen's service."

"For the queen I will do anything and everything, as Fritz would."

He took her hand and pressed it in a friendly, encouraging way.

"Then I may issue my orders?" he asked, smiling.

"They shall be obeyed."

"Then a dry cloak, a little supper, and this room to myself, except for you."

As he spoke the butler turned the handle of the door. My wife flew across the room, opened the door, and, while Rudolf turned his back, directed the man to bring some cold meat, or whatever could be ready with as little delay as possible.

"Now come with me," she said to Rudolf, directly the servant was gone.

She took him to my dressing-room, where he got dry clothes; then she saw the supper laid, ordered a bedroom to be prepared, told the butler that she had business with the baron and that he need not sit up if she were later than eleven, dismissed him, and went to tell Rudolf that the coast was clear for his return to the sitting-room. He came, expressing admiration for her courage and address; I take leave to think that she deserved his compliments. He made a hasty supper; then they talked together, Rudolf smoking his cigar. Eleven came and went. It was not yet time. My wife opened the door and looked out. The hall was dark, the door locked and its key in the hands of the butler. She closed the door again and softly locked it. As the clock struck twelve Rudolf rose and turned the lamp very low. Then he unfastened the shutters noiselessly, raised the window and looked out.

"Shut them again when I'm gone," he whispered. "If I come back, I'll knock like this, and you'll open for me."

"For heaven's sake, be careful," she murmured, catching at his hand.

He nodded reassuringly, and crossing his leg over the windowsill, sat there for a moment listening. The storm was as fierce as ever, and the street was deserted. He let himself down on to the pavement, his face again wrapped up. She watched his tall figure stride quickly along till a turn of the road hid it. Then, having closed the window and the shutters again, she sat down to keep her watch, praying for him, for me, and for her dear mistress the queen. For she knew that perilous work was afoot that night, and did not know whom it might threaten or whom destroy.

From the moment that Mr. Rassendyll thus left my house at midnight on his search for Rupert of Hentzau, every hour and almost every moment brought its incident in the swiftly moving drama which decided the issues of our fortune. What we were doing has been told; by now Rupert himself was on his way back to the city, and the queen was meditating, in her restless vigil, on the resolve that in a few hours was to bring her also to Strelsau. Even in the dead of night both sides were active. For, plan cautiously and skillfully as he might, Rudolf fought with an antagonist who lost no chances, and who had found an apt and useful tool in that same Bauer, a rascal, and a cunning rascal, if ever one were bred in the world. From the beginning even to the end our error lay in taking too little count of this fellow, and dear was the price we paid.

Both to my wife and to Rudolf himself the street had seemed empty of every living being when she watched and he set out. Yet everything had been seen, from his first arrival to the moment when she closed the window after him. At either end of my house there runs out a projection, formed by the bay windows of the principal drawing-room and of the dining room respectively. These projecting walls form shadows, and in the shade of one of them—of which I do not know, nor is it of moment—a man watched all that passed; had he been anywhere else, Rudolf must have seen him. If we had not been too engrossed in playing our own hands, it would doubtless have struck us as probable that Rupert would direct Rischenheim and Bauer to keep an eye on my house during his absence; for it was there that any of us who found our way to the city would naturally resort in the first instance. As a fact, he had not omitted this precaution. The night was so dark that the spy, who had seen the king but once and never Mr. Rassendyll, did not recognize who the visitor was, but he rightly conceived that he should serve his employer by tracking the steps of the tall man who made so mysterious an arrival and so surreptitious a departure from the suspected house. Accordingly, as Rudolf turned the corner and Helena closed the window, a short, thickset figure started cautiously out of the projecting shadow, and followed in Rudolf's wake through the storm. The pair, tracker and tracked, met nobody, save here and there a police constable keeping a most unwilling beat. Even such were few, and for the most part more intent on sheltering in the lee of a friendly wall and thereby keeping a dry stitch or two on them than on taking note of passers-by. On the pair went. Now Rudolf turned into the Konigstrasse. As he did so, Bauer, who must have been nearly a hundred yards behind (for he could not start till the shutters were closed) quickened his pace and reduced the interval between them to about seventy yards. This he might well have thought a safe distance on a night so wild, when the rush of wind and the pelt of the rain joined to hide the sound of footsteps.

But Bauer reasoned as a townsman, and Rudolf Rassendyll had the quick ear of a man bred in the country and trained to the woodland. All at once there was a jerk of his head; I know so well the motion which marked awakened attention in him. He did not pause nor break his stride: to do either would have been to betray his suspicions to his follower; but he crossed the road to the opposite side to that where No. 19 was situated, and slackened his pace a little, so that there was a longer interval between his own footfalls. The steps behind him grew slower, even as his did; their sound came no nearer: the follower would not overtake. Now, a man who loiters on such a night, just because another head of him is fool enough to loiter, has a reason for his action other than what can at first sight be detected. So thought Rudolf Rassendyll, and his brain was busied with finding it out.

Then an idea seized him, and, forgetting the precautions that had hitherto served so well, he came to a sudden stop on the pavement, engrossed in deep thought. Was the man who dogged his steps Rupert himself? It would be like Rupert to track him, like Rupert to conceive such an attack, like Rupert to be ready either for a fearless assault from the front or a shameless shot from behind, and indifferent utterly which chance offered, so it threw him one of them. Mr. Rassendyll asked no better than to meet his enemy thus in the open. They could fight a fair fight, and if he fell the lamp would be caught up and carried on by Sapt's hand or mine; if he got the better of Rupert, the letter would be his; a moment would destroy it and give safety to the queen. I do not suppose that he spent time in thinking how he should escape arrest at the hands of the police whom the fracas would probably rouse; if he did, he may well have reckoned on declaring plainly who he was, of laughing at their surprise over a chance likeness to the king, and of trusting to us to smuggle him beyond the arm of the law. What mattered all that, so that there was a moment in which to destroy the letter? At any rate he turned full round and began to walk straight towards Bauer, his hand resting on the revolver in the pocket of his coat.

Bauer saw him coming, and must have known that he was suspected or detected. At once the cunning fellow slouched his head between his shoulders, and set out along the street at a quick shuffle, whistling as he went. Rudolf stood still now in the middle of the road, wondering who the man was: whether Rupert, purposely disguising his gait, or a confederate, or, after all, some person innocent of our secret and indifferent to our schemes. On came Bauer, softly, whistling and slushing his feet carelessly through the liquid mud. Now he was nearly opposite where Mr. Rassendyll stood. Rudolf was well-nigh convinced that the man had been on his track: he would make certainty surer. The bold game was always his choice and his delight; this trait he shared with Rupert of Hentzau, and hence arose, I think, the strange secret inclination he had for his unscrupulous opponent. Now he walked suddenly across to Bauer, and spoke to him in his natural voice, at the same time removing the scarf partly, but not altogether, from his face.

"You're out late, my friend, for a night like this."

Bauer, startled though he was by the unexpected challenge, had his wits about him. Whether he identified Rudolf at once, I do not know; I think that he must at least have suspected the truth.

"A lad that has no home to go to must needs be out both late and early, sir," said he, arresting his shuffling steps, and looking up with that honest stolid air which had made a fool of me.

I had described him very minutely to Mr. Rassendyll; if Bauer knew or guessed who his challenger was, Mr. Rassendyll was as well equipped for the encounter.

"No home to go to!" cried Rudolf in a pitying tone. "How's that? But anyhow, Heaven forbid that you or any man should walk the streets a night like this. Come, I'll give you a bed. Come with me, and I'll find you good shelter, my boy."

Bauer shrank away. He did not see the meaning of this stroke, and his eye, traveling up the street, showed that his thoughts had turned towards flight. Rudolf gave no time for putting any such notion into effect. Maintaining his air of genial compassion, he passed his left arm through Bauer's right, saying:

"I'm a Christian man, and a bed you shall have this night, my lad, as sure as I'm alive. Come along with me. The devil, it's not weather for standing still!"

The carrying of arms in Strelsau was forbidden. Bauer had no wish to get into trouble with the police, and, moreover, he had intended nothing but a reconnaissance; he was therefore without any weapon, and he was a child in Rudolf's grasp. He had no alternative but to obey the suasion of Mr. Rassendyll's arm, and they two began to walk down the Konigstrasse. Bauer's whistle had died away, not to return; but from time to time Rudolf hummed softly a cheerful tune, his fingers beating time on Bauer's captive arm. Presently they crossed the road. Bauer's lagging steps indicated that he took no pleasure in the change of side, but he could not resist.

"Ay, you shall go where I am going, my lad," said Rudolf encouragingly; and he laughed a little as he looked down at the fellow's face.

Along they went; soon they came to the small numbers at the station end of the Konigstrasse. Rudolf began to peer up at the shop fronts.

"It's cursed dark," said he. "Pray, lad, can you make out which is nineteen?"

The moment he had spoken the smile broadened on his face. The shot had gone home. Bauer was a clever scoundrel, but his nerves were not under perfect control, and his arm had quivered under Rudolf's.

"Nineteen, sir?" he stammered.

"Ay, nineteen. That's where we're bound for, you and I. There I hope we shall find—what we want."

Bauer seemed bewildered: no doubt he was at a loss how either to understand or to parry the bold attack.

135

"Ah, this looks like it," said Rudolf, in a tone of great satisfaction, as they came to old Mother Holf's little shop. "Isn't that a one and a nine over the door, my lad? Ah, and Holf! Yes, that's the name. Pray ring the bell. My hands are occupied."

Rudolf's hands were indeed occupied; one held Bauer's arm, now no longer with a friendly pressure, but with a grip of iron; in the other the captive saw the revolver that had till now lain hidden.

"You see?" asked Rudolf pleasantly. "You must ring for me, mustn't you? It would startle them if I roused them with a shot." A motion of the barrel told Bauer the direction which the shot would take.

"There's no bell," said Bauer sullenly.

"Ah, then you knock?"

"I suppose so."

"In any particular way, my friend?"

"I don't know," growled Bauer.

"Nor I. Can't you guess?"

"No, I know nothing of it."

"Well, we must try. You knock, and—Listen, my lad. You must guess right. You understand?"

"How can I guess?" asked Bauer, in an attempt at bluster.

"Indeed, I don't know," smiled Rudolf. "But I hate waiting, and if the door is not open in two minutes, I shall arouse the good folk with a shot. You see? You quite see, don't you?" Again the barrel's motion pointed and explained Mr. Rassendyll's meaning.

Under this powerful persuasion Bauer yielded. He lifted his hand and knocked on the door with his knuckles, first loudly, then very softly, the gentler stroke being repeated five times in rapid succession. Clearly he was expected, for without any sound of approaching feet the chain was unfastened with a subdued rattle. Then came the noise of the bolt being cautiously worked back into its socket. As it shot home a chink of the door opened. At the same moment Rudolf's hand slipped from Bauer's arm. With a swift movement he caught the fellow by the nape of the neck and flung him violently forward into the roadway, where, losing his footing, he fell sprawling face downwards in the mud. Rudolf threw himself against the door: it yielded, he was inside, and in an instant he had shut the door and driven the bolt home again, leaving Bauer in the gutter outside. Then he turned, with his hand on the butt of his revolver. I know that he hoped to find Rupert of Hentzau's face within a foot of his.

Neither Rupert nor Rischenheim, nor even the old woman fronted him: a tall, handsome, dark girl faced him, holding an oil-lamp in her hand. He did not know her, but I could have told him that she was old Mother Holf's youngest child, Rosa, for I had often seen her as I rode through the town of Zenda with the king, before the old lady moved her dwelling to Strelsau. Indeed the girl had seemed to haunt the king's foot-steps, and he had himself joked on her obvious efforts to attract his attention, and the languishing glances of her great black eyes. But it is the lot of prominent personages to inspire these strange passions, and the king had spent as little thought on her as on any of the romantic girls who found a naughty delight in half-fanciful devotion to him—devotion starting, in many cases, by an irony of which the king was happily unconscious, from the brave figure that he made at his coronation and his picturesque daring in the affair of Black Michael. The worshipers never came near enough to perceive the alteration in their idol.

The half then, at least, of Rosa's attachment was justly due to the man who now stood opposite to her, looking at her with surprise by the murky light of the strong-smelling oil-lamp. The lamp shook and almost fell from her hand when she saw him; for the scarf had slid away, and his features were exposed to full view. Fright, delight, and excitement vied with one another in her eyes.

"The king!" she whispered in amazement. "No, but—" And she searched his face wonderingly.

"Is it the beard you miss?" asked Rudolf, fingering his chin. "Mayn't kings shave when they please, as well as other men?" Her face still expressed bewilderment, and still a lingering doubt. He bent towards her, whispering:

"Perhaps I wasn't over-anxious to be known at once."

She flushed with pleasure at the confidence he seemed to put in her.

"I should know you anywhere," she whispered, with a glance of the great black eyes. "Anywhere, your Majesty."

"Then you'll help me, perhaps?"

"With my life."

"No, no, my dear young lady, merely with a little information. Whose home is this?"

"My mother's."

"Ah! She takes lodgers?"

The girl appeared vexed at his cautious approaches. "Tell me what you want to know," she said simply.

"Then who's here?"

"My lord the Count of Luzau-Rischenheim."

"And what's he doing?"

"He's lying on the bed moaning and swearing, because his wounded arm gives him pain."

"And is nobody else here?"

She looked round warily, and sank her voice to a whisper as she answered:

"No, not now—nobody else."

"I was seeking a friend of mine," said Rudolf. "I want to see him alone. It's not easy for a king to see people alone."

"You mean—?"

"Well, you know whom I mean."

"Yes. No, he's gone; but he's gone to find you."

"To find me! Plague take it! How do you know that, my pretty lady?"

"Bauer told me."

"Ah, Bauer! And who's Bauer?"

"The man who knocked. Why did you shut him out?"

"To be alone with you, to be sure. So Bauer tells you his master's secrets?"

She acknowledged his raillery with a coquettish laugh. It was not amiss for the king to see that she had her admirers.

"Well, and where has this foolish count gone to meet me?" asked Rudolf lightly.

"You haven't seen him?"

"No; I came straight from the Castle of Zenda."

"But," she cried, "he expected to find you at the hunting lodge. Ah, but now I recollect! The Count of Rischenheim was greatly vexed to find, on his return, that his cousin was gone."

"Ah, he was gone! Now I see! Rischenheim brought a message from me to Count Rupert."

"And they missed one another, your Majesty?"

"Exactly, my dear young lady. Very vexatious it is, upon my word!" In this remark, at least, Rudolf spoke no more and no other than he felt. "But when do you expect the Count of Hentzau?" he pursued.

"Early in the morning, your Majesty—at seven or eight."

Rudolf came nearer to her, and took a couple of gold coins from his pocket.

"I don't want money, your Majesty," she murmured.

"Oh, make a hole in them and hang them round your neck."

"Ah, yes: yes, give them to me," she cried, holding out her hand eagerly.

"You'll earn them?" he asked, playfully holding them out of her reach.

"How?"

"By being ready to open to me when I come at eleven and knock as Bauer knocked."

"Yes, I'll be there."

"And by telling nobody that I've been here to-night. Will you promise me that?"

"Not my mother?"

"No."

"Nor the Count of Luzau-Rischenheim?"

"Him least of all. You must tell nobody. My business is very private, and Rischenheim doesn't know it."

"I'll do all you tell me. But—but Bauer knows."

"True," said Rudolf. "Bauer knows. Well, we'll see about Bauer."

As he spoke he turned towards the door. Suddenly the girl bent, snatched at his hand and kissed it.

"I would die for you," she murmured.

"Poor child!" said he gently. I believe he was loath to make profit, even in the queen's service, of her poor foolish love. He laid his hand on the door, but paused a moment to say:

"If Bauer comes, you have told me nothing. Mind, nothing! I threatened you, but you told me nothing."

"He'll tell them you have been here."

"That can't be helped; at least they won't know when I shall arrive again. Good-night."

Rudolf opened the door and slipped through, closing it hastily behind him. If Bauer got back to the house, his visit must be known; but if he could intercept Bauer, the girl's silence was assured. He stood just outside, listening intently and searching the darkness with eager eyes.

CHAPTER XI. WHAT THE CHANCELLOR'S WIFE SAW

THE night, so precious in its silence, solitude, and darkness, was waning fast; soon the first dim approaches of day would be visible; soon the streets would become alive and people be about. Before then Rudolf Rassendyll, the man who bore a face that he dared not show in open day, must be under cover; else men would say that the king was in Strelsau, and the news would flash in a few hours through the kingdom and (so Rudolf feared) reach even those ears which we knew to be shut to all earthly sounds. But there was still some time at Mr. Rassendyll's disposal, and he could not spend it better than in pursuing his fight with Bauer. Taking a leaf out of the rascal's own book, he drew himself back into the shadow of the house walls and prepared to wait. At the worst he could keep the fellow from communicating with Rischenheim for a little longer, but his hope was that Bauer would steal back after a while and reconnoitre with a view to discovering how matters stood, whether the unwelcome visitor had taken his departure and the way to Rischenheim were open. Wrapping his scarf closely round his face, Rudolf waited, patiently enduring the tedium as he best might, drenched by the rain, which fell steadily, and very imperfectly sheltered from the buffeting of the wind. Minutes went by; there were no signs of Bauer nor of anybody else in the silent street. Yet Rudolf did not venture to leave his post; Bauer would seize the opportunity to slip in; perhaps Bauer had seen him come out, and was in his turn waiting till the coast should be clear; or, again, perhaps the useful spy had gone off to intercept Rupert of Hentzau, and warn him of the danger in the Konigstrasse. Ignorant of the truth and compelled to accept all these chances, Rudolf waited, still watching the distant beginnings of dawning day, which must soon drive him to his hiding-place again. Meanwhile my poor wife waited also, a prey to every fear that a woman's sensitive mind can imagine and feed upon.

Rudolf turned his head this way and that, seeking always the darker blot of shadow that would mean a human being. For a while his search was vain, but presently he found what he looked for—ay, and even more. On the same side of the street, to his left hand, from the direction of the station, not one, but three blurred shapes moved up the street. They came stealthily, yet quickly; with caution, but without pause or hesitation. Rudolf, scenting danger, flattened himself close against the wall and felt for his revolver. Very likely they were only early workers or late revelers, but he was ready for something else; he had not yet sighted Bauer, and action was to be looked for from the man. By infinitely gradual sidelong slitherings he moved a few paces from the door of Mother Holf's house, and stood six feet perhaps, or eight, on the right-hand side of it. The three came on. He strained his eyes in the effort to discern their features. In that dim light certainty was impossible, but the one in the middle might well be Bauer: the height, the walk, and the make were much what Bauer's were. If it were Bauer, then Bauer had friends, and Bauer and his friends seemed to be stalking some game. Always most carefully and gradually Rudolf edged yet farther from the little shop. At a distance of some five yards he halted finally, drew out his revolver, covered the man whom he took to be Bauer, and thus waited his fortune and his chance.

Now, it was plain that Bauer—for Bauer it was—would look for one of two things: what he hoped was to find Rudolf still in the house, what he feared was to be told that Rudolf, having fulfilled the unknown purpose of his visit, was gone whole and sound. If the latter tidings met him, these two good friends of his whom he had enlisted for his reinforcement were to have five crowns each and go home in peace; if the former, they were to do their work and make ten crowns. Years after, one of them told me the whole story without shame or reserve. What their work was, the heavy bludgeons they carried and the long knife that one of them had lent to Bauer showed pretty clearly.

But neither to Bauer nor to them did it occur that their quarry might be crouching near, hunting as well as hunted. Not that the pair of ruffians who had been thus hired would have hesitated for that thought, as I imagine. For it is strange, yet certain, that the zenith of courage and the acme of villainy can alike be bought for the price of a lady's glove. Among such outcasts as those from whom Bauer drew his recruits the murder of a man is held serious only when the police are by, and death at the hands of him they seek to kill is no more than an every-day risk of their employment.

"Here's the house," whispered Bauer, stopping at the door. "Now, I'll knock, and you stand by to knock him on the head if he runs out. He's got a six-shooter, so lose no time."

"He'll only fire it in heaven," growled a hoarse, guttural voice that ended in a chuckle.

"But if he's gone?" objected the other auxiliary.

"Then I know where he's gone," answered Bauer. "Are you ready?"

A ruffian stood on either side of the door with uplifted bludgeon. Bauer raised his hand to knock.

Rudolf knew that Rischenheim was within, and he feared that Bauer, hearing that the stranger had gone, would take the opportunity of telling the count of his visit. The count would, in his turn, warn Rupert of Hentzau, and the work of catching the ringleader would all fall to be done again. At no time did Mr. Rassendyll take count of odds against him, but in this instance he may well have thought himself, with his revolver, a match for the three ruffians. At any rate, before Bauer had time to give the signal, he sprang out suddenly from the wall and darted at the fellow. His onset was so sudden that the other two fell back a pace; Rudolf caught Bauer fairly by the throat. I do not suppose that he meant to strangle him, but the anger, long stored in his heart, found vent in the fierce grip of his fingers. It is certain that Bauer thought his time was come, unless he struck a blow for himself. Instantly he raised his hand and thrust fiercely at Rudolf with his long knife. Mr. Rassendyll would have been a dead man, had he not loosed his hold and sprung lightly away. But Bauer sprang at him again, thrusting with the knife, and crying to his associates,

"Club him, you fools, club him!"

Thus exhorted, one jumped forward. The moment for hesitation had gone. In spite of the noise of wind and pelting rain, the sound of a shot risked much; but not to fire was death. Rudolf fired full at Bauer: the fellow saw his intention and tried to leap behind one of his companions; he was just too late, and fell with a groan to the ground.

Again the other ruffians shrank back, appalled by the sudden ruthless decision of the act. Mr. Rassendyll laughed. A half smothered yet uncontrolled oath broke from one of them. "By God!" he whispered hoarsely, gazing at Rudolf's face and letting his arm fall to his side. "My God!" he said then, and his mouth hung open. Again Rudolf laughed at his terrified stare. "A bigger job than you fancied, is it?" he asked, pushing his scarf well away from his chin. The man gaped at him; the other's eyes asked wondering questions, but neither did he attempt to resume the attack. The first at last found voice, and he said, "Well, it'd be damned cheap at ten crowns, and that's the living truth."

His friend—or confederate rather, for such men have no friends—looked on, still amazed. "Take up that fellow by his head and his heels," ordered Rudolf. "Quickly! I suppose you don't want the police to find us here with him, do you? Well, no more do I. Lift him up."

As he spoke Rudolf turned to knock at the door of No. 19. But even as he did so Bauer groaned. Dead perhaps he ought to have been, but it seems to me that fate is always ready to take the cream and leave the scum. His leap aside had served him well, after all: he had nearly escaped scot free. As it was, the bullet, almost missing his head altogether, had just glanced on his temple as it passed; its impact had stunned, but not killed. Friend Bauer was in unusual luck that night; I wouldn't have taken a hundred to one about his chance of life. Rupert arrested his hand. It would not do to leave Bauer at the house, if Bauer were likely to regain speech. He stood for a moment, considering what to do, but in an instant the thoughts that he tried to gather were scattered again.

"The patrol! the patrol!" hoarsely whispered the fellow who had not yet spoken. There was a sound of the hoofs of horses. Down the street from the station end there appeared two mounted men. Without a second moment's hesitation the two rascals dropped their friend Bauer with a thud on the ground; one ran at his full speed across the street, the other bolted no less quickly up the Konigstrasse. Neither could afford to meet the constables; and who could say what story this red-haired gentleman might tell, ay, or what powers he might command?

But, in truth, Rudolf gave no thought to either his story or his powers. If he were caught, the best he could hope would be to lie in the lockup while Rupert played his game unmolested. The device that he had employed against the amazed ruffians could be used against lawful authority only as a last and desperate resort. While he could run, run he would. In an instant he also took to his heels, following the fellow who had darted up the Konigstrasse. But before he had gone very far, coming to a narrow turning, he shot down it; then he paused for a moment to listen.

The patrol had seen the sudden dispersal of the group, and, struck with natural suspicion, quickened pace. A few minutes brought them where Bauer was. They jumped from their horses and ran to him. He was unconscious, and could, of course, give them no account of how he came to be in his present state. The fronts of all the houses were dark, the doors shut; there was nothing to connect the man stretched on the ground with either No. 19 or any other dwelling. Moreover, the constables were not sure that the sufferer was himself a meritorious object, for his hand still held a long, ugly knife. They were perplexed: they were but two; there was a wounded man to look after; there were three men to pursue, and the three had fled in three separate directions. They looked up at No. 19; No. 19 remained dark, quiet, absolutely indifferent. The fugitives were out of sight. Rudolf Rassendyll, hearing nothing, had started again on his way. But a minute later he heard a shrill whistle. The patrol were summoning assistance; the man must be carried to the station, and a report made; but other constables might be warned of what had happened, and despatched in pursuit of the culprits. Rudolf heard more than one answering whistle; he broke into a run, looking for a turning on the left that would take him back into the direction of my house, but he found none. The narrow street twisted and curved in the bewildering way that characterizes the old parts of the town. Rudolf had spent some time once in Strelsau; but a king learns little of back streets, and he was soon fairly puzzled as to his whereabouts. Day was dawning, and he began to meet people here and there. He dared run no more, even had his breath lasted him; winding the scarf about his face, and cramming his hat over his forehead again, he fell into an easy walk, wondering whether he could venture to ask his way, relieved to find no signs that he was being pursued, trying to persuade himself that Bauer, though not dead, was at least incapable of embarrassing disclosures; above all, conscious of the danger of his tell-tale face, and of the necessity of finding some shelter before the city was all stirring and awake.

At this moment he heard horses' hoofs behind him. He was now at the end of the street, where it opened on the square in which the barracks stand. He knew his bearings now, and, had he not been interrupted, could have been back to safe shelter in my house in twenty minutes. But, looking back, he saw the figure of a mounted constable just coming into sight behind him. The man seemed to see Rudolf, for he broke into a quick trot. Mr. Rassendyll's position was critical; this fact alone accounts for the dangerous step into which he allowed himself to be forced. Here he was, a man unable to give account of himself, of remarkable appearance, and carrying a revolver, of which one barrel was discharged. And there was Bauer, a wounded man, shot by somebody with a revolver, a quarter of an hour before. Even to be questioned was dangerous; to be detained meant ruin to the great business that engaged his energies. For all he knew, the patrol had actually sighted him as he ran. His fears were not vain; for the constable raised his voice, crying, "Hi, sir—you there—stop a minute!"

Resistance was the one thing worse than to yield. Wit, and not force, must find escape this time. Rudolf stopped, looking round again with a surprised air. Then he drew himself up with an assumption of dignity, and waited for the constable. If that last card must be played, he would win the hand with it.

"Well, what do you want?" he asked coldly, when the man was a few yards from him; and, as he spoke, he withdrew the scarf almost entirely from his features, keeping it only over his chin. "You call very peremptorily," he continued, staring contemptuously. "What's your business with me?"

With a violent start, the sergeant—for such the star on his collar and the lace on his cuff proclaimed him—leant forward in the saddle to look at the man whom he had hailed. Rudolf said nothing and did not move. The man's eyes studied his face intently. Then he sat bolt upright and saluted, his face dyed to a deep red in his sudden confusion.

"And why do you salute me now?" asked Rudolf in a mocking tone. "First you hunt me, then you salute me. By Heaven, I don't know why you put yourself out at all about me!"

"I—I—" the fellow stuttered. Then trying a fresh start, he stammered, "Your Majesty, I didn't know—I didn't suppose—"

Rudolf stepped towards him with a quick, decisive tread.

"And why do you call me 'Your Majesty'?" he asked, still mockingly.

"It—it—isn't it your Majesty?"

Rudolf was close by him now, his hand on the horse's neck.

He looked up into the sergeant's face with steady eyes, saying:

"You make a mistake, my friend. I am not the king."

"You are not—?" stuttered the bewildered fellow.

"By no means. And, sergeant—?"

"Your Majesty?"

"Sir, you mean."

"Yes, sir."

"A zealous officer, sergeant, can make no greater mistake than to take for the king a gentleman who is not the king. It might injure his prospects, since the king, not being here, mightn't wish to have it supposed that he was here. Do you follow me, sergeant?"

The man said nothing, but stared hard. After a moment Rudolf continued:

"In such a case," said he, "a discreet officer would not trouble the gentleman any more, and would be very careful not to mention that he had made such a silly mistake. Indeed, if questioned, he would answer without hesitation that he hadn't seen anybody even like the king, much less the king himself."

A doubtful, puzzled little smile spread under the sergeant's moustache.

"You see, the king is not even in Strelsau," said Rudolf.

"Not in Strelsau, sir?"

"Why, no, he's at Zenda."

"Ah! At Zenda, sir?"

"Certainly. It is therefore impossible—physically impossible—that he should be here."

The fellow was convinced that he understood now.

"It's certainly impossible, sir," said he, smiling more broadly.

"Absolutely. And therefore impossible also that you should have seen him." With this Rudolf took a gold piece from his pocket and handed it to the sergeant. The fellow took it with something like a wink.

"As for you, you've searched here and found nobody," concluded Mr. Rassendyll. "So hadn't you better at once search somewhere else?

"Without doubt, sir," said the sergeant, and with the most deferential salute, and another confidential smile, he turned and rode back by the way he had come. No doubt he wished that he could meet a gentleman who was—not the king—every morning of his life. It hardly need be said that all idea of connecting the gentleman with the crime committed in the Konigstrasse had vanished from his mind. Thus Rudolf won freedom from the man's interference, but at a dangerous cost—how dangerous he did not know. It was indeed most impossible that the king could be in Strelsau.

He lost no time now in turning his steps towards his refuge. It was past five o'clock, day came quickly, and the streets began to be peopled by men and women on their way to open stalls or to buy in the market. Rudolf crossed the square at a rapid walk, for he was afraid of the soldiers who were gathering for early duty opposite to the barracks. Fortunately he passed by them unobserved, and gained the comparative seclusion of the street in which my house stands, without encountering any further difficulties. In truth, he was almost in safety; but bad luck was now to have its turn. When Mr. Rassendyll was no more than fifty yards from my door, a carriage suddenly drove up and stopped a few paces in front of him. The footman sprang down and opened the door. Two ladies got out; they were dressed in evening costume, and were returning from a ball. One was middle-aged, the other young and rather pretty. They stood for a moment on the pavement, the younger saying:

"Isn't it pleasant, mother? I wish I could always be up at five o'clock."

"My dear, you wouldn't like it for long," answered the elder. "It's very nice for a change, but—"

She stopped abruptly. Her eye had fallen on Rudolf Rassendyll. He knew her: she was no less a person than the wife of Helsing the chancellor; his was the house at which the carriage had stopped. The trick that had served with the sergeant of police would not do now. She knew the king too well to believe that she could be mistaken about him; she was too much of a busybody to be content to pretend that she was mistaken.

"Good gracious!" she whispered loudly, and, catching her daughter's arm, she murmured, "Heavens, my dear, it's the king!"

Rudolf was caught. Not only the ladies, but their servants were looking at him.

Flight was impossible. He walked by them. The ladies curtseyed, the servants bowed bareheaded. Rudolf touched his hat and bowed slightly in return. He walked straight on towards my house; they were watching him, and he knew it. Most heartily did he curse the untimely hours to which folks keep up their dancing, but he thought that a visit to my house would afford as plausible an excuse for his presence as any other. So he went on, surveyed by the wondering ladies, and by the servants who, smothering smiles, asked one another what brought his Majesty abroad in such a plight (for Rudolf's clothes were soaked and his boots muddy), at such an hour—and that in Strelsau, when all the world thought he was at Zenda.

Rudolf reached my house. Knowing that he was watched he had abandoned all intention of giving the signal agreed on between my wife and himself and of making his way in through the window. Such a sight would indeed have given the excellent Baroness von Helsing matter for gossip! It was better to let every servant in my house see his open entrance. But, alas, virtue itself sometimes leads to ruin. My dearest Helga, sleepless and watchful in the interest of her mistress, was even now behind the shutter, listening with all her ears and peering through the chinks. No sooner did Rudolf's footsteps become audible than she cautiously unfastened the shutter, opened the window, put her pretty head out, and called softly: "All's safe! Come in!"

The mischief was done then, for the faces of Helsing's wife and daughter, ay, and the faces of Helsing's servants, were intent on this most strange spectacle. Rudolf, turning his head over his shoulder, saw them; a moment later poor Helga saw them also. Innocent and untrained in controlling her feelings, she gave a shrill little cry of dismay, and hastily drew back. Rudolf looked round again. The ladies had retreated to the cover of the porch, but he still saw their eager faces peering from between the pillars that supported it.

"I may as well go in now," said Rudolf, and in he sprang. There was a merry smile on his face as he ran forward to meet Helga, who leant against the table, pale and agitated.

"They saw you?" she gasped.

"Undoubtedly," said he. Then his sense of amusement conquered everything else, and he sat down in a chair, laughing.

"I'd give my life," said he, "to hear the story that the chancellor will be waked up to hear in a minute or two from now!"

But a moment's thought made him grave again. For whether he were the king or Rudolf Rassendyll, he knew that my wife's name was in equal peril. Knowing this, he stood at nothing to serve her. He turned to her and spoke quickly.

"You must rouse one of the servants at once. Send him round to the chancellor's and tell the chancellor to come here directly. No, write a note. Say the king has come by appointment to see Fritz on some private business, but that Fritz has not kept the appointment, and that the king must now see the chancellor at once. Say there's not a moment to lose."

She was looking at him with wondering eyes.

"Don't you see," he said, "if I can impose on Helsing, I may stop those women's tongues? If nothing's done, how long do you suppose it'll be before all Strelsau knows that Fritz von Tarlenheim's wife let the king in at the window at five o'clock in the morning?"

"I don't understand," murmured poor Helga in bewilderment.

"No, my dear lady, but for Heaven's sake do what I ask of you. It's the only chance now."

"I'll do it," she said, and sat down to write.

Thus it was that, hard on the marvelous tidings which, as I conjecture, the Baroness von Helsing poured into her husband's drowsy ears, came an imperative summons that the chancellor should wait on the king at the house of Fritz von Tarlenheim.

Truly we had tempted fate too far by bringing Rudolf Rassendyll again to Strelsau.

CHAPTER XII. BEFORE THEM ALL!

GREAT as was the risk and immense as were the difficulties created by the course which Mr. Rassendyll adopted, I cannot doubt that he acted for the best in the light of the information which he possessed. His plan was to disclose himself in the character of the king to Helsing, to bind him to secrecy, and make him impose the same obligation on his wife, daughter, and servants. The chancellor was to be quieted with the excuse of urgent business, and conciliated by a promise that he should know its nature in the course of a few hours; meanwhile an appeal to his loyalty must suffice to insure obedience. If all went well in the day that had now dawned, by the evening of it the letter would be destroyed, the queen's peril past, and Rudolf once more far away from Strelsau. Then enough of the truth—no more—must be disclosed. Helsing would be told the story of Rudolf Rassendyll and persuaded to hold his tongue about the harum-scarum Englishman (we are ready to believe much of an Englishman) having been audacious enough again to play the king in Strelsau. The old chancellor was a very good fellow, and I do not think that Rudolf did wrong in relying upon him. Where he miscalculated was, of course, just where he was ignorant. The whole of what the queen's friends, ay, and the queen herself, did in Strelsau, became useless and mischievous by reason of the king's death; their action must have been utterly different, had they been aware of that catastrophe; but their wisdom must be judged only according to their knowledge.

In the first place, the chancellor himself showed much good sense. Even before he obeyed the king's summons he sent for the two servants and charged them, on pain of instant dismissal and worse things to follow, to say nothing of what they had seen. His commands to his wife and daughter were more polite, doubtless, but no less peremptory. He may well have supposed that the king's business was private as well as important when it led his Majesty to be roaming the streets of Strelsau at a moment when he was supposed to be at the Castle of Zenda, and to enter a friend's house by the window at such untimely hours. The mere facts were eloquent of secrecy. Moreover, the king had shaved his beard—the ladies were sure of it—and this, again, though it might be merely an accidental coincidence, was also capable of signifying a very urgent desire to be unknown. So the chancellor, having given his orders, and being himself aflame with the liveliest curiosity, lost no time in obeying the king's commands, and arrived at my house before six o'clock.

When the visitor was announced Rudolf was upstairs, having a bath and some breakfast. Helga had learnt her lesson well enough to entertain the visitor until Rudolf appeared. She was full of apologies for my absence, protesting that she could in no way explain it; neither could she so much as conjecture what was the king's business with her husband. She played the dutiful wife whose virtue was obedience, whose greatest sin would be an indiscreet prying into what it was not her part to know.

"I know no more," she said, "than that Fritz wrote to me to expect the king and him at about five o'clock, and to be ready to let them in by the window, as the king did not wish the servants to be aware of his presence."

The king came and greeted Helsing most graciously. The tragedy and comedy of these busy days were strangely mingled; even now I can hardly help smiling when I picture Rudolf, with grave lips, but that distant twinkle in his eye (I swear he enjoyed the sport), sitting down by the old chancellor in the darkest corner of the room, covering him with flattery, hinting at most strange things, deploring a secret obstacle to immediate confidence, promising that to-morrow, at latest, he would seek the advice of the wisest and most tried of his counselors, appealing to the chancellor's loyalty to trust him till then. Helsing, blinking through his spectacles, followed with devout attention the long narrative that told nothing, and the urgent exhortation that masked a trick. His accents were almost broken with emotion as he put himself absolutely at the king's disposal, and declared that he could answer for the discretion of his family and household as completely as for his own.

"Then you're a very lucky man, my dear chancellor," said Rudolf, with a sigh which seemed to hint that the king in his palace was not so fortunate. Helsing was immensely pleased. He was all agog to go and tell his wife how entirely the king trusted to her honor and silence.

There was nothing that Rudolf more desired than to be relieved of the excellent old fellow's presence; but, well aware of the supreme importance of keeping him in a good temper, he would not hear of his departure for a few minutes.

"At any rate, the ladies won't talk till after breakfast, and since they got home only at five o'clock they won't breakfast yet awhile," said he.

So he made Helsing sit down, and talked to him. Rudolf had not failed to notice that the Count of Luzau-Rischenheim had been a little surprised at the sound of his voice; in this conversation he studiously kept his tones low, affecting a certain weakness and huskiness such as he had detected in the king's utterances, as he listened behind the curtain in Sapt's room at the castle. The part was played as completely and triumphantly as in the old days when he ran the gauntlet of every eye in Strelsau. Yet if he had not taken such pains to conciliate old Helsing, but had let him depart, he might not have found himself driven to a greater and even more hazardous deception.

They were conversing together alone. My wife had been prevailed on by Rudolf to lie down in her room for an hour. Sorely needing rest, she had obeyed him, having first given strict orders that no member of the household should enter the room where the two were except on an express summons. Fearing suspicion, she and Rudolf had agreed that it was better to rely on these injunctions than to lock the door again as they had the night before.

But while these things passed at my house, the queen and Bernenstein were on their way to Strelsau. Perhaps, had Sapt been at Zenda, his powerful influence might have availed to check the impulsive expedition; Bernenstein had no such authority, and could only obey the queen's peremptory orders and pathetic prayers. Ever since Rudolf Rassendyll left her, three years before, she had lived in stern self-repression, never her true self, never for a moment able to be or to do what every hour her heart urged on her. How are these things done? I doubt if a man lives who could do them; but women live who do them. Now his sudden coming, and the train of stirring events that accompanied it, his danger and hers, his words and her enjoyment of his presence, had all worked together to shatter her self-control; and the strange dream, heightening the emotion which was its own cause, left her with no conscious desire save to be near Mr. Rassendyll, and scarcely with a fear except for his safety. As they journeyed her talk was all of his peril, never of the disaster which threatened herself, and which we were all striving with might and main to avert from her head. She traveled alone with Bernenstein, getting rid of the lady who attended her by some careless pretext, and she urged on him continually to bring her as speedily as might be to Mr. Rassendyll. I cannot find much blame for her. Rudolf stood for all the joy in her life, and Rudolf had gone to fight with the Count of Hentzau. What wonder that she saw him, as it were, dead? Yet still she would have it that, in his seeming death, all men hailed him for their king. Well, it was her love that crowned him.

As they reached the city, she grew more composed, being persuaded by Bernenstein that nothing in her bearing must rouse suspicion. Yet she was none the less resolved to seek Mr. Rassendyll at once. In truth, she feared even then to find him dead, so strong was the hold of her dream on her; until she knew that he was alive she could not rest. Bernenstein, fearful that the strain would kill her, or rob her of reason, promised everything; and declared, with a confidence which he did not feel, that beyond doubt Mr. Rassendyll was alive and well.

"But where—where?" she cried eagerly, with clasped hands.

"We're most likely, madam, to find him at Fritz von Tarlenheim's," answered the lieutenant. "He would wait there till the time came to attack Rupert, or, if the thing is over, he will have returned there."

"Then let us drive there at once," she urged.

Bernenstein, however, persuaded her to go to the palace first and let it be known there that she was going to pay a visit to my wife. She arrived at the palace at eight o'clock, took a cup of chocolate, and then ordered her carriage. Bernenstein alone accompanied her when she set out for my house about nine. He was, by now, hardly less agitated than the queen herself. In her entire preoccupation with Mr. Rassendyll, she gave little thought to what might have happened at the hunting lodge; but Bernenstein drew gloomy auguries from the failure of Sapt and myself to return at the proper time. Either evil had befallen us, or the letter had reached the king before we arrived at the lodge; the probabilities seemed to him to be confined to these alternatives. Yet when he spoke in this strain to the queen, he could get from her nothing except, "If we can find Mr. Rassendyll, he will tell us what to do."

Thus, then, a little after nine in the morning the queen's carriage drove up to my door. The ladies of the chancellor's family had enjoyed a very short night's rest, for their heads came bobbing out of window the moment the wheels were heard; many people were about now, and the crown on the panels attracted the usual small crowd of loiterers. Bernenstein sprang out and gave his hand to the queen. With a hasty slight bow to the onlookers, she hastened up the two or three steps of the porch, and with her own hand rang the bell. Inside, the carriage had just been observed. My wife's waiting-maid ran hastily to her mistress; Helga was lying on her bed; she rose at once, and after a few moments of necessary preparations (or such preparations as seem to ladies necessary, however great the need of haste may be) hurried downstairs to receive her Majesty—and to warn her Majesty. She was too late. The door was already open. The butler and the footman both had run to it, and thrown it open for the queen. As Helga reached the foot of the stairs, her Majesty was just entering the room where Rudolf was, the servants attending her, and Bernenstein standing behind, his helmet in his hand.

Rudolf and the chancellor had been continuing their conversation. To avoid the observations of passers-by (for the interior of the room is easy to see from the street), the blind had been drawn down, and the room was in deep shadow. They had heard the wheels, but neither of them dreamt that the visitor could be the queen. It was an utter surprise to them when, without their orders, the door was suddenly flung open. The chancellor, slow of movement, and not, if I may say it, over-quick of brain, sat in his corner for half a minute or more before he rose to his feet. On the other hand, Rudolf Rassendyll was the best part of the way across the room in an instant. Helga was at the door now, and she thrust her head round young Bernenstein's broad shoulders. Thus she saw what happened. The queen, forgetting the servants, and not observing Helsing—seeming indeed to stay for nothing, and to think of nothing, but to have her thoughts and heart filled with the sight of the man she loved and the knowledge of his safety—met him as he ran towards her, and, before Helga, or Bernenstein, or Rudolf himself, could stay her or conceive what she was about to do, caught both his hands in hers with an intense grasp, crying:

"Rudolf, you're safe! Thank God, oh, thank God!" and she carried his hands to her lips and kissed them passionately.

A moment of absolute silence followed, dictated in the servants by decorum, in the chancellor by consideration, in Helga and Bernenstein by utter consternation. Rudolf himself also was silent, but whether from bewilderment or an emotion answering to hers, I know not. Either it might well be. The stillness struck her. She looked up in his eyes; she looked round the room and saw Helsing, now bowing profoundly from the corner; she turned her head with a sudden frightened jerk, and glanced at my motionless deferential servants. Then it came upon her what she had done. She gave a quick gasp for breath, and her face, always pale, went white as marble. Her features set in a strange stiffness, and suddenly she reeled where she stood, and fell forward. Only Rudolf's hand bore her up. Thus for a moment, too short to reckon, they stood. Then he, a smile of great love and pity coming on his lips, drew her to him, and passing his arm about her waist, thus supported her. Then, smiling still, he looked down on her, and said in a low tone, yet distinct enough for all to hear:

"All is well, dearest."

My wife gripped Bernenstein's arm, and he turned to find her pale-faced too, with quivering lips and shining eyes. But the eyes had a message, and an urgent one, for him. He read it; he knew that it bade him second what Rudolf Rassendyll had done. He came forward and approached Rudolf; then he fell on one knee, and kissed Rudolf's left hand that was extended to him.

"I'm very glad to see you, Lieutenant von Bernenstein," said Rudolf Rassendyll.

For a moment the thing was done, ruin averted, and safety secured. Everything had been at stake; that there was such a man as Rudolf Rassendyll might have been disclosed; that he had once filled the king's throne was a high secret which they were prepared to trust to Helsing under stress of necessity; but there remained something which must be hidden at all costs, and which the queen's passionate exclamation had threatened to expose. There was a Rudolf Rassendyll, and he had been king; but, more than all this, the queen loved him and he the queen. That could be told to none, not even to Helsing; for Helsing, though he would not gossip to the town, would yet hold himself bound to carry the matter to the king. So Rudolf chose to take any future difficulties rather than that present and certain disaster. Sooner than entail it on her he loved, he claimed for himself the place of her husband and the name of king. And she, clutching at the only chance that her act left, was content to have it so. It may be that for an instant her weary, tortured brain found sweet rest in the dim dream that so it was, for she let her head lie there on his breast and her eyes closed, her face looking very peaceful, and a soft little sigh escaping in pleasure from her lips.

But every moment bore its peril and exacted its effort. Rudolf led the queen to a couch, and then briefly charged the servants not to speak of his presence for a few hours. As they had no doubt perceived, said he, from the queen's agitation, important business was on foot; it demanded his presence in Strelsau, but required also that his presence should not be known. A short time would free them from the obligation which he now asked of their loyalty. When they had withdrawn, bowing obedience, he turned to Helsing, pressed his hand warmly, reiterated his request for silence, and said that he would summon the chancellor to his presence again later in the day, either where he was or at the palace. Then he bade all withdraw and leave him alone for a little with the queen. He was obeyed; but Helsing had hardly left the house when Rudolf called Bernenstein back, and with him my wife. Helga hastened to the queen, who was still sorely agitated; Rudolf drew Bernenstein aside, and exchanged with him all their news. Mr. Rassendyll was much disturbed at finding that no tidings had come from Colonel Sapt and myself, but his apprehension was greatly increased on learning the untoward accident by which the king himself had been at the lodge the night before. Indeed, he was utterly in the dark; where the king was, where Rupert, where we were, he did not know. And he was here in Strelsau, known as the king to half a dozen people or more, protected only by their promises, liable at any moment to be exposed by the coming of the king himself, or even by a message from him.

Yet, in face of all perplexities, perhaps even the more because of the darkness in which he was enveloped, Rudolf held firm to his purpose. There were two things that seemed plain. If Rupert had escaped the trap and was still alive with the letter on him, Rupert must be found; here was the first task. That accomplished, there remained for Rudolf himself nothing save to disappear as quietly and secretly as he had come, trusting that his presence could be concealed from the man whose name he had usurped. Nay, if need were, the king must be told that Rudolf Rassendyll had played a trick on the chancellor, and, having enjoyed his pleasure, was gone again. Everything could, in the last resort, be told, save that which touched the queen's honor.

At this moment the message which I despatched from the station at Hofbau reached my house. There was a knock at the door. Bernenstein opened it and took the telegram, which was addressed to my wife. I had written all that I dared to trust to such a means of communication, and here it is:

"I am coming to Strelsau. The king will not leave the lodge to-day. The count came, but left before we arrived. I do not know whether he has gone to Strelsau. He gave no news to the king."

"Then they didn't get him!" cried Bernenstein in deep disappointment.

"No, but he gave no news to the king," said Rudolf triumphantly.

They were all standing now round the queen, who sat on the couch. She seemed very faint and weary, but at peace. It was enough for her that Rudolf fought and planned for her.

147

"And see this," Rudolf went on. "'The king will not leave the lodge to-day.' Thank God, then, we have to-day!"

"Yes, but where's Rupert?"

"We shall know in an hour, if he's in Strelsau," and Mr. Rassendyll looked as though it would please him well to find Rupert in Strelsau. "Yes, I must seek him. I shall stand at nothing to find him. If I can only get to him as the king, then I'll be the king. We have to-day!"

My message put them in heart again, although it left so much still unexplained. Rudolf turned to the queen.

"Courage, my queen," said he. "A few hours now will see an end of all our dangers."

"And then?" she asked.

"Then you'll be safe and at rest," said he, bending over her and speaking softly. "And I shall be proud in the knowledge of having saved you."

"And you?"

"I must go," Helga heard him whisper as he bent lower still, and she and Bernenstein moved away.

CHAPTER XIII. A KING UP HIS SLEEVE

The tall handsome girl was taking down the shutters from the shop front at No. 19 in the Konigstrasse. She went about her work languidly enough, but there was a tinge of dusky red on her cheeks and her eyes were brightened by some suppressed excitement. Old Mother Holf, leaning against the counter, was grumbling angrily because Bauer did not come. Now it was not likely that Bauer would come just yet, for he was still in the infirmary attached to the police-cells, where a couple of doctors were very busy setting him on his legs again. The old woman knew nothing of this, but only that he had gone the night before to reconnoitre; where he was to play the spy she did not know, on whom perhaps she guessed.

"You're sure he never came back?" she asked her daughter.

"He never came back that I saw," answered the girl. "And I was on the watch with my lamp here in the shop till it grew light."

"He's twelve hours gone now, and never a message! Ay, and Count Rupert should be here soon, and he'll be in a fine taking if Bauer's not back."

The girl made no answer; she had finished her task and stood in the doorway, looking out on the street. It was past eight, and many people were about, still for the most part humble folk; the more comfortably placed would not be moving for an hour or two yet. In the road the traffic consisted chiefly of country carts and wagons, bringing in produce for the day's victualling of the great city. The girl watched the stream, but her thoughts were occupied with the stately gentleman who had come to her by night and asked a service of her. She had heard the revolver shot outside; as it sounded she had blown out her lamp, and there behind the door in the dark had heard the swiftly retreating feet of the fugitives and, a little later, the arrival of the patrol. Well, the patrol would not dare to touch the king; as for Bauer, let him be alive or dead: what cared she, who was the king's servant, able to help the king against his enemies? If Bauer were the king's enemy, right glad would she be to hear that the rogue was dead. How finely the king had caught him by the neck and thrown him out! She laughed to think how little her mother knew the company she had kept that night.

The row of country carts moved slowly by. One or two stopped before the shop, and the carters offered vegetables for sale. The old woman would have nothing to say to them, but waved them on irritably. Three had thus stopped and again proceeded, and an impatient grumble broke from the old lady as a fourth, a covered wagon, drew up before the door.

"We don't want anything: go on, go on with you!" she cried shrilly.

The carter got down from his seat without heeding her, and walked round to the back.

"Here you are, sir," he cried. "Nineteen, Konigstrasse."

A yawn was heard, and the long sigh a man gives as he stretches himself in the mingled luxury and pain of an awakening after sound refreshing sleep.

"All right; I'll get down," came in answer from inside.

"Ah, it's the count!" said the old lady to her daughter in satisfied tones. "What will he say, though, about that rogue Bauer?"

Rupert of Hentzau put his head out from under the wagon-tilt, looked up and down the street, gave the carter a couple of crowns, leapt down, and ran lightly across the pavement into the little shop. The wagon moved on.

"A lucky thing I met him," said Rupert cheerily. "The wagon hid me very well; and handsome as my face is, I can't let Strelsau enjoy too much of it just now. Well, mother, what cheer? And you, my pretty, how goes it with you?" He carelessly brushed the girl's cheek with the glove that he had drawn off. "Faith, though, I beg your pardon." he added a moment later, "the glove's not clean enough for that," and he looked at his buff glove, which was stained with patches of dull rusty brown.

"It's all as when you left, Count Rupert," said Mother Holf, "except that that rascal Bauer went out last night—"

"That's right enough. But hasn't he returned?"

"No, not yet."

"Hum. No signs of—anybody else?" His look defined the vague question.

The old woman shook her head. The girl turned away to hide a smile. "Anybody else" meant the king, so she suspected. Well, they should hear nothing from her. The king himself had charged her to be silent.

"But Rischenheim has come, I suppose?" pursued Rupert.

"Oh, yes; he came, my lord, soon after you went. He wears his arm in a sling."

"Ah!" cried Rupert in sudden excitement. "As I guessed! The devil! If only I could do everything myself, and not have to trust to fools and bunglers! Where's the count?"

"Why, in the attic. You know the way."

"True. But I want some breakfast, mother."

"Rosa shall serve you at once, my lord."

The girl followed Rupert up the narrow crazy staircase of the tall old house. They passed three floors, all uninhabited; a last steep flight that brought them right under the deep arched roof. Rupert opened a door that stood at the top of the stairs, and, followed still by Rosa with her mysterious happy smile, entered a long narrow room. The ceiling, high in the centre, sloped rapidly down on either side, so that at door and window it was little more than six feet above the floor. There was an oak table and a few chairs; a couple of iron bedsteads stood by the wall near the window. One was empty; the Count of Luzau-Rischenheim lay on the other, fully dressed, his right arm supported in a sling of black silk. Rupert paused on the threshold, smiling at his cousin; the girl passed on to a high press or cupboard, and, opening it, took out plates, glasses, and the other furniture of the table. Rischenheim sprang up and ran across the room.

"What news?" he cried eagerly. "You escaped them, Rupert?"

"It appears so," said Rupert airily; and, advancing into the room, he threw himself into a chair, tossing his hat on to the table.

"It appears that I escaped, although some fool's stupidity nearly made an end of me." Rischenheim flushed.

"I'll tell you about that directly," he said, glancing at the girl who had put some cold meat and a bottle of wine on the table, and was now completing the preparations for Rupert's meal in a very leisurely fashion.

"Had I nothing to do but to look at pretty faces—which, by Heaven, I wish heartily were the case—I would beg you to stay," said Rupert, rising and making her a profound bow.

149

"I've no wish to hear what doesn't concern me," she retorted scornfully.

"What a rare and blessed disposition!" said he, holding the door for her and bowing again.

"I know what I know," she cried to him triumphantly from the landing. "Maybe you'd give something to know it too, Count Rupert!"

"It's very likely, for, by Heaven, girls know wonderful things!" smiled Rupert; but he shut the door and came quickly back to the table, now frowning again. "Come, tell me, how did they make a fool of you, or why did you make a fool of me, cousin?"

While Rischenheim related how he had been trapped and tricked at the Castle of Zenda, Rupert of Hentzau made a very good breakfast. He offered no interruption and no comments, but when Rudolf Rassendyll came into the story he looked up for an instant with a quick jerk of his head and a sudden light in his eyes. The end of Rischenheim's narrative found him tolerant and smiling again.

"Ah, well, the snare was cleverly set," he said. "I don't wonder you fell into it."

"And now you? What happened to you?" asked Rischenheim eagerly.

"I? Why, having your message which was not your message, I obeyed your directions which were not your directions."

"You went to the lodge?"

"Certainly."

"And you found Sapt there?—Anybody else?"

"Why, not Sapt at all."

"Not Sapt? But surely they laid a trap for you?"

"Very possibly, but the jaws didn't bite." Rupert crossed his legs and lit a cigarette.

"But what did you find?"

"I? I found the king's forester, and the king's boar-hound, and—well, I found the king himself, too."

"The king at the lodge?"

"You weren't so wrong as you thought, were you?"

"But surely Sapt, or Bernenstein, or some one was with him?"

"As I tell you, his forester and his boar-hound. No other man or beast, on my honor."

"Then you gave him the letter?" cried Rischenheim, trembling with excitement.

"Alas, no, my dear cousin. I threw the box at him, but I don't think he had time to open it. We didn't get to that stage of the conversation at which I had intended to produce the letter."

"But why not—why not?"

Rupert rose to his feet, and, coming just opposite to where Rischenheim sat, balanced himself on his heels, and looked down at his cousin, blowing the ash from his cigarette and smiling pleasantly.

"Have you noticed," he asked, "that my coat's torn?"

"I see it is."

"Yes. The boar-hound tried to bite me, cousin. And the forester would have stabbed me. And—well, the king wanted to shoot me."

"Yes, yes! For God's sake, what happened?"

"Well, they none of them did what they wanted. That's what happened, dear cousin."

Rischenheim was staring at him now with wide-opened eyes. Rupert smiled down on him composedly.

"Because, you see," he added, "Heaven helped me. So that, my dear cousin, the dog will bite no more, and the forester will stab no more. Surely the country is well rid of them?"

A silence followed. Then Rischenheim, leaning forward, said in a low whisper, as though afraid to hear his own question:

"And the king?"

"The king? Well, the king will shoot no more."

For a moment Rischenheim, still leaning forward, gazed at his cousin. Then he sank slowly back into his chair.

"My God!" he murmured: "my God!"

"The king was a fool," said Rupert. "Come, I'll tell you a little more about it." He drew a chair up and seated himself in it.

While he talked Rischenheim seemed hardly to listen. The story gained in effect from the contrast of Rupert's airy telling; his companion's pale face and twitching hands tickled his fancy to more shameless jesting. But when he had finished, he gave a pull to his small smartly-curled moustache and said with a sudden gravity:

"After all, though, it's a serious matter."

Rischenheim was appalled at the issue. His cousin's influence had been strong enough to lead him into the affair of the letter; he was aghast to think how Rupert's reckless dare-deviltry had led on from stage to stage till the death of a king seemed but an incident in his schemes. He sprang suddenly to his feet, crying:

"But we must fly—we must fly!"

"No, we needn't fly. Perhaps we'd better go, but we needn't fly."

"But when it becomes known?" He broke off and then cried:

"Why did you tell me? Why did you come back here?"

"Well, I told you because it was interesting, and I came back here because I had no money to go elsewhere."

"I would have sent money."

"I find that I get more when I ask in person. Besides, is everything finished?"

"I'll have no more to do with it."

"Ah, my dear cousin, you despond too soon. The good king has unhappily gone from us, but we still have our dear queen. We have also, by the kindness of Heaven, our dear queen's letter."

"I'll have no more to do with it."

"Your neck feeling—?" Rupert delicately imitated the putting of a noose about a man's throat.

Rischenheim rose suddenly and flung the window open wide.

"I'm suffocated," he muttered with a sullen frown, avoiding Rupert's eyes.

"Where's Rudolf Rassendyll?" asked Rupert. "Have you heard of him?"

"No, I don't know where he is."

"We must find that out, I think."

Rischenheim turned abruptly on him.

"I had no hand in this thing," he said, "and I'll have no more to do with it. I was not there. What did I know of the king being there? I'm not guilty of it: on my soul, I know nothing of it."

"That's all very true," nodded Rupert.

"Rupert," cried he, "let me go, let me alone. If you want money, I'll give it to you. For God's sake take it, and get out of Strelsau!"

"I'm ashamed to beg, my dear cousin, but in fact I want a little money until I can contrive to realize my valuable property. Is it safe, I wonder? Ah, yes, here it is."

He drew from his inner pocket the queen's letter. "Now if the king hadn't been a fool!" he murmured regretfully, as he regarded it.

Then he walked across to the window and looked out; he could not himself be seen from the street, and nobody was visible at the windows opposite. Men and women passed to and fro on their daily labors or pleasures; there was no unusual stir in the city. Looking over the roofs, Rupert could see the royal standard floating in the wind over the palace and the barracks. He took out his watch; Rischenheim imitated his action; it was ten minutes to ten.

"Rischenheim," he called, "come here a moment. Here—look out."

Rischenheim obeyed, and Rupert let him look for a minute or two before speaking again.

"Do you see anything remarkable?" he asked then.

"No, nothing," answered Rischenheim, still curt and sullen in his fright.

"Well, no more do I. And that's very odd. For don't you think that Sapt or some other of her Majesty's friends must have gone to the lodge last night?"

"They meant to, I swear," said Rischenheim with sudden attention.

"Then they would have found the king. There's a telegraph wire at Hofbau, only a few miles away. And it's ten o'clock. My cousin, why isn't Strelsau mourning for our lamented king? Why aren't the flags at half-mast? I don't understand it."

"No," murmured Rischenheim, his eyes now fixed on his cousin's face.

Rupert broke into a smile and tapped his teeth with his fingers.

"I wonder," said he meditatively, "if that old player Sapt has got a king up his sleeve again! If that were so—" He stopped and seemed to fall into deep thought. Rischenheim did not interrupt him, but stood looking now at him, now out of the window. Still there was no stir in the streets, and still the standards floated at the summit of the flag staffs. The king's death was not yet known in Strelsau.

"Where's Bauer?" asked Rupert suddenly. "Where the plague can Bauer be? He was my eyes. Here we are, cooped up, and I don't know what's going on."

"I don't know where he is. Something must have happened to him."

"Of course, my wise cousin. But what?"

Rupert began to pace up and down the room, smoking another cigarette at a great pace. Rischenheim sat down by the table, resting his head on his hand. He was wearied out by strain and excitement, his wounded arm pained him greatly, and he was full of horror and remorse at the event which happened unknown to him the night before.

"I wish I was quit of it," he moaned at last. Rupert stopped before him.

"You repent of your misdeeds?" he asked. "Well, then, you shall be allowed to repent. Nay, you shall go and tell the king that you repent. Rischenheim, I must know what they are doing. You must go and ask an audience of the king."

"But the king is—"

"We shall know that better when you've asked for your audience. See here."

Rupert sat down by his cousin and instructed him in his task. This was no other than to discover whether there were a king in Strelsau, or whether the only king lay dead in the hunting lodge. If there were no attempt being made to conceal the king's death, Rupert's plan was to seek safety in flight. He did not abandon his designs: from the secure vantage of foreign soil he would hold the queen's letter over her head, and by the threat of publishing it insure at once immunity for himself and almost any further terms which he chose to exact from her. If, on the other hand, the Count of Luzau-Rischenheim found a king in Strelsau, if the royal standards continued to wave at the summit of their flag staffs, and Strelsau knew nothing of the dead man in the lodge, then Rupert had laid his hand on another secret; for he knew who the king in Strelsau must be. Starting from this point, his audacious mind darted forward to new and bolder schemes. He could offer again to Rudolf Rassendyll what he had offered once before, three years ago—a partnership in crime and the profits of crime—or if this advance were refused, then he declared that he would himself descend openly into the streets of Strelsau and proclaim the death of the king from the steps of the cathedral.

"Who can tell," he cried, springing up, enraptured and merry with the inspiration of his plan, "who can tell whether Sapt or I came first to the lodge? Who found the king alive, Sapt or I? Who left him dead, Sapt or I? Who had most interest in killing him—I, who only sought to make him aware of what touched his honor, or Sapt, who was and is hand and glove with the man that now robs him of his name and usurps his place while his body is still warm? Ah, they haven't done with Rupert of Hentzau yet!"

He stopped, looking down on his companion. Rischenheim's fingers still twitched nervously and his cheeks were pale. But now his face was alight with interest and eagerness. Again the fascination of Rupert's audacity and the infection of his courage caught on his kinsman's weaker nature, and inspired him to a temporary emulation of the will that dominated him.

"You see," pursued Rupert, "it's not likely that they'll do you any harm."

"I'll risk anything."

"Most gallant gentleman! At the worst they'll only keep you a prisoner. Well, if you're not back in a couple of hours, I shall draw my conclusions. I shall know that there's a king in Strelsau."

"But where shall I look for the king?"

"Why, first in the palace, and secondly at Fritz von Tarlenheim's. I expect you'll find him at Fritz's, though."

"Shall I go there first, then?"

"No. That would be seeming to know too much."

"You'll wait here?"

"Certainly, cousin—unless I see cause to move, you know."

"And I shall find you on my return?"

"Me, or directions from me. By the way, bring money too. There's never any harm in having a full pocket. I wonder what the devil does without a breeches-pocket?"

Rischenheim let that curious speculation alone, although he remembered the whimsical air with which Rupert delivered it. He was now on fire to be gone, his ill-balanced brain leaping from the depths of despondency to the certainty of brilliant success, and not heeding the gulf of danger that it surpassed in buoyant fancy.

"We shall have them in a corner, Rupert," he cried.

"Ay, perhaps. But wild beasts in a corner bite hard."

"I wish my arm were well!"

"You'll be safer with it wounded," said Rupert with a smile.

"By God, Rupert, I can defend myself."

"True, true; but it's your brain I want now, cousin."

"You shall see that I have something in me."

"If it please God, dear cousin."

With every mocking encouragement and every careless taunt Rischenheim's resolve to prove himself a man grew stronger. He snatched up a revolver that lay on the mantelpiece and put it in his pocket.

"Don't fire, if you can help it," advised Rupert. Rischenheim's answer was to make for the door at a great speed. Rupert watched him go, and then returned to the window. The last his cousin saw was his figure standing straight and lithe against the light, while he looked out on the city. Still there was no stir in the streets, still the royal standard floated at the top of the flag staffs.

Rischenheim plunged down the stairs: his feet were too slow for his eagerness. At the bottom he found the girl Rosa sweeping the passage with great apparent diligence.

"You're going out, my lord?" she asked.

"Why, yes; I have business. Pray stand on one side, this passage is so cursedly narrow."

Rosa showed no haste in moving.

"And the Count Rupert, is he going out also?" she asked.

"You see he's not with me. He'll wait." Rischenheim broke off and asked angrily: "What business is it of yours, girl? Get out of the way!"

She moved aside now, making him no answer. He rushed past; she looked after him with a smile of triumph. Then she fell again to her sweeping. The king had bidden her be ready at eleven. It was half-past ten. Soon the king would have need of her.

CHAPTER XIV. THE NEWS COMES TO STRELSAU

ON leaving No. 19, Rischenheim walked swiftly some little way up the Konigstrasse and then hailed a cab. He had hardly raised his hand when he heard his name called, and, looking round, saw Anton von Strofzin's smart phaeton pulling up beside him. Anton was driving, and on the other seat was a large nosegay of choice flowers.

"Where are you off to?" cried Anton, leaning forward with a gay smile.

"Well, where are you? To a lady's, I presume, from your bouquet there," answered Rischenheim as lightly as he could.

"The little bunch of flowers," simpered young Anton, "is a cousinly offering to Helga von Tarlenheim, and I'm going to present it. Can I give you a lift anywhere?"'

Although Rischenheim had intended to go first to the palace, Anton's offer seemed to give him a good excuse for drawing the more likely covert first.

"I was going to the palace to find out where the king is. I want to see him, if he'll give me a minute or two," he remarked.

"I'll drive you there afterwards. Jump up. That your cab? Here you are, cabman," and flinging the cabman a crown, he displaced the bouquet and made room for Rischenheim beside him. Anton's horses, of which he was not a little proud, made short work of the distance to my home. The phaeton rattled up to the door and both young men got out. The moment of their arrival found the chancellor just leaving to return to his own home. Helsing knew them both, and stopped to rally Anton on the matter of his bouquet. Anton was famous for his bouquets, which he distributed widely among the ladies of Strelsau.

"I hoped it was for my daughter," said the chancellor slyly. "For I love flowers, and my wife has ceased to provide me with them; moreover, I've ceased to provide her with them, so, but for my daughter, we should have none."

Anton answered his chaff, promising a bouquet for the young lady the next day, but declaring that he could not disappoint his cousin. He was interrupted by Rischenheim, who, looking round on the group of bystanders, now grown numerous, exclaimed: "What's going on here, my dear chancellor? What are all these people hanging about here for? Ah, that's a royal carriage!"

"The queen's with the countess," answered Helsing. "The people are waiting to see her come out."

"She's always worth seeing," Anton pronounced, sticking his glass in his eye.

"And you've been to visit her?" pursued Rischenheim.

"Why, yes. I—I went to pay my respects, my dear Rischenheim."

"An early visit!"

"It was more or less on business."

"Ah, I have business also, and very important business. But it's with the king."

"I won't keep you a moment, Rischenheim," called Anton, as, bouquet in hand, he knocked at the door.

"With the king?" said Helsing. "Ah, yes, but the king—"

"I'm on my way to the palace to find out where he is. If I can't see him, I must write at once. My business is very urgent."

"Indeed, my dear count, indeed! Dear me! Urgent, you say?"

"But perhaps you can help me. Is he at Zenda?"

The chancellor was becoming very embarrassed; Anton had disappeared into the house; Rischenheim buttonholed him resolutely.

"At Zenda? Well, now, I don't—Excuse me, but what's your business?"

"Excuse me, my dear chancellor; it's a secret."

"I have the king's confidence."

"Then you'll be indifferent to not enjoying mine," smiled Rischenheim.

"I perceive that your arm is hurt," observed the chancellor, seeking a diversion.

"Between ourselves, that has something to do with my business. Well, I must go to the palace. Or—stay—would her Majesty condescend to help me? I think I'll risk a request. She can but refuse," and so saying Rischenheim approached the door.

"Oh, my friend, I wouldn't do that," cried Helsing, darting after him. "The queen is—well, very much engaged. She won't like to be troubled."

Rischenheim took no notice of him, but knocked loudly. The door was opened, and he told the butler to carry his name to the queen and beg a moment's speech with her. Helsing stood in perplexity on the step. The crowd was delighted with the coming of these great folk and showed no sign of dispersing. Anton von Strofzin did not reappear. Rischenheim edged himself inside the doorway and stood on the threshold of the hall. There he heard voices proceeding from the sitting-room on the left. He recognized the queen's, my wife's, and Anton's. Then came the butler's, saying, "I will inform the count of your Majesty's wishes."

The door of the room opened; the butler appeared, and immediately behind him Anton von Strofzin and Bernenstein. Bernenstein had the young fellow by the arm, and hurried him through the hall. They passed the butler, who made way for them, and came to where Rischenheim stood.

"We meet again," said Rischenheim with a bow.

The chancellor rubbed his hands in nervous perturbation. The butler stepped up and delivered his message: the queen regretted her inability to receive the count. Rischenheim nodded, and, standing so that the door could not be shut, asked Bernenstein whether he knew where the king was.

Now Bernenstein was most anxious to get the pair of them away and the door shut, but he dared show no eagerness.

"Do you want another interview with the king already?" he asked with a smile. "The last was so pleasant, then?"

Rischenheim took no notice of the taunt, but observed sarcastically: "There's a strange difficulty in finding our good king. The chancellor here doesn't know where he is, or at least he won't answer my questions."

"Possibly the king has his reasons for not wishing to be disturbed," suggested Bernenstein.

"It's very possible," retorted Rischenheim significantly.

"Meanwhile, my dear count, I shall take it as a personal favor if you'll move out of the doorway."

"Do I incommode you by standing here?" answered the count.

"Infinitely, my lord," answered Bernenstein stiffly.

"Hallo, Bernenstein, what's the matter?" cried Anton, seeing that their tones and glances had grown angry. The crowd also had noticed the raised voices and hostile manner of the disputants, and began to gather round in a more compact group.

Suddenly a voice came from inside the hall: it was distinct and loud, yet not without a touch of huskiness. The sound of it hushed the rising quarrel and silenced the crowd into expectant stillness. Bernenstein looked aghast, Rischenheim nervous yet triumphant, Anton amused and gratified.

"The king!" he cried, and burst into a laugh. "You've drawn him, Rischenheim!"

The crowd heard his boyish exclamation and raised a cheer. Helsing turned, as though to rebuke them. Had not the king himself desired secrecy? Yes, but he who spoke as the king chose any risk sooner than let Rischenheim go back and warn Rupert of his presence.

"Is that the Count of Luzau-Rischenheim?" called Rudolf from within. "If so, let him enter and then shut the door."

There was something in his tone that alarmed Rischenheim. He started back on the step. But Bernenstein caught him by the arm.

"Since you wish to come in, come in," he said with a grim smile.

Rischenheim looked round, as though he meditated flight. The next moment Bernenstein was thrust aside. For one short instant a tall figure appeared in the doorway; the crowd had

155

but a glimpse, yet they cheered again. Rischenheim's hand was clasped in a firm grip; he passed unwillingly but helplessly through the door. Bernenstein followed; the door was shut. Anton faced round on Helsing, a scornful twist on his lips.

"There was a deuced lot of mystery about nothing," said he. "Why couldn't you say he was there?" And without waiting for an answer from the outraged and bewildered chancellor he swung down the steps and climbed into his phaeton.

The people round were chatting noisily, delighted to have caught a glimpse of the king, speculating what brought him and the queen to my house, and hoping that they would soon come out and get into the royal carriage that still stood waiting.

Had they been able to see inside the door, their emotion would have been stirred to a keener pitch. Rudolf himself caught Rischenheim by the arm, and without a moment's delay led him towards the back of the house. They went along a passage and reached a small room that looked out on the garden. Rudolf had known my house in old days, and did not forget its resources.

"Shut the door, Bernenstein," said Rudolf. Then he turned to Rischenheim. "My lord," he said, "I suppose you came to find out something. Do you know it now?"

Rischenheim plucked up courage to answer him.

"Yes, I know now that I have to deal with an impostor," said he defiantly.

"Precisely. And impostors can't afford to be exposed." Rischenheim's cheek turned rather pale. Rudolf faced him, and Bernenstein guarded the door. He was absolutely at their mercy; and he knew their secret. Did they know his—the news that Rupert of Hentzau had brought?

"Listen," said Rudolf. "For a few hours to-day I am king in Strelsau. In those few hours I have an account to settle with your cousin: something that he has, I must have. I'm going now to seek him, and while I seek him you will stay here with Bernenstein. Perhaps I shall fail, perhaps I shall succeed. Whether I succeed or fail, by to-night I shall be far from Strelsau, and the king's place will be free for him again."

Rischenheim gave a slight start, and a look of triumph spread over his face. They did not know that the king was dead.

Rudolf came nearer to him, fixing his eyes steadily on his prisoner's face.

"I don't know," he continued, "why you are in this business, my lord. Your cousin's motives I know well. But I wonder that they seemed to you great enough to justify the ruin of an unhappy lady who is your queen. Be assured that I will die sooner than let that letter reach the king's hand."

Rischenheim made him no answer.

"Are you armed?" asked Rudolf.

Rischenheim sullenly flung his revolver on the table. Bernenstein came forward and took it.

"Keep him here, Bernenstein. When I return I'll tell you what more to do. If I don't return, Fritz will be here soon, and you and he must make your own plans."

"He sha'n't give me the slip a second time," said Bernenstein.

"We hold ourselves free," said Rudolf to Rischenheim, "to do what we please with you, my lord. But I have no wish to cause your death, unless it be necessary. You will be wise to wait till your cousin's fate is decided before you attempt any further steps against us." And with a slight bow he left the prisoner in Bernenstein's charge, and went back to the room where the queen awaited him. Helga was with her. The queen sprang up to meet him.

"I mustn't lose a moment," he said. "All that crowd of people know now that the king is here. The news will filter through the town in no time. We must send word to Sapt to keep it from the king's ears at all costs: I must go and do my work, and then disappear."

The queen stood facing him. Her eyes seemed to devour his face; but she said only: "Yes, it must be so."

"You must return to the palace as soon as I am gone. I shall send out and ask the people to disperse, and then I must be off."

"To seek Rupert of Hentzau?"

"Yes."

She struggled for a moment with the contending feelings that filled her heart. Then she came to him and seized hold of his hand.

"Don't go," she said in low trembling tones. "Don't go, Rudolf. He'll kill you. Never mind the letter. Don't go: I had rather a thousand times that the king had it than that you should.... Oh, my dear, don't go!"

"I must go," he said softly.

Again she began to implore him, but he would not yield. Helga moved towards the door, but Rudolf stopped her.

"No," he said; "you must stay with her; you must go to the palace with her."

Even as he spoke they heard the wheels of a carriage driven quickly to the door. By now I had met Anton von Strofzin and heard from him that the king was at my house. As I dashed up the news was confirmed by the comments and jokes of the crowd.

"Ah, he's in a hurry," they said. "He's kept the king waiting. He'll get a wigging."

As may be supposed, I paid little heed to them. I sprang out and ran up the steps to the door. I saw my wife's face at the window: she herself ran to the door and opened it for me.

"Good God," I whispered, "do all these people know he's here, and take him for the king?"

"Yes," she said. "We couldn't help it. He showed himself at the door."

It was worse than I dreamt: not two or three people, but all that crowd were victims of the mistake; all of them had heard that the king was in Strelsau—ay, and had seen him.

"Where is he? Where is he?" I asked, and followed her hastily to the room.

The queen and Rudolf were standing side by side. What I have told from Helga's description had just passed between them. Rudolf ran to meet me.

"Is all well?" he asked eagerly.

I forgot the queen's presence and paid no sign of respect to her. I caught Rudolf by the arm and cried to him: "Do they take you for the king?"

"Yes," he said. "Heavens, man, don't look so white! We shall manage it. I can be gone by to-night."

"Gone? How will that help, since they believe you to be the king?"

"You can keep it from the king," he urged. "I couldn't help it. I can settle with Rupert and disappear."

The three were standing round me, surprised at my great and terrible agitation. Looking back now, I wonder that I could speak to them at all.

Rudolf tried again to reassure me. He little knew the cause of what he saw.

"It won't take long to settle affairs with Rupert," said he. "And we must have the letter, or it will get to the king after all."

"The king will never see the letter," I blurted out, as I sank back in a chair.

They said nothing. I looked round on their faces. I had a strange feeling of helplessness, and seemed to be able to do nothing but throw the truth at them in blunt plainness. Let them make what they could of it, I could make nothing.

"The king will never see the letter," I repeated. "Rupert himself has insured that."

"What do you mean? You've not met Rupert? You've not got the letter?"

"No, no; but the king can never read it."

Then Rudolf seized me by the shoulder and fairly shook me; indeed I must have seemed like a man in a dream or a torpor.

"Why not, man; why not?" he asked in urgent low tones. Again I looked at them, but somehow this time my eyes were attracted and held by the queen's face. I believe that she was the first to catch a hint of the tidings I brought. Her lips were parted, and her gaze eagerly strained upon me. I rubbed my hand across my forehead, and, looking up stupidly at her, I said:

"He never can see the letter. He's dead."

There was a little scream from Helga; Rudolf neither spoke nor moved; the queen continued to gaze at me in motionless wonder and horror.

"Rupert killed him," said I. "The boar-hound attacked Rupert; then Herbert and the king attacked him; and he killed them all. Yes, the king is dead. He's dead."

Now none spoke. The queen's eyes never left my face. "Yes, he's dead." said I; and I watched her eyes still. For a long while (or long it seemed) they were on my face; at last, as though drawn by some irresistible force, they turned away. I followed the new line they took. She looked at Rudolf Rassendyll, and he at her. Helga had taken out her handkerchief, and, utterly upset by the horror and shock, was lying back in a low chair, sobbing half-hysterically; I saw the swift look that passed from the queen to her lover, carrying in it grief, remorse, and most unwilling joy. He did not speak to her, but put out his hand and took hers. She drew it away almost sharply, and covered her face with both hands.

Rudolf turned to me. "When was it?"

"Last night."

"And the.... He's at the lodge?"

"Yes, with Sapt and James."

I was recovering my senses and my coolness.

"Nobody knows yet," I said. "We were afraid you might be taken for him by somebody. But, my God, Rudolf, what's to be done now?"

Mr. Rassendyll's lips were set firm and tight. He frowned slightly, and his blue eyes wore a curious entranced expression. He seemed to me to be forgetful of everything, even of us who were with him, in some one idea that possessed him. The queen herself came nearer to him and lightly touched his arm with her hand. He started as though surprised, then fell again into his reverie.

"What's to be done, Rudolf?" I asked again.

"I'm going to kill Rupert of Hentzau," he said. "The rest we'll talk of afterwards."

He walked rapidly across the room and rang the bell. "Clear those people away," he ordered. "Tell them that I want to be quiet. Then send a closed carriage round for me. Don't be more than ten minutes."

The servant received his peremptory orders with a low bow, and left us. The queen, who had been all this time outwardly calm and composed, now fell into a great agitation, which even the consciousness of our presence could not enable her to hide.

"Rudolf, must you go? Since—since this has happened—"

"Hush, my dearest lady," he whispered. Then he went on more loudly, "I won't quit Ruritania a second time leaving Rupert of Hentzau alive. Fritz, send word to Sapt that the king is in Strelsau—he will understand—and that instructions from the king will follow by midday. When I have killed Rupert, I shall visit the lodge on my way to the frontier."

He turned to go, but the queen, following, detained him for a minute.

"You'll come and see me before you go?" she pleaded.

"But I ought not," said he, his resolute eyes suddenly softening in a marvelous fashion.

"You will?"

"Yes, my queen."

Then I sprang up, for a sudden dread laid hold on me.

"Heavens, man," I cried, "what if he kills you—there in the Konigstrasse?"

Rudolf turned to me; there was a look of surprise on his face. "He won't kill me," he answered.

The queen, looking still in Rudolf's face, and forgetful now, as it seemed, of the dream that had so terrified her, took no notice of what I said, but urged again: "You'll come, Rudolf?"

"Yes, once, my queen," and with a last kiss of her hand he was gone.

The queen stood for yet another moment where she was, still and almost rigid. Then suddenly she walked or stumbled to where my wife sat, and, flinging herself on her knees, hid her face in Helga's lap; I heard her sobs break out fast and tumultuously. Helga looked up at me, the tears streaming down her cheeks. I turned and went out. Perhaps Helga could comfort her; I prayed that God in His pity might send her comfort, although she for her sin's sake dared not ask it of Him. Poor soul! I hope there may be nothing worse scored to my account.

CHAPTER XV. A PASTIME FOR COLONEL SAPT

THE Constable of Zenda and James, Mr. Rassendyll's servant, sat at breakfast in the hunting-lodge. They were in the small room which was ordinarily used as the bedroom of the gentleman in attendance on the king: they chose it now because it commanded a view of the approach. The door of the house was securely fastened; they were prepared to refuse admission; in case refusal was impossible, the preparations for concealing the king's body and that of his huntsman Herbert were complete. Inquirers would be told that the king had ridden out with his huntsman at daybreak, promising to return in the evening but not stating where he was going; Sapt was under orders to await his return, and James was expecting instructions from his master the Count of Tarlenheim. Thus armed against discovery, they looked for news from me which should determine their future action.

Meanwhile there was an interval of enforced idleness. Sapt, his meal finished, puffed away at his great pipe; James, after much pressure, had consented to light a small black clay, and sat at his ease with his legs stretched before him. His brows were knit, and a curious half-smile played about his mouth.

"What may you be thinking about, friend James?" asked the constable between two puffs. He had taken a fancy to the alert, ready little fellow.

James smoked for a moment, and then took his pipe from his mouth.

"I was thinking, sir, that since the king is dead—"

He paused.

"The king is no doubt dead, poor fellow," said Sapt, nodding.

"That since he's certainly dead, and since my master, Mr. Rassendyll, is alive—"

"So far as we know, James," Sapt reminded him.

"Why, yes, sir, so far as we know. Since, then, Mr. Rassendyll is alive and the king is dead, I was thinking that it was a great pity, sir, that my master can't take his place and be king." James looked across at the constable with an air of a man who offers a respectful suggestion.

"A remarkable thought, James," observed the constable with a grin.

"You don't agree with me, sir?" asked James deprecatingly.

"I don't say that it isn't a pity, for Rudolf makes a good king. But you see it's impossible, isn't it?"

James nursed his knee between his hands, and his pipe, which he had replaced, stuck out of one corner of his mouth.

"When you say impossible, sir," he remarked deferentially, "I venture to differ from you."

"You do? Come, we're at leisure. Let's hear how it would be possible."

"My master is in Strelsau, sir," began James.

"Well, most likely."

"I'm sure of it, sir. If he's been there, he will be taken for the king."

"That has happened before, and no doubt may happen again, unless—"

"Why, of course, sir, unless the king's body should be discovered."

"That's what I was about to say, James."

James kept silence for a few minutes. Then he observed, "It will be very awkward to explain how the king was killed."

"The story will need good telling," admitted Sapt.

"And it will be difficult to make it appear that the king was killed in Strelsau; yet if my master should chance to be killed in Strelsau—"

"Heaven forbid, James! On all grounds, Heaven forbid!"

"Even if my master is not killed, it will be difficult for us to get the king killed at the right time, and by means that will seem plausible."

Sapt seemed to fall into the humor of the speculation. "That's all very true. But if Mr. Rassendyll is to be king, it will be both awkward and difficult to dispose of the king's body and of this poor fellow Herbert," said he, sucking at his pipe.

Again James paused for a little while before he remarked: "I am, of course, sir, only discussing the matter by way of passing the time. It would probably be wrong to carry any such plan into effect."

"It might be, but let us discuss it—to pass the time," said Sapt; and he leant forward, looking into the servant's quiet, shrewd face.

"Well, then, sir, since it amuses you, let us say that the king came to the lodge last night, and was joined there by his friend Mr. Rassendyll."

"And did I come too?"

"You, sir, came also, in attendance on the king."

"Well, and you, James? You came. How came you?"

"Why, sir, by the Count of Tarlenheim's orders, to wait on Mr. Rassendyll, the king's friend. Now, the king, sir... This is my story, you know, sir, only my story."

"Your story interests me. Go on with it."

"The king went out very early this morning, sir."

"That would be on private business?"

"So we should have understood. But Mr. Rassendyll, Herbert, and ourselves remained here."

"Had the Count of Hentzau been?"

"Not to our knowledge, sir. But we were all tired and slept very soundly."

"Now did we?" said the constable, with a grim smile.

"In fact, sir, we were all overcome with fatigue—Mr. Rassendyll like the rest—and full morning found us still in our beds. There we should be to this moment, sir, had we not been suddenly aroused in a startling and fearful manner."

"You should write story books, James. Now what was this fearful manner in which we were aroused?"

James laid down his pipe, and, resting his hands on his knees, continued his story.

"This lodge, sir, this wooden lodge—for the lodge is all of wood, sir, without and within."

"This lodge is undoubtedly of wood, James, and, as you say, both inside and out."

"And since it is, sir, it would be mighty careless to leave a candle burning where the oil and firewood are stored."

"Most criminal!"

"But hard words don't hurt dead men; and you see, sir, poor Herbert is dead."

"It is true. He wouldn't feel aggrieved."

"But we, sir, you and I, awaking—"

"Aren't the others to awake, James?"

"Indeed, sir, I should pray that they had never awaked. For you and I, waking first, would find the lodge a mass of flames. We should have to run for our lives."

"What! Should we make no effort to rouse the others?"

"Indeed, sir, we should do all that men could do; we should even risk death by suffocation."

"But we should fail, in spite of our heroism, should we?"

"Alas, sir, in spite of all our efforts we should fail. The flames would envelop the lodge in one blaze; before help could come, the lodge would be in ruins, and my unhappy master and poor Herbert would be consumed to ashes."

"Hum!"

"They would, at least, sir, be entirely unrecognizable."

"You think so?"

"Beyond doubt, if the oil and the firewood and the candle were placed to the best advantage."

"Ah, yes. And there would be an end of Rudolf Rassendyll?"

"Sir, I should myself carry the tidings to his family."

"Whereas the King of Ruritania—"

"Would enjoy a long and prosperous reign, God willing, sir."

"And the Queen of Ruritania, James?"

"Do not misunderstand me, sir. They could be secretly married. I should say re-married."

"Yes, certainly, re-married."

"By a trustworthy priest."

"You mean by an untrustworthy priest?"

"It's the same thing, sir, from a different point of view." For the first time James smiled a thoughtful smile.

Sapt in his turn laid down his pipe now, and was tugging at his moustache. There was a smile on his lips too, and his eyes looked hard into James's. The little man met his glance composedly.

"It's an ingenious fancy, this of yours, James," the constable remarked. "What, though, if your master's killed too? That's quite possible. Count Rupert's a man to be reckoned with."

"If my master is killed, sir, he must be buried," answered James.

"In Strelsau?" came in quick question from Sapt.

"He won't mind where, sir."

"True, he won't mind, and we needn't mind for him."

"Why, no, sir. But to carry a body secretly from here to Strelsau—"

"Yes, that is, as we agreed at the first, difficult. Well, it's a pretty story, but—your master wouldn't approve of it. Supposing he were not killed, I mean."

"It's a waste of time, sir, disapproving of what's done: he might think the story better than the truth, although it's not a good story."

The two men's eyes met again in a long glance.

"Where do you come from?" asked Sapt, suddenly.

"London, sir, originally."

"They make good stories there?"

"Yes, sir, and act them sometimes."

The instant he had spoken, James sprang to his feet and pointed out of the window.

A man on horseback was cantering towards the lodge. Exchanging one quick look, both hastened to the door, and, advancing some twenty yards, waited under the tree on the spot where Boris lay buried.

"By the way," said Sapt, "you forgot the dog." And he pointed to the ground.

"The affectionate beast will be in his master's room and die there, sir."

"Eh, but he must rise again first!"

"Certainly, sir. That won't be a long matter."

Sapt was still smiling in grim amusement when the messenger came up and, leaning from his home, handed him a telegram.

"Special and urgent, sir," said he.

Sapt tore it open and read. It was the message that I sent in obedience to Mr. Rassendyll's orders. He would not trust my cipher, but, indeed, none was necessary. Sapt would understand the message, although it said simply, "The king is in Strelsau. Wait orders at the lodge. Business here in progress, but not finished. Will wire again."

Sapt handed it to James, who took it with a respectful little bow. James read it with attention, and returned it with another bow.

"I'll attend to what it says, sir," he remarked.

"Yes," said Sapt. "Thanks, my man," he added to the messenger. "Here's a crown for you. If any other message comes for me and you bring it in good time, you shall have another."

"You shall have it quick as a horse can bring it from the station, sir."

"The king's business won't bear delay, you know," nodded Sapt.

"You sha'n't have to wait, sir," and, with a parting salute, the fellow turned his horse and trotted away.

"You see," remarked Sapt, "that your story is quite imaginary. For that fellow can see for himself that the lodge was not burnt down last night."

"That's true; but, excuse me, sir—"

"Pray go on, James. I've told you that I'm interested."

"He can't see that it won't be burnt down to-night. A fire, sir, is a thing that may happen any night."

Then old Sapt suddenly burst into a roar, half-speech, half laughter.

"By God, what a thing!" he roared; and James smiled complacently.

"There's a fate about it," said the constable. "There's a strange fate about it. The man was born to it. We'd have done it before if Michael had throttled the king in that cellar, as I thought he would. Yes, by heavens, we'd have done it! Why, we wanted it! God forgive us, in our hearts both Fritz and I wanted it. But Rudolf would have the king out. He would have him out, though he lost a throne—and what he wanted more—by it. But he would have him out. So he thwarted the fate. But it's not to be thwarted. Young Rupert may think this new affair is his doing. No, it's the fate using him. The fate brought Rudolf here again, the fate will have him king. Well, you stare at me. Do you think I'm mad, Mr. Valet?"

"I think, sir, that you talk very good sense, if I may say so," answered James.

"Sense?" echoed Sapt with a chuckle. "I don't know about that. But the fate's there, depend on it!"

The two were back in their little room now, past the door that hid the bodies of the king and his huntsman. James stood by the table, old Sapt roamed up and down, tugging his moustache, and now and again sawing the air with his sturdy hairy hand.

"I daren't do it," he muttered: "I daren't do it. It's a thing a man can't set his hand to of his own will. But the fate'll do it—the fate'll do it. The fate'll force it on us."

"Then we'd best be ready, sir," suggested James quietly. Sapt turned on him quickly, almost fiercely.

"They used to call me a cool hand," said he. "By Jove, what are you?"

"There's no harm in being ready, sir," said James, the servant.

Sapt came to him and caught hold of his shoulders. "Ready?" he asked in a gruff whisper.

"The oil, the firewood, the light," said James.

"Where, man, where? Do you mean, by the bodies?"

"Not where the bodies are now. Each must be in the proper place."

"We must move them then?"

"Why, yes. And the dog too."

Sapt almost glared at him; then he burst into a laugh.

"So be it," he said. "You take command. Yes, we'll be ready. The fate drives."

Then and there they set about what they had to do. It seemed indeed as though some strange influence were dominating Sapt; he went about the work like a man who is hardly awake. They placed the bodies each where the living man would be by night—the king in the guest-room, the huntsman in the sort of cupboard where the honest fellow had been wont to lie. They dug up the buried dog, Sapt chuckling convulsively, James grave as the mute whose grim doings he seemed to travesty: they carried the shot-pierced, earth-grimed thing in, and laid it in the king's room. Then they made their piles of wood, pouring the store of oil over them, and setting bottles of spirit near, that the flames having cracked the bottles, might gain fresh fuel. To Sapt it seemed now as if they played some foolish game that was to end with the playing, now as if they obeyed some mysterious power which kept its great purpose hidden from its instruments. Mr. Rassendyll's servant moved and arranged and ordered all as

162

deftly as he folded his master's clothes or stropped his master's razor. Old Sapt stopped him once as he went by.

"Don't think me a mad fool, because I talk of the fate," he said, almost anxiously.

"Not I, sir," answered James, "I know nothing of that. But I like to be ready."

"It would be a thing!" muttered Sapt.

The mockery, real or assumed, in which they had begun their work, had vanished now. If they were not serious, they played at seriousness. If they entertained no intention such as their acts seemed to indicate, they could no longer deny that they had cherished a hope. They shrank, or at least Sapt shrank, from setting such a ball rolling; but they longed for the fate that would give it a kick, and they made smooth the incline down which it, when thus impelled, was to run. When they had finished their task and sat down again opposite to one another in the little front room, the whole scheme was ready, the preparations were made, all was in train; they waited only for that impulse from chance or fate which was to turn the servant's story into reality and action. And when the thing was done, Sapt's coolness, so rarely upset, yet so completely beaten by the force of that wild idea, came back to him. He lit his pipe again and lay back in his chair, puffing freely, with a meditative look on his face.

"It's two o'clock, sir," said James. "Something should have happened before now in Strelsau."

"Ah, but what?" asked the constable.

Suddenly breaking on their ears came a loud knock at the door. Absorbed in their own thoughts, they had not noticed two men riding up to the lodge. The visitors wore the green and gold of the king's huntsmen; the one who had knocked was Simon, the chief huntsman, and brother of Herbert, who lay dead in the little room inside.

"Rather dangerous!" muttered the Constable of Zenda as he hurried to the door, James following him.

Simon was astonished when Sapt opened the door.

"Beg pardon, Constable, but I want to see Herbert. Can I go in?" And he jumped down from his horse, throwing the reins to his companion.

"What's the good of your going in?" asked Sapt. "Herbert's not here."

"Not here? Then where is he?"

"Why, he went with the king this morning."

"Oh, he went with the king, sir? Then he's in Strelsau, I suppose?"

"If you know that, Simon, you're wiser than I am."

"But the king is in Strelsau, sir."

"The deuce he is! He said nothing of going to Strelsau. He rose early and rode off with Herbert, merely saying they would be back to-night."

"He went to Strelsau, sir. I am just from Zenda, and his Majesty is known to have been in town with the queen. They were both at Count Fritz's."

"I'm much interested to hear it. But didn't the telegram say where Herbert was?"

Simon laughed.

"Herbert's not a king, you see," he said. "Well, I'll come again to-morrow morning, for I must see him soon. He'll be back by then, sir?"

"Yes, Simon, your brother will be here to-morrow morning."

"Or what's left of him after such a two-days of work," suggested Simon jocularly.

"Why, yes, precisely," said Sapt, biting his moustache and darting one swift glance at James. "Or what's left of him, as you say."

"And I'll bring a cart and carry the boar down to the castle at the same time, sir. At least, I suppose you haven't eaten it all?"

Sapt laughed; Simon was gratified at the tribute, and laughed even more heartily himself.

"We haven't even cooked it yet," said Sapt, "but I won't answer for it that we sha'n't have by to-morrow."

"All right, sir; I'll be here. By the way, there's another bit of news come on the wires. They say Count Rupert of Hentzau has been seen in the city."

"Rupert of Hentzau? Oh, pooh! Nonsense, my good Simon. He daren't show his face there for his life."

"Ah, but it may be no nonsense. Perhaps that's what took the king to Strelsau."

"It's enough to take him if it's true," admitted Sapt.

"Well, good day, sir."

"Good day, Simon."

The two huntsmen rode off. James watched them for a little while.

"The king," he said then, "is known to be in Strelsau; and now Count Rupert is known to be in Strelsau. How is Count Rupert to have killed the king here in the forest of Zenda, sir?" Sapt looked at him almost apprehensively.

"How is the king's body to come to the forest of Zenda?" asked James. "Or how is the king's body to go to the city of Strelsau?"

"Stop your damned riddles!" roared Sapt. "Man, are you bent on driving me into it?"

The servant came near to him, and laid a hand on his shoulder.

"You went into as great a thing once before, sir," said he.

"It was to save the king."

"And this is to save the queen and yourself. For if we don't do it, the truth about my master must be known."

Sapt made him no answer. They sat down again in silence.

There they sat, sometimes smoking, never speaking, while the tedious afternoon wore away, and the shadows from the trees of the forest lengthened. They did not think of eating or drinking; they did not move, save when James rose and lit a little fire of brushwood in the grate. It grew dusk and again James moved to light the lamp. It was hard on six o'clock, and still no news came from Strelsau.

Then there was the sound of a horse's hoofs. The two rushed to the door, beyond it, and far along the grassy road that gave approach to the hunting-lodge. They forgot to guard the secret and the door gaped open behind them. Sapt ran as he had not run for many a day, and outstripped his companion. There was a message from Strelsau!

The constable, without a word of greeting, snatched the envelope from the hand of the messenger and tore it open. He read it hastily, muttering under his breath "Good God!" Then he turned suddenly round and began to walk quickly back to James, who, seeing himself beaten in the race, had dropped to a walk. But the messenger had his cares as well as the constable. If the constable's thoughts were on a crown, so were his. He called out in indignant protest:

"I have never drawn rein since Hofbau, sir. Am I not to have my crown?"

Sapt stopped, turned, and retraced his steps. He took a crown from his pocket. As he looked up in giving it, there was a queer smile on his broad, weather-beaten face.

"Ay," he said, "every man that deserves a crown shall have one, if I can give it him."

Then he turned again to James, who had now come up, and laid his hand on his shoulder.

"Come along, my king-maker," said he.

James looked in his face for a moment. The constable's eyes met his; and the constable nodded.

So they turned to the lodge where the dead king and his huntsman lay. Verily the fate drove.

CHAPTER XVI. A CROWD IN THE KONIGSTRASSE

The project that had taken shape in the thoughts of Mr. Rassendyll's servant, and had inflamed Sapt's daring mind as the dropping of a spark kindles dry shavings, had suggested itself vaguely to more than one of us in Strelsau. We did not indeed coolly face and plan it, as the little servant had, nor seize on it at once with an eagerness to be convinced of its necessity, like the Constable of Zenda; but it was there in my mind, sometimes figuring as a dread, sometimes as a hope, now seeming the one thing to be avoided, again the only resource against a more disastrous issue. I knew that it was in Bernenstein's thoughts no less than in my own; for neither of us had been able to form any reasonable scheme by which the living king, whom half Strelsau now knew to be in the city, could be spirited away, and the dead king set in his place. The change could take place, as it seemed, only in one way and at one cost: the truth, or the better part of it, must be told, and every tongue set wagging with gossip and guesses concerning Rudolf Rassendyll and his relations with the queen. Who that knows what men and women are would not have shrunk from that alternative? To adopt it was to expose the queen to all or nearly all the peril she had run by the loss of the letter. We indeed assumed, influenced by Rudolf's unhesitating self-confidence, that the letter would be won back, and the mouth of Rupert of Hentzau shut; but enough would remain to furnish material for eager talk and for conjectures unrestrained by respect or charity. Therefore, alive as we were to its difficulties and its unending risks, we yet conceived of the thing as possible, had it in our hearts, and hinted it to one another—my wife to me, I to Bernenstein, and he to me—in quick glances and half uttered sentences that declared its presence while shunning the open confession of it. For the queen herself I cannot speak. Her thoughts, as I judged them, were bounded by the longing to see Mr. Rassendyll again, and dwelt on the visit that he promised as the horizon of hope. To Rudolf we had dared to disclose nothing of the part our imaginations set him to play: if he were to accept it, the acceptance would be of his own act, because the fate that old Sapt talked of drove him, and on no persuasion of ours. As he had said, he left the rest, and had centered all his efforts on the immediate task which fell to his hand to perform, the task that was to be accomplished at the dingy old house in the Konigstrasse. We were indeed awake to the fact that even Rupert's death would not make the secret safe. Rischenheim, although for the moment a prisoner and helpless, was alive and could not be mewed up for ever; Bauer was we knew not where, free to act and free to talk. Yet in our hearts we feared none but Rupert, and the doubt was not whether we could do the thing so much as whether we should. For in moments of excitement and intense feeling a man makes light of obstacles which look large enough as he turns reflective eyes on them in the quiet of after-days.

A message in the king's name had persuaded the best part of the idle crowd to disperse reluctantly. Rudolf himself had entered one of my carriages and driven off. He started not towards the Konigstrasse, but in the opposite direction: I supposed that he meant to approach his destination by a circuitous way, hoping to gain it without attracting notice. The queen's carriage was still before my door, for it had been arranged that she was to proceed to the palace and there await tidings. My wife and I were to accompany her; and I went to her now, where she sat alone, and asked if it were her pleasure to start at once. I found her thoughtful but calm. She listened to me; then, rising, she said, "Yes, I will go." But then she asked suddenly, "Where is the Count of Luzau-Rischenheim?"

I told her how Bernenstein kept guard over the count in the room at the back of the house. She seemed to consider for a moment, then she said:

"I will see him. Go and bring him to me. You must be here while I talk to him, but nobody else."

I did not know what she intended, but I saw no reason to oppose her wishes, and I was glad to find for her any means of employing this time of suspense. I obeyed her commands and brought Rischenheim to her. He followed me slowly and reluctantly; his unstable mind had again jumped from rashness to despondency: he was pale and uneasy, and, when he found himself in her presence, the bravado of his bearing, maintained before Bernenstein, gave place to a shamefaced sullenness. He could not meet the grave eyes that she fixed on him.

I withdrew to the farther end of the room; but it was small, and I heard all that passed. I had my revolver ready to cover Rischenheim in case he should be moved to make a dash for liberty. But he was past that: Rupert's presence was a tonic that nerved him to effort and to confidence, but the force of the last dose was gone and the man was sunk again to his natural irresolution.

"My lord," she began gently, motioning him to sit, "I have desired to speak with you, because I do not wish a gentleman of your rank to think too much evil of his queen. Heaven has willed that my secret should be to you no secret, and therefore I may speak plainly. You may say my own shame should silence me; I speak to lessen my shame in your eyes, if I can."

Rischenheim looked up with a dull gaze, not understanding her mood. He had expected reproaches, and met low-voiced apology.

"And yet," she went on, "it is because of me that the king lies dead now; and a faithful humble fellow also, caught in the net of my unhappy fortunes, has given his life for me, though he didn't know it. Even while we speak, it may be that a gentleman, not too old yet to learn nobility, may be killed in my quarrel; while another, whom I alone of all that know him may not praise, carries his life lightly in his hand for me. And to you, my lord, I have done the wrong of dressing a harsh deed in some cloak of excuse, making you seem to serve the king in working my punishment."

Rischenheim's eyes fell to the ground, and he twisted his hands nervously in and out, the one about the other. I took my hand from my revolver: he would not move now.

"I don't know," she went on, now almost dreamily, and as though she spoke more to herself than to him, or had even forgotten his presence, "what end in Heaven's counsel my great unhappiness has served. Perhaps I, who have place above most women, must also be tried above most; and in that trial I have failed. Yet, when I weigh my misery and my temptation, to my human eyes it seems that I have not failed greatly. My heart is not yet humbled, God's work not yet done. But the guilt of blood is on my soul—even the face of my dear love I can see now only through its scarlet mist; so that if what seemed my perfect joy were now granted me, it would come spoilt and stained and blotched."

She paused, fixing her eyes on him again; but he neither spoke nor moved.

"You knew my sin," she said, "the sin so great in my heart; and you knew how little my acts yielded to it. Did you think, my lord, that the sin had no punishment, that you took it in hand to add shame to my suffering? Was Heaven so kind that men must temper its indulgence by their severity? Yet I know that because I was wrong, you, being wrong, might seem to yourself not wrong, and in aiding your kinsman might plead that you served the king's honor. Thus, my lord, I was the cause in you of a deed that your heart could not welcome nor your honor praise. I thank God that you have come to no more hurt by it."

Rischenheim began to mutter in a low thick voice, his eyes still cast down: "Rupert persuaded me. He said the king would be very grateful, and—would give me—" His voice died away, and he sat silent again, twisting his hands.

"I know—I know," she said. "But you wouldn't have listened to such persuasions if my fault hadn't blinded your eyes."

She turned suddenly to me, who had been standing all the while aloof, and stretched out her hands towards me, her eyes filled with tears.

"Yet," said she, "your wife knows, and still loves me, Fritz."

"She should be no wife of mine, if she didn't," I cried. "For I and all of mine ask no better than to die for your Majesty."

"She knows, and yet she loves me," repeated the queen. I loved to see that she seemed to find comfort in Helga's love. It is women to whom women turn, and women whom women fear.

"But Helga writes no letters," said the queen.

"Why, no," said I, and I smiled a grim smile. Well, Rudolf Rassendyll had never wooed my wife.

She rose, saying: "Come, let us go to the palace."

As she rose, Rischenheim made a quick impulsive step towards her.

"Well, my lord," said she, turning towards him, "will you also go with me?"

"Lieutenant von Bernenstein will take care—" I began. But I stopped. The slightest gesture of her hand silenced me.

"Will you go with me?" she asked Rischenheim again.

"Madam," he stammered, "Madam—"

She waited. I waited also, although I had no great patience with him. Suddenly he fell on his knee, but he did not venture to take her hand. Of her own accord she came and stretched it out to him, saying sadly: "Ah, that by forgiving I could win forgiveness!"

Rischenheim caught at her hand and kissed it.

"It was not I," I heard him mutter. "Rupert set me on, and I couldn't stand out against him."

"Will you go with me to the palace?" she asked, drawing her hand away, but smiling.

"The Count of Luzau-Rischenheim," I made bold to observe, "knows some things that most people do not know, madam." She turned on me with dignity, almost with displeasure.

"The Count of Luzau-Rischenheim may be trusted to be silent," she said. "We ask him to do nothing against his cousin. We ask only his silence."

"Ay," said I, braving her anger, "but what security shall we have?"

"His word of honor, my lord." I knew that a rebuke to my presumption lay in her calling me "my lord," for, save on formal occasions, she always used to call me Fritz.

"His word of honor!" I grumbled. "In truth, madam—"

"He's right," said Rischenheim; "he's right."

"No, he's wrong," said the queen, smiling. "The count will keep his word, given to me."

Rischenheim looked at her and seemed about to address her, but then he turned to me, and said in a low tone:

"By Heaven, I will, Tarlenheim. I'll serve her in everything—"

"My lord," said she most graciously, and yet very sadly, "you lighten the burden on me no less by your help than because I no longer feel your honor stained through me. Come, we will go to the palace." And she went to him, saying, "We will go together."

There was nothing for it but to trust him. I knew that I could not turn her.

"Then I'll see if the carriage is ready," said I.

"Yes, do, Fritz," said the queen. But as I passed she stopped me for a moment, saying in a whisper, "Show that you trust him."

I went and held out my hand to him. He took and pressed it.

"On my honor," he said.

Then I went out and found Bernenstein sitting on a bench in the hall. The lieutenant was a diligent and watchful young man; he appeared to be examining his revolver with sedulous care.

"You can put that away," said I rather peevishly—I had not fancied shaking hands with Rischenheim. "He's not a prisoner any longer. He's one of us now."

"The deuce he is!" cried Bernenstein, springing to his feet.

I told him briefly what had happened, and how the queen had won Rupert's instrument to be her servant.

"I suppose he'll stick to it," I ended; and I thought he would, though I was not eager for his help.

A light gleamed in Bernenstein's eyes, and I felt a tremble in the hand that he laid on my shoulder.

"Then there's only Bauer now," he whispered. "If Rischenheim's with us, only Bauer!"

I knew very well what he meant. With Rischenheim silent, Bauer was the only man, save Rupert himself, who knew the truth, the only man who threatened that great scheme which more and more filled our thoughts and grew upon us with an increasing force of attraction as every obstacle to it seemed to be cleared out of the way. But I would not look at Bernenstein, fearing to acknowledge even with my eyes how my mind jumped with his. He was bolder, or less scrupulous—which you will.

"Yes, if we can shut Bauer's mouth." he went on.

"The queen's waiting for the carriage," I interrupted snappishly.

"Ah, yes, of course, the carriage," and he twisted me round till I was forced to look him in the face. Then he smiled, and even laughed a little.

"Only Bauer now!" said he.

"And Rupert," I remarked sourly.

"Oh, Rupert's dead bones by now," he chuckled, and with that he went out of the hall door and announced the queen's approach to her servants. It must be said for young Bernenstein that he was a cheerful fellow-conspirator. His equanimity almost matched Rudolf's own; I could not rival it myself.

I drove to the palace with the queen and my wife, the other two following in a second carriage. I do not know what they said to one another on the way, but Bernenstein was civil enough to his companion when I rejoined them. With us my wife was the principal speaker: she filled up, from what Rudolf had told her, the gaps in our knowledge of how he had spent his night in Strelsau, and by the time we arrived we were fully informed in every detail. The queen said little. The impulse which had dictated her appeal to Rischenheim and carried her through it seemed to have died away; she had become again subject to fears and apprehension. I saw her uneasiness when she suddenly put out her hand and touched mine, whispering:

"He must be at the house by now."

Our way did not lie by the house, and we came to the palace without any news of our absent chief (so I call him—as such we all, from the queen herself, then regarded him). She did not speak of him again; but her eyes seemed to follow me about as though she were silently asking some service of me; what it was I could not understand. Bernenstein had disappeared, and the repentant count with him: knowing they were together, I was in no uneasiness; Bernenstein would see that his companion contrived no treachery. But I was puzzled by the queen's tacit appeal. And I was myself on fire for news from the Konigstrasse. It was now two hours since Rudolf Rassendyll had left us, and no word had come of him or from him. At last I could bear it no longer. The queen was sitting with her hand in my wife's; I had been seated on the other side of the room, for I thought that they might wish to talk to one another; yet I had not seen them exchange a word. I rose abruptly and crossed the room to where they were.

"Have you need of my presence, madam, or have I your permission to be away for a time?" I asked.

"Where do you wish to go, Fritz?" the queen asked with a little start, as though I had come suddenly across her thoughts.

"To the Konigstrasse," said I.

To my surprise she rose and caught my hand.

"God bless you, Fritz!" she cried. "I don't think I could have endured it longer. But I wouldn't ask you to go. But go, my dear friend, go and bring me news of him. Oh, Fritz, I seem to dream that dream again!"

My wife looked up at me with a brave smile and a trembling lip.

"Shall you go into the house, Fritz?" she asked.

"Not unless I see need, sweetheart," said I.

She came and kissed me. "Go, if you are wanted," she said. And she tried to smile at the queen, as though she risked me willingly.

"I could have been such a wife, Fritz," whispered the queen. "Yes, I could."

I had nothing to say; at the moment I might not have been able to say it if I had. There is something in the helpless courage of women that makes me feel soft. We can work and fight; they sit and wait. Yet they do not flinch. Now I know that if I had to sit and think about the thing I should turn cur.

Well, I went, leaving them there together. I put on plain clothes instead of my uniform, and dropped my revolver into the pocket of my coat. Thus prepared, I slipped out and made my way on foot to the Konigstrasse.

It was now long past midday, but many folks were at their dinner and the streets were not full. Two or three people recognized me, but I passed by almost unnoticed. There was no sign of stir or excitement, and the flags still floated high in the wind. Sapt had kept his secret; the men of Strelsau thought still that their king lived and was among them. I feared that Rudolf's coming would have been seen, and expected to find a crowd of people near the house. But when I reached it there were no more than ten or a dozen idle fellows lounging about. I began to stroll up and down with as careless an air as I could assume.

Soon, however, there was a change. The workmen and business folk, their meal finished, began to come out of their houses and from the restaurants. The loafers before No. 19 spoke to many of them. Some said, "Indeed?" shook their heads, smiled and passed on: they had no time to waste in staring at the king. But many waited; lighting their cigars or cigarettes or pipes, they stood gossiping with one another, looking at their watches now and again, lest they should overstay their leisure. Thus the assembly grew to the number of a couple of hundred. I ceased my walk, for the pavement was too crowded, and hung on the outskirts of the throng. As I loitered there, a cigar in my mouth, I felt a hand on my shoulder. Turning round, I saw the lieutenant. He was in uniform. By his side was Rischenheim.

"You're here too, are you?" said I. "Well, nothing seems to be happening, does it?"

For No. 19 showed no sign of life. The shutters were up, the door closed; the little shop was not open for business that day.

Bernenstein shook his head with a smile. His companion took no heed of my remark; he was evidently in a state of great agitation, and his eyes never left the door of the house. I was about to address him, when my attention was abruptly and completely diverted by a glimpse of a head, caught across the shoulders of the bystanders.

The fellow whom I saw wore a brown wide-awake hat. The hat was pulled down low over his forehead, but nevertheless beneath its rim there appeared a white bandage running round his head. I could not see the face, but the bullet-shaped skull was very familiar to me. I was sure from the first moment that the bandaged man was Bauer. Saying nothing to Bernenstein, I began to steal round outside the crowd. As I went, I heard somebody saying that it was all nonsense; the king was not there: what should the king do in such a house? The answer was a reference to one of the first loungers; he replied that he did not know what the devil the king did there, but that the king or his double had certainly gone in, and had as certainly not yet come out again. I wished I could have made myself known to them and persuaded them to go away; but my presence would have outweighed my declarations, and been taken as a sure sign that the king was in the house. So I kept on the outskirts and worked my way unobtrusively towards the bandaged head. Evidently Bauer's hurt had not been so serious as to prevent him leaving the infirmary to which the police had carried him: he was come now to await, even as I was awaiting, the issue of Rudolf's visit to the house in the Konigstrasse.

He had not seen me, for he was looking at No. 19 as intently as Rischenheim. Apparently neither had caught sight of the other, or Rischenheim would have shown some embarrassment, Bauer some excitement. I wormed my way quickly towards my former servant. My mind was full of the idea of getting hold of him. I could not forget Bernenstein's remark, "Only Bauer now!" If I could secure Bauer we were safe. Safe in what? I did not answer to myself, but the old idea was working in me. Safe in our secret and safe in our plan— in the plan on which we all, we here in the city, and those two at the hunting-lodge, had set our minds! Bauer's death, Bauer's capture, Bauer's silence, however procured, would clear the greatest hindrance from its way.

Bauer stared intently at the house; I crept cautiously up behind him. His hand was in his trousers' pocket; where the curve of the elbow came there with a space between arm and body. I slipped in my left arm and hooked it firmly inside his. He turned round and saw me.

"Thus we meet again, Bauer," said I.

He was for a moment flabbergasted, and stared stupidly at me.

"Are you also hoping to see the king?" I asked.

He began to recover himself. A slow, cunning smile spread over his face.

"The king?" he asked.

"Well, he's in Strelsau, isn't he? Who gave you the wound on your head?"

Bauer moved his arm as though he meant to withdraw it from my grasp. He found himself tightly held.

"Where's that bag of mine?" I asked.

I do not know what he would have answered, for at this instant there came a sound from behind the closed door of the house. It was as if some one ran rapidly and eagerly towards the door. Then came an oath in a shrill voice, a woman's voice, but harsh and rough. It was answered by an angry cry in a girl's intonation. Full of eagerness, I drew my arm from Bauer's and sprang forward. I heard a chuckle from him and turned round, to see his bandaged head retreating rapidly down the street. I had no time to look to him, for now I saw two men, shoulder to shoulder, making their way through the crowd, regardless of any one in their way, and paying no attention to abuse or remonstrances. They were the lieutenant and Rischenheim. Without a moment's hesitation I set myself to push and battle a way through, thinking to join them in front. On they went, and on I went. All gave place before us in surly reluctance or frightened willingness. We three were together in the first rank of the crowd when the door of the house was flung open, and a girl ran out. Her hair was disordered, her face pale, and her eyes full of alarm. There she stood on the doorstep, facing the crowd, which in an instant grew as if by magic to three times its former size, and, little knowing what she did, she cried in the eager accents of sheer terror:

"Help, help! The king! The king!"

CHAPTER XVII. YOUNG RUPERT AND THE PLAY-ACTOR

There rises often before my mind the picture of young Rupert, standing where Rischenheim left him, awaiting the return of his messenger and watching for some sign that should declare to Strelsau the death of its king which his own hand had wrought. His image is one that memory holds clear and distinct, though time may blur the shape of greater and better men, and the position in which he was that morning gives play enough to the imagination. Save for Rischenheim, a broken reed, and Bauer, who was gone, none knew where, he stood alone against a kingdom which he had robbed of its head, and a band of resolute men who would know no rest and no security so long as he lived. For protection he had only a quick brain, his courage, and his secret. Yet he could not fly—he was without resources till his cousin furnished them—and at any moment his opponents might find themselves able to declare the king's death and raise the city in hue and cry after him. Such men do not repent; but it may be that he regretted the enterprise which had led him on so far and forced on him a deed so momentous; yet to those who knew him it seems more likely that the smile broadened on his firm full lips as he looked down on the unconscious city. Well, I daresay he would have been too much for me, but I wish I had been the man to find him there. He would not have had it so; for I believe that he asked no better than to cross swords again with Rudolf Rassendyll and set his fortunes on the issue.

Down below, the old woman was cooking a stew for her dinner, now and then grumbling to herself that the Count of Luzau-Rischenheim was so long away, and Bauer, the rascal, drunk in some pot-house. The kitchen door stood open, and through it could be seen the girl Rosa, busily scrubbing the tiled floor; her color was high and her eyes bright; from time to time she paused in her task, and, raising her head, seemed to listen. The time at which the king needed her was past, but the king had not come. How little the old woman knew for whom she listened! All her talk had been of Bauer—why Bauer did not come and what could have befallen him. It was grand to hold the king's secret for him, and she would hold it with her life; for he had been kind and gracious to her, and he was her man of all the men in Strelsau. Bauer was a stumpy fellow; the Count of Hentzau was handsome, handsome as the devil; but the king was her man. And the king had trusted her; she would die before hurt should come to him.

There were wheels in the street—quick-rolling wheels. They seemed to stop a few doors away, then to roll on again past the house. The girl's head was raised; the old woman, engrossed in her stewing, took no heed. The girl's straining ear caught a rapid step outside. Then it came—the knock, the sharp knock followed by five light ones. The old woman heard now: dropping her spoon into the pot, she lifted the mess off the fire and turned round, saying: "There's the rogue at last! Open the door for him, Rosa."

Before she spoke Rosa had darted down the passage. The door opened and shut again. The old woman waddled to the threshold of the kitchen. The passage and the shop were dark behind the closed shutters, but the figure by the girl's side was taller than Bauer's.

"Who's there?" cried Mother Holf sharply. "The shop's shut to-day: you can't come in."

"But I am in," came the answer, and Rudolf stepped towards her. The girl followed a pace behind, her hands clasped and her eyes alight with excitement. "Don't you know me?" asked Rudolf, standing opposite the old woman and smiling down on her.

There, in the dim light of the low-roofed passage, Mother Holf was fairly puzzled. She knew the story of Mr. Rassendyll; she knew that he was again in Ruritania, it was no surprise to her that he should be in Strelsau; but she did not know that Rupert had killed the king, and she had not seen the king close at hand since his illness and his beard impaired what had been a perfect likeness. In fine, she could not tell whether it were indeed the king who spoke to her or his counterfeit.

"Who are you?" she asked, curt and blunt in her confusion. The girl broke in with an amused laugh.

"Why, it's the—" She paused. Perhaps the king's identity was a secret.

Rudolf nodded to her. "Tell her who I am," said he.

"Why, mother, it's the king," whispered Rosa, laughing and blushing. "The king, mother."

"Ay, if the king's alive, I'm the king," said Rudolf. I suppose he wanted to find out how much the old woman knew.

She made no answer, but stared up at his face. In her bewilderment she forgot to ask how he had learnt the signal that gained him admission.

"I've come to see the Count of Hentzau," Rudolf continued. "Take me to him at once."

The old woman was across his path in a moment, all defiant, arms akimbo.

"Nobody can see the count. He's not here," she blurted out.

"What, can't the king see him? Not even the king?"

"King!" she cried, peering at him. "Are you the king?"

Rosa burst out laughing.

"Mother, you must have seen the king a hundred times," she laughed.

"The king, or his ghost—what does it matter?" said Rudolf lightly.

The old woman drew back with an appearance of sudden alarm.

"His ghost? Is he?"

"His ghost!" rang out in the girl's merry laugh. "Why, here's the king himself, mother. You don't look much like a ghost, sir."

Mother Holf's face was livid now, and her eyes staring fixedly. Perhaps it shot into her brain that something had happened to the king, and that this man had come because of it—this man who was indeed the image, and might have been the spirit, of the king. She leant against the door post, her broad bosom heaving under her scanty stuff gown. Yet still—was it not the king?

"God help us!" she muttered in fear and bewilderment.

"He helps us, never fear," said Rudolf Rassendyll. "Where is Count Rupert?"

The girl had caught alarm from her mother's agitation. "He's upstairs in the attic at the top of the house, sir," she whispered in frightened tones, with a glance that fled from her mother's terrified face to Rudolf's set eyes and steady smile.

What she said was enough for him. He slipped by the old woman and began to mount the stairs.

The two watched him, Mother Holf as though fascinated, the girl alarmed but still triumphant: she had done what the king bade her. Rudolf turned the corner of the first landing and disappeared from their sight. The old woman, swearing and muttering, stumbled back into her kitchen, set her stew on the fire, and began to stir it, her eyes set on the flames and careless of the pot. The girl watched her mother for a moment, wondering how she could think of the stew, not guessing that she turned the spoon without a thought of what she did; then she began to crawl, quickly but noiselessly, up the staircase in the track of Rudolf Rassendyll. She looked back once: the old woman stirred with a monotonous circular movement of her fat arm. Rosa, bent half-double, skimmed upstairs, till she came in sight of the king whom she was so proud to serve. He was on the top landing now, outside the door of a large attic where Rupert of Hentzau was lodged. She saw him lay his hand on the latch of the door; his other hand rested in the pocket of his coat. From the room no sound came; Rupert may have heard the step outside and stood motionless to listen. Rudolf opened the door and walked in. The girl darted breathlessly up the remaining steps, and, coming to the door, just as it swung back on the latch, crouched down by it, listening to what passed within, catching glimpses of forms and movements through the chinks of the crazy hinge and the crevices where the wood of the panel sprung and left a narrow eye hole for her absorbed gazing.

Rupert of Hentzau had no thought of ghosts; the men he killed lay still where they fell, and slept where they were buried. And he had no wonder at the sight of Rudolf Rassendyll. It told him no more than that Rischenheim's errand had fallen out ill, at which he was not surprised, and that his old enemy was again in his path, at which (as I verily believe) he was more glad than sorry. As Rudolf entered, he had been half-way between window and table; he came forward to the table now, and stood leaning the points of two fingers on the unpolished dirty-white deal.

"Ah, the play-actor!" said he, with a gleam of his teeth and a toss of his curls, while his second hand, like Mr. Rassendyll's, rested in the pocket of his coat.

Mr. Rassendyll himself has confessed that in old days it went against the grain with him when Rupert called him a play-actor. He was a little older now, and his temper more difficult to stir.

"Yes, the play-actor," he answered, smiling. "With a shorter part this time, though."

"What part to-day? Isn't it the old one, the king with a pasteboard crown?" asked Rupert, sitting down on the table. "Faith, we shall do handsomely in Ruritania: you have a pasteboard crown, and I (humble man though I am) have given the other one a heavenly crown. What a brave show! But perhaps I tell you news?"

"No, I know what you've done."

"I take no credit. It was more the dog's doing than mine," said Rupert carelessly. "However, there it is, and dead he is, and there's an end of it. What's your business, play-actor?"

At the repetition of this last word, to her so mysterious, the girl outside pressed her eyes more eagerly to the chink and strained her ears to listen more sedulously. And what did the count mean by the "other one" and "a heavenly crown"?

"Why not call me king?" asked Rudolf.

"They call you that in Strelsau?"

"Those that know I'm here."

172

"And they are—?"

"Some few score."

"And thus," said Rupert, waving an arm towards the window, "the town is quiet and the flags fly?"

"You've been waiting to see them lowered?"

"A man likes to have some notice taken of what he has done," Rupert complained. "However, I can get them lowered when I will."

"By telling your news? Would that be good for yourself?"

"Forgive me—not that way. Since the king has two lives, it is but in nature that he should have two deaths."

"And when he has undergone the second?"

"I shall live at peace, my friend, on a certain source of income that I possess." He tapped his breast-pocket with a slight, defiant laugh. "In these days," said he, "even queens must be careful about their letters. We live in moral times."

"You don't share the responsibility for it," said Rudolf, smiling.

"I make my little protest. But what's your business, play-actor? For I think you're rather tiresome."

Rudolf grew grave. He advanced towards the table, and spoke in low, serious tones.

"My lord, you're alone in this matter now. Rischenheim is a prisoner; your rogue Bauer I encountered last night and broke his head."

"Ah, you did?"

"You have what you know of in your hands. If you yield, on my honor I will save your life."

"You don't desire my blood, then, most forgiving play-actor?"

"So much, that I daren't fail to offer you life," answered Rudolf Rassendyll. "Come, sir, your plan has failed: give up the letter."

Rupert looked at him thoughtfully.

"You'll see me safe off if I give it you?" he asked.

"I'll prevent your death. Yes, and I'll see you safe."

"Where to?"

"To a fortress, where a trustworthy gentleman will guard you."

"For how long, my dear friend?"

"I hope for many years, my dear Count."

"In fact, I suppose, as long as—?"

"Heaven leaves you to the world, Count. It's impossible to set you free."

"That's the offer, then?"

"The extreme limit of indulgence," answered Rudolf. Rupert burst into a laugh, half of defiance, yet touched with the ring of true amusement. Then he lit a cigarette and sat puffing and smiling.

"I should wrong you by straining your kindness so far," said he; and in wanton insolence, seeking again to show Mr. Rassendyll the mean esteem in which he held him, and the weariness his presence was, he raised his arms and stretched them above his head, as a man does in the fatigue of tedium. "Heigho!" he yawned.

But he had overshot the mark this time. With a sudden swift bound Rudolf was upon him; his hands gripped Rupert's wrists, and with his greater strength he bent back the count's pliant body till trunk and head lay flat on the table. Neither man spoke; their eyes met; each heard the other's breathing and felt the vapor of it on his face. The girl outside had seen the movement of Rudolf's figure, but her cranny did not serve her to show her the two where they were now; she knelt on her knees in ignorant suspense. Slowly and with a patient force Rudolf began to work his enemy's arms towards one another. Rupert had read his design in his eyes and resisted with tense muscles. It seemed as though his arms must crack; but at last they moved. Inch by inch they were driven closer; now the elbows almost touched; now the wrists joined in reluctant contact. The sweat broke out on the count's brow, and stood in

173

large drops on Rudolf's. Now the wrists were side by side, and slowly the long sinewy fingers of Rudolf's right hand, that held one wrist already in their vise, began to creep round the other. The grip seemed to have half numbed Rupert's arms, and his struggles grew fainter. Round both wrists the sinewy fingers climbed and coiled; gradually and timidly the grasp of the other hand was relaxed and withdrawn. Would the one hold both? With a great spasm of effort Rupert put it to the proof.

The smile that bent Mr. Rassendyll's lips gave the answer. He could hold both, with one hand he could hold both: not for long, no, but for an instant. And then, in the instant, his left hand, free at last, shot to the breast of the count's coat. It was the same that he had worn at the hunting-lodge, and was ragged and torn from the boar-hound's teeth. Rudolf tore it further open, and his hand dashed in.

"God's curse on you!" snarled Rupert of Hentzau.

But Mr. Rassendyll still smiled. Then he drew out a letter. A glance at it showed him the queen's seal. As he glanced Rupert made another effort. The one hand, wearied out, gave way, and Mr. Rassendyll had no more than time to spring away, holding his prize. The next moment he had his revolver in his hand—none too soon, for Rupert of Hentzau's barrel faced him, and they stood thus, opposite to one another, with no more than three or four feet between the mouths of their weapons.

There is, indeed, much that may be said against Rupert of Hentzau, the truth about him well-nigh forbidding that charity of judgment which we are taught to observe towards all men. But neither I nor any man who knew him ever found in him a shrinking from danger or a fear of death. It was no feeling such as these, but rather a cool calculation of chances, that now stayed his hand. Even if he were victorious in the duel, and both did not die, yet the noise of the firearms would greatly decrease his chances of escape. Moreover, he was a noted swordsman, and conceived that he was Mr. Rassendyll's superior in that exercise. The steel offered him at once a better prospect for victory and more hope of a safe fight. So he did not pull his trigger, but, maintaining his aim the while, said:

"I'm not a street bully, and I don't excel in a rough-and-tumble. Will you fight now like a gentleman? There's a pair of blades in the case yonder."

Mr. Rassendyll, in his turn, was keenly alive to the peril that still hung over the queen. To kill Rupert would not save her if he himself also were shot and left dead, or so helpless that he could not destroy the letter; and while Rupert's revolver was at his heart he could not tear it up nor reach the fire that burnt on the other side of the room. Nor did he fear the result of a trial with steel, for he had kept himself in practice and improved his skill since the days when he came first to Strelsau.

"As you will," said he. "Provided we settle the matter here and now, the manner is the same to me."

"Put your revolver on the table, then, and I'll lay mine by the side of it."

"I beg your pardon," smiled Rudolf, "but you must lay yours down first."

"I'm to trust you, it seems, but you won't trust me!"

"Precisely. You know you can trust me; you know that I can't trust you."

A sudden flush swept over Rupert of Hentzau's face. There were moments when he saw, in the mirror of another's face or words, the estimation in which honorable men held him; and I believe that he hated Mr. Rassendyll most fiercely, not for thwarting his enterprise, but because he had more power than any other man to show him that picture. His brows knit in a frown, and his lips shut tight.

"Ay, but though you won't fire, you'll destroy the letter," he sneered. "I know your fine distinctions."

"Again I beg your pardon. You know very well that, although all Strelsau were at the door, I wouldn't touch the letter."

With an angry muttered oath Rupert flung his revolver on the table. Rudolf came forward and laid his by it. Then he took up both, and, crossing to the mantelpiece, laid them there;

between there he placed the queen's letter. A bright blaze burnt in the grate; it needed but the slightest motion of his hand to set the letter beyond all danger. But he placed it carefully on the mantelpiece, and, with a slight smile on his face, turned to Rupert, saying: "Now shall we resume the bout that Fritz von Tarlenheim interrupted in the forest of Zenda?"

All this while they had been speaking in subdued accents, resolution in one, anger in the other, keeping the voice in an even, deliberate lowness. The girl outside caught only a word here and there; but now suddenly the flash of steel gleamed on her eyes through the crevice of the hinge. She gave a sudden gasp, and, pressing her face closer to the opening, listened and looked. For Rupert of Hentzau had taken the swords from their case and put them on the table. With a slight bow Rudolf took one, and the two assumed their positions. Suddenly Rupert lowered his point. The frown vanished from his face, and he spoke in his usual bantering tone.

"By the way," said he, "perhaps we're letting our feelings run away with us. Have you more of a mind now to be King of Ruritania? If so, I'm ready to be the most faithful of your subjects."

"You honor me, Count."

"Provided, of course, that I'm one of the most favored and the richest. Come, come, the fool is dead now; he lived like a fool and he died like a fool. The place is empty. A dead man has no rights and suffers no wrongs. Damn it, that's good law, isn't it? Take his place and his wife. You can pay my price then. Or are you still so virtuous? Faith, how little some men learn from the world they live in! If I had your chance!"

"Come, Count, you'd be the last man to trust Rupert of Hentzau."

"If I made it worth his while?"

"But he's a man who would take the pay and betray his associate."

Again Rupert flushed. When he next spoke his voice was hard, cold, and low.

"By God, Rudolf Rassendyll," said he, "I'll kill you here and now."

"I ask no better than that you should try."

"And then I'll proclaim that woman for what she is in all Strelsau." A smile came on his lips as he watched Rudolf's face.

"Guard yourself, my lord," said Mr. Rassendyll.

"Ay, for no better than—There, man, I'm ready for you." For Rudolf's blade had touched his in warning.

The steel jangled. The girl's pale face was at the crevice of the hinge. She heard the blades cross again and again. Then one would run up the other with a sharp, grating slither. At times she caught a glimpse of a figure in quick forward lunge or rapid wary withdrawal. Her brain was almost paralyzed.

Ignorant of the mind and heart of young Rupert, she could not conceive that he tried to kill the king. Yet the words she had caught sounded like the words of men quarreling, and she could not persuade herself that the gentlemen fenced only for pastime. They were not speaking now; but she heard their hard breathing and the movement of their unresting feet on the bare boards of the floor. Then a cry rang out, clear and merry with the fierce hope of triumph: "Nearly! nearly!"

She knew the voice for Rupert of Hentzau's, and it was the king who answered calmly, "Nearly isn't quite."

Again she listened. They seemed to have paused for a moment, for there was no sound, save of the hard breathing and deep-drawn pants of men who rest an instant in the midst of intense exertion. Then came again the clash and the slitherings; and one of them crossed into her view. She knew the tall figure and she saw the red hair: it was the king. Backward step by step he seemed to be driven, coming nearer and nearer to the door. At last there was no more than a foot between him and her; only the crazy panel prevented her putting out her hand to touch him. Again the voice of Rupert rang out in rich exultation, "I have you now! Say your prayers, King Rudolf!"

"Say your prayers!" Then they fought. It was earnest, not play. And it was the king—her king—her dear king, who was in great peril of his life. For an instant she knelt, still watching. Then with a low cry of terror she turned and ran headlong down the steep stairs. Her mind could not tell what to do, but her heart cried out that she must do something for her king. Reaching the ground floor, she ran with wide-open eyes into the kitchen. The stew was on the hob, the old woman still held the spoon, but she had ceased to stir and fallen into a chair. "He's killing the king! He's killing the king!" cried Rosa, seizing her mother by the arm. "Mother, what shall we do? He's killing the king!"

The old woman looked up with dull eyes and a stupid, cunning smile.

"Let them alone," she said. "There's no king here."

"Yes, yes. He's upstairs in the count's room. They're fighting, he and the Count of Hentzau. Mother, Count Rupert will kill—"

"Let them alone. He the king? He's no king," muttered the old woman again.

For an instant Rosa stood looking down on her in helpless despair. Then a light flashed into her eyes.

"I must call for help," she cried.

The old woman seemed to spring to sudden life. She jumped up and caught her daughter by the shoulder.

"No, no," she whispered in quick accents. "You—you don't know. Let them alone, you fool! It's not our business. Let them alone."

"Let me go, mother, let me go! Mother, I must help the king!"

"I'll not let you go," said Mother Holf.

But Rosa was young and strong; her heart was fired with terror for the king's danger.

"I must go," she cried; and she flung her mother's grasp off from her so that the old woman was thrown back into her chair, and the spoon fell from her hand and clattered on the tiles. But Rosa turned and fled down the passage and through the shop. The bolts delayed her trembling fingers for an instant. Then she flung the door wide. A new amazement filled her eyes at the sight of the eager crowd before the house. Then her eyes fell on me where I stood between the lieutenant and Rischenheim, and she uttered her wild cry, "Help! The king!"

With one bound I was by her side and in the house, while Bernenstein cried, "Quicker!" from behind.

CHAPTER XVIII. THE TRIUMPH OF THE KING

THE things that men call presages, presentiments, and so forth, are, to my mind, for the most part idle nothings: sometimes it is only that probable events cast before them a natural shadow which superstitious fancy twists into a Heaven sent warning; oftener the same desire that gives conception works fulfilment, and the dreamer sees in the result of his own act and will a mysterious accomplishment independent of his effort. Yet when I observe thus calmly and with good sense on the matter to the Constable of Zenda, he shakes his head and answers, "But Rudolf Rassendyll knew from the first that he would come again to Strelsau and engage young Rupert point to point. Else why did he practise with the foils so as to be a better swordsman the second time than he was the first? Mayn't God do anything that Fritz von Tarlenheim can't understand? a pretty notion, on my life!" And he goes off grumbling.

Well, be it inspiration, or be it delusion—and the difference stands often on a hair's breadth—I am glad that Rudolf had it. For if a man once grows rusty, it is everything short of impossible to put the fine polish on his skill again. Mr. Rassendyll had strength, will, coolness, and, of course, courage. None would have availed had not his eye been in perfect familiarity with its work, and his hand obeyed it as readily as the bolt slips in a well-oiled groove. As the thing stood, the lithe agility and unmatched dash of young Rupert but just missed being too much for him. He was in deadly peril when the girl Rosa ran down to bring him aid. His practised skill was able to maintain his defence. He sought to do no more, but endured Rupert's fiery attack and wily feints in an almost motionless stillness. Almost, I say; for the slight turns of wrist that seem nothing are everything, and served here to keep his skin whole and his life in him.

There was an instant—Rudolf saw it in his eyes and dwelt on it when he lightly painted the scene for me—when there dawned on Rupert of Hentzau the knowledge that he could not break down his enemy's guard. Surprise, chagrin, amusement, or something like it, seemed blended in his look. He could not make out how he was caught and checked in every effort, meeting, it seemed, a barrier of iron impregnable in rest. His quick brain grasped the lesson in an instant. If his skill were not the greater, the victory would not be his, for his endurance was the less. He was younger, and his frame was not so closely knit; pleasure had taken its tithe from him; perhaps a good cause goes for something. Even while he almost pressed Rudolf against the panel of the door, he seemed to know that his measure of success was full. But what the hand could not compass the head might contrive. In quickly conceived strategy he began to give pause in his attack, nay, he retreated a step or two. No scruples hampered his devices, no code of honor limited the means he would employ. Backing before his opponent, he seemed to Rudolf to be faint-hearted; he was baffled, but seemed despairing; he was weary, but played a more complete fatigue. Rudolf advanced, pressing and attacking, only to meet a defence as perfect as his own. They were in the middle of the room now, close by the table. Rupert, as though he had eyes in the back of his head, skirted round, avoiding it by a narrow inch. His breathing was quick and distressed, gasp tumbling over gasp, but still his eye was alert and his hand unerring. He had but a few moments' more effort left in him: it was enough if he could reach his goal and perpetrate the trick on which his mind, fertile in every base device, was set. For it was towards the mantelpiece that his retreat, seeming forced, in truth so deliberate, led him. There was the letter, there lay the revolvers. The time to think of risks was gone by; the time to boggle over what honor allowed or forbade had never come to Rupert of Hentzau. If he could not win by force and skill, he would win by guile and by treachery, to the test that he had himself invited. The revolvers lay on the mantelpiece: he meant to possess himself of one, if he could gain an instant in which to snatch it.

The device that he adopted was nicely chosen. It was too late to call a rest or ask breathing space: Mr. Rassendyll was not blind to the advantage he had won, and chivalry would have turned to folly had it allowed such indulgence. Rupert was hard by the mantelpiece now. The sweat was pouring from his face, and his breast seemed like to burst in the effort after breath; yet he had enough strength for his purpose. He must have slackened his hold on his weapon, for when Rudolf's blade next struck it, it flew from his hand, twirled out of a nerveless grasp, and slid along the floor. Rupert stood disarmed, and Rudolf motionless.

"Pick it up," said Mr. Rassendyll, never thinking there had been a trick.

"Ay, and you'll truss me while I do it."

"You young fool, don't you know me yet?" and Rudolf, lowering his blade, rested its point on the floor, while with his left hand he indicated Rupert's weapon. Yet something warned him: it may be there came a look in Rupert's eyes, perhaps of scorn for his enemy's simplicity, perhaps of pure triumph in the graceless knavery. Rudolf stood waiting.

"You swear you won't touch me while I pick it up?" asked Rupert, shrinking back a little, and thereby getting an inch or two nearer the mantelpiece.

"You have my promise: pick it up. I won't wait any longer."

"You won't kill me unarmed?" cried Rupert, in alarmed scandalized expostulation.

"No; but—"

The speech went unfinished, unless a sudden cry were its ending. And, as he cried, Rudolf Rassendyll, dropping his sword on the ground, sprang forward. For Rupert's hand had shot out behind him and was on the butt of one of the revolvers. The whole trick flashed on

Rudolf, and he sprang, flinging his long arms round Rupert. But Rupert had the revolver in his hand.

In all likelihood the two neither heard nor heeded, though it seemed to me that the creaks and groans of the old stairs were loud enough to wake the dead. For now Rosa had given the alarm, Bernenstein and I—or I and Bernenstein (for I was first, and, therefore, may put myself first)—had rushed up. Hard behind us came Rischenheim, and hot on his heels a score of fellows, pushing and shouldering and trampling. We in front had a fair start, and gained the stairs unimpeded; Rischenheim was caught up in the ruck and gulfed in the stormy, tossing group that struggled for first footing on the steps. Yet, soon they were after us, and we heard them reach the first landing as we sped up to the last. There was a confused din through all the house, and it seemed now to echo muffled and vague through the walls from the street without. I was conscious of it, although I paid no heed to anything but reaching the room where the king—where Rudolf—was. Now I was there, Bernenstein hanging to my heels. The door did not hold us a second. I was in, he after me. He slammed the door and set his back against it, just as the rush of feet flooded the highest flight of stairs. And at the moment a revolver shot rang clear and loud.

The lieutenant and I stood still, he against the door, I a pace farther into the room. The sight we saw was enough to arrest us with its strange interest. The smoke of the shot was curling about, but neither man seemed wounded. The revolver was in Rupert's hand, and its muzzle smoked. But Rupert was jammed against the wall, just by the side of the mantelpiece. With one hand Rudolf had pinned his left arm to the wainscoting higher than his head, with the other he held his right wrist. I drew slowly nearer: if Rudolf were unarmed, I could fairly enforce a truce and put them on an equality; yet, though Rudolf was unarmed, I did nothing. The sight of his face stopped me. He was very pale and his lips were set, but it was his eyes that caught my gaze, for they were glad and merciless. I had never seen him look thus before. I turned from him to young Hentzau's face. Rupert's teeth were biting his under lip, the sweat dropped, and the veins swelled large and blue on his forehead; his eyes were set on Rudolf Rassendyll. Fascinated, I drew nearer. Then I saw what passed. Inch by inch Rupert's arm curved, the elbow bent, the hand that had pointed almost straight from him and at Mr. Rassendyll pointed now away from both towards the window. But its motion did not stop; it followed the line of a circle: now it was on Rupert's arm; still it moved, and quicker now, for the power of resistance grew less. Rupert was beaten; he felt it and knew it, and I read the knowledge in his eyes. I stepped up to Rudolf Rassendyll. He heard or felt me, and turned his eyes for an instant. I do not know what my face said, but he shook his head and turned back to Rupert. The revolver, held still in the man's own hand, was at his heart. The motion ceased, the point was reached.

I looked again at Rupert. Now his face was easier; there was a slight smile on his lips; he flung back his comely head and rested thus against the wainscoting; his eyes asked a question of Rudolf Rassendyll. I turned my gaze to where the answer was to come, for Rudolf made none in words. By the swiftest of movements he shifted his grasp from Rupert's wrist and pounced on his hand. Now his forefinger rested on Rupert's and Rupert's was on the trigger. I am no soft-heart, but I laid a hand on his shoulder. He took no heed; I dared do no more. Rupert glanced at me. I caught his look, but what could I say to him? Again my eyes were riveted on Rudolf's finger. Now it was crooked round Rupert's, seeming like a man who strangles another.

I will not say more. He smiled to the last; his proud head, which had never bent for shame, did not bend for fear. There was a sudden tightening in the pressure of that crooked forefinger, a flash, a noise. He was held up against the wall for an instant by Rudolf's hand; when that was removed he sank, a heap that looked all head and knees.

But hot on the sound of the discharge came a shout and an oath from Bernenstein. He was hurled away from the door, and through it burst Rischenheim and the whole score after him. They were jostling one another and crying out to know what passed and where the king was.

High over all the voices, coming from the back of the throng, I heard the cry of the girl Rosa. But as soon as they were in the room, the same spell that had fastened Bernenstein and me to inactivity imposed its numbing power on them also. Only Rischenheim gave a sudden sob and ran forward to where his cousin lay. The rest stood staring. For a moment Rudolf eyed them. Then, without a word, he turned his back. He put out the right hand with which he had just killed Rupert of Hentzau, and took the letter from the mantelpiece. He glanced at the envelope, then he opened the letter. The handwriting banished any last doubt he had; he tore the letter across, and again in four pieces, and yet again in smaller fragments. Then he sprinkled the morsels of paper into the blaze of the fire. I believe that every eye in the room followed them and watched till they curled and crinkled into black, wafery ashes. Thus, at last the queen's letter was safe.

When he had thus set the seal on his task he turned round to us again. He paid no heed to Rischenheim, who was crouching down by the body of Rupert; but he looked at Bernenstein and me, and then at the people behind us. He waited a moment before he spoke; then his utterance was not only calm but also very slow, so that he seemed to be choosing his words carefully.

"Gentlemen," said he, "a full account of this matter will be rendered by myself in due time. For the present it must suffice to say that this gentleman who lies here dead sought an interview with me on private business. I came here to find him, desiring, as he professed, to desire, privacy. And here he tried to kill me. The result of his attempt you see."

I bowed low, Bernenstein did the like, and all the rest followed our example.

"A full account shall be given," said Rudolf. "Now let all leave me, except the Count of Tarlenheim and Lieutenant von Bernenstein."

Most unwillingly, with gaping mouths and wonder-struck eyes, the throng filed out of the door. Rischenheim rose to his feet.

"You stay, if you like," said Rudolf, and the count knelt again by his kinsman.

Seeing the rough bedsteads by the wall of the attic, I touched Rischenheim on the shoulder and pointed to one of them. Together we lifted Rupert of Hentzau. The revolver was still in his hand, but Bernenstein disengaged it from his grasp. Then Rischenheim and I laid him down, disposing his body decently and spreading over it his riding cloak, still spotted with the mud gathered on his midnight expedition to the hunting-lodge. His face looked much as before the shot was fired; in death, as in life, he was the handsomest fellow in all Ruritania. I wager that many tender hearts ached and many bright eyes were dimmed for him when the news of his guilt and death went forth. There are ladies still in Strelsau who wear his trinkets in an ashamed devotion that cannot forget. Well, even I, who had every good cause to hate and scorn him, set the hair smooth on his brow; while Rischenheim was sobbing like a child, and young Bernenstein rested his head on his arm as he leant on the mantelpiece, and would not look at the dead. Rudolf alone seemed not to heed him or think of him. His eyes had lost their unnatural look of joy, and were now calm and tranquil. He took his own revolver from the mantelpiece and put it in his pocket, laying Rupert's neatly where his had been. Then he turned to me and said:

"Come, let us go to the queen and tell her that the letter is beyond reach of hurt."

Moved by some impulse, I walked to the window and put my head out. I was seen from below, and a great shout greeted me. The crowd before the doors grew every moment; the people flocking from all quarters would soon multiply it a hundred fold; for such news as had been carried from the attic by twenty wondering tongues spreads like a forest-fire. It would be through Strelsau in a few minutes, through the kingdom in an hour, through Europe in but little longer. Rupert was dead and the letter was safe, but what were we to tell that great concourse concerning their king? A queer feeling of helpless perplexity came over me and found vent in a foolish laugh. Bernenstein was by my side; he also looked out, and turned again with an eager face.

"You'll have a royal progress to your palace," said he to Rudolf Rassendyll.

Mr. Rassendyll made no answer, but, coming to me, took my arm. We went out, leaving Rischenheim by the body. I did not think of him; Bernenstein probably thought that he would keep his pledge given to the queen, for he followed us immediately and without demur. There was nobody outside the door. The house was very quiet, and the tumult from the street reached us only in a muffled roar. But when we came to the foot of the stairs we found the two women. Mother Holf stood on the threshold of the kitchen, looking amazed and terrified. Rosa was clinging to her; but as soon as Rudolf came in sight, the girl sprang forward and flung herself on her knees before him, pouring out incoherent thanks to Heaven for his safety. He bent down and spoke to her in a whisper; she looked up with a flush of pride on her face. He seemed to hesitate a moment; he glanced at his hands, but he wore no ring save that which the queen had given him long ago. Then he disengaged his chain and took his gold watch from his pocket. Turning it over, he showed me the monogram, R. R.

"Rudolfus Rex," he whispered with a whimsical smile, and pressed the watch into the girl's hand, saying: "Keep this to remind you of me."

She laughed and sobbed as she caught it with one hand, while with the other she held his.

"You must let go," he said gently. "I have much to do."

I took her by the arm and induced her to rise. Rudolf, released, passed on to where the old woman stood. He spoke to her in a stern, distinct voice.

"I don't know," he said, "how far you are a party to the plot that was hatched in your house. For the present I am content not to know, for it is no pleasure to me to detect disloyalty or to punish an old woman. But take care! The first word you speak, the first act you do against me, the king, will bring its certain and swift punishment. If you trouble me, I won't spare you. In spite of traitors I am still king in Strelsau."

He paused, looking hard in her face. Her lip quivered and her eyes fell.

"Yes," he repeated, "I am king in Strelsau. Keep your hands out of mischief and your tongue quiet."

She made no answer. He passed on. I was following, but as I went by her the old woman clutched my arm. "In God's name, who is he?" she whispered.

"Are you mad?" I asked, lifting my brows. "Don't you know the king when he speaks to you? And you'd best remember what he said. He has servants who'll do his orders."

She let me go and fell back a step. Young Bernenstein smiled at her; he at least found more pleasure than anxiety in our position. Thus, then, we left them: the old woman terrified, amazed, doubtful; the girl with ruddy cheeks and shining eyes, clasping in her two hands the keepsake that the king himself had given her.

Bernenstein had more presence of mind than I. He ran forward, got in front of both of us, and flung the door open. Then, bowing very low, he stood aside to let Rudolf pass. The street was full from end to end now, and a mighty shout of welcome rose from thousands of throats. Hats and handkerchiefs were waved in mad exultation and triumphant loyalty. The tidings of the king's escape had flashed through the city, and all were there to do him honor. They had seized some gentleman's landau and taken out the horses. The carriage stood now before the doors of the house. Rudolf had waited a moment on the threshold, lifting his hat once or twice; his face was perfectly calm, and I saw no trembling in his hands. In an instant a dozen arms took gentle hold of him and impelled him forward. He mounted into the carriage; Bernenstein and I followed, with bare heads, and sat on the back seat, facing him. The people were round as thick as bees, and it seemed as though we could not move without crushing somebody. Yet presently the wheels turned, and they began to drag us away at a slow walk. Rudolf kept raising his hat, bowing now to right, now to left. But once, as he turned, his eyes met ours. In spite of what was behind and what was in front, we all three smiled.

"I wish they'd go a little quicker," said Rudolf in a whisper, as he conquered his smile and turned again to acknowledge the loyal greetings of his subjects.

But what did they know of any need for haste? They did not know what stood on the turn of the next few hours, nor the momentous question that pressed for instant decision. So far from hurrying, they lengthened our ride by many pauses; they kept us before the cathedral, while some ran and got the joy bells set ringing; we were stopped to receive improvised bouquets from the hands of pretty girls and impetuous hand-shakings from enthusiastic loyalists. Through it all Rudolf kept his composure, and seemed to play his part with native kingliness. I heard Bernenstein whisper, "By God, we must stick to it!"

At last we came in sight of the palace. Here also there was a great stir. Many officers and soldiers were about. I saw the chancellor's carriage standing near the portico, and a dozen other handsome equipages were waiting till they could approach. Our human horses drew us slowly up to the entrance. Helsing was on the steps, and ran down to the carriage, greeting the king with passionate fervor. The shouts of the crowd grew louder still.

But suddenly a stillness fell on them; it lasted but an instant, and was the prelude to a deafening roar. I was looking at Rudolf and saw his head turn suddenly and his eyes grow bright. I looked where his eyes had gone. There, on the top step of the broad marble flight, stood the queen, pale as the marble itself, stretching out her hands towards Rudolf. The people had seen her: she it was whom this last rapturous cheer greeted. My wife stood close behind her, and farther back others of her ladies. Bernenstein and I sprang out. With a last salute to the people Rudolf followed us. He walked up to the highest step but one, and there fell on one knee and kissed the queen's hand. I was by him, and when he looked up in her face I heard him say:

"All's well. He's dead, and the letter burnt."

She raised him with her hand. Her lips moved, but it seemed as though she could find no words to speak. She put her arm through his, and thus they stood for an instant, fronting all Strelsau. Again the cheers rang out, and young Bernenstein sprang forward, waving his helmet and crying like a man possessed, "God save the king!" I was carried away by his enthusiasm and followed his lead. All the people took up the cry with boundless fervor, and thus we all, high and low in Strelsau, that afternoon hailed Mr. Rassendyll for our king. There had been no such zeal since Henry the Lion came back from his wars, a hundred and fifty years ago.

"And yet," observed old Helsing at my elbow, "agitators say that there is no enthusiasm for the house of Elphberg!" He took a pinch of snuff in scornful satisfaction.

Young Bernenstein interrupted his cheering with a short laugh, but fell to his task again in a moment. I had recovered my senses by now, and stood panting, looking down on the crowd. It was growing dusk and the faces became blurred into a white sea. Yet suddenly I seemed to discern one glaring up at me from the middle of the crowd—the pale face of a man with a bandage about his head. I caught Bernenstein's arm and whispered, "Bauer," pointing with my finger where the face was. But, even as I pointed, it was gone; though it seemed impossible for a man to move in that press, yet it was gone. It had come like a cynic's warning across the scene of mock triumph, and went swiftly as it had come, leaving behind it a reminder of our peril. I felt suddenly sick at heart, and almost cried out to the people to have done with their silly shouting.

At last we got away. The plea of fatigue met all visitors who made their way to the door and sought to offer their congratulations; it could not disperse the crowd that hung persistently and contentedly about, ringing us in the palace with a living fence. We still heard their jests and cheers when we were alone in the small saloon that opens on the gardens. My wife and I had come here at Rudolf's request; Bernenstein had assumed the duty of guarding the door. Evening was now falling fast, and it grew dark. The garden was quiet; the distant noise of the crowd threw its stillness into greater relief. Rudolf told us there the story of his struggle with Rupert of Hentzau in the attic of the old house, dwelling on it as lightly as he could. The queen stood by his chair—she would not let him rise; when he finished by telling how he had burnt her letter, she stooped suddenly and kissed him off the brow. Then she looked straight across at Helga, almost defiantly; but Helga ran to her and caught her in her arms.

Rudolf Rassendyll sat with his head resting on his hand. He looked up once at the two women; then he caught my eye, and beckoned me to come to him. I approached him, but for several moments he did not speak. Again he motioned to me, and, resting my hand on the arm of his chair, I bent my head close down to his. He glanced again at the queen, seeming afraid that she would hear what he wished to say.

"Fritz," he whispered at last, "as soon as it's fairly dark I must get away. Bernenstein will come with me. You must stay here."

"Where can you go?"

"To the lodge. I must meet Sapt and arrange matters with him."

I did not understand what plan he had in his head, or what scheme he could contrive. But at the moment my mind was not directed to such matters; it was set on the sight before my eyes. "And the queen?" I whispered in answer to him.

Low as my voice was, she heard it. She turned to us with a sudden, startled movement, still holding Helga's hand. Her eyes searched our faces, and she knew in an instant of what we had been speaking. A little longer still she stood, gazing at us. Then she suddenly sprang forward and threw herself on her knees before Rudolf, her hands uplifted and resting on his shoulders. She forgot our presence, and everything in the world, save her great dread of losing him again.

"Not again, Rudolf, my darling! Not again! Rudolf, I can't bear it again."

Then she dropped her head on his knees and sobbed.

He raised his hand and gently stroked the gleaming hair. But he did not look at her. He gazed out at the garden, which grew dark and dreary in the gathering gloom. His lips were tight set and his face pale and drawn.

I watched him for a moment, then I drew my wife away, and we sat down at a table some way off. From outside still came the cheers and tumult of the joyful, excited crowd. Within there was no sound but the queen's stifled sobbing. Rudolf caressed her shining hair and gazed into the night with sad, set eyes. She raised her head and looked into his face.

"You'll break my heart," she said.

CHAPTER XIX. FOR OUR LOVE AND HER HONOR

RUPERT of Hentzau was dead! That was the thought which, among all our perplexities, came back to me, carrying with it a wonderful relief. To those who have not learnt in fighting against him the height of his audacity and the reach of his designs, it may well seem incredible that his death should breed comfort at a moment when the future was still so dark and uncertain. Yet to me it was so great a thing that I could hardly bring myself to the conviction that we had done with him. True, he was dead; but could he not strike a blow at us even from beyond the gulf?

Such were the half-superstitious thoughts that forced their way into my mind as I stood looking out on the crowd which obstinately encircled the front of the palace. I was alone; Rudolf was with the queen, my wife was resting, Bernenstein had sat down to a meal for which I could find no appetite. By an effort I freed myself from my fancies and tried to concentrate my brain on the facts of our position. We were ringed round with difficulties. To solve them was beyond my power; but I knew where my wish and longing lay. I had no desire to find means by which Rudolf Rassendyll should escape unknown from Strelsau; the king, although dead, be again in death the king, and the queen be left desolate on her mournful and solitary throne. It might be that a brain more astute than mine could bring all this to pass. My imagination would have none of it, but dwelt lovingly on the reign of him who was now king in Strelsau, declaring that to give the kingdom such a ruler would be a splendid fraud, and prove a stroke so bold as to defy detection. Against it stood only the suspicions of Mother Holf—fear or money would close her lips—and the knowledge of Bauer; Bauer's mouth also could be shut, ay, and should be before we were many days older. My reverie led me far; I saw the future years unroll before me in the fair record of a great king's sovereignty. It seemed to me that by the violence and bloodshed we had passed through, fate, for once penitent, was but righting the mistake made when Rudolf was not born a king.

For a long while I stood thus, musing and dreaming; I was roused by the sound of the door opening and closing; turning, I saw the queen. She was alone, and came towards me with timid steps. She looked out for a moment on the square and the people, but drew back suddenly in apparent fear lest they should see her. Then she sat down and turned her face towards mine. I read in her eyes something of the conflict of emotions which possessed her; she seemed at once to deprecate my disapproval and to ask my sympathy; she prayed me to be gentle to her fault and kind to her happiness; self-reproach shadowed her joy, but the golden gleam of it strayed through. I looked eagerly at her; this would not have been her bearing had she come from a last farewell; for the radiance was there, however much dimmed by sorrow and by fearfulness.

"Fritz," she began softly, "I am wicked—so wicked. Won't God punish me for my gladness?"

I fear I paid little heed to her trouble, though I can understand it well enough now.

"Gladness?" I cried in a low voice. "Then you've persuaded him?"

She smiled at me for an instant.

"I mean, you've agreed?" I stammered.

Her eyes again sought mine, and she said in a whisper: "Some day, not now. Oh, not now. Now would be too much. But some day, Fritz, if God will not deal too hardly with me, I—I shall be his, Fritz."

I was intent on my vision, not on hers. I wanted him king; she did not care what he was, so that he was hers, so that he should not leave her.

"He'll take the throne," I cried triumphantly.

"No, no, no. Not the throne. He's going away."

"Going away!" I could not keep the dismay out of my voice.

"Yes, now. But not—not for ever. It will be long—oh, so long—but I can bear it, if I know that at last!" She stopped, still looking up at me with eyes that implored pardon and sympathy.

"I don't understand," said I, bluntly, and, I fear, gruffly, also.

"You were right," she said: "I did persuade him. He wanted to go away again as he went before. Ought I to have let him? Yes, yes! But I couldn't. Fritz, hadn't I done enough? You don't know what I've endured. And I must endure more still. For he will go now, and the time will be very long. But, at last, we shall be together. There is pity in God; we shall be together at last."

"If he goes now, how can he come back?"

"He will not come back; I shall go to him. I shall give up the throne and go to him, some day, when I can be spared from here, when I've done my—my work."

I was aghast at this shattering of my vision, yet I could not be hard to her. I said nothing, but took her hand and pressed it.

"You wanted him to be king?" she whispered.

"With all my heart, madam," said I.

"He wouldn't, Fritz. No, and I shouldn't dare to do that, either."

I fell back on the practical difficulties. "But how can he go?" I asked.

"I don't know. But he knows; he has a plan."

We fell again into silence; her eyes grew more calm, and seemed to look forward in patient hope to the time when her happiness should come to her. I felt like a man suddenly robbed of the exaltation of wine and sunk to dull apathy. "I don't see how he can go," I said sullenly. She did not answer me. A moment later the door again opened. Rudolf came in, followed by Bernenstein. Both wore riding boots and cloaks. I saw on Bernenstein's face just such a look of disappointment as I knew must be on mine. Rudolf seemed calm and even happy. He walked straight up to the queen.

"The horses will be ready in a few minutes," he said gently. Then, turning to me, he asked, "You know what we're going to do, Fritz?"

"Not I, sire," I answered, sulkily.

"Not I, sire!" he repeated, in a half-merry, half-sad mockery. Then he came between Bernenstein and me and passed his arms through ours. "You two villains!" he said. "You two unscrupulous villains! Here you are, as rough as bears, because I won't be a thief! Why have I killed young Rupert and left you rogues alive?"

I felt the friendly pressure of his hand on my arm. I could not answer him. With every word from his lips and every moment of his presence my sorrow grew keener that he would not stay. Bernenstein looked across at me and shrugged his shoulders despairingly. Rudolf gave a little laugh.

"You won't forgive me for not being as great a rogue, won't you?" he asked.

Well, I found nothing to say, but I took my arm out of his and clasped his hand. He gripped mine hard.

"That's old Fritz!" he said; and he caught hold of Bernenstein's hand, which the lieutenant yielded with some reluctance. "Now for the plan," said he. "Bernenstein and I set out at once for the lodge—yes, publicly, as publicly as we can. I shall ride right through the people there, showing myself to as many as will look at me, and letting it be known to everybody where I'm going. We shall get there quite early to-morrow, before it's light. There we shall find what you know. We shall find Sapt, too, and he'll put the finishing touches to our plan for us. Hullo, what's that?"

There was a sudden fresh shouting from the large crowd that still lingered outside the palace. I ran to the window, and saw a commotion in the midst of them. I flung the sash up. Then I heard a well-known, loud, strident voice: "Make way, you rascals, make way."

I turned round again, full of excitement.

"It's Sapt himself!" I said. "He's riding like mad through the crowd, and your servant's just behind him."

"My God, what's happened? Why have they left the lodge?" cried Bernenstein.

The queen looked up in startled alarm, and, rising to her feet, came and passed her arm through Rudolf's. Thus we all stood, listening to the people good-naturedly cheering Sapt, whom they had recognized, and bantering James, whom they took for a servant of the constable's.

The minutes seemed very long as we waited in utter perplexity, almost in consternation. The same thought was in the mind of all of us, silently imparted by one to another in the glances we exchanged. What could have brought them from their guard of the great secret, save its discovery? They would never have left their post while the fulfilment of their trust was possible. By some mishap, some unforeseen chance, the king's body must have been discovered. Then the king's death was known, and the news of it might any moment astonish and bewilder the city.

At last the door was flung open, and a servant announced the Constable of Zenda. Sapt was covered with dust and mud, and James, who entered close on his heels, was in no better plight. Evidently they had ridden hard and furiously; indeed they were still panting. Sapt, with a most perfunctory bow to the queen, came straight to where Rudolf stood.

"Is he dead?" he asked, without preface.

"Yes, Rupert is dead," answered Mr. Rassendyll: "I killed him."

"And the letter?"

"I burnt it."

"And Rischenheim?"

The queen struck in.

"The Count of Luzau-Rischenheim will say and do nothing against me," she said.

Sapt lifted his brows a little. "Well, and Bauer?" he asked.

"Bauer's at large," I answered.

"Hum! Well, it's only Bauer," said the constable, seeming tolerably well pleased. Then his eyes fell on Rudolf and Bernenstein. He stretched out his hand and pointed to their riding-boots. "Whither away so late at night?" he asked.

"First together to the lodge, to find you, then I alone to the frontier," said Mr. Rassendyll.

"One thing at a time. The frontier will wait. What does your Majesty want with me at the lodge?"

"I want so to contrive that I shall be no longer your Majesty," said Rudolf.

Sapt flung himself into a chair and took off his gloves.

"Come, tell me what has happened to-day in Strelsau," he said.

We gave a short and hurried account. He listened with few signs of approval or disapproval, but I thought I saw a gleam in his eyes when I described how all the city had hailed Rudolf as its king and the queen received him as her husband before the eyes of all. Again the hope and vision, shattered by Rudolf's calm resolution, inspired me. Sapt said little, but he had the air of a man with some news in reserve. He seemed to be comparing what we told him with something already known to him but unknown to us. The little servant stood all the while in respectful stillness by the door; but I could see by a glance at his alert face that he followed the whole scene with keen attention.

At the end of the story, Rudolf turned to Sapt. "And your secret—is it safe?" he asked.

"Ay, it's safe enough!"

"Nobody has seen what you had to hide?"

"No; and nobody knows that the king is dead," answered Sapt.

"Then what brings you here?"

"Why, the same thing that was about to bring you to the lodge: the need of a meeting between yourself and me, sire."

"But the lodge—is it left unguarded?"

"The lodge is safe enough," said Colonel Sapt.

Unquestionably there was a secret, a new secret, hidden behind the curt words and brusque manner. I could restrain myself no longer, and sprang forward, saying: "What is it? Tell us, Constable!"

He looked at me, then glanced at Mr. Rassendyll.

"I should like to hear your plan first," he said to Rudolf. "How do you mean to account for your presence alive in the city to-day, when the king has lain dead in the shooting-box since last night?"

We drew close together as Rudolf began his answer. Sapt alone lay back in his chair. The queen also had resumed her seat; she seemed to pay little heed to what we said. I think that she was still engrossed with the struggle and tumult in her own soul. The sin of which she accused herself, and the joy to which her whole being sprang in a greeting which would not be abashed, were at strife between themselves, but joined hands to exclude from her mind any other thought.

"In an hour I must be gone from here," began Rudolf.

"If you wish that, it's easy," observed Colonel Sapt.

"Come, Sapt, be reasonable," smiled Mr. Rassendyll. "Early to-morrow, we—you and I—"

"Oh, I also?" asked the colonel.

"Yes; you, Bernenstein, and I will be at the lodge."

"That's not impossible, though I have had nearly enough riding."

Rudolf fixed his eyes firmly on Sapt's.

"You see," he said, "the king reaches his hunting-lodge early in the morning."

"I follow you, sire."

"And what happens there, Sapt? Does he shoot himself accidentally?"

"Well, that happens sometimes."

"Or does an assassin kill him?"

"Eh, but you've made the best assassin unavailable."

Even at this moment I could not help smiling at the old fellow's surly wit and Rudolf's amused tolerance of it.

"Or does his faithful attendant, Herbert, shoot him?"

"What, make poor Herbert a murderer!"

"Oh, no! By accident—and then, in remorse, kill himself."

"That's very pretty. But doctors have awkward views as to when a man can have shot himself."

"My good Constable, doctors have palms as well as ideas. If you fill the one you supply the other."

"I think," said Sapt, "that both the plans are good. Suppose we choose the latter, what then?"

"Why, then, by to-morrow at midday the news flashes through Ruritania—yes, and through Europe—that the king, miraculously preserved to-day—"

"Praise be to God!" interjected Colonel Sapt; and young Bernenstein laughed.

"Has met a tragic end."

"It will occasion great grief," said Sapt.

"Meanwhile, I am safe over the frontier."

"Oh, you are quite safe?"

"Absolutely. And in the afternoon of to-morrow, you and Bernenstein will set out for Strelsau, bringing with you the body of the king." And Rudolf, after a pause, whispered, "You must shave his face. And if the doctors want to talk about how long he's been dead, why, they have, as I say, palms."

Sapt sat silent for a while, apparently considering the scheme. It was risky enough in all conscience, but success had made Rudolf bold, and he had learnt how slow suspicion is if a deception be bold enough. It is only likely frauds that are detected.

"Well, what do you say?" asked Mr. Rassendyll. I observed that he said nothing to Sapt of what the queen and he had determined to do afterwards.

Sapt wrinkled his forehead. I saw him glance at James, and the slightest, briefest smile showed on James's face.

"It's dangerous, of course," pursued Rudolf. "But I believe that when they see the king's body—"

"That's the point," interrupted Sapt. "They can't see the king's body."

Rudolf looked at him with some surprise. Then speaking in a low voice, lest the queen should hear and be distressed, he went on: "You must prepare it, you know. Bring it here in a shell; only a few officials need see the face."

Sapt rose to his feet and stood facing Mr. Rassendyll.

"The plan's a pretty one, but it breaks down at one point," said he in a strange voice, even harsher than his was wont to be. I was on fire with excitement, for I would have staked my life now that he had some strange tidings for us. "There is no body," said he.

Even Mr. Rassendyll's composure gave way. He sprang forward, catching Sapt by the arm. "No body? What do you mean?" he exclaimed.

Sapt cast another glance at James, and then began in an even, mechanical voice, as though he were reading a lesson he had learnt, or playing a part that habit made familiar:

"That poor fellow Herbert carelessly left a candle burning where the oil and the wood were kept," he said. "This afternoon, about six, James and I lay down for a nap after our meal. At about seven James came to my side and roused me. My room was full of smoke. The lodge was ablaze. I darted out of bed: the fire had made too much headway; we could not hope to quench it; we had but one thought!" He suddenly paused, and looked at James.

"But one thought, to save our companion," said James gravely.

"But one thought, to save our companion. We rushed to the door of the room where he was. I opened the door and tried to enter. It was certain death. James tried, but fell back. Again I rushed in. James pulled me back: it was but another death. We had to save ourselves. We gained the open air. The lodge was a sheet of flame. We could do nothing but stand watching, till the swiftly burning wood blackened to ashes and the flames died down. As we watched we knew that all in the cottage must be dead. What could we do? At last James started off in the hope of getting help. He found a party of charcoal-burners, and they came with him. The flames were burnt down now; and we and they approached the charred ruins. Everything was in ashes. But"—he lowered his voice—"we found what seemed to be the body of Boris the hound; in another room was a charred corpse, whose hunting-horn, melted to a molten mass, told us that it had been Herbert the forester. And there was another corpse, almost shapeless, utterly unrecognizable. We saw it; the charcoal-burners saw it. Then more peasants came round, drawn by the sight of the flames. None could tell who it was; only I and James knew. And we mounted our horses and have ridden here to tell the king."

Sapt finished his lesson or his story. A sob burst from the queen, and she hid her face in her hands. Bernenstein and I, amazed at this strange tale, scarcely understanding whether it were jest or earnest, stood staring stupidly at Sapt. Then I, overcome by the strange thing, turned half-foolish by the bizarre mingling of comedy and impressiveness in Sapt's rendering of it, plucked him by the sleeve, and asked, with something between a laugh and a gasp:

"Who had that other corpse been, Constable?"

He turned his small, keen eyes on me in persistent gravity and unflinching effrontery.

"A Mr. Rassendyll, a friend of the king's, who with his servant James was awaiting his Majesty's return from Strelsau. His servant here is ready to start for England, to tell Mr. Rassendyll's relatives the news."

The queen had begun to listen before now; her eyes were fixed on Sapt, and she had stretched out one arm to him, as if imploring him to read her his riddle. But a few words had in truth declared his device plainly enough in all its simplicity. Rudolf Rassendyll was dead, his body burnt to a cinder, and the king was alive, whole, and on his throne in Strelsau. Thus had Sapt caught from James, the servant, the infection of his madness, and had fulfilled in action the strange imagination which the little man had unfolded to him in order to pass their idle hours at the lodge.

Suddenly Mr. Rassendyll spoke in clear, short tones.

"This is all a lie, Sapt," said he, and his lips curled in contemptuous amusement.

"It's no lie that the lodge is burnt, and the bodies in it, and that half a hundred of the peasants know it, and that no man could tell the body for the king's. As for the rest, it is a lie. But I think the truth in it is enough to serve."

The two men stood facing one another with defiant eyes. Rudolf had caught the meaning of the great and audacious trick which Sapt and his companion had played. It was impossible now to bring the king's body to Strelsau; it seemed no less impossible to declare that the man burnt in the lodge was the king. Thus Sapt had forced Rudolf's hand; he had been inspired by the same vision as we, and endowed with more unshrinking boldness. But when I saw how Rudolf looked at him, I did not know but that they would go from the queen's presence set on a deadly quarrel. Mr. Rassendyll, however, mastered his temper.

"You're all bent on having me a rascal," he said coldly. "Fritz and Bernenstein here urge me; you, Sapt, try to force me. James, there, is in the plot, for all I know."

"I suggested it, sir," said James, not defiantly or with disrespect, but as if in simple dutiful obedience to his master's implied question.

"As I thought—all of you! Well, I won't be forced. I see now that there's no way out of this affair, save one. That one I'll follow."

We none of us spoke, but waited till he should be pleased to continue.

"Of the queen's letter I need say nothing and will say nothing," he pursued. "But I will tell them that I'm not the king, but Rudolf Rassendyll, and that I played the king only in order to serve the queen and punish Rupert of Hentzau. That will serve, and it will cut this net of Sapt's from about my limbs."

He spoke firmly and coldly; so that when I looked at him I was amazed to see how his lips twitched and that his forehead was moist with sweat. Then I understood what a sudden, swift, and fearful struggle he had suffered, and how the great temptation had wrung and tortured him before he, victorious, had set the thing behind him. I went to him and clasped his hand: this action of mine seemed to soften him.

"Sapt, Sapt," he said, "you almost made a rogue of me."

Sapt did not respond to his gentler mood. He had been pacing angrily up and down the room. Now he stopped abruptly before Rudolf, and pointed with his finger at the queen.

"I make a rogue of you?" he exclaimed. "And what do you make of our queen, whom we all serve? What does this truth that you'll tell make of her? Haven't I heard how she greeted you before all Strelsau as her husband and her love? Will they believe that she didn't know her husband? Ay, you may show yourself, you may say they didn't know you. Will they believe she didn't? Was the king's ring on your finger? Where is it? And how comes Mr. Rassendyll to be at Fritz von Tarlenheim's for hours with the queen, when the king is at his hunting lodge? A king has died already, and two men besides, to save a word against her. And you— you'll be the man to set every tongue in Strelsau talking, and every finger pointing in suspicion at her?"

Rudolf made no answer. When Sapt had first uttered the queen's name, he had drawn near and let his hand fall over the back of her chair. She put hers up to meet it, and so they remained. But I saw that Rudolf's face had gone very pale.

"And we, your friends?" pursued Sapt. "For we've stood by you as we've stood by the queen, by God we have—Fritz, and young Bernenstein here, and I. If this truth's told, who'll believe that we were loyal to the king, that we didn't know, that we weren't accomplices in the tricking of the king—maybe, in his murder? Ah, Rudolf Rassendyll, God preserve me from a conscience that won't let me be true to the woman I love, or to the friends who love me!"

I had never seen the old fellow so moved; he carried me with him, as he carried Bernenstein. I know now that we were too ready to be convinced; rather that, borne along by our passionate desire, we needed no convincing at all. His excited appeal seemed to us an argument. At least the danger to the queen, on which he dwelt, was real and true and great.

Then a sudden change came over him. He caught Rudolf's hand and spoke to him again in a low, broken voice, an unwonted softness transforming his harsh tones.

"Lad," he said, "don't say no. Here's the finest lady alive sick for her lover, and the finest country in the world sick for its true king, and the best friends—ay, by Heaven, the best friends—man ever had, sick to call you master. I know nothing about your conscience; but this I know: the king's dead, and the place is empty; and I don't see what Almighty God sent you here for unless it was to fill it. Come, lad—for our love and her honor! While he was alive I'd have killed you sooner than let you take it. He's dead. Now—for our love and her honor, lad!"

I do not know what thoughts passed in Mr. Rassendyll's mind. His face was set and rigid. He made no sign when Sapt finished, but stood as he was, motionless, for a long while. Then he slowly bent his head and looked down into the queen's eyes. For a while she sat looking back into his. Then, carried away by the wild hope of immediate joy, and by her love for him and her pride in the place he was offered, she sprang up and threw herself at his feet, crying: "Yes, yes! For my sake, Rudolf—for my sake!"

"Are you, too, against me, my queen?" he murmured caressing her ruddy hair.

CHAPTER XX. THE DECISION OF HEAVEN

WE were half mad that night, Sapt and Bernenstein and I. The thing seemed to have got into our blood and to have become part of ourselves. For us it was inevitable—nay, it was done. Sapt busied himself in preparing the account of the fire at the hunting-lodge; it was to be communicated to the journals, and it told with much circumstantiality how Rudolf Rassendyll had come to visit the king, with James his servant, and, the king being summoned unexpectedly to the capital, had been awaiting his Majesty's return when he met his fate. There was a short history of Rudolf, a glancing reference to his family, a dignified expression of condolence with his relatives, to whom the king was sending messages of deepest regret by the hands of Mr. Rassendyll's servant. At another table young Bernenstein was drawing up, under the constable's direction, a narrative of Rupert of Hentzau's attempt on the king's life and the king's courage in defending himself. The count, eager to return (so it ran), had persuaded the king to meet him by declaring that he held a state-document of great importance and of a most secret nature; the king, with his habitual fearlessness, had gone alone, but only to refuse with scorn Count Rupert's terms. Enraged at this unfavorable reception, the audacious criminal had made a sudden attack on the king, with what issue all knew. He had met his own death, while the king, perceiving from a glance at the document that it compromised well-known persons, had, with the nobility which marked him, destroyed it unread before the eyes of those who were rushing in to his rescue. I supplied suggestions and improvements; and, engrossed in contriving how to blind curious eyes, we forgot the real and permanent difficulties of the thing we had resolved upon. For us they did not exist; Sapt met every objection by declaring that the thing had been done once and could be done again. Bernenstein and I were not behind him in confidence.

We would guard the secret with brain and hand and life, even as we had guarded and kept the secret of the queen's letter, which would now go with Rupert of Hentzau to his grave. Bauer we could catch and silence: nay, who would listen to such a tale from such a man? Rischenheim was ours; the old woman would keep her doubts between her teeth for her own sake. To his own land and his own people Rudolf must be dead while the King of Ruritania would stand before all Europe recognized, unquestioned, unassailed. True, he must marry the queen again; Sapt was ready with the means, and would hear nothing of the difficulty and risk in finding a hand to perform the necessary ceremony. If we quailed in our courage: we had but to look at the alternative, and find recompense the perils of what we meant to undertake by a consideration the desperate risk involved in abandoning it. Persuaded the substitution of Rudolf for the king was the only thing would serve our turn, we asked no longer whether it possible, but sought only the means to make it safe and safe.

But Rudolf himself had not spoken. Sapt's appeal and the queen's imploring cry had shaken but not overcome him; he had wavered, but he was not won. Yet there was no talk of impossibility or peril in his mouth, any more than in ours: those were not what gave him pause. The score on which he hesitated was whether the thing should be done, not whether it could; our appeals were not to brace a failing courage, but cajole a sturdy sense of honor which found the imposture distasteful so soon as it seemed to serve a personal end. To serve the king he had played the king in old days, but he did not love to play the king when the profit of it was to be his own. Hence he was unmoved till his care for the fair fame of the queen and the love of his friends joined to buffet his resolution.

Then he faltered; but he had not fallen. Yet Colonel Sapt did all as though he had given his assent, and watched the last hours in which his flight from Strelsau was possible go quickly by with more than equanimity. Why hurry Rudolf's resolve? Every moment shut him closer in the trap of an inevitable choice. With every hour that he was called the king, it became more impossible for him to bear any other name all his days. Therefore Sapt let Mr. Rassendyll doubt and struggle, while he himself wrote his story and laid his long-headed plans. And now and then James, the little servant, came in and went out, sedate and smug, but with a quiet satisfaction gleaming in his eyes. He had made a story for a pastime, and it was being translated into history. He at least would bear his part in it unflinchingly.

Before now the queen had left us, persuaded to lie down and try to rest till the matter should be settled. Stilled by Rudolf's gentle rebuke, she had urged him no more in words, but there was an entreaty in her eyes stronger than any spoken prayer, and a piteousness in the lingering of her hand in his harder to resist than ten thousand sad petitions. At last he had led her from the room and commended her to Helga's care. Then, returning to us, he stood silent a little while. We also were silent, Sapt sitting and looking up at him with his brows knit and his teeth restlessly chewing the moustache on his lip.

"Well, lad?" he said at last, briefly putting the great question. Rudolf walked to the window and seemed to lose himself for a moment in the contemplation of the quiet night. There were no more than a few stragglers in the street now; the moon shone white and clear on the empty square.

"I should like to walk up and down outside and think it over," he said, turning to us; and, as Bernenstein sprang up to accompany him, he added, "No. Alone."

"Yes, do," said old Sapt, with a glance at the clock, whose hands were now hard on two o'clock. "Take your time, lad, take your time."

Rudolf looked at him and broke into a smile.

"I'm not your dupe, old Sapt," said he, shaking his head. "Trust me, if I decide to get away, I'll get away, be it what o'clock it will."

"Yes, confound you!" grinned Colonel Sapt.

So he left us, and then came that long time of scheming and planning, and most persistent eye-shutting, in which occupations an hour wore its life away. Rudolf had not passed out of the porch, and we supposed that he had betaken himself to the gardens, there to fight his battle. Old Sapt, having done his work, suddenly turned talkative.

"That moon there," he said, pointing his square, thick forefinger at the window, "is a mighty untrustworthy lady. I've known her wake a villain's conscience before now."

"I've known her send a lover's to sleep," laughed young Bernenstein, rising from his table, stretching himself, and lighting a cigar.

"Ay, she's apt to take a man out of what he is," pursued old Sapt. "Set a quiet man near her, and he dreams of battle; an ambitious fellow, after ten minutes of her, will ask nothing better than to muse all his life away. I don't trust her, Fritz; I wish the night were dark."

"What will she do to Rudolf Rassendyll?" I asked, falling in with the old fellow's whimsical mood.

"He will see the queen's face in hers," cried Bernenstein.

"He may see God's," said Sapt; and he shook himself as though an unwelcome thought had found its way to his mind and lips.

A pause fell on us, born of the colonel's last remark. We looked one another in the face. At last Sapt brought his hand down on the table with a bang.

"I'll not go back," he said sullenly, almost fiercely.

"Nor I," said Bernenstein, drawing himself up. "Nor you, Tarlenheim?"

"No, I also go on," I answered. Then again there was a moment's silence.

"She may make a man soft as a sponge," reflected Sapt, starting again, "or hard as a bar of steel. I should feel safer if the night were dark. I've looked at her often from my tent and from bare ground, and I know her. She got me a decoration, and once she came near to making me turn tail. Have nothing to do with her, young Bernenstein."

"I'll keep my eyes for beauties nearer at hand," said Bernenstein, whose volatile temper soon threw off a serious mood.

"There's a chance for you, now Rupert of Hentzau's gone," said Sapt grimly.

As he spoke there was a knock at the door. When it opened James entered.

"The Count of Luzau-Rischenheim begs to be allowed to speak with the king," said James.

"We expect his Majesty every moment. Beg the count to enter," Sapt answered; and, when Rischenheim came in, he went on, motioning the count to a chair: "We are talking, my lord, of the influence of the moon on the careers of men."

"What are you going to do? What have you decided?" burst out Rischenheim impatiently.

"We decide nothing," answered Sapt.

"Then what has Mr.—what has the king decided?"

"The king decides nothing, my lord. She decides," and the old fellow pointed again through the window towards the moon. "At this moment she makes or unmakes a king; but I can't tell you which. What of your cousin?"

"You know that my cousin's dead."

"Yes, I know that. What of him, though?"

"Sir," said Rischenheim with some dignity, "since he is dead, let him rest in peace. It is not for us to judge him."

"He may well wish it were. For, by Heaven, I believe I should let the rogue off," said Colonel Sapt, "and I don't think his Judge will."

"God forgive him, I loved him," said Rischenheim. "Yes, and many have loved him. His servants loved him, sir."

"Friend Bauer, for example?"

"Yes, Bauer loved him. Where is Bauer?"

"I hope he's gone to hell with his loved master," grunted Sapt, but he had the grace to lower his voice and shield his mouth with his hand, so that Rischenheim did not hear.

"We don't know where he is," I answered.

"I am come," said Rischenheim, "to put my services in all respects at the queen's disposal."

"And at the king's?" asked Sapt.

"At the king's? But the king is dead."

"Therefore 'Long live the king!'" struck in young Bernenstein.

"If there should be a king—" began Sapt.

"You'll do that?" interrupted Rischenheim in breathless agitation.

"She is deciding," said Colonel Sapt, and again he pointed to the moon.

"But she's a plaguey long time about it," remarked Lieutenant von Bernenstein.

Rischenheim sat silent for a moment. His face was pale, and when he spoke his voice trembled. But his words were resolute enough.

"I gave my honor to the queen, and even in that I will serve her if she commands me."

Bernenstein sprang forward and caught him by the hand. "That's what I like," said he, "and damn the moon, colonel!" His sentence was hardly out of his mouth when the door opened, and to our astonishment the queen entered. Helga was just behind her; her clasped hands and frightened eyes seemed to protest that their coming was against her will. The queen was clad in a long white robe, and her hair hung on her shoulders, being but loosely bound with a ribbon. Her air showed great agitation, and without any greeting or notice of the rest she walked quickly across the room to me.

"The dream, Fritz," she said. "It has come again. Helga persuaded me to lie down, and I was very tired, so at last I fell asleep. Then it came. I saw him, Fritz—I saw him as plainly as I see you. They all called him king, as they did to-day; but they did not cheer. They were quiet, and looked at him with sad faces. I could not hear what they said; they spoke in hushed voices. I heard nothing more than 'the king, the king,' and he seemed to hear not even that. He lay still; he was lying on something, something covered with hanging stuff, I couldn't see what it was; yes, quite still. His face was so pale, and he didn't hear them say 'the king.' Fritz, Fritz, he looked as if he were dead! Where is he? Where have you let him go?"

She turned from me and her eyes flashed over the rest. "Where is he? Why aren't you with him?" she demanded, with a sudden change of tone; "why aren't you round him? You should be between him and danger, ready to give your lives for his. Indeed, gentlemen, you take your duty lightly."

It might be that there was little reason in her words. There appeared to be no danger threatening him, and after all he was not our king, much as we desired to make him such. Yet we did not think of any such matter. We were abashed before her reproof and took her indignation as deserved. We hung our heads, and Sapt's shame betrayed itself in the dogged sullenness of his answer.

"He has chosen to go walking, madam, and to go alone. He ordered us—I say, he ordered us not to come. Surely we are right to obey him?" The sarcastic inflection of his voice conveyed his opinion of the queen's extravagance.

"Obey him? Yes. You couldn't go with him if he forbade you. But you should follow him; you should keep him in sight."

This much she spoke in proud tones and with a disdainful manner, but then came a sudden return to her former bearing. She held out her hands towards me, wailing:

"Fritz, where is he? Is he safe? Find him for me, Fritz; find him."

"I'll find him for you if he's above ground, madam," I cried, for her appeal touched me to the heart.

"He's no farther off than the gardens," grumbled old Sapt, still resentful of the queen's reproof and scornful of the woman's agitation. He was also out of temper with Rudolf himself, because the moon took so long in deciding whether she would make or unmake a king.

"The gardens!" she cried. "Then let us look for him. Oh, you've let him walk in the gardens alone?"

"What should harm the fellow?" muttered Sapt.

She did not hear him, for she had swept out of the room. Helga went with her, and we all followed, Sapt behind the rest of us, still very surly. I heard him grumbling away as we ran downstairs, and, having passed along the great corridor, came to the small saloon that opened on the gardens. There were no servants about, but we encountered a night-watchman, and Bernenstein snatched the lantern from the astonished man's hand.

Save for the dim light thus furnished, the room was dark. But outside the windows the moon streamed brightly down on the broad gravel walk, on the formal flower-beds, and the great trees in the gardens. The queen made straight for the window. I followed her, and, having flung the window open, stood by her. The air was sweet, and the breeze struck with grateful coolness on my face. I saw that Sapt had come near and stood on the other side of the queen. My wife and the others were behind, looking out where our shoulders left space.

There, in the bright moonlight, on the far side of the broad terrace, close by the line of tall trees that fringed its edge, we saw Rudolf Rassendyll pacing slowly up and down, with his hands behind his back and his eyes fixed on the arbiter of his fate, on her who was to make him a king or send him a fugitive from Strelsau.

"There he is, madam," said Sapt. "Safe enough!"

The queen did not answer. Sapt said no more, and of the rest of us none spoke. We stood watching him as he struggled with his great issue; a greater surely has seldom fallen to the lot of any man born in a private station. Yet I could read little of it on the face that the rays of white light displayed so clearly, although they turned his healthy tints to a dull gray, and gave unnatural sharpness to his features against the deep background of black foliage.

I heard the queen's quick breathing, but there was scarcely another sound. I saw her clutch her gown and pull it away a little from her throat; save for that none in the group moved. The lantern's light was too dim to force notice from Mr. Rassendyll. Unconscious of our presence, he wrestled with fate that night in the gardens.

Suddenly the faintest exclamation came from Sapt. He put his hand back and beckoned to Bernenstein. The young man handed his lantern to the constable, who set it close to the side of the window-frame. The queen, absolutely engrossed in her lover, saw nothing, but I perceived what had caught Sapt's attention. There were scores on the paint and indentations in the wood, just at the edge of the panel and near the lock. I glanced at Sapt, who nodded his head. It looked very much as though somebody had tried to force the door that night, employing a knife which had dented the woodwork and scratched the paint. The least thing was enough to alarm us, standing where we stood, and the constable's face was full of suspicion. Who had sought an entrance? It could be no trained and practised housebreaker; he would have had better tools.

But now our attention was again diverted. Rudolf stopped short. He still looked for a moment at the sky, then his glance dropped to the ground at his feet. A second later he jerked his head—it was bare, and I saw the dark red hair stir with the movement—like a man who has settled something which caused him a puzzle. In an instant we knew, by the quick intuition of contagious emotion, that the question had found its answer. He was by now king or a fugitive. The Lady of the Skies had given her decision. The thrill ran through us; I felt the queen draw herself together at my side; I felt the muscles of Rischenheim's arm which rested against my shoulder grow rigid and taut. Sapt's face was full of eagerness, and he gnawed his moustache silently. We gathered closer to one another. At last we could bear the suspense no longer. With one look at the queen and another at me, Sapt stepped on to the gravel. He would go and learn the answer; thus the unendurable strain that had stretched us like tortured men on a rack would be relieved. The queen did not answer his glance, nor even seem to see that he had moved. Her eyes were still all for Mr. Rassendyll, her thoughts buried in his; for her happiness was in his hands and lay poised on the issue of that decision whose momentousness held him for a moment motionless on the path. Often I seem to see him as he stood there, tall, straight, and stately, the king a man's fancy paints when he reads of great monarchs who flourished long ago in the springtime of the world.

Sapt's step crunched on the gravel. Rudolf heard it and turned his head. He saw Sapt, and he saw me also behind Sapt. He smiled composedly and brightly, but he did not move from where he was. He held out both hands towards the constable and caught him in their double grasp, still smiling down in his face. I was no nearer to reading his decision, though I saw that he had reached a resolution that was immovable and gave peace to his soul. If he meant to go on he would go on now, on to the end, without a backward look or a falter of his foot; if he had chosen the other way, he would depart without a murmur or a hesitation. The queen's quick breathing had ceased, she seemed like a statue; but Rischenheim moved impatiently, as though he could no longer endure the waiting.

Sapt's voice came harsh and grating.

"Well?" he cried. "Which is it to be—backward or forward?" Rudolf pressed his hands and looked into his eyes. The answer asked but a word from him. The queen caught my arm; her rigid limbs seemed to give way, and she would have fallen if I had not supported her. At the same instant a man sprang out of the dark line of tall trees, directly behind Mr. Rassendyll. Bernenstein uttered a loud startled cry and rushed forward, pushing the queen herself violently out of his path. His hand flew to his side, and he ripped the heavy cavalry sword that belonged to his uniform of the Cuirassiers of the Guard from its sheath. I saw it flash in the moonlight, but its flash was quenched in a brighter short blaze. A shot rang out through the quiet gardens. Mr. Rassendyll did not loose his hold of Sapt's hands, but he sank slowly on to his knees. Sapt seemed paralyzed.

Again Bernenstein cried out. It was a name this time. "Bauer! By God, Bauer!" he cried.

In an instant he was across the path and by the trees. The assassin fired again, but now he missed. We saw the great sword flash high above Bernenstein's head and heard it whistle through the air. It crashed on the crown of Bauer's head, and he fell like a log to the ground with his skull split. The queen's hold on me relaxed; she sank into Rischenheim's arms. I ran forward and knelt by Mr. Rassendyll. He still held Sapt's hands, and by their help buoyed himself up. But when he saw me he let go of them and sank back against me, his head resting on my chest. He moved his lips, but seemed unable to speak. He was shot through the back. Bauer had avenged the master whom he loved, and was gone to meet him.

There was a sudden stir from inside the palace. Shutters were flung back and windows thrown open. The group we made stood clean-cut, plainly visible in the moonlight. A moment later there was a rush of eager feet, and we were surrounded by officers and servants. Bernenstein stood by me now, leaning on his sword; Sapt had not uttered a word; his face was distorted with horror and bitterness. Rudolf's eyes were closed and his head lay back against me.

"A man has shot the king," said I, in bald, stupid explanation.

All at once I found James, Mr. Rassendyll's servant, by me.

"I have sent for doctors, my lord," he said. "Come, let us carry him in."

He, Sapt and I lifted Rudolf and bore him across the gravel terrace and into the little saloon. We passed the queen. She was leaning on Rischenheim's arm, and held my wife's hand. We laid Rudolf down on a couch. Outside I heard Bernenstein say, "Pick up that fellow and carry him somewhere out of sight." Then he also came in, followed by a crowd. He sent them all to the door, and we were left alone, waiting for the surgeon. The queen came up, Rischenheim still supporting her. "Rudolf! Rudolf!" she whispered, very softly.

He opened his eyes, and his lips bent in a smile. She flung herself on her knees and kissed his hand passionately. "The surgeon will be here directly," said I.

Rudolf's eyes had been on the queen. As I spoke he looked up at me, smiled again, and shook his head. I turned away.

When the surgeon came Sapt and I assisted him in his examination. The queen had been led away, and we were alone. The examination was very short. Then we carried Rudolf to a bed; the nearest chanced to be in Bernenstein's room; there we laid him, and there all that could be done for him was done. All this time we had asked no questions of the surgeon, and he had given no information. We knew too well to ask: we had all seen men die before now, and the look on the face was familiar to us. Two or three more doctors, the most eminent in Strelsau, came now, having been hastily summoned. It was their right to be called; but, for all the good they were, they might have been left to sleep the night out in their beds. They drew together in a little group at the end of the room and talked for a few minutes in low tones. James lifted his master's head and gave him a drink of water. Rudolf swallowed it with difficulty. Then I saw him feebly press James's hand, for the little man's face was full of sorrow. As his master smiled the servant mustered a smile in answer. I crossed over to the doctors. "Well, gentlemen?" I asked.

They looked at one another, then the greatest of them said gravely:

"The king may live an hour, Count Fritz. Should you not send for a priest?"

I went straight back to Rudolf Rassendyll. His eyes greeted me and questioned me. He was a man, and I played no silly tricks with him. I bent down and said: "An hour, they think, Rudolf."

He made one restless movement, whether of pain or protest I do not know. Then he spoke, very low, slowly, and with difficulty.

"Then they can go," he said; and when I spoke of a priest he shook his head.

I went back to them and asked if anything more could be done. The answer was nothing; but I could not prevail further than to get all save one sent into an adjoining room; he who remained seated himself at a table some way off. Rudolf's eyes had closed again; old Sapt, who had not once spoken since the shot was fired, raised a haggard face to mine.

"We'd better fetch her to him," he said hoarsely. I nodded my head.

Sapt went while I stayed by him. Bernenstein came to him, bent down, and kissed his hand. The young fellow, who had borne himself with such reckless courage and dash throughout the affair, was quite unmanned now, and the tears were rolling down his face. I could have been much in the same plight, but I would not before Mr. Rassendyll. He smiled at Bernenstein. Then he said to me:

"Is she coming, Fritz?"

"Yes, she's coming, sire," I answered.

He noticed the style of my address; a faint amused gleam shot into his languid eyes.

"Well, for an hour, then," he murmured, and lay back on his pillows.

She came, dry-eyed, calm, and queenly. We all drew back, and she knelt down by his bed, holding his hand in her two hands. Presently the hand stirred; she let it go; then, knowing well what he wanted, she raised it herself and placed it on her head, while she bowed her face to the bed. His hand wandered for the last time over the gleaming hair that he had loved so well. She rose, passed her arm about his shoulders, and kissed his lips. Her face rested close to his, and he seemed to speak to her, but we could not have heard the words even if we would. So they remained for a long while.

The doctor came and felt his pulse, retreating afterwards with close-shut lips. We drew a little nearer, for we knew that he would not be long with us now. Suddenly strength seemed to come upon him. He raised himself in his bed, and spoke in distinct tones.

"God has decided," he said. "I've tried to do the right thing through it all. Sapt, and Bernenstein, and you, old Fritz, shake my hand. No, don't kiss it. We've done with pretence now."

We shook his hand as he bade us. Then he took the queen's hand. Again she knew his mind, and moved it to his lips. "In life and in death, my sweet queen," he murmured. And thus he fell asleep.

CHAPTER XXI. THE COMING OF THE DREAM

THERE IS little need, and I have little heart, to dwell on what followed the death of Mr. Rassendyll. The plans we had laid to secure his tenure of the throne, in case he had accepted it, served well in the event of his death. Bauer's lips were for ever sealed; the old woman was too scared and appalled to hint even to her gossips of the suspicions she entertained. Rischenheim was loyal to the pledge he had given to the queen. The ashes of the hunting-lodge held their secret fast, and none suspected when the charred body which was called Rudolf Rassendyll's was laid to quiet rest in the graveyard of the town of Zenda, hard by the tomb of Herbert the forester. For we had from the first rejected any idea of bringing the king's body to Strelsau and setting it in the place of Mr. Rassendyll's. The difficulties of such an undertaking were almost insuperable; in our hearts we did not desire to conquer them. As a king Rudolf Rassendyll had died, as a king let him lie. As a king he lay in his palace at Strelsau, while the news of his murder at the hands of a confederate of Rupert of Hentzau went forth to startle and appall the world. At a mighty price our task had been made easy; many might have doubted the living, none questioned the dead; suspicions which might have gathered round a throne died away at the gate of a vault. The king was dead. Who would ask if it were in truth the king who lay in state in the great hall of the palace, or whether the humble grave at Zenda held the bones of the last male Elphberg? In the silence of the grave all murmurs and questionings were hushed.

Throughout the day people had been passing and repassing through the great hall. There, on a stately bier surmounted by a crown and the drooping folds of the royal banner, lay Rudolf Rassendyll. The highest officer guarded him; in the cathedral the archbishop said a mass for his soul. He had lain there three days; the evening of the third had come, and early on the morrow he was to be buried. There is a little gallery in the hall, that looks down on the spot where the bier stood; here was I on this evening, and with me Queen Flavia. We were alone together, and together we saw beneath us the calm face of the dead man. He was clad in the white uniform in which he had been crowned; the ribbon of the Red Rose was across his breast. His hand held a true red rose, fresh and fragrant; Flavia herself had set it there, that even in death he might not miss the chosen token of her love. I had not spoken to her, nor she to me, since we came there. We watched the pomp round him, and the circles of people that came to bring a wreath for him or to look upon his face. I saw a girl come and kneel long at the bier's foot. She rose and went away sobbing, leaving a little circlet of flowers. It was Rosa Holf. I saw women come and go weeping, and men bite their lips as they passed by. Rischenheim came, pale-faced and troubled; and while all came and went, there, immovable, with drawn sword, in military stiffness, old Sapt stood at the head of the bier, his eyes set steadily in front of him, and his body never stirring from hour to hour through the long day.

A distant faint hum of voices reached us. The queen laid her hand on my arm.

"It is the dream, Fritz," she said. "Hark! They speak of the king; they speak in low voices and with grief, but they call him king. It's what I saw in the dream. But he does not hear nor heed. No, he can't hear nor heed even when I call him my king."

A sudden impulse came on me, and I turned to her, asking:

"What had he decided, madam? Would he have been king?" She started a little.

"He didn't tell me," she answered, "and I didn't think of it while he spoke to me."

"Of what then did he speak, madam?"

"Only of his love—of nothing but his love, Fritz," she answered.

Well, I take it that when a man comes to die, love is more to him than a kingdom: it may be, if we could see truly, that it is more to him even while he lives.

"Of nothing but his great love for me, Fritz," she said again. "And my love brought him to his death."

"He wouldn't have had it otherwise," said I.

"No," she whispered; and she leant over the parapet of the gallery, stretching out her arms to him. But he lay still and quiet, not hearing and not heeding what she murmured, "My king! my king!" It was even as it had been in the dream.

That night James, the servant, took leave of his dead master and of us. He carried to England by word of mouth—for we dared write nothing down—the truth concerning the King of Ruritania and Mr. Rassendyll. It was to be told to the Earl of Burlesdon, Rudolf's brother, under a pledge of secrecy; and to this day the earl is the only man besides ourselves who knows the story. His errand done, James returned in order to enter the queen's service, in which he still is; and he told us that when Lord Burlesdon had heard the story he sat silent for a great while, and then said:

"He did well. Some day I will visit his grave. Tell her Majesty that there is still a Rassendyll, if she has need of one."

The offer was such as should come from a man of Rudolf's name, yet I trust that the queen needs no further service than such as it is our humble duty and dear delight to render her. It is our part to strive to lighten the burden that she bears, and by our love to assuage her undying grief. For she reigns now in Ruritania alone, the last of all the Elphbergs; and her only joy is to talk of Mr. Rassendyll with those few who knew him, her only hope that she may some day be with him again.

In great pomp we laid him to his rest in the vault of the kings of Ruritania in the Cathedral of Strelsau. There he lies among the princes of the House of Elphberg. I think that if there be indeed any consciousness among the dead, or any knowledge of what passes in the world they have left, they should be proud to call him brother. There rises in memory of him a stately monument, and people point it out to one another as the memorial of King Rudolf. I go often to the spot, and recall in thought all that passed when he came the first time to Zenda, and again on his second coming. For I mourn him as a man mourns a trusted leader and a loved comrade, and I should have asked no better than to be allowed to serve him all my days. Yet I serve the queen, and in that I do most truly serve her lover.

Times change for all of us. The roaring flood of youth goes by, and the stream of life sinks to a quiet flow. Sapt is an old man now; soon my sons will be grown up, men enough themselves to serve Queen Flavia. Yet the memory of Rudolf Rassendyll is fresh to me as on the day he died, and the vision of the death of Rupert of Hentzau dances often before my eyes. It may be that some day the whole story shall be told, and men shall judge of it for themselves. To me it seems now as though all had ended well. I must not be misunderstood: my heart is still sore for the loss of him. But we saved the queen's fair fame, and to Rudolf himself the fatal stroke came as a relief from a choice too difficult: on the one side lay what impaired his own honor, on the other what threatened hers. As I think on this my anger at his death is less, though my grief cannot be. To this day I know not how he chose; no, and I don't know how he should have chosen. Yet he had chosen, for his face was calm and clear.

Come, I have thought so much of him that I will go now and stand before his monument, taking with me my last-born son, a little lad of ten. He is not too young to desire to serve the queen, and not too young to learn to love and reverence him who sleeps there in the vault and was in his life the noblest gentleman I have known.

I will take the boy with me and tell him what I may of brave King Rudolf, how he fought and how he loved, and how he held the queen's honor and his own above all things in this world. The boy is not too young to learn such lessons from the life of Mr. Rassendyll. And while we stand there I will turn again into his native tongue—for, alas, the young rogue loves his toy soldiers better than his Latin!—the inscription that the queen wrote with her own hand, directing that it should be inscribed in that stately tongue over the tomb in which her life lies buried.

"To Rudolf, who reigned lately in this city, and reigns for ever in her heart.—QUEEN FLAVIA."

I told him the meaning, and he spelt the big words over in his childish voice; at first he stumbled, but the second time he had it right, and recited with a little touch of awe in his fresh young tones:

RUDOLFO

Qui in hac civitate nuper regnavit In corde ipsius in aeternum regnat

FLAVIA REGINA.

I felt his hand tremble in mine, and he looked up in my face. "God save the Queen, father," said he.

THE HEART OF PRINCESS OSRA

CHAPTER I.

The Happiness of Stephen the Smith.

"Stephen! Stephen! Stephen!"

The impatient cry was heard through all the narrow gloomy street, where the old richly-carved house-fronts bowed to meet one another and left for the eye's comfort only a bare glimpse of blue. It was, men said, the oldest street in Strelsau, even as the sign of the "Silver Ship" was the oldest sign known to exist in the city. For when Aaron Lazarus the Jew came there, seventy years before, he had been the tenth man in unbroken line that took up the business; and now Stephen Nados, his apprentice and successor, was the eleventh. Old Lazarus had made a great business of it, and had spent his savings in buying up the better part of the street; but since Jews then might hold no property in Strelsau, he had taken all the deeds in the name of Stephen Nados; and when he came to die, being unable to carry his houses or his money with him, having no kindred, and caring not a straw for any man or woman alive save Stephen, he bade Stephen let the deeds be, and, with a last curse against the Christians (of whom Stephen was one, and a devout one), he kissed the young man, and turned his face to the wall and died. Therefore Stephen was a rich man, and had no need to carry on the business, though it never entered his mind to do anything else; for half the people who raised their heads at the sound of the cry were Stephen's tenants, and paid him rent when he asked for it; a thing he did when he chanced to remember, and could tear himself away from chasing a goblet or fashioning a little silver saint; for Stephen loved his craft more than his rents; therefore, again, he was well liked in the quarter.

"Stephen! Stephen!" cried Prince Henry, impatiently hammering on the closed door with his whip. "Plague take the man! Is he dead?"

The men in the quarter went on with their work; the women moved idly to the doors; the girls came out into the street and clustered here and there, looking at the Prince. For although he was not so handsome as that scamp Rudolf, his brother, who had just come back from his travels with half a dozen wild stories spurring after him, yet Henry was a comely youth, as he sat on his chestnut mare, with his blue eyes full of impatience, and his chestnut curls fringing his shoulders. So the girls clustered and looked. Moreover Stephen the smith must come soon, and the sight of him was worth a moment's waiting; for he buried himself all day in his workshop, and no laughing challenge could lure him out.

"Though, in truth," said one of the girls, tossing her head, "it's thankless work to spend a glance on either, for they do not return it. Now when Rudolf comes——"

She broke off with a laugh, and her comrades joined in it. Rudolf left no debts of that sort unpaid, however deep he might be in the books of Stephen Nados and of the others who furnished his daily needs.

Presently Stephen came, unbolting his door with much deliberation, and greeting Prince Henry with a restrained courtesy. He was not very well pleased to see his guest, for it was a ticklish moment with the nose of Saint Peter, and Stephen would have liked to finish the job uninterrupted. Still, the Prince was a prince, a gentleman, and a friend, and Stephen would not be uncivil to him.

"You ride early to-day, sir," he observed, patting the chestnut mare.

"I have a good reason," answered Henry. "The Lion rages to-day."

Stephen put up his hand to shelter his eyes from a ray of sunshine that had evaded the nodding walls and crept in; it lit up his flaxen hair, which he wore long and in thick waves, and played in his yellow beard; and he looked very grave. For when the Lion raged, strange and alarming things might happen in the city of Strelsau. The stories of his last fit of passion were yet hardly old.

"What has vexed the King?" he asked; for he knew that Prince Henry spoke of his father, Henry surnamed the Lion, now an old man, yet as fierce as when he had been young. "Is it your brother again?"

"For a marvel, no. It is myself, Stephen. And he is more furious with me than he has ever been with Rudolf; aye, even more than he was at all the stories that followed my brother home."

"And what is the cause of it all, sir, and how is it in my power to help?"

"That you will find out very soon," said the Prince with a bitter laugh. "You will be sent for to the palace in an hour, Stephen."

"If it is about the King's ring, the ring is not finished," said Stephen.

"It is not about the ring. Yet indeed it is, in a way, about a ring. For you are to be married, Stephen. This very day you are to be married."

"I think not, sir," said Stephen mildly. "For it is a thing that a man himself hears about if it be true."

"But the King thinks so; Stephen, have you remarked, among my sister Osra's ladies, a certain dark lady, with black hair and eyes? I cannot describe her eyes."

"But you can tell me her name, sir," suggested Stephen, who was a practical man.

"Her name? Oh, her name is Hilda—Hilda von Lauengram."

"Aye, I know the Countess Hilda. I have made a bracelet for her."

"She is the most beautiful creature alive!" cried Prince Henry, in a sudden rapture and so loudly (being carried away by his passion) that the girls heard him and wondered of whom he spoke with so great an enthusiasm.

"To those to whom she seems such," observed Stephen. "But, pray, how am I concerned in all this, sir?"

The Prince's smile grew more bitter as he answered:

"Why, you are to marry her. It was an idle suggestion of Osra's, made in jest; my father is pleased to approve of it in earnest."

Then he bent in his saddle and went on in a hurried urgent whisper: "I love her better than my life, Stephen—better than heaven; and my faith and word are pledged to her; and last night I was to have fled with her—for I knew better than to face the old Lion—but Osra found her making preparations and we were discovered. Then Osra was scornful, and the King mad, and Rudolf laughed; and when they talked of what was to be done to her, Osra came in with her laughing suggestion. It caught the King's angry fancy, and he swore that it should be so. And, since the Archbishop is away, he has bidden the Bishop of Modenstein be at the palace at twelve to-day, and you will be brought there also, and you will be married to her. But, by heavens, I'll have your blood if you are!" With this sudden outbreak of fury the Prince ended. Yet a moment later, he put out his hand to the smith, saying: "It's not your fault, man."

"That's true enough," said the smith; "for I have no desire to marry her; and it is not fitting that a lady of her birth should mate with a smith; she is of a great house, and she would hate and despise me."

Prince Henry was about to assent when his eye chanced to fall on Stephen the smith. Now the smith was a very handsome man—handsomer, many said, than Prince Rudolf himself, whom no lady could look on without admiration; he stood six feet and two inches in his flat working shoes; he was very broad, and could leap higher and hurl a stone farther than any man in Strelsau. Moreover he looked kind and gentle, yet was reputed to grow angry at times, and then to be very dangerous. Therefore Prince Henry, knowing (or thinking that he knew) the caprices of women, and how they are caught by this and that, was suddenly seized with a terrible fear that the Countess Hilda might not despise Stephen the smith. Yet he did not express his fear, but said that it was an impossible thing that a lady of the Countess's birth (for the House of Lauengram was very noble) should wed a silversmith, even though he were as fine a fellow as his good friend Stephen; to which gracious speech Stephen made no reply, but stood very thoughtful, with his hand on the neck of the chestnut mare. But at last he said: "In any case it cannot be, for I am bound already."

"A wife? Have you a wife?" cried the Prince eagerly.

"No; but my heart is bound," said Stephen the smith.

"The King will make little of that. Yet who is she? Is she any of these girls who stand looking at us?"

"No, she is none of these," answered Stephen, smiling as though such an idea were very ludicrous.

"And are you pledged to her?"

"I to her, but not she to me."

"But does she love you?"

"I think it most unlikely," said Stephen the smith.

"The Lion will care nothing for this," groaned the Prince despondently. "They will send for you in half an hour. For heaven's sake spare her, Stephen!"

"Spare her, sir?"

"Do not consent to marry her, however urgently the King may command you."

The smith shook his head, smiling still. Prince Henry rode sorrowfully away, spending not a glance on the bevy of girls who watched him go; and Stephen, turning into his house, shut the door, and with one great sigh set to work again on the nose of Saint Peter.

"For anyhow," said he, "a man can work." And after a long pause he added, "I never thought to tell any one; but if I must, I must."

Now, sure enough, when the clock on the Cathedral wanted a quarter of an hour of noon, two of the King's Guard came and bade Stephen follow them with all haste to the palace; and since they were very urgent and no time was to be lost, he followed them as he was, in his apron, without washing his hands or getting rid of the dust that hung about him from his work. However he had finished Saint Peter's nose and all had gone well with it, so that he went in a contented frame of mind, determined to tell the whole truth to King Henry the Lion sooner than be forced into a marriage with the Countess Hilda von Lauengram.

The Lion sat in his great chair; he was a very thin old man, with a face haggard and deeply lined; his eyes, set far back in his head, glowed and glowered, and his fingers pulled his sparse white beard. On his right Prince Rudolf lolled on a low seat, smiling at the play; on his left sat that wonderfully fair lady, the Princess Osra, then in the first bloom of her young beauty; and she was smiling scornfully. Prince Henry stood before his father, and some yards from him was the Countess Hilda, trembling and tearful, supported by one of her companions; and finally, since the Archbishop was gone to Rome to get himself a Scarlet Hat, the Bishop of Modenstein, a young man of noble family, was there, most richly arrayed in choicest lace and handsomest vestments, ready to perform the ceremony. Prince Rudolf had beckoned the Bishop near him, and was jesting with him in an undertone. The Bishop laughed as a man laughs who knows he should not laugh but cannot well help himself; for Rudolf owned a pretty wit, although it was sadly unrestrained.

The King's fury, having had a night and a morning to grow cool in, had now settled into a cold ironical mood, which argued no less resolution than his first fierce wrath. There was a grim smile on his face as he addressed the smith, who, having bowed to the company, was standing between the Countess and Prince Henry.

"The House of Elphberg," said the King, with mocking graciousness, "well recognises your worth, Stephen, my friend. We are indebted to you——"

"It's a thousand crowns or more from Prince Rudolf alone, sire," interrupted Stephen, with a bow to the Prince he named.

"For much faithful service," pursued the King, while Rudolf laughed again. "I have therefore determined to reward you with the hand of a lady who is, it may be, above your station, but in no way above your worth. Behold her! Is she not handsome? On my word, I envy you, smith. She is beautiful, young, high-born. You are lucky, smith. Nay, no thanks. It is but what you deserve—and no more than she deserves. Take her and be happy," and he ended with a snarling laugh, as he waved his lean veined hand towards the unhappy Countess, and fixed his sneering eyes on the face of his son Henry, who had turned pale as death, but neither spoke nor moved.

The Bishop of Modenstein—he was of the House of Hentzau, many of which have been famous in history—lifted up his hands in horror at Rudolf's last whispered jest, and then, advancing with a bow to the King, asked if he were now to perform his sacred duties.

"Aye, get on with it," growled the Lion, not heeding the Countess's sobs or the entreaty in his son's face. And the Princess Osra sat unmoved, the scornful smile still on her lips; it seemed as though she had no pity for a brother who could stoop, or for a girl who had dared to soar too high.

"Wait, wait!" said Stephen the smith. "Does this lady love me, sire?"

"Aye, she loves you enough for the purpose, smith," grinned the King. "Do not be uneasy."

"May I ask her if she loves me, sire?"

"Why, no, smith. Your King's word must be enough for you."

"And your Majesty says that she loves me?"

"I do say so, smith."

"Then," said Stephen, "I am very sorry for her; for as there's a heaven above us, sire, I do not love her."

Prince Rudolf laughed; Osra's smile broadened in greater scorn; the Countess hid her face in her companion's bosom. The old King roared out a gruff burst. "Good, good!" he chuckled. "But it will come with marriage, smith; for with marriage love either comes or goes—eh, son Rudolf?—and since in this case it cannot go, you must not doubt, friend Stephen, that it will come." And he threw himself back in his chair, greatly amused that a smith, when offered the hand of a Countess, should hesitate to take it. He had not thought of so fine a humiliation as this for the presumptuous girl.

"That might well be, sire," admitted Stephen, "were it not that I most passionately love another."

"Our affections," said the King, "are unruly things, smith, and must be kept in subjection; is it not so, son Rudolf?"

"It should be so, sire," answered the merry Prince.

But the Princess Osra, whose eyes had been scanning Stephen's figure, here broke suddenly into the conversation.

"Are you pledged to her whom you love so passionately?" she asked.

"I have not ventured to tell her of my love, madame," answered he, bowing low.

"Then there is no harm done," observed Prince Rudolf. "The harm lies in the telling, not in the loving."

"Tell us something about her," commanded the Princess; and the King, who loved sport most when it hurt others, chimed in: "Aye, let's hear about her whom you prefer to this lady. In what shop does she work, smith? Or does she sell flowers? Or is she a serving-girl? Come, listen, Countess, and hear about your rival."

Prince Henry took one step forward in uncontrolled anger; but he could not meet the savage mirth in the old man's eyes, and, sinking into a chair, spread his hand across his face. But Stephen, regarding the King with placid good-humour, began to speak of her whom he loved so passionately. And his voice was soft as he spoke.

"She works in no shop, sire," said he, "nor does she sell flowers, nor is she a serving-girl; though I would not care if she were. But one day, when the clouds hung dark over our street, she came riding down it, and another girl with her. The two stopped before my door, and, seeing them, I came out——"

"It is more than you do for me," remarked Prince Rudolf.

Stephen smiled, but continued his story. "I came out; and she whom I love gave me a bracelet to mend. And I, looking at her rather than at the bracelet, said, 'But already it is perfect.' But she did not hear, for, when she had given me the bracelet, she rode on again at once and took no more notice of me than of the flies that were crawling up my wall. That was the first and is the last time that I have spoken to her until this day. But she was so beautiful that there and then I swore that, until I had found means and courage to tell her my love, and until she had thrice refused it, I would marry no other maiden nor speak a word of love."

"It seems to me," said Prince Rudolf, "that the oath has some prudence in it; for if she prove obdurate, friend Stephen, you will then be able to go elsewhere; many lovers swear more intemperately."

"But they do not keep their oaths," said Stephen, with a shrewd look at the Prince.

"You had best let him alone, my son," said the old King. "He knows what all the country knows of its future King."

"Then he may go and hang with all the country," said the Prince peevishly.

But the Princess Osra leant a little forward towards Stephen, and the Countess Hilda also looked covertly out from the folds of her friend's dress at Stephen. And the Princess said:

"Was she then so beautiful, this girl?"

"As the sun in heaven, madame," said the smith.

"As beautiful as my pretty sister?" asked Rudolf in careless jest.

"Yes, as beautiful, sir," answered Stephen.

"Then," said the cruel old King, "very much more beautiful than this Countess?"

"Of that you must ask your son Henry, sire," said Stephen discreetly.

"Nevertheless," said the King, "you must put up with the Countess. We cannot all have what we want in this world, can we, son Henry?" and he chuckled again most maliciously.

"Not, sire, till my lady has thrice refused me," the smith reminded the King.

"Then she must be quick about it. For we all, and my lord Bishop here, are waiting. Send for her, Stephen—by heaven, I have a curiosity to see her!"

"And, by heaven! so have I," added Prince Rudolf with a merry smile. "And poor Henry here may be cured by the sight."

The Princess Osra leant a little further forward, and said gently:

"Tell us her name, and we will send for her. Indeed I also would like to see her."

"But if she refuses, I shall be worse off than I am now; and if she says yes, still I must marry the Countess," objected the smith.

"Nay," said the King, "if she does not refuse you three times, you shall not marry the Countess, but shall be free to try your fortune with the girl;" for the smith had put the old Lion in a better temper, and he thought he was to witness more sport.

"Since your Majesty is so good, I must tell her name," said Stephen, "though I had rather have declared my love to herself alone."

"It is the pleasantest way," said Prince Rudolf, "but the thing can be done in the presence of others also."

"You must tell us her name that we may send for her," said the Princess, her eyes wandering now from the Countess to the smith, and back to the Countess again.

"Well, then," said Stephen sturdily, "the lady who came riding down the street and took away my heart with her is called Osra, and her father is named Henry."

A moment or two passed before they understood what the smith had said. Then the old King fell into a fit of laughter, half choked by coughing; Prince Rudolf clapped his hands in merry mockery, and a deep flush spread over the face of the Princess; while the Countess, her companion, and the younger Prince seemed too astonished to do anything but stare. As for Stephen, having said what he had to say, he held his peace—a thing in him which many men, and women also, would do well to imitate; and, if they cannot, let them pray for the grace that is needful. Heaven is omnipotent.

The old King, having recovered from his fit of laughing, looked round on the smith with infinite amusement, and, turning to his daughter, he said: "Come, Osra, you have heard the declaration. It remains only for you to satisfy our good friend's conscience by refusing him three times. For then he will be free to do our pleasure and make the Countess Hilda happy."

The heart of women is, as it would seem, a strange thing; for the Princess Osra, hearing what the smith had said and learning that he had fallen passionately in love with her on the mere sight of her beauty, suddenly felt a tenderness for him and a greater admiration than she had entertained before; and although she harboured no absurd idea of listening to his madness, or of doing anything in the world but laugh at it as it deserved, yet there came on her a strange dislike of the project that she had herself, in sport, suggested: namely, that the smith should be married immediately to the Countess Hilda by the Lord Bishop of Modenstein. The fellow, this smith, had an eye for true beauty, it seemed. It would be hard to tie him down to this dusky, black-maned girl; for so the Princess described the lady whom her brother loved, she herself being, like most of the Elphbergs, rather red than black in color. Accordingly, when the King spoke to her, she said fretfully:

"Am I to be put to refuse the hand of such a fellow as this? Why, to refuse him is a stain on my dignity!" And she looked most haughty.

"Yet you must grant him so much because of his oath," said the King.

"Well, then, I refuse him," said she tartly, and she turned her eyes away from him.

"That is once," said Stephen the smith calmly, and he fixed his eyes on the Princess's face. She felt his gaze, her eyes were drawn back to his, and she exclaimed angrily:

"Yes, I refuse him," and again she looked away. But he looked still more intently at her, waiting for the third refusal.

"It is as easy to say no three times as twice," said the King.

"For a man, sire," murmured Prince Rudolf; for he was very learned in the perilous knowledge of a woman's whims, and, maybe, read something of what was passing in his sister's heart. Certainly he looked at her and laughed, and said to the King:

"Sire, I think this smith is a clever man, for what he really desires is to wed the Countess, and to do it without disobliging my brother. Therefore he professes this ridiculous passion, knowing well that Osra will refuse him, and that he will enjoy the great good fortune of marrying the Countess against his will. Thus he will obey you and be free from my brother's anger. In truth, you're a crafty fellow, Master Stephen!"

"There is no craft, sir," said Stephen. "I have told nothing but the truth."

But the King swore a loud oath, crying: "Aye, that there is! Rudolf has hit the mark. Yet I do not grudge him his good luck. Refuse him, Osra, and make him happy."

But the dark flush came anew on the Princess's face, for now she did not know whether the smith really loved her or whether he had been making a jest of her in order to save himself in the eyes of her brother Henry, and it became very intolerable to her to suppose that the smith desired the Countess, and had lied in what he said about herself, making a tool of her. Again, it was hardly more tolerable to give him to the Countess, in case he truly loved herself; so that her mind was very greatly disturbed, and she was devoured with eagerness to know the reality of the smith's feelings towards her; for, although he was only a smith, yet he was a wonderfully handsome man—in truth, it was curious that she had not paid attention to his looks before. Thus she was reluctant to refuse him a third time, when the Bishop of Modenstein stood there, waiting only for her word to marry him to the Countess; and she rose suddenly from her seat and walked towards the door of the room, and, when she had almost reached the door, she turned her head over her shoulder and cast one smile at Stephen the smith. As she glanced, the blush again mounted to her face, making her so lovely that her father wondered, and she said in arch softness: "I'll refuse him the third time some other day; two denials are enough for one day," and with that she passed through the door and vanished from their sight.

The King and Rudolf, who had seen the glance that she cast at Stephen, fell to laughing again, swearing to one another that a woman was a woman all the world over, whereat the lips of the Bishop twitched.

"But the marriage can't go on," cried Rudolf at last.

"Let it rest for to-day," said the King, whose anger was past. "Let it rest. The Countess shall be guarded; and, since this young fool" (and he pointed to his son Henry) "will not wander while she is caged, let him go where he will. Then as soon as Osra has refused the smith a third time, we will send for the Bishop."

"And what am I to do, sire?" asked Stephen the smith.

"Why, my son-in-law that would be," chuckled the King, "you may go back to where you came from till I send for you again."

So Stephen, having thanked the King, went back home, and, sitting down to the chasing of a cup, became very thoughtful; for it seemed to him that the Countess had been hardly treated, and that the Prince deserved happiness, and that the Princess was yet more lovely than his eyes had found her before.

Thus, in his work and his meditations, the afternoon wore away fast. So goes time when hand and head are busy.

The Princess Osra walked restlessly up and down the length of her bed-chamber. Dinner was done and it was eight o'clock, and, the season being late October, it had grown dark. She had come thither to be alone; yet, now that she was alone, she could not rest. He was an absurd fellow—that smith! Yes, she thought him fully as handsome as her brother Rudolf. But what did Henry find to love in the black-brown Hilda? She could not understand a man caring for such a colour; a blackamoor would serve as well! Ah, what had that silly smith meant? It must have been a trick, as Rudolf said. Yet when he spoke first of her riding down the street, there was a look in his eyes that a man can hardly put there of his own will. Did the silly fellow then really——? Nay, that was absurd; she prayed that it might not be true, for she would not have the poor fool unhappy. Nay, he was no fool. It was a trick, then! How dared the insolent knave use her for his tricks? Was there no other maiden in Strelsau whose name would have served? Must he lay his tongue to the name of a daughter of the Elphbergs? The fellow deserved flogging, if it were a trick. Ah, was it a trick? Or was it the truth? Oh, in heaven's name, which was it? And the Princess tore the delicate silk of her ivory fan to shreds, and flung the naked sticks with a clatter on the floor.

"I can't rest till I know," she cried, as she came to a stand before a long mirror let into the panel of the wall, and saw herself at full length in it. As she looked a smile came, parting her lips, and she threw her head back as she said: "I will go and ask the smith what he meant." And she smiled again at her own face in triumphant daring; for when she looked, she thought, "I know what he meant! Yet I will hear from himself what he meant."

Stephen the smith sat alone in his house; his apprentices were gone, and he himself neither worked nor supped, but sat still and idle by his hearth. The street was silent also, for it rained and nobody was about. Then suddenly came a light timid rap at the door; so light was it that the smith doubted if he had really heard, but it came again and he rose leisurely and opened the door. Even as he did so a slight tall figure slipped by him, an arm pulled him back, the door was pushed close again, and he was alone inside the house with a lady wrapped in a long riding-cloak, and so veiled that nothing of her face could be seen.

"Welcome, madame," said Stephen the smith; and he drew a chair forward and bowed to his visitor. He was not wearing his apron now, but was dressed in a well-cut suit of brown cloth and had put on a pair of silk stockings. He might have been expecting visitors, so carefully had he arrayed himself.

"Do you know who I am?" asked the veiled lady.

"Since I was a baby, madame," answered the smith, "I have known the sun when I saw it, even though clouds dimmed its face."

A corner of the veil was drawn down, and one eye gleamed in frightened mirth.

"Nobody knows I have come," said Osra. "And you do not know why I have come."

"Is it to answer me for the third time?" asked he, drawing a step nearer, yet observing great deference in his manner.

"It is not to answer at all, but to ask. But I am very silly to have come. What is it to me what you meant?"

"I cannot conceive that it could be anything, madame," said Stephen, smiling.

"Yet some think her beautiful—my brother Henry, for example."

"We must respect the opinions of Princes," observed the smith.

"Must we share them?" she asked, drawing the veil yet a little aside.

"We can share nothing—we humble folk—with Princes or Princesses, madame."

"Yet we can make free with their names, though humbler ones would serve as well."

"No other would have served at all, madame."

"Then you meant it?" she cried in sudden half-serious eagerness.

"Nay, but what, madame?"

"I don't care whether you meant it or not."

"Alas! I know it so well, that I marvel you have come to tell me."

The Princess rose and began to walk up and down as she had in her own chamber. Stephen stood regarding her as though God had made his eyes for that one purpose.

"The thing is nothing," she declared petulantly, "but I have a fancy to ask it. Stephen, was it a trick, or—or was it really so? Come, answer me! I can't spend much time on it."

"It is not worth a thought to you. If you say no a third time, all will be well."

"You will marry the Countess?"

"Can I disobey the King, madame?"

"I am very sorry for her," said the Princess. "A lady of her rank should not be forced to marry a silversmith."

"Indeed I thought so all along. Therefore——"

"You played the trick?" she cried in unmistakable anger.

Stephen made no answer for a time, then he said softly: "If she loves the Prince and he her, why should they not marry?"

"Because his birth is above hers."

"I am glad, then, that I am of no birth, for I can marry whom I will."

"Are you so happy and so free, Stephen?" sighed the Princess; and there was no more of the veil left than served to frame the picture of her face.

"So soon as you have refused me the third time, madame," bowed the smith.

"Will you not answer me?" cried the Princess; and she smiled no more, but was as eager as though she were asking some important question.

"Bring the Countess here to-morrow at this time," said Stephen, "and I will answer."

"You wish, perhaps, to make a comparison between us?" she asked haughtily.

"I cannot be compelled to answer except on my own terms," said the smith. "Yet if you will refuse me once again, the thing will be finished."

"I will refuse you," she cried, "when I please."

"But you will bring the Countess, madame?"

"I am very sorry for her. I have behaved ill to her, Stephen, though I meant only to jest."

"There is room for amends, madame," said he.

The Princess looked long and curiously in his face, but he met her glance with a quiet smile.

"It grows late," said he, "and you should not be here longer, madame. Shall I escort you to the palace?"

"And have every one asking with whom Stephen the smith walks? No, I will go as I came. You have not answered me, Stephen."

"And you have not refused me, madame."

"Will you answer me to-morrow when I come with the Countess?"

"Yes, I will answer then."

The Princess had drawn near to the door; now Stephen opened it for her to pass out; and as she crossed the threshold, she said:

"And I will refuse you then—perhaps;" with which she darted swiftly down the dark, silent, shining street, and was gone; and Stephen, having closed the door, passed his hand twice over his brow, sighed thrice, smiled once, and set about the preparation of his supper.

On the next night, as the Cathedral clock struck nine, there arose a sudden tumult and excitement in the palace. King Henry the Lion was in such a rage as no man had ever seen him in before; even Rudolf, his son, did not dare to laugh at him; courtiers, guards, attendants, lackeys, ran wildly to and fro in immense fear and trepidation. A little later, and a large company of the King's Guard filed out, and, under the command of various officers, scattered themselves through the whole of Strelsau, while five mounted men rode at a gallop to each of the five gates of the city, bearing commands that the gates should be closed, and no man, woman, or child be allowed to pass out without an order under the hand of the King's Marshal. And the King swore by heaven, and by much else, that he would lay them—that is to say, the persons whose disappearance caused all this hubbub—by the heels, and that they should know that there was life in the Lion yet; whereat Prince Rudolf looked as serious as he could contrive to look—for he was wonderfully amused—and called for more wine. And the reason of the whole thing was no other than this, that the room of the Princess Osra was empty, and the room of the Countess Hilda was empty, and nobody had set eyes on Henry, the King's son, for the last two hours or more. Now these facts were, under the circumstances of the case, enough to upset a man of a temper far more equable than was old King Henry the Lion.

Through all the city went the Guards, knocking at every door, disturbing some at their suppers, some from their beds, some in the midst of revelry, some who toiled late for a scanty livelihood. When the doors were not opened briskly, the Guard without ceremony broke them in; they ransacked every crevice and cranny of every house, and displayed the utmost zeal imaginable; nay, one old lady they so terrified that she had a fit there where she lay in bed, and did not recover for the best part of a month. And thus, having traversed all the city and set the whole place in stir and commotion, they came at last to the street where Stephen lived, and to the sign of the "Silver Ship," where he carried on the business bequeathed to him by Aaron Lazarus the Jew.

"Rat, tat, tat!" came thundering on the door from the sword-hilt of the Sergeant in command of the party.

There was no answer; no light shone from the house, for the window was closely shuttered. Again the Sergeant hammered on the door.

"This pestilent smith is gone to bed," he cried in vexation. "But we must leave no house unsearched. Come, we must break in the door!" and he began to examine the door, and found that it was a fine solid door, of good oak and clamped with iron.

"Phew, we shall have a job with this door!" he sighed. "Why, in the devil's name, doesn't the fellow answer? Stephen, Stephen! Ho, there! Stephen!"

Yet no answer came from the inside of the house.

But at this moment another sound struck sharp on the ears of the Sergeant and his men. It was the noise of flames crackling; from the house next to Stephen's (which belonged to him, but was inhabited by a fruit-seller) there welled out smoke in volumes from every window; and the fruit-seller and his family appeared at the windows calling for aid. Seeing this, the Sergeant blew very loudly the whistle that he carried and cried "Fire!" and bade his men run and procure a ladder; for plainly the fruit-seller's house was on fire, and it was a more urgent matter to rescue men and women from burning than to find the Countess and the Prince. Presently the ladder came, and a great crowd of people, roused by the whistle and the cries of fire, came also; and then the door of Stephen's house was opened, and Stephen himself, looking out, asked what was the matter. Being told that the next house was on fire, he turned very grave—for the house was his—and waited for a moment to watch the fruit-seller and his family being brought down the ladder, which task was safely and prosperously accomplished. But the Sergeant said to him: "The fire may well spread, and if there is anyone in your house, it would be prudent to get them out."

"That is well thought of," said Stephen approvingly. "I was working late with three apprentices, and they are still in the house." And he put his head in at his door and called: "You had better come out, lads, the fire may spread." But the Sergeant turned away again and busied himself in putting the fire out.

Then three lads, one being very tall, came out of Stephen's house, clad in their leather breeches, their aprons, and the close-fitting caps that apprentices wore; and for a moment they stood watching the fire at the fruit-seller's. Then, seeing that the fire was burning low— which it did very quickly—they did not stay till the attention of the Sergeant was released from it, but, accompanied by Stephen, turned down the street, and, going along at a brisk rate, rounded the corner and came into the open space in front of the Cathedral.

"The gates will be shut, I fear," said the tallest apprentice. "How came the fire, Stephen?"

"It was three or four trusses of hay, sir, and a few crowns to repair his scorched paint. Shall we go to the gate?"

"Yes, we must try the gate," said Prince Henry, gathering the hand of the Countess into his; and the third apprentice walked silently by Stephen's side. Yet once as she went, she said softly:

"So it was no trick, Stephen?"

"No trick, but the truth, madame," said Stephen.

"I do not know," said Osra, "how I am to return to the palace in these clothes."

"Let us get your brother and the Countess away first," counselled the smith.

Now when they came to the nearest gate it was shut; but at the moment a troop of mounted men rode up, having been sent by the King to scour the country round, in case the fugitives should have escaped already from the city. And the Commandant of the company bore an order from the King's Marshal for the opening of the gate. Seeing this, Stephen the smith went up to him and began to talk to him, the three apprentices standing close by. The Commandant knew Stephen well, and was pleased to talk with him while the gates were opened and the troopers filed through. Stephen kept close by him till the troopers were all through. Then he turned and spoke to the apprentices, and they nodded assent. The Commandant checked his horse for an instant when he was half-way through the gate, and bent down and took Stephen's hand to shake it in farewell. Stephen took his hand with marvellous friendliness, and held it, and would not let him go. But the apprentices edged cautiously nearer and nearer the gate.

"Enough, man, enough!" laughed the Commandant. "We are not parting for ever."

"I trust not, sir, I trust not," said Stephen earnestly, still holding his hand.

"Come, let me go. See, the gate-warden wants to shut the gate!"

"True!" said Stephen. "Good-bye then, sir. Hallo, hallo! stop, stop! Oh, the young rascals!"

For even as Stephen spoke, two of the apprentices had darted through the half-closed gate, and run swiftly forward into the gloom of the night. Stephen swore an oath.

"The rogues!" he cried. "They were to have worked all night to finish an image of Our Lady! And now I shall see no more of them till to-morrow! They shall pay for their prank then, by heaven they shall!" But the Commandant laughed.

"I am sorry I can't catch them for you, friend Stephen," said he, "but I have other fish to fry. Well, boys will be boys. Don't be too hard on them when they return."

"They must answer for what they do," said Stephen; and the Commandant rode on and the gates were shut.

Then the Princess Osra said:

"Will they escape, Stephen?"

"They have money in their purses, love in their hearts, and an angry King behind them. I should travel quickly, madame, if I were so placed."

The Princess looked through the grating of the gate.

"Yes," she said, "they have all those. How happy they must be, Stephen! But what am I to do?"

Stephen made no answer and they walked back in silence to his house. It may be that they were wondering whether Prince Henry and the Countess would escape. Yet it may be that they thought of something else. When they reached the house, Stephen bade the Princess go into the inner room and resume her own dress that she might return to the palace, and that it might not be known where she had been nor how she had aided her brother to evade the King's prohibition; and when she, still strangely silent, went in as he bade her, he took his great staff in his hand, and stood on the threshold of the house, his head nearly touching the lintel and his shoulders filling almost all the space between door-post and door-post.

When he had stood there a little while, the same Sergeant of the Guard, recollecting (now that the fire at the fruit-seller's was out) that he had never searched the house of the smith,

211

came again with his four men, and told Stephen to stand aside and allow him to enter the house.

"For I must search it," he said, "or my orders will not be performed."

"Those whom you seek are not here," said Stephen.

"That I must see for myself," answered the Sergeant. "Come, smith, stand aside."

When the Princess heard the voices outside, she put her head round the door of the inner room, and cried in great alarm to Stephen:

"They must not come in, Stephen. At any cost they must not come in!"

"Do not be afraid, madame, they shall not come in," said he.

"I heard a voice in the house," exclaimed the Sergeant.

"It is nothing uncommon to hear in a house," said Stephen, and he grasped more firmly his great staff.

"Will you make way for us?" demanded the Sergeant. "For the last time, will you make way?"

Stephen's eyes kindled; for though he was a man of peace, yet his strength was great and he loved sometimes to use it; and above all, he loved to use it now at the bidding and in protection of his dear Princess. So he answered the Sergeant from between set teeth:

"Over my dead body you can come in."

Then the Sergeant drew his sword and his men set their halberds in rest, and the Sergeant, crying, "In the King's name!" came at Stephen with drawn sword and struck fiercely at him. But Stephen let the great staff drop on the Sergeant's shoulder, and the Sergeant's arm fell powerless by his side. Thereupon the Guards cried aloud, and people began to come out of their houses, seeing that there was a fight at Stephen's door. And Stephen's eyes gleamed, and when the Guards thrust at him, he struck at them, and two of them he stretched senseless on the ground; for his height and reach were such that he struck them before they could come near enough to touch him, and having no firearms they could not bring him down.

The Princess, now fully dressed in her own garments, came out into the outer room, and stood there looking at Stephen. Her bosom rose and fell, and her eyes grew dim as she looked; and growing very eager, and being very much moved, she kept murmuring to herself, "I have not said no thrice!" And she spent no thought on the Countess or her brother, nor on how she was to return undetected to the palace, but saw only the figure of Stephen on the threshold, and heard only the cries of the Guards who assaulted him. It seemed to her a brave thing to have such a man to fight for her, and to offer his life to save her shame.

Old King Henry was not a patient man, and when he had waited two hours without news of son, daughter, or Countess, he flew into a mighty passion and sent one for his horse, and another for Rudolf's horse, and a third for Rudolf himself; and he drank a draught of wine, and called to Rudolf to accompany him, that they might see for themselves what the lazy hounds of Guards were doing, that they had not yet come up with the quarry. Prince Rudolf laughed and yawned and wished his brother at the devil, but mounted his horse and rode with the King. Thus they traversed the city, riding swiftly, the old King furiously upbraiding every officer and soldier whom he met; then they rode to the gate; and all the gate-wardens said that nobody had gone out, save that one gate-warden admitted that two apprentices of Stephen the silversmith had contrived to slip out when the gates were open to let the troopers pass. But the King made nothing of it, and, turning with his son, rode up the street where Stephen lived. Here they came suddenly into the midst of a crowd, that filled all the roadway, and would hardly let the horses move even at a foot's pace. The King cried out angrily, "What is this tumult?"

Then the people knew him, and, since common folk are always anxious to serve and commend themselves to the great, a score began all at once to tell him what had happened, some starting with the fire, some going straight to the fight; and the King could not make head or tail of the babel of voices and different stories. And Prince Rudolf dropped his reins and sat on his horse laughing. But the King, his patience being clean gone, drew his sword and cried fiercely, "Make way!" and set his spurs to his horse, not recking whether he hurt any man in life or limb. Thus he gained a passage through the crowd, and came near to Stephen's house, Prince Rudolf following in his wake, still greatly amused at all that was happening.

But the sight they saw there arrested even Prince Rudolf's smiles, and he raised himself in his stirrups with a sudden cry of wonder. For four more of the Guard had come, and there were now six standing round the doorway, and three lay stretched on the ground; but Stephen the smith still stood on the threshold, with his staff in his hand. Blood flowed from a wound in his head, but he twirled the staff to and fro, and was not weary, and none of the Guard dared to rush in and close with him. Thus he had held the threshold for an hour; yet the Princess Osra could not escape unless he could drive off the Guard for a few moments, and this he hoped to do, thinking that they might draw off and wait for reinforcements; but in any case he had sworn that they should not pass. And Osra did not pray him to let them pass, but stood motionless in the middle of the room behind him, her hands clasped, her face rigid, and her eyes all aflame with admiration of his strength and his courage.

Thus matters were when the old King and Prince Rudolf broke through the crowd that ringed the house round, and the King cried out, asking what was the meaning of all that he saw.

But when the King heard that Stephen the smith resisted the officers, would not suffer his house to be searched, had stretched three of the Guards senseless on the ground, and still more than held his own, he fell into a great rage; he roared out on them all, calling them cowards, and, before his son or any one else could stop him, he drew his sword, and dug his spurs into his horse; the horse bounded forward and knocked down one of the Guards who stood round Stephen. Then the King, neither challenging Stephen to yield, nor giving him time to stand aside, being carried away by passion, raised his sword and rode full at him. And the Princess from within caught sight of his face, and she fell on her knees with a moan and hid her face. Then Stephen saw that it was the King and none other who rode against him; and even had the King given him time, it may be that he would not have yielded, for he was a very resolute man, and he had pledged his promise to Osra the Princess. But he had no time for thought, for the King was on him in the space of a second, and he could do nothing but drop the staff that he held, and stand defenceless in the doorway; for he would neither strike the King nor yield the passage. But the King, in his fury not heeding that Stephen had dropped his staff, drew back his arm and lunged with his sword, and thrust the smith through the chest; and Stephen reeled and fell on one knee, and his blood flowed out on the stone of the doorstep. Then the King reined in his horse, and sat looking down on Stephen; but Rudolf leapt to the ground, and came and caught hold of Stephen, supporting him, and asking, "What does it mean, man, what does it mean?"

Then Stephen, being very faint with his wound, said with difficulty: "Come in alone—you and the King alone."

Prince Rudolf looked at the King, who sheathed his sword and dismounted from his horse; the Prince supported Stephen inside the house, and the King followed them, shutting the door on all the people outside.

Then King Henry saw his daughter, crouching now in the middle of the room, her face hidden in her hands. Surprise and wonder banished his rage and he could not do more than gasp her name, while the Prince, who knelt supporting Stephen, cried to her, asking how she came there; but she answered nothing. She took her hands from her face and looked at Stephen; and when she saw that he was hurt and bleeding, she fell to sobbing and hid her face again. And she did not know whether she would have him live or die; for if he lived he could not be hers, and if he died her heart would ache sorely for him. Then Stephen, being supported by the arms of Prince Rudolf, made shift to speak, and he told the King how, at his persuasion, the Princess had brought the Countess thither; how he himself had contrived the presence of the Prince at the same time, how again the Princess had been prevailed upon to aid the lovers; how they assumed the disguise of apprentices; and how, hearing the arrival of the Guard, they had escaped out into the street; and lastly, how that the Prince and the Countess had got out of the city. But he said nothing of the fire at the fruit-seller's, nor of how he himself had bribed the fruit-seller to set the hay on fire, speaking to him from the back windows of the house, and flinging a purse of gold pieces across to him; nor did this ever become known to the King. And when Stephen had said his say, he fell back very faint in the arms of the Prince; and the Prince tore a scarf from his waist, and tried to staunch the blood from Stephen's wound. But the old King, who was a hard man, smiled grimly.

"Indeed he has tricked us finely, this smith, and he is a clever fellow," said he; "but unless he would rather hang than bleed to death, let his wound be, Rudolf. For by heaven, if you cure him, I will hang him."

"Do not be afraid, sire," said Stephen; "the Prince cannot cure me. You still strike straight, though you are hard on seventy."

"Straight enough for a rascal like you," said the King well pleased; and he added, "Hold the fellow easily, Rudolf, I would not have him suffer." And this was, they say, the only time in all his life that Henry the Lion shewed a sign of pity to any man.

But Stephen was now very faint, and he cast his eyes towards the Princess; and Rudolf followed his eyes. Now Rudolf had an affection for Stephen, and he loved his sister, and was a man of soft heart; so he cried gently to Osra, "Come, sister, and help me with him." And she rose, and came and sat down by the wall, and gathered Stephen's head into her lap; and there he lay, looking up at her, with a smile on his lips. But still he bled, and his blood stained the white cloak that she wore over her robe; and her tears dropped on his face. But Rudolf took his father by the arm, and led him a little way off, saying:

"What matter, sire? The girl is young, and the man is dying. Let them be."

The old King, grumbling, let himself be led away; and perhaps even he was moved, for he forgot Prince Henry and the Countess, and did not think of sending men in pursuit of them, for which reason they obtained a fair and long start in their flight.

Then Stephen, looking up at Osra, said:

"Do not weep, madame. They will escape now, and they will be happy."

"I was not weeping for them," said the Princess.

Stephen was silent for a little, and then he said:

"In very truth it was no trick, madame; it was even as I said, from the first day that you rode along the street here; it was always the same in my heart, and would always have been, however long I had lived."

"I do not doubt it, Stephen; and it is not for doubt of it that I weep," said she.

Then, after a little while, he said:

"Do you weep, madame, because I am dying?"

"Yes, I weep for that."

"Would you have me live, madame?" he asked.

"No, I would not—no—but I do not know," she said.

Then Stephen the smith smiled, and his smile was happy.

"Yet," said he, "it would make small difference to the Princess Osra whether Stephen the smith lived or died."

At this, although he lay there a dying man, a sudden flush of red spread all over her cheeks, and she turned her eyes away from his, and would not meet his glance; she made him no answer, and he said again:

"What can it concern the Princess whether I live or die?"

Still the blush burnt on her cheek, and still she had no answer to give to Stephen, as he lay dying with his head on her lap. And a bright gleam came into his eyes, and he tried to move a hand towards her hand; and she, seeing the effort, put out her hand and held his; and he whispered very low, for he could hardly speak:

"You have not yet refused me three times, madame."

At that her eyes came back to his, and their eyes dwelt long on one another. And for a moment it seemed to them that all things became possible, life and joy and love. Yet since all could not be, they were content that none should be.

Then the Princess bent low over his head, and she whispered to him:

215

"No, I have not refused you thrice, Stephen."

His lips just moved once again, and, being very near him, she heard:

"And you will not?" he said.

"No," said she, and she kissed his lips, and he smiled and turned on his side; and he nestled his head, as it were cosily, on her lap, and he said no more.

Thus died Stephen the silversmith of Strelsau, happy in his death because Osra the Princess had not refused him thrice. And she laid him gently on the ground, and rose, and went across to where the King sat with Rudolf.

"Sire, he is dead," said she.

"It is well," said the King. And he bade Rudolf go and cause all the people to leave the streets, and return to their houses; and when all the streets were cleared, the Princess veiled herself, and her brother mounted her on his horse, and thus she rode back to the palace; and none knew that she had been in the house of Stephen the silversmith.

And after many months Prince Henry, who had made good his escape and married the lady whom he loved, was reconciled to his father and returned to the city of Strelsau. And when he heard how Stephen had died, he raised a stately monument over him, and had carved on it his name, and the day and year in which he had died; and underneath he caused to be engraved the words, "From a Friend to a Friend." But when this monument had stood three days in its place, there came thither a lady closely veiled; she prayed on her knees by the monument for a long while, and then rose and stood regarding it; and her eyes rested on the last words that Prince Henry had written on the stone. Then she came nearer, and kissed the words, and, when she had kissed them, she whispered softly, "From a Lover to a Lover"; and, having whispered this, she turned away and went back to the palace, and came no more to the tomb, for fear that the people should remark her coming. Yet often in the days that followed she would open the window of her bed-chamber by night, and she would whisper to the silent trusty darkness, that holds secrets and comforts sore hearts:

"Not thrice, Stephen, not thrice!"

Therefore it may be that there had been a sweet madness in her heart, and that Stephen the silversmith had done a great thing, a thing that would appear impossible, before he died. And, as Prince Rudolf said, what matter? For the girl was young, and the dream was sweet, and the man was dead, and in death at last are all men equal.

CHAPTER II.

The Wager of the Marquis de Mérosailles.

In the year 1734, as spring began, there arrived at Strelsau a French nobleman of high rank and great possessions, endowed also with many accomplishments. He came to visit Prince Rudolf, whose acquaintance he had made while the Prince was at Paris in the course of his travels. King Henry received M. de Mérosailles—for such was his name—most graciously, and sent a guard of honour to conduct him to the Castle of Zenda, where the Prince was then staying in company with his sister Osra. There the Marquis, on his arrival, was greeted with much joy by Prince Rudolf, who found his sojourn in the country somewhat irksome and was glad of the society of a friend with whom he could talk, and sport, and play at cards. All these things he did with M. de Mérosailles, and a great friendship arose between the young men, so that they spoke very freely to one another at all times, and most of all when they had drunk their wine and sat together in the evening in Prince Rudolf's chamber that looked across the moat towards the gardens; for the new château that now stands on the site of these gardens was not then built. And one night M. de Mérosailles made bold to ask the Prince how it fell out that his sister the Princess, a lady of such great beauty, seemed sad, and shewed no pleasure in the society of any gentleman, but treated all alike with coldness and disdain. Prince Rudolf, laughing, answered that girls were strange creatures, and that he had ceased to trouble his head about them (of his heart he said nothing) and he finished by exclaiming: "On my honour, I doubt if she so much as knows you are here, for she has not looked at you once since your arrival!" And he smiled maliciously, for he knew that the Marquis was not accustomed to be neglected by ladies, and would take it ill that even a Princess should be unconscious of his presence. In this he calculated rightly, for M. de Mérosailles was greatly vexed, and, twisting his glass in his fingers, he said:

"If she were not a Princess, and your sister, sir, I would engage to make her look at me."

"I am not hurt by her looking at you," rejoined the Prince: for that evening he was very merry. "A look is no great thing."

The Marquis, being no less merry, and knowing that Rudolf had not the regard for his dignity that a Prince should have, threw out carelessly:

"A kiss is more, sir."

"It is a great deal more," laughed the Prince, tugging his moustache.

"Are you ready for a wager, sir?" asked M. de Mérosailles, leaning across the table towards him.

"I'll lay you a thousand crowns to a hundred that you do not gain a kiss, using what means you will, save force."

"I'll take that wager, sir," cried the Marquis. "But it shall be three, not one."

"Have a care," said the Prince. "Don't go too near the flame, my lord! There are some wings in Strelsau singed at that candle."

"Indeed the light is very bright," assented the Marquis courteously. "That risk I must run, though, if I am to win my wager. It is to be three then, and by what means I will, save force?"

"Even so," said Rudolf, and he laughed again. For he thought the wager harmless, since by no device could M. de Mérosailles win so much as one kiss from the Princess Osra, and the wager stood at three. But he did not think how he wronged his sister by using her name lightly, being in all such matters a man of careless mind.

But the Marquis, having made his wager, set himself steadily to win it. Therefore he brought forth the choicest clothes from his wardrobe, and ornaments, and perfumes; and he laid fine presents at the Princess's feet; and he waylaid her wherever she went, and was profuse of glances, sighs, and hints; and he wrote sonnets, as fine gentlemen used in those days, and lyrics and pastorals, wherein she figured under charming names. These he bribed the

Princess's waiting-women to leave in their mistress's chamber. Moreover he looked now sorrowful, now passionate, and he ate nothing at dinner, but drank his wine in wild gulps, as though he sought to banish sadness. So that, in a word, there was no device in Cupid's armoury that the Marquis de Mérosailles did not practise in the endeavour to win a look from the Princess Osra. But no look came, and he got nothing from her but cold civility. Yet she had looked at him when he looked not—for Princesses are much like other maidens—and thought him a very pretty gentleman, and was highly amused by his extravagance. Yet she did not believe it to witness any true devotion to her, but thought it mere gallantry.

Then, one day, M. de Mérosailles, having tried all else that he could think of, took to his bed. He sent for a physician, and paid him a high fee to find the seeds of a rapid and fatal disease in him: and he made his body-servant whiten his face and darken his room; and he groaned very pitifully, saying that he was sick, and that he was glad of it; for death would be better far than the continued disdain of the Princess Osra. And all this, being told by the Marquis's servants to the Princess's waiting-women, reached Osra's ears, and caused her much perturbation. For she now perceived that the passion of the Marquis was real and deep, and she became very sorry for him: the longer the face of the rascally physician grew the more sad the Princess became: she walked up and down, bewailing the terrible effects of her beauty, wishing that she were not so fair, and mourning very tenderly for the sad plight of the unhappy Marquis.

Through all Prince Rudolf looked on, but was bound by his wager not to undeceive her; moreover he found much entertainment in the matter, and swore that it was worth three times a thousand crowns.

At last the Marquis sent by the mouth of his physician a very humble and pitiful message to the Princess, in which he spoke of himself as near to death, hinted at the cruel cause of his condition, and prayed her of compassion to visit him in his chamber, and speak a word of comfort, or at least let him look on her face: for the brightness of her eyes, he said, might cure even what it had caused.

Deceived by this appeal, Princess Osra agreed to go; moved by some strange impulse, she put on her choicest array, dressed her hair most splendidly, and came into the chamber looking like a goddess. There lay the Marquis, white as a ghost and languid on his pillows; and they were left, as they thought, alone. Then Osra sat down and began to talk very gently and kindly to him, glancing only at the madness which brought him to his sad state, and imploring him to summon his resolution, and conquer his sickness for his friends' sake at home in France, and for the sake of her brother, who loved him.

"There is nobody who loves me," said the Marquis petulantly; and when Osra cried out at this, he went on, "For the love of those whom I do not love is nothing to me, and the only soul alive I love——." There he stopped, but his eyes, fixed on Osra's face, ended the sentence for him. And she blushed, and looked away. Then thinking the moment was come, he burst suddenly into a flood of protestations and self-reproach, cursing himself for a fool and a presumptuous madman, pitifully craving her pardon, and declaring that he did not deserve her kindness, and yet that he could not live without it, and that anyhow he would be dead soon, and thus cease to trouble her. But she, being thus passionately assailed, showed such sweet tenderness and compunction and pity, that M. de Mérosailles came very near to forgetting that he was playing a comedy, and threw himself into his part with eagerness, redoubling his vehemence, and feeling now full half of what he said. For the Princess was to his eyes far more beautiful in her softer mood. Yet he remembered his wager, and, at last, when she was nearly in tears and ready, as it seemed, to do anything to give him comfort, he cried desperately:

"Ah, leave, leave me! Leave me to die alone! Yet, for pity's sake, before you go, and before I die, give me your forgiveness, and let your lips touch my forehead in token of it. Then I shall die in peace."

At that the Princess blushed still more, and her eyes were wet, and shone, for she was deeply touched at his misery and at the sad prospect of the death for love of so gallant a gentleman. Thus she could scarcely speak for emotion; and the Marquis seeing her emotion was himself deeply affected; and she rose from her chair, and bent over him, and whispered comfort to him. Then she leant down, and very lightly touched his forehead with her lips; he felt her eyelashes, which were wet with tears, brush the skin of his forehead; and then she sobbed and covered her face with her hands. Indeed his state seemed to her most pitiful.

Thus M. de Mérosailles had won one of his three kisses; yet, strange to tell, there was no triumph in him, but now he perceived the baseness of his device; and the sweet kindness of the Princess, working together with the great beauty of her softened manner, so affected him that he thought no more of his wager and could not endure to carry on his deception; nothing would serve his turn but to confess to the Princess what he had done, humbling himself in the dust before her, and entreating her to pardon him and let him find forgiveness.

Impelled by these feelings, after he had lain still a few moments listening to the Princess weeping, he leapt suddenly out of bed, showing himself fully dressed under the bed-gown which he now eagerly tore off; and he rubbed all the white he could from his cheeks, and then he fell on his knees before the Princess, crying to her that he had played the meanest trick on her, and that he was a scoundrel, and no gentleman, and that unless she forgave him he should in very truth die; nay, that he would not consent to live unless he could win from her pardon for his deceit. And in all this he was now absolutely in earnest, wondering only how he had not been as passionately enamoured of her from the first as he had feigned himself to be. For a man in love can never conceive himself out of it, nor he that is out of it in it; for if he can, he is half way to the one or the other, however little he may know it.

At first the Princess sat as though she were turned to stone: but when he finished his confession, and she understood the trick that had been played on her, and how not only her kiss, but also her tears, had been won from her by fraud, and when she thought, as she did, that the Marquis was playing another trick on her, and that there was no more truth or honesty in his present protestations than in those which went before, she fell into great shame and into a great rage; her eyes flashed like the eyes of her father himself, as she rose to her feet and looked down on M. de Mérosailles as he knelt imploring her. Now her face turned pale from red, and she set her lips, and she drew her gown close round her, lest his touch should defile it (so the unhappy gentleman understood her gesture) and she picked her steps daintily round him, for fear she should happen to come in contact with so foul a thing. Thus she walked to the door, and, having reached it, she turned and said to him:

"Your death may blot out the insult—nothing less." And with her head held high, and her whole air full of scorn, she swept out of the room, leaving the Marquis on his knees. He started up to follow her, but dared not; he flung himself on the bed in a paroxysm of shame and vexation, and now of love also, and he cried out loud:

"Then my death shall blot it out, since nothing else will serve!"

He was in a desperate mood. For a long time he lay there, and then, having risen, dressed himself in a sombre suit of black, and buckled his sword by his side, and, having put on his riding boots and summoned his servant, bade him saddle his horse. "For," said he to himself, "I will ride into the forest, and there kill myself; and perhaps when I am dead the Princess will forgive, and will believe in my love, and grieve a little for me."

Now as he went from his chamber to cross the moat by the drawbridge, he encountered Prince Rudolf returning from hawking. They met full in the centre of the bridge, and the Prince, seeing M. de Mérosailles dressed all in black from the feather in his hat to his boots, called out mockingly:

"Who is to be buried to-day, my lord, and whither do you ride to the funeral? It cannot be yourself, for I see that you are marvellously recovered of your sickness."

"But it is myself," answered the Marquis, coming near, and speaking low that the servants and the falconers might not overhear. "I ride, sir, to my own funeral."

"The jest is still afoot, then?" asked the Prince. "Yet I do not see my sister at the window to watch you go, and I warrant you have made no way with your wager yet."

"A thousand curses on my wager!" cried the Marquis. "Yes, I have made way with the accursed thing, and that is why I now go to my death."

"What, has she kissed you?" cried the Prince, with a merry astonished laugh.

"Yes, sir, she has kissed me once, and therefore I go to die."

"I have heard of many a better reason, then," answered the Prince.

By now the Prince had dismounted, and he stood by M. de Mérosailles in the middle of the bridge, and heard from him how the trick had prospered. At this he was much tickled, and, alas, he was even more diverted when the penitence of the Marquis was revealed to him, and was most of all moved to merriment when it appeared that the Marquis, having gone too near the candle, had been caught by its flame, and was so terribly singed and scorched that he could not bear to live. And while they talked on the bridge the Princess looked out on them from a lofty narrow window, but neither of them saw her. But when the Prince had done laughing, he put his arm through his friend's and bade him not be a fool, but come in and toast the Princess's kiss in a draught of wine. "For," he said, "though you will never get the other two, yet it is a brave exploit to have got one."

But the Marquis shook his head, and his air was so resolute, and so full of sorrow, that not only was Rudolf alarmed for his reason, but Princess Osra also, at the window, wondered what ailed him and why he wore such a long face; and now she noticed that he was dressed all in black, and that his horse waited for him across the bridge.

"Not," said she, "that I care what becomes of the impudent rogue!" Yet she did not leave the window, but watched very intently to see what M. de Mérosailles would do.

For a long while he talked with Rudolf on the bridge, Rudolf seeming more serious than he was wont to be; and at last the Marquis bent to kiss the Prince's hand, and the Prince raised him and kissed him on either cheek; then the Marquis went and mounted his horse, and rode off, slowly and unattended, into the glades of the forest of Zenda; but the Prince, with a shrug of the shoulders and a frown on his brow, entered under the portcullis, and disappeared from his sister's view.

Upon this the Princess, assuming an air of great carelessness, walked down from the room where she was, and found her brother, sitting still in his boots and drinking wine; and she said:

"M. de Mérosailles has taken his leave then?"

"Even so, madame," rejoined Rudolf.

Then she broke into a fierce attack on the Marquis, and on her brother also; for a man, said she, is known by his friends, and what a man Rudolf must be to have a friend like the Marquis de Mérosailles!

"Most brothers," she said in fiery temper, "would make him answer for what he has done with his life. But you laugh, nay, I daresay you had a hand in it."

As to this last charge the Prince had the discretion to say nothing; he chose rather to answer the first part of what she said, and shrugging his shoulders again rejoined:

"The fool saves me the trouble, for he has gone off to kill himself."

"To kill himself?" she said, half incredulous, but also half believing, because of the Marquis's gloomy looks and black clothes.

"To kill himself," repeated Rudolf. "For in the first place you are angry, so he cannot live; in the second he has behaved like a rogue, so he cannot live; and in the third place you are so lovely, sister, that he cannot live; and in the first, second, and third places he is a fool, so he cannot live." And the Prince finished his flagon of wine with every sign of ill-humour in his manner.

"He is well dead," she cried.

"Oh, as you please," said he. "He is not the first brave man who has died on your account." And he rose and strode out of the room very surlily; for he had a great friendship for M. de Mérosailles, and had no patience with men who let love make dead bones of them.

The Princess Osra, being left alone, sat for a little time in deep thought. There rose before her mind the picture of M. de Mérosailles riding mournfully through the gloom of the forest to his death. And although his conduct had been all and more than all that she had called it, yet it seemed hard that he should die for it. Moreover, if he now in truth felt what he had before feigned, the present truth was an atonement for the past treachery; and she said to herself that she could not sleep quietly that night if the Marquis killed himself in the forest. Presently she wandered slowly up to her chamber, and looked in the mirror, and murmured low, "Poor fellow!" and then with sudden speed she attired herself for riding, and commanded her horse to be saddled, and darted down the stairs and across the bridge, and mounted, and, forbidding any one to accompany her, rode away into the forest, following the marks of the hoofs of M. de Mérosailles's horse. It was then late afternoon, and the slanting rays of the sun, striking through the tree-trunks, reddened her face as she rode along, spurring her horse, and following hard on the track of the forlorn gentleman. But what she intended to do if she came up with him she did not think.

When she had ridden an hour or more, she saw his horse tethered to a trunk; and there was a ring of trees and bushes near, encircling an open grassy spot. Herself dismounting, and fastening her horse by the Marquis's horse, she stole up, and saw M. de Mérosailles sitting on the ground, his drawn sword lying beside him; and his back was towards her. She held her breath and waited a few moments. Then he took up the sword and felt the point and also the edge of it, and sighed deeply; and the Princess thought that this sorrowful mood became him better than any she had seen him in before. Then he rose to his feet, and took his sword by the blade beneath the hilt, and turned the point of it towards his heart. But Osra, fearing that the deed would be done immediately, called out eagerly, "My lord, my lord!" and M. de Mérosailles turned round with a great start. When he saw her, he stood in astonishment, his hand still holding the blade of the sword. And, standing just on the other side of the trees, she said:

"Is your offence against me to be cured by adding an offence against Heaven and the Church?"

And she looked on him with great severity, yet her cheek was flushed, and after a while she did not meet his glance.

"How came you here, madame?" he asked in wonder.

"I heard," she said, "that you meditated this great sin, and I rode after you to forbid it."

"Can you forbid what you cause?" he asked.

"I am not the cause of it," she said, "but your own trickery."

"It is true. I am not worthy to live," cried the Marquis, smiting the hilt of his sword on the ground. "I pray you, madame, leave me alone to die. For I cannot tear myself from the world so long as I see your face." And as he spoke he knelt on one knee, as though he were doing homage to her.

The Princess caught at the bough of the tree under which she stood, and pulled the bough down, so that its leaves half hid her face, and the Marquis saw little more than her eyes from among the foliage. Thus being better able to speak to him, she said softly:

"And dare you die, unforgiven?"

"I had prayed for forgiveness before you found me, madame," said he.

"Of heaven, my lord?"

"Of heaven, madame. For of heaven I dare to ask it."

The bough swayed up and down; now Osra's gleaming hair, and now her cheek, and always her eyes were seen through the leaves. And presently the Marquis heard a voice asking:

"Does heaven forgive unasked?"

"Indeed, no," he said, wondering.

"And," she said, "are we poor mortals kinder than heaven?"

The Marquis rose, and took a step or two towards where the bough swayed up and down, and then knelt again.

"A great sinner," said he, "cannot believe himself forgiven."

"Then he wrongs the power of which he seeks forgiveness; for forgiveness is divine."

"Then I will ask it, and, if I obtain it, I shall die happy."

Again the bough swayed: and Osra said:

"Nay, if you will die, you may die unforgiven."

M. de Mérosailles hearing these words sprang to his feet, and came towards the bough, until he was so close that he touched the green leaves; through them the eyes of Osra gleamed: the sun's rays struck on her eyes, and they danced in the sun; and her cheeks were reddened by the same or some other cause. And the evening was very still, and there were no sounds in the forest.

"I cannot believe that you forgive. The crime is so great," said he.

"It was great: yet I forgive."

"I cannot believe it," said he again, and he looked at the point of his sword, and then he looked through the leaves at the Princess.

"I cannot do more than say that if you will live, I will forgive. And we will forget."

"By heaven, no," he whispered. "If I must forget to be forgiven, then I will remember and be unforgiven."

The faintest laugh reached him from among the foliage.

"Then I will forget, and you shall be forgiven," said she.

The Marquis put up his hand, and held a leaf aside, and he said again:

"I cannot believe myself forgiven. Is there no token of forgiveness?"

"Pray, my lord, do not put the leaves aside."

"I still must die, unless I have sure warrant of forgiveness."

"Ah, you try to make me think that!"

"By heaven, it is true!" And again he pointed his sword at his heart, and he swore on his honour that unless she gave him a token he would still kill himself.

"Oh," said the Princess with great petulance, "I wish I had not come!"

"Then I should have been dead by now—dead, unforgiven."

"But you will still die!"

"Yes, I must still die, unless——"

"Sheathe your sword, my lord. The sun strikes it, and it dazzles my eyes."

"That cannot be: for your eyes are brighter than sun and sword together."

"Then I must shade them with the leaves."

"Yes, shade them with the leaves," he whispered. "Madame, is there no token of forgiveness?"

In the silence that followed his eyes spoke, at last she said:

"Why did you swear on your honour?"

"Because it is an oath that I cannot break."

"Indeed I wish that I had not come," sighed Princess Osra.

Again came silence. The bough was pressed down for an instant; then it swayed swiftly up again; and its leaves brushed the cheek of M. de Mérosailles. And he laughed loudly and joyfully.

"Something touched my cheek," said he.

"It must have been a leaf," said Princess Osra.

"Ah, a leaf!"

"I think so," said Princess Osra.

"Then it was a leaf of the Tree of Life," said M. de Mérosailles.

"I wish some one would set me on my horse," said Osra.

"That you may ride back to the castle—alone?"

"Yes, unless you would relieve my brother's anxiety."

"It would be courteous to do that much," said the Marquis.

So they mounted, and rode back through the forest.

In an hour the Princess had come, and in the space of something over two hours they returned; yet during all this time they spoke hardly a word: and although the sun was now set, yet the glow remained on the face and in the eyes of Princess Osra; while M. de Mérosailles, being forgiven, rode with a smile on his lips.

But when they came to the castle, Prince Rudolf ran out to meet them, and he cried almost before he reached them:

"Hasten, hasten! There is not a moment to lose, if the Marquis values life or liberty!" And when he came to them he told them that a waiting-woman had been false to M. de Mérosailles and, after taking his money, had hid herself in his chamber, and seen the first kiss that the Princess gave him, and, having made some pretext to gain a holiday, had gone to the King, who was hunting near, and betrayed the whole matter to him.

"And one of my gentlemen," he continued, "has ridden here to tell me. In an hour the Guards will be here, and if the King catches you, my lord, you will hang as sure as I live."

The Princess turned very pale, but M. de Mérosailles said haughtily, "I ask your pardon, sir, but the King dares not hang me. For I am a gentleman and a subject of the King of France."

"Man, man!" cried Rudolf. "The Lion will hang you first, and think of all that afterwards! Come now, it is dusk. You shall dress yourself as my groom, and I will ride to the frontier, and you shall ride behind me, and thus you may get safe away. I cannot have you hanged over such a trifle."

"I would have given my life willingly for what you call a trifle, sir," said the Marquis with a bow to Osra.

"Then have the trifle and life too," said Rudolf derisively. "Come in with me, and I will give you your livery!"

When the Prince and M. de Mérosailles came out again on the drawbridge the evening had fallen, and it was dark; their horses stood at the end of the bridge, and by the horses stood the Princess.

"Quick!" said she. "For a peasant who came in, bringing a load of wood, saw a troop of men coming over the crown of the hill, and he says they are the King's Guard."

"Mount, man!" cried the Prince to M. de Mérosailles, who was now dressed as a groom. "Perhaps we can get clear, or perhaps they will not dare to stop me."

But the Marquis hesitated a little, for he did not like to run away; but the Princess ran a little forward and, shading her eyes with her hand, cried, "See there! I see the gleam of steel in the dark. They have reached the top of the hill, and are riding down."

Then Prince Rudolf sprang on his horse, calling again to M. de Mérosailles, "Quick, quick! Your life hangs on it!"

Then at last the Marquis, though he was most reluctant to depart, was about to spring on his horse, when the Princess turned and glided back swiftly to them. And—let it be remembered that evening had fallen thick and black—she came to her brother and put out her hand, and grasped his hand, and said:

"My lord, I forgive your wrong, and I thank you for your courtesy, and I wish you farewell."

Prince Rudolf, astonished, gazed at her without speaking. But she, moving very quickly in spite of the darkness, ran to where M. de Mérosailles was about to spring on his horse, and she flung one arm lightly about his neck, and she said:

"Farewell, dear brother, God preserve you. See that no harm comes to my good friend, M. de Mérosailles." And she kissed him lightly on the cheek. Then she suddenly gave a loud cry of dismay, exclaiming, "Alas, what have I done? Ah, what have I done?" and she hid her face in her two hands.

Prince Rudolf burst into a loud short laugh, yet he said nothing to his sister, but again urged the Marquis to mount his horse. And the Marquis, who was in a sad tumult of triumph and of woe, leapt up; and they rode out, and turning their faces towards the forest, set spurs to their horses and vanished at a breakneck speed into the glades. And no sooner were they gone than the troopers of the King's Guard clattered at a canter up to the end of the bridge, where the Princess Osra stood. But when their captain saw the Princess, he drew rein.

"What is your errand, sir?" she asked most coldly and haughtily.

"Madame, we are ordered to bring the Marquis de Mérosailles alive or dead into the King's presence, and we have information that he is in the castle, unless, indeed, he were one of the horsemen who rode away just now."

"The horsemen you saw were my brother the Prince and his groom," said Osra. "But if you think that M. de Mérosailles is in the castle, pray search the castle from keep to cellar; and if you find him, carry him to my father, according to your orders."

Then the troopers dismounted in great haste, and ransacked the castle from keep to cellar; and they found the clothes of the Marquis, and the white powder with which he had whitened his face, but the Marquis they did not find. So the captain came again to the Princess, who still stood at the end of the bridge, and said:

"Madame, he is not in the castle."

"Is he not?" said she, and turned away, and, walking to the middle of the bridge, looked down into the water of the moat.

"Was it in truth the Prince's groom who rode with him, madame?" asked the captain, following her.

"In truth, sir, it was so dark," answered the Princess, "that I could not myself clearly distinguish the man's face."

"One was the Prince, for I saw you embrace him, madame."

"You do well to conclude that that was my brother," said Osra, smiling a little.

"And to the other, madame, you gave your hand."

"And now I give it to you," said she with haughty insolence. "And if to my father's servant, why not to my brother's?" And she held out her hand that he might kiss it, and turned away from him, and looked down into the water again.

"But we found M. de Mérosailles's clothes in the castle!" persisted the captain.

"He may well have left something of his in the castle," said the Princess.

"I will ride after them!" cried the captain.

"I doubt if you will catch them," smiled the Princess; for by now the pair had been gone half an hour, and the frontier was but ten miles from the castle, and they could not be overtaken. Yet the captain rode off with his men, and pursued till he met Prince Rudolf returning alone, having seen M. de Mérosailles safe on his way. And Rudolf had paid the sum of a thousand crowns to the Marquis, so that the fugitive was well provided for his journey, and, travelling with many relays of horses, made good his escape from the clutches of King Henry.

But the Princess Osra stayed a long time looking down at the water in the moat. Sometimes she sighed, and then, again, she frowned, and, although nobody was there, and it was very dark into the bargain, more than once she blushed. And at last she turned to go into the castle. But, as she went, she murmured softly to herself:

"Why I kissed him the first time I know; it was in pity. And why I kissed him the second time I know; it was in forgiveness. But why I kissed him the third time, or what that kiss meant," said Osra, "heaven knows."

And she went in with a smile on her lips.

CHAPTER III.

The Madness of Lord Harry Culverhouse.

"Seeing that my father Henry is dead, and that I am King; seeing also that I am no longer a bachelor, but a married man"—and here he bowed to Margaret of Tuscany, his newly wedded wife; "and seeing that Osra's turned twenty years of age—why, we are all to be sober folk at Strelsau from this day forward, and we are to play no more pranks. Here's a pledge to it!"

And having said this, King Rudolf III. took a deep draught of wine.

At this moment the ushers announced that the Lord Harry Culverhouse had come to take his leave of their Majesties and of the Princess. This gentleman had accompanied the Embassy that came from England to congratulate the King on his marriage, and he had stayed some months in Strelsau, very eagerly acceding to the King's invitation to prolong his visit. For such were his folly and headstrong passion, that he had fallen most desperately in love with the fair face of Princess Osra, and could not endure to live out of her presence. Yet now he came to bid farewell, and when he was ushered in, Rudolf received him with much graciousness, and made him a present of his own miniature set in diamonds, while the Queen gave him her miniature set in the lid of a golden casket. In return, Lord Harry prayed the King to accept a richly-mounted sword, and the Queen an ivory fan, painted by the greatest artist of France and bearing her cipher in jewels. Then he came to Princess Osra, and she, having bidden him farewell, said:

"I am a poor maid, my lord, and I can give no great gift, but take this pin from my hair and keep it for my sake."

And she drew out a golden pin from her hair, a long and sharp pin, bearing for its head her cipher in brilliants, and she gave it to him, smiling.

But he, bowing low and then falling on his knee, offered her a box of red morocco leather, and when she opened it she saw a necklace of rubies of great splendour. The Princess flushed red, seeing that the gift was most costly. And she would fain have refused it, and held it out again to Lord Harry. But he turned swiftly away, and, bowing once more, withdrew. Then the Princess said to her brother, "It is too costly."

The King, seeing how splendid the gift was, frowned a little, and then said:

"He must be a man of very great wealth. They are rich in England. I am sorry the gift is so great, but we cannot refuse it without wounding his honour."

So the Princess set the ruby necklace with her other jewels, and thought for a day or two that Lord Harry was no wiser than other men, and then forgot him.

Now Lord Harry Culverhouse, on leaving the King's presence, had mounted his horse, which was a fine charger and splendidly equipped, and ridden alone out of Strelsau; for he had dismissed all his servants and despatched them with suitable gratuities to their own country. He rode through the afternoon, and in the evening he reached a village fifteen miles away; here he stopped at a cottage, and an old man came out and escorted him in. A bundle lay on the table in the little parlour of the cottage.

"Here are the clothes, my lord," said the old man, laying his hand on the bundle.

"And here are mine," answered Lord Harry. "And the horse stands ready for you." With this he began to pull off the fine clothes in which he had had audience of the King, and he opened the bundle and put on the old and plain suit which it contained. Then he held out his hand to the old man, saying, "Give me the five crowns, Solomon, and our bargain is complete."

Then Solomon the Jew gave him five crowns and bade him farewell, and he placed the crowns in his purse and walked out of the cottage, possessing nothing in the world saving his old clothes, five crowns, and the golden pin that had fastened the ruddy hair of Princess Osra. For everything else that he had possessed, his lands and houses in England, his horses and carriages, his money, his clothes, and all that was his, he had bartered with Solomon the Jew, in order that he might buy the ruby necklace which he had given to Princess Osra. Such was the strange madness wrought in him by her face.

It was now late evening, and he walked to and fro all night. In the morning he went to the shop of a barber and, in return for one of his crowns, the barber cropped his long curls short and shaved off his moustaches, and gave him a dye with which he stained his complexion to a darker tint; and he made his face dirty, and soiled his hands and roughened the skin of them by chafing them on some flints which lay by the roadside. Then, changing a second crown, he bought a loaf of bread, and set off to trudge to Strelsau, for in Strelsau was Osra, and he would not be anywhere else in the world. And when he had arrived there, he went to a sergeant of the King's Guard, and prevailed on him by a present of three crowns to enlist him as a trooper, and this the sergeant, having found that Lord Harry could ride and knew how to use his sword, agreed to do. Thus Lord Harry became a trooper in the Guard of King Rudolf, having for all his possessions, save what the King's stores afforded him, a few pence and the golden pin that had fastened the hair of Princess Osra. But nobody knew him, except

Solomon the Jew, and he, having made a good profit, held his peace, both then and afterwards.

Many a day Lord Harry mounted guard at the palace, and often he saw the King, with the Queen, ride out and back; but they did not notice the face of the trooper. Sometimes he saw the Princess also, but she did not look at him, although he could not restrain himself from looking at her; but since every man looked at her she had grown accustomed to being gazed at and took no heed of it. But once she wore the ruby necklace, and the breath of the trooper went quick and eager when he saw it on her neck; and a sudden flush of colour spread over all his face, so that the Princess, chancing to glance at him in passing, and seeing the colour beneath and through the dye that stained him, was greatly astonished, and she reined in her horse for an instant and looked very intently at him; yet she rode on again in silence.

That evening there came to the quarters of the King's Guard a waiting-woman, who asked to see the trooper who had mounted guard at the west gate of the palace that day; and when he came the woman held out to him a box of red morocco leather, saying, "It is for you."

But he answered, "It is not for me," and, turning away, left her. And this happened on three evenings. Then, on the fourth day, it was again his turn to mount guard at the palace; and when he had sat there on his horse for an hour, the Princess Osra rode out from under the portico; she rode alone and the ruby necklace was on her neck; and she said:

"I am going to ride outside the city by the river bank. Let a trooper follow me some way behind." And she signed with her hand to Lord Harry, and he rode after her through the streets, and out of the Western Gate; and they turned along the bank of the river. When they had gone three or four miles from the city, Osra halted, and beckoned to Lord Harry to approach her; and he came. But when she was about to speak to him and tell him that she knew him, a sudden new madness came on him; he seized her bridle, and dug his spurs deep into his horse's flanks, and the horse bounded forward at a gallop. In alarm the Princess cried out, but he did not heed her. Along the bank they galloped: and when they met any one, which happened seldom (for the place was remote, and it was now evening), he bade her cover her face, and she obeyed, twisting her lace handkerchief about her face. Thus they rode till they came at nightfall to a bluff of rock high above the stream. Here Lord Harry suddenly checked the horses, flung himself from his saddle, and bade the Princess dismount. She obeyed, and stood facing him, pale with fear and apprehension, but wearing a proud and scornful air. And he cried:

"Is it not well you should die? For you live but to madden men and drive them to sin and folly."

"Nay," said she, "to men of good heart beauty leads to goodness. From yourself come the sin and folly, my lord;" and she laid hold of the ruby necklace and broke the clasp of it, and flung it on the ground before him. He took no heed of it, but seized her hand, and drew her to the edge of the bluff, saying:

"The world will be safer if I fling you down."

Then she looked in his face, and a sudden pity entered into her heart, and she said very gently:

"Sit down, my lord, and let me put my hands on your brow, for I think you are in a fever."

He sat down, all trembling and shaking like a man with ague, and she stripped off her gauntlets, and took his forehead between her hands; and he lay there quiet with his head between her hands. Presently his eyes closed, and he slept. But Osra did not know what to do, for darkness had fallen, and she dared not leave him alone there by the river. So she sat where she was, and in an hour, the night being fine and not cold, she grew weary; her hands fell away from his brow, and she sank back on the green turf, pillowing her head on a curved arm, and there she slept with the mad lord by her and the ruby necklace lying near them.

At midnight Lord Harry Culverhouse awoke, and saw Princess Osra sleeping peacefully, with a smile on her lips such as decks a child's in sleep. He rose and stood up on his feet, looking at her: and he heard nothing but the sound of the horses cropping the grass a little way off. Then he drew near her and gazed long on her face: and she opened her eyes and saw him; she smiled at him, and she said:

"Even here I am guarded by one of the gentlemen who guard me in the palace." And she closed her eyes again and turned to sleep.

A shiver ran through him. He dug his nails into the palms of his hands, and, turning, walked swiftly up and down on the bluff by the side of the river, while Osra slept.

Presently he fell on his knees beside her, beginning to murmur in a rapid rush of words: but he did not now curse her beauty, but blessed God for it, and blessed Him also for the preservation of his own honour. Thus he spent the night till day was near: then he bent over Osra, and looked once more on her: and he took up the ruby necklace and laid it lightly about her neck. Feeling the touch of it, cool and wet from the dew, she again opened her eyes, and, putting her knuckles in them, she rubbed gently; and she gasped a gentle yawn, saying: "Heigho, I am sleepy!" and sat up. And she said:

"Are you not sleepy, my lord?"

"I am on watch, madame," said Lord Harry Culverhouse.

As the Princess sat up, the ruby necklace fell from her neck into her lap. Seeing it, she held it up to him, saying:

"Take it again, and go to your own home. I am sure you gave too great a price for it."

He smiled, for she did not know how great the price was, and he asked:

"Must I, in my turn, give back the pin that fastened your hair?"

"No, keep the pin—it is worth nothing," she smiled. "Is it safe for me to go to sleep a little longer?"

"Who would harm you, madame? Even I have not harmed you."

"You!" said she, with a little laugh. "You would not harm me."

And she lay down again and closed her eyes.

Then Lord Harry Culverhouse sat down on the ground, resting his chin on his knees, and clasping his hands about his shins, and he cursed himself bitterly not now because he meditated any harm to her—for his hot fury was past, and he would have died before a hair of her head should be hurt—but because of the evil that his wild and reckless madness had brought upon her. For he knew that soon there would be a pursuit, and that, if she and he were found there, it would become known who he was, and her fame would suffer injurious rumours by reason of what he had done. Therefore he made up his mind what he must next do, and he abandoned all the dreams that had led him into the foolish adventure on which he had embarked, and put from him the wickedness that had filled his heart when first he carried her to the bluff over the river. He rose on to his knees, and prayed that if his deed were a sin—for it seemed to him to be a necessary thing—then that it might be forgiven, but that, in any case, no hurt or harm should befall the Princess Osra by reason of anything that he had done. Finally he commended his soul to God. Then he took the ruby necklace in his hand and, holding it, walked to the edge of the bluff.

But at this instant the sound of the hoofs of a horse struck on his ear; the sound was loud and close, and he had no more time than to turn round before a horse was reined in suddenly by him, and a man leapt from it and ran at him and grappled with him. And Lord Harry perceived that the man was the King. For when Osra did not return, search parties had been sent out; the King himself headed one, and, having the best horse and being urged on by love and fear for his sister, he had outridden all the rest and had chanced to come alone where Osra and Lord Harry were; and he gripped Lord Harry furiously, cursing him for a scoundrel and demanding what he had done to the Princess. Then Lord Harry said:

"Do you not know me, sire? I am Harry Culverhouse."

Greatly astonished, the King loosed his hold and fell back a pace, for he could not understand what he heard, but yet knew the voice of his friend. Then, looking down, he beheld Osra sleeping peacefully as a child on the ground, with her cloak spread under her, that she might take no harm from the damp. But Lord Harry caught him by the arm, crying:

"Are there others coming after you?"

"Aye," said the King, "many others. The whole of the Guard are roused, and seek her high and low in the city and outside. But how came you here, man?"

Then Lord Harry told the King what he had done, speaking very briefly and hastily, but yet sparing nothing; and when he told him how he had carried off the Princess, the King's hand flew to the hilt of his sword. But Lord Harry said "Not yet," and continued to tell the King how Osra had pitied him, how he had watched by her, and how she had slept again, bidding him keep the pin. Then glancing at Osra, he lowered his voice and spoke very quick and urgently, and the King held out his hand and shook Lord Harry's hand, asking: "Is there no other way?" But Lord Harry shook his head; then he kissed the King's hand; next he went and kissed Osra's hand very softly, and looked for the last time on her face; and he drew the golden pin from his purse and he put it gently and deftly among her hair. Then taking the ruby necklace in his own hand and clenching it tight, he said to King Rudolf:

"Sire, there are some in the city that knew me before, but have not known me since I have been in your Guard, because I have altered my face. Take care that you so alter it that they do not know me again."

The King's breath caught in his throat, for he had loved Lord Harry Culverhouse, and he asked again:

"Is there no other way?"

"Hark!" said the other, "I hear the horses of your Guard drawing near; I hear them to east and west and north; and do you not see shapes riding there to the south, across the river? If I ride from here alive, I shall be taken, and the truth must be known. For my sake and hers, strike, sire."

The King took Lord Harry Culverhouse by the arm and drew him to him, saying:

"Must it be so, Harry? And we have lived as friends together!"

"The sound of the hoofs is very near, sire."

The King drew himself up to his height, and he raised his hat from his head, and bowed low to Lord Harry Culverhouse, and he said:

"Now praise be to God for the restoration of this gentleman to a sound mind, and may Christ grant him mercy for the sake of his honourable death!"

And he drew his sword from its sheath, and came up to Lord Harry Culverhouse, who stood on the edge of the bluff. The King raised his sword and struck with all his strength; the head split under the blow, and Lord Harry Culverhouse fell dead from the bluff into the river, holding the ruby necklace in his clenched hand. But the King shivered, and a short sob burst from him.

On this instant there arose an eager glad cry, and twenty of the Guard rushed forward, greeting the King and rejoiced to see the Princess. Roused by the noise of their coming, she sat up again, rubbing her eyes, and cried:

"Where is he? Where is Lord Harry?"

And she looked round on the troopers, and they gazed on her, much astonished at hearing what she said. But Rudolf came to her and took her hand, saying:

"Why, Osra, you have been dreaming! There is no Lord Harry here. Lord Harry Culverhouse is far off in his own country. Did that rascal of a trooper frighten you?"

Her eyes grew wide in wonder; but before she could speak he turned to the Guard, saying:

"By heaven's pleasure I came in time to prevent any harm, except the loss of a necklace my sister wore. For as I rode up, I saw a fellow stooping down by her and fumbling with the clasp of her necklace. He was one of your troop, and had ridden out behind her, and he must have carried her off by force: now he was endeavouring to rob her, and as I rode up to him he sprang away from her, holding her necklace in his hand: but I leapt down from my horse and ran at him, and he retreated in fear. Then I drew my sword, and drove him back to the edge of the bluff: and then I split his skull, and he fell into the river, still holding the necklace. But, thanks to God, the Princess is not hurt. Let search be made for the fellow's body, for perhaps the necklace will be still in his hand."

But one cried, "How came they here?"

"Ah, sister," said the King, fixing his eyes on Osra, "how came you here?"

232

Reading in the King's eyes the answer that he would have, she said:

"The trooper compelled me to come hither with him, and he threatened to kill me if I would not give him my necklace. But I refused: then he drew a knife and menaced me with it, and I fell into a swoon, and knew no more until I awoke and found you here; and now I see that my necklace is gone."

"Bring her horse," the King commanded, "and ride in front and behind. We will return to the city at the best speed we may."

Then he mounted the Princess on her horse, and rode by her side, supporting her with his arm: and the troopers were some way off in front and behind. But the Princess felt the pin again in her hair, and putting up her hand she pulled it out, and she said:

"He has given me back my pin."

"Of whom do you speak?" asked the King.

"Of Lord Harry Culverhouse. Is he indeed dead, Rudolf?"

"Are you indeed still dreaming?" answered the King with a laugh. "What had that fellow to do with Harry Culverhouse?"

"But the pin?" she cried.

"My wife set it in your hair, before you started, for she wished to replace the one you gave to Lord Harry."

"She did not touch my hair to-day!" cried the Princess.

"Aye, but she did," said he.

The Princess suddenly fell to sobbing; and she said:

"Tell me the truth, tell me the truth. Surely it was in truth Lord Harry Culverhouse?"

Then Rudolf drew very close to her, and said softly:

"Sweet sister, the noble gentleman whom we knew, he whom I loved, and who loved you in chivalrous deference, went from us two months ago. Be not troubled about him, for now all is well with him. But there was an unhappy man with you, who was not our Harry Culverhouse, and who had murderous and mad thoughts in his heart. Yet at the end he also died as readily and as nobly as our dear friend himself would have died for your sake. I pray you ask no more of him, but be contented to know that though he died by the sword yet he died in peace and willingly. But of our dear friend, as we knew him, think as much as you will, for the love of an honest gentleman is a good thing to think of."

The Princess Osra, hearing this, laid her hand in her brother's hand, and for a long while she did not speak. Then she said:

"But our friend will not come again, Rudolf?"

"No, you will never see our friend again," answered the King.

"Then when you see him—for I think you will see him once again—lay this pin in his hand, and bid him take and keep it for the sake of the love I bear him: perhaps he will hear you."

"It may be, I cannot tell," said the King.

"And if he has the necklace," said she, "pray him to give that to you, and sell it, Rudolf, and give the value of it in gifts to the poor. Yes, to all that are unhappy and afflicted, even as the poor man who was with me to-night."

"So be it, Osra," said the King, and he kissed her. But she burst again suddenly into passionate weeping, calling God to witness that her face was a curse to her and a curse to her friends, and praying the King to suffer her to take the veil in a convent, that she might trouble honest men no more. Thus he brought her in a sad plight to the palace, and gave her into the arms of his wife, still sobbing bitterly. And he himself took the pin, and when the body of the mad trooper was found, with his own hand he covered the face, and put the pin in the hand from which he took the ruby necklace: and he sold the necklace, and used the proceeds of it as his sister had desired.

Thus the madness of Lord Harry Culverhouse, which was bred in him by the beauty of the Princess Osra, worked its way with him, and brought him first into peril of great villainy, and at last to death. And his name passed no more on the lips of any in Strelsau, nor between King Rudolf and his sister, while the story that the King had told to the troopers was believed by all, and none save the King knew what Lord Harry Culverhouse had done in his madness. But Osra mourned for him, and for a long while she would not go abroad, nor receive any of the princes or nobles who came to the Court, but lay still sick and full of grief, bewailing the harm that she had wrought. Yet, as time passed, she grew again happy, for she was young, and the world was sweet to her: and then, as King Rudolf had bidden her, she remembered Lord Harry Culverhouse as he had been before his madness came upon him. Yet still more did she remember how, even in his madness, he had done her no harm, but had watched beside her through the night, and had, as morning dawned, entreated death at the hands of the King, preferring to die rather than that the talk of a single idle tongue should fall foully on her name. Therefore she mourned for him with secret tears.

But he, although no monument marked his grave, and although men spoke only of the mad trooper who had robbed the Princess, yet slept soundly and at peace: and his right hand lay clenched upon his heart, and in it the golden pin that had fastened the ruddy hair of Princess Osra.

CHAPTER IV.

The Courtesy of Christian the Highwayman.

"I am am tired of men," cried Princess Osra, "and of suitors, and of princes. I will go to Zenda and ride in the forest all alone."

"You will meet men even there," said the King.

"How do you know that, sire?" she asked with a smile.

"At least I have found it impossible to avoid meeting women anywhere."

"I do not think it is the same thing," observed Osra, smiling again.

The King said no more, but let her go her own way; and to Zenda she went, and rode in the forest all alone, meeting for many days no man at all, though, perhaps, she thought a little of those whom she had met, and (who can tell?) now and then of one whom she should some day meet. For the mind loves to entertain itself with such idle musings, and they are hardly conscious till a sudden smile or a beat of the heart betrays them to the abashed thinker. Just in this manner a flush had chanced to rise to Osra's cheek one day as she rode in a reverie, being above ten miles from the Castle and on the very edge of the kingdom's frontier, which skirts the extremity of the forest on the east. Breaking off her thoughts, half ashamed of them, she looked up and saw a very fine and powerful horse tethered to a tree a few yards away, saddled and bridled. Then she said to herself with a sigh, "Alas, here is a man as my brother said!" And she shook her head very sorrowfully.

The next instant she saw, as she had foreboded, a man approaching her; indeed, the matter was as bad as could be, for he was young and handsome, finely dressed, carrying a good sword by his side and a brace of pistols mounted in silver in his belt. He held a feathered hat in his hand, and, advancing with a deep bow, knelt on one knee by the Princess's horse, saying:

"Madame, if you will, you can do me a great service."

"If it be in my power, sir," she answered—for since fate compelled her to meet a man, she would not show him rudeness—"I am at your service."

"You see my horse there, madame? He is as dear as my life to me; and I fear I shall lose him, unless I have your aid," and he rose and stood looking at the Princess.

"Why, what threatens him?" she asked.

"I will tell you, madame. I come from across the frontier, from a secluded village nearly ten miles from here. There I live with my mother, whom I support. There is a rich fellow there, a farmer, Otho by name, who is, saving your presence, a plaguey boastful fellow. And he is to-day to be betrothed."

"Do you also love the lady?" asked Osra, thinking she had come at the cause of his trouble.

"Not I, madame. But this Otho boasted and vaunted so intolerably of her beauty, and of his own prowess and attraction, that last night I, led away by emulation (nay, I am ashamed to say that I had also drunk a flask of wine) wagered with him my horse against a thousand crowns—though the horse is worth two thousand—that I would bring with me to the feast a girl handsomer than his Lotta. But now it is eleven o'clock, and the feast is at one o'clock, and I have no girl to show, ugly or handsome. And if I lose my horse I must hang myself, for I cannot live without him."

"You cannot live without your horse?" she asked in surprise.

"At least, madame," he answered in some confusion, "his loss would go near to breaking my heart."

"But is this Lotta so handsome that you can find none to surpass her?"

"She is, indeed, wonderfully handsome. In the village they call her the most beautiful girl in the world."

"Then, sir, it seems to me that your wager was most improvident and rash. For you are certain to lose it."

"Alas, yes!" he answered in great distress. "I am certain to lose; for there are, I think, only two ladies in the world who could save me, and one would not."

"Two ladies? Who are they?"

"Madame," said he, "before you came in sight, I sat desolate and despairing on the ground, and what I said to myself was, 'If what men say is true, there is only one lady who could save me. But how shall I, poor Christian Hantz, come at the Princess Osra? And would she put on a country girl's dress and go to the feast with me? Alas, it is impossible! And there is no other lady in the world beautiful enough.' But then——"

"Well, sir, what then?" asked Osra, playing with her whip and smothering a smile.

"Then, madame," said Christian, "I looked up and I saw you, and I cried, 'A fig for the Princess Osra! For here is a lady more beautiful than all they tell of Princess Osra; I will throw myself at her feet and pray her in pity to help me.'"

Still Osra hid her smile, and so busy was she with this task that she did not perceive that Christian also hid a smile; but she thought that he did not know her, whereas he had seen her several times, and had this day tracked her in the forest, knowing that she was accustomed to ride there.

"But where," she asked, "would the lady who went with you get the dress you speak of?"

"At my mother's cottage, madame, where my mother would wait on her."

"And when could she be back at this spot?"

"By five in the afternoon, madame. I would myself escort her."

"And why, sir, should she rescue you from the straits into which your folly has led you?"

"Alas, madame, for no reason, unless, by a divine miracle, she should prove as kind as she is beautiful."

"You have a rash tongue, sir, in other matters than the making of wagers." And she looked at him. For she was very sorely tempted to do what he prayed of her; and she said:

"Has the Princess Osra ever ridden through your village?"

"Never, madame."

"But some there may know her face, and then they will think nothing of mine."

"It is unlikely that any one there should have seen even a picture of her, for they are quiet folk and do not go abroad."

"Besides, in a peasant's dress—" began Osra meditatively. But she stopped, blushing and laughing. And Christian caught her hand and kissed it, crying:

"For heaven's sake, come, madame!"

He was so earnest, and his earnestness so became his bronzed face and bright eyes, that Osra could not deny him, but she swore him to secrecy, and agreed to ride with him, blaming herself all the while very greatly, and blaming yet more that Fate which would not allow her to be quit of the troublesome race of men even in the recesses of the forest of Zenda.

Turning their horses, therefore, towards the frontier, they set them at a smart canter, for there was little time to lose if they were to come to the feast by one o'clock; and shortly before noon, having struck a bye-path through the trees, they came on a small cottage that stood apart and by itself; and a hill rose from it.

"On the other side of the hill lies the village, madame," said Christian, jumping from his horse. "And this is my cottage. Hallo, there, mother!"

An old woman came out, neatly and cleanly clad. Christian ran up to her, spoke to her briefly, and brought her to Osra. The worthy dame, bewildered by the appearance and stately air of the Princess, did nothing but curtsey and murmur incoherent thanks, but Osra, now caught by the excitement of the enterprise, clapped her hands, crying:

"Quick, quick, or we shall be too late!"

So Christian lifted her down and led away the horses to a shed behind the cottage. But the old woman led Osra in, and took her to the bedroom, where lay a dress such as the peasant girls wore. Osra took up the skirt, and looked at it curiously.

"Must I indeed wear this?" she asked. "And I am somewhat tall, mother!"

The old woman said that nothing would serve save the dress, and Osra sighed. Yet as there was no help for it, she suffered the old woman to help her in getting it on.

So the door was shut, and Christian sat smiling in the sun outside, well pleased at the success of his audacious scheme, and feeling Otho's crowns already in his pocket.

Still less did he doubt of this most desirable result when the door of the cottage again opened and Osra came out, blushing, and yet biting her lips to keep back her laughter. Her hair was plaited in two long plaits; she wore a white bodice, and over it a jacket of black velvet, and a red skirt hung full from her waist to but a very little below her knee; then came hose of red also—for it was a holiday, and the best of all was worn—and stout square-toed shoes. Osra in her heart loved all except the shoes, yet she declared that she loathed all except the shoes. And Christian, with eyes cast most demurely on the ground, prayed her to forgive the sad necessity, yet assured her that Lotta would die of envy that very day.

"Let us go then," said Osra. "For the sooner we go, the sooner will it be done, and I can get rid of these ridiculous clothes. Heaven have mercy on me and grant that I may meet none who know me!"

They were mounting the hill now, the old woman standing at the cottage door and watching. When they reached the top Osra saw a small village nestling in the valley below, and the sound of music struck on her ear. At this a sudden fear seized her, and putting out her hand she caught Christian by the sleeve, saying:

"Will they know me?"

"Not they, madame," said he. But as he spoke his eyes fell on a ring that the Princess wore, a gem engraved with the Royal Arms. "Not they, if you conceal that ring;" and for a moment he looked in her face, and he smiled.

Osra uttered a little cry, as she hastily plucked the ring from her finger, and gave it to him, saying:

"Keep it safe, and do not forget to give it me again."

But she would not meet his glance, for she began from now to suspect that he knew who she was.

The sound of music came from a solid square-built house that stood on the outskirts of the village, and coming nearer they saw a long table spread in the shade near the house, and a company of men and women seated at it. The Princess was somewhat comforted to find that the girls' dresses were in all respects like her own, though hers seemed newer and more handsome; therefore she took courage, and put her arm inside Christian's arm, saying:

"Since I have accepted the part, I will play it. Come, sir, let us go and challenge Lotta. Your horse is at stake!"

"He is in no danger," said Christian, "and I am worth a thousand crowns." And his eyes most plainly added the reason which led him to these comfortable conclusions.

Now at this moment Otho, having toasted the company and accepted their good wishes, was standing up before them all, Lotta standing by him, her hand in his; and he vowed (as was but right) all manner of love and devotion to her, and declared that she was the prettiest girl in the world; in truth she was very pretty, being, although low of stature, most admirably formed, having golden hair, the pinkest of cheeks and large blue eyes that followed a man about in a most appealing and distracting manner. So that Otho had good reason to be content, and would have come to no harm, had it not been for that old extravagance of lovers which will not allow this world to hold more than one pretty girl—the truth being, of course, quite otherwise. But, led on by this infatuation, Otho cried:

"I dare any man to find so pretty a girl! As for Master Christian whose wager you heard— why, this evening his fine horse shall feed in my stable!"

"Softly, friend Otho, softly," came to the ears of the feasters from behind the trees. "Mistress Lotta is very pretty, but I have here a girl whom some think handsome. Well, this worthy company shall judge." And Christian came from the shelter of the trees leading Osra by the hand, and he set her opposite to Lotta, where all could see her. And all looked and beheld her with amazement. But none spoke. So they rested for a long while, Christian smiling and Osra's eyes being set on Lotta, while Otho did nothing but gaze at Osra.

Presently a low murmur began to run along the table. "Who is she?" asked some one, but none could answer. "Who is she?" called an old man to Christian, but he answered, "What's that to you? Is she not fairer?" And when the others asked whence she came, he made the same answer. But one young fellow leant from his place and plucked Christian's sleeve, saying, "Is she promised to you?" and at this Christian frowned, answering, "At least she is not for you," while Osra, overhearing, blushed mightily. Then Otho, still saying nothing, suddenly lugged out a great purse of money, and flung it violently into the middle of the table with a curse, and Christian with a mocking lift of his hat, came forward, and, taking it, tossed it up and down in his hand, crying, "Is it fair weight, neighbour Otho?" Otho did not heed him, but turned suddenly to Lotta and put his arm round her waist, saying:

"Aye, it is true. The devil must have sent her, but it is true. Yet you are pretty too, my lass." For Lotta, after looking at all the company and at Osra, had been so sorely wounded in her pride and robbed of her triumph, that, poor child, she had begun to weep, hiding her face in her hands, and Otho was trying to comfort her, though, lover as he was, he could not for the life of him declare that she was more beautiful than the girl whom Christian had brought. And they all moved from their places and came to stand round Osra. But she, after a moment, caught from Christian the bag that he tossed so exultantly, crying to him: "I'll be your debtor for it;" and bursting through the ring, she ran round the table and came to Lotta, and, pulling the girl's hands down from her face, she thrust the bag into her hands, and began to talk to her, whispering low, and looking into her frightened eyes with shining eyes.

"Ah, my dear," said Osra, "see, he still loves you, dear. Ah, why did I come? But I am going away, yes, now, and I shall never come here again. I do harm wherever I go! Yes, but you'll be the prettiest girl in the village always! Otho, Otho, kiss her, Otho! Tell her that you love her, Otho. Don't stand there dumb. Oh, how stupid men are! Don't you see what she wants? Yes, do it again. I never saw anybody so pretty, Otho. Yes, yes, dear, keep the bag. It's from me; you must keep it, and buy pretty clothes and be prettier than ever, for Otho's sake, because he loves you."

By the time the Princess Osra had ended her consolations, behold she was very nearly crying herself! But Lotta put her arms round the Princess's neck and kissed her, because she said that Otho still loved her; and in her gratitude for this, she forgot thanks for the bag of crowns, or even to wonder who this girl was that could give away a thousand crowns. But in this the rest of the company were not like her, and an eager murmuring marked the excitement with which they watched the scene; and they cried to Christian:

"Look after your crowns;" and thought him mad when he shook his head jauntily, answering:

"Let Otho do what he will with them."

Then, their interest growing more and more intense, they crowded round the Princess, scanning her very closely; and she was in great fear that she would be known, and also in some embarrassment from the ardent glances and free comments of the simple countrymen, who were accustomed to say what they thought with more plainness than were the gentlemen of the Court. So that at length, fairly alarmed, she gave Lotta a last hasty kiss, and made her way to Christian, crying: "Take me away."

"Aye, madame," said he, and he put her arm in his and turned away. But all the company followed him, staring and gossiping and crowding, so that Lotta and Otho were left alone at the feast which Otho had provided, with nothing to console them but one another's love and the happily recovered thousand crowns. And the crowd pressed hard on Osra and Christian, being full of eagerness to see where the girl went and what became of her. Thus they reached the top of the hill and came in sight of Christian's cottage. But now Christian suddenly loosed Osra's arm and, turning round, faced the throng of inquisitive folk; with either hand he drew a silver-mounted pistol from his belt; and when he had cocked the pair, he pointed them at his friends and neighbours, saying in a quiet and pleasant voice: "I shall count to twenty. Any one who means to be within range when I come to twenty had best now order his coffin."

At this a great grumbling arose among them; yet they knew Christian, and did not wait till he had counted, but one and all turned tail and ran down the hill much quicker than they had come up. But one or two fellows, resentful and malicious because of their disappointment, as soon as they found themselves out of range, turned round and shouted:

"Aye, he is ready with his pistol, is Christian. We know him. Highwayman! Whom did you last rob?" And Christian went red as the frock that Osra wore. But she turned questioning eyes on him.

"Yes," said he sullenly. "They say highwayman; it is true. I am a robber. That is why I said, madame, that I could not live without my horse."

"Come," said Osra, "let us go to the cottage."

So they returned together to the cottage, saying nothing. There Osra put on her own clothes again, and having bidden farewell to the old woman who asked no questions of her, mounted her horse. Then Christian said:

"Shall I ride with you, madame?"

She bowed her head in assent.

Till they entered the forest the Princess did not speak. But then she sighed, saying:

"I am sorry that I went with you. For if you had lost your horse maybe you would have ceased from your way of life. It is better to lose a horse than to be hanged."

"Madame," said he, "you speak prudently. Yet I had rather be hanged than lose him."

"I am in your debt a thousand crowns," said she, and, stopping her horse, she wrote for him an order for a thousand crowns, and she signed it with her own name, Osra, and gave it to him. He received it bowing very low.

"You knew me all the time?" she asked.

"Yes, madame," said he. They had now come to where he had first met her.

"Why do you live by robbery?" she asked.

"For the love of the same thing that made you come with me to-day, madame."

"But could you not find what you love in the King's service?"

"I do not like service, madame," said Christian. "I love to be free."

She paused for a moment, and then said in a lower tone:

"Could you not endure my service, sir?"

"In that I shall now live and die, madame," said he, and she felt his eyes upon her.

Again in silence they rode on; it was evening now, and had grown dark, and presently the lantern in the tower of the keep of Zenda became visible. Then Osra drew rein.

"For my sake," said she, "rob no more."

"What you command, madame, is my law. And here is your ring."

"Keep the ring," she said. "But when I can serve you, you shall send it back to me, and ask what you will in return for it."

"There is nothing," said he, very low, and looking away from her, "that I would take in exchange for it."

"A foolish man or only a foolish speech?" she asked as lightly as she could, with one fleeting glance at his face.

"A foolish man, madame, it may be, but a true speech," and he bent bareheaded in his saddle and raised her hand to his lips. And, still bareheaded, he turned away and rode back at a canter into the forest. But the Princess Osra rode on to the Castle, wondering greatly at what she had done that day.

Yet she could not be very sorry that she had saved his horse for him, and she trusted that Otho and Lotta would be happy, and she thought that one man was, after all, as good flesh and blood as another, and then that she was a Princess and he a robber, and that his eyes had been over bold. Yet there was deference in them also.

"It is a great pity that he should be a robber," sighed the Princess, as she reached the Castle.

The Princess Osra's carriage was within two miles of Strelsau when she put her head out of the window and asked the officer who rode by the wheel why such a throng of people hastened to the city.

"It is nothing, madame," answered he, saluting. "It is only that two rogues are to be hanged to-day."

"What pleasure is there in seeing men hanged?" asked Osra scornfully. "I wish I had not come to-day." And she drew her head back in disgust. Then she called: "Go slowly, and do not let me get into the middle of the wild beasts who go to gloat over men being hanged."

So the horses were checked to a walk, and thus the carriage proceeded slowly towards Strelsau. But presently the Princess put her head out of the window again and asked:

"Who are to be hanged to-day, sir?"

"The noted highwayman, Sigismund Kohl, madame," said the officer. "He robbed the Archbishop's coach in the forest of Zenda; but they pursued him over the frontier and tracked him to the cottage of the other rogue, who had a part in many previous robberies, though not in this. The second fellow hid Kohl, and tried to put off the officers, but they caught them both, and both are to be hanged."

"It seems hard," said Osra, "to hang the one who only sheltered his friend. He could do no less."

"Nay, madame, he richly deserves it. Besides his previous robberies, he is gravely suspected of a most foul murder. For a few weeks ago he was in company with a girl, and she seemed to have money and to spare, and was mighty pretty too, they say. Now he can give no account of what has become of her; but they have found all the clothes she wore hidden away in his house, and he says his mother bought the clothes. But they are a girl's clothes, not an old woman's. It looks black; but luckily the other matter is enough to hang him on. His mother's clothes, in faith! Would an old woman, who died three weeks ago, have bought a new red frock and smart red stockings for herself?"

"A red frock? Red stockings? And the mother is dead? Dead of what?"

"Of a chill, madame, such as carries old people off suddenly. Yes, it looks black, and so the people think, for when the pair were brought into the city, though the rascals cheered Kohl who had only robbed the Archbishop, they pelted and came near to killing Christian Hantz."

The Princess's face went pale, and she sank back, murmuring "Christian Hantz!" But in another moment she cried:

"At what hour is the hanging?"

"At noon, madame; that is, half an hour from now."

Then the Princess cried in a loud urgent tone:

"Faster, faster! Drive at top speed!" The officers looked at her in wonder; but she cried: "A hundred crowns to the coachman if he brings me to the place before noon! Quick, quick!" For she was all on fire at the thought that Christian Hantz was to be hanged, not for any new robbery but because he had sheltered his friend. And she knew how the red skirt and the red stockings came in his house; her breath caught in her throat, as she thought how he had suffered stoning and execration rather than betray her secret. And she cried out to herself as she was carried along, "But the ring! Why did he not send the ring?"

By now they were at the gates of the city, and now within them. The officer and the two men who were with him rode forward to clear the road for the Princess. Thus they made their way on, until they came to the street which leads from the West Gate to the Cathedral, and could see the gibbet that had been raised before the prison, between the Cathedral and the Palace. But here the whole street was blocked with people, and the officer could not get the carriage through, for the folk were thick as swarming bees all across the roadway, and even if they would have moved, they could not; so the carriage came to a dead stand, while the officer said to Princess Osra:

"Madame, it is useless, we cannot get through them." Osra sprang from the carriage, and she said:

"You have two men with you, sir. For God's sake, gentlemen, bring me through to the foot of the scaffold. I care not if it costs me my life."

"Nor we, madame, though it costs us ours, since it is your pleasure," they said, as every man in the city would have said for the Princess Osra. And the two men went ahead, while Osra followed with the officer; and pushing and struggling, and dodging in and out, aye, and when need was, hitting, and buffeting, and kicking, the three took her through into the square of the Cathedral. And the clock in the great tower struck noon.

As the bell boomed a cry went up from the thronged square; the body of a man shot from the scaffold to the top of the gibbet and hung there. The people cried aloud, some cheering, some also groaning and weeping.

"Who is it, who is it?" asked the Princess.

"It is Sigismund Kohl, madame," said the officer.

"Then on, on, on!" she commanded, and again they struggled forward. Now a louder and fiercer cry rang out as a man was brought forward on the scaffold, in his shirt and breeches. A priest was with him, holding a crucifix before his eyes. King Rudolf, who sat at a window of his palace, asked why they delayed to string the rascal up; and one of his gentlemen answered:

"Sire, the priest begged a few minutes' delay. For the obstinate rogue will not confess to the murder of the girl, and therefore cannot receive absolution, and the priest is loth to have him hanged without it."

"He shall be hanged without it, unless his conscience act quickly," said the King. But a moment later, he asked:

"What is the tumult in the corner of the square? There is a fight there. Let it be seen to."

Indeed there was a fight; for the three with Osra were bent on getting through, and the crowd would not let them through; and they struck at the crowd, and the crowd at them. But suddenly some one, peering past the Guards, exclaimed: "The Princess Osra, the Princess!" Then the blows ceased, and the crowd began slowly to give back, making way for Osra. And she walked between walls of people, yet did not seem to see or to take heed of any of them; her eyes were glued to the man on the scaffold. For even now the priest, who had held the crucifix, turned sorrowfully away, and signed with his hand to the hangman.

Again the people shouted fiercely for Christian's death; and he, stepping forward, gave himself into the executioner's hands. Those who were near him saw that there was a smile on his lips, and, as the hangman took hold of him, he kissed a little packet which he held in his right hand. But the people shrieked loudly: "Murderer, murderer! Where is the girl?" At this, stung beyond endurance, Christian cried, so loudly that his voice rose above the clamour:

"I am no murderer, I did not touch a hair of her head."

"Then where is she, where is she?" they shouted.

"I do not know," said he; and he added in a low tone, kissing his little packet again: "Wherever she is, God in his graciousness send her joy." And he turned to the executioner, saying, "Get on, man." But then he looked as it were for the last time on the living sea of faces round him, and suddenly, out of all of them, he saw one.

What Christian saw the King saw also, and he rose from his chair with an oath and a laugh.

"This sister of mine is a wonderful wench," said he. "Come, let us see why she will not have this rascal hanged. Run, some one, and tell them not to string him up till I give the word."

The King walked out of the palace and came into the square, the Guard parting the people before him; and Osra, seeing him coming, stood now quite still, blushing and smiling, although she was very ashamed and panted sorely.

Then the King came and faced her, saying nothing, but lifting his eyebrows and smiling whimsically; but at last he whispered:

"What, was there a man in the forest, Osra?"

And she answered: "Do not ask me that, sire, but ask Christian Hantz what is in the packet which he kissed as the hangman took hold of him."

"He is not only a robber, but a murderer also, though he will not own to it."

"No, he is no murderer," said she. "Look in the packet."

"Then come and look with me," said the King, and taking her hand he led her up on to the scaffold in the sight of all the people, who wondered and laughed; for they always laughed at the ways of the Princess Osra. But she flew straight across to Christian, who fell on one knee with the rope round his neck.

"Give me the packet," she cried, and she tore it open. And in it she found her order for a thousand crowns and the gem engraved with the Royal Arms. For an instant she looked at Christian, and then she said:

"You have not got money for the order? Yet my name is good for a thousand crowns."

"To me, madame, it was better than fifty thousand."

"But," she broke out eagerly; "you should have sent the ring. I could have saved you."

"But you would have kept it in return for the service, madame."

"Aye, sir, that was the bargain," said Osra, with a little low laugh.

"I knew it. And I preferred to die with it rather than live without it."

"Another foolish speech!"

"Yes, for the man is foolish, madame."

"And they cry to you, 'Where is the girl?' And you do not answer, but die under a foul charge!"

To this Christian Hantz made no answer at all, unless it were one to murmur mournfully:

244

"And, madame, they have taken from me the red skirt and——"

The Princess Osra suddenly turned from him, and went to the King, who had stood regarding her; and she knelt down before him, saying:

"Sire and dear brother, pardon this man. He did but shelter his friend, and he will rob no more."

"I might forgive him his robberies, if he would take service in my army."

"Yes, in my regiment of Guards!" she cried.

"But how shall I forgive that foul murder, of which he is certainly guilty? For where, sister, is the pretty girl, of whom no traces can be found saving her dress, her red skirt, and——?"

"Sire, these things—I pray you, sire, let your gentlemen stand back a little."

"Stand back, then, gentlemen," said the King.

"These things, sire, were, by a strange chance, in the little parcel that the poor man kissed. Though why he kissed it, I do not know."

The King took Osra's order for a thousand crowns, and also the gem engraved with the Royal Arms; he looked at them and at his sister.

"Therefore, sire," said she, "I ask life and pardon for the most courteous gentleman in your dominions. For he prized my ring above his life and my secret above his honour. Sire, such men should live and not die."

The King turned to his officers, and said:

"Gentlemen, the Princess knows that the girl is alive and well and has no complaint against this man. For he might not in honour tell who or where she was. And, for the rest, he did but shelter his friend, and my sister is surety that he will rob no more. May he live?"

When they heard this, they all declared that Christian should live, and they went into the crowd and told the people that the girl was found. Then the people suddenly veered round and began to cheer Christian, and some cried, "Who is the girl?" and laughed merrily, conceiving that it was a love affair on which Christian had been engaged; and because he preferred to die under an imputation of murder rather than endanger his love's reputation, he became a hero with them; and when they heard he was not to die, they dispersed in the utmost good temper, cheering him and the King, and above all the Princess Osra, whom they loved.

But she went again to Christian, and bade the hangman take the rope off his neck.

"Will you serve in my regiment of Guards, sir?" she asked. "Or is service still irksome to you?"

"I will serve you, madame," said Christian.

"And since you will need equipment, get money for this order," and she gave him again the order.

"I must needs obey you, madame, though reluctantly."

"It is well, sir. I trust you will serve me faithfully. I bid you farewell, sir," and she bowed slightly, and turned as if to leave him. And he said nothing, but stood looking at her, so that presently she blushed, saying:

"They will let you have those things now, sir."

Christian bowed very low, and, raising himself again, looked at her ring.

"Nay, I cannot do that," said Princess Osra. "But you will see it now and then, and, now and then, maybe, you can touch it." And she put the ring on her finger and held out her hand to him. He knelt and kissed the ring and then her hand; but he looked very glum. And the Princess laughed openly at him, her eyes dancing in delight and amusement. But he still looked more as though he were going to be hanged than he had any time before in the day. So that the King, pointing at him, said to Osra:

"An ungrateful dog! Upon my soul he looks as though he were sorry not to be hanged! Do you call that courtesy?"

But the Princess laughed softly and rubbed the ring on her finger, as she answered:

"Aye, sire, I call that the best of courtesy."

CHAPTER V.

The Sin of the Bishop of Modenstein.

In the days of Rudolf III. there stood on the hill opposite the Castle of Zenda, and on the other side of the valley in which the town lies, on the site where the château of Tarlenheim now is situated, a fine and strong castle belonging to Count Nikolas of Festenburg. He was a noble of very old and high family, and had great estates; his house being, indeed, second only to the Royal House in rank and reputation. He himself was a young man of great accomplishments, of a domineering temper, and of much ambition; and he had gained distinction in the wars that marked the closing years of the reign of King Henry the Lion. With King Rudolf he was not on terms of cordial friendship, for he despised the King's easy manners and carelessness of dignity, while the King had no love for a gentleman whose one object seemed to be to surpass and outshine him in the eyes of his people, and who never rested from extending and fortifying his castle until it threatened to surpass Zenda itself both in strength and magnificence. Moreover Nikolas, although maintaining a state ample and suitable to his rank, was yet careful and prudent, while Rudolf spent all that he received and more besides, so that the Count grew richer and the King poorer. But in spite of these causes of difference, the Count was received at Court with apparent graciousness, and no open outburst of enmity had yet occurred, the pair being, on the contrary, often together, and sharing their sports and pastimes with one another.

Now most of these diversions were harmless, or, indeed, becoming and proper, but there was one among them full of danger to a man of hot head and ungoverned impulse such as King Rudolf was. And this one was diceing, in which the King took great delight, and in which the

Count Nikolas was very ready to encourage him. The King, who was generous and hated to win from poor men or those who might be playing beyond their means in order to give him pleasure, was delighted to find an opponent whose purse was as long or longer than his own, and thus gradually came to pass many evenings with the boxes in Nikolas's company. And the more evenings he passed the deeper he fell into the Count's debt; for the King drank wine, while the Count was content with small beer, and when the King was losing he doubled his stakes, whereas the Count took in sail if the wind seemed adverse. Thus always and steadily the debt grew, till at last Rudolf dared not reckon how large it had become, nor did he dare to disclose it to his advisers. For there were great public burdens already imposed by reason of King Henry's wars, and the citizens of Strelsau were not in a mood to bear fresh exaction, nor to give their hard earnings for the payment of the King's gambling debts; in fine, although they loved the Elphbergs well enough, they loved their money more. Thus the King had no resource except in his private possessions, and these were of no great value, saving the Castle and estate of Zenda.

At length, when they had sat late one night and the throws had gone all the evening against the King and for Nikolas, the King flung himself back in his chair, drained his glass, and said impatiently:

"I am weary of the game! Come, my lord, let us end it."

"I would not urge you, sire, a moment beyond what you desire. I play but for your pleasure."

"Then my pleasure has been your profit," said the King with a vexed laugh, "for I believe I am stripped of my last crown. What is my debt?"

The Count, who had the whole sum reckoned on his tablets, took them out, and shewed the King the amount of the debt.

"I cannot pay it," said Rudolf. "I would play you again, to double the debt or wipe it out, but I have nothing of value enough to stake."

The desire which had been nursed for long in the Count's heart now saw the moment of its possible realisation.

He leant over the table, and, smoothing his beard with his hand, said gently:

"The amount is no more than half the value of your Majesty's Castle and demesne of Zenda."

The King started and forced a laugh.

"Aye, Zenda spoils the prospect from Festenburg, does it?" said he. "But I will not risk Zenda. An Elphberg without Zenda would seem like a man robbed of his wife. We have had it since we have had anything or been anything. I should not seem King without it."

"As you will, sire. Then the debt stands?" He looked full and keenly into the King's eyes, asking without words, "How will you pay it?" and adding without words, "Paid it must be." And the King read the unspoken words in the eyes of Count Nikolas.

The King took up his glass, but finding it empty flung it angrily on the floor, where it shivered into fragments at Count Nikolas's feet; and he shifted in his chair and cursed softly under his breath. Nikolas sat with the dice-box in his hand and a smile on his lips; for he knew that the

King could not pay, and therefore must play, and he was in the vein, and did not doubt of winning from the King Zenda and its demesne. Then he would be the greatest lord in the kingdom, and hold for his own a kingdom within the kingdom, and the two strongest places in all the land. And a greater prize might then dangle in reach of his grasp.

"The devil spurs and I gallop," said the King at last. And he took up the dice-box and rattled it.

"Fortune will smile on you this time, sire, and I shall not grieve at it," said Count Nikolas with a courteous smile.

"Curses on her!" cried the King. "Come, my lord, a quick ending to it! One throw, and I am a free man, or you are master of my castle."

"One throw let it be, sire, for it grows late," assented Nikolas with a careless air; and they both raised the boxes and rattled the dice inside them. The King threw; his throw was a six and a five, and a sudden gleam of hope lit up his eyes; he leant forward in his chair, gripping the elbows of it with his hands; his cheeks flushed and his breath came quickly. With a bow Count Nikolas raised his hand and threw. The dice fell and rolled on the table. The King sank back; and the Count said with a smile of apology and a shrug of his shoulders:

"Indeed I am ashamed. For I cannot be denied to-night."

For Count Nikolas of Festenburg had thrown sixes, and thereby won from the King the Castle and demesne of Zenda.

He rose from his chair, and, having buckled on his sword that had lain on the table by him, and taking his hat in his hand, stood looking down on the King with a malicious smile on his face. And he said with a look that had more mockery than respect in it:

"Have I your Majesty's leave to withdraw? For ere day dawn, I have matters to transact in Strelsau, and I would be at my Castle of Zenda to-night."

Then King Rudolf took a sheet of paper and wrote an order that the Castle, and all that was in it, and all the demesne should be surrendered to Count Nikolas of Festenburg on his demand, and he gave the paper to Nikolas. Then he rose up and held out his hand, which Nikolas kissed, smiling covertly, and the King said with grace and dignity:

"Cousin, my Castle has found a more worthy master. God give you joy of it."

And he motioned with his hand to be left alone. Then, when the Count had gone, he sat down in his chair again, and remained there till it was full day, neither moving nor yet sleeping. There he was found by his gentlemen when they came to dress him, but none asked him what had passed.

Count Nikolas, now Lord of Zenda, did not so waste time, and the matters that he had spoken of did not keep him long in Strelsau; but in the early morning he rode out, the paper which the King had written in his belt.

First he rode with all speed to his own house of Festenburg, and there he gathered together all his followers, servants, foresters, and armed retainers, and he told them that they were to ride with him to Zenda, for that Zenda was now his and not the King's. At this they were greatly astonished, but they ate the fine dinner and drank the wine which he provided, and in the evening they rode down the hill very merry, and trotted, nearly a hundred strong, through the town, making a great noise, so that they disturbed the Bishop of Modenstein, who was lying that night at the inn in the course of a journey from his See to the Capital; but nobody could tell the Bishop why they rode to Zenda, and presently the Bishop, being wearied with travelling, went to his bed.

Now King Rudolf, in his chagrin and dismay, had himself forgotten, or had at least neglected to warn the Count of Festenburg, that his sister Princess Osra was residing at the Castle of Zenda; for it was her favourite resort, and she often retired from the Court and spent many days there alone. There she was now with two of her ladies, a small retinue of servants, and no more than half a dozen Guards; and when Count Nikolas came to the gate, it being then after nine, she had gone to her own chamber, and sat before the mirror, dressed in a loose white gown, with her ruddy hair unbound and floating over her shoulders. She was reading an old story book, containing tales of Helen of Troy, of Cleopatra, of Berenice, and other lovely ladies, very elegantly related and embellished with fine pictures. And the Princess, being very much absorbed in the stories, did not hear nor notice the arrival of the Count's company, but continued to read, while Nikolas roused the watchmen, and the bridge was let down, and the steward summoned. Then Nikolas took the steward aside, and shewed him the King's order, bearing the King's seal, and the steward, although both greatly astonished and greatly grieved, could not deny the letter or the seal, but declared himself ready to obey and to surrender the Castle; and the sergeant in command of the Guard said the same; but, they added, since the Princess was in the Castle, they must inform her of the matter, and take her commands.

"Aye, do," said Nikolas, sitting down in the great hall. "Tell her not to be disturbed, but to give me the honour of being her host for as long as she will, and say that I will wait on her, if it be her pleasure."

But he smiled to think of the anger and scorn with which Osra would receive the tidings when the steward delivered them to her.

In this respect the event did not fall short of his expectations, for she was so indignant and aghast that, thinking of nothing but the tidings, she flung away the book and cried: "Send the Count here to me," and stood waiting for him there in her chamber, in her white gown and with her hair unbound and flowing down over her shoulders. And when he came she cried: "What is this, my lord?" and listened to his story with parted lips and flashing eyes, and thus read the King's letter and saw the King's seal. And her eyes filled with tears, but she dashed them away with her hand. Then the Count said, bowing to her as mockingly as he had bowed to her brother:

"It is the fortune of the dice, madame."

"Yes, my lord, as you play the game," said she.

His eyes were fixed on her, and it seemed to him that she was more beautiful in her white gown and with her hair unbound over her shoulders, than he had ever felt her to be before, and he eyed her closely. Suddenly she looked at him, and for a moment he averted his eyes; but he looked again and her eyes met his. For several moments she stood rigid and motionless. Then she said:

"My lord, the King has lost the Castle of Zenda, which is the home and cradle of our House. It was scarcely the King's alone to lose. Have I no title in it?"

"It was the King's, madame, and now it is mine," smiled Nikolas.

"Well, then, it is yours," said she, and taking a step towards him, she said: "Have you a mind to venture it again, my lord?"

"I would venture it only against a great stake," said he, smiling still, while his eyes were fixed on her face and marked every change in the colour of her cheeks.

"I can play dice as well as the King," she cried. "Are we not all gamblers, we Elphbergs?" And she laughed bitterly.

"But what would your stake be?" he asked sneeringly.

Princess Osra's face was now very pale, but her voice did not tremble and she did not flinch; for the honour of her House and of the throne was as sacred to her as her salvation, and more than her happiness.

"A stake, my lord," said she, "that many gentlemen have thought above any castle in preciousness."

"Of what do you speak?" he asked, and his voice quivered a little, as a man's does in excitement. "For, pardon me, madame, but what have you of such value?"

"I have what the poorest girl has, and it is of the value that it pleased God to make it and pleases men to think it," said Osra. "And all of it I will stake against the King's Castle of Zenda and its demesne."

Count Nikolas's eyes flashed and he drew nearer to her; he took his dice-box from his pocket, and he held it up before her, and he whispered in an eager hoarse voice:

"Name this great stake, madame; what is it?"

"It is myself, my lord," said Princess Osra.

"Yourself?" he cried wondering, though he had half guessed.

"Aye. To be the Lord of Zenda is much. Is it not more to be husband to the King's sister?"

"It is more," said he, "when the King's sister is the Princess Osra." And he looked at her now with open admiration. But she did not heed his glance, but with face pale as death she seized a small table and drew it between them and cried: "Throw then, my lord! We know the stakes."

"If you win, Zenda is yours. If I win, you are mine."

"Yes, I and Zenda also," said she. "Throw, my lord!"

"Shall we throw thrice, madame, or once, or how often?"

"Thrice, my lord," she answered, tossing back her hair behind her neck, and holding one hand to her side. "Throw first," she added.

The Count rattled the box; and the throw was seven. Osra took the box from him, looked keenly and defiantly in his eyes, and threw.

"Fortune is with you, madame," said he, biting his lips. "For a five and a four make nine, or I err greatly."

He took the box from her; his hand shook, but hers was firm and steady; and again he threw.

"Ah, it is but five," said he impatiently, and a frown settled on his brow.

"It is enough, my lord," said Osra; and pointed to the dice that she had thrown, a three and a one.

The Count's eyes gleamed again; he sprang towards her, and was about to seize the box. But he checked himself suddenly, and bowed, saying:

"Throw first this time, I pray you, madame, if it be not disagreeable to you."

"I do not care which way it is," said Osra, and she shook and made her third cast. When she lifted the box, the face of the dice showed seven. A smile broadened on the Count's lips, for he thought surely he could beat seven, he that had beaten eleven and thereby won the Castle of Zenda, which now he staked against the Princess Osra. But his eyes were very keenly and attentively on her, and he held the box poised, shoulder-high, in his right hand.

Then a sudden faintness and sickness seized on the Princess, and the composure that had hitherto upheld her failed; she could not meet his glance, nor could she bear to see the fall of the dice; but she turned away her head before he threw, and stood thus with averted face. But he kept attentive eyes on her, and drew very near to the table so that he stood right over it. And the Princess Osra caught sight of her own face in the mirror, and started to see herself pallid and ghastly, and her features drawn as though she were suffering some great pain. Yet she uttered no sound.

The dice rattled in the box; they rattled on the table; there was a pause while a man might quickly count a dozen; and then Count Nikolas of Festenburg cried out in a voice that trembled and tripped over the words:

"Eight, eight, eight!"

But before the last of the words had left his shaking lips, the Princess Osra faced round on him like lightning. She raised her hand so that the loose white sleeve fell back from her rounded arm, and her eyes flashed, and her lips curled as she outstretched her arm at him, and cried:

"Foul play!"

For, as she watched her own pale face in the mirror—the mirror which Count Nikolas had not heeded—she had seen him throw, she had seen him stand for an instant over the dice he had thrown with gloomy and maddened face; and then she had seen a slight swift movement of his left hand, as his fingers deftly darted down and touched one of the dice and turned it.

And all this she had seen before he had cried eight. Therefore now she turned on him, and cried, "Foul play!" and before he could speak, she darted by him towards the door. But he sprang forward, and caught her by the arm above the wrist and gripped her, and his fingers bit into the flesh of her arm, as he gasped, "You lie! Where are you going?" But her voice rang out clear and loud in answer:

"I am going to tell all the world that Zenda is ours again, and I am going to publish in every city in the kingdom that Count Nikolas of Festenburg is a common cheat and rogue, and should be whipped at the cart's tail through the streets of Strelsau. For I saw you in the mirror, my lord, I saw you in the mirror!" And she ended with a wild laugh that echoed through the room.

Still he gripped her arm, and she did not flinch; for an instant he looked full in her eyes; covetousness, and desire, and shame, came all together upon him, and over-mastered him, and he hissed between set teeth:

"You shan't! By God, you shan't!"

"Aye, but I will, my lord," said Osra. "It is a fine tale for the King and for your friends in Strelsau."

An instant longer he held her where she was; and he gasped and licked his lips. Then he suddenly dragged her with him towards a couch; seizing up a coverlet that lay on the couch he flung it around her, and he folded it tight about her, and he drew it close over her face. She could not cry out nor move. He lifted her up and swung her over his shoulder, and, opening the door of the room, dashed down the stairs towards the great hall.

In the great hall were six of the King's Guard, and some of the servants of the Castle, and many of the people who had come with Count Nikolas; they all sprang to their feet when they saw them. He took no heed of them, but rushed at a run through the hall, and out under the portcullis and across the bridge, which had not been raised since he entered. There at the end of the bridge a lackey held his horse; and he leapt on his horse, setting one hand on the saddle, and still holding Osra; and then he cried aloud:

"My men follow me! To Festenburg!"

And all his men ran out, the King's Guard doing nothing to hinder them, and jumping on their horses and setting them at a gallop, hurried after the Count. He, riding furiously, turned towards the town of Zenda, and the whole company swept down the hill, and, reaching the town, clattered and dashed through it at full gallop, neither drawing rein nor turning to right or left; and again they roused the Bishop of Modenstein, and he turned in his bed, wondering what the rush of mounted men meant. But they, galloping still, climbed the opposite hill and came to the Castle of Festenburg with their horses spent and foundered. In they all crowded, close on one another's heels; the bridge was drawn up; and there in the entrance they stood looking at one another, asking mutely what their master had done, and who was the lady whom he carried wrapped in the coverlet. But he ran on till he reached the stairs, and he climbed them, and entering a room in the gate-tower, looking over the moat, he laid the Princess Osra on a couch, and standing over her he smote one hand upon the other, and he swore loudly:

"Now, as God lives, Zenda I will have, and her I will have, and it shall be her husband whom she must, if she will, proclaim a cheat in Strelsau!"

Then he bent down and lifted the coverlet from her face. But she did not stir nor speak, nor open her eyes. For she had fallen into a swoon as they rode, and did not know what had befallen her, nor where she had been brought, nor that she was now in the Castle of Festenburg, and in the power of a desperate man. Thus she lay still and white, while Count Nikolas stood over her and bit his nails in rage. And it was then just on midnight.

On being disturbed for the third time, the Bishop of Modenstein, whose temper was hot and cost him continual prayers and penances from the mastery it strove to win over him, was very impatient; and since he was at once angry and half asleep, it was long before he could or would understand the monstrous news with which his terrified host came trembling and quaking to his bedside in the dead of the night. A servant-girl, stammered the frightened fellow, had run down half dressed and panting from the Castle of Zenda, and declared that whether they chose to believe her or not—and, indeed, she could hardly believe such a thing herself, although she had seen it with her own eyes from her own window—yet Count Nikolas of Festenburg had come to the Castle that evening, had spoken with Princess Osra, and now (they might call her a liar if they chose) had carried off the Princess with him on his horse to Festenburg, alive or dead none knew, and the men-servants were amazed and terrified, and the soldiers were at their wits' end, talking big and threatening to bring ten thousand men from Strelsau and to leave not one stone upon another at Festenburg, and what not. But all the while and for all their big talk nothing was done; and the Princess was at Festenburg, alive or dead or in what strait none knew. And, finally, nobody but one poor servant-girl had had the wit to run down and rouse the town.

The Bishop of Modenstein sat up in his bed and he fairly roared at the innkeeper:

"Are there no men, then, who can fight in the town, fool?"

"None, none, my lord—not against the Count. Count Nikolas is a terrible man. Please God, he has not killed the Princess by now."

"Saddle my horse," said the Bishop, "and be quick with it."

And he leapt out of bed with sparkling eyes. For the Bishop was a young man, but a little turned of thirty, and he was a noble of the old House of Hentzau. Now some of the Hentzaus (of whom history tells us of many) have been good, and some have been bad; and the good fear God, while the bad do not; but neither the good nor the bad fear anything in the world besides. Hence, for good or ill, they do great deeds and risk their lives as another man risks a penny. So the Bishop, leaving his bed, dressed himself in breeches and boots, and set a black hat with a violet feather on his head, and, staying to put on nothing else but his shirt and his cloak over it, in ten minutes was on his horse at the door of the inn. For a moment he looked at a straggling crowd that had gathered there; then with a toss of his head and a curl of his lip he told them what he thought of them, saying openly that he thanked heaven they were not of his diocese, and in an instant he was galloping through the streets of the town towards the Castle of Festenburg, with his sword by his side and a brace of pistols in the holsters of the saddle. Thus he left the gossipers and vapourers behind, and rode alone as he was up the hill, his blood leaping and his heart beating quick; for, as he went, he said to himself:

"It is not often a Churchman has a chance like this."

On the stroke of half-past twelve he came to the bridge of the Castle moat, and the bridge was up. But the Bishop shouted, and the watchman came out and stood in the gateway across the moat, and, the night being fine and clear, he presented an excellent aim.

"My pistol is straight at your head," cried the Bishop, "let down the bridge. I am Frederick of Hentzau; that is, I am the Bishop of Modenstein, and I charge you, if you are a dutiful son of the Church, to obey me. The pistol is full at your head."

The watchman knew the Bishop, but he also knew the Count his master.

"I dare not let down the bridge without an order from my lord," he faltered.

"Then before you can turn round, you're a dead man," said the Bishop.

"Will you hold me harmless with my lord, if I let it down?"

"Aye, he shall not hurt you. But if you do not immediately let it down, I'll shoot you first and refuse you Christian burial afterwards. Come, down with it."

So the watchman, fearing that, if he refused, the Bishop would spare neither body nor soul, but would destroy the one and damn the other, let down the bridge, and the Bishop, leaping from his horse, ran across with his drawn sword in one hand and a pistol in the other. Walking into the hall, he found a great company of Count Nikolas's men, drinking with one another, but talking uneasily and seeming alarmed. And the Bishop raised the hand that held the sword above his head in the attitude of benediction, saying, "Peace be with you!"

Most of them knew him by his face, and all knew him as soon as a comrade whispered his name, and they sprang to their feet, uncovering their heads and bowing. And he said:

"Where is your master the Count?"

"The Count is upstairs, my lord," they answered. "You cannot see him now."

"Nay, but I will see him," said the Bishop.

"We are ordered to let none pass," said they, and although their manner was full of respect, they spread themselves across the hall, and thus barred the way to the staircase that rose in the corner of the hall. But the Bishop faced them in great anger, crying:

"Do you think I do not know what has been done? Are you all, then, parties in this treachery? Do you all want to swing from the turrets of the Castle when the King comes with a thousand men from Strelsau?"

At this they looked at him and at one another with great uneasiness; for they knew that the King had no mercy when he was roused, and that he loved his sister above everybody in the world. And the Bishop stepped up close to their rank. Then one of them drew his sword half-way from its scabbard. But the Bishop, perceiving this, cried:

"Do you all do violence to a lady, and dare to lay hands on the King's sister? Aye, and here is a fellow that would strike a Bishop of God's Church!" And he caught the fellow a buffet with the flat of his sword, that knocked him down, "Let me pass, you rogues," said the Bishop. "Do you think you can stop a Hentzau?"

"Let us go and tell the Count that my lord the Bishop is here," cried the house-steward, thinking that he had found a way out of the difficulty; for they dared neither to touch the Bishop nor yet to let him through; and the steward turned to run towards the staircase. But the Bishop sprang after him, quick as an arrow, and, dropping the pistol from his left hand, caught him by the shoulder and hurled him back. "I want no announcing," he said. "The Church is free to enter everywhere." And he burst through them at the point of the sword, reckless now what might befall him so that he made his way through. But they did not venture to cut him down; for they knew that nothing but death would stop him, and for their very souls' sake they dared not kill him. So he, kicking one and pushing another and laying about him with the flat of his sword and with his free hand, and reminding them all the while of their duty to the Church and of his sacred character, at last made his way through and stood alone, unhurt, at the foot of the staircase, while they cowered by the walls or looked at him in stupid helplessness and bewilderment. And the Bishop swiftly mounted the stairs.

At this instant in the room in the gate-tower of the Castle overlooking the moat there had fallen a moment of dead silence. Here Count Nikolas had raised the Princess, set her on a couch, and waited till her faintness and fright were gone. Then he had come near to her, and in brief harsh tones told her his mind. For him, indeed, the dice were now cast; in his fury and fear he had dared all. He was calm now, with the calmness of a man at a great turn of fate. That room, he told her, she should never leave alive, save as his promised wife, sworn and held to secrecy and silence by the force of that bond and of her oath. If he killed her he must die, whether by his own hand or the King's mattered little. But he would die for a great cause and in a great venture. "I shall not be called a cheating gamester, madame," said he, a smile on his pale face. "I choose death sooner than disgrace. Such is my choice. What is yours? It stands between death and silence; and no man but your husband will dare to trust your silence."

"You do not dare to kill me," said she defiantly.

"Madame, I dare do nothing else. They may write 'murderer' on my tomb; they shall not throw 'cheat' in my living face."

"I will not be silent," cried Osra, springing to her feet. "And rather than be your wife I would die a thousand times. For a cheat you are—a cheat—a cheat!" Her voice rose, till he feared that she would be heard, if any one chanced to listen, even from so far off as the hall. Yet he made one more effort, seeking to move her by an appeal to which women are not wont to be insensible.

"A cheat, yes!" said he. "I, Nikolas of Festenburg, am a cheat. I say it, though no other man shall while I live to hear him. But to gain what stake?"

"Why, my brother's Castle of Zenda."

"I swear to you it was not," he cried, coming nearer to her. "I did not fear losing on the cast, but I could not endure not to win. Not my stake, madame, but yours lured me to my foul play. Have you your face, and yet do not know to what it drives men?"

"If I have a fair face, it should inspire fair deeds," said she. "Do not touch me, sir, do not touch me. I loathe breathing the same air with you, or so much as seeing your face. Aye, and I can die. Even the women of our House know how to die."

255

At her scorn and contempt a great rage came upon him, and he gripped the hilt of his sword, and drew it from the scabbard. But she stood still, facing him with calm eyes. Her lips moved for a moment in prayer, but she did not shrink.

"I pray you," said he in trembling speech, mastering himself for an instant, "I pray you!" But he could say no more.

"I will cry your cheating in all Strelsau," said she.

"Then commend your soul to God. For in one minute you shall die."

Still she stood motionless; and he began to come near to her, his sword now drawn in his hand. Having come within the distance from which he could strike her, he paused and gazed into her eyes. She answered him with a smile. Then there was for an instant the utter stillness in the room; and in that instant the Bishop of Modenstein set his foot on the staircase and came running up. On a sudden Osra heard the step, and a gleam flashed in her eye. The Count heard it also, and his sword was arrested in its stroke. A smile came on his face. He was glad at the coming of some one whom he might kill in fight; for it turned him sick to butcher her unresisting. Yet he dared not let her go, to cry his cheating in the streets of Strelsau. The steps came nearer.

He dropped his sword on the floor and sprang upon her. A shriek rang out, but he pressed his hand on her mouth and seized her in his arms. She had no strength to resist, and he carried her swiftly across the room to a door in the wall. He pulled the door open—it was very heavy and massive—and he flung her down roughly on the stone floor of a little chamber, square and lofty, having but one small window high up, through which the moonlight scarcely pierced. She fell with a moan of pain. Unheeding, he turned on his heel and shut the door. And, as he turned, he heard a man throw himself against the door of the room. It also was strong and twice the man hurled himself with all his force against it. At last it strained and gave way; and the Bishop of Modenstein burst into the room breathless. And he saw no trace of the Princess's presence, but only Count Nikolas standing sword in hand in front of the door in the wall with a sneering smile on his face.

The Bishop of Modenstein never loved to speak afterwards of what followed, saying always that he rather deplored than gloried in it, and that when a man of sacred profession was forced to use the weapons of this world it was a matter of grief to him, not of vaunting. But the King compelled him by urgent requests to describe the whole affair, while the Princess was never weary of telling all that she knew, or of blessing all bishops for the sake of the Bishop of Modenstein. Yet the Bishop blamed himself; perhaps, if the truth were known, not for the necessity that drove him to do what he did, as much as for a secret and ashamed joy which he detected in himself. For certainly, as he burst into the room now, there was no sign of reluctance or unwillingness in his face; he took off his feathered hat, bowed politely to the Count, and resting the point of his sword on the floor, asked:

"My lord, where is the Princess?"

"What do you want here, and who are you?" cried the Count with a blasphemous oath.

"When we were boys together, you knew Frederick of Hentzau. Do you not now know the Bishop of Modenstein?"

"Bishop! This is no place for bishops. Get back to your prayers, my lord."

"It wants some time yet before matins," answered the Bishop. "My lord, where is the Princess?"

"What do you want with her?"

"I am here to escort her wherever it may be her pleasure to go."

He spoke confidently, but he was in his heart alarmed and uneasy because he had not found the Princess.

"I do not know where she is," said Nikolas of Festenburg.

"My lord, you lie," said the Bishop of Modenstein.

The Count had wanted nothing but an excuse for attacking the intruder. He had it now, and an angry flush mounted in his cheeks as he walked across to where the Bishop stood.

Shifting his sword, which he had picked up again, to his left hand, he struck the Bishop on the face with his gloved hand. The Bishop smiled and turned the other cheek to Count Nikolas, who struck again with all his force, so that he reeled back, catching hold of the open door to avoid falling, and the blood started dull red under the skin of his face. But he still smiled, and bowed, saying:

"I find nothing about the third blow in Holy Scripture."

At this instant the Princess Osra, who had been half stunned by the violence with which Nikolas had thrown her on the floor, came to her full senses and, hearing the Bishop's voice, she cried out loudly for help. He, hearing her, darted in an instant across the room, and was at the door of the little chamber before the Count could stop him. He pulled the door open and Osra sprang out to him, saying:

"Save me! Save me!"

"You are safe, madame, have no fear," answered the Bishop. And turning to the Count, he continued: "Let us go outside, my lord, and discuss this matter. Our dispute will disturb and perhaps alarm the Princess."

And a man might have read the purpose in his eyes, though his manner and words were gentle; for he had sworn in his heart that the Count should not escape.

But the Count cared as little for the presence of the Princess as he had for her dignity, her honour, or her life: and now that she was no longer wholly at his mercy, but there was a new chance that she might escape, his rage and the fear of exposure lashed him to fury, and, without more talking, he made at the Bishop, crying:

"You first, and then her! I'll be rid of the pair of you?"

The Bishop faced him, standing between Princess Osra and his assault, while she shrank back a little, sheltering herself behind the heavy door. For although she had been ready to die without fear, yet the sight of men fighting frightened her, and she veiled her face with her hands, and waited in dread to hear the sound of their swords clashing. But the Bishop looked

257

very happy, and, setting his hat on his head with a jaunty air, he stood on guard. For ten years or more he had not used his sword, but the secret of its mastery seemed to revive, fresh and clear in his mind, and let his soul say what it would, his body rejoiced to be at the exercise again, so that his blood kindled and his eyes gleamed in the glee of strife. Thus he stepped forward, guarding himself, and thus he met the Count's impetuous onset; he neither flinched nor gave back, but finding himself holding his own, he pressed on and on, not violently attacking and yet never resting, and turning every thrust with a wrist of iron. And while Osra now gazed with wide eyes and close-held breath, and Count Nikolas muttered oaths and grew more furious, the Bishop seemed as gay as when he talked to the King, more gaily, may be, than Bishops should. Again his eye danced as in the days when he had been called the wildest of the Hentzaus. And still he drove Count Nikolas back and back.

Now behind the Count was a window, which he himself had caused to be enlarged and made low and wide, in order that he might look from it over the surrounding country; in time of war it was covered with a close and strong iron grating. But now the grating was off and the window open, and beneath the window was a fall of fifty feet or hard upon it into the moat below. The Count, looking into the Bishop's face, and seeing him smile, suddenly recollected the window, and fancied it was the Bishop's design to drive him on to it so that he could give back no more; and, since he knew by now that the Bishop was his master with the sword, a despairing rage settled upon him; determining to die swiftly, since die he must, he rushed forward, making a desperate lunge at his enemy. But the Bishop parried the lunge, and, always seeming to be about to run the Count through the body, again forced him to retreat till his back was close to the opening of the window. Here Nikolas stood, his eyes glaring like a madman's; then a sudden devilish smile spread over his face.

"Will you yield yourself, my lord?" cried the Bishop, putting a restraint on the wicked impulse to kill the man, and lowering his point for an instant.

In that short moment the Count made his last throw; for all at once, as it seemed, and almost in one motion, he thrust and wounded the Bishop in the left side of his body, high in the chest near the shoulder, and, though the wound was slight, the blood flowed freely; then drawing back his sword, he seized it by the blade half-way up and flung it like a javelin at the Princess, who stood still by the door, breathlessly watching the fight. By an ace it missed her head, and it pinned a tress of her hair to the door and quivered deep-set in the wood of the door. When the Bishop of Modenstein saw this, hesitation and mercy passed out of his heart, and though the man had now no weapon, he thought of sparing him no more than he would have spared any cruel and savage beast, but he drove his sword into his body, and the Count, not being able to endure the thrust without flinching, against his own will gave back before it. Then came from his lips a loud cry of dismay and despair; for at the same moment that the sword was in him he, staggering back, fell wounded to death through the open window. The Bishop looked out after him, and Princess Osra heard the sound of a great splash in the water of the moat below; for very horror she sank against the door, seeming to be held up more by the sword that had pinned her hair than by her own strength. Then came up through the window, from which the Bishop still looked with a strange smile, the clatter of a hundred feet, running to the gate of the Castle. The bridge was let down; the confused sound of many men talking, of whispers, of shouts, and of cries of horror, mounted up through the air. For the Count's men in the hall also had heard the splash, and run out to see what it was, and there they beheld the body of their master, dead in the moat; their eyes were wide open, and they could hardly lay their tongues to the words as they pointed to the body and whispered to one another, very low: "The Bishop has killed him—the Bishop has killed him." But the Bishop saw them from the window, and leant out, crying:

"Yes, I have killed him. So perish all such villains!"

When they looked up, and saw in the moonlight the Bishop's face, they were amazed. But he hastily drew his head in, so that they might not see him any more. For he knew that his face had been fierce, and exultant, and joyful. Then, dropping his sword, he ran across to the Princess; he drew the Count's sword, which was wet with his own blood, out of the door, releasing the Princess's hair; and, seeing that she was very faint, he put his arm about her, and led her to the couch; she sank upon it, trembling and white as her white gown, and murmuring: "Fearful, fearful!" and she clutched his arm, and for a long while she would not let him go; and her eyes were fixed on the Count's sword that lay on the floor by the entrance of the little room.

"Courage, madame," said the Bishop softly. "All danger is past. The villain is dead, and you are with the most devoted of your servants."

"Yes, yes," she said, and pressed his arm and shivered. "Is he really dead?"

"He is dead. God have mercy on him," said the Bishop.

"And you killed him?"

"I killed him. If it were a sin, pray God forgive me!"

Up through the window still came the noise of voices and the stir of men moving; for they were recovering the body of the Count from the moat; yet neither Osra nor the Bishop noticed any longer what was passing; he was intent on her, and she seemed hardly yet herself; but suddenly, before he could interpose, she threw herself off the couch and on to her knees in front of him, and, seizing hold of his hand, she kissed first the episcopal ring that he wore and then his hand. For he was both Bishop and a gallant gentleman, and a kiss she gave him for each; and after she had kissed his hand, she held it in both of hers as though for safety's sake she clung to it. But he raised her hastily, crying to her not to kneel before him, and, throwing away his hat, he knelt before her, kissing her hands many times. She seemed now recovered from her bewilderment and terror; for as she looked down on him kneeling, she was half-way between tears and smiles, and with curving lips but wet shining eyes, she said very softly:

"Ah, my lord, who made a bishop of you?" And her cheeks grew in an instant from dead white into sudden red, and her hand moved over his head as if she would fain have touched him with it. And she bent down ever so little towards him. Yet, perhaps, it was nothing; any lady, who had seen how he bore himself, and knew that it was in her cause, for her honour and life, might well have done the same.

The Bishop of Modenstein made no immediate answer; his head was still bowed over her hand, and after a while he kissed her hand again; and he felt her hand press his. Then, suddenly, as though in alarm, she drew her hand away, and he let it go easily. Then he raised his eyes and met the glance of hers, and he smiled; and Osra also smiled. For an instant they were thus. Then the Bishop rose to his feet, and he stood before her with bent head and eyes that sought the ground in becoming humility.

"It is by God's infinite goodness and divine permission that I hold my sacred office." said he. "I would that I were more worthy of it! But to-day I have taken pleasure in the killing of a man."

"And in the saving of a lady, sir," she added softly, "who will ever count you among her dearest friends and the most gallant of her defenders. Is God angry at such a deed as that?"

"May He forgive us all our sins," said the Bishop gravely; but what other sins he had in his mind he did not say, nor did the Princess ask him.

Then he gave her his arm, and they two walked together down the stairs into the hall; the Bishop, having forgotten both his hat and his sword, was bare-headed and had no weapon in his hand. The Count's men were all collected in the hall, being crowded round a table that stood by the wall; for on the table lay the body of Count Nikolas of Festenburg, and it was covered with a horse-cloth that one of the servants had thrown over it. But when the men saw the Princess and the Bishop, they made way for them and stood aside, bowing low as they passed.

"You bow now," said Osra, "but, before, none of you would lift a finger for me. To my lord the Bishop alone do I owe my life; and he is a Churchman, while you were free to fight for me. For my part, I do not envy your wives such husbands;" and with a most scornful air she passed between their ranks, taking great and ostentatious care not to touch one of them even with the hem of her gown. At this they grew red and shuffled on their feet; and one or two swore under their breath, and thanked God their wives were not such shrews, being indeed very much ashamed of themselves, and very uneasy at thinking what these same wives of theirs would say to them when the thing came to be known. But Osra and the Bishop passed over the bridge, and he set her on his horse. The summer morning had just dawned, clear and fair, so that the sun caught her ruddy hair as she mounted in her white gown. But the Bishop took the bridle of the horse and led it at a foot's pace down the hill and into the town.

Now by this time the news of what had chanced had run all through the town, and the people were out in the streets, gossiping and guessing. And when they saw the Princess Osra safe and sound and smiling, and the Bishop in his shirt—for he had given his cloak to her— leading the horse, they broke into great cheering. The men cheered the Princess, while the women thrust themselves to the front rank of the crowd, and blessed the Bishop of Modenstein. But he walked with his head down and his eyes on the ground, and would not look up, even when the women cried out in great fear and admiration on seeing that his shirt was stained with his blood and with the blood of Nikolas of Festenburg that had spurted out upon it. But one thing the Princess heard, which sent her cheeks red again; for a buxom girl glanced merrily at her, and made bold to say in a tone that the Princess could not but hear:

"By the Saints, here's waste! If he were not a Churchman, now!" And her laughing eye travelled from the Princess to him, and back to the Princess again.

"Shall we go a little faster?" whispered Osra, bending down to the Bishop. But the girl only thought that she whispered something else, and laughed the more.

At last they passed the town, and with a great crowd still following them, came to the Castle. At the gate of it the Bishop stopped and aided the Princess to alight. Again he knelt and kissed her hand, saying only:

"Madame, farewell!"

"Farewell, my lord," said Osra softly; and she went hastily into the Castle, while the Bishop returned to his inn in the town, and though the people stood round the inn the best part of the day, calling and watching for him, he would not shew himself.

In the evening of that day the King, having heard the tidings of the crime of Count Nikolas, came in furious haste with a troop of horse from Strelsau. And when he heard how Osra had played at dice with the Count, and staking herself against the Castle of Zenda had won it back, he was ashamed, and swore an oath that he would play dice no more, which oath he faithfully observed. But in the morning of the next day he went to Festenburg, where he flogged soundly every man who had not run away before his coming; and all the possessions of Count Nikolas he confiscated, and he pulled down the Castle of Festenburg, and filled up the moat that had run round its walls.

Then he sent for the Bishop of Modenstein, and thanked him, offering to him all the demesne of Count Nikolas; but the Bishop would not accept it, nor any mark of the King's favour, not even the Order of the Red Rose. Therefore the King granted the ground on which the Castle stood, and all the lands belonging to it, to Francis of Tarlenheim, brother-in-law to the wife of Prince Henry, who built the château which now stands there and belongs to the same family to this day.

But the Bishop of Modenstein, having been entertained by the King with great splendour for two days, would not stay longer, but set out to pursue his journey, clad now in his ecclesiastical garments. And Princess Osra sat by her window, leaning her head on her hand, and watching him till the trees of the forest hid him; and once, when he was on the edge of the forest, he turned his face for an instant, and looked back at her where she sat watching in the window. Thus he went to Strelsau; and when he was come there, he sent immediately for his confessor, and the confessor, having heard him, laid upon him a severe penance, which he performed with great zeal, exactness, and contrition. But whether the penance were for killing Count Nikolas of Festenburg (which in a layman, at least, would have seemed but a venial sin) or for what else, who shall say?

CHAPTER VI.

The Device of Giraldo the Painter.

When the twenty-first birthday of the Princess Osra approached, her brother King Rudolf, desiring to make her a present, summoned from his home at Verona, in Italy, a painter of very high fame, by name Giraldo, and commanded him to paint a portrait of the Princess, to be her brother's gift to her. This command Giraldo carried out, the Princess giving him every opportunity of studying her features and grudging no time that was spent by her in front of his easel; and the picture, when finished, being pronounced to be as faithful as beautiful the reputation of Giraldo was greatly enhanced by the painting of it. Thus it followed that in many cases, when foreign Princes had heard the widespread praises of Osra's beauty, they sent orders to Giraldo to execute for them, and despatch with all speed, miniatures or other portraits of the Princess, that they might judge for themselves whether she were in truth as lovely as report said; and they sent Giraldo large sums of money in recompense, adding not seldom some further donation on the express term and condition that Giraldo should observe absolute fidelity in his representation and not permit himself the least flattery. For some desired themselves to court her, and others intended their sons to ask her hand, if the evidence of Giraldo's portraits satisfied their hopes. So Giraldo, although but two or three years above thirty, grew in both fame and wealth, and was very often indebted to the Princess for the favour of a visit to his house, that he might again correct his memory of her face.

Now what several Princes had done before, it chanced that the King of Glottenberg also did; and Giraldo, to all appearance much pleased, accepted the command, and prayed the Princess to visit him; for, he said, this picture was to be larger and more elaborate than the rest, and therefore needed more study of her. So the Princess went many times, and the portrait destined for the King of Glottenberg (who was said to be seeking a suitable alliance for his eldest son) grew before her eyes into the most perfect and beautiful presentment of her which the skill of Giraldo had ever accomplished, surpassing even that first picture which he had painted by King Rudolf's command. The King made no doubt that, so soon as the picture had reached the Court of Glottenberg, an embassy would come from there to demand the hand of his sister for the Crown Prince, a proposal which he would have received with much pleasure and gratification.

"I do not think," said Osra, tossing her head, "that any such embassy will come, sire. For four or five pictures have been already painted by Signor Giraldo in like manner, but no embassies have come. It seems that my poor features do not find approval in the Courts of Europe."

Her tone, it must be confessed, was full of contempt. For the Princess Osra knew that she was beautiful, as indeed all beautiful ladies are, by the benevolence of heaven, permitted to know. How much greater mischief might they work, if such knowledge were denied them!

"That's true enough," cried Rudolf. "And I do not understand the meaning of it. But it will not be so at Glottenberg. For my good brother the King has eyes in his head, and his son sees no less well. I met them on my travels, and I can speak to it. Most certainly an embassy will come from Glottenberg before we are a month older!"

Yet, strange to say, the same thing followed on the despatch of the portrait (which Giraldo sent by a certain trusty messenger, whom he was accustomed to employ) as had happened before; no embassy came, and the King of Glottenberg excused himself from paying a visit to Strelsau, which he and his son had promised on the invitation of King Rudolf. Therefore Rudolf was very vexed, and Osra also, thinking herself scorned, was very sore at heart, although she bore herself more proudly than before. But, being very greatly disturbed in her mind concerning her beauty, she went herself again to Giraldo and charged him to paint her once more.

"This picture," she said, "is for my own eyes, and mine alone. Therefore, signor, paint it faithfully, and spare me not. For if a woman be ugly, it is well she should know it, and it seems that nobody in the kingdom will tell me the truth, although I get hints enough of it from abroad." And she frowned and flushed and was very sadly out of temper, as any beautiful lady would most naturally be in such a case.

Giraldo bowed very low, seeking to hide the sudden red that dyed his cheek, and to conceal the great joy which the command of the Princess gave him. For by reason of having painted the Princess so often, of having studied her face so curiously, and of having spent so much time in her company, listening to her conversation, and enjoying her wit and grace, this hapless young man had become so deeply and desperately her lover, that he no longer cared to use his brush in the service of any other lady or lord, but stayed at Strelsau solely that he might again and again depict the face that he loved; and, save when she sat before him, he seemed now unable to ply his art at all, and had he not received so many commands for pictures of her, he would have sat all day long idle, thinking of her; which, indeed, was what he did in the intervals between his labour on her portraits. But she, not imagining such presumption and folly on his part, thought that he was glad merely because she would pay him well; so she promised him more and more, if he would but paint her faithfully. And he gave her his word that he would paint her in every respect most faithfully.

"I desire to know," said she, "what I am in truth like; for my mirror says one thing, and the King of Glottenberg——"

But here she stopped, remembering that such matters were not fit for Giraldo's ears. Yet he must have understood, for a strange, cunning, exultant smile came on his lips as he turned away and set himself to mix the colours on his palette. Thus he began this last picture and the Princess came every day and stayed long, so that Giraldo might be able to render her likeness in every most minute respect with perfect fidelity.

"For," she thought resentfully, "either I have no eyes, or they have none in Glottenberg."

When she had been visiting Giraldo thus for hard on a month, and the picture was nearly finished, and was at once the most lovely and the most faithful of all that Giraldo had painted, it chanced that letters came to the King from a nobleman of France who was well known to him, and had known the Princess well also, the Marquis de Mérosailles. And the Marquis wrote to the King in the greatest indignation and scorn, upbraiding the King and saying:

"What is this, sire? Do you keep a madman at your Court, and call him a painter? I have been at Glottenberg; and when I spoke there, as it is my humble duty and true delight to speak everywhere, of the incomparable beauty of your Majesty's sister the Princess Osra, the King, his son, and all the company, did nothing but laugh. I fought three duels with gentlemen of the Court on this account, and two of them I, heaven helping me, wounded, and one, by some devil's trick, wounded me. After this, the matter coming to the King's ear, he sent for me, and excused the laughter by showing me a picture done by a rascal called Giraldo at your Court, the picture was named after your Majesty's most matchless sister; but, as I am a true son of the Church, it was like the devil's daughter, and, on my honour and conscience, it squinted most villainously. I pray you, sire, find out the meaning of this thing; and receive most humble duty and homage from your devoted servant, and, since your graciousness so wills it, most obliged and obedient friend, Henri Marquis de Mérosailles. I kiss the hand of the Princess."

When King Rudolf had read this letter, he grew very thoughtful, and, unknown to Giraldo, he sent and caught the messenger whom Giraldo was wont to entrust with the pictures, and who carried the picture of which M. de Mérosailles wrote to Glottenberg; and the King interrogated the messenger most closely, but got nothing from him, save that he himself never beheld the pictures which he carried, but received them most carefully packed from Giraldo, and so delivered them without undoing the coverings, and then by Giraldo's strict orders returned at once, and did not wait until the recipient had inspected the picture. So that the fellow did not know anything about the picture that had gone to Glottenberg, except that it was certainly the same as Giraldo had entrusted to his hands. But the King was not satisfied, and, learning that his sister was at that moment at Giraldo's house, being painted afresh by him, he called half-a-dozen of his gentlemen, and set out on horseback for the place where Giraldo lived in the street that runs from the Cathedral towards the western gate of Strelsau. To this day the house stands there.

The Princess sat and Giraldo painted. Behind the Princess was a window, looking on to the street, and behind Giraldo was a second door, which led into an inner room. On Giraldo's easel stood the nearly finished picture; Giraldo's eyes were alight both with love and with triumph, as he turned from the Princess to the picture, and from the picture to the Princess again; and she, seeing something of his admiration, said with a blush:

"Is it indeed faithful, signor?" For it seemed even to herself a marvellously lovely picture.

"No, madame," answered he. "For my imperfect hand cannot be faithful to perfection."

"I pray you, do not flatter me. Have you indeed shewn every fault of my face?"

"If there be a fault in your face, madame, there it is also in my picture," said Giraldo.

The Princess was silent for a moment, then she said:

"It is better, is it not, than the picture you painted for the King of Glottenberg?"

Giraldo painted a stroke or two before he answered carelessly:

"Indeed, madame, it is more faithful than that which the King of Glottenberg has."

"Then less beautiful?" asked Osra with a petulant smile.

"Nay, I do not say that; not less beautiful," he answered.

"Perhaps he would like this one better, and give me his in exchange; for I never saw his after it was finished. I think I will ask the King to write to him."

Giraldo had turned round suddenly as the Princess made this suggestion; she had spoken half in sport, half in continuing chagrin at the blindness shewn by the Court of Glottenberg. Now he stood staring at her with wide-open alarmed eyes; and he dropped his brushes on to the floor.

"What ails you, signor?" she cried. "I did but suggest exchanging the pictures."

He tried to regain his composure, as he stooped to pick up his brushes.

"The King of Glottenberg's picture is the best for him to have," said he sullenly. "This one, madame, I painted for you yourself, and for you alone."

"I pay the price and can do what I will with the picture," returned the Princess haughtily. "If I desire, I will give it to the King of Glottenberg."

Giraldo had now turned very pale, and, forgetful of the picture, stood gazing fixedly at the Princess. For he could no longer hold down in secrecy and silence the passion that possessed him, but it was declared in his eyes and in the trembling of his limbs; so that the Princess rose from her chair and shrank away from him in alarm, regretting that she had dismissed her ladies, in order to be less restrained in talk with the painter; and she tried to cry out, that they might hear her where they were in an adjoining room, but her cry froze on her lips at the sight of Giraldo's passion. And he cried in a hoarse whisper:

"He shall not have the picture, he shall not have it!" As he spoke he moved nearer to the Princess, who still shrank away from him, being now in very great alarm, and thinking that surely he had run mad. Yet she looked at him, and, looking, saw whence his madness came;

and she felt pity for him, and held out her clasped hands towards him, saying in a very soft voice, and with eyes that grew sad and tender:

"Ah, signor, signor, am I always to have lovers, and never a friend?"

At this the unfortunate painter was overcome, and dropping his head between his hands he gave a deep half-stifled sob, and then he cried:

"God's curse on me, for having slandered the beauty that I love!" And then he sobbed again.

But the Princess wondered greatly what he meant by his strange cry, and turned her eyes again on him in bewildered questioning; saying, as she pointed to the picture:

"There is no slander here, signor, unless too much praise be slander."

Giraldo made her no answer in words, but, springing towards her, caught her by the wrist, and drew her across the room to the door behind his easel. With feverish haste he unlocked it and passed through. The Princess, although now free from his grip, followed him in a strange fascination. Giraldo drew the door close behind him; and at that moment the Princess gave a cry, half a scream, half laughter. For facing her she saw, each on its easel, three, four, five, six pictures of herself, each beautiful and painted most lovingly; and the last of the six was the picture that had been painted by order of the King of Glottenberg. For she knew it by the attire, although the face had not been finished when she had last seen it. A sudden enlightenment pierced her mind, and she knew that Giraldo had not sent the pictures for which she had sat to him, but kept them himself, and sent others to his patrons. This strange conviction found its sure confirmation in a seventh easel which stood apart from the rest, on the other side of the room; for it supported what was in all respects a copy of the portrait on which Giraldo was now engaged, save that by cunning touches he had imparted to the face an alien and fearful aspect; for here, although the features had their shape and perfect grace, yet it was the face of a devil that looked out of the canvas, a face that a man would not have gazing at him from the wall on to the bed where he sought to sleep.

But when Giraldo saw her eyes fixed on this picture, he cried:

"That is for you—the other is mine. Are they not your features? The King of Glottenberg should not have even your features. But you shall have them, and if a devil looks out through such a fair mask, is it not so with all fair women that lead men to destruction? There is your true picture, Princess Osra!" And he flung himself on a couch with a mad cry of rage, and then a groan of despair.

The Princess Osra looked at him, and at the beautiful pictures, and then at the picture that was like her and yet like a devil. First she pitied the painter, and then marvelled at the wonderful mad skill, which so transformed her without drawing a line that could be called untrue. Thus thinking, she stood for a while, grave and puzzled. But then the humour struck her, as it struck her House always in great things and in small; it seemed to her most ludicrous that the pictures should all be resting here in Giraldo's house, while the Princes who had commanded portraits of her had received nothing but distorted parodies of her face, to the end that they might be disgusted and, abandoning the alliance they had projected, leave her still at Strelsau, to be painted times out of number and most fruitlessly by this mad painter. And these thoughts gaining the mastery over the others, in spite of the sad plight of unhappy Signor Giraldo, her lips curved into a bow, her eyes gleamed in dancing merriment, and a moment later she broke into a glad gleeful laugh, that rose and rippled, and fell to soft delighted murmurings. As she looked again at the picture that was like her and also like a devil, her mirth grew and grew at the ingenuity of the work and the mocking devilry so cunningly made out of her face. Small wonder was it to her now that the embassies had not come.

The Princess Osra thus stood laughing, and presently Signor Giraldo looked up. When he had listened and looked for a few moments, his wild mood caught the infection from her, so that, springing to his feet, he also began to laugh loudly, like a man who cannot restrain his amusement, but is carried away by it beyond all bounds and restraints. Thus Giraldo laughed loudly, long, and fiercely; for there was madness in his laugh. And the Princess heard the madness; even while she still laughed, her eyes opened in wonder; alarm came on her face, her merry laugh quivered, trembled, choked in her throat, and at last died away into dumbness; yet her lips hung apart frozen in the shape of laughter, while no laughter came. But as her laugh thus ended in mute horror, his grew louder yet and wilder, and its peal rang through the room, as he gasped between his spasms of horrid mirth, "You, you, you!" and pointed at the picture which he had touched to devilishness. But she shrank away, and stood crouched against the wall; for she knew now that he was mad, but did not know to what his fury might next lead him. Then he caught up a knife that lay on the sill of the window, and, now smiling as though in grim quiet amusement, strode across to the row of pictures, and reached up to them, knife in hand. But Osra suddenly sprang forward, crying:

"Do not hurt them."

"These?" he asked, turning to her with a sneer. "These? I'll destroy them all, for they are no longer beautiful to me, but that one only is beautiful, because it is true." And he wrenched his arm away from the detaining hand she had laid upon it. Falling back in terror, she watched him cutting and slashing each of the pictures, until the face was utterly destroyed. And she feared that when he had finished with the pictures, he would turn upon her; therefore she flung herself on the couch, hiding her face for fear of some horrible fate; she murmured low to herself, "Not my face, O God, not my face!" and she pressed her face down into the cushions of the couch, while he, muttering and grumbling to himself, cut the pictures into strips and ribbons, and strewed the fragments at his feet on the floor. This done, he turned to the devil's face that he loved, and poured out to it, as though it had been a cruel idol he worshipped, a flood of wild passionate reproachful words, that Osra shivered to hear, and the purport of which she dared tell none, though for all her prayers she could not herself forget one of them.

At last he came to her again, and plucked her roughly and rudely from the couch where she lay, and dragged her behind him back to the door again and through it; and they stood together in front of the last picture, whose paint was still wet from his hand. The painted face smiled down on the trembling pale girl with its smile of careless serene dignity, so that now even to herself it seemed hardly to be her picture. For it was the true presentment of a King's daughter, and she no better than a helpless frightened girl. It seemed to reproach her; and suddenly she drew herself to her height, and turned on Giraldo, saying: "You shall not touch it."

She stept forward, so that she stood between him and the picture, raising her hand, and forbidding him to approach it with his knife. And now the picture seemed more to be hers, although while it smiled she frowned.

But at this moment there came through the window that opened on the street the clatter of horses' hoofs. At the sound Giraldo arrested the motion that he had already made to fling himself on the Princess; whether to kill her, or only to thrust her away from in front of the picture she did not know. Running to the window, he looked out, and called in seeming glee: "It is the King come to see my pictures!" And he looked proud and happy. Going to the door of the room, he flung it open, and stood there waiting for the King and the gentlemen who attended the King. They were not long in coming, for Rudolf was full of anger, impatience, and curiosity, and ran swiftly up the staircase. His gentlemen pressed into the room behind him, and Giraldo drew back, keeping his face to the King and bowing again and again. But the King and the rest saw the knife in his hand; and ragged strips of painted canvas hung here and there on his clothes, while the Princess, pale and proud, stood guarding the picture on the easel. The King, in spite of his wonder, was not turned from the purpose which had brought him to the painter's house, but with a quick step darted up to Giraldo and thrust the letter of the Marquis de Mérosailles into his hand, bidding him in a sharp peremptory tone to read it and give what explanation he could of the contents. Giraldo fell to reading it, while the King turned to his sister in order to ask her why she seemed agitated, and stood so obstinately in front of her own picture; but at that instant one of the gentlemen, whose name was Ladislas, gave a cry of surprise; for he had looked through the door into the inner room, and seen the havoc and destruction that Giraldo had made, and also the strange and terrible picture which alone had escaped the knife. The King, wondering, followed Ladislas to the threshold of the inner room and passed it, while his gentlemen, full of curiosity, crowded close on his heels after him.

The Princess Osra, thinking herself safe, found her anger and terror pass away as her mirth had passed before. Now she felt in her heart that pity which borders on tenderness, and which she could never refuse to a man who loved her, let the folly of his love and of the extravagances into which it drove him be as great as it would. Turning towards Giraldo, she saw him fretting his puckered brow with his hand, and vainly seeking to compel his disordered brain to understand M. de Mérosailles' letter. So she was very sorry for him, and, knowing the sudden hot temper to which the careless King was subject, she glided swiftly across to the painter, and whispered: "Escape and hide. Hide for a few days. He will be furious now, but he will soon forget. Don't wait now, but escape, signor. Some harm will happen to you here;" and in her eager pleading with him she laid her hand on his arm, and looked up in his face with imploring eyes. But he looked at her with dazed vacant stare, muttering, "I cannot read the letter;" then a wistful smile came on his face, and he thrust the letter towards her, saying: "Madame, will you read it for me?" And at that moment they heard the King swear an angry oath; for he had seen the mad picture of his sister.

"No, no, not now," whispered Osra, beseeching Giraldo. "Not now, signor. Listen, the King is angry! Escape now, and we will read the letter afterwards." She was as earnest as though she had loved him and were praying him to save himself for the sake of her love.

Giraldo looked into her softened eyes; suddenly giving a little cry, as if a great joy had come to him unexpectedly and contrary to all likelihood, he dropped M. de Mérosailles' letter, and sprang to where his brushes lay on the floor; seizing them and his palette, he gave another swift glance at the Princess, and then, turning to the picture, began to paint with marvellous dexterity and deftness and with the sudden confidence of a man inspired to the work. As he worked, his brow grew smoother, the tension of his strained face relaxed, happiness dawned in his eyes, and a smile broke on his lips; and Osra watched him with a tender sorrowful gaze. Still he painted, and he was painting when the King burst in from the other room in a great rage, carrying his sword drawn in his hand; for he had sworn by Our Lady and St. Peter to kill the rogue who had done the Princess such wrong and so slandered her beauty. And his gentlemen came in with him, all very ready to see Giraldo killed, but each eager that the King should leave the task to him. Yet when they entered and saw Giraldo painting as though he were rapt by some ecstasy and had forgotten all that had passed, nay, even their very presence, they paused in unwilling and constrained hesitation. Osra raised her hand to bid them stay still where they were, and not interfere with Giraldo's painting. For now she desired above all things on earth that he should be left to finish his task. For he thought that he had read more than pity and more than tenderness in Osra's eyes; he had seemed to see love there, and thus he had cried out in joy, and thus he was now painting as never had even he, for all his skill, painted before. His unerring hand, moving lightly to and fro, imparted the sweetness of his delusive vision to the canvas, so that the eyes of the portrait glowed with wonderful and beautiful love and gentleness. Presently Giraldo began to sing very softly to himself a sweet happy old song, that peasants sang to peasant girls in the fields outside his native Verona on summer evenings. His head was thrown back in triumph and exultation as he sang and worked, tasting the luxury of love, and glorying in the tribute that his genius paid to her whom he loved. Thus came a moment of great joy to the soul of Giraldo the painter; for a man's love and a man's work are, when they seem to prosper, of all things the sweetest, and their union in one his life's consummation.

It was done. He laid down the brush, and drew back a step, looking at what he had done. The Princess came softly and slowly, as though attracted against her will, and she stood by him; for she saw that this picture was now, beyond all compare, the most perfect and beautiful of all that he or any other man had painted of her; and she loved him for thus glorifying her. But, before many moments had gone by, a sudden start and shiver ran through Giraldo's body. The spell of his entranced ecstasy broke; his eyes fell from the masterpiece that he had made, and wandered to those who stood about him—to the gentlemen who did not know whether to wonder or to laugh, to the angry face of the King and the naked sword in his hand, at last to Osra, whose eyes were still on the picture. His exultation vanished, and with it went, as it seemed to them, his madness. Reason dawned for a moment in his eyes, but was quenched in an instant by shame and despair. For he knew that all there had seen that other picture and knew now what he had done; and suddenly with a stifled cry he flung himself full length on the floor at Osra's feet.

"Let us wait," said she gently. "He will be himself again soon."

But the King was too angry to listen.

"He has made us fools before half Europe," he cried angrily, "and he shall not live to talk of it. And you—have you seen the picture yonder?"

"Yes, I have seen it," said she. "But he does not now think that picture like me, but this one." And she turned to the gentlemen, and desired them to raise Giraldo and lay him on a couch, and they obeyed. Then she knelt by his head; and, after a while he opened his eyes, seeming sound of sense in everything except that he believed she loved him, so that he began to whisper to her as lovers whisper to their loves, very tenderly and low. And the King, with his gentlemen, stood a little way off. But the Princess said nothing to Giraldo, neither refusing his love, nor yet saying what was false; yet she suffered him to talk to her, and to reach up his hand and gently touch a lock of hair that strayed on her forehead. And he, sighing in utter happiness and contentment, closed his eyes again, and lay back very quietly on the couch.

"Let us go," said she rising. "I will send a physician." And she bade one of the gentlemen lock the inner room, and give her the key, and she and the King and they all then departed, and sent his servants to tend Giraldo; and Osra caused the King's physician also to be summoned. But Giraldo did no more than linger some few days alive; for the most of them he was in a high fever, his brain being wild; and he raved about the Princess, sometimes railing at her, sometimes praising her; yet once or twice he awoke, calm and happy as he had been when she knelt by him, and having for his only delusion the thought that she still knelt there and was breathing words of love into his ear. And in this last merciful error, in respect of which the physicians humoured him, one day a week later, he passed away and was at peace.

Then the Princess came, attended by one gentleman in whom she placed confidence, and she destroyed the evil picture that Giraldo had painted, and having caused a fire to be made, burnt up the pieces of it, and all the ruins of the pictures that Giraldo had destroyed. But that on which he had last worked so happily, and with such a triumph of art, she carried with her to the palace; and presently she caused copies to be made of it, and sent one to each of the Princes by whom Giraldo had been commanded to paint her picture, and with it the money he had received, the whole of which was found untouched in a cabinet in his house. But the picture itself she hung in her own chamber, and would often look at it, feeling great sorrow for the fate of Giraldo the painter.

Yet King Rudolf could not be prevailed upon to pity the young man, saying that for his part he should have to be mad before the love of a woman should drive him mad; and he cursed Giraldo for an insolent knave, declaring that he did well to die of his own accord. And because M. de Mérosailles had gallantly defended his sister's beauty in three duels, he sent him by the hand of a high officer his Order of the Red Rose, which M. de Mérosailles wore with great pride at the Court of Versailles.

But when the copies of the last picture reached the Courts to which they were addressed, together with the money and a brief history of Giraldo's mad doings, the Princes turned their thoughts again to the matter of the alliance, and several embassies set out for Strelsau; so that Princess Osra said, with a smile that was half-sad, half-amused, and very whimsical:

"I am much troubled by reason of the loss of Signor Giraldo my painter."

CHAPTER VII.

The Indifference of the Miller of Hofbau.

There is a swift little river running by the village of Hofbau, and on the river is a mill, kept in the days of King Rudolf III. by a sturdy fellow who lived there all alone; the King knew him, having alighted at his house for a draught of beer as he rode hunting, and it was of him the King spoke when he said to the Queen, "There is, I believe, but one man in the country whom Osra could not move, and he is the Miller of Hofbau." But although he addressed the Queen, it was his sister at whom he aimed his speech. The Princess herself was sitting by, and when she heard the King she said:

"In truth I do not desire to move any man. What but trouble comes of it? Yet who is this miller?"

The King told her where the miller might be found, and he added: "If you convert him to the love of women you shall have the finest bracelet in Strelsau."

"There is nothing, sire, so remote from my thoughts or desires as to convert your miller," said Osra scornfully.

In this, at the moment, she spoke truthfully; but being left alone for some days at the Castle of Zenda, which is but a few miles from Hofbau, she found the time hang very heavy on her hands; indeed she did not know what to do with herself for weariness; and for this reason, and none other at all, one day she ordered her horse and rode off with a single groom into the forest. Coming, as the morning went on, to a wide road, she asked the groom where it led. "To Hofbau, madame," he answered. "It is not more than a mile further on." Osra waited a few moments, then she said: "I will ride on and see the village, for I have been told that it is pretty. Wait here till I return," and she rode on, smiling a little, and with a delicate tint of colour in her cheeks.

Before long she saw the river and the mill on the river; and, coming to the mill, she saw the miller sitting before his door, smoking a long pipe. She called out to him, asking him to sell her a glass of milk.

"You can have it for the asking," said the miller. He was a good-looking fair fellow, and wore a scarlet cap. "There is a pail of it just inside the door behind me." Yet he did not rise, but lay there, lolling luxuriously in the sun. For he did not know Osra, never having been to Strelsau in his life, and to Zenda three or four times only, and that when the Princess was not there. Moreover—though this, as must be allowed, is not to the purpose—he had sworn never again to go so far afield.

Being answered in this manner, and at the same time desiring the milk, the Princess had no choice but to dismount.

This she did, and passed by the miller, pausing a moment to look at him with bright curious eyes, that flashed from under the brim of her wide-rimmed feathered hat; but the miller blinked lazily up at the sun and took no heed of her.

Osra passed on, found the pail, poured out a cup of milk, and drank it. Then, refilling the cup, she carried it to the miller.

"Will you not have some?" said she with a smile.

"I was too lazy to get it," said the miller; and he held out his hand, but did not otherwise change his position.

Osra's brow puckered and her cheek flushed as she bent down, holding the cup of milk so that the miller could reach it. He took and drained it, gave it back to her, and put his pipe in his mouth again. Osra sat down by him and watched him. He puffed and blinked away, never so much as looking at her.

"What have you for dinner?" asked she presently.

"A piece of cold pie," said he. "There's enough for two, if you're hungry."

"Would you not like it better hot?"

"Oh, aye; but I cannot weary myself with heating it."

"I'll heat it," said the Princess; and, rising, she went into the house, and made up the fire, which was almost burnt out; then she heated the pie, and set the room in order, and laid the table, and drew a large jug of beer from the cask. Next she placed an arm-chair ready for the miller, and put the jug by it; then she filled the pipe from the bowl of tobacco and set a cushion in the chair. All this while she hummed a tune, and from time to time smiled gayly.

Lastly, she arranged a chair by the elbow of the miller's chair; then she went out and told him that his dinner was ready; and he stumbled to his feet with a sigh of laziness, and walked before her into the house.

"May I come?" cried she.

"Aye, there is enough for two," said the Miller of Hofbau without looking round.

So she followed him in. He sank into the arm-chair and sat there, for a moment surveying the room which was so neat, and the table so daintily laid, and the pie so steaming hot. And he sighed, saying:

"It was like this before poor mother died." And he fell to on a great portion of pie with which Osra piled his plate.

When he had finished eating—which thing did not happen for some time—she held the jug while he took a long draught; then she brought a coal in the tongs and held it while he lit his pipe from it; then she sat down by him. For several moments he puffed, and then at last he turned his head and looked at Princess Osra; she drooped her long lashes and cast down her eyes; next she lifted her eyes and glanced for an instant at the miller; and, finally, she dropped her eyes again and murmured shyly: "What is it, sir? Why do you look at me?"

"You seem to be a handy wench," observed the miller. "The pie was steaming hot and yet not burnt, the beer was well frothed but not shaken nor thickened, and the pipe draws well. Where does your father dwell?"

"He is dead, sir," said Princess Osra very demurely.

"And your mother?" pursued the miller.

"She also is dead."

"There is small harm in that," said the miller thoughtfully; and Osra turned away her head to hide her smile.

"Are you not very lonely, living here all by yourself?" she asked a moment later.

"Indeed I have to do everything for myself," said the miller sadly.

"And there is nobody to—to care for you?"

"No, nor to look after my comfort," said the miller. "Have you any kindred?"

"I have two brothers, sir; but they are married now, and have no need of me."

The miller laid down his pipe and, setting his elbow on the table, faced Princess Osra.

"H'm!" said he. "And is it likely you will ride this way again?"

"I may chance to do so," said Osra, and now there was a glance of malicious triumph in her eyes; she was thinking already how the bracelet would look on her arm.

"Ah!" said the miller. And after a pause he added: "If you do, come half an hour before dinner, and you can lend a hand in making it ready. Where did you get those fine clothes?"

"My mistress gave them to me," answered Osra. "She has cast them off."

"And that horse you rode?"

"It is my master's; I have it to ride when I do my mistress's errands."

"Will your master and mistress do anything for you if you leave your service?"

"I have been promised a present if——" said Osra, and she paused in apparent confusion.

"Aye," said the miller, nodding sagaciously, as he rose slowly from the arm-chair. "Will you be this way again in a week or so?" he asked.

"I think it is very likely," answered the Princess Osra.

"Then look in," said the miller. "About half an hour before dinner." He nodded his head again very significantly at Osra, and, turning away, went to his work, as a man goes who would far rather sit still in the sun. But just as he reached the door he turned his head and asked: "Are you sturdy?"

"I am strong enough, I think," said she.

"A sack of flour is a heavy thing for a man to lift by himself," remarked the miller, and with that he passed through the door and left her alone.

Then she cleared the table, put the pie—or what was left—in the larder, set the room in order, refilled the pipe, stood the jug handy by the cask, and, with a look of great satisfaction on her face, tripped out to where her horse was, mounted, and rode away.

The next week—and the interval had seemed long to her, and no less long to the Miller of Hofbau—she came again, and so the week after; and in the week following that she came twice; and on the second of these two days, after dinner, the miller did not go off to his sacks, but he followed her out of the house, pipe in hand, when she went to mount her horse, and as she was about to mount, he said:

"Indeed you're a handy wench."

"You say much of my hands, but nothing of my face," remarked Princess Osra.

"Of your face?" repeated the miller in some surprise. "What should I say of your face?"

"Well, is it not a comely face?" said Osra, turning towards him that he might be better able to answer her question.

The miller regarded her for some minutes, then a slow smile spread on his lips.

"Oh, aye, it is well enough," said he. Then he laid a floury finger on her arm as he continued: "If you come next week—why, it is but half a mile to church! I'll have the cart ready and bid the priest be there. What's your name?" For he had not hitherto asked Osra's name.

"Rosa Schwartz," said she, and her face was all alight with triumph and amusement.

"Yes, I shall be very comfortable with you," said the miller. "We will be at the church an hour before noon, so that there may be time afterwards for the preparation of dinner."

"That will be on Thursday in next week?" asked Osra.

"Aye, on Thursday," said the miller, and he turned on his heel. But in a minute he turned again, saying: "Give me a kiss, then, since we are to be man and wife," and he came slowly towards her, holding his arms open.

"Nay, the kiss will wait till Thursday. Maybe there will be less flour on your face then." And with a laugh she dived under his outstretched arms and made her escape. The day being warm, the miller did not put himself out by pursuing her, but stood where he was, with a broad comfortable smile on his lips; and so he watched her ride away.

Now, as she rode, the Princess was much occupied in thinking of the Miller of Hofbau. Elated and triumphant as she was at having won from him a promise of marriage, she was yet somewhat vexed that he had not shown a more passionate affection, and this thought clouded her brow for full half an hour. But then her face cleared. "Still waters run deep," she said to herself. "He is not like these Court gallants, who have learnt to make love as soon as they learn to walk, and cannot talk to a woman without bowing and grimacing and sighing at every word. The miller has a deep nature, and surely I have won his heart, or he would not take me for his wife. Poor miller! I pray that he may not grieve very bitterly when I make the truth known to him!" And then, at the thought of the grief of the miller, her face was again clouded; but it again cleared when she considered of the great triumph that she had won, and how she would enjoy a victory over the King, and would have the finest bracelet in all Strelsau as a gift from him. Thus she arrived at the Castle in the height of merriment and exultation.

It chanced that the King came to Zenda that night, to spend a week hunting the boar in the forest; and when Osra, all blushing and laughing, told him of her success with the Miller of Hofbau he was greatly amused, and swore that no such girl ever lived, and applauded her, renewing his promise of the bracelet; and he declared that he would himself ride with her to Hofbau on the wedding-day, and see how the poor miller bore his disappointment.

"Indeed I do not see how you are going to excuse yourself to him," he laughed.

"A purse of five hundred crowns must do that office for me," said she.

"What, will crowns patch a broken heart?"

"His broken heart must heal itself, as men's broken hearts do, brother!"

"In truth, sister, I have known them cure themselves. Let us hope it may be so with the Miller of Hofbau."

"At the worst I have revenged the wrongs of women on him. It is unendurable that any man should scorn us, be he king or miller."

"It is indeed very proper that he should suffer great pangs," said the King, "in spite of his plaster of crowns. I shall love to see the stolid fellow sighing and moaning like a lovesick courtier."

So they agreed to ride together to the miller's at Hofbau on the day appointed for the wedding, and both of them waited with impatience for it. But, with the bad luck that pursues mortals (even though they be princes) in this poor world, it happened that early in the morning of the Thursday a great officer came riding post-haste from Strelsau to take the King's commands on high matters of State; and, although Rudolf was sorely put out of temper by this untoward interruption, yet he had no alternative but to transact the business before he rode to the miller's at Hofbau. So he sat fretting and fuming, while long papers were read to him, and the Princess walked up and down the length of the drawbridge, fretting also; for before the King could escape from his affairs, the hour of the wedding was already come, and doubtless the Miller of Hofbau was waiting with the priest in the church. Indeed it was one o'clock or more before Osra and the King set out from Zenda, and they had then a ride of an hour and a half; and all this when Osra should have been at the miller's at eleven o'clock.

"Poor man, he will be half mad with waiting and with anxiety for me!" cried Osra. "I must give him another hundred crowns on account of it." And she added, after a pause, "I pray he may not take it too much to heart, Rudolf."

"We must try to prevent him doing himself any mischief in his despair," smiled the King.

"Indeed it is a serious matter," pouted the Princess, who thought the King's smile out of place.

"It was not so when you began it," said her brother; and Osra was silent.

Then about half-past two they came in sight of the mill. Now the King dismounted, while they were still several hundred yards away, and tied his horse to a tree in a clump by the wayside; and when they came near to the mill he made a circuit and approached from the side, and, creeping along to the house, hid himself behind a large water-butt, which stood just under the window; from that point he could hear what passed inside the house, and could see if he stood erect. But Osra rode up to the front of the mill, as she had been accustomed, and, getting down from her horse, walked up to the door. The miller's cart stood in the yard of the mill, but the horse was not in the shafts, and neither the miller nor anybody else was to be seen about; and the door of the house was shut.

"He must be waiting at the church," said she. "But I will look in and make sure. Indeed I feel half afraid to meet him." And her heart was beating rapidly and her face was rather pale as she walked up to the door; for she feared what the miller might do in the passion of his disappointment at learning who she was and that she could not be his wife. "I hope the six hundred crowns will comfort him," she said, as she laid her hand on the latch of the door; and she sighed, her heart being heavy for the miller, and, maybe a little heavy also for the guilt that lay on her conscience for having deceived him.

Now when she lifted the latch and opened the door, the sight that met her eyes was this: The table was strewn with the remains of a brave dinner; two burnt-out pipes lay beside the plates. A smaller table was in front of the fire; on it stood a very large jug, entirely empty, but bearing signs of having been full not so long ago; and on either side of it, each in an arm-chair, sat the priest of the village and the Miller of Hofbau; both of them were sleeping very contentedly, and snoring somewhat as they slept. The Princess, smitten by remorse at the spectacle, said softly:

"Poor fellow, he grew weary of waiting, and hungry, and was compelled to take his dinner; and, like the kind man he is, he has entertained the priest, and kept him here, so that no time should be lost when I arrived. Indeed I am afraid the poor man loves me very much. Well, miller, or lord, or prince—they are all the same. Heigh-ho! Why did I deceive him?" And she walked up to the miller's chair, leant over the back of it, and lightly touched his red cap with her fingers. He put up his hand and brushed with it, as though he brushed away a fly, but gave no other sign of awakening.

The King called softly from behind the water-butt under the window:

"Is he there, Osra? Is he there?"

"The poor man has fallen asleep in weariness," she answered. "But the priest is here, ready to marry us. Oh, Rudolf, I am so sorry for what I have done!"

"Girls are always mighty sorry, after it is done," remarked the King. "Wake him up, Osra."

At this moment the Miller of Hofbau sat up in his chair and gave a great sneeze; and by this sound the priest also was awakened. Osra came forward and stood between them. The miller looked at her, and tilted his red cap forward in order that he might scratch his head. Then he looked across to the priest, and said:

"It is she, Father. She has come."

The priest rubbed his hands together, and smiled uncomfortably.

"We waited two hours," said he, glancing at the clock. "See, it is three o'clock now."

"I am sorry you waited so long," said Osra, "but I could not come before. And—and now that I am come, I cannot——" But here she paused in great distress and confusion, not knowing how to break her sad tidings to the Miller of Hofbau.

The miller drew his legs up under his chair, and regarded Osra with a grave air.

"You should have been here at eleven," said he. "I went to the church at eleven, and the priest was there, and my cousin Hans to act as my groom, and my cousin Gertrude to be your maid. There we waited hard on two hours. But you did not come."

"I am very sorry," pleaded Princess Osra. The King laughed low to himself behind the water-butt, being much amused at her distress and her humility.

"And now that you are come," pursued the miller, scratching his head again, "I do not know what we are to do." He looked again at the priest, seeking counsel.

At this the Princess Osra, thinking that an opportunity had come, took the purse of six hundred crowns from under her cloak, and laid it on the table.

"What is this?" said the miller, for the first time showing some eagerness.

275

"They are for you," said Osra as she watched him while he unfastened the purse. Then he poured the crowns out on the table, and counted them one by one, till he had told all the six hundred. Then he raised his hands above his head, let them fall again, sighed slightly, and looked across at the priest.

"I warned you not to be in such a hurry, friend miller," remarked the priest.

"I waited two hours," said the miller plaintively, "and you know that she is a handy wench, and very fond of me."

He began to gather up the crowns and return them to the purse.

"I trust I am a handy wench," said Osra, smiling, yet still very nervous, "and, indeed, I have a great regard for the miller, but———"

"Nay, he does not mean you," interrupted the priest.

"Six hundred," sighed the miller, "and Gertrude has but two hundred! Still she is a handy wench and very sturdy. I doubt if you could lift a sack by yourself, as she can." And he looked doubtfully at Osra's slender figure.

"I do not know why you talk of Gertrude," said the Princess petulantly. "What is Gertrude to me?"

"Why, I take it that she is nothing at all to you," answered the priest, folding his hands on his lap and smiling placidly. "Still, for my part, I bade him wait a little longer."

"I waited two hours," said the miller. "And Gertrude urged me, saying that you would not come, and that she would look after me better than you, being one of the family. And she said it was hard that she should have no husband, while her own cousin married a stranger. And since it was all the same to me, provided I got a handy and sturdy wench———"

"What?" cried the Princess Osra; and the King was so interested that he rose up from behind the water-butt, and, leaning his elbows on the window-sill, looked in and saw all that happened.

"It being," pursued the Miller of Hofbau, "all the same to me, so that I got what I wanted, why, when you did not come———"

"He married his cousin," said the priest.

A sudden roar of laughter came from the window. All three turned round, but the King ducked his head and crouched again behind the water-butt before they saw him.

"Who was that?" cried the priest.

"A lad that came to hold my horse," answered Osra hastily, and then she turned fiercely on the miller.

"And that," she said, "was all you wanted! I thought you loved me."

"Aye, I liked you very well," said the miller. "You are a handy——" A stamp of her foot drowned the rest. "But you should have come in time," he went on.

"And this Gertrude—is she pretty?" demanded Osra.

"Gertrude is well enough," said the miller. "But she has only two hundred crowns." And he put the purse, now full again, on the table with a resigned sigh.

"And you shall have no more," cried Osra, snatching up her purse in great rage. "And you and Gertrude may——"

"What of Gertrude?" came at this moment from the door of the room where the sacks were. The Princess turned round swift as the wind, and she saw in the doorway a short and very broad girl, with a very wide face and straggling hair; the girl's nose was very flat, and her eyes were small; but her great mouth smiled good-humouredly and, as the Princess looked, she let slip to the ground a sack of flour that she had been carrying on her sturdy back.

"Aye, Gertrude is well enough," said the miller, looking at her contentedly. "She is very strong and willing."

Then, while Gertrude stood wondering and staring with wide eyes in the doorway, the Princess swept up to the miller, and leant over him, and cried:

"Look at my face, look at my face! What manner of face is it?"

"It is well enough," said the miller. "But Gertrude is——"

There was a crash on the floor, and the six hundred crowns rolled out of the purse, and scattered, spinning and rolling hither and thither all over the floor and into every corner of the room. And Princess Osra cried: "Have you no eyes?" and then she turned away; for her lip was quivering, and she would not have the miller see it. But she turned from the miller only to face Gertrude his wife; Gertrude's small eyes brightened with sudden intelligence.

"Ah, you're the other girl!" said Gertrude with much amusement. "And was that your dowry? It is large! I am glad you did not come in time. But see, I'll pick it up for you. Nay, don't take on. I dare say you'll find another husband."

She passed by Osra, patting her on the shoulder kindly as she went, and then fell on her knees and began to pick up the crowns, crawling after them all over the floor, and holding up her apron to receive the recovered treasure. And Princess Osra stood looking at her.

"Aye, you'll find another husband," nodded the priest encouragingly.

"Aye, you'll find another husband," assented the miller placidly. "And just as one girl is pretty nearly as good as another—if she is handy and sturdy—so one husband is as good as another, if he can keep a house over you."

Princess Osra said nothing. But Gertrude, having picked up the crowns, came to her with a full apron, saying:

"Hold your lap, and I'll pour them in. They'll get you a good husband."

Princess Osra suddenly bent and kissed Gertrude's cheek, and she said gently:

"I hope you have got a good husband, my dear; but let him do some work for himself. And keep the six hundred crowns as a present from me, for he will value you more with eight hundred than with two."

The eyes of all three were fixed on her in wonder and almost in fear, for her tone and manner were now different. Then she turned to the miller, and she bit her lip and dashed her hand across her eyes, and she said:

"And you, miller, are the only sensible man I have found in all the kingdom. Therefore good luck and a good wife to you." And she gave a little short laugh, and turned and walked out of the cottage, leaving them all spellbound in wonder. But the miller rose from his chair and ran to the door, and when he reached it the King was just lifting Osra on to her horse; the miller knew the King, and stood there with eyes wide and cheeks bulged in wonder; but he could gasp out no more than "The King, the King!" before Rudolf and Osra were far away. And they could, none of them, neither the miller, nor Gertrude, nor the priest, tell what the matter meant, until one day King Rudolf rode again to the mill at Hofbau, and, having sent for the priest, told the three enough of the truth, saying that the affair was the outcome of a jest at Court; and he made each of them a handsome present, and vowed them to secrecy by their fealty and attachment to his person and his honour.

"So she would not have married me, anyhow?" asked the miller.

"I think not, friend," answered Rudolf with a laugh.

"Then we are but quits and all is well. Gertrude, the jug, my lass!"

And so, indeed, it seemed to the King that they were but quits, and so he said to the Princess Osra. But he declared that she had so far prevailed with the miller as to make him desire marriage as an excellent and useful thing in itself, although she had not persuaded him that it was of great moment whom a man married. Therefore he was very anxious to give her the bracelet which he had promised, and more than once prayed her to accept it. But Osra saw the laugh that lurked in the King's eye, and would not consent to have the bracelet, and for a long while she did not love to speak of the Miller of Hofbau. Yet once, when the King on some occasion cried out very impatiently that all men were fools, she said:

"Sire, you forget the Miller of Hofbau." And she blushed, and laughed, and turned her eyes away.

One other thing she did which very greatly puzzled Queen Margaret, and all the ladies of the Court, and all the waiting-women, and all the serving-maids, and, in fine, every person high or low who saw or heard of it, except the King only. For in winter evenings she took her scissors and her needle, and she cut strips of ribbon, each a foot long and a couple of inches broad; on each of them she embroidered a motto or legend; and she affixed the ribbons bearing the legend to each and every one of the mirrors in each of her chambers at Strelsau, at Zenda, and at the other royal residences. And her waiting-women noticed that, whenever she had looked in the mirror and smiled at her own image or shewn other signs of pleasure in it, she would then cast her eyes up to the legend, and seem to read it, and blush a little, and laugh a little, and sigh a little; the reason for which things they could by no means understand.

For the legend was but this:

"Remember the Miller of Hofbau."

CHAPTER VIII.

The Love of the Prince of Glottenberg.

It was the spring of the year when Ludwig, Prince of Glottenberg, came courting the Princess Osra; for his father had sought the most beautiful lady of a Royal House in Europe, and had found none equal to Osra. Therefore the Prince came to Strelsau with a great retinue, and was lodged in the White Palace, which stood on the outskirts of the city, where the public gardens now are (for the Palace itself was sacked and burnt by the people in the rising of 1848). Here Ludwig stayed many days, coming every day to the King's palace to pay his respects to the King and Queen, and to make his court to the Princess. King Rudolf had received him with the utmost friendship, and was, for reasons of State then of great moment but now of vanished interest, as eager for the match as was the King of Glottenberg himself; and he grew very impatient with his sister when she hesitated to accept Ludwig's hand, alleging that she felt for him no more than a kindly esteem, and, what was as much to the purpose, that he felt no more for her. For although the Prince possessed most courteous and winning manners, and was very accomplished both in learning and in exercises, yet he was a grave and pensive young man, rather stately than jovial, and seemed in the Princess's eyes (accustomed as they were to catch and check ardent glances), to perform his wooing more as a duty of his station than on the impulse of any passion. Finding in herself also no such sweet ashamed emotions as had before now invaded her heart on account of lesser men, she grew grave and troubled. At last she said to the King:

"Brother, is this love? For I had as lief he were away as here, and when he is here he kisses my hand as though it were a statue's hand; and—and I feel as though it were. They say you know what love is. Is this love?"

"There are many forms of love," smiled the King. "This is such love as a Prince and a Princess may most properly feel."

"I do not call it love at all," said Osra with a pout.

When Prince Ludwig came next day to see her and told her with grave courtesy that his pleasure lay in doing her will, she broke out:

"I had rather it lay in watching my face," and then, ashamed, she turned away from him.

He seemed grieved and hurt at her words; it was with a sigh that he said: "My life shall be spent in giving you joy."

She turned round on him with flushed cheek and trembling lips:

"Yes, but I had rather it were spent in getting joy from me."

He cast down his eyes a moment, and then, taking her hand, kissed it. But she drew it away sharply. So that afternoon they parted, he back to his Palace, she to her chamber, where she sat, asking again: "Is this love?" and crying: "He does not know love," and pausing, now and again, before her mirror, to ask her pictured face why it would not unlock the door of love.

On another day she would be merry, or feign merriment, rallying him on his sombre air and formal compliments, professing that for her part she soon grew weary of such wooing, and loved to be easy and merry; for thus she hoped to sting him, so that he would either disclose more warmth or altogether forsake his pursuit. But he offered many apologies, blaming nature that had made him grave, but assuring her of his deep affection and respect.

"Affection and respect!" murmured Osra with a little toss of her head. "Oh, that I had not been born a Princess!" And yet, though she did not love him, she thought him a very noble gentleman, and trusted to his honour and sincerity in everything. Therefore, when he still persisted, and Rudolf and the Queen urged her, telling her (the King mockingly, the Queen with a touch of sadness) that she must not look to find in the world such love as romantic girls dreamt of, at last she yielded; she told her brother that she would marry Prince Ludwig; yet for a little while she would not have the news proclaimed. So Rudolf went, alone and privately, to the White Palace, and said to Ludwig:

"Cousin, you have won the fairest lady in the world. Behold, her brother says it!"

Prince Ludwig bowed low, and taking the King's hand, pressed it, thanking him for his help and approval, and expressing himself as most grateful for the boon of the Princess's favour.

"Will you not come with me and find her?" cried the King with a merry look.

"I have urgent business now," answered Ludwig. "Beg the Princess to forgive me. This afternoon I will crave the honour of waiting on her with my humble gratitude."

King Rudolf looked at him, a smile curling on his lips; and he said, in one of his gusts of impatience:

"By heaven! is there another man in the world who would talk about gratitude, and business, and the afternoon, when Osra of Strelsau sat waiting for him?"

"I mean no discourtesy," protested Ludwig, taking the King's arm, and glancing at him with most friendly eyes. "Indeed, dear friend, I am rejoiced and honoured. But this business of mine will not wait."

So the King, frowning and grumbling and laughing, went back alone and told the Princess that the happy wooer was most grateful, and would come after his business was transacted that afternoon. But Osra, having given her hand, would admit no fault in the man she had chosen, and thanked the King for the message with great dignity. Then the King came to her, and, sitting down by her, stroked her hair, saying softly:

"You have had many lovers, sister Osra, and now comes a husband!"

"Yes, now a husband," she murmured, catching swiftly at his hand; her voice was half caught in a sudden sob.

"So goes the world—our world," said the King, knitting his brows and seeming to fall for a moment into a sad reverie.

"I am frightened," she whispered. "Should I be frightened if I loved him?"

"I have been told so," said the King, smiling again. "But the fear has a way of being mastered then." And he drew her to him, and gave her a hearty brother's kiss, telling her to take courage. "You'll thaw the fellow yet," said the King, "though, I grant you, he is icy enough." For the King himself had been by no means what he called an icy man.

But Osra was not satisfied, and sought to assuage the pain of her heart by adorning herself most carefully for the Prince's coming, hoping to fire him to love. For she thought that if he loved she might, although since he did not she could not. And surely he did not, or all the tales of love were false! Thus she came to receive him very magnificently arrayed. There was a flush on her cheek and an uncertain, expectant, fearful look in her eyes; thus she stood before him, as he fell on his knee and kissed her hand. Then he rose and declared his thanks, and promised his devotion; but as he spoke the flush faded and the light died from her eyes; and when at last he drew near to her and offered to kiss her cheek, her eyes were dead and her face pale and cold as she suffered him to touch it. He was content to touch it but once, and seemed not to know how cold it was; and so, after more talk of his father's pleasure and his pride, he took his leave, promising to come again the next day. She ran to the window when the door was closed on him, and thence watched him mount his horse and ride away slowly, with his head bent and his eyes downcast; yet he was a noble gentleman, stately and handsome, kind and true. The tears came suddenly into her eyes and blurred her sight as she leant watching from behind the hanging curtains of the window. Though she dashed them away angrily, they came again, and ran down her pale cold cheeks, mourning the golden vision that seemed gone without fulfilment.

That evening there came a gentleman from the Prince of Glottenberg, carrying most humble excuses from his master, who (so he said) was prevented from waiting on the Princess the next day by a certain very urgent affair which took him from Strelsau, and would keep him absent from the city all day long; and the gentleman delivered to Osra a letter from the Prince, full of graceful and profound apologies, and pleading an engagement that his honour would not let him break; for nothing short of that, said he, should have kept him from her side. There followed some lover's phrases, scantily worded and frigid in an assumed passion. But Osra, smiling graciously, sent back a message, readily accepting all that the Prince urged in excuse. And she told what had passed to the King, with her head high in the air and a careless haughtiness, so that even the King did not rally her, nor yet venture to comfort her, but urged her to spend the day in riding with the Queen and him; for they were setting out for Zenda, where the King was to hunt in the forest, and she could ride some part of the way with them, and return in the evening. And she, wishing that she had sent first to the Prince to bid him not come, agreed to go with her brother; it was better far to go than to wait at home for a lover who would not come.

Thus the next morning they rode out, the King and Queen with their retinue, the Princess attended by one of her Guard, named Christian Hantz, who was greatly attached to her and most jealous in praise and admiration of her. This fellow had taken it on himself to be very angry with Prince Ludwig's coldness, but dared say nothing of it; yet, impelled by his anger, he had set himself to watch the Prince very closely; and thus he had, as he conceived, discovered something which brought a twinkle into his eye and a triumphant smile to his lips as he rode behind the Princess. Some fifteen miles she accompanied her brother, and then, turning with Christian, took another way back to the city. Alone she rode, her mind full of sad thoughts; while Christian, behind, still wore his malicious smile. But presently, although she had not commanded him, he quickened his pace and came up to her side, relying for excuse on the favour which she always shewed him.

"Well, Christian," said she, "have you something to say to me?"

For answer he pointed to a small house standing among the trees, some way from the road, and he said:

"If I were Ludwig and not Christian, yet I would be here where Christian is, and not there where Ludwig is," and he pointed still at the house.

She faced round in anger at his daring to speak to her of the Prince, but he was a bold fellow and would not be silenced now that he had begun to speak; he knew also that she would bear much from him. So he leant over towards her, saying:

"By your bounty, madame, I have money, and he who has money can get knowledge. So I know that the Prince is there. For fifty crowns I gained a servant of his, and he told me."

"I do not know why you should spy on the Prince," said Osra, "and I do not care to know where the Prince is;" and she touched her horse with the spur and cantered forward fast, leaving the little house behind. But Christian persisted, partly in a foolish grudge against any man who should win what was above his reach, partly in an honest anger that she, whom he worshipped, should be treated lightly by another; and he forced her to hear what he had learnt from the gossip of the Prince's groom, telling it to her in hints and half-spoken sentences, yet so plainly that she could not miss the gist of it.

She rode the faster towards Strelsau, at first answering nothing; but at last she turned on him fiercely, saying that he told a lie, and that she knew it was a lie, since she knew where the Prince was, and what business had taken him away; and she commanded Christian to be silent and to speak neither to her nor to any one else of his false suspicions; and she bade him very harshly to fall back and ride behind her again, which he did, sullen yet satisfied. For he knew that his arrow had gone home. On she rode, with her cheeks aflame and her heart beating, until she came to Strelsau; having arrived at the Palace, she ran to her own bedroom and flung herself on the bed.

Here for an hour she lay; then, it being about six o'clock, she sat up, pushing her disordered hair back from her hot aching brow. An agony of humiliation had come upon her, and a fury of resentment against the Prince, whose coldness seemed now to need no more explanation. Yet she could hardly believe what she had been told of him, for though she had not loved him, she had accorded to him her full trust. Rising, she paced in pain about the room. She could not rest; she cried out in longing that her brother were there, to aid her and find out the truth for her. But he was away, and she had none to whom she could turn. So she strove to master her anger and endure her suspense till the next day, but they were too strong for her, and she cried:

"I will go myself, I cannot sleep till I know. But I cannot go alone. Who will go with me?" But she knew of none, for she would not take Christian with her, and she shrank from speaking of the matter to any gentlemen of the Court. Yet she must know. At last she sprang from the chair into which she had sunk despondent, exclaiming:

"He is a gentleman and my friend. He will go with me." And she sent hastily for the Bishop of Modenstein, who was then in Strelsau, bidding him come dressed for riding, with a sword, and on the best horse in his stables. The Bishop came equipped as she bade him, and in very great wonder. But when she told what she wanted, and what Christian had made known to her, he grew grave, saying that they must wait and consult the King, when he returned.

"I will not wait an hour," she cried. "I cannot wait an hour."

"Then I will ride and bring you word. You must not go," he urged.

"Nay, if I go alone I will go," said she. "Yes, I will go, and myself fling his falseness in his teeth."

Finding her thus resolved, the Bishop knew that he could not turn her; so, leaving her to prepare herself, he caught Christian Hantz, and charged him to bring their horses to the most private gate of the palace, which opened on a little by-street. Here Christian waited for them with the horses, and they came presently, the Bishop wearing a great slouched hat, and swaggering like a roystering trooper, while Osra was closely veiled. The Bishop again imposed secrecy on Christian, and then, they both being mounted, said to Osra: "If you will then, madame, come," and thus they rode secretly out of the city, about seven in the evening, the gate-wardens opening the gate at sight of the Royal Arms on Osra's ring, which she gave to the Bishop in order that he might shew it.

In silence they rode a long way, going at a great speed; Osra's face was set and rigid, for she felt now no shame at herself for going, nor any fear of what she might find, but the injury to her pride swallowed every other feeling; and at last she said, in short sharp words, to the Bishop of Modenstein, having suddenly thrown the veil back from her face:

"He shall not live if it prove true."

The Bishop shook his head. His profession was peace; yet his blood also was hot against the man who had put a slight on Princess Osra.

"The King must know of it," he said.

"The King! The King is not here to-night," said Osra; and she pricked her horse and set him at a gallop. The moon, breaking suddenly in brightness from behind a cloud, shewed the Bishop her face. Then she put out her hand and caught him by the arm, whispering: "Are you my friend?"

"Yes, madame," said he. She knew well that he was her friend.

"Kill him for me, then; kill him for me."

"I cannot kill him," said the Bishop. "I pray God it may prove untrue."

"You are not my friend, if you will not kill him," said Osra; and she turned her face away and rode yet more quickly.

At last they came in sight of the little house standing back from the road; and there was a light in one of the upper windows. The Bishop heard a short gasp break from Osra's lips, as she pointed with her whip to the window. Now his own breath came quick and fast; he prayed to God that he might remember his sacred character and his vows, and not be led into great and deadly sin, at the bidding of that proud and bitter face; and he clenched his left hand and struck his brow with it.

Thus then they came to the gate of the avenue of trees that led to the house. Here, having dismounted and tied their horses to the gate-post, they stood for an instant, and Osra again veiled her face.

"Let me go alone, madame," he implored.

"Give me your sword, and I will go alone," she answered.

"Here, then, is the path," said the Bishop, and he led the way by the moonlight that broke fitfully here and there through the trees.

"He swore that all his life should be mine," she whispered. "Yet I knew that he did not love me."

The Bishop made her no answer; she looked for none and did not know that she spoke the bitterness of her heart in words which he could hear. He bowed his head and prayed again for her and for himself; for he had found his hand gripping the hilt of his sword. Thus, side by side now, they came to the door of the house, and saw a gentleman standing in front of the door, still but watchful. Osra knew that he was the Prince's Chamberlain.

When the Chamberlain saw them, he started violently and clapped a hand to his sword; but Osra flung her veil on to the ground, and the Bishop gripped his arm as with a vice. The Chamberlain looked at Osra and at the Bishop, and half drew his sword.

"This matter is too great for you, sir," said the Bishop. "It is a quarrel of Princes. Stand aside," and before the Chamberlain could make up his mind what to do Osra had passed by him and the Bishop had followed her.

Finding themselves in a narrow passage, they made out by the dim light of a lamp a flight of stairs that rose from the furthest end of it. The Bishop tried to pass the Princess, but she motioned him back, and walked swiftly to the stairs. In silence they mounted, till they had reached the top of the first stage; and facing them, eight or ten steps further up, was a door. By the door stood a groom; this was the man who had treacherously told Christian of his master's doings; but when he saw suddenly what had come of his disloyal chattering, the fellow turned white as a ghost and came tottering in stealthy silence down the stairs, his finger on his lips.

Neither of them spoke to him, nor he to them. They gave no thought to him, his only thought was to escape as soon as he might; so he passed them, and, going on, passed also the Chamberlain, who stood dazed at the house-door, and so disappeared, intent on saving the life he had justly forfeited. Thus the rogue vanished, and what became of him none knew or cared. He showed his face no more at Glottenberg or Strelsau.

"Hark, there are voices!" whispered Osra to the Bishop, raising her hand above her head, as they two stood listening.

The voices came from the door that faced them, the voice of a man and the voice of a woman; Osra's glance at her companion told him that she knew as well as he whose the man's voice was.

"It is true, then," she breathed from between her teeth. "My God, it is true!"

The woman's voice spoke now, but the words were not audible. Then came the Prince's:

"For ever, in life or death, apart or together, for ever."

The woman's answer came no more in words, but in deep low passionate sobs which struck their ears like the distant cry of some brute creature in pain that it cannot understand. Yet Osra's face was stern and cold, and her lips curled scornfully when she saw the Bishop's look of pity.

"Come, let us end it," said she, and with a firm step she began to mount the stairs that lay between them and the door.

Yet once again they paused outside the door, for it seemed as though the Princess could not choose but listen to the passionate words of love that pierced her ears like knives; yet they were all sad, speaking of renunciation, not of happiness.

But at last she heard her own name; then with a sudden start she caught the Bishop's hand, for she could not listen longer. She staggered and reeled as she whispered to him:

"The door, the door, open the door!"

The Bishop, his right hand being across his body and resting on the hilt of his sword, laid his left upon the handle of the door, and turned it. Then he flung the door open wide; at that instant Osra sprang past him, her eyes gleaming like flames from her dead white face. And she stood rigid on the threshold of the room, with the Bishop by her side.

In the middle of the room stood the Prince of Glottenberg; strained in a close embrace, clinging to him, supported by his arms, with head buried in his breast, was a girl of slight and slender figure, graceful though not tall; her body was still shaken by continual struggling sobs. The Prince held her there as though against the world, but raised his head and looked at the intruders with a grave sad air. There was no shame on his face, and hardly surprise. Presently he took one arm from about the lady, and, raising it, motioned to them to be still. Osra took one step forward towards where the pair stood; the Bishop caught her sleeve, but she shook him off. The lady looked up into the Prince's face; with a sudden startled cry she clutched him closer, and turned a terrified face over her shoulder. Then she moaned in great fear, and, reeling, fell against the Prince; she would have sunk to the ground if he had not upheld her, and her eyes closed and her lip dropped, as she swooned away. But the Princess smiled, and, drawing herself to her full height, stood watching while Ludwig bore the lady to a couch and laid her there. Then, when he came back and faced her, she asked coldly and slowly:

"Who is this woman, sir? Or is she one of those who have no names?"

The Prince sprang forward, a sudden anger in his eyes; he raised his hand as if he would have pressed it across her scornful mouth and kept back her bitter words. But she did not flinch; pointing at him with her finger, she cried to the Bishop in a ringing voice:

"Kill him, my lord, kill him."

And the sword of the Bishop of Modenstein was half way out of the scabbard.

"I would to God, my lord," said the Prince in low sad tones, "that God would suffer you to kill me and me to take death at your hands. But neither for you nor for me is the blow lawful. Let me speak to the Princess."

The Bishop still grasped his sword; for Osra's face and hand still commanded him. But at the instant of his hesitation, while the temptation was hot on him, there came from the couch where the lady lay a low moan of great pain. She flung her arms out and turned, groaning again, on her back and her head lay hanging over the side of the couch. The Bishop's eyes met Ludwig's, and with a "God forgive me!" he let the sword slip back, and, springing across the room, fell on his knees beside the couch. He broke the gold chain round his neck and grasped the crucifix which it carried in one hand, while with the other he raised the lady's head, praying her to open her eyes, before whose closed lids he held the sacred image; and he, who had come so near to great sin, now prayed softly but fervently for her life and God's pity on her; for the frailty her slight form showed could not withstand the shock of this trial.

"Who is she?" asked the Princess.

But Ludwig's eyes had wandered back to the couch, and he answered only:

"My God, it will kill her."

"I care not," said Osra. But then came another low moan. "I care not," said the Princess again. "Ah, she is in great suffering!" And her eyes followed the Prince's.

There was silence, save for the lady's low moans and the whispered prayers of the Bishop of Modenstein. But the lady opened her eyes, and in an instant, answering the summons, the Prince was by her side, kneeling and holding her hand very tenderly; and he met a glance from the Bishop across her prostrate body. The Prince bowed his head and one sob burst from him.

"Leave me alone with her for a little, sir," said the Bishop, and the Prince, obeying, rose and withdrew into the bay of the window, while Osra stood alone near the door by which she had entered.

A few minutes passed, then Osra saw the Prince return to where the lady was and kneel again beside her; and she saw that the Bishop was preparing to perform his most sacred and sublime office; the lady's eyes dwelt on him now in peace and restfulness, and she held Prince Ludwig's hand in her small hand. But Osra would not kneel; she stood upright, still and cold, as though she neither saw nor heard anything of what passed; she would not pity nor forgive the woman, even if, as they seemed to think, she lay dying. But she spoke once, asking in a harsh voice:

"Is there no physician in the house or near?"

"None, madame," said the Prince.

The Bishop began the office, and Osra stood, dimly hearing the words of comfort, peace, and hope, dimly seeing the smile on the lady's face; for gradually her eyes clouded with tears. Now her ears seemed to hear nothing save the sad and piteous sobs that had shaken the girl as she hung about Ludwig's neck. But she strove to drive away her softer thoughts, fanning her fury when it burnt low, and telling herself again of the insult that she had suffered. Thus she rested till the Bishop had performed the office. But when he had finished it, he rose from his knees and came to where Osra was.

"It was your duty," she said, "but it is none of mine."

"She will not live an hour," said he. "For she had an affection of the heart, and this shock has killed her. Indeed I think she was half dead for grief before we came."

"Who is she?" broke again from Osra's lips.

"Come and hear," said he, and she followed him obediently, yet unwillingly, to the couch, and looked down at the lady. The lady looked at her with wondering eyes, and then she smiled faintly, pressing the Prince's hand, and whispering:

"Yet she is so beautiful." And she seemed now wonderfully happy, so that they three all watched her and were envious, although they were to live and she to die.

"Now God pardon her sin!" said the Princess Osra suddenly, and she fell on her knees beside the couch, crying: "Surely God has pardoned her!"

"Sin she has none, save what clings even to the purest in this world," said the Bishop. "For what she has said to me I know to be true."

Osra answered nothing, but gazed in questioning at the Prince, and he, still holding the lady's hand, began to speak in a gentle voice:

"Do not ask her name, madame. But from the first hour that we knew the meaning of love we have loved one another. And had the issue rested in my hands, I would have thrown to the winds all that kept me from her. I remember when first I met her—ah, my sweet, do you remember? From that day to this in soul she has been mine, and I hers in all my life. But more could not be. Madame, you have asked what love is. Here is love. Yet fate is stronger. Thus I came to Strelsau to woo, and she, left alone, resolved to give herself to God."

"How comes she here, then?" whispered Osra, and she laid one hand timidly on the couch, near to the lady yet not so as to touch even her garments.

"She came here—" he began; but suddenly, to their amazement, the lady, who had seemed dead, with an effort raised herself on her elbow, and spoke in a quick eager whisper, as if she feared time and strength would fail.

"He is a great Prince," she said, "he must be a great King; God means him for greatness, God forbid that I should be his ruin. Ah, what a sweet dream he painted! But praise be to the Blessed Saints who kept me strong. Yet at the last I was weak. I could not live without another sight of his face; and so—I came. Next week I am—I was to take the veil; and I came here to see him once again. God pardon me for it. But I could not help it. Ah, madame, I know you, and I see now your beauty. Have you known love?"

"No," said Osra; and she moved her hand near to the lady's hand.

"When he found me here, he prayed me again to do what he asked; and I was half killed in denying it. But I prevailed, and we were even then parting when you came. Why, why did I come?" For a moment her voice died away in a low soft moan. But she made one more effort; clasping Osra's hand in her delicate fingers, she whispered: "I am going. Be his wife."

"No, no, no," whispered Osra, her face now close to the lady's. "You must live; you must live and be happy."

And then she kissed the lady's lips. The lady put out her arms and clasped them round Osra's neck, and again she whispered softly in Osra's ear. Neither Ludwig nor the Bishop heard what she said, but they heard only that Osra sobbed. Presently the lady's arms relaxed a little in their hold, and Osra, having kissed her again, rose and signed to Ludwig to come nearer; while she, turning, gave her hand to the Bishop, and he led her from the room, and, finding another room near, took her in there, where she sat, silent and pale.

Thus half an hour passed; then the Bishop stole out softly, and presently returned, saying:

"God has spared her the long painful path, and has taken her straight to His rest."

Osra heard him, half in a trance and as if she did not hear; she did not know where he went nor what he did, nor anything that passed, until, as it seemed after a long while, she looked up and saw Prince Ludwig standing before her. He was composed and calm; but it seemed as if half the life had gone out of his face. Osra rose slowly to her feet, supporting herself on an arm of the chair on which she had sat; and, when she had seen his face, she suddenly threw herself on the floor at his feet, crying:

"Forgive me, forgive me!"

"The guilt is mine," said he, "I did not trust you and did by stealth what your nobility would have allowed me to do openly. The guilt is mine." And he offered to raise her. But she rose, unaided, asking with choking voice:

"Is she dead?"

"She is dead," said the Prince, and Osra, hearing it, covered her face with her hands and blindly groped her way back to the chair, where she sat, panting and exhausted.

"To her I have said farewell, and now, madame, to you. Yet do not think that I am a man without eyes for your beauty, or a heart to know your worth. I seemed to you a fool and a churl. I grieved most bitterly, and I wronged you bitterly. My excuse for all is now known. For though you are more beautiful than she, yet true love is no wanderer; it gives a beauty that it does not find, and forges a chain no charms can break. Madame, farewell."

She looked at him and saw the sad joy in his eyes, an exultation over what had been, that what was could not destroy; and she knew that the vision was still with him though his love was dead. Suddenly he seemed to her a man she also might love and for whom she also, if need be, might gladly die; yet not because she loved him, for she was asking still in wonder: "What is this love?"

"Madame, farewell," said he again, and, kneeling before her, he kissed her hand.

"I carry the body of my love," he went on, "back with me to my home, there to mourn for her; and I shall come no more to Strelsau."

Osra bent her eyes on his face as he knelt, and presently she said to him in a whisper that was low for awe, not shame:

"You heard what she bade me do?"

"Yes, madame. I know her wish."

"And you would do it?" she asked.

"Madame, my struggle was fought before she died. But now you know that my love was not yours."

"That also I knew before, sir," and a slight bitter smile came on her face. But she grew grave again and sat there, seeming to be pondering, while Prince Ludwig waited. Then she suddenly leant forward and said:

"If I loved I would wait for you to love. Now what is this love that I cannot feel?"

And then she sat again silent, but at last raised her eyes again to his, saying in a voice that even in the stillness of the room he hardly heard:

"Now I nearly love you, for I have seen your love and know that you can love; and I think that love must breed love, so that she who loves must in God's time be beloved. Yet I——" She paused here, and for a moment hid her face with her hand. "Yet I cannot," she went on. "Is it our Lord Christ who bids us take the lower place? I cannot take it. He does not so reign in my heart. For to my proud heart—ah, my heart so proud!—she would be ever between us. I could not bear it. Yet I believe now that with you I might one day find happiness."

The Prince, though in that hour he could not think of love, was yet very much moved by her new tenderness and felt that what had passed rather drew them together than made any separation between them. And it seemed to him that the dead lady's blessing was on his suit; so he said:

"Madame, I would most faithfully serve you and you would be nearest and dearest to me of all living women."

She waited awhile, then she sighed heavily, looking in his face with an air of wistful longing; and she knit her brows as though she were puzzled. But at last, shaking her head, she said:

"It is not enough."

With this she rose and took him by the hand, and they two went back together to where the Bishop of Modenstein still prayed beside the body of the lady.

Osra stood on one side of the body and stretched her hand out to the Prince who stood on the other side.

"See," said she, "she must be between us." And having kissed the dead face once, she left the Prince there by the side of his love and herself went out; and, turning her head, she saw that the Prince knelt again by the corpse of his love.

"He does not think of me," she said to the Bishop.

"His thoughts are still with her, madame," he answered.

It was late night now, and they rode swiftly and silently along the road to Strelsau. On all the way they spoke to one another only a few words, both being sunk deep in thought. But once Osra spoke, as they were already near to Strelsau. For she turned suddenly to the Bishop, saying:

"My lord, what is it? Do you know it?"

"Yes, madame, I have known it," answered the Bishop.

"Yet you are a Churchman!"

"True, madame," said he, and he smiled sadly.

She seemed to consider, fixing her eyes on his; but he turned his aside.

"Could you not make me understand?" she asked.

"Your lover, when he comes, will do that, madame," said he, and still he kept his eyes averted. Osra wondered why he kept his eyes turned away; yet presently a faint smile curved her lips, and she said:

"It may be you might feel it, if you were not a Churchman. But I do not. Many men have said they loved me, and I have felt something in my heart; but not this."

"It will come," said the Bishop.

"Does it come then to every one?"

"To most," he answered.

"Heigho, will it ever come to me?" she sighed.

With this they were at home. And Osra was for a long time very sorrowful for the fate of the lady whom the Prince of Glottenberg had loved; yet, since she saw Ludwig no more, and the joy of youth conquers sadness, she ceased to mourn; but as she walked alone she would wonder more and more what it might be, this great love that she did not feel.

"For none will tell me, not even the Bishop of Modenstein," said she.

CHAPTER IX.

The Victory of the Grand Duke of Mittenheim.

King Rudolf, being in the worst of humours, had declared in the presence of all the Court that women were born to plague men and for no other purpose whatsoever under heaven. Hearing this discourteous speech, the Princess Osra rose and said that for her part she would go walking alone by the river outside the city gates, where at least she would be assailed by no more reproaches. For since she was irrevocably determined to live and die unmarried, of what use or benefit was it to trouble her with embassies, courting, or proposals from either the Grand Duke of Mittenheim or anybody else? She was utterly weary of this matter of love, and her mood would be unchanged though this new suitor were as exalted as the King of France, as rich as Crœsus himself, and as handsome as the god Apollo. She did not desire a husband, and there was an end of it. Thus she went out, while the Queen sighed, and the King fumed, and the courtiers and ladies said to one another that these dissensions made life very uncomfortable at Strelsau, the ladies further adding that he would be a bold man who married Osra, although doubtless she was not ill-looking.

To the banks of the river outside the walls then Osra went; and as she went she seemed to be thinking of nothing at all in the world, least of all of whom she might chance to meet there on the banks of the river, where in those busy hours of the day few came. Yet there was a strange new light in her eyes, and there seemed a new understanding in her mind; and when a young peasant wife came by, her baby in her arms, Osra stopped her, and kissed the child and gave money, and then ran on in unexplained confusion, laughing and blushing as though she had done something which she did not wish to be seen. Then without reason her eyes filled with tears, but she dashed them away and burst suddenly into singing. And she was still singing when, from the long grass by the river's edge, a young man sprang up, and, with a very low bow, drew aside to let her pass. He had a book in his hand, for he was a student at the University, and came there to pursue his learning in peace; his plain brown clothes spoke of no wealth or station, though certainly they set off a stalwart straight shape and seemed to match well with his bright brown hair and hazel eyes. Very low this young man bowed and Osra bent her head. The pace of her walk slowed, grew quicker, slowed again; she was past him, and with a great sigh he lay down again. She turned, he sprang up; she spoke coldly, yet kindly.

"Sir," said she, "I cannot but notice that you lie every day here by the river with your book, and that you sigh. Tell me your trouble, and if I can I will relieve it."

"I am reading, madame," he answered, "of Helen of Troy, and I am sighing because she is dead."

"It is an old grief by now," said Osra, smiling. "Will none serve you but Helen of Troy?"

"If I were a Prince," said he, "I need not mourn."

"No, sir?"

"No, madame," he said, with another bow.

"Farewell, sir."

"Madame, farewell."

So she went on her way, and saw him no more till the next day, nor after that till the next day following; and then came an interval when she saw him not, and the interval was no less than twenty-four hours; yet still he read of Helen of Troy, and still sighed because she was dead, and he no Prince. At last he tempted the longed-for question from Osra's shy smiling lips.

"Why would you not mourn, sir, if you were a Prince?" said she. "For Princes and Princesses have their share of sighs." And with a very plaintive sigh Osra looked at the rapid running river, as she waited for his answer.

"Because then I would go to Strelsau and so forget her."

"But you are at Strelsau now!" she cried with wondering surprise.

291

"Ah, but I am no Prince, madame," said he.

"Can Princes alone—forget in Strelsau?"

"How should a poor student dare to—forget in Strelsau?" As he spoke he made bold to step near her and stood close, looking down into her face. Without a word she turned and left him, going through the meadow with a step that seemed to dance and yet led her to her own chamber, where she could weep in quiet.

"I know it now, I know it now," she whispered softly that night to the tree which rose by her window. "Heigho, what am I to do? I cannot live, no, and now I cannot die. Ah me, what am I to do? I wish I were a peasant girl; but then perhaps he would not—ah, yes, but he would!" And her low long laugh rippled in triumph through the night, blending sweetly with the rustling of the leaves under a summer breeze; and she stretched her white arms to heaven, imploring the kind God with prayers that she dared not speak even to His pitiful ear.

"Love knows no Princesses, my Princess." It was that she heard as she fled from him next day. She should have rebuked him. But for that she must have stayed; and to stay she had not dared. But she must rebuke him. She would see him again in order to rebuke him. Yet all this while she must be pestered with the court of the Grand Duke of Mittenheim! And when she would not name a day on which the embassy should come, the King flew into a passion, and declared that he himself would set a date for it. Was his sister mad, he asked, that she would do nothing but walk every day by the river's bank? "Surely I must be mad," thought Osra; for no sane being could be at once so joyful and so piteously unhappy.

Did he know what it was he asked? He seemed to know nothing of it. He did not speak any more now of Princesses, only of his Princess, nor of Queens, save of his heart's queen; and when his eyes asked love, they asked as though none would refuse and there could be no cause for refusal. He would have wooed his neighbour's daughter thus, and thus he wooed the sister of King Rudolf.

"Will you love me?" was his question, not, "Though you love, yet dare you own your love?" He seemed to shut the whole world from her, leaving nothing but her and him; and in a world that held none but her and him, she could love, unblamed, untroubled, and with no trembling.

"You forget who I am," she faltered once.

"You are the beauty of the world," he answered smiling, and he kissed her hand—a matter about which she could make no great ado, for it was not the first time that he had kissed it.

But the embassy from the Grand Duke was to come in a week and to be received with great pomp. The ambassador was already on the way, carrying proposals and gifts. Therefore Osra went pale and sad down to the river bank that day, having declared again to the King that she would live and die unmarried. But the King had laughed cruelly. Surely she needed kindness and consolation that sad day; yet Fate had kept for her a crowning sorrow; for she found him also almost sad; at least she could not tell whether he was sad or not. For he smiled and yet seemed ill at ease, like a man who ventures a fall with fortune, hoping and fearing. And he said to her:

"Madame, in a week I return to my own country."

She looked at him in silence with lips just parted. For her life she could not speak; but the sun grew dark and the river changed its merry tune to mournful dirges.

"So the dream ends," said he. "So comes the awakening. But if life were all a dream?" His eyes sought hers.

"Yes," she whispered, "if life were all a dream, sir?"

"Then I should dream of two dreamers whose dream was one, and in that dream I should see them ride together at break of day from Strelsau."

"Whither?" she murmured.

"To Paradise," said he. "But the dream ends. If it did not end———" He paused.

"If it did not end?" a breathless longing whisper echoed.

"If it did not end now, it should not end even with death," said he.

"You see them in your dream? You see them riding?"

"Aye, swiftly, side by side, they two alone, through the morning. None is near; none knows."

He seemed to be searching her face for something that yet he scarcely hoped to find.

"Their dream," said he, "brings them at last to a small cottage; it is where they live."

"They live?"

"And work," he added. "For she keeps his home while he works."

"What does she do?" asked Osra, with smiling wondering eyes.

"She gets his supper for him when he comes home weary in the evening, and makes a bright fire, and———"

"Ah, and she runs to meet him at the door! Oh, farther than the door!"

"But she has worked hard and is weary."

"No, she is not weary," cried Osra. "It is for him she works!"

"The wise say this is silly talk," said he.

"The wise are fools then," cried Osra.

"So the dream would please you, madame?" he asked.

She had come not to know how she left him; somehow, while he still spoke, she would suddenly escape by flight. He did not pursue, but let her go. So now she returned to the city, her eyes filled with that golden dream; she entered her home as though it had been some strange Palace decked with unknown magnificence, and she an alien to it. For her true home seemed now rather in the cottage of the dream, and she moved unfamiliarly through the pomp that had been hers from birth. Her soul was gone from it, while her body rested there; and life stopped for her till she saw him again by the banks of the river.

"In five days now I go," said he, and he smiled at her. She hid her face in her hands. Still he smiled; but suddenly he sprang forward; for she had sobbed. The summons had sounded; he was there; and who could sob again when he was there, and his sheltering arm warded off all grief? She looked up at him with shining eyes, whispering:

"Do you go alone?"

A great joy blazed confidently in his eyes as he whispered in answer:

"I think I shall not go alone."

"But how, how?"

"I have two horses."

"You! You have two horses?"

"Yes, is it not riches? But we will sell them when we get to the cottage."

"To the cottage! Two horses!"

"I would I had but one for both of us."

"Yes."

"But we should not go quick enough."

"No."

He took his hand from her waist and stood away from her.

"You will not come?" he said.

"If you doubt of my coming, I will not come. Ah, do not doubt of my coming! For there is a great hoard of fears and black thoughts beating at the door, and you must not open it."

"And what can keep it shut, my Princess?"

"I think your arm, my Prince," said she; and she flew to him.

That evening King Rudolf swore that if a man were only firm enough and kept his temper (which, by the way, the King had not done, though none dared say so), he could bring any foolish girl to reason in good time. For in the softest voice, and with the strangest smile flitting to her face, the Princess Osra was pleased to bid the embassy come on the fifth day from then.

"They shall have their answer then," said she, flushing and smiling.

"It is as much as any lady could say," the Court declared; and it was reported through all Strelsau that the match was as good as made, and that Osra was to be Grand Duchess of Mittenheim.

"She's a sensible girl after all," cried Rudolf, all his anger gone.

The dream began then, before they came to the cottage. Those days she lived in its golden mists, that shut out all the cold world from her, moving through space which held but one form, and time that stood still waiting for one divine unending moment. And the embassy drew near to Strelsau.

It was night, the dead of night, and all was still in the Palace. But the sentinel by the little gate was at his post, and the gate-warden stood by the Western Gate of the city. Each was now alone, but to each, an hour ago, a man had come stealthily and silently through the darkness; and each was richer by a bag of gold than he had been before. The gold was Osra's—how should a poor student, whose whole fortune was two horses, scatter bags of gold? And other gold Osra had, aye, five hundred crowns. Would not that be a brave surprise for the poor student? And she, alone of all awake, stood looking round her room, entranced with the last aspect of it. Over the city also she looked, but in the selfishness of her joy did no more than kiss a hasty farewell to the good city folk who loved her. Once she thought that maybe, some day, he and she would steal together back to Strelsau, and sheltered by some disguise watch the King ride in splendour through the streets. But if not—why, what was Strelsau, and the people, and the rest? Ah, how long the hours were, before those two horses stood by the little gate, and the sentry and the gate-warden earned their bags of gold! So she passed the hours, the last long lingering hours.

There was a little tavern buried in the narrowest oldest street of the city. Here the poor student had lodged; here, in the back room, a man sat at a table, and two others stood before him. These two seemed gentlemen, and their air spoke of military training. They stroked long moustaches and smiled with an amusement that deference could not hide. Both were booted and wore spurs, and the man sitting at the table gave them orders.

"You will meet the embassy," he said to one, "about ten o'clock. Bring it to the place I have appointed, and wait there. Do not fail."

The officer addressed bowed and retired. A minute later his horse's hoofs clattered through the streets. Perhaps he also had a bag of gold, for the gate-warden opened the Western Gate for him, and he rode at a gallop along the river banks, till he reached the great woods that stretch to within ten miles of Strelsau.

"An hour after we are gone," said the man at the table to the other officer, "go warily, find one of the King's servants, and hand him the letter. Give no account of how you came by it, and say nothing of who you are. All that is necessary is in the letter. When you have delivered it, return here and remain in close hiding, till you hear from me again."

The second officer bowed. The man at the table rose and went out into the street. He took his way to where the Palace rose, and then skirted the wall of its gardens, till he came to the little gate. Here stood two horses, and at their heads a man.

"It is well. You may go," said the student; and he was left alone with the horses. They were good horses for a student to possess. The thought perhaps crossed their owner's mind, for he laughed softly as he looked at them. Then he also fell to thinking that the hours were long;

and a fear came suddenly upon him that she would not come. It was in these last hours that doubts crept in; and he was not with her to drive them away. Would the great trial fail? Would she shrink at the last? But he would not think it of her, and he was smiling again, when the clock of the Cathedral struck two, telling him that no more than an hour now parted her from him. For she would come; the Princess would come to him, the student, led by the vision of that cottage in the dream.

Would she come? She would come; she had risen from her knees and moved to and fro in cautious silence, making her last preparations. She had written a word of love for the brother she loved—for some day, of course, Rudolf would forgive her—and she had ready all that she took with her, the five hundred crowns, one ring that she would give her lover, some clothes to serve till his loving labour furnished more. That night she had wept and she had laughed; now she neither wept nor laughed; but there was a high pride in her face and gait. She opened the door of her room, and walked down the great staircase, under the eyes of crowned Kings who hung framed upon the walls. And as she went she seemed indeed their daughter. For her head was erect, and her lips set firm in haughty dignity. Who dared to say that she did anything that a King's daughter should not do? Should not a woman love? Love should be her diadem. And so with this proud step she came through the gardens of the Palace, looking neither to right nor left, nor behind, but with her face set straight for the little gate; and she walked as she had been accustomed to walk when all Strelsau looked on her, and hailed her as its glory and its darling.

The sentry slept, or seemed to sleep. Her face was not even veiled when she opened the little gate; she would not veil her proud face, it was his to look on now when he would; and thus she stood for an instant in the gateway, while he sprang to her, and, kneeling, carried her hand to his lips.

"You are come?" he cried; for though he had believed, yet he wondered.

"I am come," she smiled. "Is not the word of a Princess sure? Ah, how could I not come?"

"See, love," said he, rising, "day dawns in royal purple for you, and golden love for me."

"The purple is for my King and the love for me," she whispered, as he led her to the horses. "Your fortune!" said she, pointing to them. "But I also have brought a dowry. Fancy, five hundred crowns!" and her mirth and happiness burst out in a laugh. It was so deliciously little, five hundred crowns!

She was mounted now and he stood by her.

"Will you turn back?" he said.

"You shall not make me angry," said she. "Come, mount."

"Aye, I must mount," said he. "For if we were found here the King would kill me."

For the first time the peril of their enterprise seemed to strike into her mind, and turned her cheek pale.

"Ah, I forgot! In my happiness I forgot. Mount, mount! Oh, if he found you!"

He mounted. Once they clasped hands; then they rode swiftly for the Western Gate.

"Veil your face," he said, and since he bade her, she obeyed, saying:

"But I can see you through the veil."

The gate stood open, and the gate-warden was not there. They were out of the city, the morning air blew cold and pure over the meadows from the river. The horses stretched into an eager willing gallop. Osra tore her veil from her face, and turned on him eyes of radiant triumph.

"It is done," she cried, "it is done."

"Yes, it is done, my Princess," said he.

"And—and it is begun, my Prince," said she.

"Yes, and it is begun," said he.

She laughed aloud in absolute joy, and for a moment he also laughed.

But then his face grew grave, and he said:

"I pray you may never grieve for it."

She looked at him with eyes wide in wonder; for an instant she seemed puzzled; then she fell again to laughing.

"Grieve for it!" said she, between her merry laughs.

King Rudolf was a man who lay late in the morning, and he was not well pleased to be roused when the clock had but just struck four. Yet he sat up in his bed readily enough, for he imagined that the embassy from the Grand Duke of Mittenheim must be nearer than he thought, and, sooner than fail in any courtesy towards a Prince whose alliance he ardently desired, he was ready to submit to much inconvenience. But his astonishment was great, when, instead of any tidings from the embassy, one of his gentlemen handed him a letter, saying that a servant had received it from a stranger with instructions to carry it at once to the King; when asked if an answer were desired from his Majesty, the stranger had answered, "Not through me," and at once turned away and quickly disappeared. The King, with a peevish oath at having been roused for such a trifle broke the seal and fastenings of the letter, and opened it; and he read:

"Sire,—Your sister does not wait for the embassy, but chooses her own lover. She has met a student of the University every day for the last three weeks by the river bank." (The King started.) "This morning she has fled with him on horseback along the Western Road. If you desire a student for a brother-in-law, sleep again; if not, up and ride. Do not doubt these tidings."

There was no signature to the letter; yet the King, knowing his sister, cried:

"See whether the Princess is in the Palace. And in the meanwhile saddle my horse, and let a dozen of the Guard be at the gate."

The Princess was not in the Palace, but her women found the letter that she had left, and brought it to the King. And the King read: "Brother, whom I love best of all men in the world save one, I have left you to go with that one. You will not forgive me now, but some day forgive me. Nay, it is not I who have done it, but my love which is braver than I. He is the sweetest gentleman alive, brother, and therefore he must be my lord. Let me go, but still love me.—Osra."

"It is true," said the King; "and the embassy will be here to-day!" For a moment he seemed dazed. Yet he spoke nothing to anybody of what the letters contained, but sent word to the Queen's apartments that he went riding for pleasure. And he took his sword and his pistols; for he swore that by his own hand and by that of no other man, this "sweetest gentleman alive" should meet his death. But all, knowing that the Princess was not in the Palace, guessed that the King's sudden haste concerned her; and great wonder and speculation rose in the Palace, and presently, as the morning advanced, spread from the Palace to its environs, and from the environs to the rest of the city. For it was reported that a sentinel who had stood guard that night was missing, and that the gate-warden of the Western Gate was nowhere to be found, and that a mysterious letter had come by an unknown hand to the King, and lastly, that Princess Osra—their Princess—was gone, whether of her own will or by some bold plot of seizure and kidnapping, none knew. Thus a great stir grew in all Strelsau; men stood about the streets gossiping when they should have gone to work, while women chattered instead of sweeping their houses and dressing their children. So that when the King rode out of the courtyard of the Palace at a gallop, with twelve of the Guard behind, he could hardly make his way through the streets for the people who crowded round him, imploring him to tell them where the Princess was. When the King saw that the matter had become public, his wrath was greater still, and he swore again that the student of the University should pay the price of life for his morning ride with the Princess. And when he darted through the gate and set his horse straight along the Western Road, many of the people, neglecting all their business as folk will for excitement's sake, followed him as they best could, agog to see the thing to its end.

"The horses are weary," said the student to the Princess, "we must let them rest; we are now in the shelter of the wood."

"But my brother may pursue you," she urged, "and if he came up with you—ah, heaven forbid!"

"He will not know you have gone for another three hours," smiled he. "And here is a green bank where we can rest."

So he aided her to dismount; then, saying he would tether the horses, he led them away some distance, so that she could not see where he had posted them; and he returned to her, smiling still. Then he took from his pocket some bread, and breaking the loaf in two, gave her one half, saying:

"There is a spring just here; so we shall have a good breakfast."

"Is this your breakfast?" she asked with a wondering laugh. Then she began to eat, and cried directly: "How delicious this bread is! I would have nothing else for breakfast"; and at this the student laughed.

Yet Osra ate little of the bread she liked so well; presently she leant against her lover's shoulder, and he put his arm round her; and they sat for a little while in silence listening to the soft sounds that filled the waking woods as day grew to fulness and the sun beat warm through the sheltering foliage.

"Don't you hear the trees?" Osra whispered to her lover. "Don't you hear them? They are whispering for me what I dare not whisper."

"What is it they whisper, sweet?" he asked; he himself did no more than whisper.

"The trees whisper, 'Love, love, love.' And the wind—don't you hear the wind murmuring, 'Love, love, love'? And the birds sing, 'Love, love, love.' Aye, all the world to-day is softly whispering, 'Love, love, love.' What else should the great world whisper but my love? For my love is greater than the world." And she suddenly hid her face in her hands; and he could kiss no more than her hands, though her eyes gleamed at him from between slim white fingers.

But suddenly her hands dropped, and she leant forward as though she listened.

"What is that sound?" she asked, apprehension dawning in her eyes.

"It is but another whisper, love!" said he.

"Nay, but it sounds to me like—ah, like the noise of horses galloping."

"It is but the stream, beating over stones."

"Listen, listen, listen!" she cried springing to her feet. "They are horses' hoofs! Ah, merciful God, it is the King!" And she caught him by the hand and pulled him to his feet, looking at him with a face pale and alarmed.

"Not the King," said he. "He would not know yet. It is some one else. Hide your face, dear lady, and all will be well."

"It is the King," she cried. "Hark how they gallop on the road! It is my brother. Love, he will kill you, love, he will kill you."

"It is the King," said he, "I have been betrayed."

"The horses, the horses!" she cried. "By your love for me, the horses!"

He nodded his head, and, turning, disappeared among the trees. She stood with clasped hands, heaving breast, and fearful eyes, awaiting his return. Minutes passed and he did not come. She flung herself on her knees, beseeching heaven for his life. At last he came alone, and he bent over her, taking her hand.

"My love," said he, "the horses are gone!"

"Gone?" she cried, gripping his hand.

"Aye. This love, my love, is a wonderful thing. For I forgot to tie them, and they are gone. Yet what matter? For the King—yes, sweet, I think now it is the King—will not be here for some minutes yet, and those minutes I have still for love and life."

"He will kill you," she said.

"Yes," said he.

She looked long in his eyes; then she threw her arms about his neck, and, for the first time unasked, covered his face with kisses.

"Kiss me, kiss me," said she; and he kissed her. Then she drew back a little, but took his arm and set it round her waist. And she drew a little knife from her girdle, and showed it to him.

"If the King will not pardon us and let us love one another, I also will die," said she, and her voice was quiet and happy. "Indeed, my love, I should not grieve. Ah, do not tell me to live without you!"

"Would you obey?" he asked.

"Not in that," said she.

Thus they stood, while the sound of the hoofs drew very near. But she looked up at him and he looked at her; then she looked at the point of the little dagger, and she whispered:

"Keep your arm round me till I die."

He bent his head and kissed her once again, saying:

"My Princess, it is enough."

And she, though she did not know why he smiled, yet smiled back at him. For although life was sweet that day, yet such a death, with him, and to prove her love for him, seemed wellnigh as sweet. Thus they awaited the coming of the King.

King Rudolf and his Guards far outstripped the people who pursued them from the city, and when they came to the skirt of the wood they divided themselves into four parties, since, if they went all together, they might easily miss the fugitives whom they sought. Of these four parties one found nothing, another found the two horses, which the student himself, who had hidden them, failed to find; the third party had not gone far before they caught sight of the lovers, though the lovers did not see them; and two of them remained to watch, and if need were to intercept any attempted flight, while the other rode off to find the King and bring him where Osra and the student were, as he had commanded.

But the fourth party, with which the King was, though it did not find the fugitives, found the embassy from the Grand Duke of Mittenheim; for the ambassador, with all his train, was resting by the roadside, seeming in no haste at all to reach Strelsau. When the King suddenly rode up at great speed and came upon the embassy, an officer that stood by the ambassador—whose name was Count Sergius of Antheim—stooped down and whispered in his Excellency's ear; upon which he rose and advanced towards the King, uncovering his head and bowing profoundly; for he chose to assume that the King had ridden to meet him out of excessive graciousness and courtesy towards the Grand Duke; so that he began, to the impatient King's infinite annoyance, to make a very long and stately speech, assuring his Majesty of the great hope and joy with which his master awaited the result of the embassy; for, said he, since the King was so zealous in his cause, his master could not bring himself to doubt of success, and therefore most confidently looked to win for his bride the most exalted and lovely lady in the world, the peerless Princess Osra, the glory of the Court of Strelsau, and the brightest jewel in the crown of the King her brother. Having brought this period to a prosperous conclusion, Count Sergius took breath and began another that promised to be fully as magnificent and not a whit less long. So that, before it was well started, the King smote his hand on his thigh, and roared:

"Heavens, man, while you're making speeches, that rascal is carrying off my sister!"

Count Sergius, who was an elderly man of handsome presence and great dignity, being thus rudely and strangely interrupted, showed great astonishment and offence; but the officer by him covered his mouth with his hand to hide a smile. For the moment that the King had spoken these impetuous words he was himself overwhelmed with confusion; since the last thing that he wished the Grand Duke's ambassador to know was that the Princess, whom his master courted, had run away that morning with a student of the University of Strelsau. Accordingly he began, very hastily and with more regard for prudence than for truth, to tell Count Sergius how a noted and bold criminal had that morning swooped down on the Princess as she rode unattended outside the city and carried her off; which seemed to the ambassador a very strange story. But the King told it with great fervour, and he besought the Count to scatter his attendants all through the wood, and seek the robber; yet he charged them not to kill the man themselves but to keep him till he came. "For I have sworn to kill him with my own hand," he cried.

Now Count Sergius, however much astonished he might be, could do nothing but accede to the King's request, and he sent off all his men to scour the woods, and, mounting his horse, himself set out with them, showing great zeal in the King's service, but still thinking the King's story a very strange one. Thus the King was left alone with his two Guards and with the officer who had smiled.

"Will you not go also, sir?" asked the King.

But at this moment a man galloped up at furious speed, crying:

"We have found them, sire, we have found them!"

"Then he hasn't five minutes to live!" cried the King in fierce joy, and he lugged out his sword, adding: "The moment I set my eyes on him, I will kill him. There is no need for words between me and him."

At this speech the face of the officer grew suddenly grave and alarmed, and he put spurs to his horse and hastened after the King, who had at once dashed away in the direction in which the man had pointed; but the King had got a start and kept it, so that the officer seemed terribly frightened, and muttered to himself:

"Heaven send that he does not kill him before he knows!" And he added some very impatient words, concerning the follies of Princes, and, above all, of Princes in love.

Thus, while the ambassador and his men searched high and low for the noted robber, and the King's men hunted for the student of the University, the King, followed by two of his Guards at a distance of about fifty yards (for his horse was better than theirs), came straight to where Osra and her lover stood together; a few yards behind the Guards came the officer; and he also had by now drawn his sword. But he rode so eagerly that he overtook and passed the King's Guards, and got within thirty yards of the King by the time that the King was within twenty of the lovers. But the King let him get no nearer, for he dug his spurs again into his horse's side, and the animal bounded forward, while the King cried furiously to his sister: "Stand away from him!"

The Princess did not heed, but stood in front of her lover (for the student was wholly unarmed), holding up the little dagger in her hand. The King laughed scornfully and angrily, thinking that Osra menaced him with the weapon, and not supposing that it was herself for whom she destined it. And, having reached them, the King leapt from his horse and ran at them, with his sword raised to strike. Osra gave a cry of terror. "Mercy!" she cried, "mercy!" But the King had no thought of mercy, and he would certainly then and there have killed her lover, had not the officer, gaining a moment's time by the King's dismounting, at this very instant come galloping up; and, there being no leisure for any explanation, he leant from his saddle as he dashed by, and, putting out his hand, snatched the King's sword away from him, just as the King was about to thrust it through his sister's lover.

But the officer's horse was going so furiously that he could not stop it for hard on forty yards; he narrowly escaped splitting his head against a great bough that hung low across the grassy path, and he dropped first his own sword and then the King's; but at last he brought his horse to a standstill, and, leaping down, ran back towards where the swords lay. But at the moment the King also ran towards them; for the fury that he had been in before was as nothing to that which now possessed him. After his sword was snatched from him he stood in speechless anger for a full minute, but then had turned to pursue the man who had dared to treat him with such insult; and now, in his desire to be at the officer, he had come very near to forgetting the student. Just as the officer came to where the King's sword lay and picked it up, the King in his turn reached the officer's sword and picked up that. The King came with a rush at the officer, who, seeing that the King was likely to kill him, or he the King, if he stood his ground, turned tail and sped away at the top of his speed through the forest; but as he went, thinking that the time had come for plain speaking, he looked back over his shoulder and shouted:

"Sire, it's the Grand Duke himself!"

The King stopped short in sudden amazement.

"Is the man mad?" he asked. "Who is the Grand Duke?"

"It's the Grand Duke, sire, who is with the Princess. You would have killed him if I had not snatched your sword," said the officer, and he also came to a halt, but he kept a very wary eye on King Rudolf.

"I should certainly have killed him, let him be who he will," said the King. "But why do you call him the Grand Duke?"

The officer very cautiously approached the King, and, seeing that the King made no threatening motion, he at last trusted himself so close that he could speak to the King in a very low voice; and what he said seemed to astonish, please, and amuse the King immensely. For he clapped the officer on the back, laughed heartily, and cried;

"A pretty trick! on my life, a pretty trick!"

Now Osra and her lover had not heard what the officer had shouted to the King, and when Osra saw her brother returning from among the trees alone and with his sword, she still supposed that her lover must die; so she turned and flung her arms round his neck, and clung to him for a moment, kissing him. Then she faced the King, with a smile on her lips and the little dagger in her hand. But the King came up, wearing a scornful smile; and he asked her:

"What is the dagger for, my wilful sister?"

"For me, if you kill him," said she.

"You will kill yourself, then, if I kill him?"

"I would not live a moment after he was dead."

"Faith, it is wonderful!" said the King with a shrug. "Then plainly, if you cannot live without him, you must live with him. He is to be your husband, not mine. Therefore take him, if you will."

When Osra heard this, which, indeed, for joy and wonder she could hardly believe, she dropped her dagger, and, running forward, fell on her knees before her brother; catching his hand, she covered it with kisses, and her tears mingled with her kisses. But the King let her go on, and stood over her, laughing and looking at the student. Presently the student began to laugh also, and he had just advanced a step towards King Rudolf, when Count Sergius of Antheim, the Grand Duke's ambassador, came out from among the trees, riding hotly and with great zeal after the noted robber. But no sooner did the Count see the student, than he stopped his horse, leapt down with a cry of wonder, and, running up to the student, bowed very low and kissed his hand. So that when Osra looked round from her kissing of her brother's hand, she beheld the Grand Duke's ambassador kissing the hand of her lover. She sprang to her feet in wonder.

"Who are you?" she cried to the student, running in between him and the ambassador.

"Your lover and servant," said he.

"And besides?" she said.

"Why, in a month, your husband," laughed the King, taking her lover by the hand.

He clasped the King's hand, but turned at once to her, saying humbly:

"Alas, I have no cottage!"

"Who are you?" she whispered to him.

"The man for whom you were ready to die, my Princess. Is it not enough?"

"Yes, it is enough," said she; and she did not repeat her question. But the King, with a short laugh, turned on his heel, and taking Count Sergius by the arm walked off with him; and presently they called the officer and learnt fully how the Grand Duke had come to Strelsau, and how he had contrived to woo and win the Princess Osra, and finally to carry her off from the Palace.

It was an hour later when the whole of the two companies, that of the King and that of the ambassador, were all gathered together again, and had heard the story; so that when the King went to where Osra and the Grand Duke walked together among the trees, and taking each

303

by a hand led them out, they were greeted with a great cheer; they mounted their horses, which the Grand Duke now found without any difficulty, although when the need of them seemed far greater the student could not contrive to come upon them; and the whole company rode together out of the wood and along the road towards Strelsau, the King being full of jokes and hugely delighted with a trick that suited his merry fancy. But before they had ridden far they met the great crowd which had come out from Strelsau to learn what had happened to Princess Osra. And the King cried out that the Grand Duke was to marry the Princess, while his Guards, who had been with him, and the ambassador's people, spread themselves among the crowd and told the story; and when they heard it, the Strelsau folk were nearly beside themselves with amusement and delight, and thronged round Osra, kissing her hands and blessing her. The King drew back and let her and the Grand Duke ride alone together, while he followed with Count Sergius. Thus moving at a very slow pace, they came in the forenoon to Strelsau; but some one had galloped on ahead with the news, and the Cathedral bells had been set ringing, the streets were full, and the whole city given over to excitement and rejoicing. All the men were that day in love with Princess Osra, and, what is more, they told their sweethearts so; and these found no other revenge than to blow kisses and fling flowers at the Grand Duke as he rode past with Osra by his side. So they came back to the Palace, whence they had fled in the early gleams of the morning's light.

It was evening and the moon rose, fair and clear, over Strelsau. In the streets there were sounds of merriment and rejoicing; every house was bright with light; the King had sent out meat and wine for every soul in the city that none might be sad or hungry or thirsty in all the city that night; so that there was no small uproar. The King himself sat in his arm-chair, toasting the bride and bridegroom in company with Count Sergius of Antheim, whose dignity, somewhat wounded by the trick his master had played on him, was healing quickly under the balm of King Rudolf's graciousness. And the King said to Count Sergius:

"My lord, were you ever in love?"

"I was, sire," said the Count.

"So was I," said the King. "Was it with the Countess, my lord?"

Count Sergius's eyes twinkled demurely, but he answered:

"I take it, sire, that it must have been with the Countess."

"And I take it," said the King, "that it must have been with the Queen."

Then they both laughed; and then they both sighed; and the King, touching the Count's elbow, pointed out to the terrace of the Palace, on to which the room where they were opened. For Princess Osra and her lover were walking up and down together on this terrace. And the two shrugged their shoulders, smiling.

"With him," remarked the King, "it will have been with——"

"The Countess, sire," discreetly interrupted Count Sergius of Antheim.

"Why, yes, the Countess," said the King, and with a laugh they turned back to their wine.

But the two on the terrace also talked.

304

"I do not yet understand it," said Princess Osra. "For on the first day I loved you, and on the second day I loved you, and on the third and the fourth and every day I loved you. Yet the first day was not like the second, nor the second like the third, nor any day like any other. And to-day, again, is unlike them all. Is love so various and full of changes?"

"Is it not?" he asked with a smile. "For while you were with the Queen, talking of I know not what——"

"Nor I indeed," said Osra hastily.

"I was with the King, and he, saying that forewarned was forearmed, told me very strange and pretty stories; of some a report had reached me before——"

"And yet you came to Strelsau?"

"While of others I had not heard."

"Or you would not have come to Strelsau?"

The Grand Duke, not heeding these questions, proceeded to his conclusion.

"Love, therefore," said he, "is very various. For M. de Mérosailles——"

"These are old stories," cried Osra, pretending to stop her ears.

"Loved in one way, and Stephen the smith in another, and—the Miller of Hofbau in a third."

"I think," said Osra, "that I have forgotten the Miller of Hofbau. But can one heart love in many different ways? I know that different men love differently."

"But cannot one heart love in different ways?" he smiled.

"May be," said Osra thoughtfully, "one heart can have loved." But then she suddenly looked up at him with a mischievous sparkle in her eyes. "No, no," she cried, "it was not love. It was——"

"What was it?"

"The courtiers entertained me till the King came," she said, with a blushing laugh. And looking up at him again she whispered, "Yet I am glad that you lingered for a little."

At this moment she saw the King come out on to the terrace; with him was the Bishop of Modenstein; and after the Bishop had been presented to the Grand Duke, the King began to talk with the Grand Duke, while the Bishop kissed Osra's hand and wished her joy.

"Madame," said he, "once you asked me if I could make you understand what love was. I take it you have no need for my lessons now. Your teacher has come."

"Yes, he has come," she said gently, looking at the Bishop with friendliness. "But tell me, will he always love me?"

"Surely he will," answered the Bishop.

"And tell me," said Osra, "shall I always love him?"

"Surely," said the Bishop, again most courteously. "Yet indeed, madame," he continued, "it would seem almost enough to ask of heaven to love now and now to be loved. For the years roll on, and youth goes, and even the most incomparable beauty will yield its blossom when the season wanes; yet that sweet memory may ever be fresh and young, a thing a man can carry to his grave and raise as her best monument on his lady's tomb."

"Ah, you speak well of love," said she. "I marvel that you speak so well of love. For it is as you say; to-day in the wood it seemed to me that I had lived enough, and that even Death was but Love's servant as Life is, and both purposed solely for his better ornament."

"Men have died because they loved you, madame, and some yet live who love you," said the Bishop.

"And shall I grieve for both, my lord—or for which?"

"For neither, madame; the dead have gained peace, and they who live have escaped forgetfulness."

"But would they not be happier for forgetting?"

"I do not think so," said the Bishop, and bowing low to her again, he stood back, for he saw the King approaching with the Grand Duke; the King took him by the arm and walked on with him; but Osra's face lost the brief pensiveness that had come upon it as she talked with the Bishop, and turning to her lover, she stretched out her hands to him, saying:

"I wish there was a cottage, and that you worked for bread, while I made ready for you at the cottage, and then ran far, far, far down the road to watch and wait for your coming."

"Since a cottage was not too small, a palace will not be too large," said he, catching her in his arms.

Thus the heart of Princess Osra found its haven and its rest; for a month later she was married to the Grand Duke of Mittenheim in the Cathedral of Strelsau, having utterly refused to take any other place for her wedding. Again she and he rode forth together through the Western Gate; and the King rode with them on their way till they came to the woods. Here he paused and all the crowd that accompanied him stopped also; and they all waited till the sombre depths of the glades hid Osra and her lover from their sight. Then, leaving them thus riding together to their happiness, the people returned home, sad for the loss of their darling Princess. But for consolation, and that their minds might the less feel her absence, they had her name often on their lips; and the poets and storytellers composed many stories about her, not grounded on fact, as are those which have been here set forth, but the fabric of idle imaginings, wrought to please the fancy of lovers or to wake the memories of older folk. So that, if a stranger goes now to Strelsau, he may be pardoned if it seem to him that all mankind was in love with Princess Osra. Nay, and those stories so pass all fair bounds that if you listen to them, you will come near to believing that the Princess also had found some love for all the men who had given her their love. Thus to many she is less a woman who once lived and breathed, than some sweet image under whose name they fondly group all the virtues and the charms of her whom they love best, each man fashioning for himself from his own chosen model her whom he calls his Princess. Yet it may be that for some of them who so truly loved

306

her, her heart had a moment's tenderness. Who shall tell all the short-lived dreams that come and go, the promptings and stirrings of a vagrant inclination? And who would pry too closely into these secret matters? May we not more properly give thanks to heaven that the thing is as it is? For surely it makes greatly for the increase of joy and entertainment in the world, and of courtesy and true tenderness, that the heart of Princess Osra—or of what lady you may choose, sir, to call by her name—should flutter in pretty hesitation here and there and to and fro a little, before it flies on a straight wing to its destined and desired home. And if you be not the Prince for your Princess, why, sir, your case is a sad one. Yet there have been many such, and still there is laughter as well as tears in the tune to which the world spins round:—

But still a Ruby kindles in the Vine,

And many a Garden by the Water blows.

Wear your willow then, as the Marquis de Mérosailles wore his, lightly and yet most courteously; or like the Bishop of Modenstein (for so some say), with courage and self-mastery. That is, if wear it you must. You remember what the Miller of Hofbau thought?

Note from the Editor

Odin's Library Classics strives to bring you unedited and unabridged works of classical literature. As such this is the complete and unabridged version of the original English text. The English language has evolved since the writing and some of the words appear in their original form, or at least the most commonly used form at the time. This is done to protect the original intent of the author. If at any time you are unsure of the meaning of a word, please do your research on the etymology of that word. It is important to preserve the history of the English language.

Taylor Anderson

Made in United States
Troutdale, OR
12/16/2023

15967777R00176